MASSACHUSETTS AT WAR

World War II in the Baystate

Jeffrey Proctor
and
Paula Fitch Proctor

Contents

Introduction

The Second World War was the most horrific conflict in the history of mankind. It is estimated that between 70 and 85 million people lost their lives, over three percent of the Earth's population. Sixteen million American sons and fathers and brothers, daughters and mothers and sisters went to war. Over 400,000 never came home.

Each and every one of the forty-eight states made a significant contribution to the war effort. California built mighty ships, and Kansas produced thousands of airplanes. Millions of gallons of oil flowed from Texas and Oklahoma. From some states came heroes like Desmond Doss of Virginia or great military leaders like New Jersey's William "Bull" Halsey. Some, like New York and Missouri, would send presidents. From Massachusetts, ranked 44th in size, over 300,000 left family and friends to fight and die on foreign soil, more than 39 other states.

This book is dedicated to the citizens of Massachusetts, to those who fought and to those who died, to the mothers and fathers who waited anxiously for their return and to those who would never see their sons or daughters again, to the factory workers who helped to build an American war machine, to the housewives who baked war cakes, and the grandparents and children who tended victory gardens. This book is written for those who remember and for those who are yet to come.

This is the story of Massachusetts at war.

Author's Note

A few years ago, I suggested to my son, Jeffrey Proctor, that he consider writing his next book about Massachusetts during the Second World War. He had just completed *Blades*, a biography of Navy chopper pilot Don Broderick, and was working on a history of the Korean War. The idea came to me because libraries in Massachusetts were unquestionably more accessible than those in Asia. After a bit of hemming and hawing, this talented writer and armchair historian with a profound respect for veterans agreed, and together, we began *Massachusetts at War*. Jeff was in charge of writing, and my job was research. It was an exciting time as we uncovered the history of the heroes and ordinary folk of the state we were both born in.

Then, unexpectedly, on a warm summer day three years ago, a horrific call came in. Jeff was gone, taken from us at 42 years old by a heart attack. Many months later, when I was able to lift my head again, the idea came to me that perhaps I should keep working on the book. Unlike Jeff, beyond term papers and theses, I am not a writer and, even worse, just an amateur albeit rabid historian. But I picked up his notes and his writing anyway, thinking of it as therapy, convinced that without my son's talent and input, I'd never be able to finish the book. So I propped his picture up next to my laptop and went to work, and for the past three years, I have laughed with him, cried with him, and yelled at him for not being here as the stories of those who had experienced the war unfolded before me. Quite astonishingly, I seem to have finished the book. I am not healed...there will be no coming back from the loss of such a wonderful son...but I am stronger and in a much better place, strangely enough, thanks to Jeff.

While it may have been my suggestion, *Massachusetts at War* is Jeffrey's vision. He set the direction of the book, established a framework, named the chapters, and wrote pages and pages of text as we delved into the history of the Bay State. I can only hope that my words, as they blend together with his on the pages of this book, bring a smile to his dear face wherever he is. While the purpose of this book is to honor the efforts, the trials, the tragedies, and the triumphs of the people of Massachusetts who lived during the Second World War, to me, it will always be Jeff's book.

Paula Fitch Proctor

Special Thanks...
To my dear friends, Ken Laramee and Jack LaCroix, for your input and kind words of support.
To my wonderful son, Adam, for your encouragement, support, and tolerance for the excessive amount of WWII stories I've shared, in spite of the fact that learning about history is right next to root canals on your bucket list. Somewhere up there, your brother is having a good laugh.
And for my husband, Wayne, through tragedy and healing and through my latest unexpected adventure, my love and gratitude always.

Chapter 1

Prelude to War

This generation of Americans has a rendezvous with destiny.
Franklin Delano Roosevelt

It was the 1930s. In the United States, Franklin Delano Roosevelt signed the Fair Labor Standards Act, establishing a minimum wage of 25 cents. Orson Welles kicked off a wave of hysteria with his radio broadcast, *War of the Worlds*, and a red-caped superhero from planet Krypton made his first comic book appearance. Hollywood hit it big with blockbusters like *Gone with the Wind* and *The Wizard of Oz.* In Massachusetts, after being dry for a decade, the Prohibition Act was repealed, a Whitman baker created the first Toll House Cookie, and the ship City of Salisbury broke in half, dumping a boatload of exotic animals and venomous snakes into Boston Harbor.[1]

Off the Cape Verde islands in September 1938, a large low-pressure area began spinning its way across the Atlantic. Shortly afterward, the Great New England Hurricane slammed into Massachusetts, destroying roads, buildings, and rail lines. Winds of 186 mph hit the Blue Hill Observatory, and 50-foot waves crashed ashore at Gloucester. At the Boston Navy Yard, the USS Constitution was damaged when she slipped from her anchorage.

Downtown Lawrence flooded following
the Great New England Hurricane. September 21, 1938.[2]

And in Germany, in a speech filled with toxic racism, virulent hatred, and fomenting rabid nationalism, Adolph Hitler addressed a frenzied crowd at the annual Nuremberg Nazi Party rally. Four thousand miles to the east, another storm was rising.

In the late 1930s, eyes were also turned toward the Pacific and the Empire of Japan, where the island nation's sights were set on China. After invading Manchuria, the Japanese, angered by the alliance between Russia and China, made a deal with the devil. Under the guise of protecting their respective parts of the globe from Communism, in 1936, Japan entered into the Anti-Comintern Pact with Germany. Throughout the following spring and summer, Massachusetts newspapers reported on Japanese aggression. In July, a *Boston Globe* headline read, "Far East Crisis Grows Ominous[3]," and in December,

---

[1] *City of Salisbury.* Mass.gov. tinyurl.com/4aympuun.

[2] *Essex Street flooded* 1938. Pub domain photo. GetArchive. tinyurl.com/ycxeh5yy.

[3] *Crisis Grows Ominous.* Boston Globe 7/17/1937. Newspapers.com. tinyurl.com/5n8c6xc4.

readers of the *North Adams Transcript* were told, "Japanese in Sight of Nanking Gates[4]." Most Americans, however, still failed to make a connection between danger to their country and Japanese imperialism. Less than seven months after Nanjing was attacked, the *Transcript* published a rather complaisant article titled "War's Birthday," likening the war between China and Japan to a football game. By then, 100,000 Chinese were dead in Nanjing alone[5]. Despite the promotion of the Empire's envisioned Co-prosperity Sphere (a Pacific-based union of nations headed, of course, by Japan), the signing of the Tripartite Act between Germany, Italy, and Japan, and Japanese expansion into Indo-China, only half of Americans polled in November 1941 felt war with Japan was inevitable.[6]

America was not prepared for war. The signs were there, visions of goose-stepping boots marching into Austria, the sound of the shattering glass of Kristallnacht. But much like a distant flash of lightning or rumble of thunder, most Americans paused, listened for a moment, then went back to their daily lives. Thus, as the United States slowly inched toward the coming conflict, the country was not ready. To be fair, the Great War, the "war to end all wars," was still painfully fresh in the minds of many. Over 100,000 Americans had lost their lives, 3,000 of them from Massachusetts.

President Franklin Roosevelt, educated at Groton and Harvard, was no stranger to the Bay State. Growing up, he spent time at the home of his maternal grandfather in Fairhaven and was a frequent visitor to New Bedford.

Young Franklin Roosevelt, during a visit to
Fairhaven, Massachusetts. 1897.[7]

In 1936, FDR clarified his foreign policy vision by stating that America was interested in being a good neighbor but that we would "shun political commitments which might entangle us in foreign wars." Six months later, during a visit to Worcester, the only war mentioned was the country's struggle against the Depression. Back in Massachusetts in 1940, he praised Boston Navy Yard workers and New England farmers. Building up America's military prowess, he claimed, was justified as a measure to "keep any potential attacker as far from our continental shores as we possibly can." Surely, this man would not lead the country into war.

On the eve of World War II, the United States was already engaged in a desperate struggle. Nearly a decade before, Worcester's *Telegram and Gazette* featured a headline about a visit to Springfield by presidential candidate Franklin Delano Roosevelt. Tucked elsewhere in the newspaper was an article entitled, "Bankers Fail to Check Tumbling Stock Prices," along with another assuring readers that Wall

---

[4] *Japanese Nanking Gates.* No Adams Transcript 12/6/1937. Newspapers.com. tinyurl.com/2s4fd472.

[5] *War's Birthday.* No Adams Transcript 7/9/1938. Newspapers.com. tinyurl.com/yc7bj9wc.

[6] Saad, Lydia. *Country Unified.* Gallup Vault. GALLUP 12/5/2016. tinyurl.com/3rapdpu6.

[7] *Roosevelt, Fairhaven* 1897. Pub domain photo. NARA 195498. Picryl. tinyurl.com/2xuhz5rk.

Street had the issue under control.[8] In the days that followed, Worcester traders would sell off hundreds of thousands of shares[9], and the Boston Stock Exchange would lose 25 percent of its value. These ominous events foreshadowed a series of economic disasters that would thrust the US and eventually the world into a decade-long depression and sow seeds of discontent that would contribute to the rise of a German Nazi state.

In the early days of the Great Depression, the average citizen gave little notice to the tragedy that was unfolding. Only 10 percent of Americans owned stock, and the media did little to foment widespread panic. In Worcester, the *Telegram and Gazette* continued giving updates on the country's economic situation, but the emphasis was clearly on local news. At Clark University's request, Robert Goddard would move to Fort Devens to continue his rocketry research. Apparently, according to *T&G* columnist Albert Southwick, "His previous rocket launches had alarmed people in Worcester and Auburn." Money had been raised to purchase land near Lincoln Square for the construction of an auditorium, and Clark University sophomores had emerged victorious in the yearly rope pull across University Pond.[10]

Robert H. Goddard and a rocket
fired in Auburn. March 1926.[11]

By the end of the Great Depression, 90 percent of the national stock value was gone. In Massachusetts, heavily industrialized cities such as Lowell, Springfield, Fall River, and Worcester were devastated, and textile and shoe manufacturing nearly wiped out. One article commented, "Unemployed workers wandered barefoot outside of shoe factories that had failed." A 1934 national strike by textile employees took a violent turn. In Lowell, a riot erupted during a demonstration of 2,500 workers, 300 Fall River strikebreakers were held captive by a crowd of 10,000, and at a Dighton factory, a confrontation with an angry mob ended when they encountered a police squad bearing machine guns.[12] By the end of the year, Massachusetts' unemployment reached 25 percent, with those fortunate enough to find work earning less than ten dollars a week.

Franklin Roosevelt was a charismatic leader imbued with infectious optimism at a time when the country, struggling through an economic depression, needed to hear, "The only thing we have to fear is fear itself." However, polls showed that approximately half of the country disapproved of his presidency.

---

[8] *Crash Heralds Depression.* Massmoments. tinyurl.com/52za9m5a.

[9] Southwick, Albert. *Stock market crash Page One.* Telegram.com 1/14/2009. tinyurl.com/5y976dtz.

[10] Southwick, Albert. *Stock market crash Page One.*

[11] *Early Rockets.* Pub domain photo. NASA. Picryl. tinyurl.com/3uvua67s.

[12] Brecher, Jeremy. *Textile workers' strike.* Libcom.org. tinyurl.com/4e8acyjy.

In the 1936 election, Massachusetts voters barely gave FDR a win over his biggest opponent with a margin of only 10 percent.[13] As shanty towns sprung up and bread lines stretched out, to most Americans, the looming crisis in Europe seemed strangely disconnected from the challenges of daily life. Domestic, not foreign, policy was on their minds.

Many put their hopes in Roosevelt's New Deal and its Alphabet Agencies. One such program, the Work Progress Administration, would run for eight years, spend 11 billion dollars on the country's infrastructure, and employ 8.5 million Americans. Massachusetts was the beneficiary of many WPA projects. By 1939, two new bridges, the Buzzards Bay Railroad Bridge and the Bourne Bridge, stretched across the Cape Cod Canal.

Cape Cod Canal railroad bridge
construction, Bourne. May 1935.[14]

Athletic fields were laid out in Middleborough and Hudson, and in Lanesborough, the newly constructed Bascom Lodge perched atop Mt. Greylock. On a much larger scale, work began on the construction or rehabilitation of several airports, military bases, and arsenals, projects that would soon be of immense military value. Development of a huge air base began in Chicopee. At a cost of $750,000, the project employed over a thousand workers. Westover Field would become the largest military airfield in the Northeast.[15]

[13] *1936 Pres Election Results.* Dave Leip's Atlas Pres Elections. tinyurl.com/3zvpu63y.

[14] *Cape Cod Bridge* 5/23/1935. Pub domain photo. NARA Boston. Picryl. tinyurl.com/2fk5azy6.

[15] *Projects in MA.* Living New Deal. tinyurl.com/3yebu6wa.

WPA logging Project Orange, 1939.[16]

In 1935, with the Depression still raging and only a glimmer of hope that the economy would recover, a group of civic leaders and businessmen decided that America needed a break. A non-profit corporation was founded to develop a project that would become the New York World's Fair. Designed around the hopeful theme, "Building the World of Tomorrow," the two-year-long event attracted 45 million people. Although it would eventually end in bankruptcy, it generated millions of dollars in revenue. Featuring exhibits from nearly two dozen countries, the fair displayed iconic remnants of the past, such as an original copy of the Magna Carta, along with glimpses of the future. Spectacular inventions from the expanding field of technology could be seen in presentations by companies like Kodak and Ford. General Electric sponsored Steinmetz Hall in honor of the company's brilliant Charles Steinmetz, who pioneered the notion of experimenting with lightning in a lab. A model of the lightning generator from Pittsfield's General Electric High Voltage Lab stunned visitors as 10 million volts of multicolored lightning melted wires and crashed toward the ceiling.[17]

An extremely popular attraction created by a Connecticut company resulted in one of the country's most renowned advertising campaigns. Already a leader in the milk production industry with notable developments such as condensed milk, the latest project, a rotolactor milking machine, was the centerpiece of their World's Fair exhibit. In order to boost sales, the Borden Company began using the drawing of a charming little cow named Elsie as their mascot.

For visitors to the cow barn, the bewitching bovine was a hot topic. There was, of course, no Elsie, but there was the adorable and amiable You'll Do Lobelia. Renamed Elsie and given VIP status,

---

[16] *Logging MA Nat Forest.* Pub domain photo. NARA. Picryl. tinyurl.com/53ncw7zt.

[17] Behary, Jeff. *GE World's Fair Lightning.* GE 5/1940. Internet Archive. tinyurl.com/ynsu59z5.

this demure Jersey cow from Brookfield, Massachusetts, would become one of the most famous heifers in history.[18]

Elsie the Cow[19]

The World's Fair was not without its share of difficulties. A bomb exploded at the British pavilion, killing two police officers. Several "girlie shows" and "20,000 Legs Under the Sea," a fun house designed by Salvador Dali, were raided by the Vice Squad[20], and fairground security engaged in a lengthy search for two runaway teens from Oxford, Massachusetts.[21]

While the 1939 World's Fair was created as a diversion from the reality of life during the Great Depression, it could not escape the reality of the situation in Europe. Within months of its opening, Great Britain and France declared war on Germany. Czechoslovakia, consumed by Nazi aggression early in the conflict, halted development of its pavilion. As historian David Cope put it, "The World's Fair held an exhibit contract with a country that no longer existed.[22]" Russia suddenly withdrew from the fair shortly after signing the Non-aggression Pact with Germany and providing assistance in the invasion of Poland. In the Italian pavilion near maps, which arrogantly displayed Italy's expanding empire, a huge bronze statue of Benito Mussolini stood atop a black marble pedestal. Germany chose not to participate at all.

---

[18] *Elsie the Cow.* New Eng Hist Soc 2021. tinyurl.com/3famwntu.

[19] *Elsie the cow* 1948. Pub domain photo. Wiki Commons. tinyurl.com/yc2bfm3c.

[20] *Welcome to the Fair!* NY State Library 7-8 2014. tinyurl.com/5n8c9nkt.

[21] Cope, David J. *Opening Day* 1939 World's Fair. tinyurl.com/2updys5s.

[22] Cope, David J. *Czechoslovakia* 1939 World's Fair. tinyurl.com/3n7fpcda.

Italian Pavilion, 1939 World's Fair.[23]

When the World's Fair closed in October 1940, a puzzling question remained: what to do with the exhibits. Most were packed up and shipped home, but many were left behind. The Polish government, now in exile in London, sold off many of its treasures to the Polish Museum of America. The British, concerned with the safety of its precious Magna Carta, left the document in the care of the United States. During the war, it would be stored at Fort Knox along with the Declaration of Independence and the US Constitution and returned to England in 1946.

Perhaps the biggest dilemma concerned the two most recognizable structures located at the Fair. The Trylon, a 700-foot-tall plaster-covered metallic obelisk, had been struck by lightning four times since its creation and sustained wind damage on multiple occasions.[24] Nearby stood a giant white ball, the 180-foot-diameter Perisphere, containing a model of "Democracity, a utopian city set one hundred years in the future." For fairgoers immersed in the agony of the Depression, these immensely popular attractions symbolized the hope of a bright and shining tomorrow. In a final irony, the Trylon and Perisphere indeed pointed the way to the future. Within months, they would be torn down and scrapped, their metal used to fuel the nation's war machine during World War II.

Following the First World War, rumor and speculation abounded, fueled by books, media, and members of Congress, regarding the role of weapons manufacturers in motivating American entrance into World War I. Two years into office and ever cognizant of voter attitudes, Roosevelt supported the establishment of the Nye Committee to investigate. While the Committee failed to find evidence of wrongdoing by these "merchants of death," it put forth a shocking proposal: nationalizing the weapons industry. Manufacturers suddenly saw the handwriting on the wall. Deep cuts in munitions production followed. Dupont, for example, the largest munitions manufacturer during the First World War, dropped to 2 percent of former manufacturing levels. Arthur Herman, author of *Freedom's Forge*, stated, "Supplying America with arms was business you did not want." Gradually, due to budget cuts and popular opinion, America's military superiority vanished. Fourth largest military might in 1918, the US now ranked eighteenth, just ahead of the tiny Netherlands.[25] Our once feared fighting force now counted fewer than 200,000 in its ranks.

---

[23] *World's Fair Italian Building* 1939. Pub domain image. LOC. tinyurl.com/y6n26et4.

[24] Cope, David J. *Trylon Perisphere* 1939 World's Fair. tinyurl.com/2zuubvxz.

[25] Herman, Arthur. *Freedom's Forge*. Random House Trade Paperbacks 2013.

In an effort to avoid an arms race following the First World War, the Washington Naval Treaty was signed in 1922. This Five Power Treaty significantly limited the production of battleships, battle cruisers, and aircraft carriers and assigned tonnage restrictions for smaller class ships. The Army operated only six arsenals. Most weapons production equipment was over ten years old, and much of it dated from the Civil War. Their Air Corps contained 2,400 planes,[26] while the Luftwaffe was approaching 8,500 aircraft at its command. Military vehicles and supplies of all types were sadly lacking. In 1939, when Fort Benning attempted to repair some of its tanks, the commanding officer, General George Patton, had to order parts at his own expense from the Sears and Roebuck catalog.[27] President Roosevelt would later caution the country about its lack of readiness for war. In an interview, he painted a frighteningly realistic picture of potential danger: "Enemy ships could swoop in and shell New York; enemy planes could drop bombs on war plants in Detroit; enemy troops could attack Alaska." By then, however, two months after Pearl Harbor, it was too late.

The looming crisis in Europe was a constant point of contention for the seemingly pacifistic Roosevelt. A significant source of support came from Protestant churches, most of which had passed resolutions against the grievous sin of war. This would change, however, as clergy slowly took a stance of support for the country and its men and women at war. Surprisingly, one of the most eloquent statements came from a Protestant-centered publication, *The Christian Century*, well known for its anti-war stance. Following Pearl Harbor, an article appeared in the magazine that referred to war as "An Unnecessary Necessity." "Our government has taken a stand. It is our Government...It is our voice. The President is our President; all his official acts, even those which we disapprove, are our acts. We stand with our country; we cannot do otherwise."[28]

The Jewish community, witness to the horrors unfolding under the Hitler regime, was a vocal proponent of American intervention. The Catholic response was more unsure. Pope Pius XII was a controversial figure who refused to denounce the Nazis while thousands of Jews were dying. His nebulous responses ranged from silence to "bear adversity with serene patience," the statement made upon being informed that more than 200,000 Ukrainian Jews had been killed.[29]

In spite of the Holy Father's apparent political neutrality, slowly American Catholics began to step forward. In a 1940 letter to FDR, Massachusetts native Cardinal Francis Spellman wrote, "We really can no longer afford to be moles who cannot see, or ostriches who will not see. For some solemn agreements are no longer sacred, and vices have become virtues and truth a synonym of falsehood." In 1942, US bishops announced, "Deeply moved by the arrest and maltreatment of the Jews, we cannot stifle the cry of conscience. In the name of humanity and Christian principles, our voice is raised.[30]"

One of Roosevelt's biggest detractors was an outspoken Catholic priest from Detroit, Father Joseph Coughlin. With a radio program in 1926, his popularity grew so quickly that four years later, CBS began broadcasting his program nationally. Soon, thousands of letters per week were arriving from devoted followers. Initially aligned with the President, he became disillusioned after FDR distanced himself from the controversial priest. As a result, the disgruntled Coughlin gravitated toward radical right-wing groups and created the National Union for Social Justice. As the 1930s progressed, so did his anti-Semitic ideology. Using his nationally published newspaper, *Social Justice*, as a platform, Coughlin made groundless allegations about Jewish control of the country's banking industry and claims that Jewish leaders were plotting world domination.

---

[26] *Evolution Dept AF.* AF Hist Studies. tinyurl.com/5y94au9z.

[27] Herman, Arthur. *Freedom's Forge.*

[28] Abrams, Ray. *Churches and Clergy WWII.* Annals AAPSS 3/1948. JSTOR. www.jstor.org/stable/1027378.

[29] Bard, Mitchell. *Vatican & Holocaust.* JVL. AICE. tinyurl.com/2wy2srrb.

[30] Bard, Mitchell. *Vatican & Holocaust.*

Coughlin's raging racism did not fall on deaf ears in Massachusetts. Lynn native William Pelley, leader of the Fascist Silvershirts, was one of Coughlin's most vocal allies, loudly echoing the priest's credo that this was a "Jewish war.[31]" In addition, just over a decade earlier, the Ku Klux Klan had made significant inroads into the Bay State. A successful campaign to recruit new members resulted in active participation in Berlin, Holden, Shrewsbury, Marlborough, Upton, Paxton, Charlton, West Brookfield, and Spencer. As the number of adherents and cross-burnings continued to rise, Worcester became a hub of Klan activity. On October 19, 1924, 15,000 people, including a 400-strong Klan security force, gathered at the city's Agricultural Fairgrounds. As the evening wore on, a riot erupted that lasted for several hours. Public distaste for the violence associated with this "Klanvocation" soon led to a decline in interest in the Ku Klux Klan.[32]

With the rise of Hitler and the Nazi party, the treatment of the Jews and their purported role in the post-World War I decline of Germany became a constant dialogue in the media. In 1938, a brazen Coughlin declared that Jews, persecutors of Christians, were deserving of the horrors of Kristallnacht. His followers agreed, and an offshoot of the Social Justice Organization known as the Christian Front was created. Francis J. Moran, native of Boston, former seminary student, and disgruntled insurance company employee who lost his job over a rumored tussle with a former Jewish war veteran, was looking for a cause.[33] He soon found one, rising to the head of the Boston Chapter of the Christian Front. Working with German Consul General and SS officer Herbert Scholz to fund the group, he set up headquarters at the Copley Square Hotel. Christian Front clusters sprang up in Arlington and Ayer. In Worcester and Springfield, plans were laid to create 100-member armed units.[34] "When we get through with the Jews in America," Coughlin ranted, "they'll think the treatment they received in Germany was nothing.[35]"

Nazi flag at German consulate's house,
Chestnut Street, Boston. May 1940.[36]

The efforts of Moran and Coughlin were successful. On September 8, 1939, a rally at the Boston Arena was attended by 6,000 followers.[37] The Boston group cooperated with Nazi regime publishers to distribute books and leaflets. Many businessmen found ways to place pamphlets in the hands of their customers. Some restaurant owners printed anti-Jewish statements on their menus. Residents in areas heavily populated by members of the Jewish faith, such as Mattapan and Dorchester, reported frequent assaults as well as vandalism of synagogues and businesses. So invasive was the work of the Christian Front in Massachusetts that the *New York Post* reported, "Beating of Jews in Boston was an almost daily occurrence," and *Newsweek* and *Atlantic Monthly* published articles condemning the violence. Response

---

[31] Abrams, Ray H. *Churches and Clergy WWII.*

[32] *Ku Klux Klan Worcester 10/19/1924.* Mass Moments. tinyurl.com/5d83bwdf.

[33] Moses, Paul. *Old Resentment.* Commonwealth 1/6/2022. tinyurl.com/ym2t3n4j.

[34] Theodore Irwin. *Christian Front 3/1940.* Am Coun Public Affairs. ajcarchives.org. tinyurl.com/2jbrkvjr.

[35] Lebovic, Matt. *Am's capital anti-Semitism* 1940. Times of Israel 9/4/2017. tinyurl.com/33t6k5nb.

[36] *German Consulate Boston.* Pub domain photo. Lebovic, Matt. *Am's capital anti-Semitism.*

[37] Theodore Irwin. *Christian Front.*

by authorities to racist activities was lackluster at best. Governor Leverett Saltonstall and Police Commissioner Joseph Timilty both denied allegations of anti-Semitic violence, while Mayor Maurice Tobin called it a "strictly juvenile problem." Many press outlets followed their lead. When the popular magazine *LIFE* reported on anti-semitic incidents in Boston, the *Boston Post* and *Boston Daily Record* published denials.[38]

Coughlin finally went too far. Following Pearl Harbor and America's declaration of war, the priest continued his racist agenda, blatantly claiming the conflict was the result of a Jewish conspiracy to bring the US into the war. For US Attorney General Francis Biddle, this was the last straw. Coughlin's parish records and personal papers were seized by the FBI. He was identified by the State Department as pro-Nazi, denied a passport, and prohibited from using the US Postal Service to circulate his *Social Justice* newspaper. In May 1942, the Archbishop of Detroit ordered Coughlin to suspend all non-church-related activities or face being defrocked. In Boston, as knowledge of Nazi atrocities became public and with the elevation of the liberal-minded Richard Cushing to the position of Cardinal, the Christian Front faded into obscurity. Father Charles Coughlin's fifteen minutes of fame were over.

The world watched anxiously in 1935 as Hitler blatantly overruled the Treaty of Versailles and began to rebuild Germany's war machine. In response, Congress passed the Neutrality Act prohibiting the US export of arms and ammunition to countries at war. Within weeks, Italy committed a stunning act of aggression against Ethiopia, and President Franklin Roosevelt responded by invoking the tenets of the newly passed Neutrality Act. If war was on the horizon, the United States and her weapons wouldn't be a part of it.

Sen. Gerald Nye (left) and Sen. Henry Cabot
Lodge (right) discuss Neutrality Act. 1937.[39]

In 1938, the German army overran the Sudetenland. An American Institute of Public Opinion survey showed that the majority of respondents believed Hitler had territorial ambitions in Europe, and nearly all disapproved of his treatment of the Jews.[40] Yet when Poland fell a year later, a Gallup Poll showed 90 percent still felt the United States should not declare war on Germany.[41] America clung to her closed-door philosophy, offering sympathy but little else to her allies.

On September 3, 1939, an event transpired which would nudge the United States closer to war. Off the northwest coast of Ireland, the passenger liner SS Athenia headed westward toward Montreal. Of the 1,400 passengers, 311 were Americans, including several from Massachusetts. Listed were Mrs.

[38] Stephen Norwood. *Christian Front 6/2003.* Am Jewish Hist. tinyurl.com/2t5ec65k.

[39] *Gerald P. Nye, Henry Cabot Lodge* 11/23/1937. Pub domain photo. LOC. Wiki Commons. tinyurl.com/yc4yx3dr.

[40] *Am. Inst. Public Opinion-Surveys.* Pub Opinion Quarterly 1939. JSTOR. tinyurl.com/333knvxw.

[41] Reinhart, R.J. *Start of WWII.* Gallup Vault. GALLUP 8/29/2019. tinyurl.com/26788a2a.

Benjamin Alton of Worcester and her daughter Elizabeth, Dr. John Kirk and his family of Boston, and Mr. and Mrs. Alexander Nichol and their daughter, Marion, heading home to Andover. Captain James Cook had just received sobering news of England's declaration of war and set about the grim task of notifying those on board. Unknown to Athenia, nearby, the German sub U-30 was hunting for prey. Earlier that day, U-boats had received a message from command allowing unrestricted, unprovoked attack on enemy shipping. Prize rules dictated that no passenger ships could be sunk. At 7:00 p.m., U-30 Captain Fritz-Julius Lemp sighted what he believed was a British merchant ship and commenced the attack. One torpedo struck the passenger ship. By the following morning, the Athenia, the first ship to be sunk in the infamous U-boat War, was gone along with 112 souls, including the Nichol family and twenty-five other Americans.[42] Dr. Kirk told the *Boston Globe*, "My wife was killed in the explosion, and all I want to know now is whether my two children who were traveling with us are safe.[43]" Gladys Kirk and the Altons survived.[44]

Athenia survivors being taken aboard the SS City of Flint. September 1939.[45]

Lemp, having realized his mistake, quickly notified his superiors. Remembering the Lusitania incident and its effect on America's entry into the First World War, Hitler ordered a cover-up. Propaganda Minister Joseph Goebbels issued a statement blaming England for sinking its own ship in order to lure the United States into war. It would not be until the Nuremberg Trials that Admiral Karl Doenitz would take responsibility for the sinking of the Athenia by Germany. However, there would be consequences for Lemp's actions. In May 1941, three British destroyers spotted a German submarine in waters off Greenland. After significant damage from depth charges, the sub crew abandoned ship only to realize that U-110 was not sinking. In an attempt to protect classified information still on board, the captain jumped into the water and began swimming toward the sub. Kapitanleutnant Fritz-Julius Lemp was never

[42] Mayo, Jonathan. *Starting gun on slaughter.* Daily Mail.com 9/1/2019. tinyurl.com/24ftuxrj.

[43] *Victims Tale.* Daily Item 9/5/1939. Newspapers.com. tinyurl.com/yjc3fvkw.

[44] *Safe in Scotland.* Boston Globe 9/5/1939. Newspapers.com. tinyurl.com/2s3rv9dj.

[45] *Athenia's lifeboats* 9/1939. Pub Domain Photo. IWM. Wikipedia. tinyurl.com/9vke67hw.

seen again. When the sub was boarded, the British found an operational Enigma machine, the jewel in the crown of Nazi cryptography, along with up-to-date code books.

In the days following the Athenia tragedy, newspapers reported details of the sinking, witness accounts, and survivor lists. What is interesting about the week that followed is that newspaper headlines mostly failed to express patriotic outrage against Germany. This seemed to be England's problem. England was at war. The ship was British. Most of the passengers were Canadian and thus subjects of the British Empire. A few individuals dared to approach the line in the sand. Ten days after the sinking, an editorial in the *Boston Globe* stated, "Correspondents waiting for the Athenia survivors in Halifax make one realize that this war is right on our doorstep already.[46]" However, in a speech made at Holyoke, Senator David I. Walsh doubled down on American isolationism. Describing the "absolute necessity of...complete detachment from the diplomatic intrigue..." taking place across the globe, he stated, "Billions for defense and not one penny to send American youth to Europe to be slaughtered.[47]" In spite of the rhetoric, the fact remained that Germany had fired upon and sunk a privately owned vessel in the North Atlantic. The U-boat war had just begun.

Senator David I Walsh of Clinton.[48]

[46] *Editorial Points.* Boston Globe 9/13/1939. Newspapers.com. tinyurl.com/c49tr9ku.

[47] *US Stay Out Of War.* Republican 9/4/1939. Newspapers.com. tinyurl.com/23sucvzj.

[48] *DI Walsh.* Pub domain photo. LOC LC-DIG-ggbain. tinyurl.com/nfduusds.

Ever the politician, Roosevelt outwardly aligned himself with public opinion. The *Fitchburg Sentinel* reported on the President's response: "It is of the utmost importance that the people of this country...think things through...As long as it remains within my power to prevent it, there will be no blackout of peace in the United States.[49]" But just eighteen days after the loss of Athenia, FDR made a bold move. At his urging, Congress took up the question of whether or not to amend the Neutrality Act.

In November, the House of Representatives engaged in an extensive discussion regarding a dramatic move that would permit America to assist Britain and France. Edith Nourse Rogers, US Representative from Lowell, addressed her colleagues. "The changing of that law to aid one set of combatants after the countries had gone to war would be, in effect, unneutral. When we lift the embargo...we cross the gap from peace to war." She offered a solution. "It is far better to speed up our national defense to such a state of efficiency that no nation would dare to attack us.[50]" Her speech was met with applause from House members. Senator Walsh agreed. "Why should the United States...risk its future happiness and security by taking sides in a fight in which it has no real concern...We should have learned our lesson from the last war.[51]" Roosevelt emerged victorious from the debate. Two months after the sinking of the Athenia, Congress passed a new version of the Neutrality Act, which allowed belligerent countries to purchase, or to "cash and carry," badly needed war materials.

This historic step seems out of character for a man who, in 1940, loudly proclaimed from a podium in Boston, "Your boys are not going to be sent into any foreign wars." However, writer Peter Kross notes, "The president's rhetoric was for public consumption only.[52]" Behind the scenes, Franklin Delano Roosevelt was a very different man. Charming and affable on the surface, he was a consummate politician who kept his eye on the polls. First Lady Eleanor Roosevelt stated, "Franklin always said that no leader should get too far ahead of his followers." When a speech by popular aviator Charles Lindbergh advocated for non-intervention and warned that war would be brought to America only through "quarreling and meddling in affairs abroad," Representative George Holden Tinkham of Boston expressed his agreement. "He has given a message to the American people such as a patriotic American President should give." Roosevelt chose to remain silent.[53]

In reality, FDR had already set off down the path toward arming America. The new cash and carry policy was proclaimed a defensive measure, but as Edith Nourse Rogers had pointed out, it was a very "unneutral" act. In the background, pushing and prodding the American president toward war, was the cigar-smoking, hard-drinking, brilliant, and brusque Englishman Winston Churchill. Unlike Roosevelt, his agenda was clear. One week after becoming Prime Minister, his son Randolph asked if he thought Britain could defeat Germany. His father's response was, "Of course we can beat them. I shall drag the United States in."

In the months that followed, Churchill laid the foundation of a friendship that would save Britain and the world. Correspondence from the Prime Minister reveals carefully crafted messages aimed at leading Roosevelt to the realization that England and Europe would fall to the Nazis without American support. In May 1940: "...the scene has darkened swiftly...countries are simply smashed up, one by one, like matchwood...I trust you realize, Mr. President, that the voice and force of the United States may count for nothing if they are withheld too long." That Fall, a Destroyers for Bases Agreement was signed. In December, another communication from London: "Unless we can establish our ability to feed this island, to import the munitions of all kinds which we need...we may fall by the way, and the time needed

---

[49] *Roosevelt's Address.* Fitchburg Sentinel 9/5/1939. Newspapers.com. tinyurl.com/ycybpfn5.

[50] *House Reps 11/2/1939.* Cong Record House. tinyurl.com/mputrmhw.

[51] *America First Urges Walsh.* Harvard Crimson 11/16/1939. tinyurl.com/2th3csd8.

[52] Kross, Peter. *Roosevelt Prepared US.* Warfare Hist Network 7/2007. tinyurl.com/bdc2rhta.

[53] Meacham, Jon. *Franklin and Winston.* Random House Trade Paperback 2003.

by the United States to complete her defensive preparations may not be forthcoming.[54]" The Lend-Lease Program would follow three months later.

Spurred on by Churchill and emboldened by his own third-term re-election, Roosevelt gave a pivotal speech during his final Fireside Chat of 1940. "If Great Britain goes down, the Axis powers will control the continents of Europe, Asia, Africa, Australasia, and the high seas...It is no exaggeration to say that all of us, in all the Americas, would be living at the point of a gun." America would rise to the challenge. America would become the "Arsenal of Democracy." In spite of Roosevelt's assertiveness, the restless Churchill was impatient. He would later write that the British had "held the fort ALONE till those who hitherto had been half blind were half ready." Ironically within a year, it would not be Churchill who would catapult America into war.

As the world marched inescapably toward war, Americans held fast. In May 1940, the German Army pushed forward through the Netherlands, Belgium, and France, and Britain rushed to their defense. The nation, however, failed to heed this ominous foreshadowing. A Gallup poll taken less than one week later showed a stunning 93 percent did not support US engagement in war.[55] In the Spring of 1941, battle raged around the Libyan port of Tobruk; Hitler announced, "I have decided to destroy Yugoslavia," and Heinrich Himmler ordered the construction of a new camp for 100,000 inmates that would become known as Birkenau. In light of the horror that was sweeping across Europe, polls began to show a slight shift in attitude. Consistently throughout the next nine months, less than two-thirds of Americans favored helping her allies in some way with the war effort. All that was about to change.

In the early morning hours of Sunday, December 7, 1941, Japan staged a vicious and unprovoked attack on the US Naval Base at Pearl Harbor. Just five days later, an overwhelming 97 percent of those polled approved of going to war.[56] Overnight, the United States had undergone a radical change. An attack upon America, upon the free peoples of the world, would not be tolerated.

Shortly after the attack, Admiral Isoroku Yamamoto, Commander-in-Chief of the Japanese Combined Fleet and architect of the Pearl Harbor assault, reportedly wrote in his diary: "I fear all we have done is to awaken a sleeping giant and fill him with a terrible resolve."

---

[54] Meacham, Jon. *Franklin and Winston.*

[55] *Opinion WWII Change?* USHMM. Am and Holocaust. tinyurl.com/56t7wv66.

[56] Saad, Lydia. *Country Unified.*

Chapter 2

To Arms

Wars may be fought with weapons, but they are won by men.
General George S. Patton

In 1939, when the German Army marched into Poland, Adolph Hitler had more than three million men at his disposal. Following World War I, the Treaty of Versailles limited Germany's military force to 100,000 men and barred the development of an air force. Yet in 1935, a brazen Hitler announced to the world that Germany would rearm the Fatherland. The Luftwaffe had already become a reality, and conscription would now provide a formidable fighting force. He cautioned, "Whoever lights the torch of war in Europe can wish for nothing but chaos."

Across the Atlantic, Americans watched stoically, stubbornly clinging to their isolationist ideology, as Austria, Czechoslovakia, and Poland fell. Yet the numbers could not be denied. Should the United States be attacked, an Army of 200,000 men would face an enemy three million strong. A cautious FDR had begun slowly building up American production of war materials in the hopes of providing desperately needed weapons and supplies to the British. Within this escalation was an agenda aimed at beefing up the country's ability to defend itself. But in the months following the fall of Poland, there would be no pivotal moment, no snap of the fingers when the United States magically transformed into a massive mobilization machine. Rather, in the words of historian James Hewes, "The nation gradually drifted from neutrality to active belligerency between September 1939 and December 1941.[1]"

In the spring of 1940, with the November election looming, Roosevelt was reticent to blatantly announce a buildup. Negative press meant fewer votes and, as author Warren Kimball points out, "Roosevelt played to the numbers.[2]" In the absence of a crisis, he needed to bide his time. On June 10, an opportunity arose. In a speech to the people of Italy, Dictator Benito Mussolini proclaimed: "Fighters of the land, sea, and air, Blackshirts of the revolution and the legions, men and women of Italy...listen! The hour destined by fate is sounding for us...A declaration of war already has been handed to the Ambassadors of Great Britain and France."

On the train to his son's law school graduation, Roosevelt was irate. A copy of his typed speech reveals a last-minute edit in the President's own handwriting. As he stood at the podium in the University of Virginia Law School gymnasium later that day, he declared, "On this 10th day of June 1940, the hand that held the dagger has struck it into the back of its neighbor." He continued: "We will pursue two obvious and simultaneous courses: we will extend to the opponents of force the material resources of this nation; and, at the same time, we will harness and speed up the use of those resources in order that we ourselves in the Americas may have equipment and training equal to the task of any emergency and every defense."

"It was a curious trip," remembered Eleanor Roosevelt. "Franklin's address was not just a commencement address; it was a speech to the nation on an event that had brought us one step nearer to total war.[3]" The President's mask had slipped. He had propelled America forward, out from behind its protective isolationist wall. Before the year was out, the country would become the "arsenal of

---

[1] Hewes, James E. Jr. *Root to McNamara*. Ctr Mil Hist 1975. US Army. history.army.mil/books/root/chapter2.htm.

[2] Kimball, Warren F. *Roosevelt and WWII*. Pres Studies Quarterly 2004. JSTOR. tinyurl.com/4u72h9ct.

[3] Meacham, Jon. *Franklin and Winston*. Random House Trade Paperbacks 2004.

democracy." In his speech to the Italian nation, Mussolini spoke these prophetic words: "Italians...when one has a friend, one marches with him to the end. This we have done and will continue to do with Germany, her people, and her victorious armed forces." Mussolini had irrevocably linked the fate of the Italian nation with Hitler. So be it. America would prepare for war.

General George Marshall, US Army Chief of Staff, was well aware of the developing situation in Europe. Marshall knew that together French and English forces had been unable to overcome the Nazis in France. U-boats were ravaging shipping in the North Atlantic. War was surely on the horizon, and he cautioned Congress that enlisted ranks were too low and inadequate to respond to a national emergency. In September 1940, as a strategic precaution, President Roosevelt ordered the activation of tens of thousands of National Guardsmen across the United States for a year's worth of training. Such a massive endeavor hadn't been undertaken since the Great War. When war finally broke out over a year later, Guard units were already on active duty, and four of the first five US Army divisions to participate in offensive combat belonged to the National Guard.

When the troops were called out by FDR in September, 2,200 of them were from Massachusetts.[4] The Bay State has significant ties to the National Guard. The group traces its history to the Massachusetts Bay Colony, which established a force to protect colonists in 1636. Several Massachusetts regiments are the only units in the US Army whose predecessors fought at Lexington and Concord, and the 181st was the first federal regiment to shed blood in the Civil War. The 1940 mobilization permitted over 100 non-commissioned National Guard officers to receive the rank of second lieutenant, a chance that previously would have only occurred from a vacancy in the regular Army. The promotions created a situation where some Guard units suddenly had more officers than required. Some of the new lieutenants were assigned to fill positions in the 211th Anti-Aircraft Regiment and 241st Coast Artillery.

241st Coast Artillery at Sagamore Hill
near Cape Cod Canal. WWII.[5]

Shifting from the civilian world to army life in 1940, Coast Artillery Regiments under Brookline resident Col. Stuart G. Hall then headed to Camp Edwards in Falmouth, but like others in the northern US, the base was pressed to find suitable winter lodgings for troops. Established in the early 1930s as the Massachusetts Military Reservation between Bourne, Falmouth, and Sandwich, the camp could usually hold a thousand men. Once extra wooden tent platforms were built, Edwards could take another five hundred. However, since cold weather was just around the corner, the 211th Coast Artillery was

---

[4] *2200 Join Army Today.* Boston Globe 9/16/1940. ProQuest. tinyurl.com/n6u9kdu2.

[5] *Sagamore Hill Cape Cod.* Pub domain photo. USACE. Wikipedia. tinyurl.com/3s6kkx7a.

moved to Camp Hulen in Texas. The 241st Coast Artillery Regiment was deployed to the Boston Harbor Islands, where the First Coast Artillery District maintained tent space for 1,252 troops.[6]

Elected in 1940 to his second term, Massachusetts Governor Leverett Saltonstall was left with a severely depleted National Guard. In an effort to replace the guardsmen who had been absorbed into the Army, he proclaimed September 21st as National Guard Day and called for volunteers. It was Saltonstall's desire to "fill vacancies with the very best possible young men; rugged, bright, eager to learn.[7]" The Governor's call was met with lukewarm enthusiasm, and by November, just over 500 recruits were inducted.[8]

In spite of the fact that the call for reinforcements was made with some sense of urgency, many patriotic volunteers were deliberately ignored. Emmett J. Scott Jr., an MIT graduate, war veteran, and once the highest-ranking African American in the Wilson Administration, criticized the Army's failure to mobilize hundreds of black reservists. His words were published in the *Hartford-Springfield Chronicle*:

They resent, and they have a right to resent, the haughty attitude of army brass hats who look upon them with contempt and deny them the privilege of even having the Negro units of the National Guard brought up to authorized limits. Even now, the National Guard is nearly 12,000 under authorized strength, and here is a shortage that could be easily taken up by colored applicants if our army officials were more just and more fair than they are now.[9]

Among National Guard units mustered during World War II was the famed 26th Infantry. Prior to WWII, the "Yankee Division" trained at Fort Devens. As part of General George Patton's Third Army and under the command of Worcester native Maj. Gen. Willard S. Paul, the unit saw extensive action in the northern European theater and Germany and was present at the Battle of the Bulge. On May 5, 1945, the Yankee division entered the Gusen concentration camp. This branch of the Mauthausen Camp was established to provide slave labor for digging tunnels to a massive, undergrown industrial complex. With the approach of the Allies, the SS plan to collapse the tunnels with Gusen prisoners inside was foiled by the men of the 26th Infantry. By the end of World War II, the brave men of the 26th Infantry had sustained over 10,000 casualties.[10]

26th Infantry "Yankee" Division at
Camp Edwards. February 1941.[11]

---

[6] *Army Inspect Defenses.* Boston Globe 9/29/1940. ProQuest. tinyurl.com/rx6zcmm4.

[7] *Duty Boston Harbor.* Boston Globe 9/21/1940. ProQuest. tinyurl.com/59mz4xcw.

[8] *Volunteers Inducted Monday.* Boston Globe 11/16/1940. Newspapers.com. tinyurl.com/45nvyc94.

[9] Scott, Emmett J. *Nat Defense & Negro.* Hartford-Springfield Chron 6/15/1940. Chron Am. LOC. tinyurl.com/3mtpkuyn.

[10] *26th Infantry WWII.* Holocaust Encyc. USHMM. tinyurl.com/3p8pmekw.

[11] *Yankee Deactivated.* Pub domain photo. *On this day* 2/16/2024. MA Nat Guard. tinyurl.com/3f7ahnwm.

When war erupted in Europe, America was on a short list of countries without mandatory training for its armed forces. The concept of conscription was not unknown. The first draft law was enacted during the Civil War, and by the end of World War I, over two and a half million men had been called into service. Moving ahead with plans to ready his country for war, Roosevelt understood the need for conscription. However, the country had never held a peace time draft, and there was significant concern that this would be a controversial act. In addition to those who favored non-intervention, many members of the clergy, unions, and educators spoke out against a draft.

Behind the scenes, working diligently to advance the notion of selective service, was the extraordinary Grenville Clark. Born in New York into wealth, prestige, and promise, Clark had very strong ties to Massachusetts. A graduate of Harvard Law School, in 1931, he joined the college's governing board, the Harvard Corporation. He was a member of Boston's exclusive Somerset Club and married Bostonian Fanny Dwight. Grenville Clark was a man of conscience. His Harvard Square Library profile describes him as "a man of independence, financially and politically, who devotes himself as hard to public affairs as a private citizen as he would were he in public office." He used his connections and power to influence public policy, always in a quiet and unassuming manner, earning him the nickname "statesman incognito.[12]" Clark stated, "There is no limit to the good a man can do if he doesn't care who gets the credit.[13]"

Prior to the first World War, Clark and a group of associates established the Military Training Camps Association to assist the country in preparedness for war.[14] Now, on the eve of World War II, Clark stepped forward once again. Author John G. Clifford stated: "More than any other man, Grenville Clark deserved the title, 'father of the Selective Service.'" In May of 1940, Clark and his colleagues began designing a plan that four months later would become law. With FDR watching silently from the sidelines, Clark's team set about finding sponsors for their bill. Republican Representative James Wadsworth of New York quickly agreed. For a short time, the influential Massachusetts Senator Henry Cabot Lodge Jr. was considered, and while he would later vote for the legislation, differences of opinion led to his being excluded. Eventually, a "lame duck, Roosevelt-hating Democrat from Nebraska," Edward R. Burke, was chosen.[15] By the end of June, without White House involvement, the bill was in the hands of the Senate.

For two months, the debate droned on in Congress, but with the Democratic Convention slated for July, the President publicly remained noncommittal. As war in Europe continued to escalate, pro-draft public opinion slowly gained strength. General Lewis Hershey, who would become Director of the Selective Service, later stated, "Every time Hitler bombed London, we got another couple of [congressional] votes." By June 1940, a Gallup Poll showed 64 percent approval for a draft.[16]

Discussion continued until August 26, when Republican Party Chairman and Representative from Massachusetts Joseph Martin announced that this was no longer a partisan issue and that each member should follow his own conscience.[17] In the House of Representatives, the debate turned ugly when Congressman Martin Sweeney of Ohio claimed the legislation was a trick to get the US to enter the war. His colleague, Beverly Vincent of Kentucky, responded by calling him "a son of a bitch." Sweeney swung a fist at his colleague, and what ensued, according to the House doorkeeper, was "the best fistfight he had witnessed in his 50 years at his post.[18]"

---

[12] Clifford, J. Garry. *Clark, Grenville.* HSL. tinyurl.com/y35hf5cu.

[13] *Grenville Clark.* Global Governance Forum 2020. tinyurl.com/2tm3zjxt.

[14] Drinker, Henry S. *Mil Training Camps.* Mil Engineer 1931. JSTOR. tinyurl.com/ade3xvws.

[15] Clifford, John. *G. Clark Select Service.* Rev Politics. CUP 1973. tinyurl.com/346nxb6z.

[16] Raymond, Wm Jr. *Uncle Sam says.* US Army CMD/Gen Staff College. DTIC. tinyurl.com/4kcpsxw7.

[17] Clifford, John G. *Grenville Clark.*

[18] Persico, Joseph. *We Almost Lost the Army.* Am Heritage 2012. tinyurl.com/ykrert9k.

On September 14, 1940, the Selective Service Act passed. Massachusetts Senators Henry Cabot Lodge Jr. (Republican) and David Walsh (Democrat) split the vote. In order to join the army, Lodge would later resign his position as a United States Senator when the very law he voted for forbade members of Congress to enlist.

Veteran Senator David I. Walsh greets rookie
Senator Henry Cabot Lodge, Jr.[19]

Sixty-five percent of the Senate approved the bill. The House passed the legislation as well with a vote of 263-149. Of the Massachusetts Representatives voting, eight Republicans and four Democrats voted yea. One dissenting vote was cast by Republican George Tinkham of Boston.[20] Two days later, the Selective Service Act became law.

Roosevelt continued to portray the Selective Service Act as a purely defensive measure. A month after signing the bill during a speech in Boston to derail the campaign of Representative Joseph Martin of North Attleboro, he stated: "Your boys are not going to be sent into any foreign wars. They are going into training to form a force so strong that, by its very existence, it will keep the threat of war far away from our shores. The purpose of our defense is defense." In fact, the conditions of the Selective Service Act limited enlistment to a period of one year, with no recruits being assigned outside the Western Hemisphere. Men aged twenty-one to thirty-five would be required to register. A classification system was established to identify those who were fit to serve, those who would be deferred, and those who would be granted Conscientious Objector status. These decisions rested in the hands of draft boards comprised of residents from local communities acting under the supervision of state governors. Finally, a lottery system was instituted to determine which individuals would be called up for duty.

Established by Executive Order in April 1942, the War Manpower Commission was responsible for coordinating and facilitating the mobilization and utilization of manpower.   Joining the all-male membership was Frances Perkins. A longtime advocate for the working class, she was born in Boston, raised in Worcester, and educated at Mount Holyoke College in South Hadley. In 1933, Perkins became the first-ever female member of a US Presidential Cabinet when FDR appointed her as Labor Secretary. In addition to addressing the needs of industry, agriculture, and civilians, the Committee was charged with implementing the Selective Service Act. Draft Boards fell under this umbrella.

---

[19] *Veterans advice for Senator.* Pub domain photo. 2016871078 LOC. Wiki Commons. tinyurl.com/fd7j4k34.

[20] *Conf Report Selec Service Act* 9/14/1940. Govtrack. tinyurl.com/msvscakc.

Labor Secretary Frances Perkins (seated second from right) War Manpower Commission. May 1942.[21]

Draft board members carried a heavy burden during the war years. Among the more troubling duties was assigning classification to each registrant. From 1A to 4F, men were chosen or discarded based on a strict set of guidelines. Those holding jobs in agriculture or industries required for national defense were excluded. Marriage was not on the list for deferment, but many jumped at the chance to use it as an excuse or perhaps to ensure someone would be waiting when the war was over. In 1942 alone, weddings reached a high of 1.8 million, 83% more than had occurred a decade before.[22] Babies, however, were a different story. Classification IIIA was specifically designed to defer men with dependents, and US birth rates reached peak levels ten months after the Selective Service Act became law. Temporary deferment was available to college students.

The lingering effects of the Depression impacted the draft. Within a year after selection began, poor medical care and lack of education would lead to the rejection of nearly half of all draftees. However, bad teeth, bad eyesight, and illiteracy would soon no longer be exemptions as the government sought to fill the hungry draft quota by providing treatment and education for inductees. With fewer restrictions on medical deferment, Hollywood was affected, too. An agent was quoted as saying, "I've got a prospect for you–a young guy with a double hernia.[23]"

Members of the clergy were deferred from service. Conscientious objectors, however, were not. Originally characterized as someone who opted not to fight due to religious beliefs, during World War II, men who declined due to personal convictions were classified as conscientious objectors. The government, seeing a use for these 50,000 draftees, offered them choices: work in war-related non-combatant jobs or go to jail. Many chose to serve as medics, while some served as chaplains. Through the Civilian Public Service Program, COs were employed in forestry, farm, and public works projects throughout the country. Forest Service Camps were established in Petersham, Royalston, and Ashburnham. CPS Unit 97, an Agriculture Experiment Station located in Worcester, was supervised by the Mennonite Central Committee. Several members of this dairy farm unit were associated with the Mennonite community in Lancaster. Scientific Research and Development projects were operated in Boston and Cambridge. CPS 115 at Massachusetts General Hospital used volunteer COs as subjects of air and water temperature experiments for seawater research.[24]

Not all chose to join their country in the war effort. Six thousand COs opted for jail. Ronald Bailey, in *The Homefront: U.S.A.,* speculates that one out of six inmates in federal prison was a conscientious objector. An interesting story comes from the infamous convicted murderer Louis Lempke.

[21] *War Manpower Comm.* Pub domain photo. US OWI. LOC. Wikipedia. tinyurl.com/df2t7msh.

[22] Yellen, Emily. *Wartime Weddings.* Weddings NY Times 2/2/2017. tinyurl.com/5665bcpt.

[23] Bailey, Ronald H, and Eds. *Home Front: USA WWII.* Time-Life Books 1978.

[24] *Conscientious Objector Camps.* Civ Pub Service. Mennonite Central Comm. tinyurl.com/3zku7mbc.

While serving time in prison, Lempke had difficulty understanding the concept of conscientious objector and, amazed, asked, "You mean they put you in here for *not* killing?[25]"

The conscientious objector path was often not an easy one. Many experienced harassment or were treated as outcasts. Most, however, were loyal Americans who supported their country but who could not in good conscience kill another human being. William K. Hefner, later a professor at UMASS Amherst, was classified as a CO and spent time employed in CPS projects doing war-related work.[26] Stephen Siteman, a resident of Greenfield, spent time in prison for his beliefs and was later pardoned.[27] Both would go on to become prominent advocates for social justice. And one man, medic Desmond Doss, a Seventh-Day Adventist from Virginia, would receive the Congressional Medal of Honor for saving seventy-five lives on Hacksaw Ridge in Okinawa.

The first step toward induction occurred on R-Day, October 16, 1940, when all eligible men were required to register with local draft boards. Over 16,000,000 responded that day. Few were exempt from registration. Nearly 5,000 Harvard University staff and students, two Kennedy brothers,[28] and prisoners in the Massachusetts Department of Corrections were all placed on the rolls. Across the country, over 100,000 inmates would be called up before the end of the war.[29]

Lt. John F. Kennedy, USNR. March 1944.[30]

A few days prior to R-Day, one Massachusetts Draft Board met to begin making difficult decisions. Their experiences were recounted in a 1945 *Yank Magazine* article. Residents of the towns of Norwood, Foxboro, and Sharon fell under the umbrella of Local Board No. 119. Appointments to the board were made by Gov. Leverett Saltonstall, and in 1942, four of the five members were veterans of the First World War. Chairman Russell McKenzie owned a Foxboro car sales and service company. Ed Flaherty and Charles Houghton had government experience, the former as Chairman of the Norwood Board of Assessors and the latter who served on the draft board in World War I. The fifth member, Henry Crosby, managed a Norwood tannery.

On October 16, just over 5,500 local men and boys registered. Patriotism ran high, and most men felt duty-bound to serve. Some men went to great lengths to be inducted. Three young men who had been rejected (flat feet, punctured ear drum, ulcers) made their way to Boston, loudly proclaiming that

---

[25] Bailey, Ronald H, and Eds. *Home Front: USA WWII.*

[26] *William Hefner Papers.* Robert Cox Collections. UMASS Amherst Lib. tinyurl.com/3pctswr2.

[27] *Stephen Siteman Papers.* Robert Cox Collections. UMASS Amherst Lib. tinyurl.com/2pn24auh.

[28] Dickson, Paul. *Uncle Sam's Got Your Number.* HISTORY.NET 12/2020. tinyurl.com/46fwefz2.

[29] Bailey, Ronald H, and Ed. *Home Front: USA WWII.*

[30] *JF Kennedy.* Pub domain photo. NAID 80-G-165141. NHHC. tinyurl.com/ympzv89d.

their Draft Board didn't want them. Eventually taken in by authorities for being a public nuisance, they stated, "We thought maybe you'd make us fight if we stirred up enough trouble." Just before he was to report to the board for transport to Fort Devens, Alex Smith's wife became seriously ill. His neighbor, Jim Kelly, came up with a solution. With the Board's help, Kelly went off to war instead of Smith. Some draftees were just plain irate. Eighteen-year-old Michael Campiseno was drafted before he could finish his senior year at Norwood High School. He vowed that if he made it back, he'd march into the Draft Board, pitch his discharge papers at the Chairman, and say, "Now, ya sonuvabitch, I hope you're satisfied!" After eighteen months as a Combat Engineer in the European theater, Campiseno came home older, wiser, and humbler.

One of the more unusual stories involves Lawrence Tilton of Foxboro. An exceptionally tall and muscular young man who looked older than his fourteen years, he changed his name, lied about his age, and joined the Navy. Using his formidable swimming skills, Tilton trained for Navy Underwater Demolition duty. His remarkable journey brought him to waters off the coast of France, where he placed markers in the English Channel to guide ships on their way to the D-Day invasion. While under heavy fire, Tilton dove into the water to cut loose a group of mines that blocked the passage of his ship as it approached the shore, actions for which he would receive a Silver Star and the French Croix de Guerre. The Navy, grateful as they were, frowned upon fourteen-year-olds in their ranks and sent him back to Foxboro with an honorable discharge. When the young man reported to Draft Board No. 119 for severance from the Navy, he was told, "Sorry, son, you're not old enough to register. Come back when you're 18."

The Board's role continued after each draftee fulfilled his obligation. A Rehabilitation Committee, with members from the fields of medicine, business, and education, worked to help veterans re-acclimate to civilian life. The Committee assisted men in finding jobs, addressing medical issues, and enrolling in apprentice training, refresher courses, and colleges. The grateful state of Massachusetts provided each veteran with a $100 bonus on discharge. Of the millions of Americans who served during World War II, just over 2,000 began their journey at Draft Board 119. Sadly, 75 heroes never returned.[31]

In Washington D.C., on October 29, 1940, in an elaborately planned theatrical event, the first draft numbers were drawn. The President addressed those who were about to enter service to their country.

You who will enter this peacetime army will be the inheritors of a proud history and an honorable tradition. You will be members of an army which first came together to achieve independence and establish certain fundamental rights for all men. Ever since that first muster, our democratic army has existed for one purpose only: the defense of our freedom...You have the confidence, and the gratitude, and the love of your countrymen. We are all with you in the task which enlists the services of all Americans—the task of keeping the peace in this New World of ours.

Included in this speech were excerpts from letters sent by clergy of the Protestant, Jewish, and Catholic denominations. Massachusetts native and former Auxiliary Bishop of Boston, Francis J. Spellman, wrote in support of the draft. "I do believe it is better to have protection and not need it than to need protection and not have it. I do believe that Americans want peace but that we must be prepared to demand it, for other people have wanted peace, and the peace they received was the peace of death.[32]"

When Secretary of War Henry Stimson stepped up to the fishbowl from which numbers would be drawn, he was blindfolded with a scrap of upholstery material from a chair used during the signing

---

[31] Sleeper, Marvin. *DRAFT BOARD 119*. Yank Magazine 1945. Old Mag Articles 2008. tinyurl.com/y3f9y7ze.

[32] *Roosevelt: Drawing Selec Service*. American Presid Proj. tinyurl.com/29mysp7j.

of the Declaration of Independence. The bowl, a remnant of the 1917 draft lottery,[33] contained over 7,000 numbers in capsules and entered the hall in a procession of 500 World War I veterans. Before the drawing began, capsules were stirred using a wooden spoon taken from a beam at Philadelphia's Independence Hall. Stimson reached into the bowl, slowly withdrew a capsule, and handed it to Roosevelt. Across the country, men gasped, and mothers and wives cried. Number 158...6,175 men would be the first to go.[34] Alden C. Flagg Jr. of Boston was one of them. More than two decades before, Flagg's father had been drafted when his number, the first drawn in the World War I draft, had been pulled from the very same fishbowl.[35]

Broadcaster and Taunton native Stephen J. McCormick
points to his own number as it is posted in the Selective
Service Lottery while he was on the air. 1940.[36]

Owing to the inconsistent and, at times, confusing prewar buildup of the American war machine, difficulties existed with readiness for induction. Mobilization plans were created and discarded, and boards to oversee the process were appointed and disbanded. A sequencing problem developed. Should manpower precede material or the other way around? Thousands of men would be inducted before the end of 1940. Would the government be ready for them? In his book *Freedom's Forge,* Arthur Herman described the concerns of Army Chief of Staff General George Marshall: "Everything from rifles (the Army was still using the '03 Springfield model) and machine guns to telephone cable and medicine was in chronic short supply, and ...trainees would have to train using wooden guns and fire on wooden boxes labeled tanks, and fire salvos of artillery from tree stumps labeled artillery.[37]" The Army even counted a horse cavalry unit among its elite mobile forces. When young Col. Dwight Eisenhower suggested using horsepower generated from gasoline rather than oats, he was threatened with court martial.[38] In addition, the Selective Service Act required the government to provide quarters for the men inducted, but existing military bases lacked enough housing for incoming troops, and funding to build up camps hadn't been appropriated until August.

The government quickly went into the building business. Camp Blanding in Florida provides an illustration. During the summer of 1940, National Guard troops from New England were sent to the base

---

[33] Bailey, Ronald H, and Eds. *Home Front: USA WWII.*

[34] Dickson, Paul. *Uncle Sam's Got Your Number.*

[35] Fretts, Bruce. *Fifty Years Ago.* Am Heritage Sept/Oct 1990. tinyurl.com/ycy3wyda.

[36] *Stephen McCormick number.* Pub domain photo. US FWA. LOC. LC-USZ62-75209. tinyurl.com/yszyrs4d.

[37] Herman, Arthur. *Freedom's Forge.* Random House Trade Paperbacks 2013.

[38] Dickson, Paul. *Marshall's Preparations.* Am Heritage 9/2020. tinyurl.com/99awd4k8.

for training. Due to the lack of housing, the men were forced to stay at nearby Jacksonville Municipal Airport for a year. In the meantime, the War Department decided that a larger camp would be needed in three months, this time for 40,000 men. The local labor force fell far short of manpower needs, and eventually, men in search of employment began arriving from across the country, 300 of whom were from Boston. As construction on the camp reached its peak, $2.5 million a month flowed out of government coffers into workers' paychecks, and Stark, Florida, once a sleepy little town of 1,500 residents, became a boomtown. Due to this "draft-driven expansion of the army," over 100 new camps would be constructed to accommodate recruits.[39]

Two months after the Selective Service Act became law, the first soldiers were inducted into the US Army. Men reported to induction centers across the country. Due to time differences, New Englanders would be the first. After a physical exam, vaccinations, fingerprinting, and taking the oath of office, the newest members of the United States Army were shipped off to basic training. John Edward Lawton of Everett became the first man drafted in World War II when the four men ahead of him failed physical examination and were rejected. The previous year, the 21-year-old had been unemployed when he took a job on a WPA project. After being sworn in, the young man who had just made history stated, "The government helped me out when I needed it, and I'm only too glad to be of service to the government now.[40]"

Boot camp, named for leggings worn by soldiers in the First World War, was the next stop. It was an exciting experience for many. Bases operated across the country, and young men traveled to exotic locations like Fort Hood, Texas; Fort Ord, California; and Fort Benning, Georgia. In Massachusetts, Fort Devens and Camp Edwards taught young men the art of soldiering. During the early years of the war, the draft provided men exclusively for the Army. The Navy relied on volunteer enlistment and operated basic training camps in California, New York, Maryland, and Rhode Island.

For recruits, it was an abrupt shift to Army life. One sergeant, having difficulty quieting a new group about to be sworn in, politely requested, "Gentlemen, please be quiet." Immediately after the oath was administered, he shouted, "Now, goddam it, SHUT UP![41]" Boot camp was a school of sorts where recruits learned about following orders, unit solidarity, marching, handling weapons, and then marching some more. They dropped exhausted into bunks at night in barracks shared by a score of others just like themselves. Infectious diseases caused major disruption in basic training, and many soldiers fell ill with gastrointestinal and respiratory illnesses, measles, and malaria. Once camp was over, some went on to schools to learn specialized skills. For most, there was a final stop at a staging point like Camp Myles Standish in Taunton, where they received last-minute instructions before being moved to Ports of Embarkation such as Boston and deployed overseas.

Though he joined the military late in the war, the experience of Canadian Earl Rudolph Fitch was in some ways typical for new recruits. A citizen of Great Britain, he moved to this country from Nova Scotia during the Depression. At age seventeen, he watched as men and boys from his Worcester neighborhood were called up to serve. This quiet young man of principle felt the need to give back to his new country and stand alongside his friends in war. The local draft board quickly rejected him. "Come back when you're older," he was told, "or see if you can get your parents to agree." His father, who had served in the Canadian Army during the First World War, gave his approval. Earl joined the Navy, where one of his first acts as a sailor was to become a citizen of the United States.

Basic training at Fort Sampson in New York was followed by radar school in Norfolk, VA. One of the drawbacks of boot camp was exposure to communicable diseases, and for the young Canadian-

---

[39] Klein, Maury. *Call to Arms*. Bloomsbury Press 2013.

[40] *Army's No. 1 Conscript*. Springfield Daily Repub 11/19/1940. Newspapers.com. tinyurl.com/ mvhwyret.

[41] Bailey, Ronald H, and Eds. *Home Front: USA WWII*.

American, it meant tonsillitis and removal from the radar school roster. After being released from the hospital, Earl missed his second school assignment when he was diagnosed with measles. Early in 1945, he was sent to the Brooklyn Navy Yard, where he became a plank owner on the newly constructed USS Cone. Thankfully, Earl Fitch made it home. On his first voyage, while his ship lay at anchor in Cuba, the war ended.

Throughout World War II, the United States relied heavily on the draft to provide manpower. While millions stepped forward to register and be inducted, many neglected their duties. In May of 1943, the *North Adams Transcript* reported that J. Edgar Hoover and the FBI had tracked down over 36,000 men, and of those, 4,002 "willful violators" were sentenced to a total of 8,724 years in prison.[42] The Selective Service Act went through multiple changes. There would be six more registrations during World War II. The age span would extend from 18 to 64 years, and even FDR would be issued a draft card. Volunteer enlistments would be terminated, and all men would enter service through the registration/induction process. With the close of the war and growing stability in the world, President Harry S. Truman brought the draft to an end in 1947.

REGISTRATION CARD—(Men born on or after April 28, 1877 and on or before February 16, 1897)

SERIAL NUMBER	1. NAME (Print)			ORDER NUMBER
U.__ 2.	Franklin	Delano	Roosevelt	
	(First)	(Middle)	(Last)	

2. PLACE OF RESIDENCE (Print)
1600 Pennsylvania Avenue, N.W., Washington, District of Columbia
(Number and street) (Town, township, village, or city) (County) (State)
[THE PLACE OF RESIDENCE GIVEN ON THE LINE ABOVE WILL DETERMINE LOCAL BOARD JURISDICTION; LINE 2 OF REGISTRATION CERTIFICATE WILL BE IDENTICAL]

3. MAILING ADDRESS
1600 Pennsylvania Avenue, N.W., Washington D.C.
[Mailing address if other than place indicated on line 2. If same insert word same]

4. TELEPHONE	5. AGE IN YEARS			6. PLACE OF BIRTH
	Sixty			Hyde Park
				(Town or county)
	DATE OF BIRTH			
National 1414	January 30		1882	New York
(Exchange) (Number)	(Mo.)	(Day)	(Yr.)	(State or country)

7. NAME AND ADDRESS OF PERSON WHO WILL ALWAYS KNOW YOUR ADDRESS
Mrs. Franklin D. Roosevelt

8. EMPLOYER'S NAME AND ADDRESS
U.S.

9. PLACE OF EMPLOYMENT OR BUSINESS
1600 Penn. Ave.   Washington D.C.
(Number and street or R. F. D. number)   (Town)   (County)   (State)

I AFFIRM THAT I HAVE VERIFIED ABOVE ANSWERS AND THAT THEY ARE TRUE.

D.S.S. Form 1   (over)   16—21630—2   (signed) Franklin D. Roosevelt
(Revised 4-1-42)   (Registrant's signature)

FDR's World War II Draft Card.[43]

A 1940 book published in Japan, *The Asian Race and the Pacific*, illustrates pre-war propaganda sentiment aimed at the United States. "The Americans, at their very core, are materialistic animals. To them, the only measure of success is how much they can own. They do not have a spiritual culture, or any culture with regards to their nation...America is shallow. It is morally corrupt.[44]" On December 8, 1941, John R. Borts of Lawrence stood first in line at the Post Office in Boston, waiting to enlist. By the end of the day, he would be joined by 1,000 others.[45] The day before, over 2,000 soldiers, sailors, and marines had lost their lives at the hands of the Japanese at Pearl Harbor. They would be replaced by thousands during the last twenty-three days of December, and by the end of the war, over 16 million courageous men and women from this "shallow" and "corrupt" nation would go to war, 6 million of them volunteers.

---

[42] *FBI Arrests 552.* No Adams Transcript 5/15/1943. Newspapers.com. tinyurl.com/bkeuzbvd.

[43] *Registration Card No. 2.* Public Domain Photo. #101348621. FamilySearch. tinyurl.com/y7c9bbue.

[44] Chang, Ellie. *Asian Race and Pacific 1940.* 5/16/2016. Imp Japanese Mil Research. tinyurl.com/mry7yj4p.

[45] Taylor, Robert. *New Eng Home Front WWII.* Yankee Books 1992.

Chapter 3

Camps and Bases

To say that a city has sprung up overnight...tells the story. Here, the year's long growth of another city has been crammed into a few weeks...Captain Brown of the Constructing Quartermaster's office tells of leaving bare ground when he started an inspection trip...and returning to his starting place to find a barracks standing on what had shortly before been open space.
1940's Radio Narrator[1]

It was 1939, and the path leading to war was unfolding at a frightening rate. Hitler was gobbling up Europe, Russia signed a non-aggression pact with Germany, and across the Atlantic, the United States waffled. Henry Stimson, who would soon become Secretary of War, stated, "All this talk of wait, wait, wait, and we're confronted by an enemy who does not wait.[2]" Less than a week after England declared war, President Roosevelt authorized an increase in military personnel to 227,000, followed just over six months later by a funding request for even more troops, facilities, and equipment. Congress declined. At that moment, however, the total number of available army personnel amounted to ten percent of Germany's force of over two million men. The nation, with its bulk of isolationist voters, had hemmed and hawed its way into a dangerous lack of preparedness.

With the advent of the Selective Service Act in 1940, sixteen million registered, and in the last two months of 1940, over 18,000 were inducted. The Act passed with the stipulation that the government could induct only the number of men it could house. Unfortunately, it took another month for the same Representatives and Senators to figure out that funding was necessary to pay for the promised housing.

As was most often the case, the Army and Navy attacked the problem with their own people, plans, and budgets. For the Army, the Quartermaster General called upon the Corps of Engineers to develop buildings and camps that could be constructed quickly using unskilled labor a minimum of materials, and that could be replicated in a variety of locations. Most would be placed inland, away from danger of attack, and in relatively flat areas easily accessible by train. The majority of camps would be located in the South, where the climate was more accommodating for year-round training. Frigid cold requiring heating fuel was frowned upon, but blistering heat, humidity, and relentless mosquitoes were just fine.

Unable to produce housing quickly enough for the mass of incoming recruits, the Army outsourced, hiring local contractors and using local materials whenever possible. It was a plan that would successfully accommodate the millions of recruits who would become the Army's fighting force over the next five years. During 1940 and 1941 alone, more than fifty camps were constructed. In the meantime, men were sleeping in hotels and in tents on runways and front lawns while training for war. To provide for them, the Army would expand and modernize several existing bases. The first of these was located in Massachusetts.

Prior to the Great War, the US Army was primarily populated by part-time militia, maintained and administered by individual states. The story of Camp Edwards began during this period when troops used nearby forests for training purposes. In 1935, the government purchased land, some state-owned, like Shawme-Crowell State Forest, and some private, such as that obtained from the Coonamesset Sheep Ranch. The area that would become Camp Edwards stretched from Bourne to Falmouth. During the next

---

[1] *Through Soldier's Eyes*. MA Nat Guard. tinyurl.com/34526dyn.

[2] Klein, Maury. *Call to Arms*. Bloomsbury Press 2013.

few years, the base grew to several dozen buildings and included Otis Field with its two turf runways. The increase in recruits due to the 1940 draft resulted in a rapid expansion of facilities at the camp.[3] Mary Lou Smith reported in her history of Falmouth:

Buildings [were] springing up like mushrooms, and there were jobs...for anyone who could swing a hammer. Several cottages were requisitioned by the Army, and tents sprung up on the grounds of the Tower Heights Hotel, Falmouth Marine Railways and Waquoit Yacht Club. Local gossip abounded that the Cape would be evacuated with the outbreak of war.[4]

In an amazing triumph, the Army pulled it off. With a payroll of over a million dollars a week, 18,000 workers labored around the clock, producing a mind-boggling thirty buildings a day.[5] In four months, a complex of 1,300 buildings, including stores, chapels, and water and sewage systems, was ready to house 30,000 men.

While the speed with which the base was built is legendary, the development of Camp Edwards is perhaps most extraordinary for its contribution to the craft of military base construction. When the Quartermaster General and Army Corps of Engineers developed a standardized plan for mobilization camps, included were designs for temporary structures known as the 700 series. Simplicity and ease of construction were hallmarks of these buildings, which could be adjusted to fulfill a variety of functions. Located in the south quarter of the cantonment area, T-1310 was one such structure. Its two floors could house sixty-three recruits, had unfinished flooring and walls, separate NCO quarters, heating and electrical systems, and lavatories. Plans were revised as needed during the construction process, and the end result was so successful that T-1310 became the model unit for basic training camps during World War II. This architectural marvel of military design still stands at Camp Edwards.[6]

T-1310 building, Camp Edwards. 1940.[7]

Troops began arriving in January 1941, 30,000 in all, at a time when the population of Cape Cod was 37,000. The first group to arrive was the 26th Infantry Division, the celebrated Yankee Division of the National Guard. Within a year, the men of the 26th would move on to active duty in the European theater, replaced by thousands of others. (When the 36th Division arrived in 1943, it took forty trains to move them to the base.)[8]

As each unit arrived, the role the camp played was adjusted and refined. When the 101st Observation Squadron of the National Guard arrived at Otis Field, concrete replaced turf on the runways, and Otis became home to a reconnaissance unit for the Ninth Air Force and later for the Army's 14th

---

[3] *Camp Edwards History*. MA Nat Guard. tinyurl.com/47mzcnpb.

[4] Smith, Mary Lou. *Book of Falmouth*. Falmouth Hist Comm 1986.

[5] *Camp Edwards History*. MA Nat Guard.

[6] *Camp Edwards Building T-1310*. HABS. NPS. tinyurl.com/48vj38nc.

[7] *Camp Edwards Building T-1310*. Pub domain photo. HABS. LOC. tinyurl.com/686r384j.

[8] Cann, Donald Jr. and Galluzzo, John J. *Images Edwards and Otis AFB*. Arcadia Publ 2010.

Anti-Submarine Patrol Squadron. The efforts of this group were so important that in 1944, all reconnaissance missions at Otis were placed under the administration of the US Navy. With the 64th Coastal Artillery Regiment in 1942, the base became the Army Anti-Aircraft Artillery Training Center. Recruits shot at targets towed by airplanes and learned to locate aircraft at night using searchlights.[9] Nearby Popponessett in Mashpee and Scorton Neck in Sandwich became firing ranges. WACs trained here as well, living in tents and fields near Mashpee Woods.[10] Shortly after the North Africa campaign, a section of the camp was set aside to house POWs.

Soldiers scaling a wall during training.
Camp Edwards. 1942.[11]

Camp Edwards embraced the spirit of creativity. To train soldiers for warfare in an urban setting, a replica of a German village named Deutschedorf was constructed on site. Flower boxes and birdhouses adorned streets along which were situated shops, restaurants, a beer garden, homes, and Gestapo headquarters.[12] The village came complete with a realistic latrine and a sign over the door proclaiming, "birthplace of the Fuehrer" (in German, of course). Inside, perched atop two holes presumably taking care of business, were wooden cutouts of Hitler and Japanese Prime Minister Tojo.[13]

One of the more notable training programs involved the newly created Engineer Amphibian Command. Organized shortly after Pearl Harbor, the Army found a pressing need to train troops for amphibious assault, and Camp Edwards, located near Cape Cod beaches, was chosen. The success of the program led to the development of two adjunct bases known as Camp Candoit in Cotuit and Camp Havedoneit in Osterville. Equipment included thirty-six-foot landing craft, which arrived by rail at the rate of thirty-two per day over a period of several weeks.[14] Soldiers learned how to board assault boats, off-load trucks, and drive through deep sand, and the newly designed DUKW was put through its paces on nearby beaches, as was the Aqua Cheetah, competitor of the SEEP (Sea Jeep). Brown water ops for river assaults were practiced on dry land and in water.

Perhaps the most memorable moment for the Amphibian Command came in October of 1942 when the training program ended with an invasion of Martha's Vineyard. The mission was to capture the island and defend it from enemy attack. Jackson Murphy, in his article for the *Martha's Vineyard Times*, described the event.

---

[9] *Camp Edwards History*. MA Nat Guard.

[10] Cimino, Anthony J. *Camp Edwards WWII*. 1993.

[11] *Camp Edwards up and over wall*. Pub domain photo. USASC. LOC. tinyurl.com/4b5tbvwf.

[12] *Camp Edwards, Cape Cod's WWII City*. New Eng Hist Soc. tinyurl.com/5xvx3ffy.

[13] Cann, Donald Jr. and Galluzzo, John J. *Images Edwards and Otis AFB*.

[14] Smith, Mary Lou. *Book of Falmouth: Tricentennial Celebration*.

In the face of fake enemy fire, the soldiers broke through barriers placed in the sand. Enemy aircraft dropped "bombs" to stifle the onrush of troops...Medical units set up collecting and clearing stations to evacuate casualties. The quartermaster unit fed crucial supplies to the attacking forces after landing on the hazardous shores. A chemical unit laid down smoke screens to cloak the attacking infantrymen from enemy sight. In addition, signal units established communications and disrupted the enemies in order to facilitate the invasion. Parachute troops then swooped down on the vital enemy-held airport in Edgartown and assisted the invaders in establishing a grip on the Island.[15]

Lt. Commander Anthony Cimino, present at Camp Edwards during the assault, recalled:

So under tremendous secrecy and under cover of darkness, they left Cotuit after very sneakily – not sneakily, but secretly amassing there. They crossed the sound, and at just the right time...dawn, first light – they hit the beach at Martha's Vineyard, and everything went according to theory. They hit the beach, the boats opened, the troops went up and took positions, and at that time, most of the population of Martha's Vineyard rose up from behind the dunes and cheered them on. So, their secrecy went down the drain. They came back and then worked on more security.[16]

45th Division troops at Cape Cod. 1942.[17]

Camp Edwards was home to a 3,200-bed hospital. Also located at the base was the East Coast Processing Center, whose function was to deal with soldiers less than enthusiastic about their association with the Army. AWOLs and those with a history of difficulty following orders were sent to the Center for counseling or discipline. Of the thousands of men who spent time at the center, over 25,000 returned to battle, and 3,000 were discharged. The remaining 2,800 who flunked out of the program were sent to camps for further discipline or to federal prison.[18] As the war began to wind down, the camp became a debarkation point for returning soldiers.

The needs of an army at war quickly outpaced the facilities at Camp Edwards. Designed to house 30,000 soldiers, by the end of 1942, the base was deemed too small. The government constructed Camp Myles Standish in Taunton and a smaller 1,700-acre facility, Camp Wellfleet, to handle the overflow. Camp Edwards became one of the largest military training bases, with over 200,000 members of the US Army passing through its gates during World War II.[19]

There is a section of Interstate 495 in Massachusetts that curves gently to the southeast through Norton, Taunton, and Raynham. Standing on a hill near the southbound lanes is a huge snowball of a

[15] Murphy, Jackson. *Invasion Martha's Vineyard*. Martha's Vineyard Times 11/26/2019. tinyurl.com/yj89rn8d.

[16] *Through a Soldier's Eyes*. Video transcript. MA Nat Guard.

[17] *Amph Engineers Cape Cod* 1942. Pub domain photo. USASC. Wiki Commons. tinyurl.com/2s4jktxt.

[18] Phelan, Dr. Robert E. *Carrier Pigeons to Carrier Pilots*.

[19] Smith, Mary Lou. *Book of Falmouth: Tricentennial Celebration*.

tower, a radar system operated by the National Weather Service. The radar stands within what is known today as Myles Standish Industrial Park. Decades ago, however, the land was a US Army base, one of the largest troop embarkation areas in the country. More than thirty farms stretched across the area long before there was Camp Myles Standish. All would be taken by the government, including thirty-three homes in Taunton and seven in Norton.[20]

Main gate Camp Myles Standish. 1943.[21]

Construction began early in 1942, and within six months, thirty-five miles of road and nearly ten miles of railroad track crisscrossed the 1,620 acres of Camp Myles Standish.[22] The base was a city in its own right, containing 1,600 buildings, including barracks, warehouses, a hospital, an amphitheater, power stations, and a sewage treatment facility. A section of the camp was reserved for POWs. Facilities were staffed by African American soldiers, the Women's Army Corps, and civilian employees.

This was not a basic training camp. It was a staging area, the last stop on American soil for over a million members of the military who passed through on their way to the Boston Point of Embarkation and to war. Located less than forty miles from Standish, the BPOE was the third largest send-off port in the country. Filomena Todesco recalled troop transport trains passing through her hometown of Mansfield twenty-four hours a day. Tracks were so busy that trains were often delayed for long periods to let others go by. Soldiers were required to remain on the train during delays, but once, after a snowfall, a large number of Southern boys piled out of the rail cars. "They were like kids rolling in the snow," Todesco said. "Here we were, just little kids, and here were these grown men rolling in the snow."[23]

Troops leaving Camp Myles Standish
for Boston Port of Embarkation. World War II.[24]

---

[20] Mozzone, Peter. *Camp Myles Standish*. Taunton Daily Gazette 12/7/1993.

[21] *Camp Miles Standish*. Pub domain photo 01/09/1943. NARA Picryl. tinyurl.com/tarkcwyu.

[22] Hanna, William F. *Friends and Enemies*. Bridgewater Rev. BSU 11/2014. tinyurl.com/ycx74jbn.

[23] Gallotta, Stacy. *Path to war no more*. WICKEDLOCAL.com 6/11/2010. tinyurl.com/sb9s2ynx.

[24] *Troops Camp Myles Standish*. Pub domain photo. USASC. Wikipedia. tinyurl.com/mr3ufcy6.

The government, understandably concerned for the safety of the hundreds of thousands of men who would pass through the camp, emphasized security. MPs patrolled the streets of Taunton. For those entering camp, loudspeakers blared the message that the base was a secret facility not to be mentioned in telegrams or communications with the outside world. Soldiers were required to sit through lectures and films on security, and phone calls and mail were censored. Trains heading to Boston traveled with window shades drawn, and personnel stepped off rail cars directly onto a pier. A memo to post engineers in 1944 admonished: "The use of cameras within the camp area is prohibited. Officers will be disciplined, and cameras and films will be confiscated."[25] A US Army Signal Corps photo taken of soldiers returning home to the base in 1945 reads: "This is the first photo of inside Camp Myles Standish ever permitted to be published."[26]

For most soldiers, the visit was brief. After receiving medical checkups and vaccinations, troops were put through last-minute drills to prepare for what might be encountered in the field overseas. A mock wooden ship was constructed in Watson's Pond and used for abandon ship and lifeboat practice. Soldiers were instructed in the effects of poisonous gas and the use of gas masks. During downtime, the men could take advantage of camp movie theaters, rec halls, a library, or athletic fields.

Camp Myles Standish Library Lounge[27]

Baseball was an important pastime for soldiers, and in 1943, the camp had a special visit from the Red Sox. Johnny Pesky, Ted Williams, and Dom DiMaggio were serving in the military at the time, but the exhibition game was held anyway. The final score was Sox 8, Camp Myles Standish 3. The Boston Braves, managed by Casey Stengel, were rained out of their game a week later.[28] Attleboro resident Marion Rivers recalled the weekly dances held at Standish, one week even dancing with Mickey Rooney. Troops might receive liberty for a swing through Boston, Providence, or Taunton. After placing a quick call to home, soldiers moved out and headed to ships waiting for them in Boston Harbor.

As the country continued down the dark road into war, the festive atmosphere of the camp's early days diminished. Trains traveling back and forth to Taunton no longer held hordes of noisy soldiers eager for the fight. Now, they were all too often silent, carrying wounded survivors of battle or caskets of the fallen. Rivers remembered one night at a dance when guests were asked if anyone knew how to type.

We were taken to the camp hospital, where all the beds and stretchers were filled with the wounded. They were being shipped to hospitals near their homes, and we rolled typewriters from bed to bed, taking

[25] Ross, Albert A. *Memo Use of Cameras*. US Army. Camp Myles Standish 4/23/1944.

[26] *Soldiers freed from Nazis Camp Myles Standish*. Photo caption. USASC.

[27] *Camp Myles Standish Lounge*. Pub domain photo. NARA. tinyurl.com/mr4cy3ew.

[28] Keene, Kerry. *Red Sox Played Taunton*. Taunton Gazette 7/24/1993.

In July 1945, an eight-car passenger train from Boston to New Bedford derailed near Camp Standish, killing engineer Chester Wilson of Braintree and fireman J. L. Lyons of Jamaica Plain. Fifty-four injured passengers, including two soldiers from Fort Rodman in New Bedford, were brought to the camp hospital for treatment.[30] But the winter of 1943 was perhaps the most devastating period for residents of the camp: Hundreds of souls, including Chaplains Washington, Fox, Poling, and Goode, had perished with the sinking of the USS Dorchester. A memorial service was held shortly afterward for the seven hundred heroes who had just weeks before passed through Camp Myles Standish on their way to war.

With the end of the war approaching, in May 1945, nearly five thousand members of the Army Air Force, many veterans of the Ploesti raid, came home to Camp Myles Standish. Once in charge of sending troops to war, the camp was now in the business of welcoming them home. Men waited in long lines to make the all-important telephone call to loved ones. Soldiers received physicals, orientation on discharge procedures, and had their personnel records processed. They swapped stories with fellow soldiers-in-arms, remembered fallen friends, and shared tears of joy and pain. They had made it home.

Camp Myles Standish was decommissioned in January of 1946. During its busiest days, when the population of Taunton was just over 40,000, the camp had been home to 39,000, and a million and a half men had passed through its gates.

It was 1862, and they came from forty-eight towns across Massachusetts to a plot of land located near the border of Groton and Ayer. There were 950 of them in all, ready to fight and die to preserve their country. Two hundred and forty would never return. Camp Stevens, with its handful of buildings, was the training site of the 53rd Regiment Massachusetts Volunteer Militia during the Civil War. After the war, the camp was, for the most part, forgotten, a hay field remaining as the only testament to the men who had passed through.

Just over fifty years later, a nation at war would turn once again to the area that had become a hub for trains running through New England. After leasing property from landowners in Ayer, Shirley, Lancaster, and Harvard, a new base, Camp Devens, was established. The camp was named after Charles Devens: Charlestown native, Harvard graduate, Worcester lawyer, Civil War hero of the 15th Massachusetts Volunteers, and Attorney General of the United States under Rutherford Hayes. Construction of the base was completed in an astonishing three months, and the camp that was designed to hold 35,000 men would train more than 100,000 during the First World War. A cemetery on the property attests to the tragic loss of life at the Fort during the influenza pandemic of 1918. Of the 45,000 inhabiting the camp, 14,500 were infected, and over 700 perished.[31]

A decade later, the country found itself in the terrible grips of a depression, and to protect her constituents in the Devens area, Congresswoman Edith Nourse Rogers fought to preserve the base. Thus, in 1931, the camp, renamed Fort Devens, became a permanent US Army facility. With the institution of the draft in 1940, the camp underwent modernization and expansion. Construction proceeded down a bumpy road. Winter weather became a difficulty for contractors. Concerned that the estimated cost of $800 per soldier was too high, the supply branch of the Army decided that, among other things, buildings could do without paint, bringing the cost down to $400. FDR stepped in, and the buildings were painted.

---

[29] Brokaw, Tom. *Greatest Generation*. Random House Trade Paperbacks 1998.

[30] *Two Killed 54 hurt*. Meridian Record 7/2/1945. Newspapers.com. tinyurl.com/yc6y2twk.

[31] Durr, Eric. *Flu outbreak WW1*. Nat Guard 8/30/2018. tinyurl.com/msxtdk9h.

A dozen workers were arrested for theft, and up to 100 may have been involved in a scheme to claim unearned wages.[32]

One interesting twist to the Fort Devens story involved Mother Nature. Over 32 million board feet of lumber were required for the project at a cost of 1.3 million dollars. The Army encouraged the use of local men and materials whenever possible, and it just so happened that a huge lumber supply already existed in New England. In September of 1938, one of the worst hurricanes in recorded history had swept through the area, leveling homes and forests. The Northeastern Timber Salvage Administration was formed by Roosevelt to manage the fallen trees. The building market had significantly declined due to the Depression, and there was little call for lumber, so NETSA dumped thousands of trees into ponds, thus preserving the wood. With the sudden building boom at Fort Devens, 425 million board feet were pulled out of the water and sold to Grossman and Sons of Boston, the largest sale in the history of the lumber industry up until that time. The barracks at Fort Devens would be constructed of New England trees.[33]

Chandler Pond, New Hampshire.
February 1941[34]

In all, 1,200 buildings, two hospitals, and an airfield were built. The largest repair facility in the world at the time, the Whittemore Service Command Base Shop, was created to meet the needs of the equipment and vehicles operating at the Fort. The camp became home to the 1st, 32nd, and 45th infantry, a WAAC training center, a prisoner of war camp, and Army schools for bakers, cooks, and chaplains. One of the immediate difficulties facing the Army after the attack on Pearl Harbor was the availability of nurses. As their numbers began to rise, nurse basic training centers were created to familiarize the women with topics such as Army protocol, field sanitation, and defense during attacks. One such program was located at Fort Devens, where the first nurses arrived in July of 1943 for a one-month course.

For a period of two years, Fort Devens was home to the 101st Calvary Regiment. The former New York State regiment trained here from 1941 to 1943. The group saw action in Europe along the Saar

---

[32] Tabak, Andrew. *Fort Devens, From Boys to Men*. Andrew Tabak 2012.

[33] Tabak, Andrew. *Fort Devens, From Boys to Men*.

[34] *Landaff, NH* 2/28/1941. Pub domain photo. NARA 521509. tinyurl.com/tch3zs7a.

River and Siegfried Line and captured one of the most decorated members of the Nazi regime, Field Marshal Kesselring. During its eighty-five days of combat, the unit captured 27,000 members of the German military, fifteen times the total strength of the 101st.[35] These notable feats were accomplished by a cavalry without a single horse.

Horses were used extensively during the First World War, and estimates account for a horrifying eight million mule and horse deaths. During this time, Camp Devens was used as a training camp for cavalry units with accommodations for 10,000 horses. As technology advanced, the use of horses in the military declined amidst debate about their efficacy in war. By the Second World War, horses were used on a limited basis to carry supplies, weapons, and occasionally men. The last cavalry charge occurred in 1942 in the Philippines. Nine stables were constructed at the Fort in 1940, accommodating an estimated 300 horses. However, the equestrian age was over at Fort Devens, where trucks and tanks now moved across fields where horses had once grazed.

With its expansion in 1940, Fort Devens became a reception center for newly inducted New England draftees. During the next four years, 614,000 members of the Army would be processed through Fort Devens. As victory for the Allies approached, the camp's role reversed. The joyous moment of homecoming brought 100,000 soldiers to Devens, which now functioned as a separation center.

The United States came late to the development of air power for the military. By 1914, Britain and Germany were using airplanes in combat, but it wasn't until 1918 that President Woodrow Wilson established the Army Air Service. It was an idea that caught on quickly, and before the end of the First World War, over one hundred American pilots had achieved ace status, led by race car driver Eddie Rickenbacker with twenty-six kills. At FDR's urging, when new legislation was passed to manage the post-war military, included were provisions for an air combat arm of the US Army. Millions were appropriated for defense, including plans for 6,000 airplanes for the Army Air Corps.

Construction of an air base began shortly afterwards amid 4,500 acres of flat tobacco land in western Massachusetts. Mayor Anthony Stonina had waged a long and intense campaign to locate the facility in his hometown of Chicopee, and in April 1940, the base opened. The first plane, a B18 containing Massachusetts Representative Charles R. Clason, the first civilian to land at Westover, arrived in October. The sprawling compound was built to accommodate 1,400 men and included hospitals, warehouses, shops, rec halls, and a dozen miles of road. Within a year, the number of residents increased to 3,000, and by the end of 1942, 8,000 men were stationed at Westover. In 1944, a section of the base was set aside to house prisoners of war.

Initially planned as a base for anti-submarine patrols, Westover's role expanded to training a variety of Air Corps personnel, including pilots, navigators, and gunners. Soon, the airfield became known as a bomber base, preparing crews for an array of bombers, including B-17s and B-24s.

One of the more notable members of the Army Air Corps who spent time at Westover arrived in 1940 along with the 7th Bomber Squadron. Its commander, an Ohio native, moved his family to nearby Holyoke.[36] Curtis LeMay had shown a love for flying from his early days, joining the Army Air Corps in 1930. Considered the best navigator in the Corps, he flew as a test pilot, often acting as a mechanic for his own planes. After achieving the rank of Major, he was placed in charge of the 34th Bomber Group. LeMay's tough leadership style was legendary, leading to nicknames such as "Old Iron Pants" and "Bombs Away LeMay." He never seemed to mind. "In this racket," he said, "it's the tough guys who lead the survivors." LeMay commanded bomber groups in the European and Pacific theater during the war, earning numerous medals at home and abroad. After the war, with crisis looming in Berlin, he assumed control of US Air Forces in Europe where he developed a modern bomber force from the

---

[35] *101st Calvary WWII*. NY State Mil Mus & Vets Res Ctr. tinyurl.com/yc7nvtbv.

[36] *Fifty Years of Flying*. 1940 Golden Anniversary. 1990 Westover AFB.

remnants of the World War II Army Air Corps. LeMay eventually became head of the Strategic Air Command.

Westover Field. 1945[37]

Planning for a second major airfield began in 1941 when the Commonwealth of Massachusetts decided to develop an auxiliary airport for Boston's Jeffrey Field (later known as Logan Airport). Land was purchased in the towns of Bedford, Concord, Lincoln, and Lexington. In operation by mid-1942, the federal government leased the newly named Bedford Army Airfield from the state. Throughout the war years, it was used as a fighter squadron training base for the Army Air Corps. Renamed Hanscom Field in 1943 in honor of *Worcester Telegram-Gazette* reporter and well-known aviator Laurence G. Hanscom, it gained new importance when MIT's Rad Lab used the airfield as a testing ground for radar systems. Post-war, the Air Force, now its own branch of the US military, retained Hanscom Field, which today continues its role in the field of radar and electronics research.

The history of base expansion for the Navy took a slightly different track. Post World War I, the United States, Britain, Japan, France, and Italy agreed to the Washington Naval Treaty, an effort to stabilize worldwide naval power by limiting ship tonnage. However, the agreement was quietly pushed aside as countries began slowly beefing up their naval arsenals. By early 1930, a second attempt to limit naval power was made with the London Treaty. This, too, however, would soon be forgotten, and by the end of the year, Japan had a sizable fleet, a necessary tool in its quest to dominate the Pacific. England, recalling the ravages of the Great War, engaged in such extensive construction that she soon topped the chart with the largest navy in the world.

The US, still adhering to treaty guidelines, cautiously began to consider its place in the naval hierarchy of the globe, and while Japan and England dominated the seas, Congress discussed. In 1934, a step forward was taken. With the passage of the Vinson-Trammel Act, the United States committed to a 20 percent increase in the strength of its navy, amounting to 102 warships, full strength under the Washington Naval Treaty. It was an exercise in peacetime rearmament, but it wasn't nearly enough. Four years later, nearly to the day, Hitler would march into Austria.

By 1938, China was being devastated as Japan escalated its attempt to overcome its neighbor. Americans, however, were more concerned with the building conflict in Europe. While the majority of voters still favored isolation, there was growing discontent over Hitler's expansionism. FDR took advantage of this subtle shift to continue the buildup of the US Navy. A second Vinson Act, passed two months after the fall of Austria, increased the Navy's standing fleet by another 20 per cent and the number of its airplanes to 3,000. Unfortunately, no provision was made for shore facilities. Repeatedly warned of this lapse, Congress continued to release funds for ships while ignoring the lack of bases.

---

[37] *Westover Field MA.* Pub domain photo. USAF. Wiki Commons. tinyurl.com/mryam488.

The needs of the Navy were unique. Aircraft runways and hangars, sub-bases, ship construction and repair facilities, ammunition depots, and temporary housing for personnel, all located along coastal waters, were wanting. No problem... a board would be established to investigate. Shortly after the passage of the 1934 Act, the Shore Station Development Board opened for business. When a prospectus for a project was submitted, it was placed on a priority list that changed as new project requests arrived. From there, proposals went to House and Senate committees for approval. Those that got the thumbs up moved through a regimented series of steps, bouncing from offices to committees to more boards before going back to the House and Senate for appropriation. It took approximately eighteen months before a hammer ever hit a nail.

More discussion around planning and budgets followed. Finally, in July 1940, the Two-Ocean Navy Act, often considered the beginning of the Navy's war program, was sponsored by Representative Carl Vinson of Georgia and Massachusetts Senator David I Walsh. The largest bill in American history to fund naval expansion, it provided 4 billion dollars for the construction of battleships, cruisers, carriers, destroyers, subs, and 15,000 aircraft. Perhaps having learned from past lapses, this legislation included funding for shore facilities. The package of plans reached the desk of the President, who signed it into law in July 1941. It had taken seven years to reach this point. The attack on Pearl Harbor was five months away.

The Navy had an advantage. Naval bases and ordnance facilities with long-established practices and production processes were currently in operation. The huge increase in armament, as outlined by the Two Ocean Navy Act, required facilities to build, outfit, and repair ships, as well as to house men. So their eyes turned toward the easiest fix, expansion, and renovation of navy yards already in existence. Unlike the Army, the Navy's ranks were filled by those who enlisted. Thus, it was unhampered by the immediate pressure of housing and supplying tens of thousands of draft inductees. Four basic training centers, which together were capable of training 20,000 men every six weeks, were already in place. The brass was confident in its ability to provide for the 369,000 men expected to fill their ranks by June 1942. By the end of the year, however, the Japanese proved just how costly the slow march to preparing the Navy for war had been. In the months following the attack on Pearl Harbor, the number of enlistees jumped to a million. A pressing issue became where to put them.

Like the Army, the Navy needed a quick fix, a building that could be thrown up quickly with little manpower or skill. The design would become especially important as the war in the Pacific unfolded and sailors and Marines moved from island to island. Enter a Chicago company founded by Templeton, Massachusetts native George Fuller. Educated in Baldwinsville and Worcester,[38] Fuller joined his uncle's architecture firm in Worcester before moving on to Peabody and Stearns of Boston, designers of some of Newport's most prestigious mansions. Boston was apparently too small to contain the young architect's ambitions, and in 1882, along with Somerville resident Everett Clark, he moved to Chicago to found the George A. Fuller Company.[39] This was a wise move. Whether or not a cow had actually kicked over a lantern, the fire in the O'Leary's barn a decade before started a conflagration that wiped out thousands of buildings, and Chicago was still recovering. Fuller's company soared and became legendary with achievements such as the Chicago Opera House.

In 1941, the Navy approached the Fuller Company with a question. Could they produce a portable, lightweight structure adaptable for a variety of uses and that could be constructed quickly? Two months later, the first Quonset Hut came off the assembly line. Similar in design to the World War I Nissen Hut, the Quonset Hut ticked off all of the Navy's boxes.

---

[38] *George Fuller Dead.* NY Times 12/15/1900. tinyurl.com/nhkm5zs9.

[39] *Building Navy Bases WWII.* Navy BuDocks. tinyurl.com/yucury47.

Quonset hut, Majuro Atoll. WWII.[40]

Curved arch forms made of corrugated galvanized steel with plywood floors were relatively lightweight and required significantly less shipping space than tents with wood floors and frames. Eighty-six different interior floor plans insured the huts could be used for anything from hospitals to latrines. Packaged as a kit, the structure could be assembled with maximum speed and minimum skill. By the war's end, over 150,000 Quonset huts were fabricated, the first being constructed at the US Navy facility at Quonset Point in Rhode Island. However, as both branches of the military scurried to find housing, the Navy was concerned with an even greater issue. America needed ships, hundreds of them, and they needed them now.

Today, when one looks at the Charlestown waterfront with the USS Constitution resting comfortably at anchor and the Bunker Hill Monument rising majestically behind buildings of brick and stone, it is hard to imagine that this quiet museum-like compound was once home to one of the busiest naval installations in the United States. Long before there was a Hitler, a Hirohito, or a Franklin Roosevelt, the Boston Navy Yard was in the shipbuilding business. The first permanent US Navy was created in 1794 by President John Adams. Up until that time, shipbuilding had been consigned to private contractors. However, building a naval fleet would clearly outpace the ability of commercial shipyards, so construction began on eight government-owned yards all along the east coast. One of them was located on the banks of the Charles River in Charlestown, the Boston Navy Yard.

Along with shipyards came an order to build three ships. One would make history. Built with a hull designed for speed and a stout shape, this large ship was framed with heavy oak timbers and covered with thick planking. "Old Ironsides" was to prove herself nearly impenetrable. Following the War of 1812, when she earned an impressive record against the British, her career as a warship came to an end.

The USS Constitution would be forever linked to the Boston Navy Yard. In earlier days, ship repair was handled by men repelling over the sides of ships that were afloat, running them aground on mud flats at low tide, or careening (leaning a ship on its side). The process was time-consuming and dangerous. As a result, the Navy made the decision to invest in dry docks. Boston and Norfolk, Virginia, were chosen as sites for the first two dry docks in US Naval history. Construction took six years. The Boston Navy Yard's first customer was Old Ironsides, which floated in for overhaul during the dry dock's inauguration in 1833. During the Second World War, Old Ironsides stood her ground and remained at anchor in Boston. For a time, she housed naval officers awaiting court martial. FDR ordered her recommissioned as a flagship, a symbolic but appropriate gesture of defiance and strength. The USS Constitution, the oldest commissioned warship in the US Navy, has been assigned to the Boston Navy Yard since 1897.

During the First World War, the shipyard's activity rose to new heights, although ship construction was significantly curtailed, replaced by its new role as a repair and overhaul facility. The National Park Service estimates that during this period, fifty ships a day entered or departed the

[40]*Quonset, Majuro Atoll.* Pub domain photo. Quonset Hut Manuals. USNSM. NHHC. tinyurl.com/wtucccy2.

shipyard.[41] This war was a turning point in naval history for a variety of reasons. The age of sail was gone, and a new age of technology had begun. While wooden ships still moored alongside those made of metal, they were few in number. Clippers and schooners faded with the rise of the new titans of the sea, battleships. Powerful engines were designed, and rope walks grew quiet as mile after mile of chain stretched out across shipyards.

The Boston Navy Yard, which for a century had been the leader in rope production for the Navy, now became a leader in anchor chain production. Forges were constructed at the yard, the largest of which was built on a foundation buried thirty-five feet deep to support furnaces and twelve-ton hammers. It was here that the Die-Lock chain was invented, making links so strong that they became the sole anchor chain in use by the US Navy.[42]

Forge worker making chains at
Boston Navy Yard.[43]

The function of the Navy underwent a dramatic shift during the interwar years, and the peacetime Navy now engaged in occasional police actions to protect economic interests across the globe. With treaty limitations on the size of navies, the United States had, by and large, gone out of the shipbuilding business, and for a decade, ship construction at the Boston Navy Yard nearly ceased entirely. It would not be until 1934, with the launch of the USS McDonough, that ships would again be produced in Charlestown, eventually earning the BNY the reputation as a destroyer yard.

A month after the outbreak of war, the shipyard was charged with a crucial task: creating a new type of destroyer that would accompany convoys across the dangerous Atlantic passage to Europe. The Destroyer Escort, smaller and more maneuverable than destroyers, was heavily armed. Its function was anti-submarine warfare. At half the cost of a destroyer and requiring less time to build, Destroyer Escorts were referred to as a "poor man's destroyer." Unfortunately, its size and cost also made it expendable. Benjamin Garrison, a sailor aboard a Boston Navy Yard DE, stated: "We knew that if a submarine fixed a torpedo at, say, a troop carrier, the escort commander could tell a destroyer escort to get between that ship and the torpedo. We had fewer men, we were a smaller ship, and it was important that the larger ship survive."

With the construction of the first two DEs in April 1942, the Boston Navy Yard was about to make history again. The shipyard began a frenzy of construction and, by May of the following year,

---

[41] *Charleston Navy Yard.* US DOI Handbook 152.

[42] *Chain Forge, Building.* NPS. tinyurl.com/w6h8c2b8.

[43] *Worker Making Chain.* Pub domain photo. BOSTS-99672-1. NPS. tinyurl.com/rk8tcsx9.

became the first shipyard to complete four destroyer escorts in one month. Two months later, five would be delivered, and within a two-month period in the fall of 1943, six would be launched. The Boston Navy Yard constructed sixty-two Destroyer Escorts during the war.[44]

DE USS Mason, Boston Navy Yard. Keel laid down
October 14, 1943, launched November 17, 1943.[45]

While Destroyer Escorts in the Atlantic were making headway at keeping U-boats at bay, a new type of ship was on the drawing board. Created with the combined effort of England and the United States, this vessel would be able to move men and machines onto the beaches of Europe, the Mediterranean, and the Pacific. Ammunition, supplies, vehicles, tanks, and men could be carried on the 328-foot-long Landing Ship Tank (LST) and could be offloaded via bow doors onto beaches in shallow water.

A 1944 newspaper article written by well-known war correspondent Eddie Pyle provides a description of a Landing Ship Tank.

An LST isn't such a glorious ship to look at—it is neither sleek nor fast nor impressively big—and yet it is a good ship, and the crews aboard LST's are proud of them. The LST's are great rollers—the sailors say, "They'll even roll in drydock." They have flat bottoms, and consequently, they roll when there is no sea at all. They roll fast, too. Their usual tempo is a round-trip roll every six seconds. The boys say that in a really heavy sea you can stand on the bridge and actually see the bow of the ship twist, like a monster turning its head. It isn't an optical illusion, either, but a result of the "give" in these ships. The sailors say that when they run across a sandbar, the ship seems to work its way across like an inchworm, proceeding forward section by section.[46]

[44] *Destroyer Escorts.* NPS. tinyurl.com/4m24882a.

[45] *Launching USS Mason* 11/1943. Pub domain photo. NPS. tinyurl.com/y2ve3dkd.

[46] *Ernie Pyle Praises LST.* Invader. Evansville Vanderburgh Lib. tinyurl.com/mry6vycj.

First LST launched at Boston Navy Yard. November 1, 1942[47]

    Essentially a giant floating box, the LST's ability to cross oceans, land on a beach, move massive amounts of men and cargo without the need for cranes or piers, and its adaptability for a variety of uses from repair shop to hospital ship made it an invaluable resource for the Allies during World War II. So important was this vessel that planning for D-Day was in part based upon the number of LSTs available for the operation. Winston Churchill eloquently described their importance to the war effort: "The destinies of two great empires...seemed to be tied up in some god-damned things called LSTs." Between 1942 and 1945, LSTs whizzed out of the Boston Navy Yard. Of the thirty built in 1944, for example, each one required just one month to complete.

    Other landing craft would be constructed in Boston, many with mind-boggling speed. When the order for LSTs arrived at the shipyard, also included was a request for a small, shallow-draft vessel, fifty feet in length, to be used for moving tanks and men onto beaches. Within a few months, the first 150 Landing Crafts Mechanized (LCM) were ready. John Langan, a shopfitter at the Navy Yard, referred to it as a "crash program...We just stopped everything else and concentrated on them..."[48] LSDs (Landing Ship Dock) were also produced at the Boston Navy Yard. Like the first two landing crafts, the LSD could carry troops and vehicles onto a beach but, at sea, could function as a dock for vessels in need of repair.

LCM production line
Boston Naval Shipyard 1942[49]

    While the Boston shipyard achieved fame for the production of naval vessels during the war, it had a second equally vital function...repair. With the onset of the U-boat war, damaged ships began arriving at the shipyard with a wide assortment of needs. A short turnaround time was essential as workers rushed to figure out what repairs were necessary and mend ships before sending them back to

---

[47] *First LST BNY*. Pub domain photo. USN. NARA Boston. MA DC. tinyurl.com/2vhdyw4y.

[48] *Charleston Navy Yard*. US DOI.

[49] *Tank Lighter*. Pub domain photo. USN. NARA Boston. MA DC. tinyurl.com/2f2j7vz2.

sea. Some were barely afloat when they limped into the dock. Langan recalled one ship that had to be towed into Boston. It had been "torpedoed and cut right in halves... [They had] tied her down with big I-beams...tied them the full length, all the way around."[50]

Boston Navy Yard, 1942.
Note: USS Constitution left center.[51]

Roughly twenty years prior to World War II, the government purchased land in South Boston, not far from the Navy Yard. The area contained a dry dock owned by the Commonwealth of Massachusetts. In 1940, work began on expansion of the area with the construction of piers, a power plant, and barracks. Improvements were made on what would become Dry Dock 3, one of the largest dry docks on the Atlantic Coast. The role of the South Boston Annex was to provide repair services, thus freeing up space at the Boston Navy Yard for shipbuilding. Larger combat vessels still put into the Navy Yard for repair, while smaller ships and patrol craft made their way to the Annex. By 1945, the sprawling Annex repair yard had grown larger than the Boston Navy Yard.

When the government took control of the land that would become the Annex, a portion of the property was designated for use by the US Army. Named the South Boston Army Base, it was a major source of supply for ships heading across the Atlantic. The facility housed the Boston Port of Embarkation. During World War II, thousands of men passed through the doors of the Port on their way to Europe, making it the third-largest embarkation port in the United States. The facility also contained a hospital and a prisoner-of-war enclosure. The South Boston Navy Base and Naval Annex closed in 1974.

Boston Army Base and Boston
Port of Embarkation. 1942.[52]

[50] *Charleston Navy Yard.* US DOI.

[51] *Navy Yard Boston.* 1/1/1942. Pub domain photo. NARA. tinyurl.com/msvdafm8.

[52] *Boston Army Base.* Pub domain photo. War Dept. NAID 75430838. tinyurl.com/478jscz5.

During the Second World War, the Boston Navy Yard was the single largest employer of industrial labor in the Boston area. Six thousand ships were constructed, repaired, or overhauled by nearly 50,000 men and women who labored tirelessly to support their country during the conflict. At some point following the war, the Boston Navy Yard became known as the Charlestown Navy Yard. It continued to provide repair and refit services to a variety of vessels, including aircraft carriers, but its primary focus on destroyers remained. In 1974, the Boston Navy Yard's work came to an end. Now under the jurisdiction of the National Park Service, the shipyard is home to USS Cassin Young, a destroyer with a proud record of service during World War II. Nearby, the USS Constitution rests at anchor, back in the shipyard that she first sailed into 180 years before.

The work of the ships that came out of the Boston Navy Yard would not have been possible without the extraordinary efforts of a town of 8,000 residents twenty miles southeast of Boston. The establishment of the first naval ammunition depot in Hingham can be traced to John Davis Long, Harvard grad and former Governor of Massachusetts. As Secretary of the Navy under McKinley, Long sent the USS Maine to Havana, Cuba, where its destruction led to the outbreak of the Spanish-American War. (Ironically, Long would later express his belief that the sinking of the Maine was accidental, caused by the explosion of ammunition on board.) By 1903, the Navy began searching for a location to build a depot somewhere in the northeast, and Long, a Hingham resident, proposed his hometown. Land in Hingham and Weymouth, situated along the Back River, was purchased, and the first depot was constructed.

With the approach of war, the military needed ammunition for its guns, but thanks to the political agenda of isolationist Senator Gerald Nye, who in 1936 labeled weapons manufacturers "merchants of death," industrialists hesitated to invest in ammunition production. The situation became so dire that in 1940, Secretary of War Henry Stimson noted that the country had less than a day's supply of smokeless powder.[53] Eight coastal depots remained at the end of the First World War. To expedite the production of ammunition, the Navy began modernizing and expanding the preexisting depots and turned its attention to Camp Hingham.

The need for safety in handling ammunition had become a priority since a devastating 1926 explosion at the Picatinny Arsenal in New Jersey. During a heavy thunderstorm, a bolt of lightning ignited 650,000 tons of World War I surplus ammunition. The result was devastating. Nothing within a half mile of the blast was left standing, and explosions continued for three days. The Navy took note, and during the surge of pre-World War II construction, magazines like the approximately 200 at the Hingham Naval Ammunition Depot were semi-circular, fabricated of concrete, with earth berms and steel frames. Each roof was designed to be the weakest structural point in order to direct the trajectory of a blast. Magazines were placed at least 500 feet away from each other and limited to 143,000 pounds of high explosives. At Picatinny, a bunker containing 790,000 pounds of TNT had been situated 80 feet away from a magazine containing 1,700,000 pounds of the explosives.[54]

Depots were located a comfortable distance away from shipyards. Not only did this reduce congestion at the yards, but it also made ammunition readily available to outgoing ships and for those needing overhaul of existing ammunition. During the First World War, Halifax, Nova Scotia, was the scene of a horrific disaster when two ships, one carrying explosives, collided in the harbor. The resulting explosion killed nearly 2,000 people and wiped out one square mile of the city. As a result, World War II Navy regulations required that vessels remove all ammunition before entering port. Depots assumed responsibility for this storage. Wharves were constructed at Hingham, where barges and light ships ferried ammunition to and from ships anchored in the harbor or at the Boston Navy Yard. Several miles

---

⁵³ Goodwin, R. Christopher and Asso. *DOD Facilities WWII Construction.* USACE 5/1997. tinyurl.com/25afpdzt.
⁵⁴ *Building Navy Bases WWI 1940-1946.* Navy BuDocks.

of railroad tracks crisscrossed the Depot, and along sidings used by trains being held overnight, special concrete sidewalls were constructed to direct the force of a potential blast upward.

At its most active point in 1944, approximately 700 sailors and 400 Marines were stationed at Hingham Naval Ammunition Depot. The bulk of the work, however, was done by over 2,000 civilians who labored around the clock to do their part in the war effort. Peg Charlton was a teenager during the late 1930s when activity ramped up at the Depot. "The awareness of impending disaster and ultimate U.S. involvement was very clear to us when in 1939 the Nazis...overran Poland." By the fall of 1941, local residents were warned that if Germany attacked, Hingham would very probably be a target.[55] Security provided by the Army and Marines was very tight on land and in the harbor. Coast Guard Auxiliary vessels monitored the waters around Hingham. One 94-year-old Marine veteran remembered patrolling the Depot on horseback and sleeping in stables along with the horses.[56]

Charlton recalled the terrifying events roughly two days after Pearl Harbor when air raid sirens began to blare, and the town was put on high alert. German aircraft had supposedly been spotted off the coast and were heading toward Hingham. "As we approached Wollaston Beach...soldiers with anti-aircraft guns were out in force waving all cars through at top speed. When we reached Neck Street in Weymouth, barricades were blocking Route 3A. We were stopped and had to show an I.D. to prove we lived in Hingham before we could proceed over the Back River Bridge." The threat was felt elsewhere along the coastline. In Boston, 2,300 police were called in, and no civilian vehicles were allowed to enter the city. Fort Devens sent 400 trucks filled with soldiers and equipment to defend the Boston Navy Yard. Quincy, with its vital shipyard, saw the arrival of anti-aircraft weapons along with over a thousand soldiers from Camp Edwards. Artillery batteries were set up at Hingham and the lighter-than-air base in South Weymouth. Fortunately, the anticipated attack never took place.[57]

Depots were assigned a variety of tasks. At Hingham, ammunition was overhauled, shells were loaded with explosives, smokeless powder was packaged, and finished products were distributed. Some ammunition components, such as casings and high explosives, were produced off-site and transported to depots. Magnesium powder, for example, was manufactured at the Pilgrim Ordnance Works, operated by the National Fireworks Company of West Hanover, Massachusetts.

Powder stacking machine at the Hingham
Naval Ammunition Depot. WWII.[58]

The Hingham Naval Ammunition Depot initially specialized in loading small-caliber ammunition. As the country became more deeply involved in the war, changes were made in ammunition

[55]Charlton, Peg. *War Years Remembered*. Wompatuck News Issue 57. tinyurl.com/47y4avck.

[56] *Lasting Imprints WWI and WWII*. Video. Hingham Hist Soc. Harbor Media. YouTube. https://tinyurl.com/4nvkdk29.

[57] Charlton, Peg. *War Years Remembered*.

[58] *Powder Stacking Machine Hingham Nav Ammunition Depot*. Public domain photo. 1941-1945. US Navy. Wiki Commons. tinyurl.com/y7746p2p.

and propellants, and revision of depot assembly lines was common. By the end of the war, Hingham was producing a wide variety of ammunition, including the giant sixteen-inch shells used by battleships.

One of the more remarkable additions to the Hingham production line was the Variable Time or VT Fuze. This ammunition marvel, known as a proximity fuze, utilized radio waves to locate a target on land, at sea, or in the skies. When the projectile came within a certain range, it would explode in the air without having to make contact. In the early days of the war, it took approximately 2,400 rounds to shoot down an enemy plane. The VT fuze cut it down to 400.[59] A contract for production of the VT fuze was granted to Sylvania Electric Products of Pennsylvania. One of its plants was located in Ipswich, Massachusetts. Security was tight for this vital top-secret weapon. Women working at the plant were searched as they entered or left the building, and carrying a purse was prohibited. Even police and fire department access was restricted. None of the employees ever knew exactly what they were working on.[60]

VT fuze assembly line, Hingham
Naval Ammunition Depot.[61]

The importance of the VT fuze with its "radio brain" cannot be understated. By the end of World War II, the government had spent a billion dollars on its development and production, operated 110 plants, and assembled over 40,000 of the tiny radio transmitter tubes daily. General George Patton eloquently described its importance: "The new shell with the funny fuse is devastating...I am glad that you all thought of it first." Steeped in secrecy and accomplished through the ingenuity, relentless effort, and patriotism of the American people, the VT project was a stunning success. As surrender documents were being signed in 1945, neither Germany nor Japan was aware of the device. In the words of astronomer Ralph Baldwin, a member of the VT fuze development team, "They never knew what hit them." [62]

One of the more famous faces associated with the Hingham Depot was a young man from Maine who would capture the attention of the world. Born into wealth, Norman Cahners attended Andover and Harvard before joining the Navy and moving to the Hingham Depot. Lt. Cahners just happened to enjoy problem-solving and was assigned to improve supply problems at the facility. It was a good fit and led to the development of one of the most important inventions of the war, the four-way pallet.

---

[59] *Lasting Imprints WWI and WWII.* Hingham Hist Soc.

[60] *Proximity Fuse: How Ipswich Women Helped...* Historic Ipswich. tinyurl.com/bdeeu8p6.

[61] *VT Fuze Assembly line.* Pub domain photo. USN. NARA Boston. MA DC. tinyurl.com/mr3r9v3d.

[62] *Deadly Fuze.* Video. Engage Veterans. PBS 8/4/2004. tinyurl.com/ywjz8vn7.

During the Depression, with unprecedented levels of unemployment, labor was easy to find, and men hefted the crates and cases that moved the products of agriculture and industry. While the forklift had been in use for many years, the focus was on manpower. With a war on, however, men were now needed to carry guns rather than boxes, and Cahners saw a solution that blended muscle and machine. His invention, a pallet that could be picked up by a forklift from any direction, revolutionized the logistics of moving cargo. Loading and unloading could now be accomplished in less time with less manpower. At Quartermaster depots, for example, in a little over a year, the average number of tons handled by a single man doubled.[63] Cahners began a newsletter, *The Palletizer*, to share his methods with other naval suppliers.

Lt. Norman Cahners (right), Chairman of the
Cash Bond Drive, Hingham Depot. 1945.[64]

After the war, Norman Cahners purchased rights to *The Palletizer* from the Navy for one dollar. The rest is publishing history. The humble newsletter was reborn as *Modern Materials Handling* and became the foundation of a publishing empire that would include *Variety* and *Publishers Weekly*. Cahners lived in the Boston area for most of his life, becoming a well-known philanthropist and supporter of local institutions such as the Boston Museum of Science and the Boston Symphony Orchestra. The four-way pallet is still in use today, having changed little since its birth at Hingham. It is considered by many as the single most important development in the history of global economy. As of 2012, an estimated two billion pallets were circulating in the United States, with more in countries across the world used for shipping everything from shoes to heroin.[65]

Following England's entry into war and concerned about possible German aggression against East Coast shipping, FDR ordered the US Navy to establish Neutrality Patrols. Beginning in 1939, ships and aircraft moved up and down the Atlantic coastline and into the Caribbean, searching for potential threats. Within two years, it became clear that the Hingham Naval Ammunition Depot would be unable to keep up with the demands of a Navy at war. In 1941, the government purchased land in Cohasset, Scituate, Norwell, and Hingham, two miles away from the Hingham Depot. By the end of summer, the Annex was taking shape. Magazines, wharves to accommodate barges, and railroad tracks linked to the Depot were under construction. A newly dredged channel followed soon after.[66] During the war, concrete bunkers stored ammunition waiting to be shipped by rail to the Depot for loading onto barges and outward-bound naval vessels.

---

[63] LeBlanc, Rick. *Another Sneak Attack*. Pallet Enterprise 5/3/2002. tinyurl.com/3yhumnzn.

[64] *Norman Cahners* 7/14/1945. Pub domain photo. Shot and Shell, Nav Ammo Depot. US Navy. Wiki Commons. tinyurl.com/5ba8z4pe.

[65] Vanderbilt, Tom. *Most Imp Object Global Economy*. Slate 8/14/2012. tinyurl.com/487shsc6.

[66] *Building Navy's Bases WWII 1940-1946*. Navy BuDocks.

The Hingham Depot and Annex were just one part of the story of ammunition during the Second World War. By war's end, manufacturers and depots had produced an astounding 11 million tons of artillery ammunition, 1 million tons of mortar ammo, grenades, pyrotechnics, and mines, 6 million tons of bombs and rockets, and 39 billion rounds of small arms ammunition. In 1944, a German officer was taken prisoner at the Battle of Monte Cassino in Italy. His comment sums up the unbelievable effort of American citizens and of the munitions industry. "You people expend artillery ammunition, but mine expend only the bodies of men."

The Hingham Naval Ammunition Depot was in use until the 1970s when it passed into the ownership of the town of Hingham. In Cohasset, the Annex remained active throughout the Korean War and, in the mid-50s, stored the Navy's first nuclear depth charges. During the Vietnam conflict, land mines were produced here. The Annex served as an Army Reserve facility until 1982 and today is home to Wompatuck State Park.

An unusual incident occurred 75 years after World War II that today serves as a reminder of the importance of the work done at the Hingham Depot and Annex. On May 5, 1945, in a last gasp of the Third Reich, the 7,500-ton collier SS Blackpoint was sunk by a U-boat just off the coast of Point Judith, Rhode Island. Since then, it has become a popular dive site. In 2002, a five-inch shell from the stern-mounted deck gun of the Blackpoint was found. As the diver separated the shell from the projectile, an ammunition inspection certificate suddenly floated out. On it were the words, "Hingham Naval Ammunition Depot."[67]

By 1945, the Massachusetts landscape was peppered with a wide array of military installations. Most of the larger bases and camps were affiliated with smaller support or overflow facilities. The Army's Camp Curtis Guild, which included land in Reading, Lynnfield, and Wakefield, was a staging point for the Boston Port of Embarkation. Camp Washburn on Washburn Island in Falmouth was used as an amphibious base for troops training at Camp Edwards. For the Navy, places like the Naval Auxiliary Facility Ayer (formerly used by Fort Devens) supported activities at Naval Air Station Squantum, and a bombing range, No Man's Land, was located off the coast of Martha's Vineyard. The airfield in Hyannis operated under the control of the Army at the outbreak of war and was later transferred to the Navy. Renamed Naval Auxiliary Air Station Hyannis, it played an important role in anti-submarine reconnaissance. Thirty-seven aircraft conducted search and rescue activities out of the Coast Guard Air Station in Salem. Coastal defense gun batteries could be found at Salisbury Beach Military Reservation, Fort Taber/Rodman in New Bedford, and Plymouth Camp. Camp Framingham, also known as Camp Dalton, served as a National Guard Base.

Air Station Salem[68]

[67] Rose, Jim. *66 years ago today*. Tri-County Independent 6/11/2008. tinyurl.com/3a6pe7s4.

[68] *Air Station Salem*. Pub domain photo. 170602-G-XX000-263 USCG. tinyurl.com/yc7ykvxe.

The list of military installations, large and small, in the state of Massachusetts is astonishing. Certainly, one can hardly place a finger on a map of the Bay State coastline without touching upon the site of a quartermaster station, ammunition or fuel depot, training facility, shipyard, or coastal patrol base. The United States invested heavily in the state during the Second World War as it did in the country and its allies. It is estimated that the government spent approximately 300 billion dollars to defeat her enemies. Ammunition plants, covering acreage equal to the cities of New York, Philadelphia, and Chicago combined, cost the US approximately 3 billion dollars and accounted for a yearly operating budget of another billion.[69] Money, however, could not win the war. It took the ingenuity, dedication, and determination of one-quarter of a million ammunition workers, the millions of other civilians who built the camps and bases and shipyards, the clerks and cooks and welders, and the average citizens who labored untiringly to support their nation at war.

---

[69] Goodwin, R. Christopher and Asso. *DOD Facilities WWII Construction.*

Chapter 4

Battle for the Coast

The only thing that ever really frightened me
during the war was the U-boat peril.
Winston Churchill

The situation in the United Kingdom was bleak. Since the cowardly sinking of the passenger liner Athenia within hours of England's declaration of war, Admiral Karl Doenitz, head of the German submarine fleet, had begun waging open war on Britain. One month later, on October 13, 1939, U-boat 47 brazenly crept into the British naval stronghold at Scapa Flow and sank HMS Royal Oak, claiming the lives of 800 of her crew. Emboldened by this kill and in violation of the London Naval Treaty, three days later, Hitler gave the order for attack without warning on all enemy ships. Doenitz took full advantage of the opportunity. That October alone, 185,000 tons of shipping were destroyed in the North Atlantic. By the following August, another 1.5 million tons were gone.

In the United States, President Franklin Roosevelt made a cautious but crucial decision. With an eye toward the upcoming election, he moved quietly forward with a plan to provide aid to our Allies while publicly protecting American neutrality. The US became a signatory of the Declaration of Panama, which established a 300-mile zone of territorial waters around North and South America. In December 1940, his next term in office was secured, and FDR delivered a speech designed to appeal to the mass of largely isolationist voters. He described lending his garden hose to a neighbor whose house was on fire. His ploy was successful, and three months later, the Lend-Lease Act was approved. Fifty "garden hoses," aging American destroyers, leaky machinery in frequent need of repair, and with antiquated weapons, now became part of the British arsenal, a much-needed but at times frustrating loan. One British sailor during a storm commented, "...if we offered them a thousand Players [cigarettes], do you think they'd take this bloody sieve back?"[1] In return, England leased a number of military bases to the US for a period of ninety-nine years.

Throughout the long months of 1940 and into 1941, callously referred to by the Kriegsmarine as the Happy Time, Germany's submarine wolf packs seemed unstoppable. In May, an incident occurred which provided a temporary lull in the U-boat war. A German submarine was taken by the British in waters off Greenland. As Captain Julius Lemp, murderer of the innocent passengers of the Athenia, slipped beneath the waves, his sub floundered long enough to give up the secrets of the German Navy's Enigma code. As a result, by July, Allied ship sinkings significantly declined as wolfpacks scoured the Atlantic in search of targets that had been forewarned and relocated.

In December 1941, Convoy HG 76 headed homeward from Gibraltar. These were deadly waters. In an effort to protect supply routes to his North Africa campaign, Hitler had ordered Doenitz's subs to the Mediterranean. As the convoy's thirty-two ships moved out to sea, they came under attack by U-boats. A lengthy battle ensued, resulting in minimal losses for the Allies. Germany, however, was not so lucky. Four of the ten U-boats engaged in the action were gone. Doenitz had enough. He had opposed transferring U-boats to the Mediterranean, and now that the battle against Convoy HG 76 had proven costly, Doenitz needed to find more fertile hunting grounds for his wolves. The Battle for the Coast was about to begin.

---

[1] Pitt, Barrie and Editors. *Battle of the Atlantic.* Time Life Books 1977.

In spite of her supposed neutrality, the United States had been in an undeclared war for quite some time. Certainly, sending destroyers to a country at war had been anything but neutral. In mid-1941, Roosevelt upped the ante. US Marines assumed defense of Iceland, and the US Navy began escorting shipping on the dangerous voyage across the North Atlantic. On September 4, the US took the first step toward war. While operating in waters southeast of Greenland, two torpedoes were fired at the American destroyer Greer and missed. Greer followed the trail of the U-boat for over three hours, unsuccessfully dropping nearly two dozen depth charges. Roosevelt reported during a fireside chat, "I tell you the blunt fact that the German submarine fired first upon this American destroyer without warning and with deliberate design to sink her." In a bold move, he issued a shoot-on sight order against enemy ships, vowing Americans would no longer wait until the Axis struck a deadly blow. "When you see a rattlesnake poised to strike, you do not wait until he has struck before you crush him."

On October 16, while acting as a convoy escort in waters near Iceland, USS Kearny was attacked by a German submarine. Kearny was under the command of Anthony Danis, a meteorologist who had been raised in Attleboro. He was no stranger to crisis at sea. Twice during the pre-war years, Danis had been aboard dirigibles when they crashed into the ocean.[2] When the Kearny was torpedoed by U-568, he was one of the lucky ones. Eleven members of the crew perished in the attack. The ship limped into the Boston Navy Yard for repairs. Ten days later, in an intense radio address to the nation, FDR expressed outrage. "The U.S.S. Kearny is not just a Navy ship. She belongs to every man, woman, and child in this Nation." He stated, "...history has recorded who fired the first shot...In the long run...all that will matter is who fired the last shot."

Damage to USS Kearny. October 1941.[3]

Four days later, the USS Reuben James became the first US Navy ship sunk during the Battle for the Atlantic. While acting as a convoy escort eastbound out of Newfoundland, two torpedoes from U-552 slammed into the destroyer, creating a massive fireball and smoke column visible for miles. The end came quickly. Thanks to a rapid response by the convoy commander, forty-five men were rescued from the oily seas, but 115 souls, including several from Massachusetts, were gone forever. Joseph Parkins of Worcester had been unable to attend his mother's funeral because the Reuben James was sailing. Lawrence Cosgrove of Brockton was just nineteen years old when he joined the crew as a Gunner's Mate. Chief Petty Officer Alton Cousins, a native of Leominster and one of the older members of the crew, had

---

[2] *Skipper Misses Death.* Boston Globe 10/18/1941. Newspapers.com. tinyurl.com/yc4vnct6.

[3] *USS Kearny.* Pub domain photo. NHHC. tinyurl.com/4bmm93kb.

a premonition. On a visit two weeks prior, he'd left his gold watch at home, stating: "I'm going to leave it here; it's not going down with me." He had served sixteen years with the Navy, retired, and been called back to active duty in 1940. His wife feared for his safety aboard the Reuben James. "This is one of the old boats that won't stand up like the Kearney."[4] She was right. None of these men survived the voyage.

While the incident occurred before the US entered the war, the Reuben James is considered the first US Navy ship sunk by enemy fire during World War II. Yet Roosevelt was strangely passive on the sinking. The *Boston Globe* reported, "President Roosevelt said today he saw no possibility of severing diplomatic relations with Germany and thought there had been no change in American policy as a result of the loss of the American destroyer Reuben James, and other recent attacks on other American vessels."[5] The following day, the London newspaper, *The Daily Mail*, had a more realistic take on the situation with its headline, "United States Are on the Last Mile Into War."[6]

But the time for saber-rattling was rapidly passing. American ships were now actively engaged in warfare in the Atlantic, and FDR no doubt recognized that a declaration of hostilities would soon be necessary. He bided his time, allowing outrage to build among isolationist American voters. Six weeks later, however, thanks to the Japanese, the decision to make the controversial step into war was taken out of Roosevelt's hands. Three days after committing to conflict with Japan, the United States declared war on Germany. Four thousand miles to the east, Karl Doenitz was pleased. He had found his next hunting ground.

The Admiral was impatient to launch a new operation, Drumbeat (Paukenschlag), which would throw the might of his U-boats against the rich shipping lanes that ran up America's eastern seaboard. Unfortunately, he had only six subs at his disposal. On December 18, one week after the US entered the war, the first U-boat headed westward across the Atlantic, joined shortly after by five more. Others would follow. For nearly seven months, these submarines would conduct a reign of terror, waging unrelenting slaughter against Allied shipping in the North Atlantic and along the East Coast, their "Second Happy Time." Over 450 ships would be lost, half of them in the perilous waters off New England and the Maritime Provinces.

The horror of this period of US history, even today, boggles the mind, and many questions remain. How could the government not be prepared? In this resource-rich nation where manufacturing genius was legendary, where were the ships and guns needed to protect our coastal waters? Was it possible that our efforts at intelligence had gone for nothing? The reality is that this country was indeed unprepared and, more shockingly, had been forewarned. During the second week of January 1942, the US Navy received intelligence from the British warning that U-boats were headed toward the American coast.

The most striking feature is a heavy concentration [of U-boats] off the North American seaboard from New York to Cape Race [Newfoundland]. Two groups have so far been formed. One of 6 U-boats is already in position off Cape Race and St. John's [Newfoundland] and a second, or 5 U-boats, is apparently approaching the American coast between New York and Portland [Maine]. It is known that a total of 21 boats [are heading] west.[7]

In the search for blame for this debacle, one name has resurfaced consistently: Admiral Ernest J. King. This nearly thirty-year member of the US Navy had been appointed Commander in Chief of the US Fleet just after the attack on Pearl Harbor. While King would eventually prove to be an able leader, his personality made him a questionable choice. He was known for his hatred of the British, and his own

---

[4] *NH Man Was to Wed.* Boston Globe 11/1/1941. Newspapers.com. tinyurl.com/2x4arw8y.

[5] *No Split In Diplomatic Relations.* Boston Daily Globe, 10/31/1941. Newspapers.com. tinyurl.com/ytrn97rd.

[6] *US Last Mile to War.* Boston Globe 11/1/1941. Newspapers.com. tinyurl.com/msca8hve.

[7] Offley, Ed. *Drumbeat Mystery.* Nav Hist 2/2022. USNI. tinyurl.com/32ktadsv.

daughter described him as "the most even-tempered man in the Navy. He is always in a rage."[8] Roosevelt stated that he "shaves every morning with a blow torch," and Eisenhower wrote: "...one way to win the war is to shoot Admiral King." While U-boats wreaked havoc in the Atlantic, Americans were kept in the dark thanks to King's philosophy, "Don't tell them anything. When it's over, tell them who won." Admiral King was a man of strong opinions, and as U-boats approached North America in January of 1942, it was King's opinion that the eighteen available destroyers on the East Coast should be sent as escorts for convoys headed across the North Atlantic. The decision left shipping along the coastline nearly defenseless.

The Cyclops was the first sunk by U-123 three hundred miles east of Cape Cod with the loss of eighty-eight crew and passengers. It was January 11. On January 12, the First Naval District was warned of at least four submarines operating off Nantucket Light.[9] Two days later, now south of Rhode Island, Kapitänleutnant Reinhard Hardegen spotted a tanker. The Eastern Sea Frontier Diary of January 14, 1942, reported, "Norness Torpedoed and sunk...Three torpedoes – close range. Six officers and 24 men rescued and landed at Newport...Captain and eight men brought to New Bedford in fishing boat Malvina."[10] Hours later, approaching the coastline of New York, the tanker Coimbra appeared, highlighted against the backdrop of a brilliantly lit city. The kill went swiftly, the Coimbra exploding in a fireball that left thirty-six dead. Within just three weeks, Hardegen would send eight ships to the bottom and damage a ninth.

The tally went higher and higher. February 12, the Dixie Sword, carrying 5,000 tons of zinc and copper ore, went down off Monomoy Island on Cape Cod. No notice of the sinking appeared in the press, and while the official report later stated she had foundered during bad weather, it was suspected that she had been torpedoed.[11] The British ship Mattawin, with a cargo of supplies and airplanes, would meet the same fate in June, 190 miles southeast of Nantucket. The crew made their escape in four lifeboats heading northwest to Cape Cod. One would make it to Nauset Beach near Eastham. Another would be rescued by the Coast Guard and delivered to Nantucket.[12]

The story of U-576 illustrates the chaotic and often serendipitous intertwining of men and ships during the Battle for the Coast. For a little over a week in 1942, the U-boat left a path of destruction along the Atlantic coastline. Far to the south of Massachusetts on April 21, the Pipestone County was taken down by a torpedo, leaving enough time for the entire crew to man lifeboats. U-576 headed north. Three days later and now 43 miles off Nantucket, the Norwegian Tropic Star, two boatloads of Pipestone survivors on board, was fired upon unsuccessfully by U-576. The captain immediately ordered weapons to the ready, graciously allowing the gun crew of the Pipestone to man deck guns. In the minutes that followed, the submarine's conning tower appeared, and its periscope was struck by gunfire. Scratches on the hull of the Tropic Star would later support witness reports that the sub scraped the keel of the ship while attempting to dive. U-576 hid out on the sea floor for repairs on the 25th and laid quietly off Nauset Beach on the 28th while the search for the sub continued. Forty-eight hours later, the U-boat was on the move again, spotting the Norwegian merchant ship Taborfjell 95 miles east of Provincetown.[13] The vessel had transited the Cape Cod Canal the day before and was headed northeast to Canadian waters. Two torpedoes slammed through the hull of the Taborfjell and took her down in one minute, along with seventeen members of her crew.[14]

---

8 Chen, C. Peter. *Ernest King*. WWII Database. tinyurl.com/2ksj7p77.

9 Hickam, Jr., Homer H. *Torpedo Junction*. Bluejacket 1996.

10 *War Diary No Atlantic Coastal Frontier 1/1942*. Uboatarchive.net. tinyurl.com/59fanj3m.

11 *Dixie Sword*. Mass.gov. tinyurl.com/2s388ej3.

12 *Mattawin*. Uboat.net. tinyurl.com/nhbkyb77.

13 Wiberg, Eric. *U-Boats in New England*. Fonthill 2019.

14 *Taborfjell*. Uboat.net. tinyurl.com/5vbdkcu7.

Over the course of these ten days, the actions of U-576 involved vessels from four different countries. The sub had attacked three ships, sunk two, murdered seventeen innocent merchant mariners, and sent 49 survivors into ports at Massachusetts, Virginia, New Jersey, and Newfoundland. Her rampage was not over. She turned southward. On July 15, the sub encountered a convoy in waters east of North Carolina. Her last day would be a busy one. After sinking the tanker Bluefields and damaging two other vessels, she was destroyed by depth charges and deck guns from US aircraft and the merchant ship Unicoi. None of the crew survived. All that remains of U-576 lies on the ocean floor thirty miles off Cape Hatteras, approximately 1,000 feet from its final victim, the Bluefields.

Off the Atlantic Coast, shipping lanes were established for commercial vessels but lacked adequate protection. U-boats often attacked within sight of surprised bystanders ashore. As a young girl, M. Davis witnessed a ship being torpedoed during her visit to the Snow Inn Bluffs at Wychmere Harbor in Harwich Port.[15] George Bartlett of Hingham recalled: "I remember seeing one sub in 1943 prowling the waters off Brant Rock looking for prey. As soon as I gave the alert, it disappeared. U-boats were always on the prowl."[16] "The battle of the Eastern Coastline should soon be over," opined Henry W. Harris in a March 1942 edition of the *Daily Boston Globe*, although his enthusiasm was premature. The problems described in his column were not easily corrected. Not every skipper went into port after dark or sailed without running lights at night.[17] Some ships traveled alone. They crossed as massive silhouettes before the well-lit coastline, illuminated by countless signs, cars, and buildings. As a result, the killing spree continued. Author Eric Wiberg, in his book *U-Boats in New England*, offers a horrifying estimate: during the Spring of 1942, the German Second Happy Time, a tanker was sunk off the Atlantic coast every ten hours.[18]

Kriegsmarine Admiral Karl Doenitz was frank about their effectiveness.

The success of the first six boats in American waters was, as expected, very considerable. The American defense was inexperienced; on the other hand, the U-boat commanders were exceptionally experienced. It was possible to operate very near to the coast and on the surface. Traffic was heavy here; consequently, the results were great...Until the end of September 1942, such operations were worthwhile despite the very long inoperative passage out and back.[19]

A 1943 *Boston Globe* article commented: "Since early in the war...the Navy has had a policy of silence regarding anti-submarine operations, and no estimate of the total number of subs sunk in the Atlantic or the Pacific can even be approximated on the basis of occasional reports thus far made public."[20] In spite of the lack of information in the press, Massachusetts citizens gradually accepted that the U-boat was a genuine threat and not so far away as once reported. Thomas Leach, former harbormaster in Harwich, recalled: "The Coast Guard and Navy...kept the public in the dark about the numbers of these sinkings off Massachusetts, yet on Cape Cod, innuendo about the frequency of the bodies of dead merchantmen washing ashore was growing."[21] Jane Slater of Martha's Vineyard recalled:

---

[15] Leach, Thomas. *Lightships Nantucket Sound*. Threeharbors.com 1/2006. tinyurl.com/yck4cbe7.

[16] Rose, Jim. *66 years ago war touched MA Coast*. Patriot Ledger 6/12/2008. tinyurl.com/44dwnse9.

[17] Harris, Henry. *Battle Coastline*. Boston Globe 3/20/1942. Newspapers.com. tinyurl.com/587npv68.

[18] Wiberg, Eric. *U-Boats in New England*.

[19] Doenitz, Karl. *Conduct War at Sea* 1/15/1946. ONI. NHHC. tinyurl.com/mkawsbsd.

[20] *Cutter Rams Sinks Sub*. Boston Globe 3/18/1943. Newspapers.com. tinyurl.com/2w5z8nnf.

[21] Leach, Thomas. *Lightships of Nantucket Sound*.

Some nights there was a strange throbbing engine noise clearly heard in our living room. Those nights, my grandmother would call the Coast Guard to report hearing it. They, most often, could hear it too and agreed that, most likely, a submarine was surfaced in the lee of Squibnocket and was charging its batteries. This actually happened often.[22]

A history of Fairhaven, Massachusetts, contains this terrifying statement: "It was not uncommon to stroll along the beach on a quiet summer night and hear a deep thud in the distance followed by an orange glow on the horizon...another ship being struck by a torpedo and sent to the bottom."[23] Four destroyers and one sub were continuously on patrol near Provincetown Harbor.[24] Yachting enthusiasts wondered if their seasonal activities would come to an end when registration was required for boaters in communities like Marblehead, Salem, and Lynn, and, as the coast was fortified, channels would have to be altered to make room for torpedo ranges, practice targets, and mines.[25]

Concerned by the loss of shipping off the Massachusetts coast, in July 1942, Governor Leverett Saltonstall invoked blackout regulations in coastal areas.

WHEREAS, lights on or near the shore which shine or are reflected toward the sea or contribute to the skyglow over the sea or adjacent land have caused ships along the coast to be silhouetted during the nighttime, thereby giving substantial assistance to said submarines and promoting the success of their activities...During the period between one-half hour after sunset and one-half hour before sunrise, all lights of every nature which are visible from the sea, or...illuminate the sky, shall be extinguished or...shielded so that such lights...will not show the position or outline of any ship at sea.[26]

Some structures, however, were designed to stay lit. The coastal waters of the Bay State were known to be hazardous, marked by rocky outcrops, inlets, and constantly shifting shoals. Lighthouses, lightships, and buoys dotted the Massachusetts coastline and, during the war, were used by Allies and enemies alike to assist ships. Author Eric Wiberg notes with frightening frequency the useful role they played for German subs attempting to navigate the dangerous Bay State coastline:

February 1942 U-96: Intend to search for traffic for Boston at Cape Cod...Cape Cod lighthouse in sights. Burns as in peacetime.
March 1942 U-552: Passed lightship Pollock, closed [hugged] the coast from buoy to buoy...all lighthouses are lit. Rested on the bottom near Nauset Light.
June 1942 U-87: The city of Boston is hardly darkened. The lighthouses burn as if in peacetime.[27]

Soon, however, many of the lights went dark. A postwar report from US Coast Guard Headquarters describes steps taken to protect the shoreline. Twenty-three light stations were extinguished, and fifty-four were reduced in candlepower. Several lightships suffered the same fate. Unbelievably, the vessels Nantucket Shoals and Pollock Rip, which warned of deadly sandbars off Cape Cod, were relocated to be returned in 1945. Lights were extinguished on many buoys, and ten were discontinued entirely. A number of buoys were used for special projects, such as creating the outline of a submarine for bombing practice in the waters off Orleans.[28]

---

[22] Dresser, Thomas et al. *Martha's Vineyard WWII.* History Press 2014.

[23] Baron, M.L. *West Island's tower.* So Coast Today 5/16/2013. tinyurl.com/mr453yp4.

[24] Lawless, Debra. *Provincetown Since WWII.* History Press 2014.

[25] Fowle, Leonard. *Yachting Curtailed.* Boston Globe 12/141941. ProQuest. tinyurl.com/ye22dxnh.

[26] *Executive-order No. 31.* Mass.gov. tinyurl.com/57dmh43s.

[27] Wiberg, Eric. *U-Boats in New England.*

[28] *Coast Guard at War: Aids to Navigation XV.* USCG, 7/1/1949. DOD. tinyurl.com/45tnand7.

Boston Light on Little Brewster Island,
Boston Harbor went dark. WWII.[29]

In addition to keeping the coastline dark, a variety of defense plans were put into action along the Massachusetts shore. Observation or fire control towers located U-boats, tracked their course, and radioed information to a command center where data could be used to plot firing solutions. Stretched along the coastline, towers were located in long-established buildings, others in recently built concrete fortresses armed with gun batteries. Structures were located in Gloucester, Marshfield, and Hull. The West Island lookout tower in Fairhaven, which still stands today, included a small base for twenty-four men.[30] At Halibut Point Base End Station in Rockport, a wooden structure attached to a tower contained a Boston Harbor Defense Command post. The roof of the tower was used for anti-aircraft intelligence, and a gun battery was located below.[31]

Due to its importance to transportation and commerce, Boston Harbor has been the site of defensive fortifications since colonial days. With the outbreak of World War II, many Massachusetts harbor and coastal forts were expanded or updated, and others were newly built. In Nahant, the East Point Military Reservation was constructed with gun batteries, a fire control tower, and bunkers. Anti-Motor Torpedo Boat (AMTB) batteries were located at Fort Heath and Fort Revere in Boston Harbor, and sub-net defenses were placed at Deer Island and Windmill Point in Hull. Batteries at Fort Taber/Fort Rodman in New Bedford, Butler Point in Marion, and Plymouth Camp were among several that were armed with 16" guns.[32]

Shortly after Pearl Harbor, a German plot to send spies to America on a sabotage mission was uncovered. (In fact, approximately six months later, Germany successfully landed members of Operation Pastorius on Long Island. One day later, residents of both Beverly and Manchester-by-the-Sea reported saboteur landings.)[33] In response, the government created the US Coast Guard Beach Patrol. Beach Patrol headquarters were placed in coastal communities, including Popples Point in Gloucester, Provincetown, Salisbury, Revere, North Truro, Fairhaven, Cohasset, Chelsea, Bourne, Salem, New

[29] *Boston Light.* Pub domain photo. USCG 4766 7/9/2019. tinyurl.com/4stxczz2.

[30] Baron, M.L. *West Island's iconic tower.*

[31] *Halibut Point Station.* Northamericanforts.com. tinyurl.com/2s44u5f5.

[32] *History Boston Harbor.* State Lib MA. tinyurl.com/z9j3t7v3.

[33] Wiberg, Eric. *U-Boats in New England.*

Bedford, Plymouth, and Beverly.[34] Known as "sand" or "beach pounders," their job was detecting enemy vessels, reporting attempted landings, and preventing communication between anyone onshore and enemy vessels. Armed patrols consisting of two men would cover a two-mile stretch, reporting back every quarter mile. They scanned the ocean for U-boats, located shipwreck survivors, and searched for spies. If a suspect was encountered, they were expected to issue a halt order followed by a warning shot. Failure to comply was considered justification for guardsmen to shoot to kill. By the war's end, the Beach Patrol would expand to include over 3,000 horses and thousands of dogs.

Mounted Beach Patrol. WWII[35]

Though small in size, Massachusetts has 1,500 miles of convoluted coastline and a multitude of islands ranging from 100 square mile Martha's Vineyard to tiny three-acre Sheep Island in Boston Harbor. Protecting the expansive Massachusetts shoreline presented a problem. The Boston Headquarters of the First Naval District, under whose authority the Beach Patrol operated, understood the state's geography and adopted an operational plan specifically for Massachusetts. Cape Cod, stretching out into the Atlantic and U-boat territory, was particularly at risk.

In the summer of 1942, for example, two boys vacationing in Chatham discovered headphones hidden under a pile of brush near Morris Island. After reporting the suspicious find to local authorities, they returned to the site with a Coast Guardsman, who spotted an antenna attached to a tree. When approached by a young man wielding a bayonet, the man, later identified as a Nazi sympathizer, was taken into custody.[36] The islands, particularly those to the south, were a concern. In the early days of the war, nineteen U-boats were sighted in the waters around Martha's Vineyard alone.[37]

As the reign of U-boats in the Atlantic declined along with the Third Reich, so did the urgent need for intensive shore patrols. In 1944, the Guardsmen of the Beach Patrol were recalled from twenty-seven Massachusetts stations. By the end of the war, 24,000 sand pounders had patrolled nearly 4,000 miles of the American coastline, fulfilling their duty to the Coast Guard and their country.[38]

---

[34] *USCG Log 1943*. USCG. NARA. tinyurl.com/yj9jucmu.

[35] *Beach Patrol*. Pub domain photo. WWII USCG 170602-G-XX000-104. tinyurl.com/4dm6acev.

[36] *Chatham WWII*. At the Atwood 2020. tinyurl.com/4pz4c3n7.

[37] Schaffel, Chaiel. *Paradise Shifted*. This Week Martha's Vineyard 4/2014. tinyurl.com/37sabmej.

[38] *Beach Patrol XVII*. USCG 7/15/1945. Media.defense.gov. tinyurl.com/38c3ceb7.

By March of 1942, Allied shipping was hemorrhaging as a result of U-boat attacks and the shocking lack of preparedness on the part of the United States. At the outbreak of war, the number of vessels and aircraft available to the Navy's Eastern Sea Frontier (in charge of coastal defense from Maine to Florida) was extremely limited, with most being in less than optimal condition. The Eastern Defense Command of the Army found itself in similar circumstances, hindered by the small amount of aircraft at its disposal. During the first two months of 1942, in spite of 8,000 hours of patrol, the Army Air Force conducted just four attacks with no strikes. The Navy simply informed the public that they had the situation well in hand after hitting twenty-one subs since the outbreak of war.[39] It was a creative and encouraging notion with little concern for the truth, orchestrated by the organization whose leader, Admiral King, was a firm believer in sharing information on a need-to-know basis, and the public, he felt, simply didn't need to know. Until the United States could come up with the materials and manpower needed to counteract the U-boat menace, the country was in desperate need of help.

The idea that ordinary civilians could participate in the defense of the country had been pitched long before America entered the war, and by the time the Japanese attacked Pearl Harbor, the United States had a brand new Civil Air Patrol. What to do with it, unfortunately, was still being debated. In July 1942, *Boston Globe* reporter Joseph F. Dineen commented, "For months now, and for reasons that are still vague and obscure to me...the Civil Air Patrol has been lumbering along as a loose appendage, neither fish nor fowl."[40] Fear of enemy attack, infiltration by saboteurs, and the ever-growing U-boat threat weighed heavily on the minds of the powers that be. However, the idea that "a disorganized gang of civilians" had anything to offer was less than popular. "I don't care what those country club pilots say they can do," stated one official. "I don't want their toy planes cluttering up the air!"[41]

A history of the Civil Air Patrol, written by Robert Neprud, describes the early years. The government, in its typical bureaucratic fashion, was slow to develop a program. In what looked suspiciously like an attempt to militarize non-military citizens, officials outlined administrative hierarchies, created badges, decided on a red and yellow color palette for airplanes, and debated uniform design (slacks, skirts, or culottes for women were an issue). All the while, American factories and airfields went unguarded.

Observing from the sidelines, Earle Johnson had enough. "It gave me the creeps to think what a hundred German agents could do to a hundred power plants in just one night. They could drop their bombs, head for open country, land their planes in a field, walk away, and never be caught." A native of Great Barrington, Johnson decided to take matters into his own hands. After loading three sandbags into his Curtiss Sedan aircraft, he took off heading toward Cleveland. He spied his targets and, over the next several minutes, zoomed in to drop sandbags on the roof of three different defense-related production facilities. A horrified Washington was quick to respond. Within a week, armed guards were stationed at airports, and all civilian flights remained grounded unless provided with official clearance. Earle Johnson would soon become the National CAP Commander.

The group of civilian pilots that became the "Flying Minute Men" of the Civil Air Patrol were an eclectic bunch of patriots dressed in uniforms or everyday clothing. They flew Cessnas or Piper Cubs or Fairchilds, taking off from government airfields, private airstrips, and cow pastures. They held everyday jobs and ranged in age from teens to 81-year-old A.I. Martin of New York. They were men, and they were women. When not on duty, they slept in houses, barns, and chicken coops. They provided their own planes and supplies with minimal funding from the government.[42] One hundred pilots in Norwood, Massachusetts, parked their airplanes in front of a hangar built with their own hands, wore uniforms

---

[39] Blazich, Frank Jr. *Honorable Place Am Air Power.* AUP 12/2020. tinyurl.com/5n7n7p2t.

[40] Dineen, Joseph. *Spilling Beans CAP.* Boston Globe 7/27/1942. Newspapers.com. tinyurl.com/29x2tdz7.

[41] Neprud, Robert E. *Flying Minute Men CAP.* Duell, Sloane, Pierce 1948. DOD. tinyurl.com/mrwzrrsf.

[42] Neprud, Robert E. *Flying Minute Men CAP.*

purchased with their own money, and operated the Norwood Squadron at zero cost to the government.[43] Gordon C. Prince was a natural for the role of Commander for the Massachusetts Wing of the Civil Air Patrol. A lifelong resident of the Bay State, before his appointment, Prince had already been flying for twenty-five years, including a stint as a pilot in the First World War. Among his many hobbies was flying as a stunt pilot on Sunday afternoons at the Old Brockton Fair.[44]

Owing to the urgency of protecting the Atlantic coastline, a group of flyers known as the Coastal Air Patrol was created within the Civil Air Patrol. Twenty-one Coastal Air Patrol Bases operated from Maine to Texas, in Massachusetts, at Coonamessett Airport in Falmouth. Little to no government funds were provided for the operation of Coastal Air Patrol airfields. (In Virginia, the Base Commander told prospective members to report with "...money enough to last you a month, and picks and shovels, because there'll be no landing field until we've built one.")[45] These "puddle jumpers" hunted for submarines and radioed locations back to base, looked for and rescued survivors, and some, at the urging of then Maj. General Dwight Eisenhower carried 100-pound bombs. Larger aircraft flew with 350-pound depth charges on board.

The opportunity for civilians to serve, many of whom were disqualified from the military, was immensely popular with pilots. A CAP newsletter published two months after the organization's founding stated that as of January 28, 1942, over 16,000 applications had arrived at the Washington headquarters, with 850 more coming in daily. Nearly 400 applicants were from Massachusetts.[46] Everett L. King of Taunton was one of them. In January 1943, two coastal patrol planes manned by King, along with Louis Ferrari and Walter Murphy of Boston, were searching the ocean around Block Island when an oil slick came into view. No sub was sighted. Marker bombs were dropped over the site. The following day, a second patrol out of Falmouth spotted oil in the water and reported it. The Navy arrived shortly after, successfully locating and sinking a German U-boat.[47] In an effort to recognize the bravery and danger that the men and women of this group faced with each mission, the Duck Club was established. Unique to the Coastal Patrol, members had to have experienced a forced landing in water or bailed out of an airplane. At least one Massachusetts puddle jumper made it into the club.

The Coastal Air Patrol operated during the most devastating eighteen months of the Battle for the Coast. By the time it was ordered to stand down, its pilots had attacked 57 of the 173 U-boats sighted, sinking or damaging two, and dropped 82 bombs. Reports of sub-sightings were credited as assists for a number of U-boat kills. In addition, 17 mines, 36 dead bodies, 91 vessels in distress, and 363 survivors were located. The US Coastal Air Patrol logged over 244,000 flight hours during 86,685 missions. In the performance of their duty, 90 aircraft were downed, and 26 brave airmen lost their lives at sea.

The group was absorbed into the Civil Air Patrol, which was transferred to the Department of Defense in 1943. CAP pilots had earned the respect and gratitude of the Armed Forces. They left behind a stunning record of achievement and had flown 24,000,000 miles. One high-ranking German Navy official stated that one of the major reasons U-boats were recalled from the American coastline was "...because of those damned little red and yellow planes."[48] In 2012, the collective members of the Civil Air Patrol were awarded a Gold Medal by a grateful nation.

---

[43] Dineen, Joseph F. *Spilling the Beans CAP.*

[44] *Gordon Prince.* Daily Item 9/19/1983. Newspapers.com. tinyurl.com/5fshke49.

[45] Neprud, Robert E. *Flying Minute Men CAP.*

[46] *CAP News Letter 1/28/1942.* CAP. USAF Auxiliary. tinyurl.com/4bj4hek4.

[47] Connell, Lisa. *MA aviator WWII.* Berkshire Eagle 1/2/2016. tinyurl.com/c52fmcdv.

[48] *Gold Medal to CAP.* Cong Record Vol 157 2011. tinyurl.com/29uxw2c6.

Members of the Civil Air Patrol. WWII.[49]

Massachusetts had an abundance of privately owned airfields prior to 1941. Within days of the attack at Pearl Harbor, FDR granted the Secretary of War power to take control of any civilian aviation system deemed necessary for government use by the country at war. As a result, a number of local airports became Naval Auxiliary Air Facilities (NAAF). Airfields in Barnstable and Plum Island were used for anti-submarine patrols. Others were outlying fields that supported larger bases. Naval Air Station Squantum in South Weymouth was affiliated with Plymouth, Norwood, and Beverly. Naval Air Station Quonset Point in Rhode Island utilized airports at Plymouth and New Bedford.

During the Second World War, the Navy maintained larger air stations along the coast as well. Constructed in 1910 on the Squantum peninsula in Quincy, Naval Air Station Squantum provided air support and reconnaissance for the Massachusetts Bay area. A Coast Guard Air Station was located at Salem. The base was used for seaplanes, which conducted search and rescue missions and anti-submarine patrols.

Standing for inspection, Otis Field. 1944.[50]

The Massachusetts Military Reservation at Camp Edwards technically fell under the US Army administration. For the first two years of World War II, the Army Air Corps 14th Anti-Submarine Patrol Squadron flew missions out of the base, but in 1944, the US Navy assumed command of all reconnaissance missions out of the camp's Otis Field.

One of the most prominent airfields on the Massachusetts coastline had little to do with airplanes. The United States had used a limited number of blimps in the past, and as the war grew closer, Roosevelt approved expansion of the country's Lighter-Than-Air-Program. The Goodyear company was contracted

[49] *CAP.* Pub domain photo. USAF 5/20/2014. tinyurl.com/2s38brkc.

[50] *Inspection Otis Field* 1944. Public domain photo. NARA Boston. Picryl. tinyurl.com/ytjf33kn.

to produce a number of these "gas bags," and by 1945, the United States was home to the largest dirigible fleet in the world. The earliest of the giant K-class airships consisted of a gondola and a gigantic envelope containing 425,000 cubic feet of helium. A crew of up to ten was housed within the gondola along with equipment, cargo, four depth charges, a machine gun, and a crate full of carrier pigeons. A few of Goodyear's advertising blimps were purchased by the government for use in training.

South Weymouth Naval Air Station. 1944.[51]

In the fall of 1941, construction began on the South Weymouth Naval Air Station. Located on 1,267 acres of largely uninhabited land and at a cost of six million dollars, the base opened in March of 1942. The complex included two airship hangars, classed among the largest buildings in the world, six mooring circles, and a 2,000-foot diameter landing mat for dirigibles.[52] The sole mission of the base was to support and conduct anti-submarine warfare. Airships flew reconnaissance missions above the waters around Massachusetts and the Gulf of Maine and accompanied convoys headed northeast. In addition, blimps rescued survivors from ship and airplane disasters and scanned the water for mines.

Blimp crash, Scituate. 1943.[53]

---

[51] *Hangar So. Weymouth NAS.* Pub domain photo. USN. MADC. tinyurl.com/22d2y9mn.

[52] *NAS South Weymouth.* Patriot Squadron Asso Nav Aviation. tinyurl.com/4rbuzv5d.

[53] *Blimp crashes Scituate.* Pub domain photo. USN. Digital Commonwealth. tinyurl.com/36fn6nsb.

Wary of possible U-boat attacks, merchant captains were likely to hug the coast whenever possible, although this was never a guarantee of safety. U-boat logs frequently note hunting along the shoreline of Massachusetts. In May 1942, for example, U-566 turned to waters off Cape Cod on the 13th at the entrance to the Cape Cod Canal, then turned northeast toward the Nantucket Lightship on the 16th, and making its way to Provincetown until finally coming under attack by Navy aircraft thirty-five miles northeast of Cape Cod.[54] To shave their perilous coastal runs by a good seventy miles, merchants utilized the Cape Cod Canal, a man-made waterway of enormous strategic importance.

With the outbreak of World War II, the government took steps to protect the waterway. Submarine nets, minefields, and minesweepers protected approaches to the canal. Technically, the Canal passed into naval jurisdiction during the war, and Navy escorts shepherded merchant vessels into convoy formations as they neared the channel. The Coast Guard patrolled the entryways, sent tugs to nudge ships in the right direction, and kept an eye on seagoing traffic. The passage was also monitored by airships and radar. The Army posted guards on bridges and in nearby coastal batteries. Located at the eastern end of the Canal in an area now known as Scusset Beach, development began at Sagamore Hill shortly after the attack on Pearl Harbor. Two 155 mm cannons were installed, and a handful of buildings, including barracks and a mess hall, were constructed. Eventually, 240 men would be assigned to Sagamore Hill.[55] A similar installation guarded the western access to the Canal at Butler's Point in Marion, and the Mishaum Point Military Reservation in South Dartmouth controlled all military access to the waters of Buzzards Bay and the Cape Cod Canal.[56]

Passing through the Canal was an arduous process. After reaching one of the entrances, a ship was contacted by guardsmen via radio or blinker light. Data on the vessel's size, cargo, and speed was forwarded to stations in Sandwich and at Cleveland Ledge Light in Bourne. Harbor pilots, cleared by naval intelligence, along with guardsmen, would remain on board for the transit. Laden vessels bound for Europe were permitted to enter the Canal every eight minutes and had the right of way, while "pink ships" loaded with ammunition were let through every half hour. Bourne Selectman Donald Ellis recalled watching ships from the banks of the Canal, "80 to 100 ships passing through each day."[57]

USS Little Rock in Cape Cod Canal.[58]

Accidents were frequent. On June 29, 1944, the USS Richard W. Suesens collided in Buzzards Bay with the USS Valor, a coastal minesweeper out of Boston, with the loss of seven lives. In July 1945, the HMCS St. Francis, a Lend Lease destroyer, encountered a heavy fog bank after exiting the canal in Buzzards Bay. It collided with the collier Windward Gulf, which crushed through the hull of the old

[54] Wiberg, Eric. *U-Boats in New England.*

[55] Williams, Eric. *Big guns over canal.* Cape Cod Times 12/11/2020. tinyurl.com/5t3csf9j.

[56] Butler, Gerald. *Mil History CC Canal.* Arcadia Publ 2002.

[57] Lynch, Christine. *Wartime vantage point.* Repository 7/19/2014. tinyurl.com/f2m3c4hr.

[58] *USS Little Rock.* Pub domain photo. Don Fink. NHHC. tinyurl.com/37s264n8.

destroyer, sinking her.[59] On June 28, 1942, the collier Stephen R. Jones of the Boston Eastern Gas and Fuel Company grounded with its cargo of 6,000 tons of coal not far from the railroad bridge on the western end of the Canal. Sabotage was suspected, though never confirmed. The wreck completely shut down the man-made passage, and clearing the wreckage proved difficult. On Independence Day, the public witnessed an incredible fireworks display as the government destroyed the Jones using 17.5 tons of dynamite. Debris removal took twenty-eight days, and the Canal was reopened for business by the end of July.[60]

Stephen R. Jones, Cape Cod Canal. 1942.[61]

The disruption to traffic on the waterway caused by the Stephen R. Jones highlighted the importance of this vital shortcut. While the Canal was shut down, ships were forced to take the long, dangerous route around the outer Cape. One such vessel was the Alexander Macomb. Five days after the Jones lodged itself in the channel, the Macomb was on her maiden voyage from New York en route to Halifax. On board were 9,000 tons of equipment and materials, including tanks, planes, and explosives. The ship fell behind its convoy in heavy fog, and as she rounded the Cape 175 miles due east of Provincetown, she was spotted by U-215 on a mission to mine Boston Harbor. The U-boat fired one torpedo, striking it. A massive explosion followed, and the ship was gone in thirty minutes, along with ten men. Soon afterward, HMS Le Tiger, survivors of the Alexander Macomb on board, hunted down and sank U-215 with all hands. It was the U-boat's first patrol, and it had lasted 25 days. Thirty-one Macomb survivors were delivered to Woods Hole.[62] Sixty-two years later, the U-boat was discovered on the ocean floor where she went down, mines still on board.

Twenty-eight-year-old Kapitänleutnant Joachim Berger was having a very good war. A training officer for the Kriegsmarine, he completed U-boat school in August 1941 and was placed in command of his first submarine, U-87. It was a feather in his cap. The Unterseeboot was the latest and most advanced sub in the German arsenal, designed to be faster and more maneuverable than its predecessor. The sub could carry thirty-three more tons of fuel, increasing its range by 2,500 miles. On his first voyage, Berger sank two ships in just seventeen days and was rewarded with an Iron Cross. In May 1942, he received orders for his next patrol and headed westward to the east coast of America and Boston Harbor. U-87 was carrying mines.[63]

As Joachim Berger approached the Massachusetts coastline, his task was tricky. Massachusetts Bay was one of the busiest shipping zones on the Atlantic coast. The area was heavily traveled and

[59] Zeien, Scott. *Shipwrecks Buzzards Bay.* Kingman Yacht Center. tinyurl.com/2wdv9wpp.

[60] Butler, Gerald. *Mil History CC Canal.*

[61] *Stephen R Jones.* Pub domain photo. USACE. CC Canal Post. Facebook. tinyurl.com/3ufm9b6z.

[62] *Alexander Macomb.* Uboat.net. tinyurl.com/35jezb84.

[63] *Joachim Berger.* tinyurl.com/mpb7kzy8.

heavily defended. For submarines, the job of mining a harbor meant carrying cargo that took up space needed for torpedoes. In addition, many ports were protected by mines, putting the U-boats at further risk. Boston Harbor contained thirty defensive mine locations. Fort Warren served as a mine control center, and a mine storage facility can still be seen there today. In spite of these hazards, Berger and U-87 silently made their way into the harbor, dropped six mines near the entrance, and headed back out to sea. There is no evidence that the mines did any damage. It was June 12.[64]

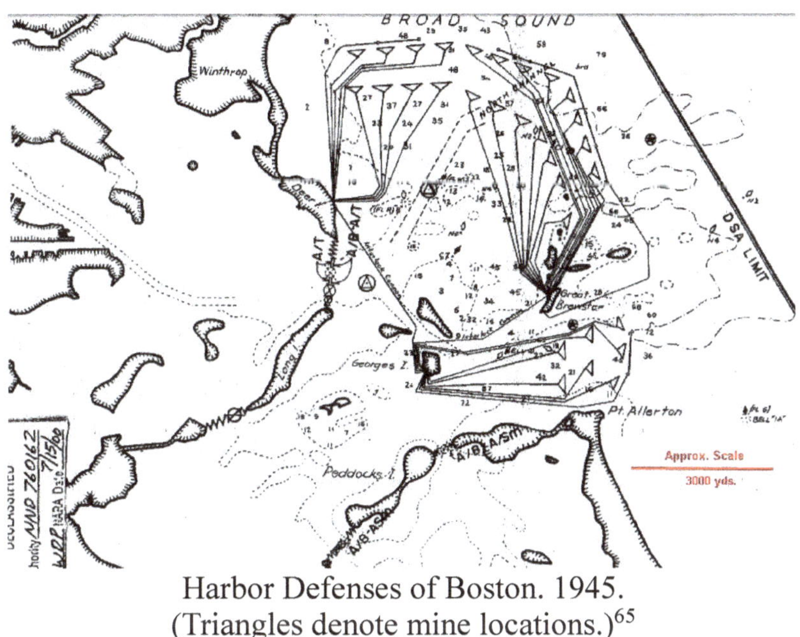

Harbor Defenses of Boston. 1945.
(Triangles denote mine locations.)[65]

The sub then headed outbound, quietly lying in wait at the busy crossroads off Cape Cod. On June 16, Convoy B-25 wandered into Berger's sights on a run from Halifax to Boston. Out in front was the Port Nicholson. At 4:17 in the morning, just off the coast of Truro,[66] two torpedoes slammed into the British merchantman, sinking her with the loss of six men. Eighty-five who survived the attack were delivered to Boston.

Four minutes after the Port Nicholson was struck, it was Cherokee's turn. The vessel carried 11 guards, 46 members of the US Army, a crew of 112, and a hold full of ballast. The first torpedo struck the port side below the bridge, lifting her right out of the water. A second torpedo slammed into the port bow and quickly took her down.[67] She was sixty-two miles northeast of Provincetown. Foul weather made launching lifeboats impossible, and only a handful of rafts made it into the water. In six minutes, eighty-six souls were gone. Survivors were picked up and taken to Boston and Providence.[68] One month later, Kapitanleutnant Joachim Berger was awarded an Iron Cross for his efforts, and nine months later, he and the entire crew of U-87 were dead, sent to the bottom of the Atlantic by Canadian warships.

"Sighted sub, sank same." It wasn't nearly as easy as this oft-heard report sounded. Sub hunting was an incredibly labor, equipment, and time-intensive business, an exercise in patience, more often than not with a negative outcome. A report of activity in April 1944 from the Secret War Diary Northern Group illustrates the difficulties facing the men searching for U-boats.

<hr>

[64] Rose, Jim. *66 years ago, world war touched MA coast.*

[65] *Mine fields Bos Harbor 1/1945.* Public domain photo. USACE. Wiki Commons. tinyurl.com/y3a2j3k4.

[66] *Port Nicholson.* U-boat.net. tinyurl.com/3u3jy9nx.

[67] *Cherokee.* U-boat.net. tinyurl.com/2s3h2zst.

[68] Linscott, Seymour. *Subs Sank Ships Off N.E.* Boston Globe 8/30/1945. Newspapers.com. tinyurl.com/59e6wawb.

April 3: A PBY flying boat out of Rhode Island reported a radar contact, a possible U-boat. Airships from NAS South Weymouth and aircraft from Salem, patrolling George's Bank at the time, were vectored to the contact's last known position. Nothing was found, and the search was suspended.

April 5: The USS Captor detected a "solid and metallic and wholly distinct" echo on sonar. A Patrol Bomber out of Salem was sent to search. The Captor began the attack. Six 300-pound depth charges were ejected into the water over the next twelve minutes. Captor's engines stopped but were unable to pick up propeller noises, so depth charges continued. The last, set for 250 feet, failed to explode. An oil slick was spotted, and Captor released a buoy to mark the location.

By morning, USS Fitch, Airship K-38, and USCG cutter Harriet Lane arrived at the scene. To determine whether the sub was on the bottom, Fitch released a spread of depth charges. Fuel immediately rose to the surface, but unfortunately, it was not the diesel used by U-boats. The Navy had struck out. All the depth charges thrown into the sea had very likely succeeded in ripping up an older shipwreck. K-38 sent out the message, "Results all contacts neg – positive wreck – CAPTOR no longer needs us," and returned to base.

April 9: While escorting the oiler USS Kaweah, airship K-11 reported magnetic anomaly detection (MAD) contacts, radar contacts, and visual sightings of a submarine periscope just east of Stellwagen Bank. Almost an hour after its first report, K-11 picked up another contact heading eastward. However, an expert onshore determined that the signal had come from geologic sources. Whales were also seen in the area. A dorsal fin may have been responsible for mimicking the visual feather typically seen in the wake of an extended periscope.

K-38 was sent to the area and discovered oil slicks. An aviation machinist's mate spotted a black cylindrical object six to eight feet high above the water. At 1700, the airship picked up a radar contact slightly southwest, closer to Cape Cod. K-38 turned to close on the contact, but visibility began to drop, and no solid evidence was discovered.

April 10: Captor returned to the site with Guinevere, a harbor patrol yacht out of Boston. In addition, a minesweeper, subchaser, and three destroyers joined in, as did a PBM out of Salem. No contacts were made, and the search was discontinued.[69]

Navy blimp on anti-submarine convoy patrol. WWII.[70]

Such was the end to a typical event, a search involving ships, aircraft, blimps, and dozens of manpower hours as the United States attempted to track down and kill a U-boat. It was an exhaustive and unproductive effort, illustrating that by 1944, in the Battle for the Coast, the hunter had clearly become the hunted.

In June 1941, a letter written by a Rhode Island fisherman arrived at the Department of the Navy. The man suggested placing radios aboard his fishing boats in order to report U-boat sightings. The British

[69] *War Diary No Group.* CDR Eastern Sea Frontier 4/1944. NARA. tinyurl.com/4euakbfm.

[70] *Blimp anti-submarine patrol.* Pub domain photo. USN. Picryl. tinyurl.com/y3y7zaau.

had been arming their fishing fleet since 1940 after Germany made its policy on the neutrality of fishing boats abundantly clear: "...U-boats frequently reported having encountered armed fishing vessels and trawlers steaming with wrongly placed lights. It seemed like the enemy hoped by this means to lure the U-boats in to attack...ships with insufficient lighting were therefore regarded with suspicion, and measures were taken against them on 17 February 1940." The United States, operating in an undeclared war, declined the fisherman's request, stating that it would set a precedent that would place civilian fishing boats in danger.[71] The sentiments were understandable but came too late. They were already in great danger.

The first to go down was the Foam, a fishing trawler out of Boston owned by General Seafoods Company. It was May 17, 1942.[72] When U-432 was spotted, the fishing boat captain ordered a full stop. In spite of this non-aggressive move, the U-boat opened fire. The attack was brutal, and as shell after shell screamed through the hull of the Foam, the crew managed to abandon her. One fisherman who was severely wounded later died, and the remainder of the men made it safely to Halifax.[73] In August, the Friars out of New Bedford was fired upon by a sub while dragging for scallops off Nantucket. No injuries were reported, and the boat returned safely to harbor.[74] The General Seafoods Company sustained a second loss in July when the Ebb was sunk on her way to the Grand Banks. Fifty rounds were fired into the boat, killing five members of the crew.[75]

The town of Gloucester felt the sting of war when two boats of the local fishing fleet were sunk on June 3, 1942. During the First World War, two ships working on Georges Bank had been lost to German subs. This time, it was the Ben & Josephine and the Aeolus. Captain Joseph Ciametaro of the Ben & Josephine recalled seeing the sub position itself 300 yards away before opening fire.

Within five minutes of the machine-gunning, the sub crew started firing from a gun fix spacing here *mounted on deck. I don't know what type it was or how big. I know that those shells came thick and fast, and there must have been anywhere from 40 to 50 shells sent at our boat. One of the shells must have banged into the foc's'tle, because we saw the stove come hurtling out through a shellhole in the port side of the boat.*

The single casualty from the loss of the two boats was Snooksie, a dog belonging to Captain John Johnson of the Aeolus. After thirty-six hours crammed into dories, the men made it to shore at Mt. Desert Island in Maine.[76]

German aggression aimed at fishing trawlers continued as late as 1944 when the Lark, owned by F.J. O'Hara Bros. of Boston, came under attack by U-107. The vessel, on a return voyage to Massachusetts, was carrying nothing but fifty tons of fish and a crew of twenty-seven. Less well reported was the presence of a government-issued radio. Captain James Abbot of Dorchester and his ship were acting as confidential observers for the Navy. No casualties were reported, and the ship survived the vicious forty-minute attack by torpedoes and deck guns.[77]

The government had reconsidered its decision to utilize fishing boats as part of an anti-submarine defense strategy. Radio equipment limited to Navy monitored frequencies was made available to qualified vessels. Government-issued weapons were placed on a limited number of larger boats. It was

---

[71] Gibson, Charles Dana. *Victim or Participant?* CNRS. No. Mariner I 10/1991. tinyurl.com/ytn46m9w.

[72] *Foam.* Uboat.net. tinyurl.com/y9wmzm32.

[73] Gibson, Charles Dana. *Victim or Participant?*

[74] Baron, M.L. *War Came New Eng Waters.* Town Beach West Haven, Fairhaven, MA. mlbaron.webs.com/west-island-w-w-ii-tower.

[75] *Ebb.* Uboat.net. uboat.net/allies/merchants/ship/1972.html.

[76] *Enemy Sub Sends Two Local...* Gloucester Daily Times. Ciaramitaro, Joey. *Sinking Ben and Josephine.* Good Morning Gloucester 1/26/2012. tinyurl.com/avd535nb.

[77] Wiberg, Eric. *FV Lark Boston fishing schooner, shelled by U-107.* Eric Wiberg, 2/26/2107. tinyurl.com/yv627xuw.

judged that the average fishing boat was too small to house guns or the Navy sailors who would be responsible for them. In addition, the government hesitated to place weapons in the hands of "unregulated and therefore largely uncontrollable civilian fishermen."[78]

With vague qualification guidelines (ships had to be capable of staying afloat on the ocean for two days), cabin cruisers, sailing yachts, skiffs, and trawlers suddenly went into the spy business. They were manned by the master of the ship and "almost anyone who could sail, including Boy Scouts, rumrunners, college kids, and beachcombers."[79] Named by the Coast Guard as the Corsair Fleet, it was commonly referred to as the Coastal Patrol or Hooligan Navy. One member of this fleet of misfits was the Roseway, a fishing yacht built in 1925 in Essex. Purchased by Harold Hathaway of Taunton in 1942, the vessel was equipped with a .50 caliber machine gun and given the task of leading ships through the minefields and anti-submarine nets of Boston Harbor.[80] Estimates vary, but before the end of the war, thousands of private citizens had become members of this patriotic American fleet of unofficial observers, over 500 of them fishermen from New England.

Armed guard on Corsair Fleet vessel WWII.[81]

The Hooligan Navy was only one part of a larger, more creative plan for the use of private vessels to counteract the U-boat threat. Using the British model, in January 1942, the Chief of Naval Operations ordered the commencement of Project LQ. Non-military boats would be acquired and converted to decoys called "Q" or "Queen Ships," heavily armed and disguised as commercial vessels. The idea was to use tankers, which would make prime U-boat targets, and small, insignificant boats that posed little threat, enticing subs to remain on the surface on approach. The project was so secret that communications were delivered face-to-face whenever possible, and funds were taken from a Navy emergency account, thus making expenditures difficult to trace.

The first vessel to become a Q-ship was waiting at the Portsmouth Navy Yard. The MS Wave was a 133-foot diesel-powered fishing trawler. Built at the Bethlehem Shipyard in Quincy for the General Sea Foods Company of Boston, the government had already earmarked her for conversion to an auxiliary minesweeper. However, in April 1942, she was assigned to the First Naval District at Boston and

---

[78] Gibson, Charles Dana. *Victim or Participant?*

[79] *Hooligan Navy.* USCG Modeling 2022. tinyurl.com/yc78nn98.

[80] *Coastal Picket Patrol.* Classic Sailboats.org 10/15/2018. tinyurl.com/3zzdw7t4.

[81] *Corsair Fleet.* Pub domain photo. 170602-G-XX000-039. USCG. tinyurl.com/59bxajxv.

renamed Captor. She carried a crew of five officers and forty-two men. On board were four machine guns, one 4"/50 gun, four depth charge throwers, five sawed-off shotguns, five Colt .45s, and twenty-five hand grenades.

Four other ships would be refitted, one of them, USS Big Horn, in Boston and sent to sea. They did almost no damage. USS Atik sank four days into her first voyage. Shortly afterward, the German High Command issued a statement: "...today a Q-boat–a heavily armed ship disguised as an unarmed vessel–was among 13 vessels sunk off the American Atlantic coast..."[82]

Q-ship Atik[83]

It was apparent that classified Project LQ was less than secret. The use of Q-ships ended in October 1943. Four of the five Q-ships survived the war, but Project LQ had been an unqualified failure.

On the morning of February 22, 1943, east of Newfoundland, Convoy ON-166 was being hunted by a ten-sub wolf pack. Among the convoy escorts was the Coast Guard Cutter Campbell. In 1939, Roosevelt ordered the formation of neutrality patrols to oversee possible enemy activity in waters off the East Coast. The Campbell, one of the first of these Grand Banks Patrols, was assigned to Boston as her permanent station and assumed the role of convoy escort. On February 22, the order was received to assist survivors of the Norwegian tanker N.T. Nielson-Alonso, which was sinking after being torpedoed by a U-boat. Fifty crewmen were rescued before the Campbell suddenly came under attack. Twenty yards off the bow, a periscope belonging to U-606 was sighted. Over the next several hours, the cutter and its convoy engaged in a terrifying battle, the Campbell alone firing more than two dozen depth charges.[84]

By morning, U-606 had sustained considerable damage and was forced to surface. Campbell's deck guns bore down on the sub, which had moved perilously close to the cutter. Two final depth charges were launched, exploding directly beneath the sub and hurling it four feet out of the water. During the action, the U-boat slammed into the Campbell, its bow plane cutting a gash through the hull. Campbell was dead in the water, but so was U-606, whose crew had abandoned ship. Commander James Hirshfield of Newton[85] was the only injured member of the crew, having sustained a shrapnel wound. The Campbell proudly served her country for the remainder of the war.

[82] *Q-ships WWII.* NHHC 11/13/2017. tinyurl.com/yshz8k66.

[83] *USS Atik.* Pub domain photo. USN. Wiki Commons. tinyurl.com/4tvudaap.

[84] *Campbell 1936.* USCG. tinyurl.com/ytma9b5f.

[85] *Cutter Rams and Sinks Sub.* Boston Globe 3/18/1943. Newpapers.com. tinyurl.com/4cwvvemm.

USCG Cutter Campbell [86]

A frightening description of the experience aboard a Coast Guard cutter during World War II appears in a letter written by Ensign Arthur Cartman of Taunton. A Deputy Air Raid Warden when he enlisted, Cartman supervised the engine room on the Campbell following the sinking of U-606. His unshakable stoicism during battle is nothing short of heroic.

An engine room is not a very pleasant place when depth charges are exploding all around you, lines letting go, floor plates jumping up as threads are stripped from the holding bolts, electric lights going out with each shock, fixtures fall all around you.
It seemed at times as though the engine was an accordion. Men watching the lines and wondering when they are going to let go and send scalding steam into an already crowded space. Men stripped to the waist – thin bodies gleaming with sweat at temperatures of 125 degrees F. and at night 150 F. It's hotter at night because the hatches are closed to conform with convoy blackout.

---

86 *USCGC Campbell.* Pub domain photo. 200401-G-G0000-001 USCG. tinyurl.com/t7n6399t.

As soon as general quarters sound, the throttle man opens her up, and I wonder if she will take it this time. The voice tube gong rings, and the Captain's voice comes down:
"Mr. Cartman. We have contact. Stand by!"
"Aye, Aye. Sir."
"You will be notified if we can ram him."
"Aye. Aye. Sir."

Down here in the bowels of the ship, all is quiet and tense. All stations are manned. All pumps going and the engines roaring at full speed and pounding for all they are worth. We can feel the ship swing as we buttercup around in search of prey. I walk from the engine room to the fire room. All eyes are on me. I always smoke or chew a cigar when the attack is coming up. I feel a cigar and quiet words have their effect on the crew. As the ship rolls around to the spot where the sub has been traced, ash cans roll off the decks and spout from the Y guns. The ship shudders and shakes until we wonder if our plates can stand anymore. Sweat is running from our bodies in little rivulets. No water is taken. You wonder about those men down below in that German sub, and as the crack of depth charges pounds against the sides of the ship, I think, "Some men might die in a sub tonight." Yet, it is we or they.[87]

The long, hideous months of 1942 passed into painful memory, and gradually, like patches on a quilt, strategies, technology, and industry came together. Admiral King devised a plan to coordinate resources in the North Atlantic. A "chop line" was established, with Canada managing waters to the west while Britain was in charge of the seas to the east, with the northeastern coastal passage to Halifax under the direction of the United States. American industry soared to new heights, building over a million tons of shipping a month at a time when U-boats sank 150,000 tons.[88]

Airplanes now flew further out to sea, able to bomb unsuspecting targets and alert convoys to the presence of submarines. German communications were being routinely deciphered after Enigma codes were broken, and advances in radar allowed the Allies to see further into the distance than the enemy imagined. In May of 1943, "Black May," forty-one U-boats went down 25 percent of Doenitz's operational fleet. The losses were too high. A recall order was issued. Subs returned to base, and Doenitz took time to reevaluate the situation. U-boats would soon return to the Atlantic and the US coast (within a year, subs would be spotted off Sandwich and Ipswich),[89] but the U-boat force would never achieve the stunning successes of the early days of the Battle for the Atlantic. Germany's Happy Time was over.

In early July 1944, the USS Card slowly pulled into the dock in Boston. On board were German sailors, survivors of the crew of U-233, sunk a few days earlier 150 miles northeast of Boston. While USS Thomas and USS Baker pummeled the sub to death with depth charges, gunfire, and eventually ramming her, nearby the men of the USS Card witnessed the attack. Sheridan Bell, Navy Chaplain, recorded his recollections in an interview with *Naval History and Heritage Command*. The death of the sub came quickly. Twenty-two minutes after being spotted by Destroyer Escorts, U-233 went down. The sub, carrying sixty-six mines bound for Halifax harbor,[90] was on the fortieth day of its first patrol. All that remained alive, thirty-one men, were brought on board the Card, which then turned southwest toward Massachusetts, where the Boston Port of Entry and its POW enclosure awaited. USS Thomas and USS Baker followed, putting into Boston for repairs.

---

[87] Parker, John. *CG No Friend of U Boats.* Taunton WWII. Drummond Printing Co 1943.

[88] Werner, Herbert A. *Iron Coffins.* Da Capo Press 1969.

[89] *War Diary No Group. Task Group.* CDR Eastern Sea Frontier.

[90] *Interrogation Survivors U-233* 9/12/1944. Chief Nav Operations. US Navy. Uboatarchive.net. tinyurl.com/36j2xv83.

U-233 being rammed by USS Thomas. 1944.[91]

U-233 sinking. 1944.[92]

Among those requiring medical attention was Kapitanleutnant Hans Steen. This was the first U-boat command for the 36-year-old sub captain who had lived in Boston for three years prior to the war.[93] Over the next twenty-four hours, he would be treated with six units of plasma, two blood transfusions, and five tanks of oxygen. Chaplain Bell remained by his side for much of the time. In spite of this medical care, Steen failed to pull through.

On July 6, he was buried at sea, his body covered by a German Lutheran Church flag (no swastikas were on board, and Bell felt a US flag would be inappropriate). Those of the U-boat crew who were well enough were brought to the deck. The Card's crew had been notified of the impending service should they choose to attend. In Bell's words, "practically the entire ship's company came." Two German officers stood at attention beside the body. Prayers were said, the crew gave a final Nazi salute to their fallen leader, and Hans Steen slipped over the side of the ship. Bell later recalled the behavior of the American crew whenever enemy survivors were taken on board. "There has been a noticed interest on the part of our own men that they share their cigarettes and their candy and their ice cream with the prisoners of war...do not look on them as enemy but as sailors who are then in need and there is no sense of bitterness or hostility."[94]

[91] *U-233 rammed.* Pub domain photo. NARA 80-G-700005. NHHC. tinyurl.com/ysr599vd.

[92] *Sinking U-233.* Pub domain photo. NARA 80-G-700007. NHHC. tinyurl.com/ysr599vd.

[93] Kellog, D.M. *USS Thomas 7/5/1944.* Interrogation Report. Uboatarchive.net. tinyurl.com/4day5ud3.

[94] *Recollections Sheridan Bell.* NHHC 9/15/2015. tinyurl.com/2frtprkf.

Burial at sea of Capt. Hans Steen. July 6, 1944.[95]

The sinking of U-233 and the subsequent treatment of its captain are in stark contrast to what Allied survivors faced at the hands of U-boats during the Battle of the Atlantic. In September of 1942, Admiral Doenitz issued the infamous Laconia Order: "No attempt of any kind must be made at rescuing members of ships sunk…Be harsh, having in mind that the enemy takes no regard for women and children in his bombing attacks on German cities." It was an idea that had been in development since Doenitz's 1939 Standing Order 154 when he admonished, "Do not rescue any men...We must be harsh in this war. The enemy began the war in order to destroy us, so nothing else matters." Hitler obligingly agreed, stating, "U-boats should surface after torpedoing and shoot up the lifeboats."[96]

In the early days of America's involvement in the Battle of the Atlantic, survivor statements document incidents of humane treatment by U-boat crews (offering water and food or assisting swimmers to reach lifeboats). The men of the SS David H. Atwater would disagree. The cargo ship, owned by Atwacoal Transportation Company of Fall River, was headed home to Massachusetts with its cargo of 4,000 tons of coal. In April 1942, just off the coast of Virginia, disaster struck. U-552 surfaced and aimed its deck guns at the unarmed collier. The bridge was struck first, and in a moment, all eight of Atwater's officers were gone. As the deadly attack continued, the crew, attempting to abandon ship and man lifeboats, was swept by machine gun fire. Three survived. Twenty-seven men, including three from Massachusetts, were murdered. Their bodies, as well as the lifeboats that held them, were riddled with bullets.[97] For victims of a U-boat attack, no help would come from Germany.

Unfortunately for those who found themselves abandoning ship off the New England coast or, worse, in the waters east of Newfoundland, chances of survival were iffy at best. Long recognized by mariners as having some of the most treacherous weather conditions in the world, the waters of the northern Atlantic could easily kill. Hurricanes were life-threatening. The Great Atlantic Hurricane of 1944, which brought eighteen-foot tides to Fall River, wiped out a destroyer, two Coast Guard cutters, and sank the Vineyard Sound Light Ship along with her crew. Hypothermia was always a threat to survivors as well as rescuers. Below 32 degrees, ice caked onto ships so thickly it had to be chopped off with axes.

---

[95] *Steen buried.* Pub domain photo. NARA 80-G-336270. *USS Card.* NavSource Online. tinyurl.com/54ujtadz.

[96] *Trial Adm Donitz.* ONI Review 10/1946. NHHC 5/26/2020. tinyurl.com/yd4d9jeh.

[97] Wimbrow, Peter Ayers III. *Atwater sank 80 years ago.* OC Today 3/31/2022. tinyurl.com/4btud28r.

USCG foul weather gear,
North Atlantic. WWII.[98]

The federal government recognized the hazards facing mariners and, in 1940, established the Atlantic Weather Observation Service. Under Coast Guard administration, weather ships monitored conditions on the surface and in the air, reporting via radio every three hours, more often during significant weather events. Duty on weather vessels consisted of twenty-five days at sea and fifteen days in port. It was dangerous work, as ships made their way to weather stations unattended, making them easy targets for subs.

The SS Cornish was built before the war as a cargo ship for the Eastern Steamship Company of Boston. Shortly after Pearl Harbor, the US Navy took possession. After refitting, she was renamed USS Muskeget and transferred to her new home base at Boston for duty as a weather ship. In August 1942, Lt. Commander Charles Toft guided the vessel out of port on her second patrol and headed toward the designated weather station 500 miles northeast of Newfoundland. She never arrived. Weather reports streamed in from August 24 until September 9, then nothing. Kapitänleutnant Walter Göing would later report that on Muskeget's last day, U-755 fired three torpedoes at a target. The sound of explosions and bulkheads bursting followed. The sub surfaced to find debris, an oil slick, and eight men in lifeboats. In response to questions about the name of the sinking vessel, Göing remembered the garbled names of Muskogee or Mukited. He then turned the sub away, leaving the crew of the Muskeget to die.[99] All 125 men aboard perished, at least twenty-nine of them fathers or sons or husbands from Massachusetts.[100] The Muskeget is the only US weather ship to be sunk during World War II.

USS Muskeget six months before she was
lost in the North Atlantic. 1942.[101]

---

[98] *Foul weather gear.* Public domain photo. 170602-G-XX000-109. USCG. tinyurl.com/4jm8caxu.

[99] Ruane, Michael. *Lost at sea WWII.* Wash Post 11/18/2015. tinyurl.com/485y4xrt.

[100] *USS Muskeget.* Uboat.net. tinyurl.com/4jwckbd9.

[101] *USS Muskeget.* Pub domain photo. 240705-G-0000-001. USCG. tinyurl.com/yw4v4ykb.

At the end of 1942 and through the early months of 1943, weather in the North Atlantic, along with U-boat attacks, turned so deadly that it was referred to as the "Bloody Winter." Stationed on the Boston-based Coast Guard Cutter Ingham, Ensign John M. Waters Jr. recalled being aboard a ship during a storm in January 1943: "Though the bridge was 35 feet above the waterline, the seas towered up at a 45-degree angle above that. As a new wave loomed up, Ingham rose to meet it, climbing steeply up the front; as the sea slid past, her bow was left momentarily hanging in the air before dropping sickeningly into the next trough...sending shock waves throughout the ship."[102] During the long, hard years of the U-boat war, what the Germans didn't take, the cruel Atlantic would.

It was the Spring of 1945, and the end of the war was in sight. Just off the coast of Truro, the tanker Atlantic States out of Boston was struck by a torpedo. The ship was abandoned with no loss of life.[103] The last major battle of World War II, the bloodiest in the Pacific, began when the US Army and Marines charged ashore on Okinawa. In Europe, the world watched in horror as Allied soldiers opened the gates of Hell at Dachau, Ravensbruk, and Buchenwald concentration camps. And on the last day of April, as Hitler cowered in his bunker in Berlin, the Third Reich crumbled into dust. The Fuhrer finalized his will and, uncaring that more Germans would die for his pathetic cause and their even more pathetic leader, appointed Admiral Karl Doenitz to carry on the fight as Commander of the Third Reich. Just hours later, Hitler killed his dog. Faithful to the end, Blondi had ingested the cyanide capsule fed to her by her beloved owner in an effort to prove that the capsules were indeed powerful enough to kill a man. Apparently not satisfied with the results and too cowardly to face punishment for his crimes against mankind, on April 30, Adolph Hitler ingested cyanide and then shot himself in the head.

Four days later, Doenitz, now Fuhrer, ordered the immediate termination of all hostile U-boat activities. In a last-ditch effort to cling to the perverted illusion of the superiority of the Third Reich, he sent a final defiant message to his men:

My U-boat men! Six years of U-boat war lie behind us. You have fought like lions. A crushing material superiority has forced us into a narrow area. A continuation of our fight from the remaining basis is no longer possible. U-boat men! Undefeated and spotless, you lay down your arms after a heroic battle without equal. We remember in deep respect our fallen comrades, who have sealed with their death their loyalty to the Fuhrer and Fatherland. Comrades! Preserve your U-boat spirit, with which you have fought courageously, stubbornly, and imperturbably through the years for the good of the Fatherland. Long live Germany![104]

Regardless of Doenitz's command, fifty miles southwest of Martha's Vineyard, Oberleutnant Helmut Fromsdorf was about to engage in the last battle of the Atlantic war. In the end, two ships would be gone, along with twelve Americans and the entire crew of U-853. Many questions remain about this senseless final act. Why had the captain disobeyed the stand-down order? Perhaps the sub never received the message. It is also possible, however, that Fromsdorf opted to score a final prize for the Third Reich. His personality supports this theory. The 24-year-old was described by his crew as a "draufganger" (a daredevil) and a "halsschmerze" (a glory seeker)[105] who had often expressed hopes of achieving a Knight's Cross. His 6' 5" height made him an unlikely candidate for a submarine, but he did well in the Kriegsmarine, and in September 1944, with defeat looming and a shortage of manpower, he was assigned to command of U-853. A firm supporter of his country and its philosophy, he wrote to his family, "I am

---

[102] Price, Scott. *CG No Atlantic Campaign.* CDRs Bulletin. DOD. tinyurl.com/y7jrum34.

[103] *Atlantic States.* Uboat.net. tinyurl.com/2zsze7nw.

[104] MacClean, French. *Karl Doenitz.* Fifth Field. tinyurl.com/397p6hcx.

[105] Kendy, Dave. *Rogue U-Boat.* HISTORYNET. tinyurl.com/mu9e3vxu.

lucky in these difficult days of my Fatherland to have the honor of commanding this submarine, and it is my duty to accept."

At 5:40 in the afternoon of May 5, 1945, Coast Guard Boatswain Joe Burbine, a Massachusetts native, stood at his post at the Point Judith Lighthouse watching the collier SS Black Point pass by. The ship, owned by the C.H. Sprague Company of Boston, carried coal destined for the Edison Power Plant in Weymouth.[106] Suddenly, Burbine heard a massive explosion. Black Point Captain Charles Prior later recalled:

I could see Point Judith light station clear as a bell, hell, we were just a couple miles offshore and a little east of the Light. It's 5:40 in the afternoon, and I just stepped out of the wheelhouse onto the bridge wing, reached in my pocket for a cigarette, put it in my mouth, and that's when it hit the fan. The clock was blown off the wall, and the barometer off the bulkhead. The wheelhouse door was blown open and I don't remember if I lit the cigarette or swallowed it. I could smell gunpowder in the air, and the stern of my ship was completely blown off.[107]

There was only time for one distress call...the ship and twelve of her crew were gone in fifteen minutes. Fourteen of the thirty-four survivors were from Massachusetts. The First Naval District Headquarters in Boston was alerted. Task Group 60.7, on the homeward-bound trip to Boston, was nearing Buzzards Bay when it was ordered to assist the Black Point. The Amick, Atherton, and Moberly responded immediately. A fourth ship, the Ericsson, was already at the western end of the Cape Cod Canal and, after turning about, headed to the scene.

The battle that followed is an exhausting tale of tragedy, determination, and retribution. From the moment the U-boat was detected in 100 feet of water, 4,000 yards to the east of the last Black Point position, a relentless hunt ensued to trap and kill U-853. Atherton's Captain Lewis Iselin stated, "It seemed everyone wanted to get in on the act. I don't think there is a hull that took a bigger beating in the war."[108] Robert Cembrola of the Naval War College Museum commented: "853 ended her life like a bull trapped in a ring with scores of ships each wanting to get at least one spear in her."[109]

A pattern of depth charge, oil slick, debris, and all quiet was enacted over and over during the next several hours. Each time, unbelievably, the sub slowly came to life again, creeping along the ocean floor, sometimes moving at just a few knots. The U-boat was now in 75 feet of water, and as a patrol bomber circled overhead, Atherton and Moberly let fly a final series of depth charges. The intensity of the explosions was so forceful that the attack paused to scan the area with searchlights. An oil slick and debris were sighted. The decision was made to suspend the assault, and Task Group 60.7 withdrew.

As if to put an exclamation point on this last gasp of the Third Reich, the Navy ordered the USS Newport, Restless, Semmes, Barney, Blakely, Action, and Breckenridge to the site to continue the search for sub contact. The following morning, Atherton, Moberly, and Ericsson returned to find a debris field that stretched for over a mile and included oil, papers, rations, equipment, and Captain Fromsdorf's cap. The three ships were ordered to attack once again. Depth charges were released. Three blimps hummed overhead to watch for further evidence of the U-boat's presence. The Task Group Commander concerned that the sub's hull hadn't been cracked open yet, decided to speed up the process and ordered a hedgehog barrage to commence. Soon afterward, he ordered the blimps to join the attack. By then, however, it was over. It was the morning of May 6, 1945. U-853 and the fifty-five members of her crew, along with the Third Reich, were dead.[110]

---

[106] Koster, John. *Tightrope Walker.* HISTORYNET 7/1/2016. tinyurl.com/3f2r7dd6.

[107] Cembrola, Bob. *Mystery U-853.* Mil History Now 12/15/2020. tinyurl.com/ycvpxfj3.

[108] *USCG History.* USCG Newsfeed 5/6/2016. tinyurl.com/yc3bu3a3.

[109] Cembrola, Robert. *Battle Point Judith.* Soundings Narragansett Bay's Nav Hist. NWC Mus Blog 5/10/2020. tinyurl.com/yc7d86vx.

[110] *Atlantic Fleet Group 60.7.* Uboat.net Arch. tinyurl.com/3wxr84h4.

USS Moberly attack on U-853. May 1945.[111]

The Battle for the Coast was over. The SS Black Point is remembered as the final Allied merchant ship lost to U-boat attack during World War II. Southeast of Newfoundland, a second U-boat went down with all hands that day. Together with U-853, they became the last German submarines sunk during the Battle for the Atlantic. Helmut Fromsdorf, who sacrificed the crew of U-853 in his quest for glory, had indeed made history. Today, what remains of the Black Point, U-853, and the men who served them lie seven miles apart on the ocean floor, fifty miles southwest of Massachusetts.

The war with Germany had come to an end, and in the following weeks, unlike Fromsdorf, 156 U-boat commanders surrendered their submarines to the Allies. For four days in May 1945, the eyes of New England were focused on the Portsmouth Naval Shipyard in New Hampshire as four German submarines made their way down the Piscataqua River on their final patrol.

Four surrendered German U-boats,
Portsmouth Navy Yard. 1945.[112]

The first to arrive was U-805, whose maiden voyage began on March 1, 1945, and ended two months later, having done no damage to Allied shipping. She formally surrendered when Commander Alexander Moffat of Boston and his crew boarded the U-boat off Casco Bay in Maine.[113] The next day, May 16, U-873, three months of sea duty and no kills, followed suit. U-1228 had a more productive run during her two patrols, sinking a Canadian corvette, yet she too made her final journey into Portsmouth Harbor on that day. A photo taken of one of the surrendered subs was accompanied by the caption, "Its

---

[111] *Sinking U-853.* Pub domain photo. 26-G-4557. NHHC. tinyurl.com/4e6nt3hr.

[112] *German subs Portsmouth.* Pub domain photo. NARA7330125. NavSource Online. tinyurl.com/3exhfywx.

[113] Banner, Earl. *Subs Taken NE Coast.* Boston Globe 5/15/1945. Newspapers.com. tinyurl.com/mpf7utwr.

fangs yanked out, the prize U-boat will prey no more upon Allied shipping in the Atlantic." U-805 would become a public relations tool featured in a series of Victory Visits to East Coast communities. U-873 achieved notoriety when word leaked out that her captain, Friedrich Steinhoff, had committed suicide after interrogation in the Charles Street Jail in Boston. The sub was scrapped in 1948. U-1228, like U-805 and several other U-boats, found its way to the bottom of the Atlantic, scuttled by the Allies off the coast of Provincetown.[114]

The fourth German sub to surrender that May yielded unexpected riches. Since mid-1943, Germany had sent submarines bearing information and materials to its ally, Japan. For these "Monsoon U-boats" headed to the Pacific, the long trip around the Cape of Good Hope and through the Indian Ocean was a perilous one, and most U-boats were lost during the voyage. In the waning days of the Third Reich, U-234 was sent on just such a mission. As the sub left Norway, in addition to Captain Johann-Heinrich Fehler and his crew, aboard were two Imperial Japanese Navy officials, several German Luftwaffe and Navy officers, and two experts in Messerschmidt technology. Fehler had gone to sea as a young man and became a devoted member of the Nazi Party in 1933. Three years later, he joined the Kriegsmarine and rose to the position of U-boat commander.[115]

Three weeks after departure, news arrived that the Third Reich had fallen, and Fehler dutifully followed the order to surrender. His decision met with little enthusiasm from some of his passengers. Luftwaffe Lt. General Ulrich Kessler, sporting a monocle, overcoat, and more than his share of arrogance, would eventually submit to his captors but not until he engaged in a heated argument with Fehler, demanding that he be delivered to South America. The two Japanese officers opted to commit suicide.

Waiting for U-234 as she approached the coast of Maine was the Argo. The ship had patrolled the coast during Prohibition and, with the outbreak of World War II, became a convoy escort. In March 1944, she was assigned to Chelsea, Massachusetts, and placed under the command of Lt. JG Eliot Winslow.[116] Winslow was a Boston boy who grew up in the area, joined the Navy in 1941, and was assigned to the USS Puffin out of Boston. By the end of the year, he applied and was accepted into the US Coast Guard. After anti-submarine warfare training, he joined the crew of the Argo, eventually taking command of the ship and her crew of 75. He would remain with the Argo for the rest of the war. Argo was one of six boats chosen by the Navy as a surrender unit in charge of escorting captured U-boats into port. Winslow and his crew delivered U-805, U-873, and U-1228 to Portsmouth and, on May 19, rendezvoused with U-234. On board was Commander Alexander Moffat. The sub's officers and crew were transferred to the Argo.

Author William H. Thiesen provides an account of what followed:

Fehler climbed over the rail cheerfully introduced himself, and extended his hand in greeting, but Moffat did not return Fehler's proffer of a handshake. Denied a warm greeting by the American, Fehler went on to remark: "Come now, commander, let's not do this the hard way. Who knows but that one of these days you'll be surrendering to me? In the meantime, I shall have a welcome rest at one of your prisoner-of-war camps with better food, I am sure, than I have had for months. Then I'll be repatriated, ready to work for a new economic empire."

Moffat was unimpressed. Fehler was sent below with his crew, where they were expected to sit on the floor with arms folded, a situation which did not suit the Kapitanleutnant, who felt free to air his complaints. After being told about the German's attitude, Lt. Winslow went below and issued an order for the guards to "shoot any prisoner who as much as scratched his head without permission. An apology

---

[114] *Surrender Nazi U-boats.* New Eng Hist Soc 2022. tinyurl.com/26n4kzmw.

[115] *Johann-Heinrich Fehler.* Uboat.net. tinyurl.com/mpz7cdt9.

[116] *Argo, 1933.* USCG. DHS 4/17/2020. tinyurl.com/59jue2uu.

must accompany every shooting."[117] Fehler wasn't through, opting to have the last word as he disembarked the Argo. A photo entitled "The Finger" from his private collection portrays Winslow's last conversation with Fehler. After listening to the U-boat officer's mumbled words of discontent in German, the interpreter told him to save it for the captain, who would be at the gangplank. When Fehler approached Winslow, he said in fluent English, "Ach – my men have been treated like gangsters." For Winslow, it was the last straw.

I had been simmering for an hour, but that remark brought me to a boil. With eyes meeting head-on, I barked, 'That's what you are! GET OFF!' My outstretched arm fix spacing here *pointed to the gangway. Strange as it may seem, there was no profanity for the moment, but I must confess the air was blue for 5 minutes while I muttered to myself. . .*[118]

Once in port, US intelligence dispatched a German-speaking officer to interview the prisoners. Fehler was cooperative, sharing information and documents with his captors. However, it was when the Kapitanleutnant gave a tour of the sub that U-boat 234 made history. Packed into the cramped confines of the ship were two rocket engines, blueprints for aircraft and missiles, and half a ton of uranium. The presence of a disassembled Messerschmidt remains debated today. Barriers were quickly thrown up around the sub to shield it from curious onlookers as the cargo was off-loaded. The uranium secretly made its way into the hands of scientists at the Manhattan Project. The officers, passengers, and crew of U-234 were determined to be of special intelligence value to the US government and sent to Washington, D.C., for further interrogation.

U-234 is torpedoed off Cape Cod. 1947.[119]

U-234 was put under a microscope and used for numerous tests until November of 1947, when she was sunk by an American sub forty miles off the coast of Cape Cod. Johann Fehler was sent to a prisoner-of-war camp for unrepentant Nazis and, after the war, returned home to his devastated Fatherland, where he lived until the age of 83. Eliot Winslow, an unrepentant American hero, retired to Maine and operated tugs and tour boats for the remainder of his life.[120] And in August of 1945, a bomb,

---

[117] Thiesen, William. *Eliot Winslow Surrender U-234*. Sea History 2013. tinyurl.com/3rhht2yt.

[118] *Argo 5/19/1945*. USCG. tinyurl.com/36dfxcmc.

[119] *U-234 torpedoed*. Pub domain photo. USN 80-G-704673. Picryl. tinyurl.com/ywu67b89.

[120] Thiesen, William. *Eliot Winslow Surrender U-234*.

rumored to contain uranium from U-234, was dropped on the city of Hiroshima. Johann Fehler had completed his mission. His cargo had successfully made it to Japan.

Grand Admiral Karl Doenitz was a devoted nationalist, a hardened anti-semitic Nazi, a vocal admirer of the Fuhrer, and a brilliant naval leader. He created a submarine fleet from the ashes of the First World War and made the Allied world tremble in fear. He waged a six-year campaign of terror to destroy Allied shipping in the Atlantic, and like Adolph Hitler and the Third Reich, he failed.

In the first months following the US declaration of war, German submarines experienced a heady string of successes, sinking over a million tons of Allied shipping. Doenitz's controlling nature and his insistence that sub captains report to base daily gave Allies the opportunity to listen in on communications. His unshaking belief in German superiority prevented him from considering the possibility that the enemy could break sub fleet secret codes. Within a year, Britain and America began to outpace German technology and productivity. Innovative strategies for defending Allied convoys at sea were implemented, significantly decreasing the effectiveness of wolfpacks. Doenitz's prowess was slipping, and for Germany, the Battle for the Atlantic took a deadly turn.

During the first four months of the war, Germany lost 22 U-boats; during the last four months, 115 were destroyed. In 1943 and 1944, 471 U-boats were lost.[121] As the Allies swarmed the beaches at Normandy, of the 1,150 U-boats that had been commissioned, only 68 remained available on the Atlantic Front.[122] In addition, Germany was having difficulty manning what remained of its fleet. In the final year of the war, among U-boat captains assigned to their first patrol, seven were 22 years old or younger.[123] A description of the crew of U-233, taken prisoner after the U-boat sunk southeast of Halifax in 1944, states: "The crew, judged from the 29 survivors, was a poor one. Most of the men were totally lacking in previous U-boat experience and a large number had never been to sea before. As a whole, they gave the impression of being in the dregs of the reserve pools in Germany and shore stations on the Baltic, with a very small sprinkling of experienced petty officers to stiffen the whole."[124] By the end of the war, 779 U-boats had been destroyed, approximately 70% of the German submarine fleet, along with 72% of the men that sailed in them.[125]

Fuhrer Karl Doenitz (center) being arrested following
the surrender of Germany. May 1945.[126]

---

[121] *U-boat Fates... Losses 1939-1945.* Uboat.net. tinyurl.com/4nr2xfwz.

[122] Werner, Herbert A. *Iron Coffins.*

[123] *Youngest... Oldest U-boat commanders.* Uboat.net. tinyurl.com/yzapbcyn.

[124] *Interrogation Survivors U-233.* CNO.

[125] Werner, Herbert A. *Iron Coffins.*

[126] *Surrender Germany.* Pub domain photo. 208-PU-52-P-7 NHHC. tinyurl.com/ycx5yme7.

Karl Doenitz would outlive the war. After his arrest, he was put on trial at Nuremberg, where his war crimes netted him a ten-year sentence in Spandau Prison, a generous retribution for the Fuhrer who reigned for twenty days. He was released from Spandau in 1956. Soon afterward, Doenitz published his memoirs, *Ten Years and Twenty Days*, a calculated and egregious recounting of the war, designed to secure his place in history as a brilliant, loyal, and guiltless son of the Fatherland. He lived out the remainder of his life in a quiet village in Germany and passed away at age 89, an unapologetic Nazi till the end.

While on trial in Nuremberg, Doenitz wrote: "So I sit here in my cell with my clear, clean conscience, and await the decision of the judges." Karl Doenitz felt no need to wash the blood off his hands. Perhaps the 30,000 German and 72,000 Allied souls who perished in the Atlantic at the hands of the Third Reich would disagree.[127]

---

[127] *Battle Atlantic. Countering U-Boat Threat.* NHHC 1/12/2021. tinyurl.com/etsbn8md.

Chapter 5

Homefront

The blackout is not a lark.
Blackout Information for General Public
January 1942[1]

Nantucket was in a perilous position. The island lay directly in the path of merchant shipping headed for New England ports and across to Europe. During the Battle of the Atlantic, merchant shipping meant U-boats, and the war was a frightening reality to the residents of Nantucket, who had become all too familiar with the boom of torpedo explosions and the hunt for survivors along beaches littered with wreckage and debris.

The threat of invasion was credible. Prior to the First World War, Germany had developed plans for landing infantry in New York Harbor and then moving northeast to Boston. A back-up plan centered on landing 100,000 German soldiers on Cape Cod. In 1941, a precedent having been set, Hitler ordered battle plans be drawn up for a submarine attack on Boston, New London, Newport, and New York.[2] In his radio broadcast on December 7, 1941, following the Pearl Harbor attack, New York City Mayor Fiorella LaGuardia had this to say:

We are in an extreme crisis...I want to warn the people of this city and along the Atlantic coast that we must not and cannot feel secure or assured because we are on the Atlantic coast, and the activities this afternoon have taken place in the Pacific. We must be prepared for anything at any time...We must toughen up. We have our homes and our lands to defend now.[3]

Two days later, a report began circulating around New England that enemy bombers were approaching the East Coast. The Hingham Naval Ammunition Depot went on high alert, Boston police and riot squads were mobilized, and civilians were advised to stay in their homes.[4] Shortly afterward, a radio broadcast warned Nantucket residents that they were "dangerously close to the war zone" and that "a single plane can release over 2,000 bombs, and the town of Nantucket has exactly five pieces of fire equipment."

All across Massachusetts, towns and cities scrambled to protect their citizens. The island of Nantucket had an edge. The Navy had leased Nobadeer Airport, operating it as an Auxiliary Air Station for Quonset Point in Rhode Island. Anti-submarine patrols flew out of the airfield, and training runs used nearby Gravelly Island for target practice. In mid-1942, the Army arrived from Camp Edwards and, for approximately six months, ran war games to prepare for the Africa campaign. The Coast Guard constructed observation stations and patrolled beaches with trained guard dogs. As an added precaution, Nantucket line steamships were painted battleship gray, and no cameras were allowed on board.[5]

---

[1] *MA Blackout Information for General Public*. MA Comm. Pub Safety 1/1942. ArchUnbound. tinyurl.com/4mntu2n4.

[2] Wiberg, Eric. *U-Boats in New England*. Fonthill Media Limited 2019.

[3] *LaGuardia Speaks About Enemy Attacks*. World War Radio 7/17/2024. tinyurl.com/2rmz7vb3.

[4] Rose, Jim. *War Years Remembered*. Wompatuck News No. 57. tinyurl.com/47y4avck.

[5] Mooney, Robert E. *Nantucket Only Yesterday*. Wesco Publ 2000.

The Nantucket ferry Nobska was
painted gray during World War II.[6]

The town of Maynard had reason to be concerned. Located just west of Boston, a local mill manufactured blankets for the Army, and on the Acton border, the American Powder Company produced gunpowder. Selectmen made the decision to build an observation tower. Within a month, a structure manned by Maynard residents stretched skyward on Summer Hill. Shortly afterward, work began on the Maynard Ordnance Supply Depot, and soon, the US Coast Guard stepped in to provide protection and assume control of the tower.[7]

Maynard Ammunition Dump. WWII.[8]

In towns less fortunate, the onus of protection fell upon the shoulders of average citizens, and local government was quick to respond. One week after Governor Leverett Saltonstall declared a state of Emergency in Massachusetts, the town of Amherst appointed a Chief Air Raid Warden, reminding citizens that 429 men and women of Amherst were already in uniform.[9] Some communities, however, were well ahead of the curve. The following statement appeared in a Bridgewater Citizens Defense Committee report a full ten months before Pearl Harbor: "We believe that we can assume that even in the event of war, the bombing of Bridgewater is extremely unlikely, but all must admit the possibility, if not the probability, of sabotage which might seriously affect the people of this community."

The Committee made impressive recommendations. "Necessities such as food, clothing, and medical attention should be planned for. Utilities might be endangered; thus, a survey of available generators and procurement of candles and hand lamps was suggested. Usable brooks and ponds should be inspected for possible use by families and fire departments, and provisions should be made for

[6] *Nobska*. Pub domain photo. NPS. Wiki Commons. tinyurl.com/4s64bbun.

[7] Mark, David. *Maynard's Observation Tower.* Maynard Life Outdoors Hidden Hist Maynard 8/22/2018. tinyurl.com/ypfcbnfr.

[8] *Maynard Ammunition Dump*. Pub domain photo. NARA. Picryl. tinyurl.com/55nye658.

[9] *Annual Reports Amherst Year 12/31/1942*. Town Amherst.

purification. Communication during a crisis would become essential, so a list of local short-wave radio operators should be obtained. Finally, in the event of an incendiary attack, plans should be developed to acquire gas masks, arrange for bomb shelters, and manage wreckage clearance."[10]

Throughout the sudden switch to a state of war and the traumatic years that followed, the Commonwealth of Massachusetts was guided by its extraordinary governor, Leverett Saltonstall. In spite of the fact that this tall Yankee politician was a blue-blood through and through, born into wealth, descended from Mayflower passengers, and educated at prestigious schools, the Governor was the real deal. After serving with the Army in France during the First World War (his son, Peter, would follow in his father's footsteps and die a hero during combat on Guam), Saltonstall entered the world of politics, joining the Massachusetts House of Representatives before being elected Governor in 1939. "Salty" kept his finger firmly on the pulse of his state during the war years. He seemed to be everywhere. Photos place him at scrap drives, victory gardens, and shaking hands on street corners. Saltonstall was quick to recognize the man on the street, all the while hobnobbing with presidents and prime ministers. He remained in office until 1944, when he moved to Washington and became a highly respected member of the United States Senate. "His engagingly homely face is his No.1 political asset," said a Time Magazine article in April 1944 when his picture appeared on its cover.[11]

Governor Leverett Saltonstall[12]

Two months before the Japanese attacked Pearl Harbor, the Massachusetts legislature adopted an act that basically appointed the Governor commander-in-chief in the event of war and granted extensive powers to manage the business of the state in any way necessary to protect its citizens. On December 29, 1941, Governor Saltonstall declared a state of emergency, thus accessing his new war powers. Two days later, he became the first governor in Massachusetts history to use an executive order when he mandated the development of civil defense agencies.

Soon, executive orders began flying out of the State House. In an effort to preserve automobile tires and decrease the consumption of rubber, the speed limit was decreased to 40 miles per hour and, six months later, to 35 miles per hour. The state pier at Bourne was closed, as was the approach road, all now under guard to protect vital shipping in the Cape Cod Canal. War production was a big concern, and executive orders addressed the sale of scrap metal and the use of convict labor. On three occasions, Saltonstall stepped in with orders to expedite war production. Handy Pad Supply Co., which held a $5.7

---

¹⁰ *Planning Comm—Citizens Defense Comm.* Town Bridgewater 2/6/1941.

¹¹ *Homely face is political asset.* Time Magazine 4/10/1944. Carberry, Christopher. Saltonstall Papers. MHS 2003. tinyurl.com/37bwfvzm.

¹² *Leverett Saltonstall.* Pub domain photo. Governor MA. Wikipedia. tinyurl.com/37ahap8w.

million government supply contract,[13] produced surgical dressings and bandages in buildings located on opposite sides of Webster Street in Worcester. After the military approached the Governor for his approval, the company was allowed to construct a bridge over the road to connect the two buildings. Additional orders granted similar permission to the Simplex Wire and Cable Co. of Cambridge, the sole US manufacturer of deep-sea submarine telegraph cable, and to Sylvania Electrical Products in Salem.

It was the executive order dealing with air raid and blackout regulations, however, that brought the reality of war into the homes and lives of Massachusetts citizens. Saltonstall's Executive Order No. 3, issued on January 18, 1942, set the tone. Civil defense agencies would appoint air raid wardens who were charged with running practice drills and patrolling streets to look for blackout offenders. The requirements were specific: "Upon the signal for a blackout or at sunset...the occupants of all premises or parts of premises, public and private, shall extinguish all lights or darken the premises so that no light is visible from the outside."[14]

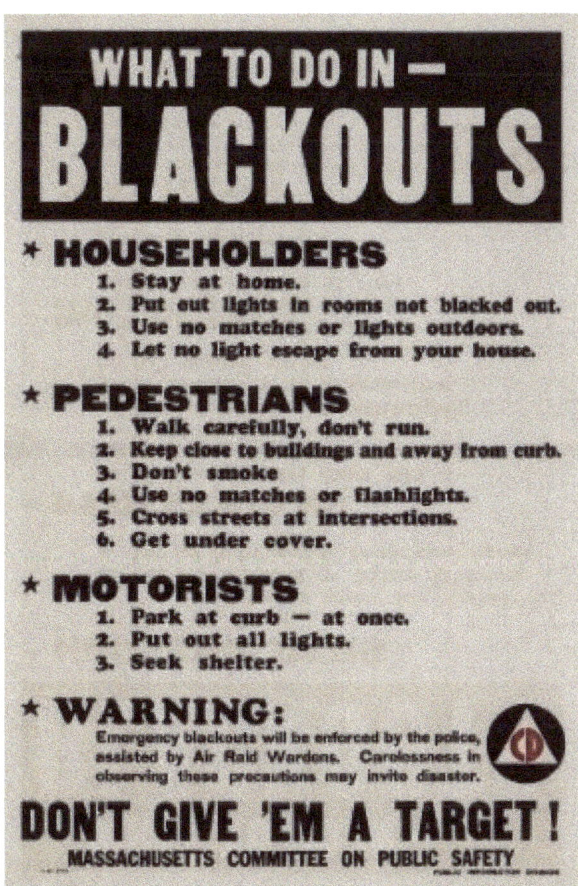

Blackout instructions, Massachusetts. WWII.[15]

The Massachusetts Committee on Public Safety released a handbook entitled *Blackout Information for the General Public,* which described the immediate need to protect the population from enemy bombers. Lights from a city, said the handbook, could be seen by a pilot from a hundred miles away. Uncovered windows were considered exposed windows, but there was also a risk of exploding glass. Thus, residents were encouraged to reinforce them with wire, tape, and cellophane. The handbook

---

[13] *War Supply Contracts.* CPA Div 1946. tinyurl.com/2p9d88re.

[14] *MA Executive Orders.* 1939-1945. MA Court System 12/31/1941. tinyurl.com/38jcb2xv.

[15] *Blackouts.* Poster. Public domain. MA Comm. Pub Safety. *Home Front WWII Blackouts.* Wright Mus WWII. tinyurl.com/5n8f9m28.

also promoted the use of blue lights almost anywhere (blue light was supposedly difficult to see from a distance): in carriage houses and stables, in garages and vestibules, in greenhouses and barns. Any large structures with numerous reflective surfaces were to be reported to the authorities. Pocket flashlights with an internal cut-off were promoted because they could switch off if pointed upward, and outdoor fires, floodlights, and advertising signs were discouraged.

Regulations weren't just rules written on paper. The blackout was very real. At the sound of a siren, citizens retreated to their homes, closed the curtains, turned off their lights, and waited for the all-clear signal. The Women's Republican Club of Boston offered a new "up-to-the-minute" seventeen-hour air raid precaution course.[16] Lecturing churchgoers at the city's Tremont Temple Baptist Church, an auxiliary policeman advised to wait a full minute before attempting to remove an incendiary bomb in the vicinity.[17] In the name of public safety, a large stained glass window depicting Christ located at the First Universalist Church in Worcester was no longer illuminated by floodlights.[18] Even what was very likely the largest reflective surface in Massachusetts went dark. The iconic dome of the Massachusetts State House was first made of wood, later resurfaced with copper by Paul Revere's company, painted yellow, and in 1874 covered with gold. With war looming, in an effort to avoid its being used as a beacon by German bombers, the dome of the Massachusetts State House was painted gray.

The Dome of Massachusetts Statehouse with
dark gray paint in 1941.[19]

Governor Saltonstall continually addressed the issue of who exactly would be expected to go dark. Executive Order No. 3: "...all premises, public and private...," basically, everybody, every air raid alarm, every sunset. Six months later, Executive Order No. 31 was good news for some and bad news for others. "The Massachusetts Committee on Public Safety may authorize a reasonable variation of the foregoing order and may relax specific provisions of the same." Dimouts became acceptable in some places but never in coastal areas. For these communities, "one-half hour after sunset and one-half hour before sunrise, all lights of every nature which are visible from the sea, or which by themselves or with others illuminate the sky, shall be extinguished." Special consideration was given to several coastal communities (Newburyport, Gloucester, Plymouth, Beverly, Salem, and New Bedford) where blackout regulations were expected to extend an additional three miles inland. For Boston, at an especially high risk of attack, requirements reached out to a radius of twelve miles from City Hall.

---

16 *Women's Defense Courses.* Boston Globe 1/3/1942. Newspapers.com. tinyurl.com/yc699jpt.

17 *Tremont Temple*. Boston Globe 1/5/1942. Newspapers.com. tinyurl.com/5h5ty8d5.

18 *First Universalist Church.* Hist Unitarian Universalist Church Worcester. tinyurl.com/3k35m2u6.

19 *MA State House* 5/23/1941. Pub domain photo. Frank Branzetti HABS MASS, 13-BOST LOC. tinyurl.com/58jehvtf.

Four months later, the blackout blanket widened. Executive Order No. 40: All parts of Massachusetts lying east of a line stretching from Lowell to Chelmsford to Sudbury to Framingham to the Rhode Island border were under the directive to cover up at sunset. This time, the new requirements included all towns within a five-mile radius of Worcester City Hall.[20]

In spite of the fact that the penalty for violation of blackout regulations (a five hundred dollar fine, imprisonment, or both) was made clear, not every citizen and business maintained a perfect record. At 9:30 p.m. on the evening of April 9, 1941, eighty-one communities in central Massachusetts went through a trial blackout. A dozen violations were reported in Worcester alone, including four downtown billboards that blazed brightly throughout the event.[21]

These regulations and advisories helped ordinary people adapt to the new reality of uncertain darkness. People were instructed to plan their day with time enough to get home before nightfall, to stay close to buildings to avoid passing vehicles, and to carry sticks or umbrellas to help with curbstones and crossings. "Go about your business quietly, and when it is over, go home," said the Public Safety Committee handbook. "Don't stand around; avoid gatherings. The blackout is not a lark. It is a grim business."[22]

The Federal Office of Civilian Defense had been in operation since May of 1941. At Its head was New York City Mayor Fiorello LaGuardia. The agency coordinated federal and state activities and resources in preparation for an enemy attack. LaGuardia's team set guidelines and monitored the progress of state Civil Defense Offices. It was good timing. Six months later, as the town of Newton was participating in a dry run of its air raid practices, 5,000 miles to the west, bombs were dropping on Pearl Harbor.

The response was swift. By the end of the following day, over a thousand Civilian Defense Offices were activated in towns and cities across New England. Two days after the attack, the town of Brighton announced a parade would be held to mark the opening of an air raid precaution school, and Natick approved a request for $2,700 to be spent for civil defense preparations. Residents were informed that a "nerve center" in the basement of the Medford City Hall would be manned by fire, police, highway, and engineering department representatives along with members of the Red Cross in case of an enemy attack. In Needham, 100 women had already been trained in Civil Defense motor transport work.[23] In light of the recent declaration of war, the American Legion post in Williamstown put a halt on plans to man the town's observation stations twenty-four hours a day until they heard from the government. The possibility existed that additional temporary housing equipped with telephone lines would have to be built to support the observation towers.[24]

At the front line were Air Raid Wardens. Wearing armbands, white helmets, and armed with whistles (often labeled "Made in Japan"), volunteers were in charge of monitoring homes and businesses to make sure blackout regulations were being complied with. Training manuals for wardens gave instructions on how to arm a grenade or administer a lethal karate chop.[25] Growing up in Quincy, Donald Burke remembered sneaking out to the front steps of his home where Mr. Gurney, the neighborhood air raid warden, roamed the streets with the occasional call for a resident to follow the rules.[26] Wardens also advised residents to place buckets of sand and pails of water near attics in case of fire caused by bombs.

---

[20] *MA Executive Orders.* 1939-1945.

[21] *Billboards Glow During Blackout.* Worcester TG 4/10/1942. Way We Were, Worcester, MA. Hist Briefs 1992.

[22] *MA Blackout Information for General Public.* MA Comm. Pub Safety.

[23] *Greater Boston Prepare Defense.* Boston Globe 12/9/1941. Newspapers.com. tinyurl.com/5fed9sum.

[24] *Post Withdraws Air Raid Wardens.* Williamstown News. No Adams Transcript 12/16/1941. Newspapers.com. tinyurl.com/ye2a4y7r.

[25] Taylor, Robert. *New Eng Home Front WWII.* Yankee Books 1992.

[26] *Conversation between author and Donald Burke* 5/9/2021.

While most citizens did their best to follow the rules, albeit with some accidental violations, air raid wardens often had to deal with disgruntled residents. In March 1942, on seeing a home in Norwood with lights ablaze during blackout hours (first offense), the warden knocked on the door. "What the hell are you—another one of those air raid wardens?" asked the resident, rude but certainly not illegal. When he was told to darken his house, the man went back inside, walked upstairs, and turned on another light (second offense). The warden fetched two police officers. This time, the upstairs light switched off, but the resident showed up on the front porch and, bold as brass, lit up a cigarette (third offense). Needless to say, the three officials were not pleased, nor was Judge Edmund Murray, who saw to it that the man became the first violator in Massachusetts to be sentenced for failure to obey blackout regulations. The gentleman was fined $500 and became a guest of the Commonwealth in the House of Corrections for a year.[27]

On December 30, 1941, the lead headline, "Wider Rationing Near," trailed across the front page of the *Daily Boston Globe*.[28] A mandatory priority system had been established for aluminum and machine tools. Nickel, nickel-steel, tungsten, and neoprene would soon be added to the list. Machine tool manufacturers were expected to prioritize orders from defense contracts, and production of consumer products containing aluminum would be cut back.

The findings of a 1941 First National Bank of Boston report supported this action. The amount of "sensitive imported raw materials" used by the US had gone up more than forty percent after developments in the Far East. The bank's analysis revealed what resources were left at hand: eight months' worth of crude rubber, 97 percent of which came from the Far East, and fifteen months' worth of tin, nine-tenths of which came from the same region. Shortages of zinc and copper could be addressed with new sources from other countries, and the bank suggested that rationing would improve the situation.[29]

But this kind of rationing was for big companies that operated multi-million-dollar businesses. Surely, it would have little impact on the average citizen. Donald Nelson was a Vice President at Sears Roebuck when he got the call from FDR to head the new Office of Production Management, later known as the War Production Board. He had a solid idea of what lay ahead. "We in America, the richest country on earth, had never really stopped to consider if we might ever be faced with serious shortages in anything...War changed this easy arrangement."[30]

The first big shock came on January 1, 1942, when Nelson suspended car sales. One month later, all production of new vehicles ended. For Massachusetts, this was a big deal. Lynn's *Daily Evening Item* called it "An Economic Tragedy." The 1,625 businesses in the Bay State that sold cars and equipment employed 13,000 people. An additional 5,500 worked in the state's nearly 7,000 gas stations. Massachusetts was looking at a loss of over $200 million, 16 percent of its total revenue.[31] Limits on tires followed.

While the restriction on cars was troublesome, most consumers were satisfied that their daily lives would continue with few changes. The President himself had told Congress on January 5, "I do not at present propose general consumer ration cards. There are not yet scarcities in the necessities of life which make such a step necessary." In spite of Roosevelt's "keep calm and carry on" propaganda, food rationing began four months later. Sugar came first. The process began with registration. In the tiny town of Warwick, registration was expected to take four days and would be held in the schoolhouse.[32] Some

---

[27] *Norwood Blackout Case*. Boston Globe 3/16/1942. Newspapers.com. tinyurl.com/yyp66bv7.

[28] *Wider Rationing Near*. Boston Globe 12/30/1941. Newspapers.com. tinyurl.com/3vx4ez26.

[29] *Radio Clip Sheet*. OPA 1/1944. Am Homefront. NARA. tinyurl.com/2xpfytfx.

[30] Klein, Maury. *A Call to Arms*. Bloomsbury Press 2013.

[31] *Economic Tragedy*. Daily Evening Item 1/20/1942. Newspapers.com. tinyurl.com/yxusf5hd.

[32] *Warwick*. Athol Daily News 5/2/1942. Newspapers.com. tinyurl.com/55fjtz7n.

towns, like Swampscott, urged registrants to show up on alphabetically designated days and reminded citizens that fraud penalties were stiff...a $10,000 fine or ten years in prison.[33] Daniel M. Wheeler, aged 95, was the first in line to have his name recorded in the sugar rationing census for Berkshire County, where a disappointing 32 percent of residents showed up.[34]

The next step was a rationing booklet. Handed out by the War Price and Rationing Board to every American man, woman, and child, it was filled with tiny perforated stamps, and printed on the back was a warning: "This book is valuable. Do not lose it."

War ration book for 2-year-old
resident of Cherry Valley. 1943.

A certain number of stamps would provide a customer with a certain amount of food. For example, four B stamps could be exchanged for one pound of ground beef. Change was issued using small fiber tokens, some red and some blue, which were also known as points. Frequent adjustments in coupon values and rules caused significant confusion. A University of Delaware article on Ration Book 1 provides a description.

Stamps #1-4—designated for sugar. Each stamp was worth 1 lb of sugar and was given a designed two-week period during which it must be used. Stamps #5-6—2 lbs of sugar each and valid for a 4-week period. Stamp #7—consumer bonus of 2 lbs of sugar for use between July 10-Aug. 22, 1942. Stamp#13—

---

[33] Swampscott. *Sugar Rationing Plans*. Daily Evening Item 5/2/1942. Newspapers.com. tinyurl.com/ufrrj5rn.

[34] *Egremont Best Showing*. Berkshire Eagle 5/5/1942. Newpapers.com. tinyurl.com/49y3yuzx.

5 lbs sugar for 2 2/3 months, expiring on Aug. 15, 1943. Stamp #14—5 lbs sugar for 2 ½ months Aug. 16-Nov. 1, 1943. Stamps #15-16—validated for 5 lbs of sugar each for home canning. Stamp #17—designated for a pair of shoes. Stamp #18—1 pair of shoes between Jun 16-Oct. 31, 1943. Stamps #19-38—designated as coffee stamps, valid for 1 lb. of coffee each for five weeks.[35]

War ration stamps. 1943.

One Texas woman was clearly overwhelmed by the rationing process. When applying for additional sugar allowances for canning, consumers needed to state how many pounds of sugar each family member required. When it was discovered that she had neglected to provide this information, the form was mailed back to her requesting that she fill in the exact weights. Shortly afterward, the local

---

[35] *WWII Ration Books.* WWII Resources HMV. UD Hist Media Center 2012. tinyurl.com/mryrbsjy.

War Price and Rationing Board received her application containing the following information: "...she weighed 210 pounds, her husband 145 and her mother-in-law 160."[36]

Not everything was in short supply. In 1941, at a cost of seventy-five cents, Christmas trees were plentiful but didn't taste very good.

Allen and Co. Fruit and Produce selling Christmas trees, Faneuil Hall. Courtesy of the Boston Public Library, Leslie Jones Collection.[37]

To compensate for the shortage of food items, cut back on tin in food cans, and decrease transportation to and from markets, the government encouraged Americans to plant gardens. Victory Gardens popped up across the country in backyards, front yards, vacant lots, and window boxes. Boston set the tone for this patriotic endeavor in Massachusetts, making forty-nine acres around the city available for growing food. On the Boston Common and in the Public Garden, vegetable patches sprouted up. Seven acres were dedicated as a growing space in the Fenway area. Still in operation today, the Fenway Garden is the oldest surviving Victory Garden in the country. There were over 200 patriotic plots in tiny Florence alone.[38]

Agriculture Secretary Claude Wickard plowing Boston Common to promote the National Victory Garden Program. 1944.[39]

[36] *Radio Clip Sheet.* OPA.

[37] *Allen and Co. Fruit and Produce selling Christmas trees, Faneuil Hall.* Leslie Jones Photo. Courtesy of the Boston Public Library, Leslie Jones Collection.

[38] Koleszar, Janice. *Florence, MA History.* Florence Civic and Bus Asso. Hatfield Printing Publ 1986.

[39] *Victory Garden.* 4/11/44. Pub domain photo. NARA 195586. Picryl. tinyurl.com/bdcvjhjw.

The results of this home-grown effort were astounding. National Geographic estimates that during the first two years of war alone, 40 percent of all vegetables and more than 4 billion jars of food consumed on the home front were grown and processed by men, women, and children in 20 million homes across the country.[40]

It made sense that what Americans did not spend or consume at home could be spent and consumed by troops, but standing in lines waiting for sugar coupons on a hot spring day rankled a bit. So, the Office of Price Administration arranged a propaganda campaign. In January of 1944, from the Tremont Street office of the OPA in Boston came this radio message to be aired across the Commonwealth:

As we sit near our radios, listening to the thrilling invasion reports, how many of us can declare with patriotic satisfaction–" I've got a hand in the fight! The gasoline I didn't use is playing its part in the invasion! Yes, the gasoline you didn't use—to drive to the country—or to go to the movies—or to the beach—together with the millions of gallons we all saved—is playing an important part in winning the war. It's flying our planes–driving our jeeps and tanks—propelling our landing barges. Yes, that gasoline you didn't use—has gone to war on all three fronts—land, sea, and air.[41]

Most Americans did their best. One loyal American from Holyoke wrote this in the local *Transcript Telegram*:

There is something fair and democratic about the sugar rationing in which 130,000,000 people of the United States are engaged today. Everybody has got to do it. Prince and pauper may have some differences about gasoline and tire rationing because there are still people who have more automobiles and tires and are in the habit of using more gasoline than others...but with sugar, it is all the same.[42]

Others, however, took advantage. A black market quickly sprung up and did a healthy business in rationed and price-controlled goods. *The Daily Item* in Lynn reported: "Illegal operators are buying animals...at above market prices and arranging for their slaughter under trees, in barns, garages and abandoned buildings."[43] *The North Adams Transcript* reported that the onion black market, headquartered in New York, was about to make a move in the local area due to the poor harvest that year.[44] *The Recorder* in Greenfield alerted readers to the presence of a thriving illegal market in horse meat and cautioned that the ceiling price was 20 cents per pound "whether it is rump, tenderloin or any other cut."[45]

During rationing, the OPA sought volunteers to serve as price panel assistants for cost checks. There was a ceiling to every item on the shelf, and investigators were charged with making sure those costs were not exceeded or part of a black market transaction. Interviewed by Boston radio station WORL, Massachusetts OPA Chief Investigator Patrick Carr stated that those who exploited the black market were not unlike their counterparts from Prohibition days. His agency was attempting to keep the lid on inflation. Carr painted a picture of what happened when customers paid above the legal price.

---

[40] Schons, Mary. *Fenway Victory Gardens*. Nat Geo 7/21/2023. tinyurl.com/mr2c28j5.

[41] *Radio Clip Sheet*. OPA.

[42] *Editorial. Democratic*. Holyoke Transcript TG 5/4/1942. Newspapers.com. tinyurl.com/yje4ewfs.

[43] *Crisis in Meat*. Daily Item 3/18/1943. Newspapers.com. tinyurl.com/32yjbv4k.

[44] *Onions Black Market*. No Adams Transcript 9/27/1943. Newspapers.com. tinyurl.com/ynfmr9vt.

[45] *Black Market Horse Meat*. Recorder 5/5/1944. Newspapers.com. tinyurl.com/mr3ecx25.

Suppose you pay a grocer a few pennies over the ceiling price for, well—poultry, for example. And so do all his other customers. The extra money enables him to go into the wholesale market and outbid his competitors. He winds up with more than his share of poultry and customers begin to flock to his store. The grocer across the street who has been sticking to ceiling prices sees his customers going there, and rather than go out of business; he is forced to charge a little more, too, so he can meet the other man on equal terms in the marketplace...If it is not checked, there is no end to it—and no limit to the prices all of us would have to pay before we get through.[46]

One challenge facing consumers was the purchase of shoes. In 1943, 53 million fewer pairs of shoes were on the shelves, and customers were cautioned to expect as much as a 75 percent decrease before the end of 1944. No prediction was made as to when the shortage would end, but "...it is apparent that it will not be until the huge demand for GI shoes falls off...and we all know why those GI shoe orders are filled first these days."[47]-A *Boston Globe* article discussed the rationing of footwear, citing lack of manpower and leather. All new shoes, rubber work boots, sneakers, and even baby shoes required ration stamps for purchase. One reader, obviously having difficulty grasping the concept, wrote in to ask if she could buy navy blue shoes to go with her new dress. Hopefully, the answer cleared it up for her: nope, not without a coupon.[48]

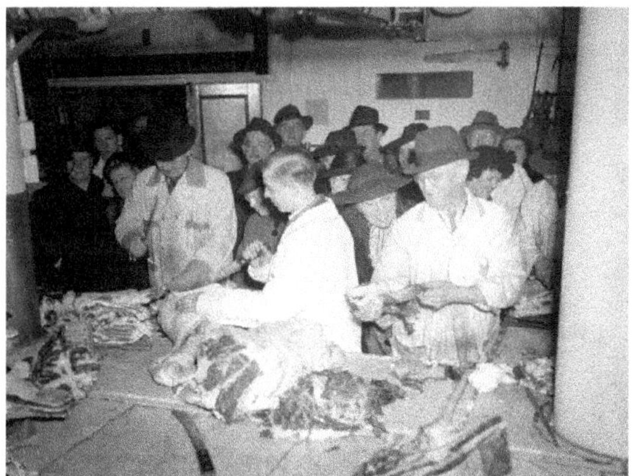

WWII: Meat shortage, Mr. Kelley, Faneuil Market.
Courtesy of the Boston Public Library Leslie Jones Collection[49]

Massachusetts made some unique contributions to the food industry during the war. Gorton's of Gloucester had been a major name in fish products since the 1800's. In 1923, when Benito Mussolini failed to cough up the money for the million-dollar shipment of Gorton's salt cod that had just arrived in Italy, it nearly sunk the company. For help, Gorton's turned to the owner of the recently opened General Seafoods Company in Gloucester. Apparently, Clarence Birdseye had developed an interest in freezing fish after spending time with the native peoples of Labrador. Within a few years, frozen fish sticks were flying out of company freezers.[50] After Pearl Harbor, fish was in high demand not only by the armed forces but as a replacement for heavily rationed beef. Gorton's sales, hampered by a lack of tin cans, relied heavily on frozen fish. It is ironic that thanks to Mussolini, this Gloucester company survived the war and remains an industry leader to this day.

---

[46] *Talking About Black Markets 12/5/1943.* Radio Transcripts. Fed Agencies New Eng. NARA. tinyurl.com/58u7sapd.

[47] *Radio Clip Sheet.* OPA.

[48] *Rationing Shoes.* Boston Globe 2/8/1943. Newspapers.com. tinyurl.com/y5zc4tbd.

[49] *WWII: Meat shortage, Mr. Kelley Faneuil Market.* Leslie Jones Photo. Courtesy of the Boston Public Library, Leslie Jones Collection.

[50] *Mussolini Stiffed Gloucester.* New Eng Hist Soc. tinyurl.com/yanfzuvm.

One of the oldest operating candy companies in the United States, the New England Confectionery Company of Cambridge, produced rations for the military during World War II. Its melt-proof Necco wafers, described as "practically indestructible during transit," became a sweet treat for the men and women of the armed forces.[51]

Shortly after they were first created by Toll House Inn owner Ruth Graves of Wakefield, Nestle Company began production of delicious Toll House Cookies. Despite wartime shortages, the company waged a major advertising campaign to keep the cookies coming. Ads encouraged housewives to consider it their duty to send the delectable treat to those serving in the war. Even cookie tins carried patriotic sentiments: "Dear Mom, The boys will make you an honorary general if you'll just send us more Tollhouse Cookies."[52]

Some companies suffered from the pressure of rationing and lack of manpower. Marshmallow Fluff, manufactured by a company in Lynn, was forced to make significant changes, sugar rationing being a major factor. While the origin of the recipe is unclear, the company, founded by Swampscott High alumni H. Allen Durkee and Fred Mower, made a hit with the sweet treat. When war broke out, the owners opted to cut sales of the gooey spread and use resources to support the war effort. A portion of Fluff manufacturing facilities were converted to wrap electronic and optical parts in waterproof casings.[53] Friendly Ice Cream of Wilbraham didn't fare as well. In 1941, owners Curtis and Presley Blake shut down after posting signs promising to reopen "when we win the war." In 1945, they did just that.[54]

Horses and chickens weren't the only hard-to-find items. One product, essential during any time of crisis, was in critically short supply. Following on the heels of prohibition (which literally drained the reserves of the magical concoction from 64 million gallons pre-prohibition to 4 million when the dry spell was over),[55] many whiskey producers were just beginning to reopen distilleries, good news for those who enjoyed a wee dram now and then but bad news because whiskey required aging before being consumed. The delay, plus the World War II government mandate that distilleries convert to industrial alcohol production, just about shut down the American whiskey industry.

Unlike hard liquor production, breweries were struggling well before Prohibition began. The First World War marked a period of intense hatred for all things German, and in this country, it included beer. The Lt. Governor of Wisconsin, a vocal Prohibitionist, stated: "We have German enemies across the water. We have German enemies in this country, too. And the worst of all our German enemies...are Pabst, Schlitz, Blatz, and Miller."[56] Sales declined, and the enactment of the 18th Amendment struck the beer industry like a one-two punch. Help was on the way, however. FDR campaigned against Prohibition in his first presidential run, calling it a "tragic failure," perhaps a bit self-serving as Roosevelt was known to enjoy a drink or three. Five months after he was elected, Congress passed the 21st Amendment, repealing Prohibition. FDR's response: "I believe this would be a good time for a beer."[57] With the country plunged into conflict, the President threw his support behind providing alcohol for our fighting men, requiring that 15 percent of beer production in the US be earmarked for the military.[58]

In New England, Narragansett had been a top seller for decades. The Rhode Island-based company survived Prohibition, in small part because of a government license to sell medicinal beer and

[51] *Candy Making Cambridge.* Necco. Cambridge Hist Soc 2011. tinyurl.com/4n9nh26a.

[52] Briggs, Tracy. *WWII vets...chocolate chip cookie.* INFORUM 8/2/2023. tinyurl.com/2exa8nyp.

[53] *Marshmallow Fluff.* Marshmallow Fluff. tinyurl.com/54ch3v8h.

[54] McDowell, Erin. *Rise fall of Friendly's.* Insider 11/4/2020. tinyurl.com/bpa44ps6.

[55] Australian Bartender. *Whiskey before after Prohibition.* Bartender 5/19/2015. tinyurl.com/29yvjhek.

[56] *WWII Saved Am Beer.* Nat WWII Mus 4/7/2021. tinyurl.com/2p6cv2vy.

[57] Abrams, Brian. *Drinking President.* Modern Drunkard Mag 7/2006. tinyurl.com/mrxeud7f.

[58] *WWII Saved Am Beer.* Nat WWII Mus.

the production of ginger ale, sarsaparilla, and root beer. But the lean years had drained the coffers of the beer company, and they turned to a competitor for help.[59]

Haffenreffer Brewery, Jamaica Plain.[60]

The Haffenreffer Brewing Company was located along the pure waters of the Stony Brook in Jamaica Plain, a company that emphasized the importance of good public relations with its neighbors. A tap installed outside the brewery invited passersby to enjoy a refreshing sip.[61] When the company was approached by Narragansett owners for financial and managerial support, Rudolph Haffenreffer Jr. said yes. In an attempt to attract the beer-craving masses, he redesigned the Narragansett logo to reflect his interest in Native American cultures. For this task, he enlisted the help of a family friend and native of Springfield. It is a bit of a stretch to imagine that the noble countenance of the proud and revered Chief Sachem of the Narragansett Tribe, Canonicus, had any relation to the rather comical (as well as cringe-worthy and politically incorrect) caricature created by Theodore Geisel. However, the Chief Gansett character (decidedly with the Dr. Seuss flare so recognizable today) did the trick, resulting in a massively successful advertising campaign. Narragansett beer surged back into popularity, the two breweries came together under President Haffenreffer, and while international upheaval raged around them, both companies survived the war.[62]

Throughout World War II, fuel was a badly needed resource for the military, and a significant portion of the country found a special challenge in the rationing of fuel oil. For residents of New England, planning for heating during the winter months began long before they felt the crispness of autumn. Fuel coupons were made available to residents who needed to fill up their oil tanks, and ration certificates were available for the purchase of coal or wood-burning stoves. In 1943, the Massachusetts Committee on Public Safety disclosed that due to low fuel stocks, a number of residences could not be heated that winter. Woolen suits, vests, and thermal underwear quickly became a necessary trend.[63]

One of the biggest shortages experienced during World War II did not come in the form of material goods but in manpower. The entrance of millions of women into the workforce would make profound changes that would impact the face of American society.

---

[59] *Narragansett Beer Survived Prohibition.* New Eng Hist Soc. tinyurl.com/4fes58ub.

[60] *Haffenreffer.* Pub domain photo. Wiki Commons. tinyurl.com/mwmtp9jk.

[61] *Rudolph Haffenreffer.* City of Boston 3/8/2022. tinyurl.com/yckx4vzh.

[62] *Narragansett Beer Survived Prohibition.* New Eng Hist Soc.

[63] *Atlantic Shivers.* Economist 1/16/1943. Economist Hist Arch. tinyurl.com/s5jzxktz.

Women working at Watertown Arsenal, World War II.[64]

Within six months after Pearl Harbor, Massachusetts became one of five states to amend labor laws enabling women to work night shifts in specific wartime production jobs. As women headed off to work, many Massachusetts retailers extended their operating schedules to include evening hours, and Filene's in Boston opened up three Slack Bars to accommodate the wardrobe of female assembly line workers.[65] Many unqualified to enter the military due to age, including elderly citizens, found a place in wartime industry.

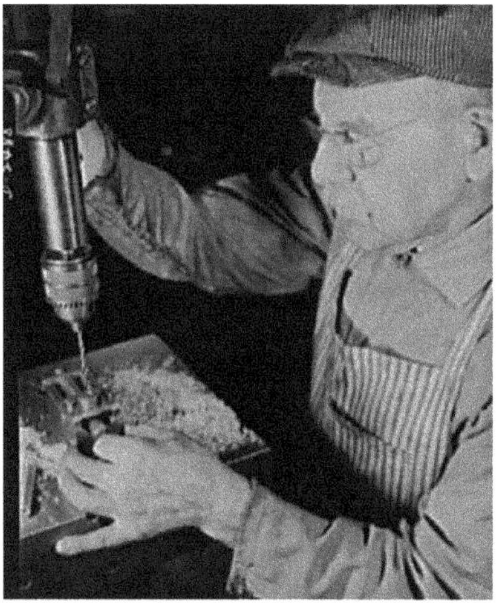

Phineas Allen, 78, who worked on submarine
parts during World War I, operates a drill at the
Cube Steak Company in Boston. 1942.[66]

Following Governor Saltonstall's 1942 Executive Order No. 36, children as young as fourteen were allowed to work at farms. Regulations required no more than six days a week and eight hours a day with two breaks, and only during the harvest season. "Absences from school shall be excused."[67] Plymouth took advantage of the change, and in 1943, the Superintendent of Schools reported that pupils in good standing had taken part in the cranberry harvest.[68]

---

[64] *Workers Watertown Arsenal.* Pub domain photo. NARA. tinyurl.com/nyjc62m4.

[65] Taylor, Robert. *New Eng Home Front WWII.*

[66] *Food machinery plant.* Pub domain photo. OWI 2/1942. LOC. tinyurl.com/wew4bfrb.

[67] *MA Executive Orders First Series.* Saltonstall.

[68] *Report Supt Schools 1943.* Annual Report, Plymouth, MA.

Schools fell victim to the manpower crunch as well. In Plymouth, a third of its teachers headed off to war during the 1942-1943 school year.[69] This was not the only change facing education in the Bay State. Officials were called upon to adjust to new priorities. In the Hadley Annual Report for 1942, the Superintendent expressed concerns over changes in curricula that were filtering down into the public schools, "whether it is liked or not." His opinion:

I believe that more boys and girls should give greater thought to the vocational courses offered right here in Hadley. Since the early days in Hadley, the livelihood of its residents in great share has been gained from the soil and its womenfolk have been in that same degree homemakers. So it seems to me that a greater share of boys and girls...should be enrolled in the respective agriculture and household arts courses.

It was the Superintendent's twelfth year heading the Hadley School Department. It would be his last.[70] One year later, the new acting Superintendent stated: "In war periods, one suddenly becomes aware of changes that affect each of us in our daily lives...It is the duty of school officials to prepare the students in our schools to meet the many problems they shall face in the immediate future..." He expressed an urgent need to provide practical courses such as woodworking and machine assembly and suggested converting the Agriculture Department building to a school shop.[71]

The Amherst Public Schools understood their new responsibilities. It was determined that two recently offered courses, Western Hemisphere History and Pre-flight Aeronautics, were simply not enough. The former Industrial Arts I and II classes were changed to Fundamentals of Machines and Electricity, respectively, both of which aligned with War Department suggestions, and a new Industrial Arts course for girls was added to assist those moving into defense industries.[72]

Schools were beginning to look different. During the 1960s, students learned to duck and cover in the hope of surviving a nuclear strike. Today's students rehearse active shooter drills. But with the call of a siren in the Second World War, children took shelter as a prelude to a German attack. The Raynham School Committee decided in 1941 that "the best policy would be to keep the pupils at school in case of an air raid siren," based upon advice from the Department of Education and the misguided belief that no school in England "had ever been hit by a bomb when the children were in it." "It is amazing," said a school official, "how seriously the pupils take these drills and how eager they are that everything shall be done just right."[73]

Schoolchildren were kept busy participating in the war effort. Students in Pittsfield collected obsolete business forms for the town's salvage committee.[74] Kapok was used in the production of life rafts, life preservers, and airplane insulation. When the supply from Southeast Asia was cut off, students in Plymouth gathered and dried 131 bags of milkweed pods to replace kapok, enough to produce sixty-five life-saving jackets.[75]

At the David Hale Fanning Trade School for Girls in Worcester, the Student Council donated one-cent stamps to go with Christmas cards made by the Print Shop. They would be sent to Fort Devens for soldiers to use. The students were, however, still just teenagers, and their *School Spirit* newsletter contained tips for stylish young women: "planning for the prom, trends in hairstyles, and how to create

---

[69] *Report Supt Schools 1945*. Annual Report, Plymouth, MA.

[70] *Report of Town Officers 1942*. Hadley, MA

[71] *Report of Town Officers 1943*. Hadley, MA.

[72] *Reports of Town of Amherst 12/31/1942*. Amherst, MA.

[73] *Report School Comm 12/31/1941*. Raynham, MA.

[74] Taylor, Robert. *New England Home Front WWII.*

[75] *Report Town of Plymouth 12/31/1944*. Plymouth, MA.

new, exciting clothes from old ones."[76] As the war darkened, so did school publications. Two years later, the Worcester Academy Bulletin carried news of the war on every one of its pages. Norman Cota, class of '13, was serving as a commander with the 29th Infantry and was "regarded as one of the most rugged characters of the US Army, always at the front of his column, moving with complete disregard for his safety, singing to himself when things go smoothly." Other alumni, like Lt. James F. O'Donoghue Jr. and Pvt. Thomas C. Power were less fortunate. Both were killed in action.[77]

Higher education stepped forward by providing curricula and programs that would prepare students to fill war-related roles. Harvard University was one of the first six universities chosen to run an Army ROTC program. The program later expanded to include the Navy, and six years later, graduates could opt for a position in the Marines. By 1941, nineteen Naval ROTC programs existed, and eight more were added to the list, including one at the College of the Holy Cross in Worcester. That fall, the first 115 ROTC students, a quarter of the incoming freshmen class, arrived.

When war came to the nation, so many young men were called to duty that colleges experienced a significant decline in enrollment. The government provided a solution. In order to prepare young men for the military, training programs were developed and assigned to schools across the country. The V1 program eventually expanded all the way to a V-12 program and served potential aviators, intelligence operators, communication specialists, and WAVES.

Holy Cross benefited from the V programs, and by 1945, the majority of the student body was enrolled in a Navy training program. Curricula aligned with Navy requirements, and math and science became the priority. War-related courses taught gunnery skills, ordnance, seamanship, engineering, military law, and naval tactics. Knowledge of the Navy was covered by studies of its history, organization, and administration. Latin was out, and Japanese, German, and French were in. The college renovated the basement of the chapel to create an armory and drill area, and an anti-aircraft gun was installed.

Like many colleges, degree programs were accelerated to allow faster turnover. Of the 400 members of the class of 1943, only 220 were left on campus when graduation time rolled around, and for the first time in its history, the college failed to hold commencement exercises. The College of the Holy Cross made their country proud during World War II. Two Medal of Honor recipients, Father Thomas O'Callahan and Lt. John Vincent Powers are counted among their alumni. Of the nearly four thousand members of the Holy Cross community who served, one hundred and nine heroes, including Lt. Powers, made the ultimate sacrifice for their country.[78]

Amherst College was also struggling with declining enrollment at the outset of the war. Early in 1942, programs that educated civilians in how to protect themselves from enemy attack became popular. They would soon be replaced by a variety of programs that eventually trained approximately 900 civilians for war. A Navy pre-flight school ran practice flights out of the airfield in Turner's Falls. Pre-Meteorology for those interested in becoming weathermen, an Army unit for language instruction, and a separate course for those headed to West Point were offered at the College.[79] The Army ran an ROTC program out of the Massachusetts State Agricultural College in Amherst. One of its students, Lt. Carl Wildner of Holyoke, would achieve fame as a navigator who participated in the Doolittle raid on Tokyo.[80]

The list of training sites in the Bay State is extensive. Programs existed at Worcester Polytechnic Institute, Boston University, Tufts, Andover Newton Theological School, Mount Holyoke College, and Wellesley College. Radar and navigation courses were offered at MIT, and Wentworth Institute taught

---

[76] *School Spirit, David Hale Fanning Trade School for Girls.* 1/14/1942.

[77] *Worcester Acad Bulletin.* Vol. X, 10/15/1944.

[78] *Holy Cross: 1900-1949.* Holy Cross. tinyurl.com/247j96wy.

[79] Rand, Frank Prentice. *Amherst Landmark of Light.* Amherst Hist Soc 1958.

[80] Carl R. Wildner. Veteran Tributes. tinyurl.com/ymwafbvy.

future machinist mates. The Navy relied on the Massachusetts Maritime Academy to turn out able seamen. The college had recently moved from its location in Boston and held classes in the former Hyannis State Teachers College in Barnstable.[81]

"900 tons of scrap metal goes into a destroyer," read a World War II poster. Early on in the war, Office of Price Administration Chairman Donald Nelson had warned that collection might become necessary. The difficulty lay in what should be defined as scrap. Nelson suggested that ornamental items like fences and statues would qualify. Two months later, FDR backed him up, adding "old cannon and bronze statues from parks" to the list. His comments met with grumbling from the public. In Westfield, citizens were divided over removing statues of a Civil War soldier and of a Revolutionary War hero from a local park. Several residents felt that scrapping them would be sacrilegious. Another responded simply, "What statues?"[82] FDR, always hesitant to displease voters, tried humor to smooth things over, stating, "A great many probably would look better if the statues were converted into weapons." A Gallup poll suggested most citizens supported giving up historically significant items, with one respondent stating, "Let's forget the Civil War and remember Pearl Harbor."[83]

One of seventeen deck guns used in the War of 1812 being
scrapped for war effort at Boston Navy Yard. WWII.
Courtesy of the Boston Public Library, Leslie Jones Collection.[84]

The government did its best to convince Americans that used metal meant weapons. Given 30,000 razor blades, 50 machine guns could be produced. One shovel could make four hand grenades.[85] This was practical information that the average American could understand, and in Massachusetts, scrap recycling became serious business. The new Turners Falls-Gill Bridge, the longest in the state, replaced

---

[81] Dennehy, Kevin. *Change of course*. Cape Cod Times 3/9/2003. tinyurl.com/4mswfczc.

[82] *Westfield Residents Statue Proposal*. Morning Union 8/12/1942. Newspapers.com. tinyurl.com/2p9z7ek8.

[83] Hunter, Edith M. *Pounding swords into swords*. ISU 2022. dr.lib.iastate.edu/server/api/core/bitstreams/ca994eca-1ab8-469c-82c0-6c9cbdbec7f2/content.

[84] *Deck guns used in the War of 1812 being scrapped for war effort at the Navy Yard*. Leslie Jones Photo. Courtesy of the Boston Public Library, Leslie Jones Collection.

[85] Bailey, Ronald H. *Iron Will*. HistoryNet, 11/27/2017. tinyurl.com/6t2z4cnf.

the Red Suspension Bridge, which was demolished and hauled away for scrap.[86] Faxon Bowen, colorful one-term mayor of North Adams, was hard at work supporting his country. Bowen, who had fired seven members of the Public Works Department for supporting his opponent in the mayoral election,[87] attempted to raise a private army composed of men too old for the draft. After discovering he was bordering on treason, he switched his endeavors to collecting scrap and tore up the town's unused trolley tracks instead.[88]

Governor Leverett Saltonstall took a blow torch to the ornamental fence around the State House; Mrs. Russell Hamlet, Chairman of the Women's Division of the Public Safety Committee in Arlington, donned a necklace of aluminum cans and a coffee pot along with a sign, "Uncle Sam Needs Aluminum...,"[89] and in twelve hours, thirteen-year-old Gladys Morrow of Everett and nine of her friends collected 3,000 pounds of scrap metal.[90]

Governor Saltonstall takes a blow torch to the
State House fence as part of a metal scrap drive. WWII.
Courtesy of the Boston Public Library, Leslie Jones Collection.[91]

Someone came up with the idea of reenacting the Henry Knox 1775 cannon haul from Fort Ticonderoga. In March 1942, Charles Thayer of Cummington, Massachusetts, and a pair of oxen headed to Pittsfield to take part in a scrap drive along the Knox Trail that would end in Boston. The plan was to collect old cannons and military scrap metal along the way. Two thousand locals gathered to hear speakers whip the crowd into a patriotic frenzy before the big send-off. The parade was largely ceremonial. A World War I Krupp artillery piece was piled into the back of the ox-drawn wagon, hauled a few feet, and then off-loaded onto a truck. "Dick and Dime, accustomed to pulling 7,200 pounds at the annual Hilltown Agricultural Society Fair in Cummington, didn't work up a sweat."[92]

The event captured the eye of the Commonwealth. By the time Chesire resident Eugene Bowen, who had dressed up as Henry Knox and the rest of the procession reached the Boston Common, added to the original six cannons from Pittsfield were three tons of scrap, including fifty more war relics and

---

[86] Stoughton, Ralph. *Hist of Gill*. Bicentennial Proj 1978. Town of Gill.

[87] *Faxon Bowen*. Find Grave. ID 31657293 1971. tinyurl.com/bwc8b8rt.

[88] Slider, Maynard. *Gritty Berkshires*. White River Press 2019.

[89] Taylor, Robert. *New Eng Home Front WWII*.

[90] *Boys, Girls Scrap Drive*. Boston Globe 10/2/1942. Newspapers.com. tinyurl.com/ycx7kxwe.

[91] *Fence at State House, Governor starts October 5, 1942 (other fences around city)*. Leslie Jones Photo. Courtesy of the Boston Public Library, Leslie Jones Collection.

[92] Drew, Bernard A. *Henry Knox and Rev War Trail*. MacFarland & Co 2012. Google Books. tinyurl.com/mjnjkyc5.

hundreds of automobile license plates. A gun from the USS Constitution waited on the common to join the haul. The Krupp artillery piece was the largest item, weighing in at 8.5 tons and fetching $350 at the auction, which netted nearly $2,000 worth of metal for the war effort.[93]

Scrap drives for tin, aluminum, rubber, and rags became commonplace. An event in Leominster in the fall of 1943 collected over 85 tons of paper, a per capita tally of 7.7 pounds per resident.[94] The city of Lynn scheduled a paper drive for October 31, 1943, with ten thousand schoolchildren expected to attend. Unfortunately, it fell on a Sunday, something which Rev. Earton Robertson of Lynnfield Street Baptist Church was only too happy to point out. "Could anything be more of a disgrace for the city of Lynn than to have us send out boys and girls on the Lord's Day to collect scrap?"[95] Apparently, the Mayor agreed. On the following day, a front-page headline of the *Daily Item* read, "Frawley Halts Drive For Paper on Sunday."[96]

Rubber scrap at a Malden garage.
WWII: Men looking at war signs at tire facility.
Courtesy of the Boston Public Library, Leslie Jones Collection.[97]

Pittsfield did its best to collect fats, an important source of the glycerin used in explosives. Of the twenty-two local schools that scraped up 6,000 pounds of fat, Central Junior High topped the list with 799 pounds. In a statement by the School Superintendent, he praised students but expressed displeasure with local housewives, whose skimpy donations had contributed to Massachusetts achieving only 47.9 percent of its War Production Board fat quota.[98] Shellac, a necessary component for making flares and explosives, was also in short supply. Luckily, it was a major ingredient in phonograph records. To kick off the city's shellac drive, singer Vaughn Monroe made a week-long appearance at the RKO Boston Theater, where records could be exchanged for tickets to see the popular crooner and his band, The Spoilers. Music shops in forty-seven towns and cities from Boston to Worcester, including Allston, Belmont, Dorchester, Foxboro, and Lexington, were expected to participate.[99]

In 1940, with preparation for war ramping up, the United States found itself facing the crucial issue of where the money to pay for it all would come from. The cost of war would be astronomical, and in order to avoid bankrupting the country and to maintain some kind of financial postwar foundation, the US Treasury Department made the decision to sell Defense Bonds. War Bonds (the name changed after Pearl Harbor) were slow-growing promises that if you laid down $18.75 to buy a piece of Treasury

---

[93] *Cannon Brings Highest Price*. Berkshire County Eagle 3/25/1942. Newpapers.com. tinyurl.com/34s4a8p9.

[94] *Paper. Leominster*. Fitchburg Sentinel 10/25/1943. Newpapers.com. tinyurl.com/4fd3e8wj.

[95] *Sunday Salvage Drive*. Daily Item 10/18/1943. Newspapers.com. tinyurl.com/vyd4cwyd.

[96] *Frawley Halts Drive*. Daily Item 10/181943. Newspapers.com. tinyurl.com/mshs3u7a.

[97] *WWII: Men looking at war signs at tire facility*. Leslie Jones Photo. Courtesy of the Boston Public Library, Leslie Jones Collection.

[98] *Central Leads in Fats Drives*. Berkshire Eagle 3/29/1943. Newspapers.com. tinyurl.com/a4zekaw7.

[99] *Shellac Drive Starts*. Boston Globe 6/4/1942. Newspapers.com. tinyurl.com/498jz7c7.

Department paper with "$25" printed on it, in ten years, the government would buy it back for the full amount. Bonds were offered in amounts from $25 to $10,000 and could be purchased for 75 percent of their worth. Ten cent stamps were also available and could be stored in booklets and saved toward bond purchases.

German sub used for war bond drive,
Tremont Street, Boston. WWII.
Courtesy of the Boston Public Library, Leslie Jones Collection.[100]

War bond drives, enticing potential buyers with exciting entertainment, were held across the state. A January 1944 event at the Bancroft Hotel Ball Room in Worcester featured actor Charles Bickford, a native of Cambridge, along with five war heroes. The price of admission was a $25 bond.[101] Later that year, Jack Lee's Military Band was scheduled to play at a baseball game between Lynn's Fraser Stars and New York's popular Black Yankees. It was part of a war bond drive, and $25 bonds would be given away in a drawing after every inning.[102]

As part of its "Fighting Dollar Days" campaign, the Boston Navy Yard held an eight-day drive. Entertainment was provided every day around lunchtime, and a huge billboard near one of the gates showed the shipyard's progress toward the goal. Each unit was marked by one of the Navy Yard's proudest accomplishments, a destroyer, and the unit at the bottom was marked by a garbage scow. By the sixth day, nearly 100% of workers had pledged, equaling over 13 percent of the yard's total wages.[103] Jordan Marsh Company was a big supporter, and in 1943, it sponsored a rally to encourage bond sales. A military band and color guard led a parade from the Boston Common to Jordan Marsh. Among the dignitaries attending was Mrs. Joseph O'Connell of Brighton, whose seventh son had just joined the military. Celebrities were also on hand to dazzle the crowd. Actors Phyllis Thaxter and Donald Cook, who played lead roles in the Colonial Theater production of *Claudia*, appeared along with comedian Jan Murray and singer Kay Ivers, a regular on radio station WBZ.[104]

With all due respect to Ms. Thaxter and Mr. Cook, a constellation of glittering stars appeared in Boston in 1943 when the Hollywood Cavalcade of Stars rolled into town. The government put the entertainment industry to good use, keeping support for the war running high. In 1942, the Treasury

<hr>

[100] *German sub used for war bond drive during WWII, on Tremont St.* Leslie Jones Photo. Courtesy of the Boston Public Library, Leslie Jones Collection.

[101] *Bond Battalion Bancroft.* Sunday TG 1/23/1944. Way We Were. Worcester, MA. Hist Briefs 1992.

[102] Southward, Harvey. *Itemizing Sports.* Daily Item 7/12/1944. Newspapers.com tinyurl.com/mra3zrhw.

[103] Jones, Janet. *Navy Yard Bond Drive.* Boston Globe 11/17/1941. Newspapers.com. tinyurl.com/zwbdr2uf.

[104] *Jordan Marsh Bond Drive.* Boston Globe 4/12/1943. Newspapers.com. tinyurl.com/4rt67d89.

Department came up with the idea to gather a group of well-known actors, put them on a train, and haul them across the country to convince citizens to buy war bonds.

Olivia de Havilland visits Boston with the Cavalcade of Stars.
Courtesy of the Boston Public Library, Leslie Jones Collection.[105]

It was an immediate success. Tours were loaded with flashy, eye-catching moments to draw the attention of potential bond buyers. During one performance at Madison Square Garden, a blushing Betty Hutton announced her impending nuptials. Bandleader Kay Kyser turned auctioneer in Cleveland and sold two pounds of butter and a three-pound steak for $100,000 each.[106] When the train huffed into South Station in Boston on May 1, 1942, on board were Bob Hope, Claudette Colbert, Laurel and Hardy, Groucho Marx, Olivia DeHavilland, James Cagney, and Springfield native Eleanor Powell.[107] The show at the Boston Garden netted $77,000 for the war bond effort.[108]

During the war, the public dug deep into their pockets. In spite of the fact that the average yearly salary was approximately $2,500, over $185 billion in war bonds were purchased by 85 million loyal Americans.

Practically every aspect of pre-war life was changing. In May 1942, Rev. John J. Connolly stood before a crowd at baccalaureate exercises at the Immaculate Conception Church in Boston. His words of wisdom for the 250 Boston College seniors included a warning about the increasingly common practice of divorce. "Upon the Christian home, ruthless hands have been laid." He likened the current increase in broken marriages to that of ancient Rome, whose civilization died, he claimed, at the hands of rampant practices such as divorce and birth control. "Shall America's history be that of Rome?"[109] Father Connolly was in for a shock.

When America went to war, men in the heat of patriotic fervor flocked to enlist. In an effort to ensure that their sweethearts would be waiting when they came home, marriages to men in the military skyrocketed, 1.2 million in 1942 alone.[110] One source estimated as many as 1,000 women a day married

---

[105] *Cavalcade of Stars comes to Boston with actresses on parade*. Leslie Jones Photo. Courtesy of the Boston Public Library, Leslie Jones Collection.

[106] Betty at War. Betty Hutton Estate Website. tinyurl.com/ykf5r6w5.

[107] Dineen, Joseph F. *Stars Arrive*. Boston Globe 5/1/1942. Newspapers.com. tinyurl.com/24secwxh.

[108] Heffernan, Harold. *Caravan Adds to Funds*. Boston Globe 5/15/1942. Newspapers.com. tinyurl.com/2bx6cuj8.

[109] *Divorce Ruined Am Home*. Boston Globe, 5/11/1942. Newspapers.com. tinyurl.com/msb674z3.

[110] Yellin, Emily. *Wartime Weddings*. Committed. NYT 2/2/2017. tinyurl.com/5665bcpt.

their men in uniforms during the first six months of the war.[111] The government was aware of the importance of good morale among its fighting men. Thus, one of Governor Saltonstall's more interesting directives was Executive Order No. 20, which allowed all Armed Forces chaplains, whether they were Massachusetts residents or not, to "solemnize marriages."[112] It was basically an effort to speed it up, get them married, and get them over there.

However, in January of 1945, the Worcester Telegram reported record-high divorces...1,205. The increase was blamed on let-down of the moral tone due to war conditions...and war marriages that got off to a bad start."[113] Less than a year later, in "an almost inevitable sequel to the wartime wedding boom," said a New York Times article, war ended, and so did one out of every four marriages.[114]

Everywhere, citizens showed their support for the men and women in the military. Newsletters were mailed overseas, and patriotic residents wrote letters and sent packages. Radio broadcasts, newspapers, and celebrations remembered those in service. Often, citizens were eloquent in expressing their opinions about the war. On July 26, 1943, the Italian American community of the Shrewsbury Street neighborhood in Worcester celebrated the downfall of Mussolini with a bonfire.[115] The irate and ever-colorful former governor of the state and soon-to-be mayor of Boston for the fourth time, James Curley, let the world know which side he stood on. In 1917, Japan presented him with a medal commemorating a visit to Boston by their ambassadors. The day after the attack on Pearl Harbor, Curley saw fit to mail it back to this ally-turned-enemy.[116] Several residents of the town of Bridgewater were particularly vocal in their messages to those in the military.

Letter August 30, 1943: Hi Ya Feller, We are not going to ask you "How Ya Doin'?" because we know and all the world knows. As far as the Axis are concerned, they know, too, but they probably don't get the same kick out of it as we do. They are getting theirs in a different place.

Letter December 31, 1943: Dear Folks...1943 is on the way out. What a job you have all done! Before 1944 is too far along, you are going to blow that itching Nazi ape and that four-eyed bucktoothed cartoon of a human Hirohito to hell in a hack. Keep slugging...[117]

In Rochdale, a tiny suburb of Leicester, the Rochdale News began sending words of encouragement and local news to those in uniform while providing town residents with updates from overseas. Each month, the editors dutifully published the names of every single resident serving in the Armed Forces. In March of 1943, the paper reported on two sad milestones. The town's first loss, Pvt. John A. Davis was killed in action in North Africa. Later that month, word came that Rochdale's first air hero, Technical Sgt. Charles "Sonny" Perry, recipient of an Air Medal and Oak Leaf Cluster, had been shot down while participating in a raid over France and was being held captive in Germany.[118] By January 1944, the town had a five-star family, Mr. and Mrs. Clement Gallant.[119] The very first issue of the Rochdale News recounted this hot off the press snippet: "Joe Robidoux is still gunning for the 'grey' who let down the bars in his cow pasture during blueberry season and let all his cows out. Joe said, 'I

---

[111] Bailey, Ronald H. et al. *Home Front: USA WWII.*

[112] *MA Executive Orders First Series.* Saltonstall.

[113] *Divorce Set Record.* Worcester TG 1/3/1945. Way We Were, Worcester, MA. Hist Briefs 1992.

[114] *And Then... Divorces.* Committed. NYT 2/2/2017. tinyurl.com/593738tn.

[115] Feid, Lawrence. *Shrewsbury Street Bonfire.* Worcester TG 7/26/1943. Way We Were, Worcester, MA. Hist Briefs 1992.

[116] *Curley Return Medal.* Boston Globe 12/8/1941. Newspapers.com. tinyurl.com/ydypkvt7.

[117] *News from Bridgewater, MA.* Correspondence 1943-1945.

[118] *Rochdale News.* Vol. 1 11/1943. Rochdale News 11/43-10/45.

[119] *Rochdale News.* Vol. 1 1/1944. Rochdale News 11/43-10/45.

don't mind 'em picking my blueberries or taking shortcuts through my land, but when it comes to letting down the bars and my cows go astray, well, that's the last straw..."'[120] Another noteworthy item appeared early in 1944. Back in those days, the train stopped in town to pick up passengers at a local depot. On one particularly busy day,

A stranger butted into the waiting line before the ticket window of the Rochdale Station. "I want a ticket for Boston," said the man, and he put 50 cents on the counter. "You can't go to Boston for 50 cents," said Gabe Meyers. "Well, then," asked the stranger, "where can I go for 50 cents?" And each of the ten people in that waiting line told him.[121]

Perhaps the most remembered, certainly the most dreaded, communication during World War II was the telegram. It became the job of telegraph operators to deliver the tragic news of the death of a loved one. In Grafton, Henry Ainsworth Jr. recalled his father's paper store in the Town House Building. "They used to hate to hear the teletype machine 'wake up' and start running, as it always meant terrible news for some poor family." His father "rued the day, years before the war, when he set up the place to be a Western Union Office."[122]

In spite of shortages, blackouts, and rationing, life went on in Massachusetts. Christmas still rolled around, although hints of the war raging overseas could be seen everywhere. Exterior holiday lights and window candles were outlawed. At Central Church in Jamaica Plain, Rev. Edgar Chandler was expected to deliver a sermon entitled, "Still the Prince of Peace," and later that day, there was to be a decidedly internationally themed "Christmas Pageant of All Nations."[123] Montgomery Ward advised readers of the *Berkshire County Eagle* to shop early as many items could not be replaced.[124] In Boston, still reeling from a fire at Luongo's Tap Cafe, which took the lives of six firefighters[125] followed a week later by the Cocoanut Grove disaster, shopping slogans were poignant and patriotic.

Filene's: Make it a Red, White and Blue Christmas
Hovey's: Christmas cheer means more this year
Jordan Marsh: Make it an American Christmas
RH Stearns: We'll Keep Our Christmas Merry Still[126]

If shopping wasn't your cup of tea for entertainment, locals could take their pick of the many amusement parks available in the Bay State. Trolley parks, built at the end of trolley lines to keep the cars filled on weekends, were popular destinations. White City on Shrewsbury's Lake Quinsigamond was known as the "Land of Fifty Thousand Electric Lights." It was a busy venue throughout the war years, even though the illegal beano games were suspended in 1942.[127]

[120] *Rochdale News.* Vol. 1 11/1943. Rochdale News 11/43-10/45.

[121] *Rochdale News.* Vol. 1 1/1944. Rochdale News 11/43-10/45.

[122] Wilson, Jayne Carroll and Keeras, Joseph *Wilderness to Information Age.* Van/Go Graphics 2016.

[123] *Central Church Jamaica Plain.* Boston Globe 12/20/1941. Newspapers.com. tinyurl.com/5daj8t3k.

[124] *Early Bird Ad.* Berkshire County Eagle 11/11/942. Newspapers.com. tinyurl.com/bdhw3x49.

[125] *Firemen Killed.* Boston Globe 11/16/1942. Newspapers.com. tinyurl.com/2s4c6nzn.

[126] Boston, Charles. *Boston's Bittersweet Christmas.* Shopping Days Retro Boston 12/5/2012. tinyurl.com/yhn3bmna.

[127] *Defendant Innocent Plea.* No Adams Transcript 2/12/1942. Newspapers.com. tinyurl.com/24c88t3h.

White City Amusement Park, Worcester.[128]

Riverside Park in Springfield with its recently constructed Cyclone roller coaster (later renamed Thunderbolt), Paragon Park at Nantasket Beach in Hull, and the thirteenth oldest continually operating amusement park in the country, Whalom Park in Lunenburg, were exciting stops for locals and servicemen home on leave.

As always, radio was a popular pastime. It was a hobby for Walter Lemmon, who purchased an expanse of beach in Scituate in 1936. He envisioned constructing a radio station powerful enough to send signals across the Atlantic to Europe. Little did he know, his idea would pique the interest of officials in Washington DC and England. In 1939, the government created station WRUL (World Radio University Listeners) and, with Lemmon's permission, used the Scituate transmitter to broadcast secret information involving a British spy scheme. Within a year, Norway fell to the Germans. To subvert a Nazi order that all Norwegian ships should return to the now-enemy country, the Norwegian ambassador used WRUL to warn ship captains. As a result, not one Norwegian vessel returned to port. Time Magazine credited the Scituate station with delaying the fall of Yugoslavia to Axis forces in 1941. Soon afterwards, the government leased the property, and Voice of America broadcasts from Boston "...news of the day, radio lectures, entertainment, and code to occupied countries—with their American agents— in as many as 12 different languages..." began zipping through transmitters in Scituate and out into the world beyond.[129]

Radio played a pivotal role in World War II, and Massachusetts had more than its share of broadcasting stations. From Boston's WBZ, WEEI, WHDH, and Worcester's WTAG, WORC, and WAAB, information about the progress of the war, fatalities, rationing, and the all-important FDR Fireside Chats went out to audiences along with local news and entertainment programs. In an effort to keep patriotic support running high, radio programs shared moving tales of combat survivors.

One such story aired on WEEI as part of its "Life to the Front" broadcast. Boatswain's Mate Second Class Julius R. Mays was holding onto a floating powder can in the Spring of 1942 when he was plucked out of the ocean and dropped into the bottom of a Higgins boat. His ship, the Northampton, had gone down in battle off Guadalcanal. Navy Chaplain Arthur F. McQuaid of Lowell was already on board, lying on the deck, covered in gauze with a plasma bottle attached to his arm after being severely burned on board the Minneapolis. The Higgins boat was headed to the island of Tulagi. Radio host Anastasia Kirby Lundquist of Auburndale would state, "The boatswain's mate went there to get first aid and dry clothes...The Chaplain was being put ashore to die." Once on dry land, McQuaid was rushed to an emergency unit where Mays watched as doctors silently shook their heads, acknowledging that the Chaplin's time was near.

---

[128] *White City Worcester.* Pub domain photo. BPL. MADC. inyurl.com/6xazumcx.

[129] O'Keefe, Jim. *Scituate's radio station.* Patriot Ledger 8/8/2010. tinyurl.com/mwzzzz3w.

When WEEI decided eight months later to interview members of the military who had seen fighting in the Pacific, they called Julius Mays. Apparently, the two men selected for the broadcast had both spent time on Tulagi. The other man was the Chaplain. Mays was aghast. "I can't believe you're here, Padre. I can't believe it's you. It seems like a miracle." McQuaid had been on a long, hard journey since the two men last met. During his recuperation in New Zealand, he temporarily lost his eyesight and the ability to walk. Mays had news, too. He had received a Silver Star for his heroic lifesaving efforts aboard the sinking Northampton. Lundquist, who worked at the Boston Blood Donor Center, was hoping the WEEI broadcast would motivate listeners to donate blood. Father McQuaid was a good choice for the program. He'd found his way back to life after being given three pints of plasma. "I wish I knew who the three people were who donated the blood...that saved my life," said the Chaplain. "I'd like to thank them."

There is a follow-up to this inspiring story. Two years later, the priest was about to hold mass on a military base in New Jersey with the help of a young Marine acting as altar boy. After the service was over, the young man noted that Father McQuaid hadn't been at the base the previous year and bet him a dollar he knew where he was. The priest dropped a dollar on the table. "You were in the hospital in Auckland, New Zealand." "How did you know?" asked the Chaplain. "You were in the bed next to mine," said the young man.[130]

Perhaps not considered entertaining for the most discerning citizen but certainly of interest to those on shore leave, Edward Liberty and sons Frank, Harold, and Ted offered a service that catered to thousands of customers during the war. Located in Scollay Square in Boston, the family's well-known tattoo parlor left its mark and scores of flags, eagles, and sweetheart names on the men in uniform who wandered through their doors. "It's really a unique story," said Derin Bray, co-author of *Loud, Naked, & in Three Colors.* "They basically had a stranglehold on tattoos (in Boston) and made it difficult for anyone to move in. If you got a tattoo in Boston, it was known it was going to be from one of the Liberty's."[131]

For those too squeamish for a tattoo, a much calmer form of entertainment was offered by the Milton Bradley Company of Springfield. The eighty-year-old business was on the verge of bankruptcy in 1941 when it was put under the management of Cambridge native James J. Shea. A nearly thirty-year employee of the Worcester Envelope Company, Shea began his career in Worcester and was working out of the Springfield division when he was approached by Milton Bradley officials.[132] He quickly made changes to the production line in order to manufacture wooden gun stocks and universal joints for fighter planes. Recognizing the need for entertainment, especially during wartime, Shea continued the manufacture of board games, including a paper/pencil version of Broadside (which would later achieve fame as Battleship) and the internationally popular Snakes and Ladders, redesigned and sold under its new name, Chutes and Ladders.[133]

Long before World Wrestling Entertainment (WWE) exploded into American pop culture, wrestling was already a popular sport in Massachusetts. In 1938, John Cheesman "Chip" Harkness, a graduate of Milton Academy with a degree from Harvard, won the 175-pound wrestling title at Penn State, perhaps not as impressive as the fact that he remained the only NCAA champion from Harvard for sixty-six years. Cheeseman was drafted into the military during World War II, classified as a conscientious objector, and drove ambulances in the European Theater of Operation. Everett resident Michael Rauseo drove trucks with the 1st Armored Division in the North Africa and Italian campaigns.

[130] Lundquist, Anastasia Kirby. *WWII Plasma Saved Lives. Excerpt from Out for Blood.* Defense Media Network 3/19/2021. tinyurl.com/5cd825tb.

[131] Scanlon, Barry. *Family tattoo industry.* Lowell Sun 12/29/2020. tinyurl.com/3w5xe8w7.

[132] *James J. Shea.* Boston Globe 1/4/1977. Newspapers.com. tinyurl.com/cpnappyy.

[133] *WWII Hist Springfield, MA.* NPS. tinyurl.com/2xfespva.

Driving trucks wasn't his only skill. Rauseo was a wrestler. In the midst of the war, he won the African middleweight contest, then moved on to Italy and did it again.[134]

Mike Rauseo. WWII.[135]

"Sharpshooting a welt over Terranova's right eye and coaxing a steady trickle of gore from the tiny champion's nose, Bartolo won a unanimous decision and an ovation from the mob." Boxing, a bit more grisly than wrestling, was also big in Massachusetts, home of the legendary bare-knuckle fighter John L. Sullivan (born in Roxbury, died in Abington). During World War II, all eyes were on Salvatore Interbartolo, "The Pride of East Boston." Better known as Sal Bartolo, the featherweight had a lengthy career, winning the National Boxing Association World Featherweight Title at Boston Garden in March 1944. Bartolo was serving in the Merchant Marines at the time.[136]

One year earlier, Rocco Francis Marchegiano of Boston joined the US Army. He served with the 150th Combat Engineers in Europe, where he took up boxing to avoid kitchen duty.[137] It was an unexpected turn of events for the young Brockton native. Rocco's dream of becoming a major league catcher was smashed when the Chicago Cubs turned him down, telling him that his right arm lacked enough strength for the job. By 1946, Marchegiano was still boxing for the Army, but on discharge, he firmed up his boxing image and his arm, naming himself Rocky Marciano and his right arm "Suzie Q."

The "Brockton Blockbuster" smashed his way into sports headlines and history. "He refused to stay down," said one ESPN reporter. "He might be bloodied, but he wouldn't be beaten... His chin seemed to be cast in concrete...He was a ceaseless aggressor, a human tank who would gladly absorb two or three punches just for the opportunity of landing one."[138] Marciano remained undefeated throughout his eight-year career and was killed in a plane crash in 1969 at the age of 45.

Today, the enthusiasm of Massachusetts residents for hockey, basketball, football, and baseball is so widely acknowledged that words like "obsession" and "rabid" often appear in the media when describing Bay State fans. But the passion for three of the four sports wasn't quite so obvious during World War II when baseball, arguably the oldest sport to be played professionally in Massachusetts, was king. Back then, the Red Sox weren't the only game in town. In 1941, the Boston Braves had their own Braves Field (later known as Boston University's Nickerson Field) and were doing pretty well, finishing seventh in National League rankings. The Red Sox, in spite of suffering the "Curse of the Bambino," finished second in the American League the same year.

---

[134] Marcellus, Matthew. *Legacy of excellence*. US Army 5/29/2020. tinyurl.com/3wz6yxac.

[135] *Mike Rauseo*. Pub domain photo. 1946. NARA. Getarchive. tinyurl.com/526kr73h.

[136] Nason, Jerry. *Bartolo Featherweight Title*. Boston Globe 3/11/1944. Newspapers.com. tinyurl.com/4fb8y4ac.

[137] *Rocky Marciano WWII*. Familyphile.com 9/2/2017. tinyurl.com/y33vpvv7.

[138] Schwartz, Larry. *Marciano glorified boxing*. ESPN.com. tinyurl.com/mpenn2ra.

Opening day at Braves Field, 1915.[139]

It is the accomplishment of the players who went to war, however, that is more noteworthy. Dom DiMaggio, Joe's baby brother, was an unlikely candidate for baseball due to his poor eyesight, which excluded him from the Army. The Navy had fewer concerns, and in 1942, "The Little Professor" went to war. After spending time managing a naval supply depot in Australia, he returned to Boston and the Red Sox, the team he'd joined in 1939. In spite of his eyeglasses, he became one of the best center fielders in BoSox history and would later be inducted into their Hall of Fame.[140] It was football, however, where he would make a more lasting mark. A few years after hanging up his uniform, Dominic DiMaggio and a group of investors founded a football team known as the Boston Patriots. The rest, as they say, is history.

John Paveskovich, a native of Oregon, signed with the Red Sox in 1940, and was showing significant promise when the government requested the pleasure of his company. He joined the Navy, was posted to a training school in Amherst, and achieved the rank of ensign. He played ball for the Navy throughout his military service.[141] Paveskovich returned to Boston after the war, where he enjoyed a lengthy career with the Red Sox as an infielder, coach, and, now known as Johnny Pesky, a radio and TV commentator. He passed away in Danvers in 2012 at age 93.[142]

One of his teammates did a bit better. Ted Williams spent nineteen years with the Red Sox, almost always playing left field and setting numerous records. When duty called during World War II, Williams opted for the Navy and, along with teammate Johnny Pesky, headed to the Navy's Training School at Amherst College. His goal was to become a pilot. For the next two years, Ted moved from one training school to another, eventually earning his wings in May 1944. He was discharged in 1946, having never seen combat.[143] The military, however, wasn't finished with Williams. He was called back to active duty during the Korean War, flew thirty-nine missions, and was hit three times, one resulting in a crash landing. Baseball didn't seem to be as big of a deal to Williams as it was to his fans. Stationed with him in Korea, future astronaut and senator John Glenn remembered, "He didn't shirk his duty at all. He got in there and dug 'em out like everybody else. He never mentioned baseball unless someone else brought it up. He was there to do a job. We all were. He was just one of the guys."[144] Williams himself would

---

[139] *Braves Field 8/1915*. Pub domain photo. Electric Railway J. Wiki Commons. tinyurl.com/2p9tf25j.

[140] Shettle, M.L. *Ted Williams Baseball Legend, MC Aviator*. Californians & Mil. 2/2016. www.militarymuseum.org/Williams.html.

[141] Bedingfield, Gary. *Johnny Pesky*. Gary Bedington's Baseball Wartime 5/27/2007. tinyurl.com/53bhtpff.

[142] *Johnny Pesky*. Find Grave ID 95304690 2012. tinyurl.com/3h96s9r5.

[143] Shettle, M.L. *Ted Williams Baseball Legend, MC Aviator*.

[144] Harrigan, Thomas. *Ted Williams back to war.* MLB.com. 1/9/2023. tinyurl.com/5awwr49h.

later say, "I hope someone hits .400 soon. Then people can start pestering that guy with questions about the last guy to hit .400."[145]

Ted Williams (right) while flight training
at Turners Falls Airport. WWII.[146]

Williams' accomplishments are legendary. He ranks among the top ten highest career batting average holders in history, was the American League batting champion six times, earned their MVP status twice, and hit over 500 home runs. No one in the long history of the Boston Red Sox has ever achieved a higher batting average. He passed away in Florida in 2002 at the age of 83.

"There is one front and one battle where everyone in the United States—every man, woman, and child—is in action and will be privileged to remain in action throughout this war. That front is right here at home, in our daily lives, and in our daily tasks." FDR's words rang true. For four long years, Americans did without, worked long hours often at dangerous jobs, rolled bandages, and planted Victory Gardens. They went to church, sat around the table at Sunday dinners, and clung to the radio for news of the war. When letters arrived from sons and husbands, like this one from young Albert Southwick of Leicester: "I guess I told you that we are now studying machine guns. In actual combat, the average life of a gunman is nine seconds, our instructor says...,"[147] families managed to respond with calm words of support and news from back home. All the while, they waited in fear of the dreaded ring of a doorbell and a telegram: "I regret to inform you...."

They did this with the unfailing belief that their sacrifices and losses would somehow preserve the world they once knew, the world that they desperately hoped their loved ones would soon return to. "They are not dead who live in lives they leave behind. In those whom they have blessed, they live a life again," wrote Eleanor Roosevelt.[148] When the enemy was defeated in 1945 and servicemen and women came back "to live their lives again," they did indeed have homes to return to and a familiar way of life, thanks to the undaunted courage and resilience of the American people.

---

[145] Paige, Woody. *Dear Ted: Todd's tearing it up.* Denv Post 8/18/2000. tinyurl.com/yam7h5ry.

[146] *Ted Williams.* Pub domain photo. Ronald Zschau. Wiki Commons. tinyurl.com/y498m6c5.

[147] Southwick, Albert B. *WWII Correspondence Albert B. Southwick and Maple Hill Farm: 9/1942 to 6/1942.* Marshall Street 2013.

[148] Roosevelt, Eleanor. *My Day 4/26/1945.* E. Roosevelt Papers, Digital Ed. tinyurl.com/bdefkrmp.

Chapter 6

The Industrial State

Reichsmarschall Hermann Goring: *That's impossible! The Americans only know how to make razor blades.*
Field Marshal Erwin Rommel: *We could do with some of those razor blades.*

Franklin D. Roosevelt: *You cannot buy a battleship from a mail-order catalogue.*

In August of 1939, residents of Plattsburgh, New York, were abuzz with excitement. The US Army had come to town. Government officials and representatives of foreign nations, including Germany and Japan, had come to witness the first war games to take place on American soil since the Great War. It was a festive atmosphere as locals lined the edges of fields, some selling snacks and drinks out of wagons and wheelbarrows. There were 52,000 participants in all, the majority from National Guard units such as the Massachusetts 26th Division. It was not their finest hour. The group performed so poorly that more training was ordered. In November, 400 guardsmen from the Berkshires along with members from other western Massachusetts communities, gathered at a former CCC camp on West Mountain. Their task was to defend their ground, which they did "against all comers...and suffered no casualties."[1]

The Plattsburgh event, an exercise designed to assess the state of the country's armed forces, provided officials with valuable information. The nation was clearly unprepared for war. In his book *Freedom's Forge,* author Arthur Hermann described the mock battle:

Fifty thousand men were put on the field...they quickly lost their direction as units haplessly bumped into each other. Without radios to issue orders, soldiers began wandering in search of officers to give them. Some stumbled on lines of Good Humor trucks parked in a field. The Army had been forced to hire them to serve as decoy tanks because there weren't enough real tanks or armored cars to go around.

Seven days after the maneuvers ended, Germany invaded Poland. FDR's response: "God help us all."[2]

With war looming on the horizon, Franklin Roosevelt faced an uphill battle. In spite of the fact that the country was slowly becoming the arsenal of democracy that he'd advocated for, not everyone in industry was cooperating. The president had a long-standing contentious relationship with big business, whom he felt was more interested in profit than in helping move the unemployed and poverty-stricken masses out of an economic depression. Business leaders looked with disfavor upon Roosevelt and his New Deal policies as an attempt to interfere with the country's free market. Concerns about a war that hadn't happened yet were just another ploy to manipulate industry.

The government didn't see it that way, however, and in 1940, it granted FDR substantial power to control industry. Manufacturers could be required to produce any materials deemed necessary for war. Many companies agreed to government contracts while maintaining the production of consumer goods. Some showed a lack of enthusiasm for FDR's policies, halfheartedly complying due to concerns over

---

[1] Willison, George. *Hist Pittsfield.* Pittsfield 1957. Sun Printing Corp.

[2] Hermann, Arthur. *Freedom's Forge.* Random House Trade Paperbacks 2012.

retooling equipment and the effect on their post-war businesses when the machines that had turned out war goods were no longer needed.

All that radically changed, however, when bombs dropped on Pearl Harbor. Historian V.R. Cardozier wrote, "Patriotism flooded out of industries all over America."[3] In his January 1942 State of the Union Address, Roosevelt voiced outrageous expectations for production: 60,000 aircraft and 45,000 tanks. "These figures...," said the President, "will give the Japanese and the Nazis a little idea of just what they accomplished in the attack at Pearl Harbor." The task that lay ahead seemed undoable. Unbelievably, the goals would be met. By the end of the war, the country would give Roosevelt over 300,000 planes and more than 80,000 tanks. The President also called for ships, big ships, 16,000,000 tons of them, and Massachusetts answered.

Long before the age of sail ended, Japan had established itself as a major naval power in Asia. By 1904, it began exploring the use of a developing naval technology, submarines, to enhance its military might in the Russo-Japanese conflict. When the country reached the apex of its naval superiority in December of 1941, it plunged a hesitant American nation into war. This was a mistake. Perhaps due to overestimation of its own superiority or underestimation of the might and determination of its enemy, six months later, Japan began its decline. On June 7, 1942, when the Battle of Midway drew to a close, four of the six Japanese aircraft carriers involved in the attack on Pearl Harbor, nearly half of its heavy carrier fleet, were either at the bottom of the ocean or irreparable. Japan would never fully replace the loss of equipment and manpower suffered at the hands of an American naval war machine in its ascendancy. Heavy cruisers Vincennes, Northampton, and Portland were present during those four days in June. They, along with three of the eighteen US destroyers at the Battle of Midway, all began their journey at the Fore River Shipyard in Quincy.

In March of 1876, Alexander Graham Bell called his young assistant, Thomas Watson, into his Boston laboratory, uttering the famous words, "Mr. Watson, come here–I want you." While controversy still exists as to who actually was the first to invent the telephone (Bell was, however, the first to receive a patent for it), both men would go on to make history. Bell, the more famous of the two, would patent several more inventions, many in the field of communications. Thomas Watson, a native of Salem, Massachusetts, would use his brilliance and restless energy to invent a variety of telephone and switchboard gadgets, obtain nearly twice as many patents as Bell, and become a member of the National Inventors Hall of Fame. Along the way, he developed a fascination with engines, marine engines in particular, and turned a stretch of farmland along the Weymouth Fore River in Braintree into an industrial site so that he could build boats.

---

[3] Cardozier, V.R. *Mobilization of US WWII*. McFarland & Co 1995.

FORE RIVER ENGINE COMPANY,

Engineers and Shipbuilders,

WEYMOUTH, MASS., U. S. A.
(Suburb of Boston.)

Fast Steam Yachts.
Merchant Vessels.
Marine Engines.
Water-Tube Boilers.

U. S. Torpedo-Boat Destroyers "Lawrence" and "Macdonough" now under construction.

1899 advertisement for Fore River Engine Company.[4]

By 1901, Watson's Fore River Ship and Engine Building Company had received several Navy contracts and become so successful that it needed more space. Although the move to Quincy provided more acreage, was closer to the ocean, and offered deeper water than the original site upriver, it was risky. The company built tall ships, many of which wouldn't fit under the bridge that spanned the Fore River from Quincy to Weymouth. Untroubled by this glitch, Watson agreed to build the Navy cruiser Des Moines at the new site, knowing it would never make it out to sea. He patiently waited until the town decided to build a new bridge, made a bid, and won the contract. Soon after, a swing bridge that had been constructed at the shipyard made its way downriver, settling into the river bed with the falling tide.[5]

The early years at the new location were busy ones. In addition to numerous US naval projects, a variety of private and merchant vessels, along with five submarines for the Japanese Navy, were constructed. The ever-restless Watson began to look for new and more interesting challenges. He invested heavily in railroads, depleted the company's cash, and, at fifty years of age, was ousted from his position as President of the Fore River Ship and Engine Building Company. Watson later wrote: "I had started the business 22 years before in my little kindergarten building, with a single helper, and left it with a plant covering with its great structures 100 acres and employing 4,000 men on a payroll of many millions of dollars a year."[6] Without much fanfare, he simply moved on to the next adventure. Thomas

---

[4] *Fore River Engine Co.* Pub domain photo. ASNE. Wiki Commons. tinyurl.com/pmw6knw2.

[5] Drummond, Dave. *Shipyard. Will It Float?* iUniverse 2003.

[6] Miller, Wayne. *Quincy MA Shipbuilding Tradition.* Quincy Hist Soc 2017.

Watson went on to study geology and art, became a painter and a Shakespearean actor, and passed away at the age of eighty. He was laid to rest in a cemetery in North Weymouth overlooking the shipyard that he had founded fifty years before.[7]

In 1913, Bethlehem Steel purchased the Fore River Shipyard for $4.8 million dollars. It was a huge amount back then, but it was a good deal. At the time of the sale, twenty-three ships were under construction with an estimated worth of $20 million. In addition, the shipyard had the ability to produce 60,000 tons of shipping a year.

The First World War was a period of extensive activity for the Quincy company. By 1917, the uptick in Navy contracts spurred the building of a second adjunct shipyard a few miles to the north, the Squantum Victory Yard. The Fore River Shipyard became one of the country's most prolific producers of WWI US Naval vessels. As expected, however, a post-war decline in activity followed. Construction jobs for the Navy were at a low point. Six South Dakota class battleships were laid down in 1920 and 1921, but due to cutbacks and limitations of the Washington Naval Treaty, work was suspended. The six ships lay silent on the ways at the Fore River facility and were scrapped in 1923.[8] Luckily, private contracts and repair jobs kept the company in business.

When the Japanese attacked Pearl Harbor, they unleashed a furor of activity that would make Fore River one of the busiest shipyards in the United States. By the second year of the war, Bethlehem Steel was in need of more space, so it opened a new facility in Hingham specifically for the construction of LSTs and destroyer escorts. Company employment rose to an all-time high of 32,000 workers. Unable to keep up with the loss of manpower slipping away to the military, the shipyard began hiring men disqualified from serving, women (over 2,700 of them), and teenagers under draft age. One of them was sixteen-year-old Ralph Pipile of Hingham, whose job involved pipe fitting, welding, and sheet metal cutting. Later, while serving on a destroyer escort, Pipile used the skills he'd learned at Bethlehem Hingham to save 122 lives when he was able to weld the crack in an engine block after his ship went dead in the water.[9]

Of the many accomplishments for which Fore River would become known, perhaps the most amazing was production speed. Shortly after purchasing the shipyard in 1913, a friendly competition developed between the Bethlehem facilities in Quincy and San Francisco to determine who could build the most destroyers in a given time. The final tally: San Francisco 6, Quincy 18. Not to be overlooked were the ten submarines and six merchant ships also constructed at Quincy within the same time frame. In 1919, the keel of USS Reid was laid down at Squantum, and forty-five days later, she launched. It was a record. It would be outdone many times during World War II.[10] During one twenty-five-month period, seventy-one destroyers were launched, more than all other US shipyards combined,[11] five LSTs were built in fifty hours at the Squantum facility, and a destroyer escort was completed in twenty-three days. In 1943, after receiving orders from the Navy for sixty ships, the men and women of the Fore River Shipyard delivered ninety.[12]

---

[7] *Thomas Watson.* Find Grave ID 5554 5/30/1999. tinyurl.com/yx9t9c3m.

[8] *South Dakota Class.* NHHC. tinyurl.com/ytjhrw2e.

[9] Buckley, Will. *Bethlehem Hingham Shipyard.* USNI 6/2021. tinyurl.com/wmmcsars.

[10] *General Dynamics Shipyard.* Photographs. HAER MA-26. NPS. tinyurl.com/4d3rahzu.

[11] Drummond, Dave. *Shipyard. Will It Float?*

[12] Buckley, Will. *Bethlehem Hingham Shipyard WWII.*

Launch of USS San Diego,
Fore River Shipyard. July 1941.[13]

The shipyard made its mark on history in another unexpected way. In order to ensure that riveting gangs were getting the job done, Fore River employed inspectors whose job was to count the number of rivets after a crew had completed its work. One of these was a man from Halifax, Massachusetts, James J. Kilroy. After each inspection, he would inscribe a notation in bright yellow chalk to indicate the work had been approved. With the speed of construction and launch, many areas on ships didn't get painted, and so the inspector's words, "Kilroy was here," launched with ships and made their way around the world. By the end of the war, the Kilroy phrase along with a goofy-faced character peering over a wall, could be found on everything from destroyers to tanks to bombs. Dave Drummond, in his excellent history of the shipyard, relates that for the 1945 Potsdam conference, a special toilet was built for use by Churchill, Stalin, and FDR. After his first visit to the porcelain potty, Stalin came out and promptly asked an aide who Kilroy was.[14]

Kilroy was here, too.

The men and women of Bethlehem Fore River were proud of their ships and protective of the men who sailed on them. When the Quincy-built Lexington became the first aircraft carrier lost in World War II, workers at the shipyard quickly requested permission to rename the Cabot which was under

---

[13] *Launching USS San Diego.* Pub domain photo. Picryl. tinyurl.com/mr466ts4.

[14] Drummond, Dave. *The Shipyard. Will It Float?*

construction at the time. Secretary of the Navy Frank Knox agreed, and in February 1943, a second USS Lexington was launched four months after her sister went to her grave.

USS Lexington steams through ice
in Boston Harbor. February 1943.[15]

A similar story involves the ill-fated aircraft carrier Wasp. Because of the size of the ships constructed at Bethlehem Fore River, deep water was required. Therefore, the river was dredged 2,000 feet out from the launchways, and massive loops of anchor chains were situated in a U around the boat so that the drag would slow ships as they slid downwards. Apparently, during her launch in 1939, the 15,000-ton Wasp didn't have enough anchor chains. When she hit the water, she floated to the opposite shore and landed in the mud. After several unsuccessful attempts to free the carrier, high tide finally raised her up and set the Wasp free. Old-timers whispered about bad omens.[16] It was. In September 1942, while transporting a regiment of Marines to Guadalcanal, she was hit by the Japanese. Too proud to die by enemy hands, she remained afloat until all survivors were evacuated and was then scuttled. Nearly two hundred brave men lost their lives with the sinking of the Wasp. Once again, the men and women of Bethlehem Fore River rose to honor the memory of the fallen, and the ship, Oriskany, under construction, was renamed Wasp. She launched in 1943 and survived the war.

Sinking of USS Wasp. September 15, 1942.[17]

After the war, Bethlehem Fore River Shipyard was sold to General Dynamics and closed in 1986, but not before it had made a significant mark in history. One of the largest sailing vessels without an auxiliary engine ever built, the seven-masted Thomas W. Lawson, was launched by Watson's company

---

[15] *USS Lexington.* Pub domain photo. 80-G-35657. NHHC. tinyurl.com/3vadvehv.

[16] Drummond, Dave. *Shipyard. Will It Float?*

[17] *80-G-16331 USS Wasp.* Public domain photo. NARA, NHHC. tinyurl.com/4pydptk3.

in 1902. In 1910, the Quincy built USS Birmingham was the site of the first launch of an airplane from the deck of a warship. In 1913, while waiting in Quincy to assume command of the USS Snapper, Chester Nimitz met and married Catherine Freeman of Wollaston. Fore River's USS Nevada was the only destroyer to get underway during the attack at Pearl Harbor in 1941, and the battleship Massachusetts became famous for firing the first and last 16" shells of World War II. By the war's end, thirty Quincy-built ships were lost.[18] Bethlehem Hingham Shipyard had held $395,840,000 in government contracts for destroyer escorts (DE), tank landing craft (LCT), and tank landing ships (LST),[19] and the men and women of Bethlehem's Fore River facility had produced more US Navy tonnage than any other American shipyard.[20]

USS Snapper. Note: autograph of Admiral Nimitz.[21]

In 1945, with the bloody battle for Okinawa, the final death knell of the Imperial Japanese Navy sounded. As US Navy battleships, destroyers, and cruisers circled in for the kill, the Japanese unleashed Operation Ten-Go, which included the suicidal destruction of the most powerful ship in Japanese history, the Yamato. Japan's systematically planned and executed journey toward naval superiority that began with the production of five submarines at the Fore River Ship and Engine Company in 1904 ended forty-one years later at the hands of the Quincy-constructed Massachusetts, New Jersey, Baltimore, Pittsburgh, Vincennes, and a score of other proud ships.

Like shipbuilding, some industries will be forever associated with Massachusetts, one of which began with fifty-eight English cannons and a bookstore owner from Boston. Henry Knox was no stranger to armaments and war. In 1775, he famously hauled a cache of captured enemy artillery from Fort Ticonderoga across icy water, over mountains, and through blizzards to assist the colonial army in breaking the British siege of Boston. By 1776, General Knox had advised George Washington that the Army needed a facility for storing and repairing weapons and making cartridges. Washington agreed and suggested Hartford, Connecticut. Congress favored Brookfield, Massachusetts.[22] Knox had other ideas. Located along the Connecticut River at a crossroads that reached toward Albany, New York City, and

---

[18] Miller, Wayne G. *Quincy MA a Shipbuilding Tradition*.

[19] *War Supply Contracts 1940-1945*. CPA 1946. tinyurl.com/2p9d88re.

[20] *MA Fore River*. Destroyer Hist Fdn 2000-2023. htinyurl.com/bdd8pf28.

[21] *USS Snapper*. Pub domain photo. NH 58102. NHHC. tinyurl.com/2s3erab5.

[22] Moore, Thomas, Goss, William. *Springfield Armory*. ASME 2/19/1980. tinyurl.com/mrxef6ws.

Boston, Springfield would be the best choice. By 1777, the arsenal at Springfield was storing cannon and muskets. Seventeen years later, Congress, concerned over having to rely on foreign companies for weapons, authorized the creation of two federal armories, one in Springfield and the other at Harper's Ferry in West Virginia.

Springfield Armory[23]

With the destruction of the West Virginia facility by federal troops in 1861, Springfield became the sole federal weapons producer in the United States, and a crisis ensued. With half of the weapon stockpile gone and a civil war impending, Springfield would have to make up for the loss. It did. The Armory became a model of innovation and industry. By focusing the majority of production on one specific type of rifle, Model 1861, and developing interchangeable parts for rifles manufactured there, the Springfield facility was able to increase output. When guns fired on Fort Sumter, a worker at the Armory could turn out forty-three rifles per month. Two years later, the number had risen to 120. By the end of the war, 800,000 rifles had been manufactured, a marvel that even Henry Ford applauded. "The initial achievement of mass production has often been credited to self-publicized 20th-century makers of automobiles...[But] it is hard to see the wartime Armory as engaged in anything other than mass production."[24]

Canadian John Garand's experience working in New England mills led to an interest in how machines worked. Soon, his attention turned to rifles, and shortly after the First World War, the young

[23] *Springfield Armory*. Pub domain photo. NPS. Wiki Commons. tinyurl.com/3a5svwdz.

[24] Giaimo, Cara. *Civil War Heroics*. Atlas Obscura 3/7/2017. tinyurl.com/ykd27upa.

man took a job as an engineer at the Springfield Armory, where he designed what Patton would call "the best battle implement ever devised." Garand's M1 rifle was lightweight and fired bullets from an eight-shot clip after a simple trigger pull without the need for a bolt-loading mechanism. It was dubbed "semi-automatic" and led the way for the development of a variety of rapid-firing weapons. During the war, the Armory increased its labor force to 7,500 men and women capable of producing over 164 rifles an hour.[25] The Springfield Armory manufactured over three million of Garand's M1 rifles, the primary weapon used in battle by American troops during World War II.

Assembly of M1 Garand rifles,
Springfield Armory. WWII.[26]

The presence of the Springfield Armory in western Massachusetts became a focal point for the development of the weapon-making industry along the Connecticut River in what would be known as "Gun Valley." Daniel Wesson of Worcester was already trained as a gunsmith when he met Cheshire native Horace Smith. Smith had a long-standing history of working with guns and had been employed at the Springfield Armory. The two men met in Worcester in 1852,[27] and together, they formed one of the most famous gun manufacturing companies in the world. Known for its line of handguns, Smith and Wesson produced a .38 caliber revolver that was used extensively by police for forty years. When war broke out, one million of these "Victory Models" would be made for the US and its Allies, in addition to a variety of guns and pistols totaling $26,346,000 in government contracts. The J. Stevens Arms Company had been producing guns in Chicopee since the Civil War. During the Second World War, now under the ownership of Savage Arms, the company produced Browning automatic weapons, Lee-Enfield rifles, and Thompson submachine guns to fulfill $52,755,000 in federal contracts.[28]

By the First World War, two federal armories were manufacturing weapons in Massachusetts. Built along the Charles River in 1816 as a storage facility for arms and ammunition, the government developed the Watertown Arsenal into a manufacturing center for gun carriages during the Civil War. So

---

[25] *Springfield WWII Heritage City.* Springfield 12/06/2022. tinyurl.com/2c755p5e.

[26] *M1 Garand Rifles.* Pub domain photo. NPS. tinyurl.com/mp4akh69.

[27] Metesh, T. Logan. *Horace Smith Born.* Free Range Am 10/26/2021. tinyurl.com/cnsx3kk5.

[28] *War Supply Contracts.*

successful was the undertaking that in 1917, one of the largest steel-framed structures in the world, Building #311, was constructed to accommodate the work. During the Second World War, the Arsenal produced railway and anti-aircraft gun mounts, guns, and ammunition. The Watertown Arsenal, however, was unique. Early on in the war, several instances of catastrophic failure in metal products began to attract attention. One of the most famous involved the Liberty Ship SS Schenectady. Built by Kaiser Shipyards in Oregon, she launched in October 1942, returning to port following sea trials on a cold January day in 1943.

Without warning and with a report which was heard for at least a mile, the deck and sides of the vessel fractured just aft of the bridge superstructure. The fracture extended almost instantaneously to the turn of the bilge port and starboard. The deck side shell, longitudinal bulkhead, and bottom girders fractured. Only the bottom plating held. The vessel jack-knifed, and the center portion rose so that no water entered. The bow and stern settled into the silt of the river bottom.[29]

SS Schenectady hull fracture. 1943.[30]

Elsewhere, metal fractures had been reported in cannons, rifles, motor cases, and mortars. To find a solution, the government turned to the Watertown Arsenal. As a result, the Arsenal became a center for materials testing and metallurgy. In addition to developing new processes for casting, welding, and machining of metal alloys, the facility also tested paints, lubricants, and cartridges. By the end of the war, the Watertown Arsenal covered 131 acres and employed 10,000 workers.[31] The facility became a major research laboratory for the US Army during the postwar years, and in the 1960s, a nuclear reactor was constructed on-site. The Watertown Arsenal closed in 1995.

With a landscape peppered by mills, textile manufacturing is synonymous with Massachusetts, a proud industry that made an essential contribution to war production. With over 100 mills holding government contracts of $50,000 or more,[32] Bay State textiles found their way into nearly every aspect of life during World War II. The demand for canvas reached new heights. Miles of the heavy woven

[29] Pinell, Rob. *Liberty Ships Fracture Mechanics.* Linkedin 5/27/2016. tinyurl.com/4e6d6hzx.

[30] *Schenectady.* Pub domain photo. GPO 1947. Wikimedia Commons. tinyurl.com/mnr4vr9b.

[31] *Laboratory Watertown Arsenal.* Global Security.org. tinyurl.com/39363x7r.

[32] *War Supply Contracts.*

cotton fabric were required for tents, tarpaulins, and covers for Jeeps and trucks. Camouflage canvas became a big item when, shortly after Pearl Harbor, the Lockheed Martin Company covered its entire Burbank, California facility with it. For good measure, after painting the fabric in camouflage colors, a War Department general was flown over at 5,000 feet, but the sprawling plant went undetected.[33] Smaller items such as magazine bags, rucksacks, rifle bags, bandoliers, holsters, and canteen covers were mass-produced by companies like L.C. Chase of Watertown, Warren Leather Goods of Worcester,[34] and Andrew Dutton Company of Boston.[35]

Parachutes flowed out of mills as well. William Skinner & Sons of Holyoke made parachute silk and New England Bedding of Medford parachute parts. By the thousand, finished parachutes were fabricated by the William E. Wright Co. of West Warren, Textron of Lowell, and Shawmut Woolen Mills of Stoughton. Bomb parachutes were produced by Royal Curtain Manufacturing of Boston.[36x]

Many textile mills like this one in New Bedford
worked 24 hours a day during WWII.[37]

The central Massachusetts town of Uxbridge cannot be overlooked in any discussion of wartime textile manufacturing. In 1907, Louis Bachman of New York and Charles Root of Webster established the Bachman Uxbridge Worsted Company. While maintaining its headquarters in Uxbridge, the business expanded rapidly and was successful enough to survive the depression by then operating thirteen plants in four states. Six thousand workers produced enough fabric to make six million suits of clothing a year.

By the time Pearl Harbor was attacked, 50 percent of the Uxbridge Company was already engaged in war production. After December 7, the company maintained its government-approved limit on the manufacture of cloth for civilian clothing while producing fabric for a variety of military uses. The Army received 10,000 blankets in 1942 alone, and its Quartermaster Corps would receive an additional 17 million yards of material by 1945. Specialized fabric was developed to meet demand for the British 21-ounce worsted known as "Tommy knit," heavier 32-ounce coated fabric to be used in Russian Army overcoats, water-repellent cotton for field jackets, and lightweight fabric for tropical use.[38] From its plants in Uxbridge and Lowell poured $35 million in cloth, and with the addition of products from its Georgia, Rhode Island, and Connecticut facilities, the company manufactured nearly $43 million in cloth for the war effort.[39]

---

[33] *Lockheed WWII*. Lockheed Martin 10/1/2020. tinyurl.com/2ndfsy28.

[34] *WW2 Medical Equipment*. WW2 MRC. tinyurl.com/4aak36u4.

[35] Taylor, Robert. *New Eng Home Front WWII*. Yankee Books 1992.

[36] *War Supply Contracts*.

[37] *Textile mill New Bedford*. Pub domain photo. 2017793296. LOC. tinyurl.com/4pa4fc7v.

[38] *Uxbridge Worsted Company*. Robert B. Grady Co 1945.

[39] *War Supply Contracts*.

The Bachman Uxbridge Worsted Company found a market after the war, continuing successful research and production in the use of synthetic blends. It seemed natural that the government would turn to Uxbridge for help in the development of uniforms when the Army Air Corps became an independent branch of the military. The company offered a fabric distinctly different from the drab olive and khaki colors of the war years, and since 1949, members of the United States Air Force have been issued uniforms of Uxbridge blue.

Early on in our nation's history, Massachusetts established a reputation for shoe manufacturing. Shoemakers, of course, could be found across all across the thirteen colonies, but what made Massachusetts special was Welsh immigrant John Adam Dagyr. His organization of local cobblers into small production units, which turned out shoes in tiny ten-footer shops, turned the city of Lynn into what President George Washington called "the greatest shoe town in the country."[40]

Enter five enterprising and creative Massachusetts natives, each adding innovation to the burgeoning industry. In 1846, Spencer's Elias Howe invented a sewing machine with lock stitch ability, which was quickly adopted by John Brooks Nichols of South Reading and used to stitch the upper part of shoes. The idea looked good to Lyman Blake of South Abington, who developed his own version, a machine that could fasten uppers to soles. Entrepreneur Gordon McKay of Pittsfield saw an opportunity, purchased Blake's patent, made changes to his stitching machines, and turned Massachusetts shoemaking into a 120 million pair-a-year industry. In 1885, the Boston Globe reported that businesses in twenty-three towns produced over a million dollars in shoes a year, the top being Lynn ($20.9 million) and the tenth relatively small Spencer ($2.3 million).[41]

Shoemaker John W. French, Weymouth.[42]

With a new conflict looming, the government turned to Massachusetts to fill its gigantic quota of shoes. Prior to the First World War, Charles Goodyear Jr. developed a process for using rubber for replaceable soles, and the Hood Rubber Co. of Watertown roared into business, employing 10,000 workers for the production of shoe and boot soles.[43] By 1945, Hood Rubber, now a subsidiary of B. F.

[40] Mulligan, William. *Am Shoe Industry Lynn*. JEH 1981. JSTOR. tinyurl.com/4xb96pcj.

[41] *Natick Shoe Industry*. Natick Hist Soc. tinyurl.com/y8dvkbw6.

[42] *John French*. Public domain photo. Weymouth & Tufts Libs. Picryl. tinyurl.com/hnd9na9t.

[43] Fahey-Flynn, Anna. *Best Foot Forward*. DPLA 9/2015. tinyurl.com/n62dk7vk.

Goodrich, produced a wide range of rubber products, from aviator boots, rubber overshoes, jungle boots, and basketball shoes to life rafts and self-sealing fuel tanks, fulfilling a federal contract worth $47 million.[44]

Twenty-five miles southwest in Millis, the Joseph M. Herman Shoe Co. was making a name for itself in the manufacture of boots. The Marines had been issuing Herman's garrison shoes as their primary footwear since 1940, but when the design changed to a more serviceable field shoe, the company accommodated their needs. John C. Herman's shoes and boots accompanied men into battle at Wake Island, the Philippines, and Guam.[45] Over the course of the war, Herman plants in Boston and Millis turned out over $15 million in footwear for those who went to war. The town of Stoughton also made a contribution when a high leather boot designed specifically for the needs of paratroopers was produced by the Joseph F. Corcoran Company. Corcoran boots, also referred to as jump boots were manufactured by the Stoughton business as part of a $5.7 million federal contract. During the war years, approximately ninety companies in Massachusetts held contracts of over $50,000 or more for the production of shoes and boots.[46]

While certain industries will be forever associated with the Bay State, a few individual companies will be as well. Robert Goddard is known for his groundbreaking achievements in the field of rocketry. He was a true son of Massachusetts, born in Worcester and educated at South High School, Worcester Polytechnic Institute, and Clark University. Among his many accomplishments was the rudimentary design of a weapon, which was listed by Eisenhower as one of the four tools that led to victory in World War II. However, plans for this invention were never finalized. The war ended, and the need for new weapons became obsolete.

Two decades later, Germany began carving up the landscape of Europe and Africa with its deadly Panzer corps, and the Allies were in desperate need of an effective anti-tank weapon. Author Maury Klein, in his book A Call to Arms, states: "A rule of thumb was that it took five Shermans to kill one Panzer."[47] While the M10 grenade could penetrate 60 mm of armor, its weight prevented it from being effectively shot by a rifle or thrown by a man. They needed a new weapon with either lighter mass or different propulsion. "I was walking by this scrap pile," recalled Second Lieutenant Edward Uhl, "and there was a tube that... happened to be the same size as the grenade that we were turning into a rocket. I said, That's the answer! Put the tube on a soldier's shoulder with the rocket inside, and away it goes."[48] Unknowingly, in May of 1942, the Lieutenant had taken up where Robert Goddard left off.

Uhl's idea turned into sketches, sketches into plans, plans into models. The Launcher, Rocket, AT, M-1 could possibly be the weapon the military needed. Time was of the essence. Men were dying, and countries were being gobbled up. The Army immediately ordered 5,000 to be delivered within thirty days. Before production could begin, however, launchers had to be tested, and samples given the okay. The process took twenty-two days. It was a scramble. With just eight days left, materials were rushed to plants; machines retooled to accommodate designs, assembly lines organized, and unbelievably, the first "bazooka" rolled out of the plant with 89 minutes to spare.[49]

---

[44] *War Supply Contracts.*

[45] *USMC Men's Shoes.* US Mil Uniforms WWII. tinyurl.com/yp9tf9w6.

[46] *War Supply Contracts.*

[47] Klein, Maury. *Call to Arms.* Bloomsbury Press 2015.

[48] *Bazooka.* Beaches Normandy Tours. tinyurl.com/mvhy4mmb.

[49] Miller, John. *Men Volts and War.* McGraw Hill Book Co 1947.

Soldier holding an M1 bazooka. 1943.[50]

The new weapon was a success, and the Army began to consider its potential for use by their Air Corps. Could groups of bazookas somehow be attached under an airplane wing? Yes was the answer, and no. The tube bazookas, basically rocket launchers, could be mounted but would weigh in at 200 pounds, too much for fighter planes. The problem was presented to engineers at the Plastics Division of a Pittsfield, Massachusetts company. The solution, a new type of fire-resistant plastic developed from high-strength paper impregnated with resin, shaved forty pounds off the weapon, essentially turning airplanes into flying artillery.[51]

The miracle of the bazooka was made possible by General Electric, a company with deep roots in the state of Massachusetts. Elihu Thomson, born in England but raised in Lynn, had an extraordinary mind and equally extraordinary interest in electricity. He co-founded the Thomson-Houston Company, which became one of the three most successful lighting companies in the United States. Following a merger with Edison Electric Illuminating Company of Boston, General Electric was formed. While GE headquarters operated in Boston, Thomson chose to remain at his research laboratory in Lynn.[52]

By 1941, the company was an industry leader, so when General Hap Arnold, Chief of the Army Air Force, needed a new type of engine, he turned to GE. Joseph Sorota, who grew up in Dorchester, was an engineering student at Northeastern University's night school when the FBI came knocking on his door. "I almost died. I didn't do anything wrong, but I thought he was there maybe to arrest me. It was the war." They put him to work at GE's Lynn facility. Sorota recalled the high level of secrecy surrounding the project. "Our colleagues called us the Hush-Hush Boys...The FBI man warned me that if I gave away any secrets, the penalty was death."[53]

---

[50] *M1 Bazooka* 1943. Pub domain photo. USAC. Wikipedia. tinyurl.com/5cwx8t6j.

[51] Miller, John A. *Men Volts and War.*

[52] Elihu Thomson. *Advances Electric Lighting.* Lemelson-MIT. tinyurl.com/yrrbt9xj.

[53] *1st US Jet Engine.* GE Aerospace 3/22/2021. MarketScreener. tinyurl.com/bdeh4y5z.

Someone Talked! Poster. 1942.[54]

Using British plans as a starting point, the company got to work, and in March 1942, the first US-made jet engine was fired up at GE's River Works Plant in Lynn. It had taken ten months for General Electric to change the face of American aviation. General Electric would continue turbo supercharger production throughout the war, manufacturing over 100,000 for aircraft such as B-17 bombers and P-38s.[55] The River Works Plant became a leader in turbo supercharger technology and became known as Air Force Plant 29, the Aircraft Gas Turbine Division.

Meanwhile, work at GE in Pittsfield continued to diversify, and it can be supposed that with the frenzy of activity, few stopped to wonder about the recently constructed Building 3, a structure with armed guards and only one door. It was wartime, and the entire facility operated under the watchful eyes of a security force that had been trained by the US Army in judo, marksmanship, and anti-sabotage methods. But the work being done within was something special. Ed Kopf, who became a part of the top-secret project, stated that numbered sections of plans were handed out to staff to be returned at the end of the day. Very few people ever saw the complete drawings, and most never knew what they were working on. As it turns out, the men of the Pittsfield lab were producing rectifier transformers used to accelerate ions through a magnetic field, separating U235 from U238, the very same uranium that would be used in the development of the atomic bomb.[56]

The government turned again and again to GE during the war, and the company never hesitated to respond. With literally tons of mortar shells being expended in both the Pacific and European theaters, the need to replenish the supply was hampered due to the shortage of aluminum. GE provided the solution. Plastic would replace the aluminum used for fuses in the nose of the shells. The Pittsfield plant, with its plastics expertise, was already functioning at capacity and unable to fill the demand, so the company opened a new facility in Holyoke for the sole purpose of manufacturing the fuses. Over the

---

[54] *Someone Talked*. Poster. Public domain. NARA 513672. Wiki Commons. tinyurl.com/yc6ssetj.

[55] Herwick, Edgar. *GE a MA Story*. GBH 1/18/2016. tinyurl.com/yvp6rwxw.

[56] Blalock, Thomas J. *Transformers, Pittsfield*. Gateway Press. 1998.

course of the war, 26 million would be produced by General Electric.[57] Concerns over extreme temperatures experienced by high-altitude pilots led the War Department to approach GE. Twelve days later, the prototype of a heated flight suit was ready for testing. To keep up with the demand for the suits, the company opened another plant in Lowell. GE would manufacture 400,000 by the war's end.[58]

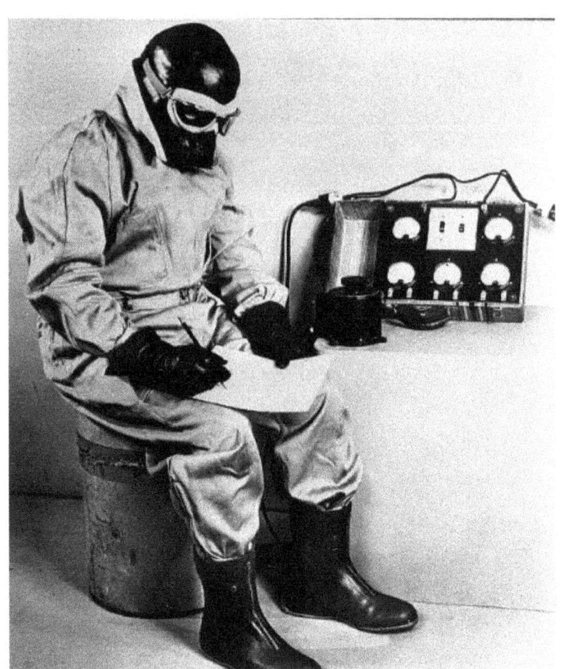
GE testing electronically heated flight suits. WWII.[59]

The work done by General Electric during the Second World War is legendary. In Massachusetts, plants in Boston, Everett, Lynn, Lowell, East Hampton, Pittsfield, and Fitchburg participated in the manufacture of a dizzying array of materials and equipment valued at approximately eight billion dollars in today's currency.[60] During a visit to the GE plant in Syracuse, New York, Secretary of the Navy Frank Knox paid tribute to the efforts of the men and women of General Electric.

No single industry in America has made a better response, a quicker response to our appeal for help than General Electric. I don't think what you've done here can be duplicated anywhere in the world...so lift up your heads with pride—the same kind of pride that men who wear the uniforms of this country have when they go forth to do battle for us—because, in the truest possible sense, you are battling for everything that America stands for.[61]

Long before December 7, 1941, several cities in Massachusetts already held long-standing reputations for manufacturing specialty products, industries that would make significant contributions to war production in unexpected ways. Not long after Arizona became the forty-eighth state, Reed & Barton Silversmiths of Taunton offered to create a silver service for the Battleship Arizona, which, at the time, was under construction at the Brooklyn Navy Yard. Due to delays, one stumbling block being the First World War, the finished set, a magnificent tribute to the new state and its battleship, was delivered

---

[57] Miller, John A. *Men Volts and War.*

[58] Leonard, Chris. *WWII at 75.* Daily Gazette 7/27/2020. tinyurl.com/37bazx8f.

[59] *Heated flying suits.* Pub domain photo. Office Emer Mgmt 2017700232. LOC. tinyurl.com/4zjj9j43.

[60] *War Supply Contracts.*

[61] Miller, John A. *Men and Volts and War.*

in 1919. In 1940, while preparing the battleship for war, the silver service was removed from the Arizona prior to its fateful tour of duty at Pearl Harbor.

Today, what remains of the Reed & Barton complex
is listed on the National Register of Historic Places.[62]

It would be quite some time before Reed & Barton would be back in the silversmith business. Shortly after Pearl Harbor, the War Production Board in Washington issued a statement: The use of strategic metals for civilian use was prohibited. Tin, aluminum, copper, silver, and zinc were to be used in government-sanctioned products only. In an effort to alleviate the shortage of these metals, copper in particular, the Treasury approved a plan to lend silver to companies engaged in war defense production. At General Electric's Pittsfield plant, where the manufacture of power transformers was a company staple, production quickly ran afoul of the copper crisis. Twelve transformers slated for an Alcoa aluminum plant were held up until GE decided to use silver instead. The government released 75 tons of the precious metal from the US Treasury to be used in transformer windings. After the war, the machinery was dismantled, and the silver was removed.[63] Reed & Barton remained in business throughout World War II, producing stainless steel products for the military, such as flatware and surgical instruments, and returned to silversmithing after the war. Taunton, known as the Silver City due to the presence of its silver companies, thrived during the war owing to its vast industrial base and the presence of Camp Miles Standish within its borders.

Less than twenty miles away from the Silver City, Attleboro was struggling. Many businesses in the Jewelry Capital of the World, a title also claimed by Providence, Rhode Island, had come to an abrupt halt when the government clamped down on metal use by private industry. Gold, silver, and platinum

---

[62] *Reed Barton*. Pub domain photo. Marc Belanger. Wiki Commons. tinyurl.com/34sp4sak.

[63] Blalock, Thomas J. *Transformers, Pittsfield.*

were essential materials for the creation of jewelry, putting manufacturers like Swank, L.G. Balfour, and Makepeace Company at risk.

In addition, these were not industrial giants like Boeing or General Motors. Seventy-five percent of government contracts before December 31, 1941, had gone to the 100 largest companies in the United States. There was a reason for this. Historian V.R. Cardozier points out: "All the small plants in the country combined could not produce the army's daily need for ammunition." The Army and Navy, however, saw a use for the thousands of failing small companies. Late in 1941, Defense Special Trains traveled the country displaying samples of 60,000 items needed by the military. Fifty thousand small businessmen viewed the exhibits, and with the ingenuity that characterized the nation's response to the war effort, toy train companies began producing airplane stabilizer equipment, lipstick manufacturers produced shell casings, and brassiere factories made mosquito netting. The Army and Navy began awarding contracts to small manufacturers, and six months later, the federal government authorized $150 million to help fill war production quotas and keep small businesses afloat.[64]

For the jewelry companies of Attleboro, the question was, what could they offer the government that would make them contenders for War Production Board contracts? The answer was themselves. Jewelers' adept fingers, familiarity with metal plating and soldering, and experience with the assembly of small items made them a perfect match for working with electronics. Soon, Attleboro began churning out war goods at an astonishing rate: circuit breakers, torpedo parts, radio equipment, radar components, ammunition, and incendiary bomb components. It didn't end there. This was the Jewelry Capital of the World, after all. Sweet Manufacturing Company made dog tags,[65] and several companies, like L.G. Balfour, began manufacturing the most coveted wartime jewelry of all: medals. Swank Company produced Bronze Stars, the Robbins Company made Distinguished Service Crosses and Army Good Conduct medals, and the Williams & Anderson Company created Silver Stars.[66]

Otto von Bismarck once said, "History is simply a piece of paper covered with print: the main thing is to make history, not to write it." The city of Holyoke might disagree. Paper, indeed, had an essential role to play during the war. From FDR's "Day of Infamy" speech to a soldier's draft card to his discharge papers or until a painful telegram found its way to loved ones, to the signing of a surrender on the decks of the USS Missouri, the story of World War II is recorded on paper. Holyoke's success in war production did not come as a surprise. Located on the banks of the Connecticut River and originally established as a center for textile manufacturing, by the late 1800s, the community became so successful at creating paper that 80 percent of all writing paper used in the United States came from Holyoke.[67]

[64] Cardozier, V.R. *Mobilization of US WWII.*

[65] *WW2 Dog Tags.* WW2 US MRC. tinyurl.com/yesbvwy5.

[66] *Manufacturers Awards & Medals.* Usmilawards.com. tinyurl.com/bdfbjvfj.

[67] *Love affair: Walsh Holyoke.* MHP. 7/26/2018. tinyurl.com/ajeh2ub7.

Holyoke paper mills. 1941.[68]

During the Second World War, eleven companies located in "The Paper City" held government contracts of $50,000 or more for paper goods. One of the largest, Marvellum Company, manufactured $1.2 million in wrapping and grease-proof paper. Paper was a big story in Massachusetts in general, and from mills and industries across the Commonwealth poured lithograph paper, writing paper, portfolios, binders, and office supplies. Some companies manufactured specific items like McLaurin-Jones of Ware (wrapping paper for crates and boxes) and Hollingsworth & Vose of East Walpole (paper tags).[69] Maps that guided men into battle were an essential item for a country at war. The Army Map Service estimated that for D-Day alone, 3,000 different maps were printed, requiring 70 million sheets of paper, a small number compared to the half-billion sheets (31 miles worth) used for maps over the course of the war.[70] In Massachusetts, map paper was produced by the Keith Paper Co. of Turners Falls ($1 million contract) and Crocker Burbank Co. of Fitchburg ($5,485,000 contract). Massachusetts companies produced paper products for the War Production Board, fulfilling nearly $20 million in contracts.[71]

The story of New Bedford is, in some ways, typical of the Massachusetts mill cities that helped to fill war production quotas. Built around the fishing industry, by the mid-1800s, the city had eclipsed Nantucket to become the country's number one whaling port. Textile production, firmly established in New England by that time, was late to take hold in this coastal city, rising to fill the void created by the decline in demand for whale oil. By 1875, dozens of mills had popped up throughout New Bedford, and by the end of the First World War, the Whaling City was the third-largest consumer of cotton in the country. Industry began to diversify based on the needs of the mills. Metalworks, machine shops, and

[68] *Holyoke city of canals*. 01/09/1941. Pub domain photo. USDA. tinyurl.com/nhbwdn5d.

[69] *War Supply Contracts*.

[70] *D Day remembered*. Medium. NGA 6/6/2016. tinyurl.com/yp27a8d5.

[71] *War Supply Contracts*.

electric companies provided materials and services.[72] As the era of textiles began to fade in New England, New Bedford went into decline. The infrastructure was in place, however, and with the advent of a second global conflict, the city flexed its creative industrial muscle to support the war effort.

Dorchester native and MIT grad Philip "Skipper" Young was a tinkerer, an inventor, and a problem solver. A friend recalled, "If it doesn't work, he will take it apart to find out why, and if it does work, he will take it apart to find out what makes it work." Young was working as an engineer at Goodyear Rubber in 1910 when he and a colleague, Frank Peabody, decided to start their own company. The plan was to locate it in Ohio, close to the rubber company giants. All they lacked was cash, and for this, they turned to Young's former MIT fraternity brother, Allen Weeks from Marion. Weeks agreed to become a partner with a stipulation. He was an avid sailor with a big boat and would only join up if the company set up shop near Buzzards Bay so he could keep sailing. They agreed, and soon Peabody, Young, and Weeks opened for business in Acushnet, Massachusetts. When their first success, a process for extracting rubber from plants, went down the tubes with a war in Mexico, they found a new source by recycling rubber, and the company began production of a variety of goods from toys to hot water bottles.

Twenty years later, Young, an avid golfer upset over losing a bet on the links (drinks at the nineteenth hole were on the line), blamed it on his golf ball. He convinced one of the players, a doctor from St. Luke's Hospital in New Bedford, to x-ray the traitorous sphere. Young's son later described the results. "Lo and behold, all the balls were cockeyed...So that afternoon, with no Sunday dinner and about six rounds of drinks under his belt, Skipper decided that if he could make a round golf ball, he could sell a few." Young designed a process that would create the perfect golf ball, the Titleist. The success of the new product helped the Acushnet Process Company survive the Depression. In 1938, due to a lack of space, the company opened a facility in New Bedford. The country would benefit from the talents of this brilliant entrepreneur when Young designed a gas-mask mold, making his New Bedford company the sole provider of the product during World War II.[73]

In spite of the lack of raw materials, rubber continued to be an important New Bedford product throughout the war years. During the run-up to the war, half of the world's natural rubber supply was consumed annually by the US, but as Japan began to gobble up the Pacific, the primary source of this vital commodity was gone. By mid-1940, the country had less than a six-month supply of rubber left. A manmade alternative would have to be found similar to that routinely used by Germany. According to historian Maury Klein, "Nearly all of Hitler's vaunted blitzkrieg units and aircraft rolled on tires that never saw a rubber tree."[74] Roosevelt set up a team of scientists and industrialists to work on the problem, and in a relatively short period of time, synthetic rubber was rolling out of plants. The first year saw the manufacture of 731 tons of synthetic rubber. By the end of the war, the number would increase to 70,000 tons per month.[75] In New Bedford, the Goodyear Tire and Rubber Factory produced fuel cells and cording for tires. The Goodyear Fabric Company turned out over $21 million in life vests, barrage balloons, parachutes, life rafts, and gas tanks that could seal themselves when struck by a bullet. The Firestone Company, whose Fall River Plant had lost nearly 15,000 tons of rubber in a fire just weeks before Pearl Harbor, produced gun stocks and cord tires.

Industries across New Bedford participated in war production. Cornell Dublier Company and Aerovox specialized in capacitors and electrical parts. Wamsutta Mills, once the largest cotton

---

[72] Richard Voyer, et al. *New Bedford, MA.* UCP J. tinyurl.com/muvvx8d5.

[73] Young, Richard B. *Hist Acushnet Company* 1991. Gifts to Give. tinyurl.com/3ws8j72v.

[74] Klein, Maury. *A Call to Arms.*

[75] *ACS Chemical Landmarks.* USSRP. tinyurl.com/4bxpcvrz.

manufacturer in the world, fabricated hot air balloons and canvas products,[76] and from Revere Copper Brass Inc. came sheets of brass, copper, nickel, and bronze along with shell parts and cartridge cases.[77]

Just as it did in World War II when Coastal Artillery Forces manned its ramparts, today Fort Tabor-Fort Rodman stands watch over the city of New Bedford, quiet now, still in recovery after the economic boom of the war years turned to silence. Throughout the city, many mill and factory buildings remain unoccupied, a fading memorial to the men and women of the Whaling City and the industries that helped to win the war.

When Congress passed the War Powers Act, it gave the President the awesome power to basically manage the United States in any way necessary to execute the war. Three months later, now with a better handle on what would be required to carry out a conflict on two fronts, a Second War Powers Act extended FDR's control of materials, resources, and manufacturing. One of Roosevelt's first moves was to appoint a War Production Board. Working with Secretary of War Henry Stimson, the Board's job was to convert American industry to wartime production. Resources were inventoried, and materials in short supply were assigned as high priorities. Companies were asked to retool operations to provide everything from ammunition to airplanes. Contracts were granted, and a workforce was mustered from a nation whose manpower was significantly depleted.

The government made the decision early on that management of private industry was not feasible. Instead, the United States opted to provide financial backing. With GOCOs (Government Owned Contractor Operated), the government constructed factories and hired individuals from the private sector to manage war production companies. Most often, however, when a product was needed, loans were provided for renovation or expansion of existing facilities and retooling or purchase of machines. Once contracts were granted, the owner was left to manage his own business. It was not a request. Under the tenets of the War Powers Act, when the government came knocking, companies were expected to comply. If, by chance, there was pushback on the part of owners, the government had the frightening power to step in and assume control of the business.

In 1943, the Massachusetts Leather Manufacturing Association fell under the watchful eye of the National War Labor Board (NWLB), a committee designed to resolve labor issues and keep war production running smoothly. Thirteen of the thirty Association companies, all of which were located within Salem, Peabody, and Danvers, had gone on strike, preventing production of essential leather goods. Repeated attempts to settle differences, including an appeal by the President, failed, and in November, all thirteen companies fell under government control.[78] The following year, in a highly publicized case, retailer Montgomery Ward was taken over after failure to comply with government fiats. After disgruntled Sewell Avery shared his feelings with War Production Board officials ("I want none of your damned advice. . .To hell with the government!"),[79] the country was treated to front-page photos of the company CEO being carried out of the Montgomery Ward building in his own chair.

The power to seize property, which had been granted by the War Powers Act, was challenged only once during the course of the war. A Massachusetts company under the management of President H. C. Dodge manufactured woodworking machinery and induction motors in South Boston. In 1940, an additional plant with 650 workers opened at the S. A. Woods company for the production of shells and shots. The War Department held $20 million in contracts with S. A. Woods. In April of 1942, the company began contract talks with its employees and their union. When negotiations fell apart, the NWLB intervened. Mediators were assigned and failed. Governor Leverett Saltonstall stepped in to no avail. In spite of repeated government warnings about potential consequences should Dodge fail to settle

[76] Briody, Sean. *Wamsutta Mills.* rhodetour.org/items/show/72.

[77] *War Supply Contracts.*

[78] Ohly, John. *Industrialists Olive Drab.* CMH 2000. Army.mil. tinyurl.com/5bzb3d3r.

[79] Ross, Tara. *FDR vs. Montgomery Ward.* Tara Ross 12/27/2020. tinyurl.com/2p9sr3ju.

the contract, he stubbornly held his ground demanding that the legality of the government's power to take over his company be brought before the courts.[80] On August 18, the President was notified. He responded a day later.

EXECUTIVE ORDER 9225

The Secretary of War is authorized and directed immediately to take possession of and operate the plant of the S. A. Woods Machine Company located at South Boston, Massachusetts, through and with the aid of such person or persons or instrumentality as he may designate, and, in so far as may be necessary or desirable, to produce the war materials called for by the Company's contracts with the United States, its departments and agencies...
Franklin D. Roosevelt
The White House
August 19, 1942

It was a done deal. By 8:00 p.m., the military arrived on the property. S. A. Woods was now in the hands of the government. But FDR had left Dodge an opening: "Possession and operation hereunder shall be terminated by the President as soon as he determines that the plant of the S. A. Woods Machine Company at South Boston, Massachusetts, will be privately operated in a manner consistent with the war effort."[81] Dodge declined to take advantage of the opportunity. For the remainder of the war, S. A. Woods produced ammunition under the control of the Murray Co., which contracted with the government to manage the business. Dodge didn't fade quietly into the background, however, and after enthusiastically advocating for the investigation of War Department seizure practices, Congress addressed the matter in 1943. Nothing changed. The company was handed back to H.C. Dodge in the fall of 1945.

A total of sixty-four companies came under government control during World War II. Most labor-related seizures, as was the case with the Leather Manufacturers in the Salem area and a similar case involving several Fall River textile mills, were resolved in a relatively short period of time, and businesses were returned to owners. Like S.A. Woods and Montgomery Ward, the vast majority of long-term government confiscations were the result of management's failure to comply with government demands.[82]

---

[80] Ohly, John H. *Industrialists Olive Drab.*

[81] Roosevelt, Franklin D. *Exec Order 9225.* FD. NARA. tinyurl.com/36ebxcnu.

[82] Ohly, John H. *Industrialists Olive Drab.*

S.A. Woods Machine Co., South Boston,
after being seized by the government. WWII.
Courtesy of the Boston Public Library, Leslie Jones Collection.[83]

In 1946, the federal government published a database of War Supply Contracts issued from June 1940 through September 1945. The 3,521-page document gives an extraordinary glimpse into the economic and industrial might of the United States during World War II. Over 1,000 companies from tiny Massachusetts are included. What makes this statistic even more startling is that the publication contains only those businesses that held government contracts of $50,000 or more. Worcester's Stafford Iron Works, which made landing craft parts, the Foxboro Company, renowned for pneumatic and electronic instruments, George H. Morrill inkworks of Norwood; and hundreds of other small companies that engaged in war production were excluded from the list.

While the database is no more than a listing of companies, products, and numbers, it paints a picture of life for those in the military during World War II. Whether recuperating in a hospital, undergoing basic training, sitting at a desk, or stationed in a combat zone, products created by the hands of average American men and women, thousands of them from Massachusetts, found their way to the 16 million who went to war. Unless otherwise noted, the information that appears below is drawn from the War Supply database.

From the moment a recruit signed on the dotted line, every step he took was managed by the military, and every need was provided for by the federal government. For many, one of the earliest memories of joining up was receiving inoculations. Smallpox, tetanus, diphtheria, and typhoid vaccines, to name a few, were delivered by syringes (MacGregor Instrument, Needham) that came at rookies fast and furious from the right and left.

Next up was government-issued clothing, and here Massachusetts made her mark. Uniforms came from a handful of Boston companies, including over $5 million worth from the Leopold Morse Co. Undershirts (Ware Knitters, Ware), drawers (Winship Boit, Wakefield), socks (Marum Knitting Mills, Lawrence), leggings (Owens Shoe, Salem), and eyelets for the leggings (United Shoe Machinery, North Brookfield) poured out of factories across the state. Trousers were a must, of course (Sun Valley Mfg., Boston), as were shirts (Shelburne Co., Fall River) and thread to hold them all together (West End Thread, Millbury). Sweaters (Old Colony Knitting Mills, Hingham) were a common item, and an amazing variety of coats and jackets (London Clothing Corp., North Abington) were shipped out of clothing companies by the thousands. Field jackets worn by the average soldier were a common item, but sheep-lined coats (Star Sportswear, Lynn), parkas (Piccariello Singer Inc., Boston), ponchos (Walker

---

Co., Middleboro), flight jackets (Knopf & Son, Boston), and raincoats (Archer Rubber, Milford) also abounded. Need a place to land your salute? Caps were made at Pelton Knitting Mills in Boston. Joining the Navy? New England Overall, Boston, and Worcester Knitting sent dungarees. Perhaps the recruit was a woman. Nurse dresses and skirts (Bernard Appfl Inc., Boston) came from the Bay State as well. Finally, the U.S. Trunk Co. in Fall River made lockers to put it all in.

Let's not forget boots and shoes. These items were considered so essential for soldiers that mobile shoe repair shops moved forward with men along combat fronts. Standard GI service shoes were handed out to recruits, but for those headed overseas, high-top leather combat boots were required. Shoes and boots whizzed out of Massachusetts, many of them from Brockton (Knapp Bros., Stacy Adams Co., Thompson Brothers), representing $22 million in contracts. Further west, Ascutney Shoe of Hudson, Well Struter Shoe in North Adams, and Anson Shoe of Athol contributed $12 million in shoes and boots. Trying to impress the brass? Whittemore Brothers of Cambridge sent shoe polish.

For recruits hungry after the first rush of shots and shirts and shoes, an astonishing array of kitchen and dining supplies (exclusive of the one million chickens provided by Red Farm of Wrentham)[84] found their way into government contracts. While Massachusetts companies actually produced kitchen equipment such as slicing machines and vegetable steamers, all that metal just couldn't go to waste. The Sexton Can Co. of Everett made baking pans and bombs, and J. C. Pitman & Sons of Lynn turned out dishwashers and torpedo cradles. When a GI headed into the mess hall, his hash was plopped onto a mess tray (Victory Plastics, Hudson) and eaten with knives, forks, and spoons made by silversmiths like those at International Silver Co. of Florence, which also turned out bomb nose bodies. Paper cups were provided by U.S. Envelope Co. in Worcester, and dabbing away the cream chipped beef was made possible by $400,000 worth of napkins from the Erving Paper Mills. Clean-up was a snap. Wiping cloths from John R. Lyman Co., Chicopee, metal sponges from Springfield Wire Tinsel Co., and whisk brooms from Spencer's Town Broom Company could handle any mess.

Tired at the end of a long day, soldiers needed to clean up and hit the sack. Massachusetts companies were on top of this as well. From the Prophylactic Brush Company of Florence came $1.6 million in toothbrushes and from Gillette Safety Razor of Boston shaving cream and razors. The chemical industry was big business in the Bay State. Lever Brothers of Cambridge and Proctor & Gamble of Quincy made laundry soap and toilet soap when they weren't making explosives. Need help taking care of business? The American Tissue Mills of Holyoke and the Statler Tissue Co. of Somerville sent toilet paper, $127,000 of it. Once cleaned up and ready to call it a day, those lucky enough to sleep in a bunk could enjoy cozy pillows (Comfort Feather Pillow Co., Somerville), clean sheets (Naumkeag Steam Cotton Co., Peabody), and blankets that rolled out of textile companies like Packard Mills in Webster by the thousands. Those who found themselves in the field might spend the night on cots (Heywood & Wakefield, Gardner), in a tent like those manufactured by the Lapierre Moore Co. of Gilbertville, or in a hammock (Selig Manufacturing, Leominster). No comfy pillows here, but plenty of sleeping bags to go around (Waterhouse Co., Webster).

With the stress of being in the military during the war, a little R&R was called for. Smith Paper Inc. of Lee provided cigarette papers for smoke, and Leominster Plastics of Leominster made cases to carry them in. Athletically inclined? Basketballs, softballs, golf balls, and tennis rackets, $13.5 million in all, along with 20 mm projectiles, were sent by A.G. Spaulding Brothers of Chicopee. Need a spot for a game of cards? Lawrence Woodworking manufactured camp tables. And for those who had a bit too much fun on leave, handcuffs came from the Peerless Handcuff Co. of Springfield.

Outfitting men for war went far beyond underwear and uniforms, however. Men going into battle often had to rely on what they carried with them to survive. Haversacks were a good fit for textile-rich Massachusetts. Companies like Arakelian Co. of Haverhill made backpacks and canteen covers. Gas masks (Sprague Electric Co., North Adams) and helmets (Horace A. Weene Co., Boston) provided

---

⁸⁴ Fiore, Jordan D. *Wrentham History.* Town Wrentham. Thomas Todd Co. 1973.

protection, and bandoliers (Robertson Factories, Taunton) and cartridge belts (Dainty Maid Shoe Co., Haverhill) carried ammunition.

The government's biggest concern was combat, and it is impossible to adequately portray the astounding amount of production dedicated to arms and ammunition in the state of Massachusetts during World War II. Exclusive of the great armories at Springfield and Watertown and the Naval Ammunition Depot at Hingham, which were government facilities, private industry stepped up to create an extraordinary array of ordnance. American Type Founders of Fitchburg made 105 mm howitzers, and Whiting Davis Co. of Plainville produced machine guns. Industry giants Smith & Wesson ($26 million contract) and Harrington Richardson & Sons of Worcester ($12 million contract) made revolvers and pistols. Limpet mines came from Tilton Cook of Leominster, grenades from Westfield Manufacturing, bayonets from Victory Plastics of Hudson, and trench knives from Pal Blade Co. in Holyoke. In addition, dozens of companies across the Commonwealth produced gun sights, stocks, magazines, and telescope parts.[85]

Cube Steak Machine Co. of Boston cutting
spouts for anti-tank guns. 1942.[86]

Wartime production of army ordnance became a $30 billion a year industry, and the country created 39 billion rounds of small arms ammunition, 475,000 tons of mortar ammunition, and 6 million tons of bombs and rockets.[87] In terms of numbers, hands down, ammunition topped the list for the most commonly produced item in Massachusetts. Everything from cartridge cases and ammunition crates to tracer bodies and shots came from the production lines of Bay State companies. From Walsh Construction in Boston and Standard Pyroxoloid Corp. of Leominster came bombs, and companies like Continental Can of Malden and Larson Tool Stamping of Attleboro made the parts that went into the bombs. Rockets were made at Westfield Manufacturing, created from parts made at the Florence Stove Co. in Gardner, and fired off by nearly $2 million in launchers from Cheney Bigelow Wire Works in Springfield. Roughly a dozen companies, like Whitin Machine Works in Whitinsville, held contracts for torpedo parts.

A variety of shells, projectiles, and cartridges spilled out of Massachusetts factories, as did the casings that held the shells, the firing pins that launched the bullets, and the detonators that exploded the

---

[85] *War Supply Contracts.*

[86] *Food machinery plant* 1/01/1942. Pub domain photo. LOC. tinyurl.com/mufrkyvz.

[87] Kropp, Cathy. *Army ammunition plants.* US Army 9/16/2020. tinyurl.com/3654xsep.

bombs. Thousands and thousands of primers and fuzes came from big companies like American Fireworks of Canton and Randolph, which specialized in ordnance equipment to fulfill its $5.6 million contract, or from unlikely sources such as the Independent Lock Co. of Fitchburg, which fabricated padlocks and bomb nose fuzes. From Murray Co., with branches in Boston, Natick, and East Bridgewater, came $16.5 million in shot and shells. Ammunition was big business in Worcester, where Worcester Taper Pin, Parker Harper Manufacturing, and Persons Majestic Manufacturing all held contracts for $1.5 million or more. Worcester's Crompton and Knowles alone produced approximately $3 million in torpedo parts and tracer bodies.

Without explosives, however, all those shells and bombs would be useless. Alcohol, supplied by New England Alcohol Co. of Everett, was a necessary ingredient for the soup that would become synthetic rubber and was also used in smokeless powder production. Incendiary bombs used to devastating effect by the Germans on London became a common part of the American arsenal, and Monsanto, with plants in Boston, Everett, Indian Orchard, and Springfield, provided phosphorous along with a variety of other chemicals.[88]

It was magnesium, however, that spurred big changes in the chemical industry. Blended into incendiary bomb casings, the combustible chemical ignited along with the thermite packed inside to create an excessively high-temperature burn, the effectiveness of which was demonstrated by the destruction of Hamburg, Germany, in 1943. As the war progressed, the magnesium industry experienced a production quota 100 times greater than ever before, introducing new manufacturing processes and making it, according to authors John Bokel and Rolf Clark, "the largest expansion of any industry" during World War II.[89] From the New England Magnesium Co. of Malden and the New England Lime Co. of Adams came $700,000 in magnesium.

Unquestionably, the big-ticket industry in the Bay State was shipbuilding. With its 1,500-mile coastline and rich maritime history, Massachusetts knew how to build boats. Scattered along the waterfront and upriver from the ocean, companies constructed a wide variety of marine vessels during World War II: boats to tug ships and boats to haul freight, boats to move men and boats to launch buoys, and boats to patrol harbor waters and keep other boats safe. Half a dozen companies, like James E. Grayes Inc. of Marblehead and J. Willis Reid Co. of Winthrop, made tugboats, and others, like Somerset Shipyards in Fall River, made barges. From Cape Cod Shipbuilding in Wareham came tow boats, and from Casey Boat Building in Fairhaven rescue vessels. Quincy Adams Yacht Yard in Quincy made motor launches, and Martha's Vineyard Shipbuilding Co. made tank lighters.

Shipbuilding drove a significant part of the state's wartime economy. Industries turned out nearly $300 million in parts that went into the ships and the tools that were needed to put all the pieces together. Over $7 million in marine engines came out of the Springfield Machine Foundry in West Springfield, and another $2.7 million from Murray and Tregurtha of Quincy. Polaroid in Cambridge built navigation equipment to guide the ships, while propellers mounted on shafts from Whitin Machine Works in Whitinsville pushed them along, and ballast weights (Feinberg Davis of Medford and Worcester Foundry) kept them on an even keel. An astonishing variety of equipment was produced by the Submarine Signal Co. of Boston and Fall River. From fathometers to sonar apparatus to $736,000 in items marked CLASSIFIED, this business held government contracts for $230 million. Known for its farm equipment, Allis Chalmers produced circuit breakers in its Boston plant but somehow managed to make hatch covers and bulkhead frames as well. Chelsea's New England Trawler Equipment Co. contributed capstans and windlasses. If all went horribly wrong, New England Bedding Co. in Medford produced shipwreck kits, and Milliken Machine in West Newton made kites that could be used by downed airmen to float radio antennas aloft.

---

[88] *War Supply Contracts.*

[89] Bokel, John E. et al. *American Logistics WWII.* NDU Press 1997. tinyurl.com/248mbtdk.

"I wish to have no connection with any ship that does not sail fast, for I intend to go in harm's way," stated legendary Captain John Paul Jones. During the Second World War, in keeping with this proud American naval tradition, Massachusetts would send hundreds of ships into battle. These were the vessels that would see combat, would humble the Japanese at the Battle of Midway, deliver tanks and supplies to the shores of Normandy, and hunt down and kill U-boats during the Battle of the Atlantic.

In addition to the federal ship works at the Charlestown Navy Yard, private companies made significant contributions. Calderwood Yacht Yard in Manchester and, Simms Brothers of Boston made subchasers, and N. A. Robinson of Ipswich made mine sweepers. The George Lawley Company, which had been a fixture along the Boston Harbor shoreline since just after the Civil War, signed an $81 million contract to fabricate a variety of boats, including subchasers, tank lighters, and landing craft. The jewel in the crown of Massachusetts wartime shipbuilding, however, was the Bethlehem Steel Corporation in Quincy ($965 million contract) and its annex, the Bethlehem Hingham Shipyard ($395 million contract). From its giant forges, factory buildings, and drydocks came LSTs, heavy and light cruisers, aircraft carriers, destroyers, and destroyer escorts.

Unlike the textile industry with mills stretching from one end of the state to the other, the number of Massachusetts businesses engaged exclusively in vessel construction with contracts exceeding $1.6 million was not extensive. By September of 1945, the government had contracted with seventeen Bay State companies to produce $1.5 billion in shipping to send into harm's way.[90]

There are other stories to be told here, but not nearly enough space to do it, like how the government discovered that the most cost-effective mode of transportation was a bicycle and entered into contracts for their production with two US manufacturers, one in Ohio and the other in Massachusetts. Westfield's Columbia Manufacturing Company produced $1.2 million worth of G159 two-wheelers for the Army, Navy, and Treasury Departments. Not to be outdone was another two-wheel vehicle company across the town line in Springfield. The Indian Motorcycle Company made nearly 40,000 motorcycles to be used by the US and its allies during the war.[91]

Indian motorcycle. WWII.[92]

A unique combination tool similar to the modern Leatherman was designed to be carried in the buttstock of an M1 Garand and used for its cleaning. As the rifle changed, so did the tool, and the very first production of the newly modified M3A1 came out of Parker Manufacturing in Worcester.[93]

---

[90] *War Supply Contracts 1940-1945*. CPA.

[91] Jackson, David. *Westfield Mfg Co.* Am Auto Indus WWII 5/27/2022. tinyurl.com/2b59mmcf.

[92] *Mil Motorcycles Second WW*. Pub domain photo. IWM UK. tinyurl.com/m6x7xbep.

[93] Ricca, Bill. *M3A1 Tool*. US Rifle~Caliber. 30~M1 Garand. tinyurl.com/8hnkpxuj.

Unfortunately, the effort put into medical supplies by the people of Massachusetts must be overlooked as well. Millions of dollars in surgical dressings, gauze pads, sutures, and surgical instruments were mass produced in companies like Sacks & Sons of Brookline (boxes, packing crates, and crutches), Allen Laws Company of Three Rivers (medical supplies and gauze bandages), and even dental supplies and smocks (Edward A. Winning, New Bedford).[94] A bit of a scandal erupted in 1942 when the government seized crates of mislabeled sanitized absorbent gauze dressings which were found to be crawling with live bacteria. Gero Products Inc. of South Boston declined to mount a defense, and the products were destroyed.[95]

December 7, 1941, caught the nation unprepared. Germany, for example, had manufactured six times more ships, planes, and weapons than the US between 1935 and 1940.[96] One month after the country declared war, Hitler predicted, "I don't see much future for the Americans...it's a decayed country." The Japanese looked down their noses at our morally and culturally decrepit society. Even War Production Board Chairman Donald Nelson had this to say: "[1941] will go down in history, I believe, as the year when we almost lost the war before we ever got into it."[97]

There was hope, however, that American industry would come to the rescue. Author Geoffrey Perrett wrote: "Perhaps there was once a time when courage, daring, imagination, and intelligence were the hinges on which wars turned. No longer. The total wars of modern history give the decision to the side with the biggest factories. The economically inferior may win battles; they do not win the all-out wars."[98]

Winston Churchill most certainly understood the crucial importance of those factories. England was already the beneficiary of ships, planes, and supplies produced by American hands when he addressed Congress three weeks after the attack on Pearl Harbor. He talked at length about the might of our country's manufacturing capability and made predictions about what would happen when American industrial potential became prowess.

The United States united as never before, has drawn the sword for freedom and cast away the scabbard...Now we are the masters of our fate; that the task which has been set us is not above our strength; that its pangs and toils are not beyond our endurance. As long as we have faith in our cause and an unconquerable will-power, salvation will not be denied us.

Stalin put it more succinctly: "The most important things in this war are machines... The United States...is a country of machines."

Finally, there was FDR. Whatever his politics and opinions behind closed doors, in public, he became a cheerleader for the men and women who moved the wheels of the American war production machine.

Guns, planes, ships, and many other things have to be built in the factories and the arsenals of America. They have to be produced by workers and managers and engineers with the aid of machines which in turn have to be built by hundreds of thousands of workers throughout the land...

---

[94] *War Supply Contracts.*

[95] *Adulteration/misbranding gauze.* NIH NLM. tinyurl.com/39ahrsjw.

[96] Meacham, Jon. *Franklin and Winston.* Random House Trade Paperbacks 2004.

[97] Klein, Maury. *A Call to Arms.*

[98] Klein, Maury. *A Call to Arms.*

I have the profound conviction that the American people are now determined to put forth a mightier effort than they have ever yet made to increase our production of all the implements of defense, to meet the threat to our democratic faith.

The people of the United States did not disappoint. They rolled up their sleeves, and approximately 20 million went to work for war production, many of them women. They cut back on consumer items, making due with a total of 139 newly manufactured cars during the war, a significant decline in the three million fabricated during the year prior to its outbreak. They increased the output of machines and materials. In 1944, airplane production was nearly five times what it had been in 1941, and they bumped up the speed of production.[99] At one Ford facility, a bomber rolled out of the factory every hour.[100] The government held up its end as well. Historian David Kennedy reported that the net value of US commerce in 1941 was surpassed by government contracts within the first six months of the war.[101]

By the time of Japan's surrender, the men and women of American industry had produced over 88,000 tanks, 325,000 aircraft, and billions of dollars in ships. In addition, 257,000 pieces of artillery, 2.6 million machine guns, and 41 billion rounds of ammunition had shipped out of privately owned factories and government installations. The United States had produced $183 billion in arms and ammunition alone,[102] exceeded FDR's expectations, and outproduced every ally and enemy in the world.

"They have given their sons to the military services," the President said. "They have stoked the furnaces and hurried the factory wheels. They have made the planes and welded the tanks. Riveted the ships and rolled the shells." Roosevelt was right to give credit to the men and women of Massachusetts and the rest of the country who toiled every day, doing their part to end the war. They may not have carried guns into battle, and they may not have single-handedly won the war, but it is certain that the war would have been lost without them.

---

[99] Burns, Ken. *War Production. The War*. PBS. tinyurl.com/3prwmxnh.

[100] *Take Closer Look: Am Goes to War*. Nat WWII Mus. tinyurl.com/yrvm6mz5.

[101] Klein, Maury. *A Call to Arms*.

[102] Herman, Arthur. *Freedom's Forge*.

Chapter 7

Republic of Science

New frontiers of the mind are before us...
Franklin D. Roosevelt

The letter was dated August 17, 1939, and addressed to F.D. Roosevelt at the White House.

It may become possible to set up a nuclear chain reaction in a large mass of uranium, by which vast amounts of power and large quantities of new radium-like elements would be generated. Now, it appears almost certain that this could be achieved in the immediate future.

The author of the letter further warned that one of the world's three accessible sources of uranium, Czechoslovakia, was under the exclusive control of Germany and that the Reich's Under-Secretary of State had ties to a university that was participating in uranium research. Nuclear fission had been discovered the previous December, and at that time, a group of scientists approached the Army and Navy in the hopes of investigating further. The military declined. When the letter reached FDR the following August, he took the information more seriously (as one should when it was written by Albert Einstein). As a result, in October 1939, the President created the Advisory Committee on Uranium, followed by the National Defense Research Committee, which was established to advance the use of science in war. Five years later, the groundwork laid by the NDRC would come full circle.

Early on the morning of 16 July 1945, Major General Leslie Groves took shelter in a trench just ten miles away from ground zero in the New Mexico desert, the spot where a device called "the Gadget," a test weapon with a plutonium core, would soon unleash its 18.6 kiloton atomic potential upon the world.

Down in the dirt with him was James Bryant Conant, National Defense Research Committee head, and Vannevar Bush, in charge of the Office of Scientific Research and Development. In a forward bunker waited project leader J. Robert Oppenheimer. Kenneth Bainbridge was also on hand, spearheading the massive test extravaganza. He would later call it "a foul and awesome display." Physicist Donald Hornig stood within reach of the "chicken switch," which could sever the bomb's electrical connection in case it all went wrong.[1] George Kistiakowsky, who supervised development of explosives for the Gadget, armed it, and was one of the last to leave the firing tower, would soon be knocked flat where he stood five miles from the blast site.[2] Not far away was his colleague, Philip Morrison, who had ridden next to the core of the bomb in the back seat of an Army sedan as it was delivered to the Trinity site.[3] Hans Bethe, on hand to determine the effect of shock waves after the blast, observed the test from Compania Hill twenty miles away. He and his colleague Victor Weisskopf, along with Enrico Fermi, would be the first civilians to tour the bomb site thirty-six hours later.[4] All but two of these men had significant ties to the Bay State.

---

[1] Ziner, Karen Lee. *Hands-on Los Alamos.* Providence Jour 8/9/2015. tinyurl.com/2fw4zwn9.

[2] *Trinity Test.* Manhattan Proj. US DOE. tinyurl.com/5xatawb5.

[3] *Philip Morrison.* AHF 2022. tinyurl.com/52zya9s3

[4] *Victor Weisskopf.* AHF 2022. tinyurl.com/5n7as9wj.

The Gadget's core arrives at the
Trinity test site. July 1945.[5]

The course of the Second World War would have looked very different without the state of Massachusetts and a singular genius from Tuxedo Park, New York. Though not a native son of the Bay State, Alfred Lee Loomis attended Philips Academy in Andover, held a law degree from Harvard, and married into the prestigious Boston Farnsworth family. From an early age, Loomis showed signs of what was to come. As a child, he was an expert at chess, able to play two games at the same time blindfolded. Convinced by friends that the legal profession could open a variety of doors, the young man embarked upon a law career, settling into practice with his cousin Henry Stimson, later Secretary of War. Having majored in mathematics at Yale, Loomis applied his considerable intellect to the world of finance, converting assets into public utility securities and emerging from the Depression spectacularly wealthy. Along the way, he spent time as a captain in the US Army, where his interest in science and weaponry earned him a position at the Aberdeen Proving Ground. Here, he fell under the influence of inventor Thomas Edison and developed a life-long friendship with a man from Concord, Massachusetts, Robert Williams Wood.[6]

Wood was a kindred spirit, easily bored, somewhat eccentric, and brilliant. Having flunked out of Roxbury Latin High School not once but twice (his path toward the priesthood went out the window when he noticed an unusual phenomenon in the night sky and decided to study science), he went on to earn a degree in chemistry at Harvard (literature and languages bored him).[7] While doing post graduate work in Germany, Wood lost interest in chemistry and moved on to physics. On his return to the states, he spent time at MIT before eventually joining the staff at Johns Hopkins. More interested in action than in collecting laurels, he never completed his PhD. Wood was several years older than Loomis, and the two developed a mentor/protegee relationship. One of Wood's pet projects, a state-of-the-art spectrograph built in his summer home on Long Island, attracted the younger man's attention. Too big for his laboratory, the 40' tall instrument was constructed in the barn, unfortunate as the device periodically got clogged by spiderwebs. No problem...Wood simply dropped his cat down one end of the tube and let him find his way out the other end.[8]

Loomis was fascinated. Despite his wide-ranging abilities, Alfred Lee Loomis was a scientist at heart, and after watching the spectrograph in operation, he asked the older man to collaborate on a

[5] *Gadge Trinity site 7/16/1945*. Pub domain photo. Manhattan Proj. US DOE. tinyurl.com/49a783kb.

[6] Alvarez, Luis. *Alfred Lee Loomis*. NAS1980. tinyurl.com/yc3ec4ea

[7] Conant, Jennet. *Tuxedo Park*. Simon and Schuster Paperbacks 2002.

[8] Dieke, G.H. *Robert Wood*. 1956. Royal Soc Publ. tinyurl.com/5xzkt7j4.

project. Utilizing Wood's knowledge and Loomis' funding, the two set about researching high-frequency sound waves. They purchased an enormous oscillator from General Electric, dismantled it, and reassembled it at Loomis' home in the village of Tuxedo Park, New York. The foundation was in place for one of the most extraordinary and unconventional research facilities in American history. Over the course of the next several years, a steady stream of scientists arrived at Tuxedo Park seeking funding and research opportunities unfettered by the bureaucracy of the military or universities. Wood and Loomis would earn a place in science history as the "fathers of ultrasonics," the EEG would be developed utilizing Loomis' research, and the Tower House laboratory would host informal seminars featuring science glitterati such as Enrico Fermi, Niels Bohr, and Albert Einstein, engaging them in a free flow of ideas and creating an environment that Einstein would later describe as a "palace of science."[9]

As the thirties unfolded, Loomis watched the rise of militarism and racism in Europe with grave concern. Einstein had left in 1933. Fermi followed in 1938. Now, with the looming threat of war, the United States was choosing to place its head in the sand. Time spent at the Aberdeen Proving Ground led Loomis to believe that the military could not be relied upon to prepare the country for war, nor could the government with its isolationist policies. Loomis aligned with Thomas Edison, a vocal advocate of creating peacetime research laboratories with the goal of developing new and more effective weapons. The next conflict, Edison believed, would be one "in which machines, not soldiers, fight."

At the suggestion of MIT President Karl Compton, Loomis developed an interest in microwave research. It was a self-serving suggestion on Compton's part as MIT was already engaged in the study of microwaves, and Loomis had deep pockets, very deep pockets. Lurking on the sidelines was Vannevar Bush, native of Everett, Massachusetts, a graduate of Chelsea High School and Tufts, with a PhD. in electrical engineering issued jointly by MIT and Harvard. Bush was a former teacher at Tufts, head of MIT's School of Engineering, and a founder of the Cambridge-based American Appliance Company, later known as Raytheon. As the three men moved forward, unleashing the secrets of microwaves across the Atlantic, Hitler set his sights on England.

When Einstein's letter warning of the danger of atomic weapons arrived at the White House, war in Britain was just a few weeks away. FDR, ever slow to take controversial steps, especially with an upcoming election year, moved cautiously, too cautiously for Vannevar Bush. In June 1940, after discussion with Karl Compton, James Bryant Conant (born in Dorchester, chemist and President of Harvard University), Richard Tolman (born West Newton, BS and PhD. from MIT), and Frank Jewett of Bell Laboratories, Bush approached the President. His proposal was four paragraphs long and laid out the necessity of organizing American scientists in an effort to prepare the country's arsenal for war.

Ten minutes into the meeting, the National Defense Research Committee was established...eight men, including Compton, Conant, Tolman, Jewett, and representatives from the Army and Navy with Bush at the helm. The hasty decision was not without controversy. Bush would later recall: "There were those who protested that the action of setting up NDRC was an end run, a grab by which a small company of scientists and engineers, acting outside established channels, got hold of the authority and money for the program of developing new weapons. That, in fact, is exactly what it was."[10]

There was more on FDR's mind than just creating a new agency. He hadn't forgotten Einstein's warning and, within six months, sent a letter to Bush sanctioning the development of an atomic bomb.

---

[9] Conant, Jennet. *Tuxedo Park.*

[10] *NDRC.* Manhattan Proj. US DOE. tinyurl.com/2v4nbrhb.

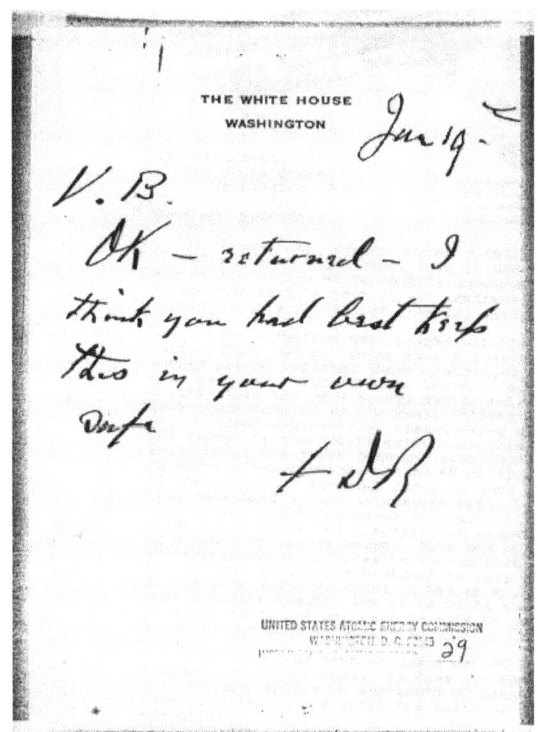

FDR's approval for the development
of the atomic bomb. June 19, 1942.[11]

Alfred Lee Loomis' role as a financial wizard who dabbled in science was about to end. Bush and Compton quickly honed in on the seminal project for the new agency, microwave radar, and asked Alfred Loomis to join them. It was a good fit. The country had only two functioning microwave radar sets at the time, one owned and built by Loomis and his people.[12] He also proved his ability to bring scientists, funding, and opportunity together with positive results at his Tuxedo Park facility. In addition, the premise of the NDRC, an independent agency that was government-funded and non-military, must have appealed to Loomis. He had a long-standing aversion to bureaucracy and to the speed with which the armed forces responded to change. As a young man working at the Aberdeen Proving Ground, Loomis witnessed a soldier whose job was to stand statue-like for long periods of time with one arm raised. Apparently, in days gone by when the caissons still rolled, a soldier was required to hold onto the lead horse and guide it to its destination. The horses had long since been put out to pasture, but the role of the soldier hadn't. So the man stood patiently, holding his arm up, waiting for the Army to change.[13] NDRC projects, funded by the government and answering only to the executive branch, would not be beholden to the military, universities or industry. Loomis accepted the offer and came on board as head of the NDRC Microwave Committee.

Across the Atlantic, England, now at war, was being subjected to brutal assaults by the Luftwaffe. For every two German planes shot down, the British lost three.[14] Radar had been in the hands of the major Allied and Axis countries since before the war. However, when the Luftwaffe began night bombings and expanded targets to industrial cities inland, England's radar network, Chain Home, began to fall short. The system utilized huge coastal towers that sent radio signals eastward across the Channel

---

[11] *Roosevelt's note to Bush.* Pub domain photo. Manhattan Proj. US DOE. tinyurl.com/2fsja3ry.

[12] Alvarez, Luis W. *Alfred Lee Loomis.*

[13] Conant, Jennet. *Tuxedo Park.*

[14] Shachtman, Tom. *Laboratory Warriors.* Perennial, HarperCollins 2002.

to detect incoming bombers. If planes managed to make it past the towers, unless they were visually sighted, they could basically fly undetected into Britain's interior. Not only that, night pilots were directed to enemy aircraft within the same range as in daylight, but they were essentially flying blind, often coming perilously close to their targets before firing. They needed a radar device small enough to fit on a plane, making aircraft interception of other aircraft possible. To accomplish this, they needed a device with the power to produce shorter radio waves...microwaves. They found one.

American scientist A.W. Hull had dabbled with his interest in controlling electricity contained within tubes as a professor at Worcester Polytechnic Institute. After a day of teaching, he conducted research into the night. "My wife often accompanied me to the laboratory in the evening and sat and read while I made glassware apparatus. Generally, we went home when the apparatus broke."[15] His work paid off when he developed a magnetron that could adjust the amount of energy within a glass tube by applying magnets. When the crisis continued to deepen in Britain, two researchers from the University of Birmingham successfully used Hull's research to create a device that could boost the power in a magnetron tube and produce microwaves.

British chemist and mathematician Sir Henry Tizard had been working on radar for several years and knew the crucial importance of this "cavity magnetron." He also knew that his country, torn by war, could produce the device only in limited quantities. England needed the United States. Author Jennet Conant, in her book *Tuxedo Park*, writes: "They had to give the magnetron to the Americans if they wanted them as partners – it would be their dowry in marriage. It was a matter of survival."[16] In spite of his distrust for Americans ("Are we going to throw our secrets into the American lap, and see what they give us in exchange? I am not in a hurry to give our secrets..."),[17] Winston Churchill agreed.

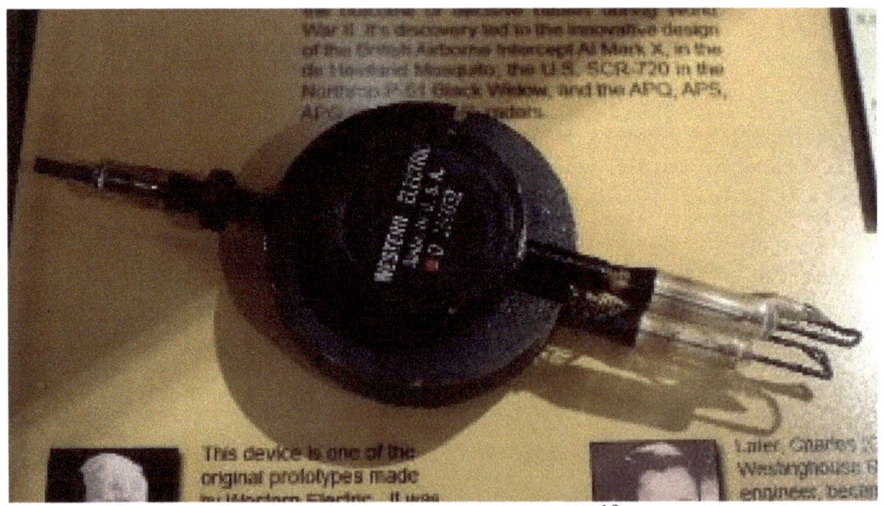
Cavity magnetron. WWII.[18]

In September 1940, Alfred Lee Loomis met with a cautious Henry Tizard. The two men hit it off. The American enthusiastically shared the current status of the country's work on microwaves. So impressed was Tizard with the willingness of the Americans to disclose information that he took a risky leap of faith. He divulged Britain's treasured secret, the cavity magnetron, and Loomis' research took a major leap forward. Plans for American development and production were laid, and a permanent bond was forged between researchers of the two nations.

---

[15] Suits, C.G. and Lafferty, J.M. *Albert Hull.* NAS 1970. tinyurl.com/rw7pu87y.

[16] Conant, Jennet. *Tuxedo Park.*

[17] Shachtman, Tom. *Laboratory Warriors.*

[18] *Cavity magnetron.* Pub domain photo. DSC00280. Nat Electronics Mus. Wiki Commons. tinyurl.com/wtxz9zwv.

One of Loomis' first jobs as Microwave Committee Chairman was to find a location for the research facility. It needed to be a place where scientists bustling in and out would go relatively unnoticed. With Compton, MIT President, and Bush, former MIT Vice-President, the Massachusetts Institute of Technology seemed an obvious choice. Now, Loomis needed a team. A month after the Tizard meeting, MIT hosted a conference on topics ranging from nuclear physics to earth science attended by hundreds of scientists. Behind the scenes, however, Loomis was busily recruiting for the new Radiation Lab. He and Compton gathered in a room at the Algonquin Club in Boston with a dozen or so confused scientists who had been lured away from the conference. The group was sworn to secrecy as they learned that what appeared to be research on long-range radar, a topic already being thoroughly investigated, actually involved a magnetron powerful enough to create microwaves.

MIT Rad Lab members represented a dizzying array of brilliant minds from the world of physics. Lee DuBridge, who had achieved notoriety for constructing a cyclotron at the University of Rochester, was placed in charge of the top-secret Rad Lab. Included were future Nobel laureates Luiz Alvarez from Berkeley, Edward Purcell of Cambridge, Massachusetts, and Columbia's Isadore Rabi, whose interest in every project began with the question, "How many Germans will it kill?"[19] The foundation of the MIT Radiation Lab had been established.

Scientists whose work would contribute to victory in
WWII. Left to right: Ernest Lawrence, Arthur Compton, Vannevar Bush, J.B. Conant, Karl Compton, Alfred Lee Loomis. March 1940.[20]

Shortly afterward, the group settled into their new research facility, a few overcrowded rooms with blackened windows in a building at MIT. Work began on their first project, airborne interception radar. They were going after Germany's night bombers. Loomis' scientists threw themselves at the task, and by December, a device was ready for testing. From a radar unit installed on the roof of the Rad Lab, microwave radar beams shot out across the city of Boston, bounced off the Christian Science Church dome, and successfully landed smack on the rooftop receiver. There were hitches to work out, but the airborne interception radar had worked. By early Spring, the aircraft interception system was ready for flight testing. A B-18 out of Logan Airport flew along the Cape Cod shoreline. With vivid detail, the AI radar detected ships and aircraft.

By now, the Battle of the Atlantic was raging, and aboard the aircraft was Welsh physicist Taffy Bowen, whose interest in submarine detection had led him to involvement with AI. He wondered if airborne microwave radar could find subs. The B-18 swung southwest to New London, and from nearly half a mile above, a handful of submarines appeared on the screen.[21] Air-to-surface vessel radar detection

---

[19] Shavelson, Michael. *Atlantic & Pacific.* COLUMBIA Mag 2010. tinyurl.com/mr32kdhr.

[20] *Lawrence Compton Bush Conant Compton Loomis 3/1940.* Pub domain photo. US DOE. Wikipedia. tinyurl.com/5ejy8773.

[21] Conant, Jennet. *Tuxedo Park.*

(ASV) would soon follow and make a devastating impact on the German navy's Atlantic assault. In the words of U-boat Commander Heinz Schaffer: "It is impossible to tell the story of the U-boat without discussing radar since it turned the tide of the Battle of the Atlantic against us at the most crucial stage of the war. For all the heroism and efficiency of our crews, the power of the U-boat was shattered overnight."[22] The work of Rad Lab scientists on the development of microwave radar systems was so effective that it would lead Lee DuBridge to comment, "Radar won the war; the atom bomb ended it."

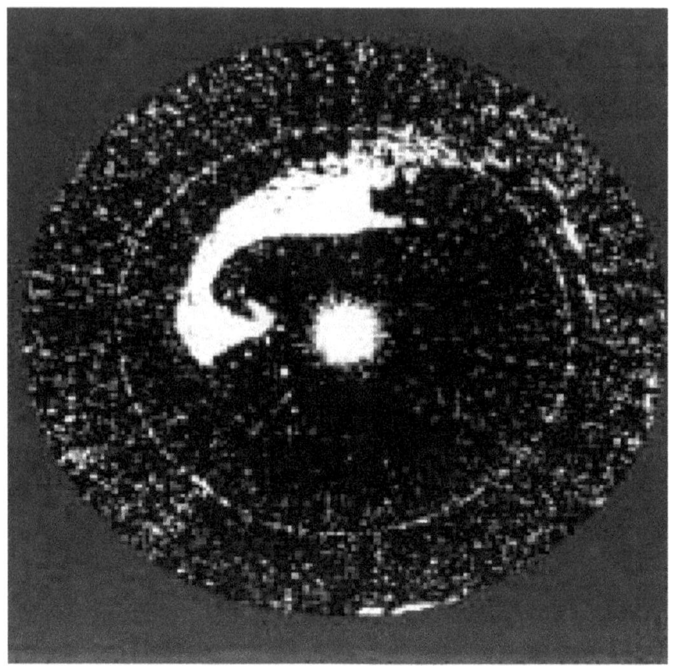

This 1942 image of Cape Cod taken with Rad Lab AI
radar revealed the exact shape of Cape Cod for the first time.
Courtesy of MIT Research Laboratory of Electronics.[23]

Early on, Loomis listed three priority projects to be tackled by the Rad Lab. Next up, after AI, was how to use microwave radar to direct weapons at enemy aircraft. Scientists developed a device that could be mounted on a trailer and detect enemy planes up to 40 miles away with a range accuracy of 75 feet. Dr. David George Briant, in his article about the gun-laying radar, reported on the performance of the first shipments of the SCR-584 system during desperate fighting at Anzio.

Two complete SCR-584s were rushed into the chaos on February 24, 1944, and dug in up to their trailer rooftops overnight. The next darkness saw twelve Nazi bombers entering beachhead air space only to lose seven of them to the 90mm guns directed by SCR-584. Air attacks stopped for a week. A single plane appeared to test the defenses, only to be destroyed. Ten more systems were emplaced that week, and eliminated the air threat to Anzio.[24]

The nearly 2,000 SCR-584s produced during the war made a devastating major impact on the enemy. In London, the radar was so successful that it essentially ended air raids overnight.

---

[22] O'Connell, Jerome *Radar and U-Boat.* USNI 9/1963. tinyurl.com/t4a6vtkr.

[23] *1942 image Cape Cod taken with experimental airborne search and bombing radar developed MIT's Rad Lab.* Photo. Courtesy of MIT RLE 9/8/2008. ethw.org/MIT_Rad_Lab.

[24] Briant, David George. *Chrysler & radar: SCR584 guns.* WPC News. tinyurl.com/57kb93rs.

SCR-584 Radar. 1945.[25]

Rad Lab Project III arose from the inability of pilots to locate themselves. Charts, compasses, and eyesight were used to get a fix on their location. However, that process was frequently inaccurate and nearly impossible at night and in heavy weather. Loomis came up with the idea of a grid spread across the globe with intersecting radio pulses a long-range navigation system. Supervising this crucial research at the Rad Lab was Melville Eastham, founder of the General Radio Company in Cambridge, one of the largest electronic instrumentation producers in the world.

The miracle of LORAN was that it could fix a position up to 700 miles, double that at night, was undetectable by the enemy, and rarely effected by weather. It required master and slave stations on land to send out intersecting signals to receivers on ships and airplanes. Operation of the first chain of this LORAN net, designed to cover the North Atlantic, was delegated to the US Coast Guard. In 1942, Unit 21 was established at the Coast Guard Station in Chatham, Massachusetts.

Unit 21 at Coast Guard Station, Chatham. WWII.[26]

---

[25] *Exterior view SCR-584.* Pub domain photo. NOAA. Wiki Commons. tinyurl.com/32rea2a7.

[26] *Busy year for SPARS.* Pub domain photo. Long Blue Line.USCG Hist Office 3/12/2021. tinyurl.com/cdejcx9z.

LORAN made a stunning impact on the efforts of the Allies in World War II. The Rad Lab, the Chatham station, and others like it provided a new, potent form of radar that could see into the clouds and over horizons, far outstripping the outdated radar of the Axis. It placed a powerful tool in the hands of those who would hunt down and kill our enemies. By the end of the war, seventy stations were in operation, and Navy charts marked LORAN coverage of 50 million square miles, roughly one-third of the planet Earth.

MIT Rad Lab hits just kept on rolling. Luis Alvarez led the search for an invention that could assist pilots in making safe landings during poor visibility. The GCA, ground control approach radar, enabled a man on the ground to talk a pilot through a blind landing. Microwave Early Warning radar (MEW) was capable of tracking aircraft at a distance of approximately 200 miles and improved upon Britain's Chain Home capabilities. In 1943, the Army Air Force was searching for a way to conduct bombing runs in bad weather. Rad Lab researchers designed H2X navigation and bombing radar and established an assembly shop at Logan Airport. So promising were the plans that the Army ordered twenty sets before production was even completed. H2X would prove vital during D-Day when poor weather shrouded the Normandy coastline. Allied bombers using H2X were able to pierce through the clouds to attack enemy coastal fortifications prior to the invasion.[27]

Beyond the walls of the Rad Lab, MIT scientists were busy on a variety of war-related projects. At the government's request, MIT opened one of the first graduate-level programs in meteorology in the country. Nearly 1,000 servicemen and women participated. MIT program director Sverre Pettersen was one of a select group of meteorologists charged with advising weather conditions for D-Day. Noting an abrupt change in the weather pattern over the Atlantic, he predicted that the storm which was impacting the Normandy coastline on June 5, 1944, would soon abate. Eisenhower took advantage of the expected break in the weather to launch the invasion a day later. Apparently, for some residents of Massachusetts, the weather was a big deal. Ten-year-old Joanne McLaughlin of Woburn chopped off her 19" braids after learning that the government was in need of blond hair for weather instruments. McLaughlin's golden tresses made it to Baltimore, where they were used for humidity recordings.[28]

The US Chemical Warfare Service rented a building from the college and, for four years, conducted research involving mustard gas, phosgene, thionyl chloride, and flame thrower fuel.[29] Under the guidance of physicist George Harrison, the MIT Spectroscopy Laboratory worked in coordination with the Manhattan Project and examined thousands of uranium specimens to be used in the development of the atomic bomb.

Not to be outdone, down the road at Harvard, Howard Aiken was working on a research program in the basement of the Cruft Laboratory that involved long and unwieldy calculations. To assist him in his work, he invented a computer. Aiken's Mark I was specifically designed to help with complicated, time-consuming computations. Operating with 750,000 parts, more than 50 feet in length, and weighing in at five tons, Aiken's gigantic calculator was capable of adding complex numbers within seconds. The Mark I was used extensively during World War II, particularly by the US Navy.

One of Harvard's more unusual research facilities was the Harvard Fatigue Laboratory. The facility worked extensively with the Army Quartermaster General to test and develop equipment and materials to be used under extreme conditions. A similar facility, the Climatic Research Laboratory, was located in Lawrence. Nicknamed the "40-40-40 Club," the Harvard Lab tested tolerance and fatigue in

---

[27] Saad, T.A. *MIT Radiation Lab*. IEEF AES Mag 10/1990. CSUS. tinyurl.com/yc2vw5ny.

[28] *Girl Cuts Off Braids*. Boston Globe 10/1/1942. Newspapers.com. tinyurl.com/ktzsrv6t.

[29] Brophy, Leo et al. *Army WWII Technical Service*. GovInfo.gov. tinyurl.com/2d69h2zd.

environments simulating temperatures of -40 degrees Fahrenheit, altitudes of 40,000 feet, and distances of 40 miles.[30]

In 1943, Dr. G. Edgar Folk Jr., born in Natick, raised in Georgetown, and a graduate of Phillips Andover Academy and Harvard, joined the Fatigue Lab and later recalled the work done there during World War II. In order to develop clothing and equipment suitable to cold weather environments, Folk joined soldiers in testing materials in a cold chamber with temperatures between 40 degrees above and 40 degrees below zero. Folk commented, "At the Fatigue Laboratory, we were all subjects in any experiments that we asked the soldiers to endure." Concerned for soldiers having to evacuate barracks in cold climates, Folk and two other subjects donned long woolen underwear and ran in minus 40-degree temperatures for half an hour. During the winter months, which followed the Battle of the Bulge, frostbite and trench foot resulted in hospitalization for 17,000 soldiers. Standard-issue boots were tested, and recommendations for sturdier footwear were made to the Quartermaster General.

Food also fell under the category of equipment. After it was suggested that dehydrated meat such as the pemmican consumed by Inuits might be a good emergency ration, several soldiers were sent to an isolated spot, Pasque Island near Woods Hole, and given nothing but pemmican to eat. On day two, they en masse refused to eat another bite of the delicacy, which caused nausea and left a greasy residue in their mouths. One-hundred percent of subjects developed severe ketosis, and the pemmican idea was discarded.

Dr. Donald Griffin, a resident of Lexington, was a biologist who had spent some of his happiest childhood moments in the Boston Museum of Natural History. He became an expert in chiropterology, the study of bats, and along with a colleague, developed the term "echolocation." His involvement with Harvard led to work on one of the Fatigue Lab's more unusual projects, bat bombs. The plan was to attach incendiary devices to bats and drop them out of airplanes over Japan. The bats were expected to find their way into the straw roofs of local houses before exploding, thus setting Japan on fire. In spite of the fact that Griffin nixed the idea, researchers in Washington actually constructed a Japanese village and tested the furry weapons before suspending the project.[31]

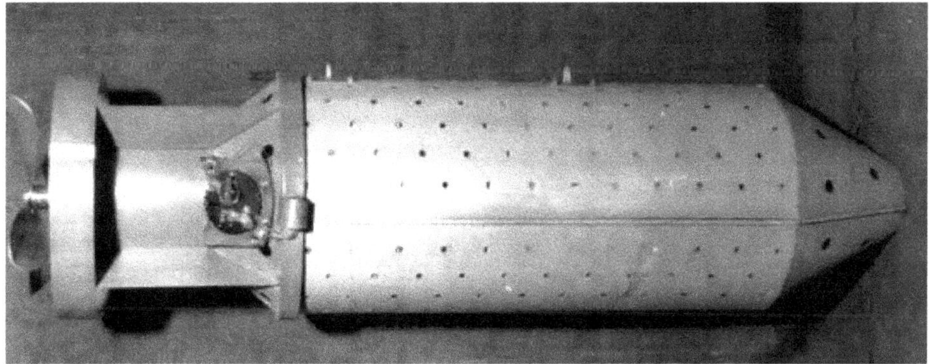

Bat bomb canister. 1942.[32]

There were others in Massachusetts who contributed to the war effort. A company founded by Sam Foster and Bill Grant in Leominster used its sunglass technology to create snow goggles for the military. Robert Van De Graff of Lexington and William Buechner of Arlington created an electrostatic generator that could detect defects in munitions. One of the more remarkable projects involved MIT geology grad and Massachusetts resident Palmer Cosslett Putnam. In 1942, the Army approached Vannevar Bush to ask if his scientists could develop a way to float tanks onto a beach. Bush, whose

[30] Bennett, B.L. *David Bruce Dill.* Wilderness and EnvMed 2006. tinyurl.com/bdfbpzf7.

[31] Folk, G. Edgar, with Thrift, Diana. *Harvard Fatigue Lab.* Advs Physiol Educ. APS 9/1/2010. tinyurl.com/3yc8yvz2.

[32] *Bat bomb canister.* Pub domain photo. USAAF. Wiki Commons. tinyurl.com/36t6d9um.

people had been trying for quite some time to get an army truck to drive through water, turned the problem over to Putman, who approached the well-known naval architecture firm of Sparkman and Stephens (the young Stephens brothers had learned to sail in the waters off Barnstable). Next to join the team was General Motors, which had been working to turn a GMC CCKW ("deuce-and-a-half") into an amphibious vehicle.[33]

Forty-two days later, a model of the first DUKW was completed. The 1942 (D) utility (U) front wheel drive truck (K) had dual rear driving axles (W) and amazingly could operate in water and on land.

Amphibious DUKW. WWII.
Courtesy US Army Transportation Museum[34]

Unfortunately, the odd-looking truck/boat, which could reach speeds of up to fifty miles per hour on land and six miles per hour in the water, was a bust with the Army. Bush and his people, however, were no strangers to the lack of vision on the part of the military. Putnam pushed and prodded, and in early December, a group of non-believers arrived in Provincetown to watch a few DUKWs demonstrate their amphibious prowess. As often happens in New England, a storm slammed into the Cape shortly before showtime, putting the display on hold. Unexpectedly, however, the Coast Guard cutter Rose, on submarine patrol in waters off the Cape, was blown onto a shoal. A DUKW charged in for the rescue, and while the Rose smashed into pieces in the surf, the members of the crew were delivered safely to shore. The storm passed, and a few days later, in high seas, Army officials watched as several DUKWs successfully completed their original mission of loading cargo and arms from a ship off the coast. Back in Washington, photos of the DUKW saving the crew of the Rose made their way into the hands of a highly placed Army official who, the story goes, was delighted to hear reports of Navy personnel being rescued by the Army. The attitude of the military suddenly changed.

Not all DUKW tests were as successful as the Provincetown experiment. Plans to carry tanks while afloat and to load half-tracks atop twin DUKWs were a no-go. In spite of its flaws, the "Duck Boat" became a permanent part of the United States war machine. General George Patton saw its potential and was the first to use it in support of the invasion of Sicily. Eisenhower also had high praise

---

[33] Gerould, Bryan. *GMC DUKW.* Haggerty Media 3/13/2020. tinyurl.com/2s3r8ahr.

[34] *2 ½ Ton DUKW.* Pub domain photo. Courtesy US ATM. 2/6/2024.

for the amphibious vehicle at war's end, calling it "one of the most valuable pieces of equipment produced by the United States during the war."

No discussion of science in war-time Massachusetts would be complete without mention of a Cambridge-based company that specialized in refrigeration. In 1922, Lawrence Marshall, born in Massachusetts and a graduate of Tufts, decided to go into the refrigeration business with another Massachusetts boy, Vannevar Bush. Together, they founded the American Appliance Company. Soon, Texan Charles Grover Smith, a gifted inventor (he would go on to hold more than 150 patents), came on board. Smith developed an interest in tubes and currents and created a radio tube that could switch power from a battery to a household current. A million dollars worth of the product was sold in the first year and revolutionized the home radio industry.[35] By the time he came to Marshall and Bush's notice, Smith was working on rectifier tubes. Recognizing the importance of this work, they welcomed Smith into the business, changed the company's focus, and renamed it Raytheon.

During World War II, Raytheon engaged in several war-related projects. Thanks to Raytheon employee Percy L. Spencer of Waban, the company essentially monopolized the production of magnetron tubes. Supposedly, Dr. Spencer was fiddling with a pile of coins at his desk when he began to wonder if he could stack magnetrons, too. Apparently, he could. By laying a line of solder between them, he could stamp out multiple tubes at one time. Raytheon's mass production of radar tubes was so successful that an estimated 80 percent of all magnetrons used by the Allies in World War II came from Raytheon.[36]

The three scientists would remain in Massachusetts until their passing, Bush in Belmont, Marshall in Cambridge, and Smith in Weston. Raytheon continued its research in microwave technology after the war, developing missile guidance systems and microwave ovens. (Percy Spencer holds the patent for the first microwave, created after he noticed that the nut cluster candy bar carried in his pocket to feed squirrels had unexpectedly melted while working with a radar magnetron.)[37] Today, Raytheon, now RTX, is an international corporation and one of the largest defense contractors in the world.

Physicist Philip M. Morse had directed MIT's Underwater Sound Project for two years. He designed hydrophones for submarine detection and a device that could confuse acoustic mines by imitating the sound of a ship's engine. When the Navy needed new weapons to counteract the U-boat threat, they looked to Harvard's Cruft Laboratory (later known as the Harvard Underwater Sound Laboratory), and Philip Morris was placed in charge. His first task was the development of an acoustic torpedo.

Germany had recently developed the GNAT, the German Naval Acoustic Torpedo, and the Navy was in search of a similar device that was small enough to be carried on an airplane, contained enough explosives to damage but not destroy a submarine, and had a relatively short running time. Several research groups were involved, and Harvard and Bell Labs collaborated on developing the homing system. Secrecy was so important that the project was referred to as the Fido mine (use of the word "torpedo" was prohibited). The resulting Mark 24 torpedo was capable of being dropped from up to 300 feet and could detect submarine noise at a distance of 1,500 feet. In May 1943, early testing by RAF and US Navy pilots resulted in the sinking of two U-boats. Fido was a success, and during the following two years, 15 percent of all submarine sinkings by aircraft involved the action of a Fido torpedo.[38]

[35] *Dr. Charles G. Smith.* Boston Sunday Globe 6/29/1960. tinyurl.com/bdzahmtk.

[36] *Radars tell story of Raytheon Company.* RTX 7/13/2022. tinyurl.com/3yf7tzuj.

[37] Livesay, Jacob. *When was microwave invented?* USA Today 6/24/2022. tinyurl.com/3m3rznck.

[38] Wildenburg, Thomas. *Sub-Hunting Bloodhound.* USNI 10/2017. tinyurl.com/uc8r69mr.

Mark 24 acoustic torpedo (Fido mine). WWII.[39]

Morse soon took on a new role that would significantly change the face of submarine warfare. One year before embarked on a ferry from Delaware to Virginia, he'd witnessed a horrifying sight...a tanker steaming for safe harbor with a ten-foot hole in its side. The hull had been ripped open by a torpedo. The ship was one of the lucky ones. U-boats had turned the Atlantic into a massive killing field, and the ninety-five merchant vessels sunk that month signified not only hundreds of lives lost but thousands of tons of vital shipping as well. Morse came up with a simple question: Had anyone stepped forward to analyze this threat? The answer was yes, but only in the UK.

America faced a steep learning curve in the hunt for enemy submarines. Early in 1942, in spite of dozens of attacks on U-boats in the Atlantic, only a few enemy subs were destroyed. Across the big pond, the British were losing ships, men, supplies, and patience. When an offer arrived from England to share their analytic practices with the Americans, it was rebuffed by Admiral Ernest King, who was known to have an off-and-on relationship with the British. In spite of King's shortsightedness, an American research group was soon formed dedicated to thwarting the U-boat menace with Philip Morse at its head. The mission of Group M was to develop plans to decrease the impact of U-boats on Allied shipping. Morse quickly recruited six people, four of whom were his associates from the Underwater Sound Laboratory at Harvard.

Initially located in Boston, within a year, Group M relocated to Washington and was renamed the antisubmarine Warfare Operations Research Group, ASWORG. At first, there was an irritable rift between soldier and academic, but in spite of it, Morse's group hunkered down with scientific precision to sift through page after page of antisubmarine reports and create a theoretical calculation for how to hunt down and sink a U-boat. They worked with remarkable speed and created the Navy's first search and attack manual within months. Among the group's contributions were recommendations for the operational use of radar in sea search, an increase in convoy size and tactics, minimum depth for detonation of depth charges, and suggestions for fleet operations. So important was their work that in 1943, Admiral King created the Tenth Fleet. Devoid of any ships, its sole mission was to coordinate information, conduct operations research, and make recommendations on how to counter the U-boat menace.

Following the war, Morse received a Presidential Medal of Merit for his work. He returned to MIT, where he remained until 1968. A resident of Winchester, Morse passed away in 1985 at age 82.[40]

---

[39] *MK 24 Fido.* Pub domain photo. US Navy AH 4/1958. Wiki Commons. tinyurl.com/mryvhen5.
[40] *Philip Morse.* NYT 9/13/1985. tinyurl.com/pd2a7z9c.

During the First World War, Germany had used mines with devastating effect. Nearly 500 Allied merchant ships and forty-four British warships were sunk by these explosive devices. With the outbreak of World War II, the British took this threat seriously and used mines extensively. The United States, however, showed little interest. In a post-war report, the US Strategic Bombing Survey stated: "Mines, perhaps more than any other weapon of equal accomplishment, were orphans during the war."[41] It would take the inspiration and enthusiasm of a young scientist from Massachusetts to nudge the United States into the development of mine technology.

Ellis Johnson, a native of Quincy, graduated from MIT with a profound fascination for the effects of magnetism on earth materials. In 1940, the United States tapped Johnson to work in the Naval Ordnance Laboratory in Washington, developing countermeasures to protect Allied shipping from mines. Johnson began work on degaussing or removing the magnetic signature from ships. However, he began to envision the use of mines as an offensive weapon. To work on this problem, he gathered together a group of other like-minded scientists to participate in a series of weekend war games. In a strange coincidence, on one winter weekend in 1941, Johnson and friends were engaged in a scenario that dealt with an aerial attack on a naval base. The date was December 6, and the men were at Pearl Harbor.[42]

Along with British researchers, Johnson and his colleagues would continue to work on the development of mine technology. A US Navy Mine Test Facility was created in Provincetown. Located on Bradford Street, the installation was responsible for testing this ordnance and, like Georges Island in Boston Harbor, for storing and distributing mines.[43] By the end of the war, Allied mines could be programmed to target specific types of vessels and were capable of arming themselves. In 1943, using intelligence information, researchers created countermeasures for newly developed German acoustic mines before the enemy was able to put them into use.

At the far southwestern corner of Cape Cod, the little village of Woods Hole was undergoing major changes. Woods Hole Oceanographic Institute Director Columbus Iselin had approached the National Defense Research Committee with ideas on how Woods Hole could help with the war effort, and in 1941, the Navy came to town. Barbed wire was thrown up around buildings, privately owned pleasure and fishing craft disappeared from the waterfront, and the Nantucket ferry was painted a drab gray. Not far from the harbor, pigeon coops sprung up to house carrier pigeons used by the Navy for communications.

Judith Stetson, in her work on Woods Hole in World War II, recalled some of the Institute's accomplishments. Athelstan Spilhaus went to work on a device that could measure underwater temperatures to a depth of several hundred feet. For submarines, because sonar detection was possible only within a certain temperature range, Spilhaus and his colleagues developed the bathythermograph.

<hr>

[41] Chilstrom, John *Mines Away!* SAAS, AU, Maxwell AFB 5/1992. tinyurl.com/bdeh7byx.

[42] Page, Thornton, et al. *Ellis Johnson.* Op Res 1974. *JSTOR.* www.jstor.org/stable/169994.

[43] *Mine Fac Provincetown.* ProPublica: Bombs Backyard Series 2015. tinyurl.com/49efakj8.

The bathythermograph was attached to a long cord and dropped off the side of a boat. As it sunk downwards, an internal needle scratched a line on a piece of glass, representing the temperature relative to water depth.[44]

While not the most popular project at WHOI (the slides used to record temperatures were smeared with skunk oil), the top-secret bathythermograph was used extensively by submarines during the war to fire torpedoes with greater accuracy and to basically hide from enemy sonar on a temperature shelf under water.

Other Woods Hole projects dealt with the acoustics of sea bottom sediment on the Atlantic and Gulf coasts, sound velocity and projection of explosion noise across ocean basins, and placement of hydrophones in harbors. Dr. George Clarke was engaged in multiple projects, including the development of anti-fouling paint, life raft drift, and using plankton as an emergency food source. Ship wakes (some illuminated by bioluminescent organisms) were a concern for the Navy, as they were detectable by aircraft in sun or moon light. Clarke came up with the idea that streaming smoke from the back of a boat might mix with the wake, decreasing its brightness. To test out his hypothesis, he borrowed Director Iselin's craft, the Risk. Things got a bit dicey when the Risk crashed into a buoy, smashing a huge hole in her side. With water gushing in, Clarke decided to beach the boat on Nonamessett Island in the Vineyard Sound. Safely stuck in the sand, he went in search of a telephone, leaving his two young sons (who feared the island might be inhabited by cannibals) with an assistant. The Risk was eventually towed back to Woods Hole. No one was injured, no cannibals were sighted, and Iselin graciously commented that there was a bit of dry rot on the vessel that needed replacing anyway. To Clarke's dismay, while awaiting repair, the Risk was left in a boat yard a few feet from Main Street, where the hole in the hull and his nautical prowess were on full display for anyone walking by.[45]

One year prior to the war's end, the Great Atlantic Hurricane of 1944 swept through Woods Hole, damaging buildings and tossing the Institute's 142-foot research vessel, Atlantis, so badly that the captain beached her on the Ram Island mud flats where she remained for three weeks.[46] WHOI survived the storm and the war and would rebuild and refocus. The US Navy continued to rely on the Institute's work in the field of oceanography and underwater research vessels. Today, Woods Hole Oceanographic Institute carries out its mission in association with the National Oceanographic and Atmospheric Administration (NOAA).

With the end of the war on the horizon, the new story in town became nuclear weapons, and Rad Lab scientists began migrating to Los Alamos and another top-secret program, the Manhattan Project. Gone were George Kistiakowsky, Hans Bethe, Kenneth Bainbridge, and Luis Alvarez. The work of the

---

[44] *Bathythermograph.* Pub domain photo. Tara M. Bell. USCA. tinyurl.com/mr27u5aw.

[45] Stetson, Judith *Woods Hole WWII.* Woods Hole Hist Mus. tinyurl.com/7txdx44s.

[46] Thayer, Mary. *Atl Hurricane 1944.* Photo caption. WHOI 9/5/2010. tinyurl.com/yc5eet42.

Rad Lab had become less relevant, and in August 1945, the doors to the MIT facility swung open, and the secrets of the MIT Rad Lab were shared with the public. Karl Compton resigned as President of MIT in 1948 to join Truman's postwar board aimed at guiding scientific research and development. After twenty years as Harvard President, James Bryant Conant became Ambassador to West Germany and participated in the reconstruction of the remnants of the fallen fatherland.

When the Rad Lab passed into history, Alfred Lee Loomis slowly began to fade away. Described by Luis Alvarez as "the last great amateur of science," Loomis left behind an amazing bulk of work. He held nearly a dozen patents ranging from gadgets such as a shoe tree, race car toy, and fishing net to chronographs and centrifuges, all the way to one of World War II's most monumental inventions, the LORAN. For the remainder of his life, he avoided involvement with government committees but continued to dabble in and fund projects of interest to him. Loomis never went back to work at his Tuxedo Park laboratory and passed away in 1975 at the age of 87. Dr. Kenneth Suslick, in his article about ultrasonics, stated: "Alfred Lee Loomis was the most important scientist of the twentieth century who almost no one has ever heard of. And from all accounts, Loomis wanted it that way."[47]

Over fifty percent of the radar used by the Allies during World War II was created at the MIT Radiation Laboratory. Nearly 4,000 people contributed to the production of over 100 different radar systems, representing $1.5 billion in radar equipment.[48] The extraordinary accomplishments of the Rad Lab were made possible by the foundation it rested upon...Loomis' freewheeling style, Conant's view that "to advance scientific knowledge, pick a man of genius, give him money, and let him alone,"[49] and Vannevar Bush's iron-clad belief that scientists "...must have independence and the opportunity to explore the bizarre."[50] The result was a free exchange of ideas unfettered by the constraints of bureaucracy and the rigidity of the military. Henry Guerlac, in his work on the history of radar, described it best when he wrote: "...the Radiation Laboratory came close to realizing a scientist's dream of a scientific republic, whose only limitation was the supply of scientists."[51]

The accomplishments of the scientists of Massachusetts during World War II are nothing short of astounding. The world was at war, their countrymen were dying, and they felt compelled to make a contribution. Australian Paul Bricknell, in his work, *The Great Escape*, wrote: "...an American only has to be sold on the idea that his cause is just and he is capable of anything."[52] Apparently, he was right.

---

[47] Suslick, Kenneth *Ultrasonics & Palace Science.* UIUC. Acoustics Today 2019. tinyurl.com/4ufem4rc.

[48] Saad, T.A. *MIT Radiation Lab.*

[49] Saad, T.A. *MIT Radiation Lab.*

[50] Bush, Vannevar. *Pieces of Action.* 1970. Goodreads. tinyurl.com/f6e3xe9a.

[51] Conant, Jennet. *Tuxedo Park.*

[52] Brickhill, Paul. *Great Escape.* W. W. Norton & Co 8/17/2004.

Chapter 8

Bridge of Ships

They faced death every mile of the way...
Marshal Georgi K. Zhukov

Early in January 1942, the body of Danish mariner Birger Oest-Larsen washed up on a beach on the Isle of Colonsay in western Scotland. It was not an unusual event. With war raging in Europe, the Atlantic had become a killing field, and Oest-Larsen's ship was another victim, sent to the bottom over a thousand miles away by a German sub. Sadly, when found, the man's body was still warm. He had endured the frigid waters of the North Atlantic for fifty-three days before succumbing.

There would be only one survivor to tell the tale of the Panamanian vessel, Crusader, that sailed under the control of the United States Maritime Commission. The ship had begun its last journey at Cape Breton, Nova Scotia, and headed eastward to join Convoy SC53. Ten days later, on November 14, 1941, she was torpedoed by a German sub and sunk.[1] With the exception of Oest-Larsen, the entire crew was lost, including 19-year-old Oskar Horowitz from Cambridge, Massachusetts.[2] His country was not at war; his fellow crewmen were nearly all Scandinavian or Canadian, and yet the young man had died aboard a ship in the service of his country. Oskar Horowitz was a Merchant Marine.

The men who served on merchant ships during the Second World War are the stuff of legend. They were men of the sea, ranging in age from 16 to 72, who stepped up to serve their country and her Allies long before bombs dropped on Pearl Harbor. They were not members of the military, nor did they receive benefits from their government. As author Felix Reisenberg points out, in the early days of the war, their fellow Americans considered Merchant Mariners "bums," whose lives were filled with "rotgut whisky and waterfront brawls."[3] Yet these men courageously braved the seas by the thousands, putting their lives at risk to provide the materials and equipment needed to wage war, and the seas ran red with their blood.

The story of the Merchant Marines is especially important to Massachusetts, a state well-known for its maritime history. Vessels from across the globe traveled to local ports carrying exotic cargoes like porcelain from China, silks from Hong Kong, and the tea, which launched a war of independence. In Boston, Salem, Newburyport, and Quincy, clipper ships rolled down the ways and into history, and by 1841, fierce Yankee whalers had made New Bedford the whaling capital of the world.

In 1914, the Great War erupted in Europe, an event that helped to enrich the coffers of American commerce. Commercial shipping assumed a new importance as the value of US exports rose by 3.8 billion dollars.[4] Goods and materials poured out of the country and headed across the Atlantic toward our Allies. In 1915, in an effort "to promote the welfare of American seamen in the merchant marine of the United States," Congress passed the Seamen's Act. It was a given that the trials of life at sea could be appalling. (Never one to be bothered by controversial statements, First Lord of the Admiralty Winston Churchill famously described life in his own Royal Navy as "rum, sodomy, and the lash.") Troubling incidents on both commercial and military vessels prompted an attempt by the US Navy to curtail

---

[1] *Mysterious Loss SS Crusader.* AMM at War 4/7/2008. USMM.org. tinyurl.com/2r2bcvjv.

[2] Howland, Ronald. *MA MMs Gave All WWII.* Made in USA. Monee IL 4/20/2022.

[3] Geroux, William. *MMs Unsung Heroes.* Smithsonian Mag 5/27/2016. tinyurl.com/yuta2jra.

[4] Michon, Heather. *US Economy WWI.* WWI Cent Comm 8/19/2019. tinyurl.com/yn5xyss8.

punishments such as flogging and tar and feathering, and in 1855, court-martial was introduced as an alternative. Even controversial Captain 'Hell Roaring' Mike Healy was suspect. Healy, who had attended Holy Cross in Worcester and lived in Boston for a time, was the first African American Coast Guard ship captain. He was court-martialed twice for brutality. Acquitted in 1890, he was found guilty at his second trial in 1896 and temporarily removed from command.[5]

"Hell Roaring" Mike Healy.[6]

In addition to physical discipline, merchant mariners were the only civilians at risk of imprisonment or hanging for desertion if they failed to fulfill their contracts. The 1915 Seamen's Act, which ostensibly was designed to protect merchant seamen against these evils, was undeniably designed to ensure seamen's continued flow into the merchant fleet and, thus, dollars into the coffers of American commerce. By the end of World War I, US profits had increased by 41 percent.[7]

Two days before Britain declared war on Germany, the United States merchant fleet consisted of roughly 1,300 dry cargo vessels and tankers, and America was in a bind. As long as isolationists held sway over public opinion, the United States was not expected to see armed conflict anytime soon. However, the country had begun to flex its industrial muscle in an effort to aid Britain and her allies. The US could make the goods and materials needed for the war in Europe, but could we deliver them?

In an effort to bulk up the merchant fleet, the US Maritime Commission was created. Millions were spent on the construction of vessels for commercial transport of such specifications as to make them usable by the US Navy should the necessity arise. The president was granted power to seize (with compensation) foreign ships lying idle in US waters, which was not much of a controversy as, by 1940, many merchant vessels had already anchored in American safe harbors rather than returning home to a country at war. The Ships Warrant Act was a clever piece of legislation by which foreign vessels entered into an agreement placing them at the disposal of the United States in return for priority use of docking and repair facilities as well as monetary compensation. The sale of maritime vessels to foreign governments required authorization from the Maritime Commission. Infrastructure was beefed up. At the Boston Terminal, repair expenses in 1940 increased by 40 percent over the previous year. Gantry cranes were installed, and the harbor near the docking area was dredged. As a result, net revenues of $10,000 in 1940 expanded to $101,000 in 1941.[8]

Preparation of men to sail the ships was also required, and the government established several training schools across the country. A few facilities were already in existence by the time war broke out.

[5] O'Toole, James. *Case Capt Healy.* Prologue Mag 1997. NARA. tinyurl.com/4puz9hed.

[6] *Michael Healy.* Pub domain photo. 190515-G-G0000-3001 USCG. tinyurl.com/3ksthp4x.

[7] *Exports Before After War.* FRB 10/1/1919. NBER 1/2005. tinyurl.com/47fm3ayf.

[8] *US Maritime Comm 10/25/1941.* House Document 554. FMC 2019. tinyurl.com/3duz8wb9.

The Massachusetts Nautical Training School opened in 1891 in Boston with its first class of forty students. In 1942, now known as the Massachusetts Maritime Academy, the campus was relocated to Hyannis, and students completed their course of study in sixteen months rather than the usual two years. After the war, the Academy would once again move this time to Buzzards Bay to accommodate their new World War II surplus training vessel, the USS Charleston, whose 13' draft was too much for Hyannis Harbor.[9]

Massachusetts Maritime Academy training ship
USS Charleston at the state pier, Cape Cod Canal. Late 1940s.[10]

On tiny Gallops Island in Boston Harbor, a former quarantine hospital for the port of Boston was used by the United States Maritime Service as a radio training school. In the summer of 1940, the first group of trainees, 500 former members of the Civilian Conservation Corps, arrived on the island to begin Merchant Marine radio training.[11] Several thousand Merchant Marines would pass through Gallops Island before the war's end. An interesting event occurred in April of 1944 when Georgia Mae Harp was voted "Life Boat Girl" by the Merchant Marine Cadets of Gallops Island. Chosen as the girl they would most prefer to be stranded on an island with, Georgia Mae of Walpole, known as the "Singing Cowgirl," hosted her own morning show on WBZ.[12]

A listing of merchant ships engaged with the enemy in the North Atlantic paints a grim picture of the escalation of events prior to America's declaration of war. During the years 1939 and 1940, of the eight ships listed which came into contact with German U-boats, all were released, and no crew member was harmed. By August 1941, nearly all ships were reported as damaged or sunk by torpedoes after encountering U-boats, most with the loss of multiple members of the crew.[13]

Cargo ships weren't the only vessels at risk. In October 1941, the tugboat Turecamo Boys out of New York put into Boston to avoid heavy seas offshore. She was bound for a northern naval base, carrying a small tug on her deck and towing a barge loaded with oil.[14] The crew of the Turecamo Boys, including Charles Ross Brown of Boston,[15] would never see home again. There is no record of her last moments in the North Atlantic during the early weeks of November, and speculation about the cause of the tugboat's loss ran from bad weather to U-boats. It was an oft-repeated story. Largely overlooked in the images of World War II, these seafaring workhorses went everywhere that surface ships did but were

---

[9] *MA Maritime Athletics.* MMA. tinyurl.com/3ed463je.

[10] *State pier CC Canal 1940s.* Pub domain photo. NH 77120. NHHC. tinyurl.com/mr3jyhpa.

[11] *CCC Boys Train Gallops Isl.* Boston Globe 6/14/1940. Newpapers.com. tinyurl.com/4mm8asvn.

[12] *Georgia Mae Life Boat Girl.* Boston Globe 4/9/1944. Newpapers.com. tinyurl.com/6je8fce4.

[13] *Ships Sunk, Damaged, Detained, No. Atlantic WWII.* AMM at War. tinyurl.com/y8h2de75.

[14] *Port of Boston 10/1.* Boston Globe 10/1/1941. Newspapers.com. tinyurl.com/2vv8cx99.

[15] Howland, Ronald. *MA MMs Gave All WWII.*

much easier targets, moving slower than other vessels and often towing ships behind them. While they were assigned to convoys, they frequently fell behind, leaving them unprotected.

A tugboat takes charge of the destroyer USS Earle after launching from the Boston Navy Yard.[16]

At home, merchant tugboats were essential to shipyards, moving vessels in and out of the harbor for docking and repairs, assembling convoys, and often rescuing ships in open water after U-boat attacks. Even this stateside activity put tugboats at risk during wartime. The John R. Williams was lost after striking a German mine near Cape May. Four Massachusetts men went down with her.[17] One of the most famous tugs, the Luna, built for the Boston Tow Boat Company in 1930, was a familiar sight along the Boston waterfront. She was one of the first tugboats to operate with a diesel-electric engine and one of the last to be constructed with a wooden hull. During World War II, the commercially owned vessel was taken by the US Navy and worked extensively with the Boston Navy Yard. Famous for being the tug that moved the USS Constitution into her final berth in Charlestown, Luna, the last American wood-hulled tugboat and a National Historic Landmark, is docked at Commonwealth Pier in South Boston.[18]

Not all ships traveled the North Atlantic route. The Astral, owned by the Socony Mobil Company and flying the American flag, went down on December 2, 1941, after being torpedoed somewhere in waters off Spain. On board were Joseph Bosse (Fitchburg), John Browne (West Newton), Burton Webberson (Readville), Harry Wescott (Fall River), and Charles Woods (Boston). The story of the Astral is a tale of tragedy and retribution, and her loss is shrouded in mystery. No records of her sinking exist, and no crewmen survived to tell her story. Piecing the events of her voyage together, it is known that she traveled from the Caribbean to Lisbon bearing 78,000 barrels of fuel[19] but never made it to her destination. She most likely arrived somewhere west of the Spanish coast, an area heavily populated by Allied ships seeking to deliver supplies to North Africa and a hunting ground for U-boats. The log of German sub-U-43 under the command of Wolfgang Lueth indicates torpedoes fired on December 2 scored a double hit on a tanker fitting Astral's description.

As the days and months passed, no identifying debris washed ashore, no survivors stepped forward, and eventually, the ship was declared lost. A year and a half after her disappearance and approximately 500 miles away, U-43 would join the Astral in death with all hands aboard, compliments of US Navy fighter aircraft. By that time, however, Wolfgang Lueth was no longer a member of the crew. He had become somewhat of a hero and risen through the ranks to assume command of the Naval School at Flensburg, Germany. In May 1945, as the Third Reich crumbled, Lueth, who had fired on and sunk a

[16] *USS Earle*. Pub domain photo. USN NY23168-40. NPS. NavSource. tinyurl.com/4rsz2bdr.

[17] *John R. Williams Tug*. Uboat.net. tinyurl.com/y8cx85h2.

[18] *Luna*. NPS. www.nps.gov/nr/travel/maritime/lun.htm.

[19] Howland, Ronald. *MA MMs Gave All WWII*.

vessel whose country had yet to declare war, murdering thirty-seven souls in the process, was shot and killed by one of his own sentries.[20]

Although with much less frequency, merchant shipping along the Pacific coastline drew the attention of Japanese subs. Two weeks after Pearl Harbor, the merchant tanker Emidio was torpedoed off the California coast. In spite of the surrender flag waved by Emidio's captain, gunfire struck crewmen in the process of lowering a lifeboat. Rescue was hampered when the sub twice attempted to ram a Coast Guard vessel trying to assist the Emidio. Approximately seventy-five other vessels would sustain damage or be lost off Alaska and the west coast of the US during the war.[21]

SS Emidio crashed into rocks and sank off
California coast after being torpedoed. 1942.[22]

The wide expanse of the Pacific Ocean, roughly twenty million square miles larger than the Atlantic, meant that vessels were less likely to encounter enemy ships. When they did, however, the experience was equally horrific. The John A. Johnson was carrying supplies, ammunition, and explosives from San Francisco to Hawaii in October 1944 when she was struck by two torpedoes. Young Harold Clark, a seaman aboard the Johnson, recalled what happened after abandoning the ship for a life raft.

The ship was now in two separate sections. We paddled away from the bow of the ship. We saw an object about three hundred feet away from us. We signaled the object, thinking it was another raft, and it returned the signal. It came to the surface and turned out to be the submarine, and it started coming toward us. About one hundred and fifty feet from us, the submarine machine-gunned us. I could see tracers going over our heads. We jumped into the water. The submarine passed by about one hundred and fifty feet. We swam back and got on the raft. The submarine circled and came back at us again. We dove into the water again. This time, the submarine hit the raft, and as it passed by, they fired again with machine guns, tracers hitting the water near me...Men on the submarine were yelling 'Bonzi' and cursing at us[23].

Ten members of the crew lost their lives. Thankfully, Arthur Miles of Malden, Richard Duest of Watertown, and John Considine of New Bedford survived.[24]

One terrifying aspect of war never experienced by Atlantic mariners was the Divine Wind. In October 1944, the Japanese, facing a declining number of aircraft and possible defeat, resorted to suicide missions. Kamikaze pilots, human bombs, successfully struck over 100 Allied ships in the Pacific.

---

[20] Gordon, Arthur. *Day Astral Vanished.* USNI 10/1965. tinyurl.com/4wz864vz.

[21] *Merchant Ships Sunk Damaged WWII.* USMM.org 1/21/2004. tinyurl.com/2zpezn2w.

[22] *NH 89910* 1942. Pub domain photo. NHHC. Picryl. tinyurl.com/7edurjmv.

[23] *Sunk By Submarine 1944.* Eyewitness to Hist 1999. tinyurl.com/ynr6ds9x.

[24] *Sub Rammed Lifeboats.* Boston Globe 1/20/1945. Newspapers.com. tinyurl.com/53sznuux.

USS Bunker Hill hit by two Kamikazes in 30
seconds off Kyushu, killing 372. 11 May 1945.[25]

In his book *Fragments of War,* Massachusetts Marine veteran of the Pacific conflict Bertram Yaffee recounted a conversation with Warrant Officer Martin Newton as their LST was approaching the shores of Iwo Jima. Newton stated: "The problem is, it isn't enough to hit the damn kamikazes. You have to <u>destroy</u> them. They're so fuckin' close and low and on a direct line for you. Even if you hit the bastard, he can still take you with him. That's what he came for."[26]

Merchant shipping was a rich target. The Gilbert Stuart had just delivered her cargo of fuel and five hundred troops to the Philippines when she was slammed by a kamikaze in 1944. While the ship did not sink, the cargo ignited, and eleven men on board were killed, among them Richard Daly of Haverhill. In January 1945, the Lewis L. Dyche, carrying ammunition near the Philippines, was hit by a kamikaze and simply disappeared. Michael Moriarity of Holyoke was lost along with the rest of the crew. On April 6, 1945, the Logan Victory arrived in waters off Okinawa. Kamikazes swarmed the skies, and one struck the vessel as she lay at anchor, her hold loaded with ammunition, causing catastrophic damage. The ship remained afloat while explosions continued to rock the ship, but she was deemed a danger to other

---

[25] *Bunker Hill Kamikazes 5/11/1945.* Pub domain photo. NAID 520678. NARA. tinyurl.com/yakva89x.

[26] Yaffe, Bertram A. *Fragments of War.* USNI Press 1999.

vessels nearby and was deliberately sunk. Among the dead was Edison Cates of Edgartown, Captain of the Logan Victory.[27]

On January 13, 1942, Alex K. McLeod of Newtonville lost his life along with thirty other members of the crew aboard the Friar Rock. The merchant vessel had been assigned to a convoy heading across the North Atlantic but fell behind and was returning to port in Newfoundland. Just before 10:00 a.m., the ship was torpedoed by U-130 and sunk approximately 100 miles south of Cape Race. The Friar Rock was unarmed.

Three weeks later, the W.L. Steed, a tanker carrying crude oil, met the same fate east of Delaware. After being struck by two torpedoes, the ship sank quickly, leaving four lifeboats afloat in rough seas during a snowstorm. Of the thirty-eight men aboard, eight were from Massachusetts. Second mate Sydney Wayland of Winthrop and Seaman Ralph Mazzucco, a native of Massachusetts, survived. Elmer Maihiot Jr. of Melrose was the Second Assistant Engineer on the W.L. Steed and the last crewman to be removed from a life raft. Unfortunately, he passed away three days later. Massachusetts native Ernest Hawkins, Oliver Andrade of New Bedford, Harold McAvenia (Greenbush), Joseph Santosuosso (Dorchester), and Francis Wagner (Roslindale) all lost their lives. Like the Friar Rock, the W.L. Steed carried no weapons.[28]

According to the tenets of the Neutrality Pact of 1939, carrying arms on neutral merchant ships was prohibited. However, the carnage in the North Atlantic continued, and the United States was unwilling to simply do nothing. In the fall of 1941, Congress approved a plan for placing weapons on merchant vessels. The process, heavily steeped in Navy bureaucracy, went grindingly slow. Unfortunately for the Friar Rock and W.L. Steed, the plan had taken too long, and the ships went down unprotected. Eventually, 145,000 guards and communication specialists, along with 53,000 weapons, were placed aboard merchant vessels.[29]

With the passage of the Merchant Marine Act in 1936, the government ordered the construction of fifty ships to expand America's merchant fleet. However, as the Battle of the Atlantic raged, it became clear that if the country was to be the arsenal of democracy, more ships would be needed. (Admiral Nimitz commented on the importance of merchant marines to the war effort: "A bridge of ships is the short line to Tokyo.") The plan was to produce ships faster than the Germans could sink them, and $350 million dollars was allocated for the merchant navy. Ships constructed with government funds would be chartered out to private merchants and operated for war-related business while sailing under the American flag.

One type of vessel, the T2 tanker, became famous because of its fatal design flaw. Between 1943 and 1945, ten of the 523 T2s built were lost due to shell fracture. The USS Schenectady broke open on a cold morning in January 1943, and the USS Ponaganset ruptured while moored dockside in Boston. The Pendleton, launched in Oregon in 1944, sailed the North Atlantic as part of a convoy and survived the war. She would become a Cape Cod landmark after foundering during a storm in February of 1952 ten miles off Chatham and cracking in half, leaving her stern protruding from the water. In a strange coincidence, the Fort Mercer had gone down earlier the same day, 30 miles southeast of Chatham. The T2 had broken into two pieces, her bow sinking below the waves, taking five members of the crew with her.[30]

---

[27] Howland, Ronald. *MA MMs Gave All WWII.*

[28] *W.L. Steed.* Uboat.net. tinyurl.com/4urdem4t.

[29] *Merchant Ships Armed Guard.* USN Admin WWII. Ibiblio. tinyurl.com/3utex7vv.

[30] *Pendleton.* Mass.gov. tinyurl.com/bdt4dkhu.

USS Ponaganset at General Ship and Iron Works in
Boston after breaking in half. December 9, 1947.[31]

Pendleton sinking. February 1952.[32]

Another more successful vessel design was also approved. Apparently, the profile of the Liberty Ship was a bit offensive to the president, an amateur sailor, who promptly nicknamed it "the Ugly Duckling." A miracle of production occurred, the US turning out over 2,700 Liberty ships over the next few years. Capable of carrying 10,000 tons, the first Liberty ship took nearly eight months to build, a record that would be smashed in 1942 when the Patrick E. Peary was completed in four days, fifteen hours, and thirty minutes. However, the bulky, slow-moving Liberty ships soon proved to be easy targets, leading to the development of faster, larger Victory ships.

---

[31] *USS Ponaganset* 12/9/1947. Public domain photo. USN. NavSource Online. tinyurl.com/hekxkzp9.

[32] *Pendleton Sinking.* Pub domain photo. USCG. Wiki Commons. tinyurl.com/yeymjwvy.

A miracle of American industrial might. A line
of Victory ships waiting for launch. Ca. 1944.[33]

The recently constructed Sumner I. Kimball, owned by the Mystic SS Company of Boston, was traveling home across the North Atlantic when she fell behind her convoy. Just after dawn on January 16, 1944, the Liberty ship was detected by German sub U-960 under the command of Oberleutnant Gunther Heinrich. Over the next several hours, seven torpedoes were fired, in the midst of which the gallant captain, Harry Atkins of East Boston, attempted to ram the sub. Four torpedoes hit their mark, and the ship and her crew held out until 3:15 a.m. on the 17th when, dead in the water, the Kimball broke in half. When it was ordered back to the site in daylight, U-960 spotted the forward section of the vessel, fired one torpedo, and sank it.[34] The tough Liberty ship refused to die, however, and the stern of the Sumner I. Kimball was located the following day. By then, however, all sixty-nine members of the crew were gone, including twenty-nine souls from Massachusetts.[35]

Four months later, while operating in Mediterranean waters, U-960 came to periscope depth to find herself in the midst of a convoy. A chase ensued, and on May 18, the attack began. Survivors recalled hearing seventy-six depth charge explosions over a three-hour period. The sub began taking on water, and the engine shut down. Heinrich ordered the engine compartment sealed off, called all crew forward, and ordered the tanks blown. U-960 shot to the surface. What awaited was a line of seven destroyers.

According to the 1944 secret U-960 Interrogation Report, the attack lasted forty-two hours. At one point, Heinrich climbed to the conning tower to wave his white cap, only to be blown overboard. The final moment came with a volley of depth charges from the USS Niblack, the destroyer that had fired the first American shots of the Battle for the Atlantic three years earlier.[36] U-960 slipped beneath the waves along with thirty-one members of her crew. Gunther Heinrich, however, was not among them. Only 24 years old at the time, he was well-liked by his men and said to be an able commander, cool-headed during battle. His charm, however, escaped those who interrogated him after his capture. "...Heinrich reacted in a very stiff and haughty manner and was considered as undesirable a Nazi as had yet been encountered."[37] It didn't matter, though. U-960 was gone, her captain would spend the rest of the war as a prisoner, and the men of the Sumner I. Kimball had been avenged.

---

[33] *Victory ships 1944.* Pub domain photo. NARA 208-YE-2B7. Wikipedia. tinyurl.com/3a3ajpuu.

[34] *Sumner I. Kimball.* Uboat.net. tinyurl.com/4t8jajmz.

[35] Howland, Ronald. *MA MMs Gave All WWII.*

[36] *Pre-U.S. Entry WWII.* NMUSN. NHHC. tinyurl.com/jyubxhy8.

[37] *Interrogation Survivors U-960.* USN CNO 9/15/1944. U-boat Arch. tinyurl.com/5fyr4xkx.

For the men of the Merchant Marines, being torpedoed was such a common occurrence (one seaman was torpedoed ten times) that the head of the Boston Seamen's Club created the 40-Fathom Club for those who lived through the experience.[38] Perhaps most dangerous of all merchant marine ships were those whose cargo literally turned them into floating bombs. Ammunition and explosives were so powerful that when disaster struck, ships simply ceased to exist. The Mary Luckenback, carrying TNT on the run to Murmansk in Russia in 1942, basically vaporized after being torpedoed. Four Massachusetts mariners, along with the rest of the crew, were lost.[39]

Tankers were especially dangerous as they ferried, on average, 140,000 barrels of kerosene, gasoline, and a variety of petroleum products. One of the ironies of these tankers is that despite their tendency to explode once hit, due to the presence of many compartments, they were relatively difficult to sink when empty. This was not the case with the tanker Jacksonville, however, which was nearing her destination in August 1944 when she was torpedoed just north of the Irish coast. She was carrying 141,000 barrels of gasoline. Within seconds, flames covered the ship, spewing fire 300 feet into the air. In less than five minutes, the tanker split in half. Two Massachusetts seamen went down with the Jacksonville.[40] Frank Hodges, a fireman on board, was one of two from the crew of eighty to survive. He later described the horror of the death of a tanker.

I ran on deck and found the ship enveloped in flames and smoke. I tried to reach the boat deck, but a wall of fire roared up in front of me...In a few seconds, the flames were coming at me there, and the smoke was so thick I could hardly breathe. I jumped over the side, and when I came to the surface, there was fire around me in the water...Flames on the ship were shooting higher than the masts. I heard men screaming. There were some bodies floating around, but they were all badly burned.

For many who survived the explosion of a tanker, excruciating burns awaited as they jumped off ships into flaming oil-soaked water. For others, it meant death. Frank Terry was aboard the W.D. Anderson as it went down.

Suddenly, there was an explosion. I knew it must be a torpedo. There were flames almost instantly. They blocked the way to my boat station, so I ran to the side and jumped over. When I came to the surface and looked back, the ship was a mass of flames, and burning oil was pouring out of the tanks onto the sea. I swam away from the oil as hard as I could...The heat from the burning oil was intense...I didn't see any of my shipmates alive in the water. I think they were trapped aboard the ship.

Frank Terry, twenty-three years old, was the sole survivor of the W.D. Anderson.[41]

---

[38] Geroux, William. *MMs Unsung Heroes WWII.*

[39] Howland, Ronald. *MA MMs Gave All WWII.*

[40] *Jacksonville.* Uboat.net. tinyurl.com/yjvszz33.

[41] Bunker, John. *Heroes in Dungarees.* USNI Press 1995.

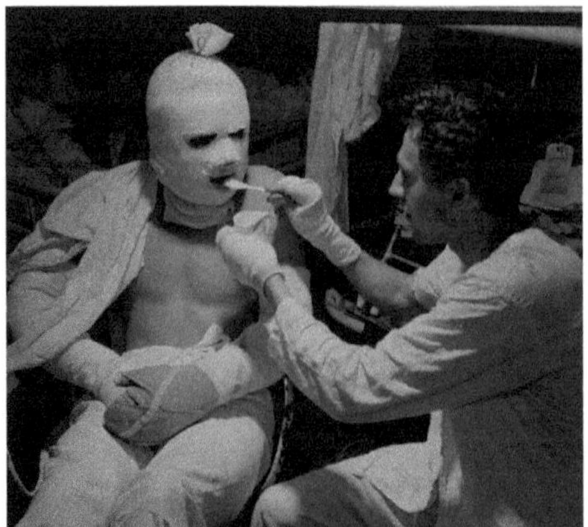

Burn victims from a kamikaze attack on their ship. WWII.[42]

For ships, being in port did not guarantee safety either. Ports in war zones were always high on the list of enemy targets. On December 2, 1943, the British-held port of Bari, Italy was savagely attacked, resulting in one of the most costly shipping losses of the war. Moored along the docks were several American merchant ships with US Navy guards aboard.

Gabriel Casavant of Oxford, a fireman and water tender in the Merchant Marines, was there. He would later describe his experience that night as "forty minutes of hell." At 7:30 p.m., approximately thirty German aircraft began their attack, and a bomb hit Casavant's ship directly on top of 4,000 barrels of high-test gasoline. The vessel was rocked by an explosion, burst into flames, and Casavant was blown overboard. Eleven fellow crew members were killed, and more sustained injuries. Docked nearby was an ammunition ship, which exploded soon after Casavant was thrown into the water. "The loss of our ship was bad enough," he recalled, "but that explosion of the ammunition ship seemed like the end of the world." In an odd twist of fate, within the town of Bari, buildings were damaged and people killed, but Casavant, floating in the water right next to the ship, was uninjured.[43]

Raid on the harbor, Bari, Italy. December 2, 1943.[44]

The *Fitchburg Sentinel* reported two weeks later that thirty merchant ships were present in the harbor when enemy aircraft came in low, completely taking local defenses by surprise. They targeted the dock area where vessels were in various stages of unloading, describing them as "sitting ducks." When it was over, seventeen ships had been destroyed or severely damaged, at least five of them American and

---

[42] *Bandaged after burns* 1940-1945. Pub domain photo. NARA 520693. tinyurl.com/ycxxwwtb.

[43] *Oxford MA. 300 Years of History.* Oxford Bus Ass., Oxford, MA 2013.

[44] *Atak lotniczy na flote w Bari.* Pub domain photo. 12/2/1943 Archiwa Panstwowe. Wiki Commons. tinyurl.com/cc2w62xp.

1,000 souls were either dead or injured.[45] Contributing to the list of casualties were 628 victims, the majority of them American Merchant Mariners, who required hospitalization due to poison gas exposure. Apparently, one of the ships, the SS John Harvey, had been carrying mustard gas, which would soon claim sixty-nine lives.[46]

Beyond the expected wartime cargo of troops, bombs, ammunition, petroleum products, and weapons, merchant vessels carried a fascinating array of goods. The list below provides a sampling of ships and their cargo.

Jack – sugar
Arkansan – coffee
Carrabulle – liquid asphalt
Raceland – tanks, trucks, airplanes
City of New York – ore, wood, hides, asbestos
Meriweather Lewis – tires, ammunition
Flora Macdonald – cocoa, mahogany

All seven of these vessels were sunk between March 1942 and May 1943, resulting in multiple fatalities. Massachusetts Merchant Marines died aboard each one of these ships.[47]

In October 1944, the *Daily Evening Item* in Lynn noted some frightening statistics: 160,000 Merchant Marines were currently in service to their country, 5,700 had perished, and an additional 500 more had been disabled.[48] The war had ten more months to go, and the numbers would go higher. From the opening shots of the Battle of the Atlantic to Operation Torch in North Africa to the beaches of Normandy and until the last campaign on Okinawa, Merchant Marines were there. MacArthur said, "I hold no branch in higher esteem than the Merchant Marine." They moved more than 200,000,000 tons of cargo and carried ten million men into war, earning the praise of admirals and generals, presidents, and politicians. According to the Department of Defense, of the 250,000 fearless Merchant Marines who served during the war, 9,521 never came home.[49] One out of twenty-six died in frigid waters and fiery wrecks from bullets, bombs, and torpedoes, a higher mortality rate than any branch of the military. Over 600 of them became prisoners of war.

In spite of their service and sacrifice, the government was slow to officially embrace these brave men. In 1944, when the GI Bill was signed, they were excluded. FDR expressed his hope that Congress would soon extend benefits to include the Merchant Marines. Congress declined. There was a litany of excuses. Yes, some of their duty was hazardous, but they weren't members of the military. (Merchant seamen were excluded from the draft due to their war-related jobs.) Not only that, mariners were free to leave the fleet when they wanted and could choose which voyages to participate in (very un-military). They didn't pay income tax, and they were paid more than the average soldier or sailor (they received none of the benefits that those in the military received.) In addition, the independent-minded mariners had also made a few enemies among the brass for their refusal to bend to the iron will of the Navy. So Congress did nothing for forty-three years. In 1988, veteran status, along with benefits, was finally granted, and in 2020, the Congressional Gold Medal was awarded to the Merchant Marines of World

---

[45] Hightower, John. *Assault On Bari.* Fitchburg Sentinel 12/16/1943. Newspapers.com. tinyurl.com/26k725vk.

[46] *Nav Armed Guard Bari, Italy.* NHHC 9/1/2022. tinyurl.com/53dtbknp.

[47] Howland, Ronald. *MA MMs Gave All WWII.*

[48] *Post Will Honor Mothers.* Daily Item 10/18/1944. Newspapers.com. tinyurl.com/3vjxfxs6.

[49] Cronk, Terri Moon. *WWII MMs Receive Cong Gold Medal.* DOD News 5/19/2022. tinyurl.com/yef3heae.

War II. At the ceremony held at the United States Capital, 94-year-old Dave Yoho, a Merchant Marine veteran, addressed the crowd.

I'm speaking for 248,500 guys that are already dead. One out of 26 of us died... And, so, when you're with others, say to them of what we did; urge them to read about us and find out about us. Greet us today if you can [and] then say to those, "We gave up our yesterdays for your better tomorrow."[50]

---

[50] Cronk, Terri Moon. *WWII MMs Receive Cong Gold Medal.*

Chapter 9

Secrets

In wartime, truth is so precious that she should
always be attended by a bodyguard of lies.
Winston Churchill

April 1943, the order thundered out of Admiral Bull Halsey's headquarters and into the annals of history: "TALLY HO. LET'S GET THE BASTARD." Within two days, Isoroku Yamamoto, visionary leader of the Japanese Imperial Navy and architect of the attack on Pearl Harbor, was dead, his plane shot down by America fighters in waters over Bougainville. A month went by before the government of Japan announced that Yamamoto had met a glorious hero's death during combat with the enemy.

When the news broke, Americans reacted with jubilation. Yamamoto, who had supposedly boasted that he was looking forward to dictating terms of peace in the White House, was despised. An editorial in the *Athol Daily News* stated that the Japanese admiral had escaped his chance to see FDR accept his country's surrender as a prisoner at the White House. "Death was too good for Yamamoto," it stated.[1] In Holyoke, the *Daily Transcript* ran a notice of Yamamoto's death under the headline, "Trip Canceled."[2] From the President, the response was less dignified. In an undelivered letter to Yamamoto's wife, FDR wrote:

Dear Widow Yamamoto:
Time is a great leveler, and somehow, I never expected to see the old boy at the White House anyway.
Sorry, I can't attend the funeral because I approve of it. Hoping he is where we know he ain't.
Very sincerely yours,
Franklin D. Roosevelt

Yamamoto's death, a major coup for the United States, would not have taken place had it not been for the efforts of American codebreakers. They had identified Yamamoto's location, the type of plane he would be traveling in, and the escort aircraft. They had cracked the Purple code.

England had long had Japan in its sights. With significant holdings in the Far East, Britain kept a wary eye on Japan, a country hungry for resources necessary to fuel future military actions. The island nation had already begun to claw its way into China with the incident at the Marco Polo Bridge in 1937, followed by the horrifying Rape of Nanjing five months later. British cryptographers had been relatively successful in breaking into communications, but in February 1939, the Japanese suddenly replaced earlier encryption devices with a new M3B machine, and access to Japanese information hit a road block. While codebreakers struggled, Japan revealed her true colors. In September 1940, Germany, Italy, and Japan became allies with the signing of the Tripartite Act, and the ability to decipher Japan's codes assumed a new urgency. For the British, however, already at war, Germany would remain the priority, and few resources were available to devote to breaking Japanese codes.

While well-developed pre-war espionage networks existed in England, France, Russia, Germany, and Japan, the United States came late to the intelligence table. The Black Chamber, a secret unit

---

[1] *No Washington Visit.* Ed. Athol Daily News 5/22/1943. Newspapers.com. tinyurl.com/2c5z8jwn.

[2] *Trip Canceled.* Transcript-TG 5/22/1943. Newspapers.com. tinyurl.com/3r8yyr23.

designed to decipher communications of foreign governments, had been created shortly after the First World War. In 1929, however, Herbert Hoover's newly appointed Secretary of State, Henry Stimson, was not a fan of such tactics. "Gentlemen," he famously stated, "do not read each other's mail." Government funding was cut, and the doors to the first American Black Chamber slammed shut. Progress was slow. By 1940, intelligence agencies existed within the Army and Navy, but due to an agreement between them, decrypted documents were read on alternate days, with reports going to the White House on alternate months. Within the government, little effort was made to engage in clandestine investigations outside of primarily domestic FBI probes or information garnered through diplomatic connections.

In the US, Japan's recent aggression and their switch to a new type B machine, code-named Purple, became a significant concern. The US Army developed a special cryptology group to focus on cracking Purple's secrets. Codebreakers set about their task armed with pencils and paper, unaware that the code machine had the potential to yield billions of different codes. "You can start from here," said one codebreaker, "and go to the end of the world and never have a repetition."[3] On September 20, 1940, after eighteen months of exhaustive labor, Genevieve Grotjan, a twenty-seven-year-old math teacher from New York, made a crucial discovery. Of more than a thousand messages examined, Grotjan discovered a repeating sequence of letters in six different texts.[4] Within a week, Purple was broken. By the end of the year, the team had created a machine that could produce the codes, an American-made version of Purple.

A portion of the Japanese Purple machine recovered from
the wreckage of the Japanese Embassy in Berlin. 1945.[5]

The story of the Enigma machine is an oft-told tale filled with international intrigue, tragedy, and brilliant intellectual achievement. Invented in Germany in 1918, the device was designed to jumble words into unreadable text using a series of rotors, all of which could change position to create

---

[3] *Breaking Purple.* George Marshall Fdn 9/23/2020. tinyurl.com/58n4pury.

[4] Gentzke, Ann Whitcher. *American Hero.* At Buffalo 2018. UB. tinyurl.com/ywsa62fn.

[5] *Purple.* Pub domain photo. NSA. 190531-D-IM742-9013. NSA/CSS. tinyurl.com/9mvmndvm.

150,000,000,000,000,000,000 possible solutions. Those receiving messages used a pass code or cipher to untangle letters. During World War II, secure in the belief that their codes were unbreakable, the German military relied heavily on Enigma machines to protect communications.

Unbeknownst to the Germans, operational plans for the precious machine were already in the hands of the Allies. In 1928, a Polish customs agent noticed a curious-looking package headed to the German Embassy in Warsaw and handed it over to the Polish Intelligence Agency. It was an Enigma machine. Within a few days, the device was examined, diagrams recorded, and the package rewrapped and shipped back on its way to Warsaw. The Germans suspected nothing.[6] Three years later, debt-ridden Hans-Thilo Schmidt, who was working in a cipher department in Germany, approached the French government with an offer to sell information. Unsure of the importance of this information but seeing the potential value of a man whose brother was highly placed in Nazi circles (Rudolph Schmidt would become a General and command the 2nd Panzer Army), Schmidt became known as agent Asche, a spy for the French Intelligence Agency, and promptly handed over several months-worth of German ciphers. This stunning discovery made its way to England and the team at Bletchley Park, the country's top-secret cryptanalysis facility, where the riddle of the Enigma machine began to unravel.[7]

Enigma machine. WWII.[8]

During World War II, the alliance between England and the United States was a cautious one. Churchill's dislike of Americans was well known. One politician recalled Churchill's comments during

---

[6] Harper, Stephen. *Capturing Enigma*. Sutton Publ Ltd 1999.

[7] Hagerty, Edward. *Spy Hitler's Inner Circle*. JSS 2017. tinyurl.com/8mhzv4yn.

[8] *Enigma Machine*. Pub domain photo. CIA. Picryl. tinyurl.com/34kya7sc.

a dinner party in 1928: "He thinks they are arrogant, fundamentally hostile to us, and that they wish to dominate world politics." Shortly afterward, Clementine Churchill cautioned: "I am afraid your known hostility to America might stand in the way... try and understand and master America and make her like you." He did just that.

Churchill at Harvard.[9]

Taking multiple trips to the US, he explored the country and its citizens, stopping in Boston to receive an honorary degree from Harvard, and emerged with a newfound, if somewhat grudging respect: "Picture...the American people as a great lusty youth — who treads on all your sensibilities, perpetrates every possible horror of ill manners — whom neither age nor tradition inspire with reverence — but who moves about his affairs with a good-hearted freshness which may well be the envy of older nations of the earth."[10] Roosevelt's initial meeting in 1918 with the man who would become Prime Minister added to the already shaky foundation. He would later share his recollections with Joseph P. Kennedy, saying Churchill "acted like a stinker." In 1940, when Neville Chamberlain was replaced by the cigar-smoking, hard-drinking Churchill, Roosevelt "...supposed Churchill was the best man England had even if he was drunk half of his time."[11]

While Churchill and FDR slowly developed bonds of friendship that would eventually help to win the war, behind the scenes, the two nations spied on one another and listened in on each other's communications. Boston, with its well-publicized anti-Semitic activity and large Irish population, was a frequent target of the British, who engaged in propaganda designed to lure the country into an alliance against Germany. In 1941, a Boston rally was held featuring isolationist Senator Gerald Nye. In an attempt to stir up anti-Nazi pro-war fervor, 25,000 pamphlets accusing Nye of being a Nazi sympathizer were distributed by members of Fight for Freedom, a pro-English activist group under the influence of

[9] *Churchill receives degree.* Pub domain photo. War Office WWII Coll. Wiki Commons. tinyurl.com/mrarz2e5.

[10] Roberts, Andrew. *Churchill's Anti-Americanism.* Time 11/15/2018. tinyurl.com/44xef9er.

[11] Hamby, Alonzo *Democracy's Champions.* Finest Hour 172, 2016, ICS 6/8/2016. tinyurl.com/3jbp58ru.

the British Security Coordination.[12] Feeling the need for secrecy, both countries held back on important developments that might have significantly helped with the war effort.

In June 1940, England approached the United States with a proposal to share cryptology practices. But Congress had just approved the Walsh Amendment, sponsored by Massachusetts Senator David I. Walsh, prohibiting the sale of military equipment deemed necessary for national defense. Isolationist fervor was running high, and the US declined the offer to become more involved in England's problems. By the end of the year, however, with Japan now a German ally, an agreement was reached. A few months later, the battleship HMS King George V waited In waters off Chesapeake Bay to pick up four Canadian diplomats. The men, wearing civilian clothing, bore diplomatic passports and were bound for England. However, all was not as it appeared. The passengers were actually US servicemen, two Navy and two Army, and they carried with them American codebreaking secrets.[13]

One of these men was the remarkable Prescott Currier. Born in Holbrook, Massachusetts, shortly after joining the Navy, he was assigned to an elite training program known as the "On the Roof Gang." The school was designed to produce Navy and Marine cryptographers who could analyze Japanese codes and was held in a concrete structure on the roof of a Navy Department building in Washington, D.C. After graduating, Currier was sent to the Philippines, where he took it upon himself to learn the Japanese language while performing various duties, including intercept operator, cryptanalyst, and translator. His activities were so diverse that the suspicious Office of Naval Intelligence monitored them. After four years in the military, he was discharged.[14]

Capt. Prescott Currier, USN (Ret)[15]

In December 1940, Currier had his "first inkling that something might be afoot" when he was called up from the Naval Reserves and moved to active duty. One month later, Currier and Robert Weeks of the Navy, along with their Army counterparts, Abraham Sinkhov and Leo Rosen, boarded the HMS

[12] Ignatius, David. *Churchill's Agents Manipulated US.* Wash Po 9/17/1989. tinyurl.com/5b9zmdn5.

[13] Sherman, David. *First Americans.* CCH 2016. tinyurl.com/yve27h3e.

[14] Mariovulcano. *Prescott Currier.* Station HYPO. Cryptology Info Warfare 6/4/2023. tinyurl.com/82f2b4e7.

[15] *Prescott Currier.* Pub domain photo. NSA/CSS. *Voices NSA's Past.* tinyurl.com/5e5xpp7s.

King George V. Currier and Weeks carried their luggage and three boxes of documents. Unknown to them, stacked in the hold under armed guard was nearly half a ton of Army material, including a Purple machine.

The team arrived at Bletchley in early February, and soon afterward, the most guarded secrets of English and American cryptography were unlocked. First came Purple. Plans, ciphers, and an American-made machine were placed in the hands of the British. The English had no intention of releasing any significant information about Enigma, but with this unexpected and dramatic concession by the Americans, their attitude softened. By the time Currier and his colleagues headed home, Engima plans, codes, and operational information about the Bombe, the computer designed by Alan Turing, were in the hands of the Americans. The top-secret trip to Bletchley had accomplished much. Leo Rosen would build his own American version of the Bombe, vastly improving the speed with which messages could be decrypted, and Abraham Sinkhov would later say the British disclosure saved two years of work for the United States.

When not in meetings, Currier and Sinkhov spent time touring London in the watchful company of a British attaché. Currier recalled seeing bombed-out buildings, a crater where an underground station had been the day before, and the vicious destruction at the London Dockyards. One evening during a visit to a popular nightclub, Currier watched actor David Niven and officers of the British Rifle Brigade having a tricycle race on the dance floor of the club. One week later, it too would be bombed, killing many.[16]

The crucial exchange of information came during the Battle for the Atlantic, one of Britain's darkest moments. With communications now being decrypted, Allied sinkings were on the decline. In February 1942, however, three months after America declared war, Admiral Karl Doenitz suddenly ordered a fourth wheel added to the German Navy's enigma machines. Shark, as it was code-named by the Allies, dropped a curtain in front of the Bletchley codebreakers for ten devastating months. In 1941, 496 ships had gone down, but by the end of 1942, 1,006 were lost.[17]

During the Second World War, Chatham, Massachusetts, played a pivotal role in the Enigma story. Located on the elbow of the Cape, the town was chosen by Guglielmo Marconi prior to World War I as the site of a wireless communication center. Shortly after the outbreak of the Second World War, the US Government quickly moved in and took over the operation at Ryder's Cove. The function of this top secret Naval installation was to intercept U-boat communications from the Atlantic and transmit them to Washington, D.C., where Enigma messages could be decrypted and U-boats targeted. Radio messages from U-boats operating in the Atlantic were trapped in a communications network that stretched from Greenland in the north to Brazil in the south.

Known as Station C, the Chatham facility monitored radio transmissions twenty-four hours a day and became the most active intercept station in the country. A staff of 600 operated Station C over the course of the war. While many Chatham residents were aware of the existence of the facility off Pleasant Bay, the role it played in ending the Battle of the Atlantic remained secret. Charles Bartlett of the Chatham Marconi Maritime Center stated, "I don't think any of us knew what they did, only that they were there. And most of us just said, 'Well, it's not my business.'"[18]

By the Fall of 1942, the situation in the Atlantic had become desperate. After Admiral Doenitz ordered adjustments made to the Kriegsmarine's enigma machine, German communications were nearly unreadable. U-boat wolfpacks hunted the Atlantic freely, and the loss of Allied lives and shipping reached devastating highs.

---

[16] Sherman, David. *First Americans.*

[17] *Cost of Battle.* NML. tinyurl.com/5x4ekabx.

[18] Nelson, Laura J. *Chatham station WWII.* Boston Globe 6/28/2011. tinyurl.com/jwfrm7y6.

German forces relied heavily on Enigma machines.
Note Enigma machine far left. WWII.[19]

On October 30, 1942, HMS Petard sank German U-559 in Mediterranean waters off Port Said. As the U-boat crew surrendered, three brave British seamen swam to the sub, returning to the Petard carrying confiscated documents. Two of them would not survive. (So secretive was this action that, in an effort to cover up this all-important find, medals awarded for their heroism were civilian rather than the military honors they deserved.) The materials, crucial ciphers for the elusive Shark, were quickly forwarded to England. Once Shark messages were decoded, the efforts of the Navy and Station C paid off. There was a sharp turn in the fortunes of the German war at sea. In a 1946 declassified report written while on trial for war crimes at Nuremberg, Grand Admiral Karl Doenitz, Supreme Commander of the German Navy, described the situation facing the Kriegsmarine in the spring of 1943.

It was evident that the enemy's aircraft and destroyers must now be fitted with new radar. The U-boat losses, which previously had been 13 percent of all the boats at sea, rose rapidly to 30 to 50 percent. In May 1943 alone, 43 U-boats were lost. These losses were suffered not only in convoy attacks but everywhere at sea. There was no part of the Atlantic where the boats were safe from being located day and night by aircraft.

Doenitz's essay reveals the extraordinary truth of the impact of the men and women of Station C and of British and American codebreakers. At various points, the Admiral places the blame for the failure of the U-boat war on the Luftwaffe, the Italian Navy, Hitler and his cronies, enemy air power and radar capabilities, and even the weather. Nowhere in the approximately fifty-page document does Doenitz recognize the fallibility of the German Enigma machine or the ability of the Allies to break its codes.[20] It would take nearly thirty years for the world to learn one of the best-kept secrets of World War II.

Under the command of legendary codebreaker Joseph Rochefort, the Navy's recently created Station HYPO at Pearl Harbor was keeping track of Japan's activities. On December 7, not far away, was the USS Tennessee and her Executive Officer Joseph Finnegan of Dorchester. One of Finnegan's colleagues would later say that bombing the Tennessee was the worst mistake the Japanese ever made because it freed up Joseph Finnegan for a decryption position in the Station HYPO group. Described as "a professional Boston Irishman," Finnegan would become a legend.[21] His dogged determination soon led to uncovering crucial information on the date, time, and bearing of the Japanese attack at Midway.

---

[19] *German Enigma machines.* Pub domain photo. USAF. NMUSAF. tinyurl.com/5n6r55at.

[20] Doenitz, Admiral Karl. *Conduct War At Sea 1/1946.* U-Boat Arch. tinyurl.com/34t7pu5n.

[21] Amos, Bill. *Pacific Duty Part III.* No Star Monthly 3/14/2019. tinyurl.com/ycx6jhah.

Captain Joseph Finnegan[22]

But in November of 1941, while all was still calm in Hawaii, Rochefort's team intercepted messages indicating that a Japanese attack was imminent. Unfortunately, while Rochefort was listening to the Japanese, nobody at Pearl Harbor was listening to Rochefort. On December 3, Commander in Chief of the Pacific Fleet Admiral Husband E. Kimmel was informed that the Japanese were destroying their secret documents, a sure indication of war. Kimmel did nothing. His counterpart in Hawaii, General Walter Short, was told by his superior, Army Chief George Marshall, to expect an imminent attack. Like Kimmel, he made no effort to prepare.

On the morning of December 7, Kimmel rose at 7 a.m. for a golf date with Short. He was informed that a submarine had fired upon USS Ward at the entrance to Pearl Harbor. Just before 8 a.m., he sent out a radiogram: "Air raid on Pearl Harbor. This is no drill." However, within fifteen minutes, the USS West Virginia was in flames, the USS Oklahoma lay on her side, the Battleship Arizona and her crew were gone, and over 2,000 Americans were dead or dying.

Radiogram reporting Pearl Harbor attack.
December 7, 1941.[23]

---

[22] *Joseph Finnegan.* Pub domain photo. USN. Wiki Commons. tinyurl.com/3aym5eeb.

[23] *Air Raid Pearl Harbor.* Pub domain photo. Am Originals. NARA 3/1996. tinyurl.com/yc8j3shf.

The December 7, 1941, attack on Pearl Harbor left the US in a state of confusion. The notion that a hostile nation could stage an unsuspected attack on American soil was unfathomable. In Washington, numerous investigations were held, conclusions drawn, scapegoats targeted, and puffed-up chests indignantly adopted a never-again persona. The reality was, however, that, for the most part, Pearl Harbor was a US intelligence failure. As early as August 1941, information about a Japanese naval intelligence operative and interest in Pearl Harbor defenses and battleships was detected, reported, and failed to elicit a response. It was time for the United States to pull its head out of the proverbial isolationist sand and take a careful look around. The country needed to do a better job of spying on its allies and its enemies, and it desperately needed codebreakers.

The Navy took the first step forward. In their search for cryptologists, they tapped into a hitherto rarely utilized resource: women. At the Seven Sisters, a group of prestigious East Coast women's colleges, letters began arriving in mailboxes, all vague, all containing the same intriguing questions: Do you like crossword puzzles? Are you engaged to be married? From Massachusetts, home to four of the Seven Sisters, dozens of women responded. Ann Williams and Elizabeth Colby of Wellesley College, Anne Barus of Smith College,[24] and Helen R. Allegrone of Radcliffe[25] would join other women from Mount Holyoke College. They were math, science, history, and language majors. They were intelligent, they were patriotic, and they could keep their mouths shut. None of them really understood what they had signed up for.

Not to be outdone, the Army made its move but quickly bumped heads with the Navy at colleges where students were already being recruited. The message was clear. This was Navy territory. Keep your hands off. (The rivalry between the two branches of the service is legendary. Navy codebreaker Prescott Currier commented, "Nobody cooperated with the Army, under pain of death.")[26] Army recruiters set their sights on those in teacher training programs or targeted women like BU graduate Fran Perlmutter from Brookline specifically for their abilities. Others answered newspaper ads or volunteered.

Once accepted, their experiences were similar. They traveled to Washington D.C., gave a pledge of secrecy (revealing their work could be considered an act of treason punishable by death), took code and cipher courses, and were assigned a role in the top-secret world of American cryptology. Some were asked to learn Japanese. Many joined the WAVES or the WAACs. Many maintained their jobs as civilians. Like Perlmutter, who was told to say she sharpened pencils for a living, all were expected to lie about their occupations.[27]

Though not as noticeable but equally important, there were thousands of codebreakers whose work included cataloging, translation, and secretarial tasks. Churchill referred to them as "geese that laid the golden eggs – but never cackled." For others, however, the war years would be spent cracking secret codes. Fran Perlmutter recalled her experience in an interview with Boston University's *Arts Sciences Magazine*. After learning Japanese, she took messages and translated them into dots and dashes, then into Japanese, and then into English. She and other women like her provided the location of Imperial Army units,[28] helped to sink enemy ships, and find and kill Yamamoto. One of them would decode the message revealing the Japanese intention to surrender.

In a speech to the House of Representatives at the close of the war, New York Representative Clarence Hancock praised the efforts of American codebreakers. "They are entitled to glory and national gratitude, which they will never receive. I believe that our cryptographers ... in the war with Japan did

---

[24] Mundy, Lisa. *Code Girls*. Hachette Books 2017.

[25] Mayton, Marlana. *Collegiate Codebreakers*. Dig Commons @ WU 5-2020. tinyurl.com/2pvap8c9.

[26] *Interview Prescott Currier*. DOCID: 425608 11/14/1980. tinyurl.com/2j9z89t4.

[27] Erlich, Lara. *WWII Codebreaker*. BU Arts Sci Mag. BU 2018. tinyurl.com/yw6xyun6.

[28] Ehrlich, *Lara. She was WWII Codebreaker.*

as much to bring that war to a successful and early conclusion as any other group of men."[29] He was right. By the war's end, the United States counted 20,000 cryptologists in their ranks, and more than half of them would never receive the recognition that they deserved...11,000 of them were women.

During the Spring of 1944, there was a noticeable flurry of Allied activity in the UK. The hero of El Alamein, British General Bernard Montgomery, had unexpectedly arrived. Troops, supplies, and equipment were massing in Scotland, and in the south of England, airwaves were abuzz with news of troop support activity and movement. Even King George had visited Dover to inspect a recently constructed oil storage facility. Also noteworthy was the presence of the man considered the most dangerous by his enemies, General George Patton. It appeared the Allies were on the move.

Germany had long prepared for invasion, and construction of a 2,000-mile-long Atlantic wall, their first line of defense, had begun in 1942. Now, with Allied bombing increasing in the area of Calais, a stone's throw from the English Coast, Hitler was convinced that the Allies would soon attack. So sure was the Fuhrer that the assault would begin in Calais, that he denied Rommel's request to reinforce defenses in Normandy with Panzer divisions. The stage was set for a massive assault by the Allies, and Hitler planned to emerge the victor.

The Fuhrer, however, had missed one important point...the whole thing was a hoax, described by author David Roos as "one of the most successful military deception schemes since the Trojan Horse."[30] The invasion of German-occupied Europe had been agreed upon at the Tehran Conference by Roosevelt, Stalin, and Churchill less than a year earlier, and planning for Operation Overlord began with an eye toward implementation in 1944. One branch of the British team, the London Controlling Section, was given an unusual task...to confuse and deceive the Germans. As a result, Operation Fortitude was put into place.

A burst of activity in Scotland and in the south of England was aimed at diverting enemy troops from the French coastline at Normandy. Radio messages broadcast phony information. Dummy buildings were constructed, including an oil supply depot in Dover. Spies spread misinformation, some at the highest levels. One double agent, Juan Pujol Garcia, would be awarded the Iron Cross by a grateful Germany. Mock barges floated in channels and canals, and inflatable tanks dotted fields. A British actor hired to impersonate General Montgomery departed England for North Africa. Surely, the Allies wouldn't begin their cross-channel invasion if Monty was a whole continent away. Best of all, the German's most feared foe, General George Patton, had suddenly appeared in the UK. Patton had recently landed himself on his commanding general's bad side, Eisenhower telling him, "I am thoroughly weary of your failure to control your tongue." Thus, Patton was a perfect choice for the job. He wandered about southern England, visiting his fake Army, the First United States Army Group, FUSAG, spreading rumor, innuendo, and even announcing, "See you in Pas de Calais!"[31]

While the Allies were unable to completely mask the impending invasion, its location and time remained a mystery. Hitler went to bed late on the evening of June 5, comfortable in the belief that bad weather would delay an enemy assault. He was awoken at noon the next day with the news that D-Day, the largest invasion in history, had begun at Normandy. It is estimated that over 4,000 brave Allies were lost during the battle, but the secrets, lies, and deception had worked, and the hoax known as Operation Fortitude ultimately saved thousands of lives.

This was not the first nor would it be the last sting operation perpetrated by the Allies. The story of the 23rd Headquarters Special Troops began in January 1944 when a specialized unit of artists, actors, and engineers was pulled together to form the "Ghost Army." Their job was to deceive the enemy. Capt.

[29] Delloye, Tate. *PA woman deciphered Enigma.* Daily Mail.com 8/7/2020. tinyurl.com/3mpj3fvz.

[30] Roos, David. *Hitler Wrong About D-Day.* History 6/5/2019. tinyurl.com/5arx3ydd.

[31] Macintyre, Ben. *Double Cross.* Broadway Books/Random House 2012.

Ralph Ingersoll, one of the men who had come up with the idea, referred to them as "my con artists."[32] The 23rd deployed to England in May of 1944, and while it was not a part of D-Day's Operation Fortitude, it followed the Allies toward the Rhine after the Normandy invasion and participated in over twenty major deception schemes. A second group operated in Italy.

The men of the Ghost Army used their skills to create the illusion that large armed forces of up to 30,000 men existed close to combat areas in the hopes of distracting and confusing the enemy. One of the more famous members of the group had significant ties to Massachusetts. Well-known artist Ellsworth Kelly's experience painting camouflage for the Army influenced his later work. After discharge, Kelly moved to Boston and attended school at the Museum of Fine Arts. He would go on to teach art at the Norfolk House Center in Roxbury, earn an honorary degree from Harvard, and achieve fame for his work as an abstract painter.[33] One member of the Ghost Army recalled painting fake tanks to make them look realistic and making phony posters and signs to be placed in nearby towns. "Like Coca-Cola signs, so they'll say, 'Oh, yeah, the Americans are here.'"[34]

Members of the Ghost Army carrying a tank. WWII.[35]

One of the more important productions staged by the 23rd took place at the edge of the Rhine River, ten miles south of where Patton and two Ninth Army divisions waited to cross. Ghost Army crews set up tanks, artillery, and vehicles. Radios spread misinformation, and sound equipment mimicked troop activity. In a letter to his wife, Patton remarked, "There is one rather bad spot in my line, but I don't think the Huns know it. Hiding it now by the grace of God and a lot of guts."[36] The Germans turned their attention and guns toward the 23rd, and Patton's Army successfully made it across the river.

Toward the end of the war, Sebastian Medina, back in Worcester on leave, told a *Worcester Telegram and Gazette* reporter of his experiences in the Ghost Army. The story was quickly censored by the War Department. Two weeks later, however, with the war over and the Censorship Department now defunct, the story went public. Word of this unique unit began to spread, but soon afterward, the Pentagon stepped in, and the story of the Ghost Army was kept secret for fifty years, and it was finally declassified in 1996.[37]

In 2016, Massachusetts Senators Edward Markey and Elizabeth Warren proposed legislation that would honor the men of the unit. One of them, Jack McGlynn of Medford, was surprised. "I can assure you that none of us volunteered because of a hope of receiving a medal, but rather we volunteered to fight to protect the freedoms that our family, friends, and coworkers here in the United States

<hr>

[32] *The Unit: Ghost Army.* Ghost Army Legacy Proj. tinyurl.com/4vnyjjkf.

[33] *Ellsworth Kelly.* Biography. Ellsworth Kelly. tinyurl.com/3ja8x5m2.

[34] Patel, Vimal. *Ghost Army Wins Recognition.* NYT 2/3/2022. tinyurl.com/uymrwers.

[35] *Inflatable tank.* Pub domain photo. US Army. Sullivan, Amanda. *WWII Ghost Army tactics.* US Army 6/9/2021. tinyurl.com/2p9dpwxr.

[36] *The Unit: The Ghost Army.* Ghost Army Legacy Proj.

[37] Teng, Jhemmylrut. *US Audio Engineers…Actors Outsmarted Adolf Hitler.* Ghost Army Legacy Proj. 5/15/2021. tinyurl.com/mr7w3ujw.

enjoyed..."[38] On February 1, 2022, President Joseph Biden awarded the Congressional Gold Medal to the Ghost Army and its soldiers, the "con artists" who saved thousands of lives during World War II.

Mother Nature had not been kind to Japan. In 1933, a devastating earthquake and the tidal wave that followed claimed 3,000 lives. One year later, typhoon Muroto swept across the island nation, killing another 3,000, and shortly afterward, the Great Hakodate Fire took an estimated 2,000 lives. Politically, Japan fared little better. When a 1934 scandal erupted, threatening senior government officials with imprisonment, Prime Minister Saito disbanded his cabinet. A 1936 revolt by members of the military led to assassinations and, eventually, executions. In addition, the country's invasion of Manchuria had placed US-Japanese relations on shaky ground. In an effort to bolster goodwill, the United States gathered together a team of the brightest stars in American baseball and sent them on a public relations tour of Japan.

Baseball was developing into a popular pastime in Japan when Babe Ruth, Lou Gehrig, and a host of others landed for the eighteen-game tour. It was an uneasy visit. The US was wary of the country's recent expansionist actions, and Japan found fault with American interference. A close watch was kept over the team's activities. East Brookfield native Connie Mack complained that his hotel room was wiretapped. At some point during the tour, one member of the team donned a kimono, tucked a camera inside, and headed to St. Luke's Hospital to visit the American ambassador's daughter, who had just given birth. His path led him not to the new mom but to the roof of the hospital. The man scaled a tower atop the building, pulled out the camera, and carefully filmed the Tokyo landscape below, including railway and refinery sites and military vessels anchored in the port. He returned to the US soon afterward, carefully tucking the video away. Moe Berg had just taken his first step to becoming a spy.[39]

Over 20,000 American men and women worked in the shadowy realm of espionage during the Second World War. Their reasons for doing such a dangerous job varied. Famous for her charismatic personality and a wooden leg named Cuthbert, Virginia Hall was looking forward to a career with the diplomatic corps. After attending Radcliffe in Cambridge, a hunting accident left her relegated to a desk job, an unacceptable option for the plucky Hall, so she became a secret agent. Patricia Warner of Lincoln lost her husband at Guadalcanal. "I wanted to do something useful," she said and went to work for America's spy network. Warner would earn a Congressional Gold Medal for her efforts.[40] Physicist Samuel Goudsmit held a teaching position at Harvard when the war broke out. It wasn't enough. His parents had been lost when Germany invaded the Netherlands. He wanted a more active role in stopping the Nazi madness. His espionage efforts were aimed at putting an end to Axis atomic research. Goudsmit would later become a member of the MIT Rad Lab.

Some became spies for the thrill of it all. Legendary William Donovan may have been one of these. Born into a working-class Irish Catholic family in Buffalo, he fought in the First World War. Known for having an impetuous side, he once led his men into battle wearing insignia and a chest full of medals, making him a prime target and shouting, "They can't hit me, and they won't hit you!" Donovan would become one of the most highly decorated soldiers in US history. In 1944, he and his colleagues created a device that, when attached to a gun, significantly diminished the sound of the gunfire. He rushed to demonstrate this new "silencer" for his buddy, the President, who unfortunately was in a meeting. To get his attention, Donovan dragged a sandbag into the White House and fired off ten rounds.[41] During World War II, "Wild Bill" took multiple unofficial information-gathering trips for his friend, FDR. As a result of these secret assignments, together they developed the Office of Strategic Services, the US espionage agency and forerunner of the CIA.

---

[38] *Markey, Warren Honor Ghost Army.* E. Markey US Senate 3/21/2016. tinyurl.com/5n6253fr.

[39] Kean, Sam. *Bastard Brigade.* Little Brown Co 2019.

[40] Hughes, Lisa. *Lincoln Woman Cong Gold Medal.* WBZ 4 CBS Boston 5/28/2019. tinyurl.com/yfv6tjm5.

[41] *Legend of Wild Bill.* CIA 11/11/2020. tinyurl.com/39k6cxps. Web 2 Dec 2024.

For Moe Berg, it was a bit more complicated. Certainly, his Jewish faith placed him in opposition to the Nazis. Born to immigrant parents in New York, the young man loved baseball and early on showed considerable prowess. More remarkable was the fact that Moe Berg was brilliant. He attended Princeton and the Sorbonne in Paris, and he earned a law degree from Columbia. He spoke close to a dozen languages and read as many newspapers a day. Author Sam Kean, in his book *The Bastard Brigade,* speculates it was this love of learning that led Berg down the path to espionage. "He hated persecution of intellectuals. The Nazis jailed professors and harassed scientists, smashed printing presses and burned books. It infuriated him."[42]

The only baseball card on display at CIA headquarters.[43]

Berg made his mark in major league baseball as a catcher with the Chicago White Sox. While he had several good seasons, he never achieved A-list status. A fellow ballplayer commented that Moe "could speak a dozen languages but couldn't hit in any one of them."[44] Known as the "brainiest guy in baseball," he enjoyed sharing stories from the newspapers that he read voraciously, rattling off baseball trivia, and entertaining in several different languages. He became popular with players, the press, and the public. In 1935, he joined the Boston Red Sox as a player and coach, ending his career in 1942. His glory days were over by that time, but Moe Berg wasn't finished yet. "Europe is in flames," he said, "withering in a fire set by Hitler...And what am I doing? Sitting in the bullpen, telling jokes to relief pitchers."[45] He dusted off the movie footage of Tokyo taken from the roof of St. Luke's Hospital and handed it over to authorities.

The invasion of Czechoslovakia by Germany caused concern for a number of reasons, one of which was pointed out in a letter from Albert Einstein to FDR in 1939. The country contained some of the richest uranium deposits on Earth, an element which, according to Einstein, could be used to create weapons of unimaginable power. With the attack on Pearl Harbor, the need for the development of more accurate and powerful weaponry assumed a new urgency. In response, the newly created National Defense Research Committee and the US Army organized the Manhattan Project. If the world were to have weapons of mass destruction, the first would belong to the Americans.

Leslie R. Groves, an engineer with an education from MIT and a diploma from West Point, was selected to manage the top-secret program. "General Groves is the biggest S.O.B. I have ever worked for." Manhattan Project engineer Colonel Kenneth Nichols painted a picture of an energetic leader who was "demanding...abrasive and sarcastic...egotistical...extremely intelligent." He also had guts, he said,

---

[42] Kean, Sam. *Bastard Brigade.*

[43] *MoeBergGoudeycard.* Pub domain image. Goudey. Wikipedia. tinyurl.com/msjnyuwm.

[44] Fitts, Rob. *1934 All-American Tour Japan.* SABR. tinyurl.com/28d75z7w.

[45] Daley, Arthur. *Berg Man of Many Facets.* Buffalo Courier-Expr 6/2/1972. NYS Hist Newspapers. tinyurl.com/y8bkssju.

and if he made a decision, he stuck with it. "If I had to do my part of the atomic bomb project over again...I would pick General Groves."[46] Among his many tasks was to ensure the secrecy of the Manhattan Project and to seek out information about ongoing research. To do this, General Groves got into the spy game.

It was Army Chief of Staff George Marshall who made the suggestion that a completely separate intelligence unit should be formed to find out how far Germany had gotten in developing atomic weapons. Placed under the umbrella of Grove and his Manhattan Project, a group code-named Alsos was created. Its members were charged with tracking down Germany's nuclear scientists, interviewing them, confiscating related documents, and locating any stashes of material that could be used for atomic research. Leading Alsos was Lt. Col. Boris Pash, a graduate of Springfield College in western Massachusetts, along with Dr. Samuel Goudsmit, recently of Harvard, who would manage the science component.

Samuel Goudsmit (far left) and members of ALSOS. 1944.[47]

Choosing the spies of Alsos proved to be difficult. They needed agents who had enough knowledge of nuclear physics to interrogate scientists but not enough knowledge of the Manhattan Project, lest they be captured and interrogated themselves. Groves turned to Wild Bill Donovan to find someone to investigate a German heavy water production facility. Donovan chose a relatively new OSS recruit who spoke several languages and had a rudimentary knowledge of physics. Soon afterward, Moe Berg jumped out of a plane in Norway, gathered the required information about the Vermork hydroelectric power plant, and returned home.[48]

The work of Alsos led Berg and his colleagues through Italy, France, and, as the Allies pushed eastward, Germany. He spent his days seeking out scientists, extracting whatever information he could, and reporting back to his superiors. Project Larson was one of his assignments, designed specifically to kidnap or coerce Italian physicists to join the Americans. Germany had built an entire town outside of Rome, Guidonia, for the purpose of conducting aeronautics research. It was here that Italian physicist Antonio Ferri had constructed one of the most advanced wind tunnels in Europe. Alsos wanted Ferri, and when Moe Berg found him, he used his ever-present charm and knowledge of Petrarch to insert himself into the trust of the poetry-loving scientist. When FDR learned that the baseball player had coerced Ferri into joining the Allies, he stated: "I see Berg is still catching pretty well."[49]

As the war wound to a close, Berg's skills were needed less and less. Added to this was his wanderlust, which caused him to disappear for weeks at a time, leaving superiors anxious. After a few moderately successful Cold War jobs, Moe was out of work. He drifted from friend to friend, often

---

[46] *Leslie Groves.* AHF 2022. tinyurl.com/3dvmtr6w.

[47] *ALSOS members* 11/1944. Pub domain photo. US Army. Wiki Commons. tinyurl.com/bdf9n6tz.

[48] Kean, Sam. *Bastard Brigade.*

[49] Zimmerman, Dwight Jon. *Berg Batted 1.000 for America.* Defense Media Network 10/23/2014. tinyurl.com/ycyhfffy.

jobless and homeless, still getting by on his intellect and charm. One constant in his life was his friend, Samuel Goudsmit. It was Goudsmit who gave Moe his last secret assignment. In 1960, when the scientist was seeking a divorce, his wife said no thank you and disappeared. Berg tracked her down on Cape Cod, Goudsmit got his divorce, and married wife number two shortly afterward.[50] Moe Berg passed away in 1972, a man of many talents who led a full and adventurous life. His last words hearkened back to where it all began, "How'd the Mets do today?"[51]

By the time Moe Berg was ending his baseball career, German spies had been at work in the US for quite some time. Just prior to the war, consul Herbert Scholz hung a swastika flag outside the German embassy in Boston. While not a crime and certainly not covert, Scholz, a friend of Heinrich Himmler, was described by historian Charles R. Gallager as "a very capable, devious spy who was able to recruit targets, using a psychology that moved them toward Nazi Lines."[52] The 35-year-old ambassador was a slick, glib operative who, on the surface, was effusive in his praise of Boston (he and his wife enjoyed the city's cultural advantages, in particular, performances of Wagner at the Boston Symphony)[53] but could be arrogant and disrespectful of his host country's laws. In 1940, after failing to appear for a parking violation, his license was suspended. Scholz claimed that as a consul, he was immune from any consequences for law-breaking and that international complications would arise should he face penalties. His attorney arrived at the Registry of Motor Vehicles hearing with a large collection of former treaties between the US and Germany to support his opinion. Registrar Frank Goodwin ignored the documents and the lawyer, warning instead that the only complication that might arise would be if Scholz chose to drive his car in Massachusetts again.[54]

The German tanker Pauline Freiderich was just off the coast of Nova Scotia on her way home in September 1939 when the captain received alarming news. England had declared war on Germany. Fearing he had little chance of making it across the Atlantic, he turned the ship around and headed to Boston. With the US not yet at war, the ship was allowed to remain docked at Battery Wharf in the North End, and its crew traveled freely back and forth into the city. The FBI, however, was watching. Of particular interest was a painter aboard the ship, Connecticut-born William Colepaugh, who had had multiple interactions with Scholz and his staff. Unhappy with life in the States, he was hoping to travel to Germany to study engineering. The FBI investigation seemed to support his story. Colepaugh had briefly been a student of naval architecture and engineering at MIT but left after failing academically. At school, he'd shown an interest in German newspapers, journals, and the correspondence he frequently received from the German Embassy in Boston.

For the next few years, Colepaugh popped in and out of the United States. He worked as a laborer at Lawley's Shipyard in Boston, joined the crew of a few outbound ships, and attended a party at Boston's German Embassy in honor of Hitler's birthday. When he signed aboard a ship hailing from Buenos Aires, his draft record became an issue. While he had registered for the draft, his failure to complete paperwork and notify the draft board of his whereabouts was a breach of federal law. He was taken into custody, but rather than being prosecuted at the suggestion of the US Attorney in Boston, he joined the Naval Reserves. After a brief eight months, he was booted out "for the convenience of the government." He bumped around Massachusetts, working at a poultry farm in Concord and at a watch company. Early in 1944, Colepaugh notified the draft board that he would be shipping out aboard the Gripsholm, a ship known by the FBI to be carrying passengers for repatriation to the Fatherland.

---

[50] Kean, Sam. *Bastard Brigade.*

[51] Francis, Bill. *Moe Berg's Life in Baseball.* NBHOF. tinyurl.com/je3p3hcn.

[52] O'Malley, JP. *FBI on Nazi plot WWII.* Times of Israel 1/28/2022. tinyurl.com/527avv4z.

[53] Wayman, Dorothy. *German Consul Ousting.* Boston Globe 6/20/1941. Newspapers.com. tinyurl.com/bxke7dnh.

[54] *German Consul Protests.* Springfield Daily Repub 10/11/1940. Newspapers.com. tinyurl.com/bxke7dnh.

William Colepaugh would soon return. Accompanied by fellow spy Erich Gimpel, the two climbed out of a German sub onto a beach in Maine on November 29, 1944. They carried guns, secret ink, plans for building a radio, $60,000, and a packet of diamonds. The men hiked to Route 1, found a taxi to take them to Bangor, and then hopped a train to Boston, where they spent the night before moving on to New York. One month later, it was all over. Colepaugh turned himself over to authorities and willingly spilled details of the mission. A few days later, a man identified as Edward George Green of 582 Massachusetts Avenue in Boston was arrested at a newsstand in New York City. He was carrying $10,000 and a package containing 99 diamonds. Erich Gimpel's story had ended as well. The two spies were placed on trial, found guilty, and sentenced to death (which would later be changed to life in prison, a gift from President Truman). Germany's short-lived Operation Elster had been a complete failure.[55]

Erich Gimpel thanks President Harry Truman for paroling
him after being sentenced to death for espionage. Munich, 1956.[56]

The FBI kept a watchful eye on the comings and goings in the Bay State. Located on Sassamon Road in Natick, a quiet, unobtrusive farm on Pegan Hill was busy receiving radio signals. The mission of the nine agents stationed there was to listen in on enemy conversations and identify potential espionage activity. In 1944, counterintelligence agent W. Mark Felt assumed the identity of German spy Helmut Goldschmidt. The real Goldschmidt, a member of the German spy agency Abewhar, was being held captive in England when Felt began sending deceptive information to the Fatherland under his name. Information relayed to Germany is rumored to have been transmitted through the Natick post.[57] Felt, whose job it was to keep secrets, would later achieve fame for telling them when it was revealed that as "Deep Throat," he had helped to dethrone President Richard Nixon.

Among the thousands of men and women who covertly operated under the Office of Strategic Services umbrella were several with ties to Massachusetts. Many would live inconspicuous lives after the war; many would achieve fame, and none would readily give up their secrets. Harvard graduate Arthur Schlesinger failed to meet the military's medical standards when the US went to war, so he took a position with the OSS as an intelligence analyst. He returned to Harvard after the war, this time as a professor. Schlesinger went on to become a Pulitzer Prize-winning author and speechwriter for John F. Kennedy. Schlesinger is buried in Mount Auburn Cemetery in Cambridge. Carleton Coon, born in Wakefield, led a privileged life, attending Phillips Academy and Harvard University, where he later became a professor of anthropology. His knowledge of Egyptian history led him to the OSS and weapons smuggling in North Africa, where, it is speculated, he participated in the assassination of a Vichy

[55] *Counterintelligence WWII.* NCSC. tinyurl.com/axfd2t7x.

[56] *1956-erich-gimpel.* Pub domain photo. Wiki Commons. tinyurl.com/3t7jr7ps.

[57] Johnston, David. *Deep Throat's Clandestine Ways.* NYT 6/4/005. tinyurl.com/nh4szyyd.

Admiral. His book, *A North African Story,* provides details of his time with the OSS.[58] Coon spent the remainder of his life in the Gloucester area.

Every few years, a racing event is held to determine which sailing craft and crew will take home the coveted America's Cup. During the 1930s, the lesser-known International Fishing Challenge Cup, described by *Sail Magazine* as "effectively a grudge match sailed between Canadian and American Grand Banks fishermen," featured only two vessels, the iconic, much-beloved Bluenose of Canada and the Gertrude L. Thebaud out of Gloucester, Massachusetts. The 1938 race was a stunner. Thebaud barely squeaked across the finish line ahead of Bluenose in the first of five races, but the navigator followed this triumph in the second race by getting lost. In a huff, the skipper gave the job to a young sailor who happened to be hanging overhead off a mast. In a raging gale, the twenty-two-year-old guided the American ship to victory. Unfortunately, the trophy eventually went to the Canadians, but the fame of the young navigator would soon surpass the short-lived International Fishing Challenge.

This was not his first boating experience. The young man had grown up along the New England coast, lived in towns from Maine to Massachusetts, and worked the Grand Banks fleet out of Gloucester. He developed a life-long love of sailing.[59] Those gathered on the shore that day in 1938 weren't just looking at the sailboats. It was hard not to notice the blond, 6'5" sailor who navigated the Thebaud across the finish line. Soon afterward, his picture appeared in the *Boston Post* with the caption, "Thebaud Sailor Like Movie Idol," and Hollywood came knocking on his door.[60] Sterling Hayden was about to become a movie star.

When war broke out, Hayden, who preferred sailing to acting, left behind the glitz and glamour of the film industry and opted for the US Marines. After breaking his ankle, he picked up a new name, John Hamilton, and a new career with the OSS. Of particular interest to Wild Bill Donovan, who would develop a long friendship with the actor, was Hayden's sailing ability. He was assigned to a covert mission involving shipping weapons and supplies to operatives in Eastern Europe. During an incident in Yugoslavia in 1943, his team took a boat across the Adriatic to rendezvous with a group of Marshal Tito's rebels. Under fire by Germans and after the loss of one of the team members, the group pulled back. In spite of the continued attack, Hayden was able to complete the mission successfully, for which he received a Silver Star.[61] After the war, Sterling Hayden returned to the movie business to become one of Hollywood's most popular leading men and a successful author, never losing his love of the sea.

Sterling Hayden, US Marine Corps. WWII.[62]

[58] *Coon, Carleton Stevens.* Encyclopedia.com 7/11/2024. tinyurl.com/3e3nvm3j.

[59] Doane, Charles *Sterling Hayden.* Sail 4/6/2018. tinyurl.com/27ptujps.

[60] Lefavour, EJ. *Sterling Hayden.* Good Morning Gloucester 6/22/2011. tinyurl.com/2uz6ujc6.

[61] *Sterling Hayden.* CIA 7/9/2021. *Sterling Hayden.* Pub domain photo. tinyurl.com/2cd5pc2a.

[62] *Sterling Hayden.* Pub domain photo. CIA. *Sterling Hayden.* CIA 7/9/2021. tinyurl.com/2cd5pc2a.

Julia McWilliams was raised in comfort in California. Her grandparents owned the Weston Paper Company in Massachusetts, a state where she would spend much of her life. With the outbreak of war, the young Smith graduate wanted to do her part. The WAVES and WAACs said no thank you. Julia was too tall. Not to be discouraged, she turned to the OSS, which saw a use for the bright, well-spoken young lady. Here, her skills came in handy as she moved through several different positions, from clerk to research assistant. Under the direction of Harvard's Museum of Comparative Zoology Chief, Captain Harold Coolidge, she participated in the development of shark repellent. For a time, she was assigned to General Mountbatten's staff. While never engaged in any undercover espionage (it would be difficult for a 6'2" female to be inconspicuous), her work was at times truly secretive in nature. Sensitive communications, agents' names, and war plans routinely passed through her hands.[63] After the war, Julia McWilliams Child moved to Cambridge and became an internationally famous chef, author, TV personality, and a staple of PBS programming for over twenty years.

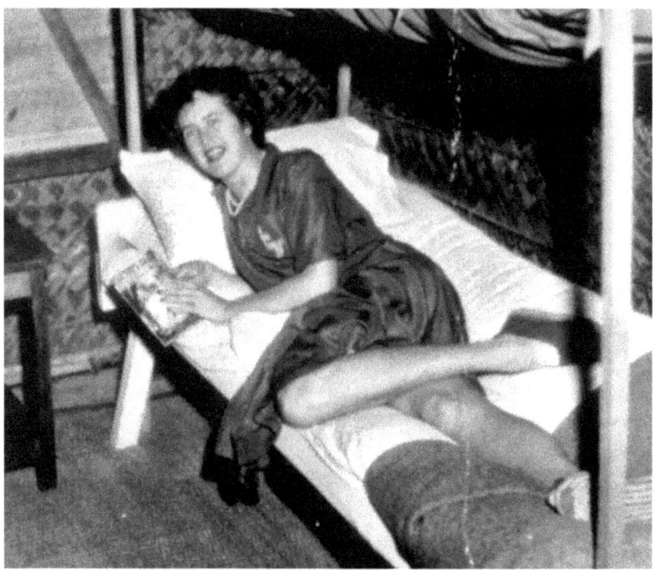

Julia Child, Ceylon. WWII.[64]

In 1907, a young scientist from Worcester, Massachusetts, nearly blew up the basement of the physics building at Worcester Polytechnic Institute. To its credit, WPI saw potential in the young man, and Robert Goddard was allowed to continue his research. The rest is history. However, while Goddard is considered the father of rocketry, American superiority in rocket science actually began in a toilet in Poland in the Spring of 1945.

Two years earlier, Germany had experienced a significant setback. Operation Barbarossa, Hitler's grand plan to overtake Russia, had failed at the cost of nearly 800,000 men, and the focus now switched to developing a rocketry program. Walter Osenberg, an official in the German Defense Research Association, compiled a list of important scientists, engineers, and technicians necessary for the initiative. These individuals were recalled from mundane positions in the military and moved to specialized research and development sites such as Peenemunde, where its technical director, twenty-five-year-old Wernher von Braun, had just joined the Nazi Party. The Program was a success, and less than a year later, V2 rockets began raining terror on the citizens of Britain. Unfortunately for the Third Reich, the story was about to change. A Polish laboratory worker at Bonn University discovered a

---

[63] Frost, Natasha. *Julia Child's Spy Days.* History 8/31/2018. tinyurl.com/4awc8x8f.

[64] *Julia Child.* Pub domain photo. CIA. *Recipe for Adventure.* NWHM 11/8/2017. tinyurl.com/y6xjudzm.

crumpled piece of paper in a toilet. Thinking it might be of importance, he quietly turned it over to the Allies. It was the Osenberg list.

At this point late in the war, the United States already had a well-developed program for interrogation of enemy prisoners. Centers like top secret Post Office Box 1142 at Fort Hunt in Virginia were in charge of debriefing potentially valuable captives such as U-boat captains. As the war in Europe was headed to an end, far-thinking Air Force General Clayton Bissell, working in intelligence out of Fort Hunt, came up with an idea...to take from the ashes of the crumbling Third Reich the best of their scientific minds and bring them to America. He was met, however, with a firm no from the State Department. Enemy aliens would not be allowed into the country. Bissell was determined. Gathering a handful of carefully selected individuals, he addressed the group:

Gentlemen, I need to take an action that is illegal and which might wind me up in jail, but a general is supposed to risk his life on the battlefield if required, and I figure I'm obligated to risk my freedom at home to do what I consider right. There are dozens, perhaps hundreds of German scientists, and if we don't bring them into this country, they will go to Russia, they'll go to England, they will go elsewhere, and we will lose all of that technology. So I have decided to do it illegally...we will take over an island in Boston Harbor, which is under control of the military for the duration, and we will import these scientists illegally and take them to the island before the immigration people see the boat.[65]

The result was Operation Overcast, a top-secret program that sought to bring 350 scientists and engineers to the United States in "an extralegal manner." The Black List was developed, containing a short list of critically important men who, if encountered, would be immediately transported for interrogation. Intelligence units proposed individuals based on the Osenberg List and recommendations from universities and private industries such as the American Optical Company of Southbridge.[66]

Wernher Von Braun, tops on the Black List, and a handful of his colleagues would be the first group to set foot on American soil as guests of the United States government. By Spring 1945, the Russian Army was closing in around Peenemunde, a facility that had been repeatedly bombed by the Allies with devastating effect.

Bomb craters after raid, Peenemunde. 1943.[67]

Peenemunde scientists were rounded up by the SS and transported to a town in the Bavarian Alps. Orders had been given to execute the group if necessary rather than let them fall into enemy hands. Von Braun, however, personable and persuasive, convinced his keepers that allowing the scientists to separate and move into the surrounding countryside would increase their chances of survival. Shortly afterward, two men approached a young US Army private in an Allied-held portion of Bavaria. "My name is Magnus von Braun," said one man. "My brother invented the V-2. We want to surrender."

[65] Bies, Brandon and Swersky, Sam. *Interview Hans Fichtner.* Fort Hunt Oral Hist. NPS 4/22/2010. tinyurl.com/w6bn4f8v.

[66] Gimble, John. *Proj Paperclip.* Dipl Hist, OUP 1990. tinyurl.com/2kxpsdt5.

[67] *Craters Peenemunde* 1943. Pub domain photo. RAF. *Peenemunde Raid.* 7/31/2023. tinyurl.com/43ftuhbr.

Once Operation Overcast began netting results, the issue of how to handle these men arose. Secrecy was of the utmost importance. Nearly all of them were German, and in the eyes of the American public, welcoming a group of Nazis with open arms, whatever their talents, would be frowned upon. How many Americans had died at their hands? How many families would love to pay the Germans back in kind? In addition, publicizing the capture of von Braun and his colleagues meant that their families back in Germany were at risk of retribution by the Third Reich, a situation that could seriously affect their interest in collaborating with the United States. Intricate plans were developed to ensure the safety and secrecy of Operation Overcast and its captives.

Henry Kolm, who would become a long-time resident of Wayland, was twenty-one when he met von Braun. Born in Austria and of the Jewish Faith, his father had moved his family to the States shortly after the Anschluss. Henry enlisted in the US Army, served with Patton, and found his way into the intelligence branch, eventually becoming a member of General Bissell's Operation Overcast team. He shared his remarkable story with the National Park Service.

Kolm was charged with preparing a site used during the Civil War, Fort Strong on Long Island in Boston Harbor. Scavenging materials from abandoned structures and with new supplies from Fort Devens, Kolm's men renovated a barracks that could hold 300 residents. It would be referred to as "the house of German science." No hidden wiring and no listening devices were installed. The Germans, claimed Kolm, gave up their secrets readily. Concerned with secrecy, Kolm declined to use the American military to work on the island. He feared they would go on leave, get liquored up, and tell stories. Instead, he hand-picked forty German POWs from Fort Meade and moved them up to Boston.

In September 1945, Von Braun and the first small group arrived in Boston. In those days, ships would wait off a tiny chunk of rock, Nixes Mate, for pilot boats to guide them into Boston Harbor. "Corky" Corkham, a seventh-generation fisherman, and his well-worn, weather-beaten, cod-stinking boat were hired by the government to take incoming Germans from ships off Nixes Mate and ferry them to Long Island. His other job was to keep secrets. During a howling storm, von Braun and his colleagues, one by one, climbed down a boatswain's ladder, boarded Corkham's boat, and made it safely to Fort Strong. The scene would be enacted over and over again as more German scientists defected to the US.[68]

Fort Strong was not a prisoner of war camp, far from it. Prisoners were treated well. Not exactly enemies, not exactly acceptable members of society, they were considered collaborators with precious secrets to tell. Medical and dental care were provided at Fort Devens. MPs guarded the POWs, but the scientists needed none. They were not allowed to leave the island but were taken on field trips into Boston, where they purchased hard-to-obtain items for families back in Germany. The US obliged them by sending the gifts to Europe in official government mail pouches. During the holidays, the German POW baker decided to make stollen, which apparently required six bottles of scotch for the recipe. His request was granted.[69] One very unusual incident occurred at Christmas when Edward Rowe Snow made a surprise visit to the island. This World War II veteran and local legend for many years made a habit of dressing up as Santa Claus and flying to remote lighthouses and islands delivering presents. This particular year, he unknowingly landed at the top-secret government installation on Long Island. After a holiday visit, he left the island, its secrets in safe hands.[70]

Kolm did his best to meet the needs of his guests. A group of Catholics asked to have a mass said on the island, so he arranged for a priest to visit. The English-speaking priest's words, however, required translation. Kolm, a member of the Jewish faith who spoke fluent German, was less than appreciative of the role that the Catholic Church played in World War II. He recalled Cardinal Innizer, who collaborated with the Nazis and gave up information about Jews, calling him "a real son of a bitch." "So whenever

---

[68] Boeri, David. *Nazis On Harbor.* Wbur 8/19/2010. tinyurl.com/5dzttj8s.

[69] Bies, Brandon and Swersky, Sam. *Interview Hans Fichtner.*

[70] Critchley, Nicole. *Edward Rowe Snow.* Boston Athanaeum 1/2017. tinyurl.com/5ha533mz.

this priest gave his sermon and referred to the great deeds of the Catholic Church, I watered it down somewhat in my translation."

Interrogation at Fort Strong was more like a conversation across the table at lunch or during a game of chess. These men had willingly gone over to the Allies with the understanding that they would be allowed to continue their research. Most of them were German. Not one, according to Kolm, was dedicated to the Nazi Party, even though many were members. Their loyalty, if they had any, seems to have been directed toward science. They had opted to bend to the will of the Third Reich rather than lose their jobs or risk imprisonment in concentration camps. It was Kolm's job to create dossiers on each man and send them to Washington, where a decision on placement would be made.[71]

The work at Fort Strong lasted for nearly a year. The war would come to an end while German scientists still inhabited the secret government facility on Long Island. Henry Kolm went on to become a noted faculty member at MIT and the founder of the MIT National Magnet Laboratory. As President Truman took control of the government, the State Department was ordered to cooperate with Bissell's people. The name "Overcast" began to slip slowly into public notice and was quickly changed to "Paperclip."

The project was not without controversy. In 1951, Janina Iwanska was approached by the FBI while recovering at Beth Israel Hospital in Boston from her experience as a prisoner at Ravensbruck Concentration Camp. She was asked to identify a man in a photograph. It was Maj. General Walter Schreiber. Although he was not the individual who had carried out horrific experiments on her, she clearly remembered him. His subordinate at Ravensbruck, Dr. Karl Gebhardt, had been blamed for failing to adequately treat SS Officer Reinhard Heydrich after an assassination attempt on Hitler. To prove his innocence, Gebhardt carried out a series of experiments on prisoners at the concentration camp. Janina Iwanska was one of them. Her legs were broken, bits of shin bone removed, and bacteria introduced into the wound. Once infection set in, it was treated with sulfa to gauge its effect on gas gangrene, basically to prove that the drug would not have saved Heydrich's life.[72] Gebhardt would be found guilty of war crimes at Nuremberg and die by the hangman's noose. Walter Schreiber's life took a different path.

Brought into the US through Operation Paperclip, Schreiber's secrets were safe with the government. He was installed in a research position at Randolph Air Force Base in Texas, and news of Schreiber's addition to Army Air Force Aviation Medicine was highlighted in a journal. Unfortunately for the government, the journal was read by Dr. Leo Alexander, Boston resident, instructor at Harvard University, and consultant to the Allies at the Nuremberg War Trials. He recognized the name and alerted the Director of the Massachusetts Medical Society, telling him that Schrieber was an "intolerable addition to American Medicine." Unhappy with their response, Alexander contacted the *Boston Globe*, and the story began to spread.

---

[71] Bies, Brandon and Swersky, Sam. *Interview Hans Fichtner.*

[72] Silver JR. *Karl Gebhardt.* RCPE 2011. Wayback Machine. tinyurl.com/yskda2y6.

Dr. Leo Alexander at Nuremberg War Crimes Trial. 1946.[73]

The FBI questioned Iwanska, and soon afterward, the government dropped Schreiber's contract, and he moved to California. However, the controversy continued. Dr. Alexander wrote directly to the President. The Physicians Forum, with affiliates in 36 states, expressed outrage, demanding that the process by which the former Nazi had been assigned to a government position be investigated. Alarm bells suddenly sounded. Public knowledge of Schreiber's story could have a devastating effect on a number of government agencies, officials, and programs that operated under the veil of secrecy provided by Operation Paperclip. Schreiber had to go and go quietly. After being given a travel allowance and police protection, the doctor and his family moved to Argentina. Walter Schreiber would spend the rest of his life in relative comfort and die in Argentina in 1970.

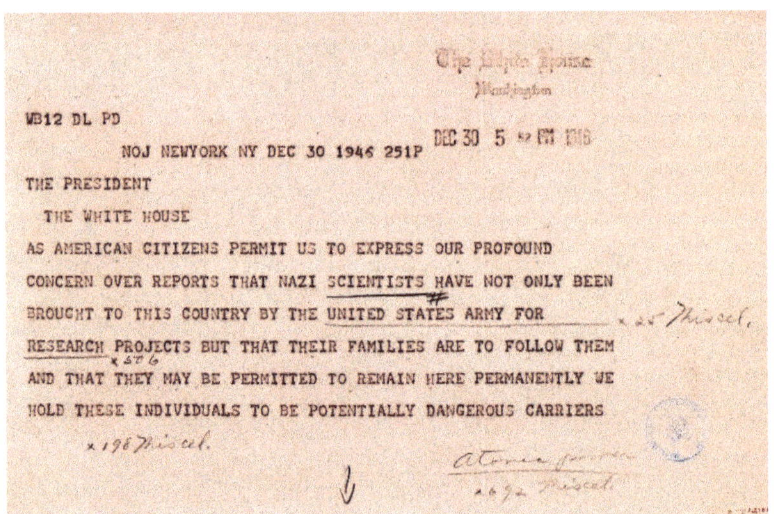

"Profound concern" over Nazi scientists in the US expressed in
telegram to Truman. The message is from Albert Einstein and over two dozen scientists,
mathematicians, educators, and clergymen, eight of them with ties to Massachusetts.[74]

The Nazi doctor from Ravensbruck was one of many who would cause public relations problems for Operation Paperclip. Luftwaffe Colonel Hubertus Strughold was sought by the Allies as a war criminal after evidence showed that he had actively participated in human medical experiments.

---

[73] *Dr. Leo Alexander.* Pub domain image. 169155574. NARA. Wiki Commons. tinyurl.com/43mj2kd2.

[74] *Truman Einstein… Transcript* 12/30/1946. Pub domain photo. Truman PPF. Wiki Commons. tinyurl.com/yhh4uw8p

Hubertus Strughold would later rise to the position of Chief Scientist of NASA's Aerospace Medical division and became known as the father of space medicine. During the war, Arthur Rudolph used slave labor from the Dora-Nordhausen concentration camp to assist in his work at the Mittelwerk rocket factory in Germany. He would lead the Saturn V rocket development program at Marshall Space Flight Center and was integral in placing the first man on the moon. Perhaps the most publicized case is that of Wernher von Braun, father of modern space science and Director of NASA's Marshall Space Flight Center. While his duties for the Third Reich primarily encompassed management of rocket research and development, it is well known that SS Sturmbannführer von Braun personally made visits to Buchenwald to hand-pick concentration camp prisoners to work at his Peenemunde facility.

The government would develop a faulty memory with some; a few would be exiled. Truman would be criticized but, in his typical no-nonsense fashion, responded that because of looming Russian aggression, "this had to be done and was done." Before the program ended, hundreds of scientists, including all of von Braun's Peenemunde people, were in the United States. These men would go on to develop American space science, become founding members of NASA, and bring the nation to a position of power that would carry the US through the Cold War and into the future.

Among the Peenemunde scientists who made their way to a new life through Operation Paperclip was Dr. Ernst Steinhoff. His extensive work on German missile guidance systems would yield a lengthy career at US rocketry and weapon development sites such as the White Sands Proving Grounds in New Mexico. However, the physicist was not the first member of the Steinhoff family to make his way to America.

In May 1942, the German U-511 was chosen for a special mission to test an experimental weapon system that could launch rockets from the deck of a submarine. The project was the brainchild of Dr. Steinhoff. Huge metal frames designed to shoot 275-pound rockets as far as five miles were welded to the deck. In spite of the fact that trials done on the surface and from fifty feet below were somewhat successful, the project was discarded. U-511 was deployed to a training group, and the sub captain, Friedrich Steinhoff, brother of Ernst Steinhoff, was assigned a desk job at Flotilla Headquarters.

The service record of this controversial figure gives clues to his personality. Within the first fifteen months of the war, he commanded a minesweeping flotilla followed by a coastal defense group. For three months, he was an officer aboard U-96. His next assignment, command of U-511, lasted thirteen months before he was removed from active duty for a year. In January 1944, he was placed in command of U-873.[75] The story of the Kapitänleutnant Friedrich Steinhoff would soon take a tragic turn.

The submarine began its final mission in March 1945. It was assigned to deliver an important cargo of mercury and optical glass to Japan. A little over one month later, the devastating news arrived...the Third Reich had collapsed. Admiral Doenitz was now in charge. All subs were ordered to return to Norway. Two days later, new orders indicated that U-873 should proceed to an Allied port. Steinhoff declined to obey. Much heated disagreement followed among the crew, some demanding to follow orders, some wanting to sail to South America with hopes of selling the material on board. On May 11, the order was given by the engineering officer. U-873 would head to America. After instruments and official documents were destroyed, the sub met with USS Vance and was escorted to Portsmouth Naval Base in New Hampshire on May 17.[76]

---

[75] Weiberg, Eric. *U-873 surrendered Portsmouth 5/1945*. Eric Weiberg 10/26/2015. tinyurl.com/322xu6be.

[76] *INTERROGATION U-873* 6/26/1945. Indiv U-boats. U-boat Arch. tinyurl.com/uevzdp2p.

The crew of U-873 after surrender at Portsmouth Navy Yard.
Note Friedrich Steinhoff, front row with white cap. May 1945.[77]

Two days later, Friedrich Steinhoff was dead. The controversy surrounding his death continues to this day. While the public was aware of the surrender of U-873, what followed was carefully hidden from view. Secret government reports document the series of unusual events that followed the sub's surrender. After initial questioning, the crew was transferred not to a military facility but to the Charles Street Jail in Boston, where they were confined with common criminals. Interrogation continued. The U-Boat captain, a hardened Nazi, was assigned a Marine guard. Jack Alberti, the civilian interrogator, wore a naval uniform during the two-and-a-half-hour interview. U-873 Petty Officer Georg Seitz would later report that the U-boat captain's face was swollen and bleeding after interrogation.[78] Alberti later explained his actions:

In regard to the Commander of the U-873, it is true that I caused him to be slapped <u>ONCE </u>by a marine guard. The Commander was of considerable physical proportions, threatening in his attitude and insolent in his demeanor. I was in the uniform of a Lt. Comdr. His attitude was not in keeping with the terms of the surrender, nor was it respectful of the uniform. He alone could furnish the answers to certain questions...the prisoner became extremely menacing and hysterically arrogant. In keeping with well-known psychological principles, I instructed the guard to slap him once. It was done entirely because of his menacing attitude and arrogance, which ceased after the slapping, and I was thereafter treated with the respect of the Commander.[79]

Several hours later, Steinhoff was found dead in his cell at the Charles Street Jail. The Medical Examiner's report stated that he was found bleeding from a wound on his right wrist and died on the way to the hospital.[80] The official government report ruled that he "committed suicide on 19 May 1945 by severing an artery in his wrist with a broken piece of eyeglass and a wire which apparently came from his cap."[81]

---

[77] *Prisoners U-873*. Pub domain photo. USN. NAID 6036884. Wiki Commons. tinyurl.com/5duahpcd.

[78] *U-873 surrendered 5/11/1945*. U-Boat Arch. tinyurl.com/yb7vb6tu.

[79] Alberti, Jack H. *Memo to V. CNO 7/27/1945*. U-Boat Arch. tinyurl.com/yxkssy9w.

[80] *ME Certificate Death Fritz Steinhoff 5/25/1945*. U-Boat Arch. tinyurl.com/4zsa5mf3.

[81] *Transfer German POWs U-873 5/21/1945*. U-Boat Arch. tinyurl.com/39h5ued9.

SUFFOLK
BOSTON

(County)
(City or Town)

The Commonwealth of Massachusetts
OFFICE OF THE SECRETARY
DIVISION OF VITAL STATISTICS
MEDICAL EXAMINER'S
CERTIFICATE OF DEATH

1 PLACE OF DEATH

No. _en route to Mass. Gen'l Hosp._ St. (If death occurred in a hospital give its NAME instead of street)

(Physician — Important)
(Was deceased a U. S. War Veteran, if so specify WAR)

2 FULL NAME _Fritz Steinhoff_
(If deceased is a married, widowed or divorced woman, give also maiden name.)

(a) Residence, No. _Germany_ St.
(Usual place of abode)
(If nonresident, give city or town and State)

Length of stay: in hospital or institution __________ years __________ months __________ days. In this community __________ yrs. __________ mos. __________ days
(Before death) (Specify whether)

PERSONAL AND STATISTICAL PARTICULARS	MEDICAL CERTIFICATE OF DEATH

3 SEX **Male** | 4 COLOR OR RACE **white** | 5 SINGLE MARRIED WIDOWED or DIVORCED (write the word) **Unknown**

18 DATE OF DEATH _May 19, 1945_ (Month) (Day) (Year)

19 I HEREBY CERTIFY that I have investigated the death of the person above-named and that the CAUSE AND MANNER thereof are as follows: (If an injury was involved, state fully.)

Incised wound right wrist

5a If married, widowed, or divorced HUSBAND of __________ (Give maiden name of wife in full)

(or) WIFE of __________ (Husband's name in full)

6 Age of husband or wife if alive __________ years

7 IF STILLBORN, enter that fact here.

8 AGE **25 ?** Years __________ Months __________ Days | If less than 1 day __________ Hours __________ Minutes

20 Accident, suicide, or homicide (specify) _Suicidal_
Date of occurrence _May 19_ 19 _46_
Where did Injury occur? _Boston_ (City or town and State)
Did Injury occur in or about home, on farm, in industrial place, or in public place? _Jail_ (Specify type of place)

9 Usual Occupation: _Officer (Submarine)_

10 Industry or Business: _German Army_

11 Social Security No. __________

Manner of Injury _Found bleeding while a prisoner_
Nature of Injury _or at Charles St Jail May 19/45_
While at work? _---_ Was there an autopsy? _Yes_

12 BIRTHPLACE (City) (State or country) __________

13 NAME OF FATHER __________

14 BIRTHPLACE OF FATHER (City) (State or country) __________

21 Was disease or injury in any way related to occupation of deceased? If so, specify __________

15 MAIDEN NAME OF MOTHER __________

(Signed) _W J Brickley_ M.D.
(Address) _Boston Mass_ Date _5-19-1945_

16 BIRTHPLACE OF MOTHER (City) (State or country) __________

22 Place of Burial, Cremation or Removal _Post Cem-Fort Devens_ (City or Town)
DATE OF BURIAL _May 24/45_ 19

17 Informant _Hosp Records_ (Relation, if any)
(Address)

23 NAME OF FUNERAL DIRECTOR _H L Farmer & Son_
ADDRESS _Ayer Mass_

I HEREBY CERTIFY that a satisfactory standard certificate of death was filed with me BEFORE the burial or transit permit was issued:

Received and filed _May 25/45_

(Signature of Agent of Board of Health or other)

(Official Designation) (Date of Issue of Permit)

A TRUE COPY ATTEST: (Registrar)

Death certificate of Friedrich Steinhoff. 1945.[82]

Had Steinhoff been brutally beaten and crumbled under the weight of a harsh investigation? The sailors of U-873 gave another clue. "He was described by his crew as an excellent seaman but totally unable to exercise his command. The engineer officer and the doctor aboard seemed to have influenced the Commanding Officer to such an extent that they were, for all practical purposes, in command of the boat."[83] Perhaps the blame should rest with Jack Alberti, who was condemned by the government following an investigation for violating the Geneva Convention. But perhaps the truth of it is that Steinhoff, a belligerent Nazi with a fragmented service record and fragile emotional state, willingly chose

---

[82] *ME Certificate Death Fritz Steinhoff.*

[83] *INTERROGATION U-873.*

to follow the Third Reich to death. He was buried at the Fort Devens Cemetery in Ayer on American soil, surrounded by his enemies.

After the final shot was fired, the dead buried, and the world settled into quiet, stories began to unfold. But, as is the way of history, the more the world began to know, the more questions that arose. Had the government engaged in coverups to keep important information from the public? Was Hitler really dead, or had he crawled out of his Berlin bunker and slithered away to Argentina with his other Nazi cronies? Or had he jumped on a German-invented anti-gravity machine and taken off on a UFO for parts unknown? Was Patton murdered? Did General Yamashita really leave a kazillion-dollar treasure trove somewhere in the Philippines? How about this whopper...did Winston Churchill know about the Japanese plan to attack Pearl Harbor and do nothing?

Today, questions and theories remain about why the United States was caught unaware on December 7, 1941. For many years, the primary target was Franklin Roosevelt, who supposedly had the decrypted Japanese attack message in his hand prior to the event yet chose to ignore it in an effort to shock his isolationist country into war. As years passed, however, this particular conspiracy theory was debunked, defused, deflated, and relegated to the domain of Sasquatch and the aliens who built the pyramids. Winston Churchill, however, remains under scrutiny. It is well known that England had the ability to read Japanese coded messages and that the Prime Minister was losing patience with Roosevelt's indecision about joining the conflict. Almost certainly, an attack on the primary US naval base in the Pacific would result in America's entry into the war. And Churchill himself described his feeling after learning of the attack as being "...to me the greatest joy."

The Prime Minister's possible treachery is an interesting point of discussion, still often challenged by journalists and historians who feel the need to protect his legacy even after all these years. If he was guilty of this betrayal, we will never know. Churchill took the truth of it to the grave with him. The reality is that, like Jimmy Hoffa, Stonehenge, and the lost Roanoke Colony, the story will most likely forever remain within the realm of secrets.

Chapter 10

Hospitals and Healers

I remember one poignant moment. As one patient was being wheeled into the O.R., he looked up at me; I smiled and gently touched his cheek...The patients were so young and so far away from family and home. Sometimes I forgot that we were young, too...
2nd Lt. Lena R. Gelott, Army Nurse Corps
48th Station Hospital, Guadalcanal 1944[1]

The Langley, the first aircraft carrier in American history, had gone down in waters off Java. Aboard the USS Pecos, medical officer Lt. Joseph Yon, a young doctor from Pennsylvania, and the ship's chief pharmacist mate were treating a survivor on the operating table when the Japanese attacked. As the ship quaked, they carefully placed the man on the floor and, kneeling beside him, carried on with the procedure. Yon recalled:

When I heard the machine guns and the anti-aircraft guns begin to rattle, I knew that we had about thirty seconds before we either had another hit or a near-miss. We would give them about ten seconds and then drop down alongside the patient, the chief on one side and I on the other, and wait for the ship to jump...As soon as the ship ceased shuddering, we got onto our knees and began to work on the injured [man] until the next bomb was due.[2]

Many of those who survived the sinking of the Langley, including Chief Petty Officer Russell W. Demarais of Adams, would perish hours later when USS Pecos met the same fate at the hands of Japanese bombers.[3]

This was the face of medicine in World War II. Gone were the horse-drawn cannons and open-cockpit biplanes of World War I, replaced by machines equipped with the technology of killing. Bombs could now wipe out hundreds at one drop, airplanes could spray bullets across a wide path, and radar could pinpoint a target miles away. The United States was not inexperienced in the art of war. The First World War was a horrific saga. In less than two years of involvement, nearly 120,000 Americans lost their lives. Tragically, however, the lessons of the War to End All Wars went unheeded, and twenty-three years later, World War II would obliterate the lives of over 400,000 Americans.

The development of the science of warfare and the truly worldwide scope of the conflict brought with it a frightening array of challenges for the medical profession. The sheer numbers involved were staggering, and those wounded in battle more than tripled from World War I to World War II. With theaters of operation in remote areas of the world, providing access to medical care was problematic. Jungle warfare brought with it oppressive humidity and temperatures and the rise of a new enemy, tropical diseases.

---

[1] Gelott, Lena R. *Veteran's Testimony.* WW2 US Med Res Ctr. tinyurl.com/mr23k673.

[2] Cowdrey, Albert E. *Fighting for Life.* Free Press/Division MacMillan 1994.

[3] *Demarais.* No Adams Transcript 12/22/1945. Newspapers.com. tinyurl.com/ms845pe2.

Soldier using a hammer for pest control, India. WWII.[4]

Powerful and accurate torpedoes caused men to abandon ship through oily water and fire. Flamethrowers now vomited forth napalm and could cover an area twice as large as in the first war. As a result, the number of burn and shock cases radically expanded. Through it all, it was up to healers to sustain the lives of the 16 million Americans who specialized in death.

A deeper look at the appalling losses the United States has sustained in war reveals some startling statistics. The Civil War, which resulted in more than 620,000 deaths, was by far the bloodiest of all conflicts. Of every eight men struck down, three were killed in action, and five lost their lives to wounds or illness. Roughly one in thirteen soldiers who returned home was an amputee.[5] In the two global conflicts that followed, US deaths thankfully fell far behind those of the Civil War. Eleven million more Americans served in the Second World War than the First, and nearly 300,000 more lost their lives, incomprehensible statistics and unspeakable losses. What is glaringly notable, however, is that the survival rate from wounds or illness increased from a shocking 4 percent in the First World War to 50 percent in World War II.[6] In *Fighting for Life,* Albert Cowdrey states, "American soldiers were now as likely to die by shells, bullets or poison gas as by disease."[7] This was a direct result of the planning, implementation, and innovation of the medical community and the awe-inspiring heroism and dedication of thousands of doctors, nurses, medics, corpsmen, and all others who fought to preserve life in a desperate time of war.

As the world steadily moved toward war, America, shrouded in an isolationist fog, failed to upgrade its medical care for the military. The Navy Bureau of Medicine and Surgery counted just over 100 servicemen and 225 civilians under its command.[8] The task that faced the US Army was more challenging. By the end of the war, more than twice the number of Navy and Marines combined would serve in the Army's ranks. Unfortunately, in 1939, the Army Medical Department consisted of less than 50,000 members. (At its highest point in the First World War, 340,000 had served in the department.)[9]

Both the military and the medical profession in general were facing a crisis. When the draft became a reality in 1940, it created an instantaneous need for physicians. Doctors now would be required by local draft boards to determine fitness for classification, by the federal government to examine inductees, and by the private sector to provide medical care for millions of Americans. One year after

---

[4] *Wham!* 1945. Pub domain photo. 111-SC-35334. Wong, Phillip. *Once Bitten, Forever Archival.* NARA tinyurl.com/39kb6py4.

[5] *Civil War Casualties.* Am Battlefield Trust 11/16/2012. tinyurl.com/em7xh4f6.

[6] Vergun, David. *Med Improvements WWII.* DOD News 3/17/2020. tinyurl.com/9n9b85ft.

[7] Cowdrey, Albert E. *Fighting for Life.*

[8] Schwartz, Joseph. *Hist US Med Dept WWII.* tinyurl.com/4479juwh.

[9] *Overview Med Dept.* WW2 US Med Red Ctr. tinyurl.com/ytyk2a7n.

war broke out, the government made plans to induct over 50,000 physicians. Given that the US had only 180,000 licensed physicians, 25,000 of them retired, the numbers just didn't add up.[10]

A conspicuous void opened in the medical profession once physicians joined the war effort and deployed overseas. The patient-doctor ratio in the US soon ballooned to 1,700:1,[11] and many left the comfort of retirement to go back into the medical field. Dr. Roger Kinnicutt had practiced medicine as an Army captain in the last war and retired from his work as a Chief Pathologist in 1933. During World War II, he once again joined the staff at Worcester Memorial Hospital.[12] In North Adams, local physicians asked the public for help by requesting fewer house calls. Due to the shortage of professionals, if doctors weren't notified before 6 p.m., they most likely wouldn't make it to the home appointment until after 9 o'clock. The privilege of the call now cost $4.00, a whopping increase of one dollar.[13]

As the shortage of doctors grew, so did health problems. Diabetes, for example, rose from twenty-seventh to tenth as a cause of death. As war production ramped up, the need for doctors in industry greatly expanded along with the number of accidents in the workplace. In 1940, over 1.5 million on-the-job injuries resulted in 18,000 deaths.[14] The government responded by encouraging state medical boards to license physicians after just three years of medical training. Applications for admission to medical schools soared.

The role of women in medicine was changing as well. The country had been at war for well over a year before female physicians were granted temporary commissions in the military, although few in number. Dr. Hazel Richards, a native of Longmeadow with a practice in Malden, became the first woman from New England to be called to duty with the Army in March 1943.[15] Opportunities for women in the medical profession in general were limited. In 1940, less than 5 percent of all American doctors were women. Now, with the approach of war, women were increasingly being admitted to medical schools.

Despite the fact that the first women's medical college in America was founded in Boston nearly a century before, Harvard University was slow to embrace this precedent, excluding women from its prestigious medical school. Dr. Joseph Aub, in 1942, cautioned: "If this proves to be a long war, we will have increasing need for such graduates." In 1943, John T. Williams, Assistant Professor of Gynecology, disagreed. "The pro-feminists are apt to overlook the fundamental biological law that the primary function of woman is to bear and raise children, and the first social duty of woman is to develop and perpetuate the home." One month later in spite of a Harvard faculty vote to support female admissions, the President and Fellows of Harvard College refused to admit women into the ranks of the medical school.[16] The policy would change.

Dora Benedict wanted to do her part in the war effort. The young woman from Milton was a student at Bryn Mawr College when she made the decision to suspend her education in order to do research for the government.[17] Soon, however, Benedict would make history. She was one of twelve women who were finally allowed to enter Harvard Medical School on September 24, 1945,[18] ninety-eight years after the first woman applied for entrance[19] and, unfortunately for the country, three weeks after World War II ended.

<hr>

[10] Klein, Maury. *Call to Arms.* Bloomsbury Press 2013.

[11] *1940s Medicine and Health.* Encyclopedia.com. tinyurl.com/4dv94wrf.

[12] *Roger Kinnicutt.* Proceedings AAS 4/1961. AAS. tinyurl.com/y32s4ahj.

[13] *Help doctors.* No Adams Transcript 2/9/1943. Newspapers.com. tinyurl.com/mwh8ebsr.

[14] Klein, Maury. *A Call to Arms.*

[15] Rice, Olive Pearson. *Woman Doctor Called.* Springfield Daily Republican 3/28/1943. Newspapers.com. tinyurl.com/2a5uabnt.

[16] Brown, Laura et al. *Matriculation Women HMS. Hist Women HMS.* HMS. tinyurl.com/yjv49m2d.

[17] Richter, Ruthann. *Dora Goldstein Dies.* SUMC News Center 10/7/2011. tinyurl.com/5n6xpb49.

[18] *Raquel Cohen.* OnView. Ctr Hist Med. Harvard Countway Lib. tinyurl.com/bddnxh6y.

[19] Brown, Laura et al. *Matriculation of Women HMS.*

In addition to medical care, among the responsibilities of the Army Medical Corps was to provide evacuation services. Thus, during World War II, a complex evacuation chain was established. Trains, ambulances, and, for the first time, aircraft were used for evacuation. Ships painted white and bearing a large, easily identifiable red cross were specifically designed to become floating hospitals. The Navy Hospital Corps maintained fifteen hospital ships and a small number of ambulance vessels. The Army operated twenty-four hospital ships, mostly for evacuation purposes.

The USAHS Acadia, refitted and supplied in Boston, became the first in 1943. Two years later, the largest hospital ship in the world, USAHS Louis A. Milne, launched from the Bethlehem Shipyard in Quincy. The vessel had space for 1,427 wounded. On board were Chief Dental Officer Major John Nesson of Boston and Brookline and 1st Officer Commander Gordon Mackie of Watertown. The ship's crew, including twenty-three Merchant Marines from Massachusetts, had spent ten months at Camp Myles Standish preparing. At least a dozen of the forty-four nurses aboard, including Lt. Hazel Chipman of Springfield, hailed from Massachusetts as well. When the Milne sailed, Chipman headed eastward across the Atlantic at the very same time that her fiance, Sgt. William Craves was returning home from Europe after having been wounded three times.[20]

Wounded being transported aboard an LCT. D-Day.[21]

The Geneva Convention protected these ships from enemy fire. It was an agreement signed by Japan but never ratified; thus, in the Pacific, hospital ships were fair game. On April 30, 1945, a front-page article in the *Springfield Union* read, "U.S. Hospital Ship Is Hit By Jap Suicide Flier in Deliberate, Vicious Attack." The USS Comfort carrying wounded from Okinawa had been struck by a kamikaze in the surgical area of the ship while doctors were tending to casualties.[22] According to Pfc. George Krohne of West Springfield, on board after being wounded in battle; the attack was deliberate retaliation for the recent sinking of a Japanese relief ship.[23] The government of Japan defiantly announced to the world, "We are justified in bombing hospital ships as they are being used as repair ships for returning wounded men back to the fighting front." Twenty-eight souls lost their lives in the attack on the Comfort. During World War II, enemy fire would sink two dozen hospital ships.

---

[20] Burns, Frances. *Hosp Ship Trial Run.* Boston Globe 3/15/1945. Newspapers.com. tinyurl.com/3dn8n4rk.

[21] *Casualties LST.* Public domain photo. Navy Med 09-7912-47. Flickr. tinyurl.com/mr3kf6hw.

[22] Haugland, Vern. *Hosp Ship Hit By Jap.* Springfield Union 4/30/1945. Newspapers.com. tinyurl.com/3dyekenc.

[23] *Survives Raid Hosp Ship.* Springfield Evening Union 7/20/1945. Newspapers.com. tinyurl.com/yc4hwyrb.

Operating room, USS Comfort, after kamikaze
attack. April 1945.[24]

The military established a series of zones that defined the level of care and extended outward from the battlefield all the way to the Zone of the Interior in the United States. Within the innermost zone on the battlefield, medical personnel provided first aid and moved the wounded to points outside the immediate combat area for more extensive treatment. For the Army, medics, often unarmed in order to carry as many supplies as possible, followed soldiers to the battlefield and into harm's way. Col. Robert Carpenter of North Adams had nothing but praise for them. "They go out under all kinds of gunfire and pick up the wounded men, give them first aid, and somehow get them back to safety. You go into any army hospital in the world and ask a soldier how soon he received aid after he was hit, and nine chances out of ten, he'll tell you a medical man caught me almost before I fell to the ground."[25]

In an interview with the *Transcript Telegram*, Army medic Anthony Donorowitz of Holyoke recalled his haunting experience at Vielsam in Belgium. With the battle raging around them, the wounded came in so quickly and in such great numbers that his clearing station was turned into a hospital. "The wounded needed blood. We were on our feet 24 hours a day and were in no shape to give it. Men less seriously injured offered what they could afford to give." He recalled seeing those injured.

Across the hall is a 16-year-old German boy with one arm blown off. And not far from him, an American in the same condition. "My fingers feel stiff," says the American. "I play a guitar. They won't stay stiff, will they?" In the dark turn of the hall are five men who will never speak again. But there is no time for brooding, a wound needs redressing. No time for questions, a man in pain needs morphine. No time for fear. If anyone is afraid he does not show it.[26]

Army medic Peter Fantasia of Somerville was another such hero. In 1944 while providing aid to wounded from the 26th Infantry Division, he was captured and spent the rest of the war in a POW camp. In 2020, 103-year-old Fantasia received long overdue medals for his service and sacrifice.[27]

---

[24] *USS Comfort Kamikaze.* Pub domain photo. NavSource Online. NARA 80-G-315912. tinyurl.com/34uexha7.

[25] *Tribute Paid Medics.* No Adams Transcript 6/19/1945. Newspapers.com. tinyurl.com/4uxwpv5p.

[26] *Medic Story.* Transcript TG 6/21/1945. Newspapers.com. tinyurl.com/2yfbwy5z.

[27] Nakrin, Joy and Kaitlin Becker. *WWII Vet Receives Medals.* 10Boston Local 1/6/2020. tinyurl.com/mr6bdxzb.

Medics helping injured soldier in France, 1944.[28]

Medics treated enemies as well as their own. According to the War Department's *Rules of Land Warfare*, belligerents who fell into the hands of the Allies during combat were considered prisoners of war. In compliance with the Geneva Convention, they were provided with medical care. It was a responsibility taken seriously by the medical corps.

A captured German soldier is treated by a US
1st Army medic. February 1945.[29]

An illustration of American treatment of prisoners occurred in September 1945. The Japanese Empire had conceded defeat, and the Allies went looking for those who had driven the world into war, chief among them General Hideki Tojo. They found him less than two weeks later, sprawled in a chair at his home, a self-inflicted gunshot wound to the gut. "I wanted to die by the sword, but the pistol had to do...banzai!" he stated between bouts of unconsciousness. When he saw his captor, General Robert Eichelberger, Tojo apologized for the trouble he was causing. The General responded wryly, "...the trouble tonight, or the last four years?"[30]

In an effort to prolong his life, Tojo was given blood transfusions, American blood, blood he had spilled so callously since December 7, 1941. Taken to a clearing station, five medics including Ernest Wrobleski of Westfield, continued treatment until the General stabilized. He was then transferred to a hospital by ambulance, accompanied by Lt. Col. Richard Reynolds of Quincy.[31] "Why don't they let him

---

[28] *Medics helping soldier.* Pub domain photo. 535973 NARA tinyurl.com/bdej5n2t.

[29] *German prisoner.* Pub domain photo. SC 201479. USASC. Wiki Commons. tinyurl.com/2p9zh65v.

[30] *Tojo receives blood.* Smithsonian. tinyurl.com/p39x89zh.

[31] *Medics Aid War Lord.* Boston Globe 9/12/1945. Newspapers.com. tinyurl.com/56d8rw3c.

die?" asked one soldier who had been present when Tojo was captured. "He helped kill some of my buddies."[32] After Tojo's trial for war crimes, the Allies would take care of that too.

In the Navy, Pharmacist's Mates, known as corpsmen, performed the same function. Being stationed at sea brought distinct challenges. The isolation of being aboard a vessel meant that medical care would have to be found on board, and with the shortage of doctors, everything from tooth extractions to broken bones became the responsibility of pharmacist's mates. Albert E. Cowdrey in his book, *Fighting for Life*, described the experience facing corpsmen during combat:

A ship was home and fortress when whole, but a steel coffin packed with explosives and fuel oil when enemy fire tore its skin. Then it became a hellish place. Lighting systems failed, the dark compartments were shut off from one another, fires burned, and the injured lay in pools of oily water among mangled corpses and fragments of jagged steel. Medics worked in gas masks as the passages filled with poisonous fumes.[33]

One of the first to lose his life in World War II was 25-year-old Merle C. J. Hillman of Holyoke. The young man was serving aboard the USS California at Pearl Harbor when it was struck by the Japanese on December 7, 1941. Listed as missing, Hillman's body was recovered and laid to rest among other unknown heroes at the National Memorial Cemetery of the Pacific in Hawaii. In 2023, DNA analysis successfully identified the young man's remains, and he was returned home to his family.[34] Pharmacist's Mate 2nd Class Merle Hillman rests at Saint Jerome Cemetery in Holyoke.[35]

During battle on Iwo Jima, a Navy Corpsman (back right)
tends to a wounded Marine while others keep down amidst
a terrific barrage. February 19, 1945.[36]

Navy corpsmen who were earmarked to provide medical services for Marines went through basic training with them and developed a strong sense of unit solidarity. Navy surgeon Gordon Bruce was stationed with a Marine unit on Bougainville. While performing surgery in a field hospital, it was attacked by Japanese. Bruce, along with several corpsmen, located and removed three machine guns from the wreckage of nearby boats and found a handful of Marines to stand guard. News of the threat to the hospital spread, and soon Marines began to arrive, setting up a defensive line around the hospital.

[32] Hurwitz, Hy. *Nippon…Cameramen Field Day.* Boston Globe 9/12/1945. Newspapers.com. tinyurl.com/56d8rw3c.

[33] Cowdrey, Albert E. *Fighting for Life.*

[34] *Hillman, M.* DPAA 1/18/2024. tinyurl.com/5yz2zbp2.

[35] *Merle C.J. Hillman 1916-2023.* Republican 1/18-21/2024. MASSLIVE. tinyurl.com/5fkwmfax. Web 3 Dec 2024.

[36] *Corpsman…wounded Marine.* Pub domain photo. NH 104288. Crunk, Lisa et al. *Battle of Iwo Jima.* NHHC 4/16/2020. tinyurl.com/56f9657k.

Through the long night as doctors and corpsmen operated, bullets ripped through the tent around them. Not one patient was lost. One corpsman, however, was seriously wounded when a sniper's bullet struck him in the chest.[37]

While on Guadalcanal, Alfred W. Cleveland, a Pharmacist's Mate from Dartmouth, encountered a Marine who had lost part of his arm when a shell exploded. Using a pen knife, Cleveland, along with another corpsman, successfully amputated the ragged remnants of the man's arm, bandaged him, and left him in a foxhole to be evacuated. The Marine lived to tell the story, and Cleveland would be awarded a Silver Star for his actions.[38]

Henry O'Neil, a Navy Pharmacist's Mate from Pittsfield, recounted a terrifying event two days after arriving on Tarawa. At around three in the morning, O'Neil was hunkered down in a trench with members of his Marine Corps Unit. "The Japs attacked our positions with about 30 tanks. The tanks were straddling the trench and firing down at us, when one of them fired a shell which went into my left arm." A Marine came to O'Neil's aid. "While he applied a tourniquet to stop the bleeding, he put my arm on the edge of the trench. The noise around there was terrific and the next thing I knew a Jap tank rumbled across my arm and brushed against the Marine who was treating my wound. The weight of the tank crushed my forearm." O'Neil went on to describe Marines throwing grenades through openings in the front of the tanks and climbing on top to lob grenades inside onto the crews. With an obvious sense of pride, he reported, "Our company accounted for 26 tanks that night."[39]

Nowhere, however, was providing medical care more unique than aboard a submarine. Pharmacist's mates needed to understand the demands of living underwater, breathing in a sub size pool of oxygen and carbon dioxide for long periods, providing potable water, and safe disposal of waste. Treating patients could be fraught with complications.

On Christmas Eve 1942, Pharmacist's Mate T.A. Moore was about to perform an appendectomy aboard the USS Silversides. The ward room with its stainless steel table was hastily cleaned and an ironing board attached to give enough length to allow the patient to lay down. Moore's instruments included two spoons from the galley, bent in order to hold the incision open. The captain ordered the sub to submerge to a depth of 100 feet in to provide more stability. While the patient was being operated on, the anesthetic began to wear off, so ether was administered "following directions on the can." Unfortunately, a bit leaked into the enclosed ward room leaving the men drowsy and causing a delay.

The operation took four hours to complete. Soon afterwards, batteries in need of charging, the sub surfaced to find a Japanese destroyer bearing down on it. "The patient convalesced the morning following his amateur appendectomy to the tune of a torpedo firing, two depth charge attacks, two crash dives and an aerial bombing which knocked him out of his bunk..." During the days ahead, Moore tended to the patient's wound and needs, which included making a bed pan, as the sub's only real bedpan was being used in the engine room as an oil pan. The patient survived, and Pharmacist's Mate Moore made history.[40]

---

[37] Haugland, Vern. *Japs Repulsed.* Morning Union 11/15/1943. Newspapers.com. tinyurl.com/mrytw5h9.

[38] Tregaskis, Richard. *Guadalcanal Diary.* Modern Lib 2000.

[39] *Youth Run Over by Tank.* Berkshire Eagle 8/15/1944. Newspapers.com. tinyurl.com/45y4a6jf.

[40] *Holiday Appendectomy.* Sub Force Lib Mus Asso 12/24/2013. tinyurl.com/53pcj73m.

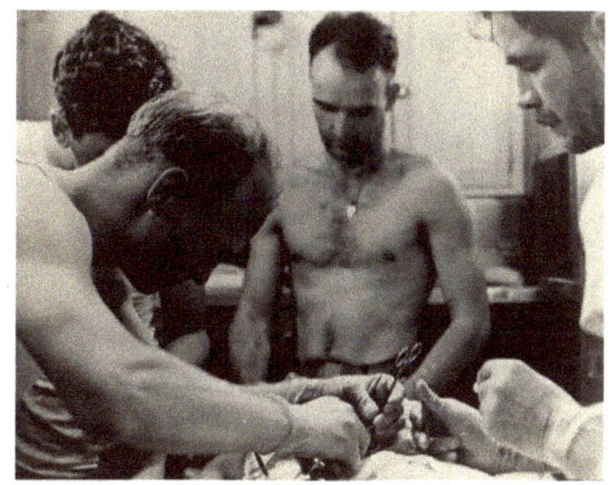

Navy corpsman performs appendectomy
aboard USS Silversides. 1942.[41]

Silversides went on to achieve fame in other ways. The sub was credited with destroying 23 ships, ranking her in the top five for enemy vessels sunk during the war. In July 1943, USS Silversides was placed under the command of John S. Coye of Worcester and Stockbridge. For his efforts, Coye was awarded the Navy cross and two gold stars.[42] Also aboard was engineering officer John Bienia of New Bedford, recipient of Silver and Bronze Stars for gallantry in action.[43]

Whether on land or at sea, being a corpsman was dangerous business. Eight months after Pearl Harbor, the *Boston Globe* published the names of eleven New Englanders reported dead or missing in action. Three of them, including Abel Gomes from Cape Cod, were pharmacists mates.[44] By that time, Frank Fenn (Great Barrington) and Edwin Custer (Fall River) along with two other New England corpsmen had been in a Japanese POW camp for six months.[45] Pharmacist Mate William Collinge of Fairview had two ships shot out from under him. Stationed aboard the USS Langley when it went down off Java in 1942, he and other survivors were rescued by the tanker USS Pecos. The following day, the Pecos was sunk by Japanese aircraft. Forced to abandon ship again, Collinge jumped into the water wearing a life belt. He later joked, "I guess the bombs scared the sharks away." After six hours in oil-soaked water, Collinge was rescued for a second time.[46]

For those wounded in combat, field hospitals performed surgery and treated those in most dire need, and evacuation hospitals could hopefully patch up soldiers well enough to send them back into combat. General hospitals, a safer distance from the front, provided longer term care. From here, many would return to the front, others would be shipped home.

In January 1942, the 5th General Hospital, affiliated with Harvard Medical School, shipped out for the European Theater of Operation. The hospital was staffed by 73 officers, 120 nurses, and 400 enlisted.[47] Associated with the Massachusetts General Hospital, recruitment for the 6th General Hospital began in 1940 under the command of New Bedford native Colonel Thomas R. Goethals. MGH contributed 40 percent of its active doctors, 48 percent of its medical school graduates, and 33 percent of its nurses.[48] The group arrived in Morocco in February 1943 and set up in a former school building.

[41] *Holiday Appendectomy.* Pub domain photo. NUM 12/22/2018. Facebook. tinyurl.com/3sv8972s.

[42] *Sub Sank 14 Vessels.* Berkshire County Eagle 1/6/1944. Newspapers.com. tinyurl.com/5cx3swpx.

[43] *A.C. Smith Commands Sub.* Fitchburg Sentinel 11/17/1944. Newspapers.com. tinyurl.com/3ze2j6vy.

[44] *2 New Eng Dead, 9 Missing.* Boston Globe 8/5/1942. Newspapers.com. tinyurl.com/pwrr2mp9.

[45] *New Eng Men Prisoners.* Boston Globe 2/20/1942. Newspapers.com. tinyurl.com/4zbedzte.

[46] *Survivor Langley & Pecos Sinkings.* Transcript TG 4/27/1943. Newspapers.com. tinyurl.com/3w7nv6jj.

[47] Lyons Louis. *Harvard Base Hospital.* Boston Globe 12/30/1941. ProQuest. tinyurl.com/2s3bnfa5.

[48] Briggs, Susan *Disaster Med Response MGH Surgeons.* MGH Surg Soc Newsl 2002. tinyurl.com/mv8t82pt.

The hospital would eventually have a capacity of 1,300 beds and was part of a large network which supported Allied operations in North Africa.

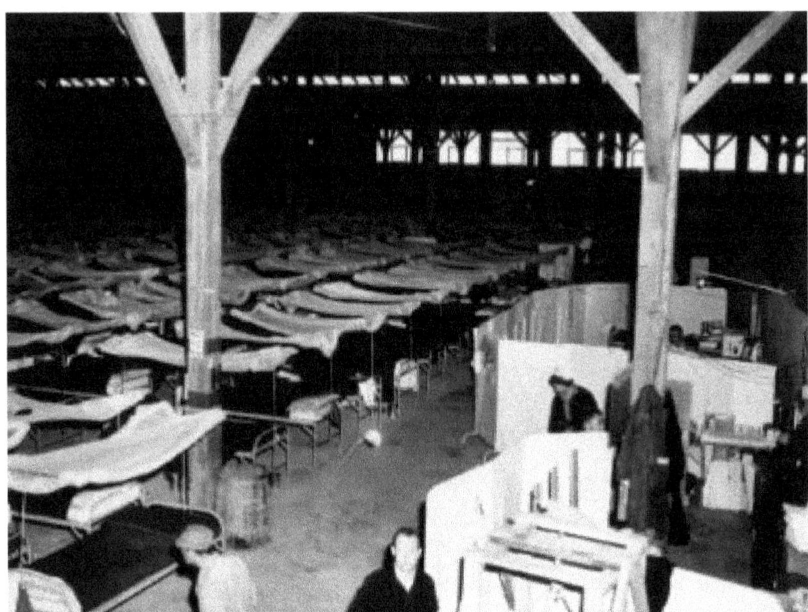

500-bed ward of the 6th General Hospital, Casablanca, Morocco. 1943.[49]

Personnel at the 6th General Hospital had to deal with a lack of water and plagues of locusts but were never under enemy fire. They found time for recreation, forming the Casablanca Yankees baseball team, which won the North Africa World Series of Baseball. The trophy was made of an unexploded Italian bomb, and each player received a baseball autographed by General Eisenhower. During the war, hospital staff provided treatment for Winston Churchill, General George Patton, and Britain's Lord Beaverbrook. The 6th would remain under the leadership of Colonel Geothals until March 1945, when he transferred to command the Joseph Lovell General Hospital at Fort Devens.[50]

An expansive array of healthcare facilities existed in Massachusetts and within the Zone of the Interior. Members of the Army received care at Fort Devens' Lovell General Hospital, Camp Edwards, and the Boston Port of Embarkation. For years, sailors and marines had come to an aging hospital in Chelsea. To accommodate the increased number of patients, in 1940, the Chelsea facility was officially replaced by the US Marine Hospital in Brighton. What remains is known as Brighton Marine, a local network with veteran housing, medical, and social services.

Chelsea Naval Hospital was one of the first three naval hospitals authorized by Congress in 1836. The facility, which closed in 1974, was a longtime fixture on the Mystic River. Chelsea admitted a number of famous figures over the years, including Ted Williams, John F. Kennedy, and Franklin D. Roosevelt Jr. Hospital staff also witnessed the passing of well-known Dr. Allan Stuart, USN Retired, a Chatham resident, veteran of the Spanish-American War, and longtime staff member at the Boston Navy Yard. Stuart died at Chelsea in 1940 at the age of seventy-five.[51] As the war drew to a close, injured personnel were admitted to Chelsea as a point of debarkation, and a helping hand was extended to assist them in transitioning to the civilian world. Dr. Saul Hertz, longtime associate of Massachusetts General

---

[49] *6th Gen Hosp*. Pub domain photo. Hist Medicine. ID A015404. NLM. tinyurl.com/25hnkc9b.

[50] *6th Gen Hosp Hist*. WW2 US Med Res Ctr. tinyurl.com/nh9syte3.

[51] *Dr. Allan Stuart Dies*. Evening Star. 8/20/1940. Newspapers.com. tinyurl.com/3n3um8u5.

Hospital who would become a legend for using radioactive iodine in the treatment of hyperthyroidism, served here as a commissioned officer in 1945.[52]

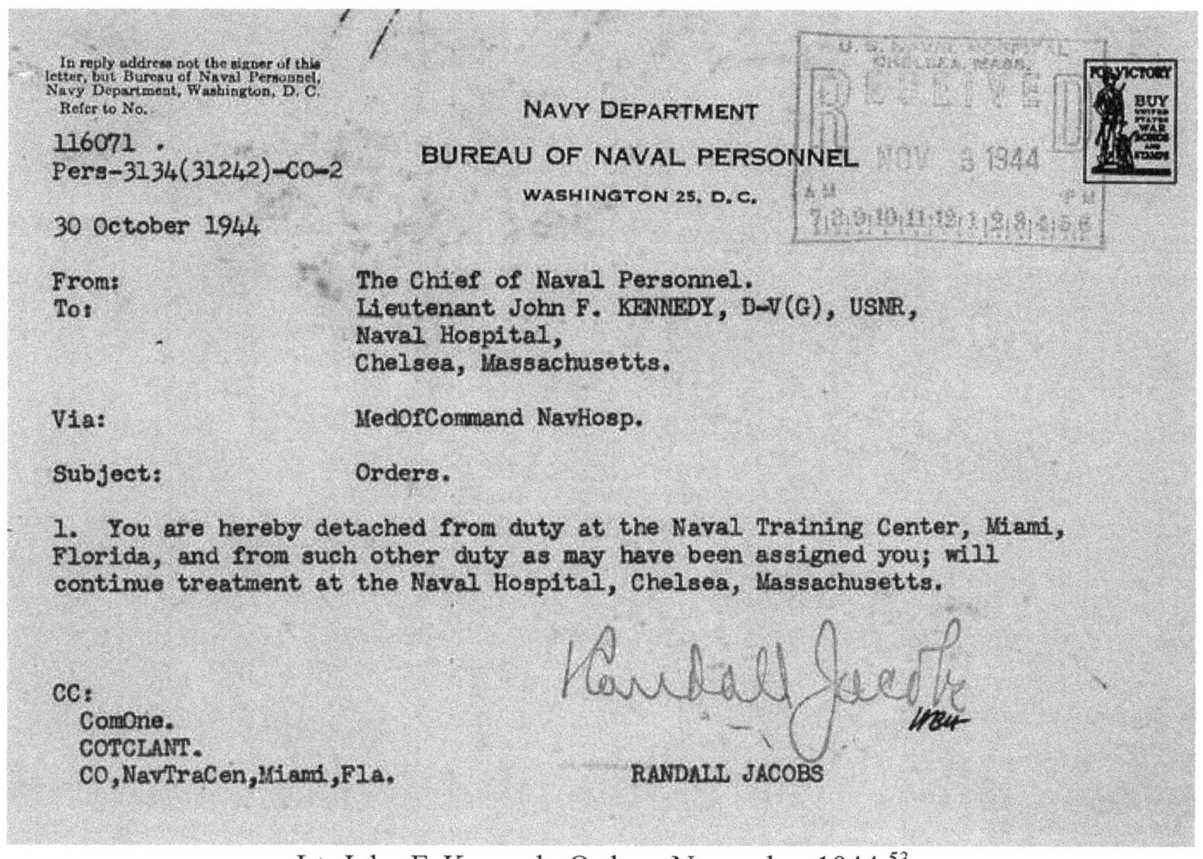

Lt. John F. Kennedy Orders. November 1944.[53]

A large piece of land between Framingham Reservoir and Farm Pond was once the home of Cushing General Hospital. During World War II, this Army hospital specialized in neurosurgery. Construction of the large complex began in 1943, and nine months later, 95 buildings were operational including surgeries, a dental clinic, x-ray facilities, physical therapy suites, and a prosthetic device shop. The complex, known as Times Square by patients and staff, required 4.3 million board feet of lumber, eleven million bricks, and encompassed 2.5 miles of roads. Named after Dr. Harvey Cushing, former Chief of Surgery at Brigham Hospital and renowned for his work with combat related brain injuries, Cushing General Hospital contained more than 2,000 beds and treated over 13,000 patients during World War II. Post-war, the facility became a veterans' hospital and a geriatric care facility and finally closed its doors in 1991. Today, all that remains is Cushing Memorial Park and a small chapel still used for occasional services.[54]

Renowned English physician Sir Thomas Clifford Allbutt once said of war: "How varied was our experience of the battlefield and how fertile the blood of warriors in rearing good surgeons." World War II was a surgeon's war. Surgeons in foxholes, standing in the mud of rain-soaked jungles, crouched on the floor of operating rooms aboard ships under attack, performing surgery while bullets whizzed through tents...their efforts saved thousands of lives. Here are some of their stories.

---

[52] Ehrhardt, John Jr. and Seza Gulec. *Radioactive Iodine Theranostics* 10/2020. NLM. tinyurl.com/ynr8jwpt.

[53] *JF Kennedy Orders.* Public domain photo. NARA 192723. Picryl. tinyurl.com/yyeb83s9.

[54] *Cushing Mem Hosp.* City Framingham, MA. tinyurl.com/zpe46xbp.

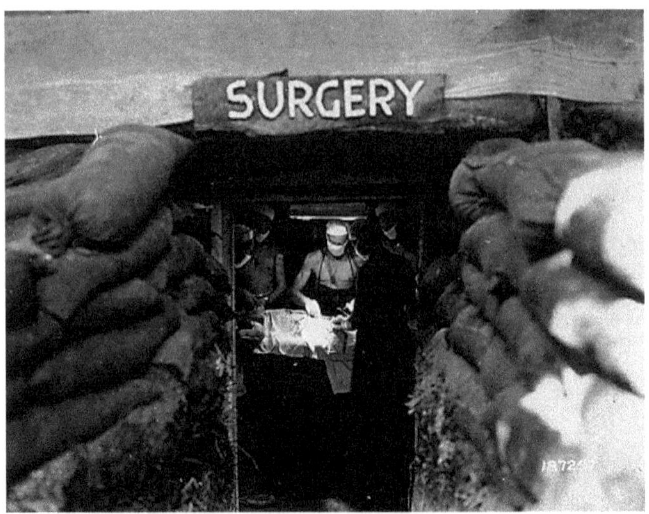
An Army surgeon operates on a soldier wounded
by a sniper on Bougainville. December 1943.[55]

Born in Salem, William McDermott carried memories of war with him throughout his life. The Harvard-educated McDermott described his wartime experience "...like running a full-time emergency room twenty-four hours a day." He was stationed in Europe and was present at Normandy and the Battle of the Bulge.[56] In May 1945, McDermott was present when the US Third Army liberated more than 18,000 prisoners at the Ebensee Concentration Camp in Austria. After the Allied bombing of German rocket production facilities at Peenemunde, the Nazis made plans to construct underground facilities for continuing rocket development. Slave labor from Ebensee provided the manpower to excavate tunnels. Prisoners suffered unspeakable hardship. The living were discarded along with the dead in a crematorium that moved too slowly to keep up with the piles of bodies. McDermott recalled: "You never in your life could imagine what it was like...I went into a barracks, and there were two men to every cot. They could barely move, but they got themselves up somehow and saluted me. I just about burst into tears."

McDermott returned home after the war and continued to practice at Massachusetts General Hospital and as a faculty member at Harvard Medical School. While he shared his experiences of the war in a book entitled *A Surgeon in Combat*, Dr. McDermott was reticent to talk about his memories of Ebensee. "I didn't share this much with my medical students. I was a little restrained, but if the war came up during discussions, I would remind them of the levels to which humans can sink. It's important for medical students to know those imperfections of the human race."[57]

Unlike general hospitals, which were relatively fixed, some medical units were designed to be mobile, following soldiers from battle to battle, never in one place too long, always tearing down and setting up. Dr. Philip Morrison's story is an exhaustive tale of bravery and dedication. A graduate of Holy Cross College and Harvard Medical School, Morrison was a member of the surgical staff at Massachusetts General Hospital when he joined the US Army. He shipped out on the Queen Mary, now a troop transport, and arrived in England in January 1944. Six months later, unaware of what lay ahead, he boarded a ship for France. He recalled, "Anti-submarine nets opened...allied aircraft zoomed overhead...escort ships dropped a few depth charges just in case." The following day, he landed on Omaha Beach.

[55] *Underground surgery.* Pub domain photo. 531177. NARA. tinyurl.com/25dmm8k5.

[56] Saxon, Wolfgang. *William McDermott.* NYTimes 7/25/2001. tinyurl.com/55wkmhve.

[57] Brokaw, Tom. *Greatest Generation.* Random House Trade Paperbacks 2005.

Morrison's first job was with the 51st Field Hospital, operating under heavy bombing and anti-aircraft fire. He moved on to the 45th Evacuation Hospital where his experience was similar, "friendly and enemy fire buzzing hospital tents almost daily, nightly raid by Germans." Once the hell of D-Day passed, the Allies moved forward, and so did Morrison's unit. The next hospital was set up in a field deep in the French countryside, but here too the roar of battle was ever present. Nearly 3,000 men received medical attention, many returning to battle. One group of men who had recently been treated was waiting in a Reinforcement Department area when it was hit by a German bomb. All perished.

Constantly on the move and now with the 24th Evacuation Hospital, Dr. Morrison found himself in Belgium. The medical staff received patients from combat areas and prepared them for evacuation Next up was Holland, where the building containing the operating theater was bombed, wounding many. It was 1945, and now Morrison and the Allies pushed further into Germany, placing a heavy strain on medical personnel. Casualties were much higher here, and terrible weather conditions resulted in leaky tents and floors deep in mud. In less than two weeks, over a thousand patients received treatment, including both American soldiers and German prisoners of war, and Morrison's hospital patients now included liberated American POWs.

Finally, in May 1945, word arrived of the surrender of Germany. Dr. Morrison remained in Europe for four more months before returning home. Soon afterward, he was awarded the Bronze Star. His citation reads: "Dr. Morrison worked untiringly during the entire combat operations...contributing in a great measure toward the superior functioning of the Hospital under shellfire and trying conditions." Out of 23,000 casualties treated and nearly 11,000 operations, less than 1 percent had perished in his unit's care. Dr. Morrison rejoined the medical community after the war, retiring in 1979, and spent his remaining years in East Orleans, Massachusetts.[58]

Boston-born Captain Albert I. Davis was a graduate of Boston's Massachusetts College of Pharmacy and the Middlesex College of Medicine and Surgery in Waltham. Memories of his time with the 105th Evacuation Hospital are a reminder of the violence of war. In October 1944, Dr. Davis landed at Omaha Beach. He recalled, "Shipwrecks dotted the water as well as steel anti-landing obstacles, reminding everyone that this had been a bloody battlefield only a few months ago." Three weeks later, his hospital moved to Maastricht, Holland, where intense fighting around Aachen resulted in an increasingly heavy caseload of wounded. "To this was added the threat of becoming surrounded or cut off. Tank columns rumbled past day and night, and moving convoys blocked the road." Dr. Davis described a frightening event that occurred on the last day of 1944.

Early in the evening, the antiaircraft battery a block away started firing. Everyone could hear planes droning overhead, and occasionally, a zooming sound was heard as if one came down to strafe...Then, the noise outside began to increase as more batteries joined in. Suddenly, there was a loud drone as a bomber came in low and a penetrating scream terminated in a terrible explosion that shook the whole building. Glass and debris flew all over the place. Some members of the command rushed to the dispensary to take care of those who had been wounded...still others went into the wreckage and chaos of the Officers' wing to help Officers and Nurses out. Glass, broken furniture, and rubble of collapsed masonry filled the wing. Lights streamed through holes blown by the bombs... Noise grew less and less; excitement dropped, order was restored...

The 105th Evacuation Hospital followed the eastward push into Germany, crossing the Rhine in March. Two weeks later, Capt. Davis and members of his unit were detached and sent to provide medical

---

care at the recently liberated Bergen-Belsen Concentration Camp. On January 7, 1946, Dr. Albert I. Davis returned to Fort Devens for separation from the US Army.[59]

There were thousands of others who stood beside surgeons, or next to dying men in battle, or by the bedside of those in pain. Wherever there was a need, a member of the Army Medical Corps stepped forward. Medics, nurses, pharmacists, dentists, and dietitians all went to war. Born in Cohasset, George McLaughlin was assigned to the 59th Evacuation Hospital in North Africa. When the unit moved on to Italy, France, and eventually Germany, McLaughlin, an x-ray technician, went with it. He described some of the injuries sustained by his patients. As troops moved into forested areas, casualties often presented with head trauma after being hit by shattered trees that had been shelled. It was discovered that many German patients had metal screws and pins in their arms and legs, a phenomenon that aroused much interest on the part of doctors.[60]

In April 1945, the Dachau Concentration Camp was liberated. One soldier with the 42nd Division when the gates opened later recalled: "I saw thousands of people...that looked like skeletons with skin stretched over them...some of them half dead. Just one look at them, something happened, and we realized what this war was all about. We now knew why we were participating in this war."[61]

A few days later, the 59th Evacuation Hospital was assigned to Dachau. In an interview after the war, George McLaughlin said little about what must have been a hellish experience. His description primarily focused on the work of the unit. "Vaccinations and dusting were completed, and box cars filled with bodies, as well as bodies lying about the inner compound, had been removed for cremation and burial." Nurses arrived to control a typhus outbreak at the camp, and a special facility was opened to contain these patients. George McLaughlin survived, and after nearly three years in war zones, he returned home in October of 1945.[62]

Lena R. Gelott's memories of war provide a nurse's perspective. After joining the Army Nurse Corps, this West Peabody native underwent basic training where she and her colleagues marched, drilled, did calisthenics, and learned to use a flamethrower. Assigned to the 48th Station Hospital, Gelott shipped out in October 1942 and spent the rest of the war in the Pacific Theater. While waiting in New Caledonia for the completion of a hospital, Gelott described an unexpected picture of life in war, tents set up in a coconut grove near the beach, USO appearances by Jack Benny and Artie Shaw, and a visit by First Lady Eleanor Roosevelt. Things were soon to change as the 48th Station Hospital moved on to the tiny island of Guadalcanal, where "hulks of sunken Japanese ships with multiple debris were gruesome reminders of war." Casualties began arriving immediately.

Gelott's memories are diverse and poignant. One day, she was asked to present Purple Hearts to four of her patients. "I thought they deserved better recognition for their bravery, so I asked them to step out on the beach. As there was no one else to observe, I asked a fellow Nurse to join us. The four men stood in line for this little ceremony, and I pinned the medals on their pajamas, except for one I had to pin onto a cast." At Christmas, Gelott and her fellow nurses decorated wards and sang Christmas carols. A wounded lieutenant asked a special favor. Could he have a bottle of soda? She poured out some of the soda, refilled the bottle with bourbon, and gave it back to him. The young nurse recalled seeing a Japanese soldier in her ward. He was restrained and guarded, and female personnel were not allowed near him. "I couldn't help thinking that he was just another scared young soldier." For some, the wounds of war would never go away. One soldier's hand was so severely mangled it would never completely

[59] *Veteran's Testimony-Albert Davis.* WW2 US Med Res Ctr. tinyurl.com/mrxcb8k7.

[60] *Veteran's Testimony-George McLaughlin.* WW2 US Med Res Ctr. tinyurl.com/52htsdfd.

[61] *Liberation Dachau: James Rose.* Timeline Events. USHMM. tinyurl.com/mrkvvfry.

[62] *Veteran's Testimony – George P. McLaughlin.* WW2 US Med Res Ctr.

recover. While changing his bandage, the nurse asked what job he did back home. "I'm a surgeon," he replied.

Lena Gelott spent three long years in the midst of horrific warfare in the Pacific. Nowhere in her recollections does she describe personal discomfort, anger, or regret. Her memories paint a picture of dedication and a different kind of heroism. She returned home in September of 1945 and was discharged three months later.[63]

The story of medical care during any war is a story about blood. Loss of fluids from wounds, surgery, and burns has consistently been the leading cause of death in modern warfare.

Wounded soldier being given blood by
Army medic in Sicily. August 1943.[64]

Prior to World War II, plasma was the primary tool in fluid replacement therapy. In 1940, Harvard Professor Walter Cannon, Chairman of the government committee investigating the treatment of shock, recommended "that the [US] Armed Forces should use whole blood in the treatment of shock whenever possible." In spite of this report, US military progress toward the use of whole blood was significantly delayed, in part due to the fact that Cannon's recommendations weren't made official for three years. Army practices dictated the use of plasma rather than whole blood in most patients. Blood was administered only sporadically and most often in patient-to-patient transfusion, a dangerous practice often resulting in clotting and death. Navy policy was inadequate as well. When war broke out, ships often had only enough plasma to treat one or two burn patients.[65]

The work of Dr. Charles Drew is another reminder of this unnecessary lapse on the part of the military. A graduate of Amherst College, in 1940, Drew created England's first blood bank. By using bloodmobiles and refrigerated trucks for donation sites, blood was made available to those injured during the Blitz. Returning to New York, the American Red Cross appointed him to oversee the provision of blood for the US military. But when the War Department required African American blood to be separated from white donor blood, he stepped down. Unfortunately, much of Charles Drew's work would go unnoticed by the US Government. By the time of the attack on Pearl Harbor, no blood banks existed in the Army.

The experiences of Massachusetts resident Edward Delos Churchill in the European Theater led to crucial changes. After noting that many shock cases required whole blood rather than just plasma, Churchill instituted whole-blood donor transfusion procedures and established regional blood banks. Not everyone agreed with these innovations. As late as November 1943, the Army Surgeon General would

[63] *Veteran's Testimony – Lena R. Gelott.* WW2 US Med Res Ctr.

[64] *Humphrey given blood.* Public domain photo. 531161 NARA. tinyurl.com/cs294yye.

[65] Cowdrey, Albert E. *Fighting for Life.*

not allow whole blood to be sent into combat areas. Churchill found fault with this ruling and went public, telling the *New York Times* that the government's attitude was "unacceptable."[66] This time, things would change. With Churchill's assistance before the war's end, the US military would have in place a successful system for blood collection, storage, delivery, and transfusion, crucial as the war in Europe alone was consuming one pint of blood for every two casualties.[67]

Blood being delivered for use on D-Day. 1944.[68]

Massachusetts was a beneficiary of these new developments in the science of blood. Thanks to a young doctor from Boston, Lamar Soutter, the first blood bank at Massachusetts General Hospital opened in April 1942. Soutter became the very first donor and would be followed by scores of others who came forward, motivated by the tragedy at Pearl Harbor. According to Elizabeth Soutter Schwarzer, granddaughter of the noted surgeon, once an old woman confronted him and asked why she wasn't allowed to give blood. Her grandson, he learned, had been on the battleship Arizona. Soutter arranged to collect a pint from the special donor, but the woman fainted on her way out, and the surgeon had to give the pint back to her.[69] Soutter later joined the US Army, where he served in the European Theater and earned a Silver Star for his actions at the Battle of the Bulge. He returned to Massachusetts after the war and became Dean of the Massachusetts Medical School in Worcester.[70]

Seven months after the Mass General Blood Bank opened, Soutter's efforts would be put to the test. Today, on a quiet lane in Boston where an apartment building now stands, a bronze plaque set into the bricks of the sidewalk marks the spot of a horrific episode in Massachusetts history. The Cocoanut Grove Night Club was a top destination for nocturnal Boston partygoers, and on a busy Thanksgiving weekend in 1942, half the world seemed to be at the famous oasis on Piedmont Street. Patrons talked about the unexpected Holy Cross victory over Boston College at Fenway Park, an upset that likely kept BC fans from showing up that night. In town for a publicity tour, cowboy western actor Buck Jones had come for a party. The theater crowd had just shown up for a late meal, as had soldiers and sailors who sought distraction from the churning war. It was business as usual for one of the city's liveliest establishments.

Downstairs in the Melody Lounge, a busboy lit a match to help him see while changing a light bulb. Moments later, people noticed fire coming from a nearby artificial palm tree and a suspended cloth ceiling. It didn't take long for the basement room to fill with smoke and flames. An emergency exit at the top of the stairs wouldn't open. Those who tried to leave through the foyer on the ground floor joined

[66] Barr, Justin et al. *Nat Med Response to Crisis.* NEJM 8/13/2020. tinyurl.com/52ennta7.

[67] Service, Haskin. *Answers to questions.* Daily Item 1/2/1945. Newspapers.com. tinyurl.com/3mp9ch3f.

[68] *Blood Bank marmites.* Pub domain photo. NARA. Jules Ashley. *Hist Depends on Historian.* Quora. tinyurl.com/muv5rxfy.

[69] *Dr. Lamar Soutter, M.D.* Schwarzer, Elizabeth Soutter. Soutter Rev Newsl. 2009. UMMS. tinyurl.com/ysdrf8a6.

[70] *Lamar Soutter.* Lamar Soutter Lib. UMASS 9/16/2015. tinyurl.com/2sz62tch.

a stampede that jammed the club's revolving doors. Another door in the vestibule that swung inward was blocked by patrons. Meanwhile, the fire spread into the dining room, wreaking even more havoc.

By chance, the Boston Fire Department was responding to a car fire on nearby Stuart Street when smoke was seen spilling out of the Cocoanut Grove. By 11:00 p.m., the emergency reached five alarms, drawing firefighters from all over the city. Firefighter Patrick Connolly of Boston's Ladder 15 recalled opening the staircase door to the Melody Lounge. "We were the ones that knocked down the metal-clad door. Inside, there were five goddam locks; every one was different. We worked like a son of a bitch with the battering ram. We had to split that door in every direction."[71] Those who reached the building encountered a mob of ghastly survivors who spilled out into the street. The Lynn Fire Department was summoned, and the Boston Police Department called for help from the military. The Boston Navy Yard sent nine vehicles loaded with Marines and corpsmen.[72]

While the blaze itself was put out in a short time, firefighters and investigators spent hours sifting through the wreckage and its corpses. The final death toll was 492. Actor Buck Jones died that night, as did the husband of Ruth Martell of Southbridge.[73] John O'Neil and his bride of three hours, Claudia Nadeau, both of Cambridge, were celebrating their wedding with the best man and maid of honor. None of them escaped.[74] Many bodies were discovered under club furniture. When Joe Connolly picked a woman up off a piano, she disintegrated in his arms. The Cocoanut Grove fire was a tragedy shared by the whole of the Commonwealth, with victims hailing from places like Winchester, Plymouth, Dorchester, Springfield, Framingham, Ashmont, Beverly, Uxbridge, Worcester, and Clinton. Many of the dead were military personnel.[75] Thirty-nine servicemen died that night; twenty-seven were injured.[76]

Military caps near the scene of the blaze, a grim
reminder of the Cocoanut Grove tragedy.
Courtesy of the Boston Public Library, Leslie Jones Collection.[77]

At area hospitals, doctors and nurses received cases, many of which were carbon monoxide poisoning and respiratory injuries. Of the 114 sent to Massachusetts General Hospital, seventy-five people were declared dead on arrival.[78] More than 300 were delivered to Boston City Hospital, arriving

[71] *Firefighter Pat Connolly.* BFD Hist Soc. tinyurl.com/3sywz69b.

[72] *BNYD Log Entry 11/28/1942.* NARA RG 181. *USN Records Fire 75 Years Ago.* Fleming, Daniel. Prologue Mag 2017. NARA tinyurl.com/php8z29v.

[73] *Ruth Martell.* Cocoanut Grove Fire. BFD. tinyurl.com/3n7m9hrz.

[74] *Wedding Party Killed.* Transcript TG 11/30/1942. Newspapers.com. tinyurl.com/mr45ttu9.

[75] *Cocoanut Grove Fatalities.* BFD. tinyurl.com/3mmyuv2f.

[76] Fleming, Daniel. *Cocoanut Grove Revisited.* Prologue Mag 2017. NARA. tinyurl.com/ydv4st44.

[77] *Military caps, a grim reminder of the Cocoanut Grove tragedy.* November 29, 1942. Leslie Jones Photo. Courtesy of the Boston Public Library, Leslie Jones Collection.

[78] *MA General Victim Statistics. Cocoanut Grove Fire.* BFD. tinyurl.com/ymc5ydrf.

at a rate of one every eleven seconds within the first two hours, the largest intake of patients in civilian hospitals in history.[79]

Performer Dorothy Myles, a seventeen-year-old singer at the end of a three-week engagement at the Grove, was buried by customers near an exit while fire consumed the air around her. Thrusting her hand out of the bodies, she was rescued by a fireman and placed inside a police vehicle for a trip to the hospital. Myles was the only one of the five victims in the vehicle left alive upon arrival. After enduring burns that covered 45 percent of her body, this courageous young woman survived, earning her the nickname Dauntless Dotty. The name would later be painted on the nose of a B-29 bomber that flew missions in the Pacific. During her two-year recovery and between procedures, she performed over the air on WEEI and WBZ.[80]

Martin Sheridan was a freelance writer and public relations rep who managed Buck Jones' Boston tour. After a busy day of public appearances, Sheridan followed the actor to the Cocoanut Grove. In a 1962 *Chicago Tribune* article, Sheridan recalled hearing someone yell "Fire!" before the lights went out:

I shall never forget the screams and cries of the trapped, the crash and clatter of overturning tables and chairs, the smashing of dishes and glasses. I began to choke from the mysterious fumes that swept the Grove, and then the world caved in on me... When I came to I was barely able to gasp in the terrific heat and thick smoke. I could hear weak moans about me, the blows of the firemen's axes, and the splashing of water.

Sheridan's eyes and hands were terribly burned. He remembers being pulled from the building by an unknown man, "walking over debris and soft bodies," and being placed in a taxi cab that delivered him to Mass General.[81]

After a lengthy hospitalization, his hopes of joining the Coast Guard were gone. Sheridan became a reporter for the *Boston Globe* and was sent to cover the war in the Pacific. One day, while interviewing servicemen, he was approached by a young sailor, Howard Sotherden. "You're Martin Sheridan, aren't you? I pulled you from the wreckage at the Cocoanut Grove fire." Sotherden was in Boston that night on leave from the Newport, Rhode Island Navy base when he overheard a police officer talking about the fire. He raced to the scene and found firefighters removing victims from the building. "I didn't wait," said Sotherden. "Lights from the fire trucks illuminated the interior, and I stumbled over overturned tables and wreckage until my foot struck something soft. It was a man." He later learned that the victim he'd placed in the taxi was Martin Sheridan.

Sotherden made it home after the war, and the two men remained in contact for the rest of their lives.[82] Sheridan went on to fame as one of the first noncombatant reporters attached to the Army during combat missions, as the first civilian correspondent allowed on a sub during the war, and as the only reporter to fly on a B-29 bomber raid of Tokyo, where a bottle of Sheridan's beer was rumored to have ended up in a bomb load before being dropped on a target.[83]

The tragedy at the Boston nightclub made a critical impact on medical care during World War II. Because of the massive number of casualties, it became a laboratory of sorts for the study of burns. Twenty-two-year-old Coast Guardsman Clifford Johnson had rescued customers from one of the club lounges and sustained burns over 67 percent of his body,[84] leaving him with little chance of survival.

---

[79] Saffle, Jeffrey. *Fire Cocoanut Grove.* Am J Surg 12/1993. tinyurl.com/2npd5upm.

[80] *Singer Dorothy Myles.* Cocoanut Grove Fire. BFD tinyurl.com/5n9be889.

[81] Sheridan, Martin. *30 Seconds in Hell.* CT 11/25/1962. SCVHistory.com. tinyurl.com/m9jzzv9b.

[82] Croyle, Jonathan. *No Syracuse native saves journalist.* Syracuse.com 11/30/2017. tinyurl.com/36enuch6.

[83] Oliver, Myrna. *Martin Sheridan.* LA Times 1/12/2004. tinyurl.com/5n8ajfjm.

[84] *Joseph Dreyfus.* Cocoanut Grove. BFD tinyurl.com/2kvvnfdz.

Miraculously, after six months, the young man was released. Johnson's treatment would lead to several advances in burn therapy.

The use of triple analin dye would reduce burn morbidity from 34 to 8 percent at Boston City Hospital.[85] Understanding of inhalation injury began here, and new techniques in skin grafting would become common practice. A chart developed by doctors Charles Lund and Newton Brodeur to estimate the area of burns is still in use today. The fire resulted in fluid replacement innovations during shock, and doctors relied heavily on the recently established Mass General Hospital Blood Bank. The massive volume of plasma that was administered during the aftermath of the emergency exceeded that used at Pearl Harbor.[86] Clifford Johnson alone received one hundred transfusions.[87]

Today, the cause of the Cocoanut Grove fire, one of the deadliest in American history, remains unsolved, but the nearly 500 souls who lost their lives that night did not die in vain. Their sacrifice would save the lives of thousands who sustained burns while in service to their country during the Second World War.

Author Brian J. Ford described the effect of war on medicine:

If any good can be said to come of war, then the Second World War must go on record as assisting and accelerating one of the greatest blessings that the 20th Century has conferred on Man – the huge advances in medical knowledge and surgical techniques.
War, by producing so many and such appalling casualties and by creating such widespread conditions in which disease can flourish confronted the medical profession with an enormous challenge – and the doctors of the world rose to the challenge of the last war magnificently.[88]

By far, one of the most beneficial advances was the development of antibiotics. Five years prior to Pearl Harbor, sulfonamides were discovered in Germany and were used with some success against everything from sore throats to gonorrhea, achieving notoriety when it was prescribed to Winston Churchill during a bout with pneumonia. During World War II, medics and corpsmen routinely carried packets of yellow sulfa powder to sprinkle on wounds in the field, but as the unending line of casualties streamed into field hospitals, researchers began to consider alternatives for sulfonamides.

Penicillin had been discovered in 1929, yet as war raged, the drug was largely overlooked. During the Second World War, Waldemar Kaempffert, former Editor of *Scientific American*, claimed: "The history of penicillin is one of the disgraces of medical research...An antiseptic, which is almost ideal...was allowed to slumber for ten years. Had it not been for the exigencies of the present war, it might be slumbering still."[89] When scientists turned to look at Fleming's wonder drug, research yielded positive results. However, pharmaceutical companies were investing heavily in sulfonamides, and finding enough penicillin for both civilian and military use was problematic. The immediate need was to provide the antibiotic to America's fighting forces. Not only would the wounded benefit (2.3 million doses were earmarked for D-Day alone),[90] but thousands in the military (in 1942, 42 out of 1,000 in the Army and 36 out of 1,000 in the Navy) who suffered from venereal disease[91] treatable with penicillin. For those civilians in desperate need, it was scarce.

---

[85] *Medicine: Dye for Burns.* Time 6/16/1941. tinyurl.com/3sxbsrdt.

[86] Saffle, Jeffrey A. *Fire Cocoanut Grove.*

[87] *Medicine: Out of the Fire.* Time Mag 8/16/1943. tinyurl.com/25x9n4r9.

[88] *War Casualties Have Changed.* Med Daily 5/29/2016. tinyurl.com/yx3m7edd.

[89] Kaempffert, Waldemar. *History of penicillin...* Quotes. Today Sci Hist 3/21. tinyurl.com/5cruxpve.

[90] *Thanks to Penicillin...!* Nat WW2 Mus. tinyurl.com/3kedszcd.

[91] Fleming, William. *Venereal Disease WWII.* J Elisha Mitchell Sci Soc 1945. JSTOR. tinyurl.com/2mjtcpex.

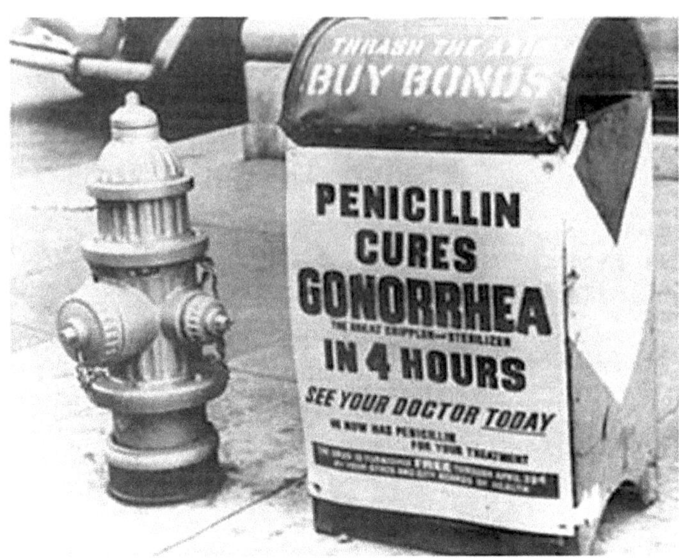

A poster describing one of the uses for Penicillin
and urging Americans to buy war bonds. World War II.[92]

Enter Dr. Chester Scott Keefer, Physician-in-Chief at Massachusetts Memorial Hospital and Chairman of the National Research Council's Committee on Chemotherapeutics. What this grand title meant was that the difficult task of determining how the precious supply of penicillin would be doled out to US citizens fell upon his shoulders. Keefer would become known as the "penicillin czar." Newspaper accounts tell the story of how, with Keefer's authorization, the antibiotic was shipped to critically ill patients in Massachusetts. Bernard Denault of Adams, suffering from a severe blood infection for ten days, was reported to be "100 percent improved" after being given penicillin.[93] A seven-year-old boy with osteomyelitis was in serious condition on admission to a hospital. Keefer released dosages of the drug, and the child's condition was upgraded to fair the following morning. Richard Green was the first resident in Williamstown history to be given the "miracle drug."[94]

Keefer's authority stretched well beyond the borders of the Bay State. Shirley Carter, sixteen-years-old from Georgia, was near death from a streptococcal infection when her father contacted the local newspaper for help. After the *Macon News* located Dr. Keefer, a shipment of the drug was flown by Army bomber to Georgia and delivered to the hospital by police escort. "Almost from the moment the penicillin entered her veins," Shirley Carter's condition improved.[95]

Nostalgia, soldier's heart, shell shock, and combat fatigue are terms historically used to describe the impact of trauma on an individual's mental health. The sights, sounds, and emotions of war have stricken thousands who served, wounding them in ways that bandages and antibiotics cannot cure. Members of the military accounted for over one million neuropsychiatric hospitalizations in World War II. At the Rigg's Clinic in Stockbridge, war became the number one source of concern for patients struggling with depression. During 1944, 24 percent of the clinic's caseload were enlisted, and an additional 33 percent were war-related.[96]

Psychiatrists John Spiegel of Cambridge, Massachusetts, and his colleague, Roy Grinker, researching the breakdown of common soldiers after exposure to combat, found that these were not

---

[92] *Penicillin cures gonorrhea.* Pub domain photo. Wiki Commons. Picryl. tinyurl.com/48r6ewc5.

[93] *Penicillin For Blood Infection.* Springfield Daily Republican 3/9/1944. Newspapers.com. tinyurl.com/mvcnz8j3.

[94] *Penicillin For Williamstown Youngster.* No Adams Transcript 3/7/1944. Newspapers.com. tinyurl.com/yc59yuz6.

[95] *Penicillin Girl Deeply Grateful.* Macon News 6/2/1944. Newspapers.com. tinyurl.com/4j6bmxne.

[96] *Riggs Patients War-Connected.* Berkshire Eagle 4/12/1945. Newspapers.com. tinyurl.com/bde9eyz7.

cowards but ordinary men who experienced difficulty dealing with the horrors of war. They stated: "It would seem to be a more rational question to ask why the soldier does not succumb to anxiety, rather than why he does."[97] In spite of the evidence, the topic was controversial. Lt. Mary Kennedy of Swampscott recalled a conversation with a Medical Corps major while stationed in North Africa. Shell shock, he believed, stemmed from childhood exposure to parents fighting, which had made them "allergic to noise." Thus, "Fear of explosions finally develops into an 'anxiety neurosis,' which is the modern military name for what the old timers call shell shock."[98] (Apparently, those who had not been diagnosed with "anxiety neurosis" must have enjoyed the combat experience.)

In his regular *Boston Globe* feature, "Let's Explore Your Mind," Albert Edward Wiggam put in his two cents. He described shell shock as: "a device, usually unconscious—of playing sick and incompetent to escape the necessity of going bravely through danger."[99] Undoubtedly, twenty-four-year-old Alexander Santilli of Everett would have found fault with Wiggam's comments. The young Marine lieutenant was killed in 1944 during combat on Saipan and earned a Silver Star for bravery. Santilli had been diagnosed with shell shock the day before and was scheduled to be evacuated to a hospital when he snuck back to his unit in order to join them in battle.[100]

For the Army, psychiatry was very much a developing science. A Division of Neuro-Psychiatry existed under the command of Dr. Roy D. Halloran of Tufts Medical School.[101] However, the US Army counted a total of thirty-five psychiatrists in its ranks, and only twenty-four of those with formal training.[102] While the military recognized the effects of stress in war, acceptance of it was another thing. General George Patton was reprimanded after calling a traumatized soldier "a god-damned coward...son of a bitch," striking him and threatening to have him shot. Whether it was Patton's actions, reported in the press as the "slap heard round the world," or the military's need to send men back into combat rather than discharge them for mental health reasons, treatment began to change.

Seeing his commander refer to these cases as cowards, Colonel Martin A. Berezin, born Wrentham and resident of Norwood, developed a plan famously known as "P&S." He gave a pick and shovel to patients who then dug trenches, allowing them quiet time to process their difficulties. He provided nourishment and treated them with respect and kindness.[103] The battlefield became a laboratory for doctors struggling to develop new ways to deal with these troubled souls. Much of the credit for a new model of treatment goes to Dr. Frederick Hanson, who, understanding that the job of psychiatrists was to return soldiers to war, moved treatment forward into combat zones, treated patients humanely and compassionately, placing blame for the trauma on war, not on the patient. The approach worked. Approximately 60% of shell shock cases returned to combat,[104] and by 1943, the military had approved the appointment of a psychiatrist for every division. No longer would men be deemed cowards, and no longer would they be left alone, untreated, to deal with the emotional scars of war. The science of psychiatry had taken a major leap forward.

The horrors of war echo in the memories of those who served in all conflicts and in all corners of the globe. The timeless remembrances of those in the medical corps who experienced combat and the recollections of those who were beneficiaries of their care reflect a unique experience. Civil War nurse Clara Barton, born in North Oxford, recalled after the battle at Cold Harbor, "We are waiting at the cot

[97] Pols, Hans and Oak, Stephanie. *War & military mental health.* Am J Publ Health 12/2007. tinyurl.com/8zdsa3j3.

[98] MacGowan, Gault. *Nurses Cared for Wounded.* Boston Globe 8/3/1943. Newspapers.com. tinyurl.com/s4ukv8xw.

[99] Wiggam, Albert. *Men More Likely to Develop Shell Shock.* Boston Globe 6/2/1942. Newspapers.com. tinyurl.com/75n7kc2v.

[100] Cuddy, Jack. *Santilli Died All-American.* Boston Globe 8/18/1944. Newspapers.com. tinyurl.com/bdez6xae.

[101] *R. D. Halloran.* Boston Globe 11/10/1943. Newspapers.com. tinyurl.com/2ev234fe.

[102] Marble, Sanders. *Rehabilitating Wounded.* Med Hist, OSG 6/28/2008. tinyurl.com/54m9c4ja.

[103] Cowdrey, Albert E. *Fighting for Life.*

[104] Lovelace, Alexander. *Slap Heard around World.* USAWC Parameters 9/1/2019. tinyurl.com/y6mkdfkc.

side and closing their eyes one by one as they pass away…I cannot but think that we shall win at last, but oh, the cost…"[105] Author Eugene B. Sledge, in his World War II memoirs, wrote of a battlefield encounter with a Navy corpsman. "Doc kept at his work. In a quiet, calm voice, he told me to get a battle dressing out of his pouch and press it firmly against his face to stop the bleeding while he finished work on the wounded arm. Such was the selfless dedication of the Navy hospital corpsmen who served in Marine infantry units."[106] From Adam Fenner, Marine Corps veteran of Iraq and Afghanistan: "An infantryman's job is to deliver his enemies into the waiting hands of Death. It is Doc's job to protect his brothers from Death, to knock him aside and say, 'Not today.'"[107]

By the close of the Second World War, 535,000 medics, corpsmen, and members of the Medical Corps, 57,000 nurses, and 47,000 physicians had served their country. Hospitals near theaters of operation numbered close to 700, and nearly 100 more within the Zone of the Interior provided care and rehabilitation for nearly 600,000 returning servicemen and women.[108] Not all who served as medical specialists survived. Over 1,700 Navy corpsmen[109] and nearly 2,500 Army medical personnel perished during the war.[110]

The men and women of the Medical Corps, regardless of the branch of service, served honorably. Frederick Coleman Murphy of Quincy was serving as a US Army medic when he was struck in the shoulder during an assault on the Siegfried Line in Germany on March 18, 1945.

He refused to withdraw for treatment and continued forward, administering first aid under heavy machine-gun mortar and artillery fire. When the company ran into a thickly sown antipersonnel minefield and began to suffer more and more casualties, he continued to disregard his own wound and unhesitatingly braved the danger of exploding mines, moving about through heavy fire and helping the injured until he stepped on a mine which severed one of his feet. In spite of his grievous wounds, he struggled on with his work, refusing to be evacuated and crawling from man to man, administering to them while in great pain and bleeding profusely. He was killed by the blast of another mine, which he had dragged himself across in an effort to reach still another casualty.

Pvt. Murphy was awarded the Congressional Medal of Honor.[111] He joined seventeen other US Army and Navy medical personnel who earned the Congressional Medal of Honor for their service during the Second World War.[112]

Harvard-educated Richard Tregaskis began his career as a reporter in Boston and became a well-known war correspondent. His memories of war would later become the classic account of World War II in the Pacific, *Guadalcanal Diary*. Tregaskis recalled a walk through a hospital tent in 1944: "I saw them, the man with the deep hole in the front of the skull, his nose gone, whose mind would eventually come back to normal, whose face would be restored by plastic surgery; the man who could neither talk nor register words...He, too, with neurological care, should be able to climb back to normal..."[113] The war would end a year later. More would die, but due to the efforts of the men and women of the Medical Corps, heroes all, most would live.

---

[105] Barton, Clara. *Letter to Mr. Baldwin.* 5/30/1964. C Barton Missing Soldiers Mus. tinyurl.com/3z95wd9t.

[106] Sledge, Eugene. *With the Old Breed.* Presidio Press Paperback Ed 2010.

[107] Nickels, Lance. *Camp Pendleton: Field Med Training.* DVIDS 9/18/2019. tinyurl.com/3mwk54as.

[108] Manring, M.M. et al. *Treatment War Wounds.* Clin Orthop Relat Res. NLM, NIH 2/14/2009. tinyurl.com/yc433v4c.

[109] Littletown, Mark and Wright, Charles. *Doc.* Zenith Press, MBI Publ Co 1/1/2005.

[110] *Overview Med Dept.* US Med Res Ctr. tinyurl.com/3t33zaap.

[111] *Frederick Coleman Murphy.* Stories Sacrifice. Cong MOH Soc. tinyurl.com/2nr2rsxu.

[112] *79 Med Aid & Corpsman MOH Recipients.* Cong MOH Soc. tinyurl.com/yu7xn25b.

[113] Tregaskis, Richard. *Invasion Diary.* Random House 1994.

<h1 align="center">Chapter 11</h1>

<h2 align="center">Second Class Citizens</h2>

*By the way, Captain, I hear the Japs done
declared war on you white folks.*
Black sharecropper to his landlord World War II[1]

The Navy Cross citation reads:

For exceptional courage, presence of mind, and devotion to duty, and disregard for his personal safety...While at the side of his Captain on the bridge...despite enemy strafing and bombing and, in the face of serious fire, assisted in moving his Captain, who had been mortally wounded, to a place of greater safety and later manned and operated a machine gun directed at enemy Japanese attacking aircraft until ordered to leave the bridge.

The date of the action was December 7, 1941, the location was aboard the Battleship West Virginia at Pearl Harbor, and the sailor who reflected "great credit upon himself...in keeping with the highest traditions of the United States Naval Service"[2] was a young man from Texas, Doris "Dorie" Miller. Today, over eighty years later, the sheer hypocrisy of this statement is baffling. The United States Navy, who supposedly held Miller in the highest esteem, deemed him unfit for combat. Dorie Miller, who would die for his country a little over a year later aboard an escort carrier in the Pacific, was black.

Doris Miller, Navy Cross recipient. May 1942.[3]

Like the majority of other African Americans who enlisted at the outbreak of war, Miller, a messmate, held a menial job. Black servicemen, however, should have been allowed to do more. They were promised more. The Selective Service Act of 1940, which required all men to register, clearly stated: "Within limits of the quota...any person, regardless of race or color...shall be afforded opportunity

---

¹ Dalfiume, Richard. *Forgotten Years Negro Rev. J Am Hist* 1968. JSTOR. tinyurl.com/z7hnrddp.

² *Doris Miller.* Veteran Tributes. tinyurl.com/39bw8ham.

³ *Doris Miller.* Pub domain photo. 55/27/1942. 12009092 NARA. tinyurl.com/mry2nccw.

to volunteer for induction..." In addition, "There shall be no discrimination against any person on account of race and color." Unfortunately, for those in charge of the armed forces, it was an unpopular decision.

The assignment of African Americans to limited roles in the military did not go unnoticed, and pressure was placed upon all branches of the service to change their policies. Four months after Pearl Harbor, *The Guardian* of Boston reported on the announcement by Navy Secretary Frank Knox, a native of Massachusetts, that blacks would be admitted to the Navy Reserves and used to perform general duties at naval bases. The headline read, "U.S. Navy Open to Colored Recruits in Jim Crow Set-Up." The Navy did not expect to commission African Americans as officers. All recruits, however, would be held to the same enlistment standards as whites. "The whole thing will be carried along in a cordial spirit of experimentation," said Knox, "to make the maximum use of colored men in the most effective way to avoid difficulties of racial character."[4]

General Thomas Holcomb, head of the Marines, stated his position with a bit less finesse. "If it were a question of having a Marine Corps of 5,000 whites or 250,000 Negroes, I would rather have the whites."[5] The Army did little better. Its Chief of Staff, George Marshall, let it be known that the Army would not be used as a platform for social experimentation.

The attitude of the military boggles the mind. The country was at war. Every branch of the service was in need of men. Yet the government chose to overlook an entire population of eligible candidates because of the color of their skin. It wasn't as if black talent was lacking in this country. Joseph Dunning of Milton had already earned degrees in Aeronautical/Astronautical Engineering, advanced degrees from Harvard and Stanford and would be recognized as the first black aeronautical engineer in the United States. Had he joined the military, he might have been assigned to empty wastebaskets.[6] Richard Barksdale of Winchester was a graduate of Bowdoin College who qualified as a sharpshooter. The Army apparently saw no use for his rifle skills during the war and assigned him to a desk job in Georgia.[7] In June 1940, the 8th Illinois Negro Regiment became the best marksmanship unit in the US National Guard. Certainly, their abilities would have been useful...if they had been allowed into combat.[8]

As the war progressed, however, it was clear that due to the growing number of casualties, replacements would have to be found.

Grim humor on Tarawa. December 1943.[9]

Whites were moved forward into battle, and their non-combatant positions were filled by African Americans who were increasingly deployed overseas. From Winchester, Ellsworth West became a

[4] *Navy Open to Colored Recruits.* Guardian 4/10/1942. Chron Am LOC. tinyurl.com/yne8a3vu.

[5] Nalty, Bernard. *Right To Fight.* Marines WWII Series, MCH and Mus Div. tinyurl.com/mvnutken.

[6] *MIT Grad Gets Vocation.* Chronicle 6/15/1940. Chron Am LOC. tinyurl.com/3bx84e22.

[7] Knight, Ellen. *Black Veterans WWII.* Winchester Hist Online. tinyurl.com/bdh9zkzs.

[8] *Illinois Best Riflemen.* Chronicle 6/15/1940. Chronicling Am LOC. tinyurl.com/3mtpkuyn.

[9] *Grim Humor Tarawa* 12/1943. Pub domain photo. USN. 520984 NARA. tinyurl.com/3dpj7jkn.

Sergeant and was sent to the Ryukyu Islands, Clifford Latham served in Germany, and Reginald Guy worked on the construction of the Ledo Road in India.[10] It was becoming clear that the Army would have to tolerate African Americans in their ranks. What they would not tolerate, however, was dissension.

In January 1944, *The Guardian* reported on a recent meeting at a church in Chelsea. The topic of discussion was Lt. Luther Marion Fuller, a young Army chaplain from Boston. Fuller was an outspoken critic of the inequality faced by black soldiers. His comments caused such a stir that he became the victim of a lynching attempt in Georgia. When the chaplain returned from the South Pacific with letters for the War Department written by soldiers complaining of their unfair treatment, Fuller was brought before a reclassification board and placed on inactive status. Present at the Chelsea meeting was newspaperman Martin D. Richardson, whose brother, another Army chaplain, had been forced to resign from his position under similar circumstances.[11] While Lt. Fuller was not discharged from the Army for his actions, he lost his commission. Author Ronit Stahl commented: "So even if spirituality transcended the color line, chaplain assignments did not."[12]

As fighting continued, in spite of the fact that over half of all African Americans in service were deployed overseas, very few intact regiments would see actual combat. Fort Devens in Ayer was home to the segregated 372nd Infantry. The unit had fought extensively in France during the First World War as part of the storied Red Hand Division and was awarded the Croix de Guerre by a grateful French nation. During the next war, the regiment would be broken into separate battalions, with the third assigned to Fort Devens.

An article in *The Guardian* decried the fate of the 372nd, blaming Jim Crow policies, which were responsible for breaking up the men of the proud Fort Devens battalion and turning it into a "replacement pool for combat troops." While acknowledging that many black men were at last fighting for their country, they were no longer a part of the "trigger-trained, polished regiment that we in Boston gloried in… To see these hard, painful gains lavishly assigned to other outfits is not an easy pill to swallow." The article continued, "What we need now…is a complete elimination of this Jim Crow evil and create a system wherein brothers in Democracy can fight and share their commands side by side. Is not this the Democracy we are fighting for?"[13]

The Colonel in charge of Deven's 372nd Infantry most likely agreed. Born in Florida, Edward O. Gourdin was an exceptionally gifted student and athlete who made his way to Harvard, where he attained a law degree. The young manmade history for his athletic prowess with a world record long jump of over twenty-five feet during a Harvard track meet in 1921 and went on to win a silver medal in the 1924 Olympics. Gourdin's record as a lawyer was even more impressive. Shortly after his Olympic win, he was admitted to the Massachusetts Bar but forced to keep his job at the Post Office as he had difficulty finding a firm willing to hire a black attorney. The young man persevered, however, eventually becoming a member of the bench in Roxbury, an assistant United States Attorney for Massachusetts, and the first African American justice in the Massachusetts Superior Court. Gourdin joined the National Guard in 1925 and, when World War II broke out, was assigned to command the 372nd Infantry.[14] Approximately 10,000 African American men trained under Gourdin during World War II. More than 1,500 of them would become Buffalo Soldiers.[15]

---

[10] Knight, Ellen. *Black Veterans Earned Respect WWII.*

[11] *Army Ousting Fuller.* Guardian 1/29/1944. Chronicling Am LOC. tinyurl.com/ekd26f8h.

[12] Stahl, Ronit. *War Stories.* Danforth Ctr on Religion and Pol 1/28/2016. tinyurl.com/52y8wrx9.

[13] *372nd on Many Battlefronts.* Guardian 12/16/1944. LOC. tinyurl.com/y73zr6kv.

[14] Greenwald, Diana. *Ned Gourdin.* Isabella Stewart Gardner Mus 9/2020. tinyurl.com/yvkjzf39.

[15] *Gen. Edward Gourdin.* Commw MA Arch. tinyurl.com/4fh6pefe.

Edward Gourdon during a long jump
at the 1924 Olympic Games.[16]

    The 366th Infantry, a group that fought in the Great War, trained at Fort Devens under Col. Ned Gourdin. A medic with the unit later remembered, "Our regiment was separate and unique as it had no white officers...The 366th was all African American from our bird colonel commanding officer down. The regiment was a political headache for the government."[17] In Europe, by the Fall of 1944, the slow-moving drive up the Italian Peninsula had bogged down at the Gothic Line in northern Italy. Casualties were high, and fighting men were being tied down when they could have reinforced other combat units in the push toward Germany. The government made the decision to send in black soldiers. The 366th arrived in Italy and was placed under a white commander, Major General Edward Almond. He welcomed his reinforcements. "I did not send for you. Your Negro newspapers, Negro politicians, and white friends have insisted on your seeing combat, and I shall see that you get combat and your share of the casualties."[18]

    Soon, the 366th was split up and dispersed into various units of the 92th Infantry. These "Buffalo Soldiers" were named after men of color who fought with the cavalry in the western United States after the Civil War. The 92nd Infantry would make history as the only African American infantry division to see combat in Europe during World War II. The fighting was heavy, and the losses were great. The *Fitchburg Sentinel* traced their long road up the Italian peninsula, taking Mt. Casala "...after a savage battle, much to the embarrassment of the defenders." They captured the ports of La Spezia and Genoa while simultaneously holding two German divisions at bay. After Italy, they moved on to Germany. The article stated the Buffalo soldiers caused "...thoughtful Nazis a good deal of dismay at witnessing the strength and determination of an 'inferior race.'"[19]

---

[16] *Edward Gourdin.* Pub domain photo. Wiki Commons. tinyurl.com/bdhsxaup.

[17] Guise, Kim. *Rothacker Smith.* Nat WWII Mus 7/28/2020. tinyurl.com/5n7wr4rn.

[18] Waite, Daniel. *William Paskins, Jr.* DE's WWII Fallen 5/23/2022. tinyurl.com/4rdcj3zn.

[19] *Your Fighting Divisions.* Fitchburg Sentinel 11/24/1945. Newspapers.com. tinyurl.com/3dfebya6.

Buffalo soldiers in combat, Italy. 1944.[20]

The Division suffered nearly 3,000 killed and wounded. Fifty-six men became prisoners of war.[21] Many, like Joseph B. Bracy of Roxbury, hailed from Massachusetts. Due to bravery on the battlefield in Italy, he was made a second lieutenant and became a platoon leader.[22] Young Arthur Guy fought with the 92nd Infantry in Italy. Three years after leaving his home in Winchester, his mother received sad news. An Army chaplain wrote:

Your son, in a critical situation against the enemy, volunteered to stay behind and cover the withdrawal of his platoon to better-prepared positions. He was discovered by the enemy and killed by machine gun fire...You have, in the death of your son, an example of valor, courage, and self-sacrifice. In attempting to save the lives of his comrades, he lost his own life.

Guy was awarded a Silver Star for gallantry in action.[23] Edward William Brooke III rose to the rank of Captain and was awarded a Bronze Star for his action against a heavily armed artillery battery. He returned home after the war, earned a law degree from Boston University, and became the first black Attorney General in Massachusetts. In 1967, Edward Brooke took the oath of office as the first African American in nearly a century to join the US Senate. Two Buffalo Soldiers became recipients of the most revered recognition their country could offer, the Congressional Medal of Honor. One was a young man from Wyoming, lst Lt. Vernon J. Baker. The other was John Robert Fox.

---

[20] *Buffalo Soldiers Italy.* Pub domain photo. US Army. Bultman, Lori. *92nd Infantry Div.* US Army 2/18/2021. tinyurl.com/3bv3bxt6.

[21] Guise, Kim. *Rothacker Smith.*

[22] *Bracy Promoted.* Guardian 12/9/1944 LOC. tinyurl.com/wv7nk4d7.

[23] Knight, Ellen. *Black Veterans Earned Respect WWII.*

John R. Fox.[24]

Fox grew up in Ohio, but after ROTC and promotion to 2nd Lieutenant was assigned to the 366th Infantry at Fort Devens. He settled in Brockton and shipped out to Italy in 1944. On Christmas Day, Fox was acting as a forward observer in the town of Semmocolonia when they were attacked by German troops. By early morning on the following day, the town was in enemy hands. Allied forces pulled out while Fox and his observation crew remained to direct artillery fire. He continuously radioed in targets that grew closer and closer to his own position. Fox ordered his squad to retreat, remaining behind and calling for a strike perilously close. "Fox," his commander replied, "that will be on you!" The last communication from Lt. Fox was, "Fire it! There's more of them than there are of us. Give them hell!"

The body of John Robert Fox was found several days later, surrounded by approximately one hundred dead enemy soldiers. He had delayed the Germans and given his unit time to organize a counterattack. For his sacrifice and heroism, Lt. Fox was awarded the Congressional Medal of Honor.[25] His widow, Arlene, stated of her husband, "We never needed any medals. John just felt that we were as good as anybody else, and he was going to prove it, and he did." John Robert Fox was laid to rest in Colebrook Cemetery in Whitman, Massachusetts.[26]

A million men came ashore during the Normandy invasion, and Allied forces were now making slow progress eastward, facing tough German resistance. Their greatest foe, however, was a lack of supplies, ammunition, and fuel. Patton's army was gobbling up five hundred thousand gallons of gasoline every fifty miles,[27] and the General, with his characteristic lack of finesse, felt free to complain about it. "Maybe there are 5,000, 10,000 Nazi bastards in their concrete foxholes before the Third Army. Now if Ike stops holding Monty's hand and gives me some supplies, I'll go through the Siegfried Line like shit goes through a goose." The irony was that Patton's badly needed supplies were sitting on the beach at Normandy or floating offshore in ships. Getting them inland was the problem. Most coastal ports were still held by Germany, and Eisenhower had blown up rail lines to sever the flow of enemy supplies, inadvertently interfering with his own.

---

[24] *John R. Fox.* Pub domain photo. NPS 6/17/2022. tinyurl.com/mm34c2zc.

[25] *John Robert Fox.* Cong MOH Soc. tinyurl.com/2h6mwvs5.

[26] Graff, Cory. *John Fox's MOH.* Nat WWII Mus9/16/2022. tinyurl.com/4yx8djzp.

[27] Sasser, Charles W. *Patton's Panthers.* Pocket Books 2004.

Lt. Col. Loren Ayers was in charge of fixing the problem. He had thousands of trucks and needed men to drive them. He found them in mess halls, laundry rooms, and motor pools. Black soldiers, like 24-year-old Merton Collins of Athol,[28] suddenly became members of the Red Ball Express, so named because of the red dot displayed on vehicles, and played a pivotal role in bringing the Third Reich to an end. For many months, 6,000 deuce-and-a-half trucks filled with everything from ammunition and fuel to medical supplies and food rolled out from beaches toward the troops and back to reload, sometimes under enemy fire, twenty-four hours a day, running without lights at night to avoid enemy detection, never stopping.

Red Ball Express, Normandy. 1944.[29]

Said Patton, "The 2 ½ truck is our most valuable weapon." One tank division commander remembered fuel being delivered by drivers under heavy fire. "Damned if I'd want their job. They have what it takes."[30]

Red Ball Express gas cans being filled.
Courtesy US Army Quartermaster Museum[31]

The courage and determination of the men of the Red Ball Express did not go unnoticed, and when the need for reinforcements reached a tipping point during the Battle of the Bulge, Eisenhower took a bold step. On December 26, 1944, the General asked for African American volunteers to go into battle alongside white troops. Over 4,000 stepped forward. As fighting at the Bulge continued, 2,500 black Americans fought shoulder to shoulder with white Americans in desegregated units. These men, non-commissioned officers who agreed to a rank reduction, were older than the average African American soldier and held a higher proportion of high school diplomas. Their performance exceeded

---

[28] *Promoted.* Athol Daily News 9/25/1945. Newspapers.com. tinyurl.com/3u2bsryd.

[29] *Red Ball Express.* Pub domain photo. Archivesnormandy. Picryl. tinyurl.com/2djuheax.

[30] Delmont, Matthew. *Black soldiers Red Ball Express.* Conversation 4/7/2022. tinyurl.com/5fyz4p9e.

[31] *Red Ball gas cans.* Pub domain photo. V1213. Courtesy US Army Quartermaster Mus.

white soldiers in many ways, with fewer absences and rule infractions. A commanding officer would later describe them: "... in courage, coolness, dependability, and pride, they are on a par with any white troops I have ever had occasion to work with. In addition, they were, during combat, possessed with a fierce desire to meet with and kill the enemy, the equal of which I have never witnessed in white troops."[32]

When the 761st segregated African American Tank Battalion landed at Omaha Beach in October 1944, General Patton was in a bind. With the number of dead and wounded rising at an alarming rate on his eastward push into Germany, he was in desperate need of reinforcements. Patton's distaste for blacks in combat is well documented. In 1944, he contacted the War Department to ask for more tanks, and the request was approved. When Patton discovered he would soon have the African American 761st under his command, he responded: "Who the fuck asked for color? I asked for tankers." He didn't have much choice in the matter. The 761st was the only tank unit left.[33] Regardless of his personal opinions, he made the best of the situation. He greeted the 761st in November.

Men, you're the first Negro tankers to ever fight in the American Army. I would never have asked for you if you weren't good. I have nothing but the best in my Army. I don't care what color you are as long as you go up there and kill those Kraut sonsofbitches. Everyone has their eyes on you and is expecting great things from you. Most of all, your race is looking forward to your success. Don't let them down, and damn you, don't let me down!

They didn't. Patton's Black Panthers, after ferocious fighting, captured Morville-les-Vic in Belgium in November 1944. Casualties were high. Captain John B. Long later described the efforts of his men. "The town of Morville-les-Vic was supposed to be a snap, but it was an inferno; my men were tigers, and they fought like seasoned veterans. We got our lumps, but we took that f***ing town."[34] The record of the 761st is extraordinary. They remained with Patton's Third Army until the end of the war, took part in campaigns in six different countries, earned seven Silver Stars, 246 Purple Hearts, and one Congressional Medal of Honor.[35] But perhaps the most fitting tribute came from a captured German soldier when he stated, "Such bravery I've never before seen."[36]

The Air Force sector of the Army grudgingly admitted African Americans into their corps, assigning them to support roles. As an excuse for overlooking potential flight candidates, the Army Air Force used the Army General Classification Test. Black candidates routinely scored lower on this general knowledge assessment than their white counterparts, thereby excluding most from flight training. While considering the results an indication of the socioeconomic and educational conditions experienced by most black Americans of the time (a later study noted that white and black candidates of similar backgrounds had shown comparable scores),[37] the Army felt its job was to produce pilots, not fix the ills of society. Thus, African Americans were excluded.

However, bowing to public pressure, the support of the formidable Eleanor Roosevelt, and, much to the dismay of the Army Air Force, FDR, the War Department soon required a training program be developed for African American pilots. A segregated program opened in Tuskegee, Alabama, and just over a year later, five men became the first black fighter pilots in US military history. In addition to

---

[32] Calhoun, Mark. *Black Volunteer Infantry WWII.* Nat WWII Mus 2/28/2023. tinyurl.com/4946xvps.

[33] Charles W. Sasser. *761st Tank Battalion.* History Reader. tinyurl.com/4rsen7wm.

[34] Lengel, Ed. *Black Panthers Enter Combat.* Nat WWII Mus 9/18/2020. tinyurl.com/3v79enxb.

[35] *761st Tank Battalion.* NPS. tinyurl.com/c5yt7px4.

[36] Martin, David. *Rescuing Black WWII tank battalion from obscurity.* Sunday Morning. CBS News 9/13/2023. tinyurl.com/mvn786xx.

[37] Lee, Ulysses. *Employment Negro Troops.* US Army CMH 1966. tinyurl.com/rasehtjt.

14,000 navigators, bombardiers, mechanics, and control tower operators, the Tuskegee program would train over 1,000 pilots.[38] At least fifteen of the Tuskegee Airmen had ties to Massachusetts.

Tuskegee Airmen credited with shooting down eight
German planes in dogfights on January 27, 1944 in Italy.[39]

Born in Roxbury, Leo Robert Gray joined the Army after graduating from Boston English High School and made his way to Tuskegee. He flew fifteen combat missions in Europe during World War II and chalked up 750 flight hours. Lt. Col. Gray returned to the Bay State after the war, earned a B.S. from the University of Massachusetts, and remained a member of the United States Air Force Reserve for forty-one years.[40]

One of only three African American men to achieve ratings as pilot, navigator, and bombardier, Daniel Keel spent part of his childhood in Massachusetts and graduated from Boston Latin High School. While studying aeronautical engineering at Northeastern University, Keel joined the Army.[41] His extensive training in Alabama, Texas, and Mississippi led to certification in a variety of flight roles, but it also exposed him to the senseless bigotry tolerated by the Army Air Force.

On arrival at Midland Air Force Army Base, Keel and others in his group were met by the white deputy base commander. Keel recalled, "He told us...that he was born in Texas, raised in Texas, and expects to die in Texas. And if we ... did not know our place while we were in his state of Texas, he'd spell it out for us." Keel and his colleagues were barred from the officer's club and were told that if they needed to travel by bus, they'd sit in the back and would be served in the mess hall only after whites had been fed. Outraged by their treatment, he and several other men wrote a letter informing the Inspector General in Washington of the discrimination. As a result, an unsuccessful attempt was made to have Keel court-martialed,[42] an incident classified by the government until 2015.

---

[38] History.com Eds. *Tuskegee Airmen* 1/26/2021. tinyurl.com/5de25uaw.

[39] *Pilots of USAAF* 2/1944. Pub domain photo. 535763 NARA. tinyurl.com/4tw6m8t2.

[40] *Leo Gray.* CAF Rise Above 4/28/2020. tinyurl.com/34w3453m.

[41] *Daniel Keel.* CAF Rise Above 4/6/2023. tinyurl.com/46vyv8zc.

[42] *Airman talks about service.* WKMG ClickOrlando.com 2/14/2017. tinyurl.com/4kpw5pd8.

Daniel Keel[43]

There were repercussions for the young flier. "I didn't want to be a bomber pilot," Keel remembered. "As far as I'm concerned, they were sitting ducks. I would much rather be a fighter pilot…A fighter pilot had something interesting to do." But he had made an enemy of his commanding officer and ended up as a bomber pilot. The war ended before Keel could be deployed. He returned to Massachusetts, opened an electrical contracting business, and retired to Florida in 1998.[44]

Lt. Maceo Antonio Harris, Jr. never made it home. Raised in Boston, he was an engineering student at Northeastern University when he enlisted and entered the flight program at Tuskegee. On July 17, 1944, while escorting B-24s in southern France, the group was attacked. Unable to engage an enemy target, Harris fixed instead on a struggling American bomber whose engines had been damaged. When radio communication proved unsuccessful, he used hand signals to guide the B-24 pilot to a Corsican airstrip. When radio contact failed once again, this time with the control tower, the young flyer buzzed the airfield to clear the runway. The B-24 landed safely. Sadly, Harris' time was nearly up. Four months later, during another escort mission, his plane developed engine trouble. Nearby pilots noted that he failed to eject before they lost visual contact with the P-51 Mustang. Maceo Harris was awarded the Purple Heart.[45]

The Tuskegee Airmen, also known as Red Tails for the color painted on the tails of their planes, flew with the 332nd Fighter Group in Italy. Often requested as escorts by bomber pilots due to their exceptional performance, the Tuskegee Airmen flew over 15,000 sorties during their time in Europe. They are credited with downing 111 German planes during flight, another 150 on the ground,[46] and the destruction of hundreds of enemy railcars and motor vehicles. Sixty-six heroes perished for their country. The Tuskegee Airmen earned 150 Distinguished Flying Crosses, 8 Purple Hearts, 14 Bronze Stars, 744 Air Medals,[47] and an honored place in American history.

All went well when the Harvard University lacrosse team traveled to Annapolis in April 1941 for an intercollegiate game against the Navy until it was discovered that Lucian Alexis Jr., an African American student on the Harvard team, was set to play. The Superintendent of the US Naval Academy offered options: get rid of him or forfeit the game. Alexis was put on a bus and sent back to Cambridge.[48]

[43] *Daniel Keel.* Pub domain photo. US Army. CAF Rise Above 4/6/2023. tinyurl.com/46vyv8zc.

[44] Quesinberry, Amy. *Tuskegee Airman Daniel Keel.* Observer 5/26/2016. tinyurl.com/4sxpm88k.

[45] *Maceo Harris Jr.* CAF Rise Above 10/21/2021. tinyurl.com/mr3e9y7f.

[46] *First Air Force Afr-Am general.* USAF 2/6/2012. tinyurl.com/445e9dkz.

[47] *Tuskegee Airmen.* SDASM. tinyurl.com/4d5hkfa3.

[48] *Team Should Be Loyal.* Boston Globe 4/10/1941. Newspapers.com. tinyurl.com/cke2w7er.

Apart from questionable decision-making on the part of Harvard's lacrosse coach, the incident made one thing abundantly clear...racism was a systemic issue in the United States Navy.

Secretary of the Navy Frank Knox and the maritime branch of the military had shown dogged resistance to allowing blacks into its ranks beyond unskilled jobs. On March 14, 1942, the headline of the *Pittsburgh Courier* screamed, "'Messman Hero' Identified." Immediately following the attack on Pearl Harbor, a list of names was released by the government, which identified those whose heroic actions were deserving of medals. Included on the list was an "unnamed Negro messman." After an exhaustive search of three months, the newspaper had discovered the name of the sailor. "Thus is revealed the first Negro hero of World War No. 2..."[49] The government had willfully withheld the identity of Doris Miller. A public outcry followed, and with increasing pressure from the White House, Knox was forced to expand the role of black sailors.

One man from Wakefield observed this progress first-hand. The Navy Lieutenant was a former construction worker who had been sent to Camp Peary in Virginia to prepare black sailors for assignment to segregated construction battalions. Discrimination and racial unrest were rampant. Whites were allotted six training days in the drill hall and rewarded with weekend passes. Blacks could train in the hall only one day and never left the base.

The lieutenant, a first-generation American whose parents had emigrated from Italy, likened it to the treatment of Italians that he had witnessed during his youth in Wakefield and Malden. He didn't like it. He convinced his superior officers that using African American drill instructors to guide the men through basic training would relax tensions. This was problematic, however, as no candidates could pass the DI test. The Lieutenant started a basic literacy class, and forty-eight men became drill instructors. He gathered together a group of experienced men to teach basic carpentry, plumbing, and masonry skills in order to raise black sailors up from the realm of mess laborers. The program was a success. The young man remained stateside during the war, training sailors for the Seabees and earning the rank of Lt. Commander. He returned to the Bay State on discharge, and in 1960, John A. Volpe became the 63rd Governor of the State of Massachusetts.[50]

John A. Volpe[51]

In spite of the growing number of African Americans in the Navy, the Department's stance remained rigid and biased. "There will be no mixing of crews on large combatant ships other than personnel of the Stewards Mates branch."[52] In an effort to quell mounting criticism and at the suggestion

---

[49] *Messman Hero Identified.* Pittsburgh Courier 3/14/1942. Newspapers.com. tinyurl.com/2w3265h6.

[50] Knight, Ellen. *Black Veterans Earned Respect WWII.*

[51] *Volpe.* Pub domain photo. Volpe Center. Wiki Commons. tinyurl.com/2cammbdp.

[52] Harrod, Frederick. *Integration of Navy.* USNI 10/1979. tinyurl.com/49d76j7e.

of First Lady Eleanor Roosevelt, the Navy decided on a grand experiment. In October 1943, the destroyer escort USS Mason launched at the Boston Navy Yard. Named after Newton Mason, who met a hero's death after deliberately turning his aircraft directly into a group of Japanese Zeros during the Battle of the Coral Sea, the ship was typical of its type. What was unusual was its crew. Under the command of white officers, 160 of the 204 men aboard were African Americans. For eleven months, USS Mason, known as "Eleanor's Folly," traveled the dangerous passage across the Atlantic as an escort, accompanying tugboats and barges while battling Mother Nature.

Two sailors stand in front of the USS Mason,
Boston Navy Yard. March 1944.[53]

USS Mason, the first Navy fleet vessel crewed predominantly by African Americans, survived the war, its men having overcome the threat of weather, U-boats, and the senseless bigotry of their own government. The Navy's experiment was proving successful much to their dismay.

By the end of 1943, there were 100,000 African American sailors in the US Navy. Zero of them were officers. Pressure was mounting from black civil and religious leaders to change policies. Another experiment was called for. In January 1944, sixteen black sailors gathered together at the Great Lakes Naval Training Center in Illinois. They had been selected to attend officer candidate school. It is an inspirational story of perseverance and dedication, a tale of sixteen men who vowed not to fail in spite of the leadership of the United States Navy, who expected them to do just that.

The men participated in an officer training program which for white candidates took sixteen weeks. They were given eight.[54] From the outset, they were segregated into a building that held sixteen cots, and after lights out, they covered the windows with blankets and hunkered down in the bathroom to study by flashlight. When it came time for final exams, the men exceeded expectations, performing so well that officials in Washington had doubts. Clearly, somebody had cheated. The men were required to retake some of the tests. This time, the numbers went up. They had scored the highest average of any officer training class in naval history.

[53] *USS Mason* 3/20/1944. Pub domain photo. 3829723 NARA. tinyurl.com/4kabkkaa.

[54] Cressman, Robert et al. *Golden Thirteen.* NHHC 11/25/2020. tinyurl.com/bdzervx5.

The Golden Thirteen of the U.S. Navy. February 1944.[55]

The end result should have been sixteen newly commissioned naval officers. It wasn't. One hundred percent of the black candidates had passed. Yet without explanation, three men were overlooked, and the rest, the "Golden Thirteen," became officers. (Twelve received commissions and one became a warrant officer.) It is interesting to note that by commissioning only twelve men, the success rate for the graduating class of African American officers became the same as for their white counterparts. None of these men ever saw combat. They were assigned domestic roles as instructors or crewing coastal patrols, and the Navy never saw reason to publicly acknowledge their achievement.

Dalton Louis Baugh Sr. was one of them. He had been an instructor of auto mechanic classes at Arkansas State College before joining the Navy in 1942. The Navy took advantage of his skills and sent him to the Great Lakes Naval Training Center as a Machinist's Mate. It was clear, however, that Baugh was a very bright young man, and in 1944, he became one of the Golden Thirteen. He was assigned to the lst Naval District in Boston and placed aboard the USS Migrant, a yacht that had been constructed at George Lawley & Sons in Neponset and reconditioned for the Navy. In his position as Chief Engineering Officer, Baugh patrolled the New England coastline in search of enemy subs.

He returned to Massachusetts after the war, earned a graduate degree in mechanical engineering from MIT, and became an instructor in the college's gas turbine lab. Later in life, Baugh worked for the Massachusetts Department of Public Health and started his own architectural firm. He remained a member of the Naval Reserves until 1964, achieving the rank of Lt Commander. Dalton Baugh Sr. passed away in Boston at age 72 and rests at Mount Auburn Cemetery in Cambridge.[56]

The launching of the USS Mason and the appointment of African American officers were major steps forward, but a month later, an event occurred which dramatically changed the future of blacks in the Navy. Secretary of the Navy Frank Knox died. He had done an admirable job of waging war against the enemies of the United States but had maintained discriminatory policies which deliberately excluded thousands of African Americans from serving in positions equal to whites. His successor would change that.

James Vincent Forestal was elevated from his position as Undersecretary of the Navy by FDR and appointed Knox's successor. Shortly afterward, Forestal began a series of changes with such rapidity that it appears almost to have been a checklist of wrongs to be righted. June 1944 saw the appointment of the first black Navy chaplain. Soon afterward, blacks who were not working steward jobs would be integrated into white auxiliary crews up to the level of 10%, and eight months later, they were stationed

[55] *Negro officers.* Pub domain photo. 2/1944. USN. NAID 520671. tinyurl.com/39k9za38.

[56] *Dalton Baugh Sr.* USN RTC 2022. tinyurl.com/yc427cdm.

as regular crew members on Navy ships. In February 1945, the Navy released the following policy statement: "The Navy accepts no theories of racial differences in inborn ability, but expects that every man wearing its uniform be trained and used in accordance with his maximum individual capacity determined on the basis of individual performance..." Although Forestal meant well, of the 187,000 African American sailors who served during World War II, only sixty-four became officers. The rest remained relegated to the level of stewards and laborers.[57]

The Marines of World War II fell under the jurisdiction of the Secretary of the Navy, and Marine chief General Thomas Holcomb was totally on board with Frank Knox's policies. With a bit less polish than the SECNAV, Holcomb clearly stated his views about blacks in the Marine Corps. They "...were trying to break into a club that doesn't want them." As the Navy's position began to weaken, Holcomb wasn't having it, saying basically, let them join the Army. In June 1942, however, an order was sent down from Knox. The Marines would have to accept African Americans into their ranks.

Much to the surprise of Marine leadership, black Americans did not rush to enlist in the Corps. Why should they? The government had excluded them from their branch of the military since the Revolutionary War. After several weeks, only sixty-three African Americans had signed on the dotted line. One Marine officer commented that perhaps only those willing to die would join because Marines die young. So recruiters went in search of truck drivers, cooks, and typists. When Obie Hall approached a recruiter in Boston, he was told he could join on the spot if he had the right specialty. Hall told the man he was a truck driver when truth be told, he could "no more drive a truck than the man in the moon," but felt he couldn't get away with saying he was a typist or a cook. Six months later, blacks were joining up at the rate of 1,000 per month.[58]

A segregated facility at Montfort Point, a section of Camp LeJeune in North Carolina, was in charge of training black Marines. The plan was to turn out service unit Marines, blacks who could cook, bake, and cut hair. Given the grand title, 51st Composite Defense Battalion (composite referring to African American Marines commanded by white officers), the unit was not expected to see battle. Obie Hall, the first black Marine from New England, was one of them. "Obie joined the Marines because they were a fighting force," said his brother, Gerry. "He wanted to fight for his country. But...he wasn't allowed to be the Marine he wanted to be."[59]

The majority of African American Marines in World War II shipped out to battlefronts in the Pacific, where their support jobs included moving supplies, ammunition, and fuel. In the heat of battle, however, the lines between black and white and combat and support became muted. Black Marines cared for and carried wounded under fire, defended foxholes, repelled Japanese attacks, killed and were killed. On Okinawa, 2,000 black Marines in ammunition and depot companies arrived to support the III Marine Amphibious Corps. Soon, nearly all would see combat.[60] Lt. General Alexander Vandegrift, who had replaced General Holcomb, issued a statement: "The Negro Marines are no longer on trial. They are Marines, period." Nearly 20,000 African Americans proudly served their country as Marines during World War II.

---

[57] Lee-Smith, Hughie. *Afr Am Sailors USN*. NHHC 6/11/2024. tinyurl.com/3z9ve6ch.

[58] Nalty, Bernard C. *Right to Fight*.

[59] Cullen, Kevin. *Trailblazer gets medal*. Boston Globe 11/15/2016. Newspapers.com. tinyurl.com/3dfbmep2.

[60] Nalty, Bernard C. *Right to Fight*.

Men of African American 12th Marine Ammunition
Company rest at a monument overrun in Okinawa. 1945.[61]

Revenue cutters, forerunners of the Coast Guard, were authorized to employ free blacks as cooks or stewards in 1843. With few exceptions, the policy remained in place until 1942, when SECNAV Frank Knox determined blacks could be used in general service. This was interpreted by the Coast Guard a bit more liberally than the Navy, and while mess men were still among the ranks, African Americans were also trained as radiomen, pharmacists, yeomen, coxswains, electricians, and boatswains mates. One year later, Lt. Carlton Skinner made a bold move.

Born in Boston, Skinner joined the military in order to participate in the defeat of fascism. His experiences aboard the Cutter Northland would impact his future course. "Their technology appeared to be superb," he later wrote of the enemy. "Their military and naval skills are extraordinarily effective, and their economic capacity to support these successful. To combat and defeat these would require the use of every resource of our economy, technology, skills and manpower."[62] During a voyage off Greenland, Northland's engine cut out, and the ship went dead in the water. After the white crew failed to fix the problem, a steward stepped forward and repaired the motor. Skinner attempted to have the guardsman promoted and was told no. The man was black. It didn't sit well with the Lieutenant, who considered it a waste of resources.

In June 1943, now Captain of the Sea Cloud, a weather ship out of Boston, Skinner pitched an idea...integrate his ship. His request was approved. Shortly afterward, when the Sea Cloud left port, fifty-four of the 173 aboard were black. The Coast Guard had quietly taken a giant step away from discrimination. Skinner would later serve as Captain aboard the integrated USS Hoquiam. After the war, he served his country as the Governor of Guam returned to Massachusetts, and passed away in Boston at the age of 91.[63]

The entrance of black women into the various branches of the military was made a bit easier by the thousands of African American men who served during the war. While these women experienced discrimination, were kept down in menial jobs, and struggled to make their way up the chain of command, the groundwork had already been laid. Of all the armed forces, the Army alone had included blacks from the moment the WACs came into being. Regardless, for women in the Army, the journey to equality was often fraught with difficulties.

---

[61] *Marine Co. Okinawa.* Pub domain photo. USMC 117624. DOD. Nalty, Bernard C. *Right to Fight.*

[62] Skinner, Carlton. *USS Sea Cloud.* USCG Historian's Office. tinyurl.com/3ktt4bkn.

[63] Tanenbaum, Jessica. *Carlton Skinner.* Boston Globe 7/7/2004. Newspapers.com. tinyurl.com/yc3tyed5.

Lured into joining with promises of nursing and technical opportunities, black WACs watched while whites were assigned to coveted jobs, and they became kitchen workers and cleaning staff. In March of 1945, a group of African American women made national news when they staged a strike at Lovell General Hospital at Fort Devens. Fifty-four women refused to work, protesting their unequal work status, until they were informed that mutiny during wartime could result in execution. Four were sent to court-martial. Boston's *Guardian* newspaper reported the outcome: "WACs Convicted. Get Year At Hard Labor." In addition, the women would forfeit pay and be dishonorably discharged. Yes, the women had been insubordinate. However, during the trial, it was reported that Col. Walter Crandell of Vinal Haven, in charge of the hospital, had made racially charged comments. "I don't want black WACS here as medical technicians. They are here to mop walls, scrub floors, and do all the dirty work." Interestingly, Crandell was absent from the trial, having suddenly taken a 30-day leave.[64]

The public was not pleased. The NAACP got involved. Thurgood Marshall, famed civil rights attorney, arrived in Boston. Letters of protest went out to FDR and Secretary of War Stimson. One month later, the Army dropped all charges against the women and returned them to duty. They had weathered the storm, brought awareness to the reality of being black in the Women's Army Corps, and went back to being kitchen staff and orderlies without the mopping and scrubbing. Crandell was removed from his position, but not much had changed.

One group of women, however, was already making history. The 6888th WAC Battalion was formed in December 1944 and became the only African American WAC unit to serve abroad during World War II. Its seemingly mundane mission, postal work, played a crucial role in maintaining morale in the European Theater of Operation. The Department of Defense tells the interesting history of these dedicated women and of the daunting task that they faced. The 850 WACs of the 6888th arrived in Birmingham, England, to find several warehouses filled with undelivered mail. Items returned after the Battle of the Bulge were stored in six airplane hangars chock full of letters, unopened packages filled with Christmas goodies, and rats...lots of rats. Difficulties encountered included 7,500 pieces of mail addressed to soldiers named Robert Smith and the constant return of items that had been sent to soldiers whose addresses changed as troops moved eastward toward Germany. The DOD estimates that during each eight-hour shift, the women processed 65,000 pieces of mail. Within six months, they completed their task and moved on to France.[65]

688th members sorting mail, France. World War II.[66]

---

[64] *WAC's Convicted.* Guardian 3/24/1945. Chron Am LOC. tinyurl.com/4pypswkn.

[65] Lange, Katie. *All-Black Female Unit Receive Gold Medal.* DOD 3/18/2022. tinyurl.com/mvk8fmhy.

[66] *6888th Rouen.* Pub domain photo. US Army. Melissa. *6888th Postal Battalion* 7/2020. George Marshall Fdn. tinyurl.com/yuz6rknb.

Nine women from Massachusetts were members of the 6888th Postal Battalion. Elsie Oliver wrote directly to Eleanor Roosevelt to ask for help in joining the group.[67] After the war, she moved to Cambridge and passed away at age 89. Proud of her service to her country, PFC Oliver is buried at the National Cemetery in Bourne.[68] Mildred Davenport Carter was 40 when she completed officer training and joined the unit. She managed a dance studio before joining the WACs.[69] A resident of Southie, Carter was the first African American WAC officer from Boston.[70] Eloise McNeeley spent three years as a WAC. She would later recall one of the highlights of her time with the 6888th, traveling through the French and English countryside. "Socializing with the French was no problem, and the English were wonderful to us."[71] Having been productive participants in the war effort and experienced acceptance in Europe, many African American WACs of the 6888th Postal Battalion came home to the US to hold meaningful jobs. Many came back to sit on the back of the bus.

The Army's resistance to women pilots in the Army Air Force pales in comparison to its record of minority integration once the WASPs were established. Only five minority women (two Asian Americans, one Native American, and two Hispanic Americans) became WASPs. No African American woman was allowed to join.

In spite of the persistent urging of Mildred McAfee, head of the WAVES, Frank Knox said no to the admission of African Americans into the women's branch of the Navy. With his passing and replacement by James Forestal, the WAVES finally became integrated. On November 18, 1944, the headline for the *Guardian* newspaper in Boston read, "Hub Girl First Wave Recruit." The article reported that on November 13, three African American women had been sworn into the WAVES. The first event took place in Boston, where Jane A. Freeman, a young woman from Roxbury, became a member of the United States Navy. Two hours later, in New York, Harriet Pickens, a Smith alumnus, and Frances Wills were accepted into the ranks as officers.[72] They were sent to Smith College in North Hampton for training. The attitude of WAVES leadership toward discrimination was clear. Those taking a racist stance would be discharged. Wills recalled an officer stating, "...should either of them sit by her in the mess hall, she would get up and walk out." Lt. Elizabeth Reynaud, Massachusetts native and commanding officer, told the woman that she should stop by her office on the way out to submit her resignation."[73]

The Coast Guard followed Navy precedent, and the SPARS opened enlistment to African American women in the fall of 1944. A total of five black women served with the Coast Guard during the war. The Marines, with outspoken General Holcomb now gone, handled the issue with much less bluster but a consistent lack of enthusiasm. A history of Women Reservists published by the Marines sums up their approach: "Black women were not specifically barred from the segregated Marine Corps, but...they were not knowingly enlisted."[74] As a result, zero black women entered the Women's Reserves of the Marine Corps during World War II.

Nurses were in short supply as the country entered the war, yet thousands of African American candidates were turned down. "Your application to the Army Nurse Corps cannot be given favorable consideration as there are no provisions in Army regulations for the appointment of colored nurses in the Corps," read the rejection.[75] This was not exactly true. The Army had permitted black women to join the

---

[67] *6888th Postal Directory Battalion.* Research Guides. LOC. tinyurl.com/c9w3sjca.

[68] *Elsie Jeannetta Oliver.* Find Grave ID128991701 5/1/2014. tinyurl.com/2n3582ha.

[69] *Women in Army.* Women & Am Story. NY Hist Soc Mus & Lib. tinyurl.com/5n64yj2x.

[70] *Major at 21.* Boston Globe 9/3/1945. Newspapers.com. tinyurl.com/yc8c6zfu.

[71] Mullenbach, Cheryl. *Double Victory.* CRP 2013. tinyurl.com/4b7sd94y.

[72] *Hub Girl First Wave Recruit.* Guardian 11/18/1944. Chron Am LOC. tinyurl.com/yc7kh4ds.

[73] Martin, Kali. *We Made it.* Nat WWII Mus /24/2021. tinyurl.com/ye2ajbcn.

[74] Stremlow, Mary. *Free A Marine To Fight.* Marines WWII Comm Series. USMC Hist and Mus. tinyurl.com/5fh3h38w.

[75] Clark, Alexis. *Army's First Black Nurses.* Smithsonian Mag 5/15/2018. tinyurl.com/edtrujje.

6,000 white members of the Army Nurse Corps in 1941...all fifty-six of them. They were sent to segregated installations and allowed to treat only black soldiers and later, prisoners of war. In response to civilian concerns, the quota was adjusted in 1943, and 160 were allowed to join. A December 1944 article in the *Guardian* newspaper noted the Army was in need of 10,000 nurses for war service.[76] Despite the constant call for nurses, by the end of the conflict, over 59,000 nurses served in the Army, only 500 of them black.

At just about the time when the Army was raising its quota, the Navy, ultra conservative in matters of race, had no black nurses in its ranks. Letters of application from African American nurses slowly became more assertive, voicing concerns and asking for explanations. From Cambridge, Massachusetts, Grace C. Scott wrote directly to Secretary of the Navy Frank Knox.

As a nurse, I am writing in protest against your refusal of colored American women being taken into the navy as nurses and waves. Is not this country managed on a democratic basis with freedom and justice for all regardless of race creed or color? Is there not a place in the navy that our women can fill in rendering service to our own sailors and other navy men? How, then, can we, as good law-abiding citizens, as fellow Americans share in this great conflict if you refuse to allow us the privilege of doing so?

Ever a supporter of the underdog, Eleanor Roosevelt had something to say as well. In a one-sentence letter to the Secretary of the Navy, she wrote: "I have had several protests lately that due to the shortage of nurses, colored nurses should be allowed to serve where there is no serious objection to it. Very sincerely yours..." The First Lady's concerns were passed along to the Acting Chief of Navy Nurses, who admitted that the Navy had fallen short by 500 nurses. But do not to worry; there were 500 nurses in training, and, even better, they were all white. As she put it, "...the question relative to the necessity for accepting colored personnel in this category is not apparent."[77] The Navy's wall of discrimination began to crumble on March 8, 1945, when Phyllis Daley became the first African American nurse in the US Navy. The war would end in Europe just two months later.

Being a nurse did not protect African American women from racism. Apparently due to excessive fraternization with enemy POWs, the Army felt white nurses providing their medical care needed to be replaced.

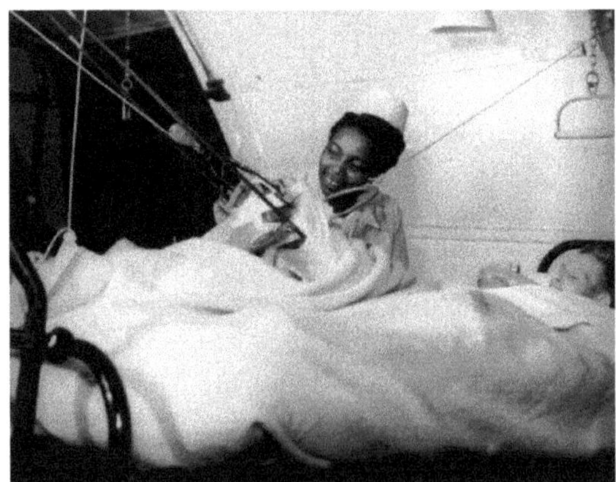

African American nurse treating
a German POW. 1945.[78]

[76] *10,000 Nurses For War Service.* Guardian 12/8/1944. Chronicling Am LOC. tinyurl.com/yc7nd829.

[77] Henneberry, Alicia. *Closed Door of Justice.* Text Message. NARA 2/4/2020. tinyurl.com/ywbj28y6.

[78] *Nurse providing care to POW.* Pub domain photo. US Army. AMEDD ACHH. tinyurl.com/nhewsew9.

African American women were the perfect choice to tend to members of the Aryan master race. It was a slap in the face for women who had joined up to support their countrymen at war. Strangely enough, the women often felt more accepted by prisoners than by their fellow Americans. Elinor Powell of Milton was stationed at a POW camp stateside. She formed a relationship with a POW who would become her husband after the war. Powell recalled treatment by white Americans as often being less respectful. She was refused service at a lunch counter near the camp because of the color of her skin. Another nurse remembered being called "nigger" at the camp and the commander tolerating it.[79]

Most POW and basic training camps were located in the South, a section of the country where nearly seventy-five lynchings took place during the war years alone.[80] The treatment of African Americans was decidedly different than that experienced by those from the North. The discrepancy was keenly felt by thousands of young men sent south for boot camp. Obie Hall of Boston, traveling to his training base in North Carolina, was forced out of his assigned seat on the train when he arrived in Washington, D.C. He had reached the "black line," an African American porter told him. From D.C. on, southward bound trains were segregated.[81] William Robinson of Winchester was sent to Alabama for basic training in 1942. He recalled having read about the treatment of blacks. On his arrival at Fort McClellan, he threw his duffle bag into the back of the truck like everyone else and was told, "Bags ride, you walk."[82] Bert B. Babero, who had been stationed at an Army base in Texas, transferred north to Camp Reynolds in Pennsylvania. "I am at present in Pennsylvania," he wrote, "on the brink of embarkation for overseas duty. Leaving the south was like coming back to God's country."[83]

But all was not well in God's country. In his State of the Union address in 1941, Roosevelt sought to convince the United States that its efforts in supporting her Allies at war were essential to protecting America's four freedoms: the freedom of speech, the freedom of worship, the freedom from want, and the freedom from fear. It was a rousing speech. For the average African-American, however, the definition of freedom looked slightly different. The NAACP (National Association for the Advancement of Colored People) expressed the attitude of many of its adherents: "...the hysterical cries of the preachers of democracy for Europe leave us cold. We want Democracy in Alabama, in Mississippi and Michigan, in the District of Columbia—*in the Senate of the United States.*"[84]

As more and more men and women of color found their way into the armed forces and the workplace, tensions began to rise. A "Double V" campaign sprang up to express the quest for victory by African Americans on two fronts, abroad and at home. J. Edgar Hoover attempted to stifle the nation's black press by invoking the Espionage Act for what he deemed was seditious behavior. Not only was the color of African American skin a focus of bias, but, according to the Smithsonian, so was the color of their blood. At the outset of the war, the military refused to use African American blood. It could be collected but not given to white servicemen. Dr. Charles Drew, graduate of Amherst College, whose groundbreaking work with blood storage and mobile blood banks would save hundreds of thousands of lives, resigned in 1942 from his position as Director of Blood Banks for the Red Cross when the organization failed to denounce racist blood replacement policies. The Red Cross would eventually reverse its decision. Unfortunately, by then, the war had been over for three years.

---

[79] Clark, Alexis. *Army's First Black Nurses.*

[80] Burran, James. *Racial Violence South WWII.* UTK 12/1977. tinyurl.com/yj25687s.

[81] Nalty, Bernard. *Right to Fight.*

[82] Knight, Ellen. *Black Veterans Earned Respect WWII.*

[83] Barbero, Bert B. Letter 3/13/1944. *Segregation Army Bases.* Am Soc Hist Proj. tinyurl.com/3dwt6c4e.

[84] Dalfiume, Richard M. *Forgotten Years of Negro Revolution.*

Massachusetts has a long history of recognizing the plight of blacks. As early as 1855, legislation dealing with anti-discrimination in the Bay State was passed. Thousands of people, black and white, gathered on the Boston Common in 1870 to celebrate the passage of the 15th Amendment granting black men the right to vote. (As late as 1942, eight southern states required a poll tax in order to vote, an effort to disenfranchise the black population.) In spite of its history, prejudice in the Bay State was still very real. On the evening of August 17, 1941, seven men got into a taxi for a trip to Fort Devens. The ride back to the base cost ten cents each...if you were white. The two black soldiers in the vehicle were expected to pay seventy-five cents. Apparently, the scam occurred only in the evening after the buses finished their last run to the base.[85]

Navy veteran J.B. Mills of Whitman remembered being segregated into a black barrack across the street from the white barracks during his time at the Hingham Naval Ammunition Depot. He was also barred from a USO club on Boylston Street in Boston and told, "There is a place for your people at the club in Roxbury."[86] In December 1943, the front page headline of Boston's *Guardian* screamed, "Hub Moves to Halt Jim Crow." The article reported on a move made by the Buddies Club on the Boston Common and the United Nations Service House in the downtown area to bar "colored hostesses" from their establishment. It stated: "Boston is considerably agitated over the expression of anti-race sentiment...it is known that Southern bias is creeping into Boston. Many persons fear that the proscription of colored hostesses at the Buddies' Club foreshadows more violent anti-race hostility, and they want to stop the Jim Crow invasion before it can gain further headway."[87]

Discrimination was present in wartime industry as well. Stanley Desmond was born in Nova Scotia and moved to Everett, Massachusetts. After apprenticing at the GE Riverworks Plant in Lynn, Desmond became a talented tool and die maker. There were few, if any, tool and die makers of color at the plant, and he recalled encountering difficulties. "The atmosphere...was too bad, you know...a good many times, even at nineteen or twenty years old, I would cry when I got home because I had been hurt during the day...And I'd say, 'I want to be a die and tool maker, and that's all there is to it.' So I'll put up with it."[88] Later, after an investigation of the Pittsfield plant, Rev. Harold Leslie Nevers of the local Second Congregational Church gave General Electric a thumbs up. The company "considers each jobholder and applicant individually, on merit," he said, "and has no blanket policy concerning Negroes."[89]

Heavily industrialized Springfield met with interesting challenges. A 1943 *Springfield Daily News* article pointed out that due to the sudden lack of white male employees, the city had experienced a 43 percent increase in the black population. Incidents of racism were on the rise. While praising the city's record of having "...proved a boon to Springfield Negroes, for whom it has opened the door to the hundreds of employment opportunities traditionally closed to 'colored' people," the article also noted employer concerns: African American workers take too many days off and treated their wages as if they were a "gift." However, while patting the city of Springfield on the back for its magnanimity, the report went on to say that some blacks "..saved up enough money to purchase homes in the restricted sections of the city *where they were allowed* to own real estate."[90]

While charges of discrimination were reported against the Springfield Armory, the facility was remembered by many as having been inclusive.

---

[85] *Taximen Accused of Unfairness.* Boston Globe 8/18/1941. Newspapers.com. tinyurl.com/bdetandd.

[86] Rose, Jim. *Segregation Hingham Navy post.* Hingham J 1/8/2015. Wickedlocal.com. tinyurl.com/5n8ytdj9.

[87] *Hub Halt Jim Crow.* Guardian 12/18/1943. Chronicling Am LOC. tinyurl.com/9kj8rw4d.

[88] Aubrey, Barbara. *Stanley Desmond.* Forge of Innovation. NPS 8/11/1986. tinyurl.com/2p9n9v44.

[89] *No Discrimination Found.* Berkshire Eagle 6/13/1941. Newspapers.com. tinyurl.com/2tbhx9s2.

[90] Doyle, Annette. *Discrimination Fails to End.* Springfield Daily News 11/15/1943. Forge of Innovation. tinyurl.com/3ybvbchw.

The Snackery at Springfield Armory. Men and women,
black and white, worked at the Armory during World War II.[91]

Dorothy Pryor recalled her time at the Armory, stating, "...race and gender became much less important than what you could do for the war effort...Cause you know...a bullet has no racial connotations."[92] For many blacks, working at the Armory was a worthwhile experience. Women especially remembered friendships, many forming bonds with white co-workers who waged their own struggle against gender bias. On her final day of employment there, Marion Wimberly wrote this poem for her friend, Nellie Dottie.

The experience I've gained can ne're be lost
The cross I've had to bear was worth the fight
You too, I know forgot, amid the fight
That we were different hues: I black, you white[93]

Stanley Desmond eventually made his way to the Springfield Armory, where he later recalled that the bulk of his co-workers were white, older men, "prima donnas," who had been with the Armory for years. They had never been asked to work with an African American before, and he experienced some resistance. However, Stanley Desmond was a very talented tool and die-maker, and he soon found acceptance based on his skills. The Armory hand-picked the 26-year-old to work with an engineer in developing a new process for making dies. The engineer would sketch a design, and it was Desmond's job to interpret the sketch and create the dies. Within a few years, he received a promotion, which involved supervising some of the very men who had been reluctant to accept him. One was the manager of the forge. "I [was] supposed to tell him what to do. One had to be very diplomatic. You wouldn't say do this or do that. You would say do you want to give us a hand on this or something like that." The manager retired soon afterward. In spite of his difficulties, Stanley Desmond later summed up his time in Springfield. "My relationship with the Armory," he recalled, "was beautiful."[94]

---

[91] *Snackery SA*. Pub domain photo. NPS SA NHS Neg 4729-SA. *Places Hist Springfield*. NPS. tinyurl.com/2xfespva.

[92] *Dorothy Pryor*. Mem Hall Mus Online. Am Centuries. tinyurl.com/4djb38da.

[93] Russell, Alison. Quoted in Wilson. *Crossing Gender, Color Lines SA*. *Places Hist Springfield*. NPS 9/22/2023. tinyurl.com/2xfespva.

[94] Aubrey, Barbara Higgins. *Stanley T. Desmond. Oral History Interview.*

And then after four long years, the war was over. Tug boats displaying welcome banners, brass bands, Red Cross stands with coffee and donuts, and ticker tape parades awaited homecoming servicemen. For thousands of African American veterans, however, it was a very different experience. Benjamin O. Davis Jr. was a West Point graduate and Tuskegee airman when he was shot down in Italy and spent eight months in a German POW camp. Thankfully, he made it home, his transport ship docking in New York Harbor, where he was told which side of the gangplank he should disembark on. "Whites to the right, niggers to the left."[95] Massachusetts resident J.B. Mills, who'd left Louisiana to join the military during the war, spoke of his homecoming from Okinawa to a *Boston Globe* reporter several years later. "There were no bands or parades...only screens saying 'whites only' that marked how far forward he could sit on his bus ride home."[96]

The bravery of the African Americans who fought in World War II far too often went unacknowledged. In June 1942, General Douglas MacArthur was awarded the Congressional Medal of Honor. The citation cited "heroic conduct of defensive and offensive operations on the Bataan Peninsula. He...led an army which has received world acclaim for its gallant defense against a tremendous superiority of enemy forces" (he showed up on the Bataan Peninsula only once after the Japanese attack on the Philippines), "his utter disregard of personal danger under heavy fire and aerial bombardment" (he sheltered in the bombproof Malinta Tunnel on Corregidor during the invasion and evacuated to Australia three months after the attack), "his calm judgment...inspired his troops," (demoralized by his lack of presence during the invasion, soldiers nicknamed him ''Dugout Doug").[97] Apparently, the government felt no black man had performed up to these questionable standards, and thus, not one was awarded a Congressional Medal of Honor during World War II.

In 1993, at the request of the Department of Defense, a committee was established to examine the distribution of medals during the war. The findings noted that 433 courageous men, all white, had received Medals of Honor for extraordinary acts of bravery. After having offered up their lives to their country, racism had prevented African American heroes from receiving the recognition they were due. Amends would have to be made. In 1997, Vernon J. Baker, a former Buffalo Soldier, stood before President Bill Clinton to receive the Congressional Medal of Honor. Of the seven black MOH recipients, among them John Fox of Massachusetts, Baker was the only surviving honoree. Clinton spoke of these brave men, calling them heroes, saying, "In the tradition of African-Americans who have fought for our nation as far back as Bunker Hill, they were prepared to sacrifice everything for freedom even though freedom's fullness was denied to them."

In spite of facing certain prejudice, African Americans, over a million of them, loyally served in the military during World War II, and when given the chance, their accomplishments and sacrifices transcended the color barriers set up by their own government. Over 700 of them made the ultimate sacrifice. Their efforts and the efforts of those who stayed home to hold jobs that would help to win the war and keep the country intact through the dark years of conflict would create unexpected changes in the social fabric. African Americans had fought side by side with whites, stood next to them in factories, earned decent wages, and stood tall and proud as American citizens. There would be no going back, no more bowing down to racism and discrimination. The foundation for the Civil Rights movement had been laid. Said General Colin Powell, "I know in the depth of my heart that the only reason I'm able to stand proudly before you today is because you stood proudly for America sixty years ago."[98]

---

[95] Delmont, Matthew F. *Half American*. Viking 2022.

[96] Latour, Francie. *Hero Recognized*. Boston Globe 1/11/1997. Newspapers.com. tinyurl.com/24wfj3kz/.

[97] *D. MacArthur. Stories of Sacrifice*. Cong MOH Soc. tinyurl.com/kmfd3fvj.

[98] Delmont, Matthew F. *Half American*.

Two African American soldiers guard a
bridge over the Rhine River. 1945.[99]

---

[99] *Pvts. guard bridge 3/30/1945.* Pub domain photo. USAC. 531273 NARA. tinyurl.com/297hjvtv.

Chapter 12

Prisoners of War

I was reminded of Dante's Inferno –
abandon all hope all ye who enter here.
Major Robert Peaty
Mukden POW Camp[1]

It was just after midnight when Kazuo Sakamaki and a second officer slipped into the water. They and four other teams were part of a secret mission to enter the enemy's harbor undetected and destroy ships. It was pretty much a suicide mission. In fact, the five small vessels were equipped with self-destruct devices along with guns and swords to ensure that the men would achieve a glorious death for their Emperor. Of the ten men, only Sakamaki would survive. His mini sub encountered difficulties early on, and unable to navigate toward the target, it collided with coral reefs before being detected and fired upon. By the time Sakamaki regained consciousness, the mini sub had run aground near Pearl Harbor. The date was December 8, 1941, and Sakamaki had just become America's first prisoner of World War II.

Kazuo Sakamaki's two-man submarine beached
on Oahu, Hawaii. December 7, 1941.[2]

Providing for prisoners of war was far down the list of priorities for a country which had just become embroiled in war. Sakamaki and a handful of other Japanese were the only militants held in captivity by the US government until an agreement was struck with England to accept captives being taken in North Africa. It was a commitment designed to benefit the island nation which was struggling in its third year of war. Unlike the United States, Britain was limited by land mass and resources to house prisoners. The move was largely unpopular as the US country feared that American POWs being held by the enemy would be the target of retaliation.

---

[1] Peaty, Robert. *I was reminded of…*. Quote. Michael, Tom. *Pure Evil*. US Sun 8/14/2020. tinyurl.com/28xe6tk4.

[2] *Two-Man Submarine* 12/7/1941. Pub domain photo. 12008982 NARA. tinyurl.com/2t3znyhu.

The first 50,000 prisoners, German and Italian, arrived in the fall of 1942 and were moved to temporary placements such as fairgrounds or former Civilian Conservation Corps camps while more permanent facilities were being constructed. Most would be located across the southern United States or in the Midwest in largely underpopulated areas far from coastlines and industrial sites. Not only did officials fear prison escapes or enemy attempts to liberate captives, but there was also a need to keep camps out of the public eye. Americans were rightfully angered by Axis aggression. Their loved ones were dying at the hands of Hitler and his cronies, and the government hesitated to add fuel to the fire. One angry letter stated, "Put them in Death Valley, chuck in a side of beef, and let them starve."[3] They might possibly need protection from Americans. Thus, the presence of camps was kept out of the press, and most Americans were initially unaware of their existence. When word eventually began to leak out that enemy prisoners were being well-fed and had access to recreation and medical care, outrage followed. The term "Fritz Ritz" found its way into the POW conversation. One historian reported that "German soldiers jokingly called the 'PW' stamped on the backs of their shirts and trousers Pensionierte Wehrmacht, or 'military retiree.'"[4]

As war plodded on and more and more members of the US military were imprisoned in POW camps, the government became very cautious about treatment of prisoners on American soil, fearing retribution aimed at US servicemen being held by the enemy. In 1929 under the watchful eye of the International Red Cross, Britain, the United States, Germany, and thirty-eight other countries signed and ratified the updated version of the Geneva Convention which had first come into being in 1899. The United States rarely wavered from her commitment. Germany's human rights violations aimed at members of the military and civilians have been recorded by history. However, most Allied prisoners of war seemed to have been treated with the barest adherence to the tenets of the Convention. Red Cross boxes, for example, were delivered to POW camps but were often disseminated among guards rather prisoners. Russia was not a signatory, and Germany took full advantage. Russian prisoners were starved, used for chemical warfare experiments, and worked to death in labor camps. Russia responded in kind, one soldier writing home, "We are taking revenge for everything, and our revenge is just. Fire for fire, blood for blood, death for death."[5] Japan, which had signed the 1929 agreement, declined to ratify it making its pledge worthless. With brutality towards members of its own military a way of life, the Empire saw no need to extend courtesy to its enemies.

---

[3] Farquhar, Michael. *Enemies Among Us.* Wash Post 9/10/1997. tinyurl.com/kcs43ase.

[4] Schwier, Ryan. *Eden for Enemy Prisoners.* ILA 8/31/2015. tinyurl.com/nhdje4nm.

[5] Morgan, Martin *Wretched Misconduct Red Army.* Hist Network 2012. tinyurl.com/53cbezd5.

A long line of German prisoners captured
at Aaachen. October 1944.[6]

When captive enemy soldiers flowed in from Africa (there would be over 300,000 German POWs by war's end), America entered into an agreement which placed Japanese prisoners into the custody of Australia, with the United States detaining only those deemed to be of intelligence value. Of over 500 prisoner of war camps in the US, only a handful were designated for the approximately 4,000 Japanese imprisoned here.

There was a more disturbing reason for the smaller number of Japanese captives. For these soldiers, surrender was not an option. It indicated failure to protect the Empire and brought shame to one's family. The preferred solution was suicide.

Two Japanese Imperial Marines who chose
suicide rather than surrender on Tarawa. 1943.[7]

---

[6] *German prisoners Aachen* 10/1944. Pub domain photo. 541597 NARA. tinyurl.com/bd68wxxa.

[7] *Japanese suicide*. Pub domain photo. USMC LOC. Wiki Commons. tinyurl.com/cmu49786.

Horrific reports from the island of Saipan testify to the Japanese fanatic belief in self-sacrifice. Of the 30,000 Japanese troops engaged in battle, less than 1,000 were taken prisoner. Roughly 29,000 of the enemy died during the twenty-four-day-long battle, and it is estimated that 5,000 of them died due to suicide. One month later, Sergeant Shoichi Yokoi failed to take his own life after Americans overran the Japanese-held island of Guam. Instead, he remained hidden in the jungle for twenty-seven years. When he finally returned to Japan in 1972, he stated, "It is with much embarrassment that I return."[8] Kazuo Sakamaki, America's first WWII prisoner of war, would later write: "Our desire for suicide, however, was thwarted on every hand. We had no knives to cut our throats. We had no ropes to hang ourselves with. Some of us banged our heads fix the spacing here against every object in sight; some men refused to eat. And yet we did not die..."[9]

As prisoners began to arrive at a rate of approximately 20,000 a month in the Spring of 1943,[10] a housing crunch developed, and established bases not initially designated to hold POWs began to fill the gap. Several of them were located in Massachusetts. Renovation began at Camp Edwards in Bourne for POW housing near the end of the airfield runway, and soon afterward prisoners began arriving from North Africa. Up to 2,000 German soldiers could be held at any given time within a stockade that was surrounded by guard towers and two rows of barbed wire, one of them electrified. Approximately 5,000 would spend time at Edwards by the end of the war.[11] POWs at the camp were typically 23 to 25 years of age and included a large number of mechanics as well as a small number of professionals. All spoke German, 10 percent were fluent in English, and another 25 percent understood it.

A 1944 article written by one of the first reporters allowed inside described life within the POW camp at Edwards.

The stockade is a group of buildings once occupied by a unit of the 26th division. The Geneva-Convention...requires each captor to provide housing equal to that of its own men. This was achieved at Camp Edwards by...enclosing a barracks group which could well have been chosen by chance among any in camp.
All mail to POWs is censored. Prisoners tell their families they find Cape Cod cooler than earlier camps, and they like that. They say they are well cared for. They urge that no food be sent to them. Often, they enjoin home folks not to worry. They express hope the war will soon end. Some of them tell mothers and fathers that the writers enjoy their work...Fair and humane are tenets of the Geneva Convention. To picture Americans in the confines of the Cape Cod stockade is to feel pity for them. Appearance of the Germans at Camp Edwards calls out for no pity. They are well-fed, healthy-looking men. The visitors saw that they can smile...The War Department's policy is, as it avows, "fair but firm." Fairness recognizes these men are soldiers of an enemy army, not criminals. Firmness permits no pampering.[12]

Some prisoner-of-war camps held a mixed Axis population. Once comrades in war, they now looked upon each other with hostility, and German, Italian, and Japanese inmates had to be isolated from one another. Germans of differing political affiliations were lumped together in camps, and officials quickly learned that protecting them from outside threats was, in some ways, easier than protecting them from other Germans. The first group of POWs, hardened fighters from Hitler's Afrika Korps and devoted followers of Nazi doctrine, established ground rules for the conduct of those comrades who would

[8] Solly, Meilan. *Soldier Refused to Surrender.* Smithsonian Mag 1/21/2022. tinyurl.com/42uuvytd.

[9] Bath, David. *Captive Samurai.* UND Scholarly Commons. tinyurl.com/bdf9zzv4.

[10] Paschal, Alfred W. *Enemy in Colorado.* Hist Colorado 12/13/2023. tinyurl.com/mrnm72sk.

[11] Taylor, Matt. *Prisoners on peninsula.* Cape Cod Life Publ 2016. tinyurl.com/4zsdxkz4.

[12] *Life in Edwards Stockade.* Enterprise 7/14/1944. Capenews.net. 2023. tinyurl.com/4jcf7t8x.

follow. German prisoners who failed to show appropriate obedience to the Nazi party line could expect to be blacklisted and disciplined. In a 1944 article, James H. Powers of the *Boston Globe* described the presence of secret police with ties to the Gestapo within prisoner-of-war camps. "Here, admittedly, is a hard nut to crack. Prisoners themselves are so firmly under the thumbs of these fanatics, and so cowed by past experience, that they seldom reveal the existence of the terror until secret disciplinary punishments inflicted upon them by their Nazi noncoms become intolerable."[13]

At Camp Edwards, typical of American POW camp hierarchies, a German sergeant held the position of leader within the stockade, an administrative role whose function did not include discipline. Any prisoner requiring discipline was treated in the same manner as American soldiers, and POWs were allowed access to American officers in order to lodge complaints. Such safeguards often failed to prevent violence among the inmates. On one occasion, two months after their arrival at Fort Devens, four men identified themselves as members of the Gestapo who had concealed themselves in the prison population in order to gather information on Nazi dissenters.[14] Powers further reported two instances of riots between factions, hanging deaths "apparently from suicide," and more than a dozen cases of outright murder.[15] Fourteen rabid supporters of the Third Reich were executed at Fort Leavenworth for such crimes, one who denounced a fellow prisoner as a traitor for collaborating with American guards, and then stood aside to watch his followers beat the man to death.[16]

Fort Devens housed 5,000 POWs before the end of the war, 450 of them Italian. As the need to separate Germans from Germans became clear, the camp was earmarked for a specific population. Hardcore Nazis were isolated, and in March 1944, a group of leftist anti-Nazis arrived in Ayer. These individuals were liberal-minded German citizens who had rejected the Nazi regime. (One POW camp commander stated, "About the only way to distinguish a Nazi from an anti-Nazi is when you see a man being pursued by a crowd of fifty others who are howling for murder, you can be sure that the man who is running is an anti-Nazi.")[17] Their philosophy, as stated on posters at the camp, read: "As soldiers of the German Army, we see this war as nothing more than the Nazi leadership clique's desperate struggle for survival, for which they are prepared to sacrifice the entire German people." Of the 3,100 transferred to Devens, 400 had spent time in a German concentration camp due to dissident activities.[18] At the other end of the political spectrum, 300 POWs who espoused an extremist communist agenda were exiled from Devens to Camp Stark near the Canadian border in New Hampshire.[19]

Many members of this anti-Nazi population were activists who fit well with the American way of life, albeit within the confines of a prison camp. They were allowed to publish a periodical, *PW. Halbmonatsblatt Deutscher Gefangener.* The magazine, which was shared with other POW camps, dealt kindly with the treatment of German prisoners in the US while pointing fingers at the Third Reich and honoring those who had suffered at its hands. It was an organic propaganda campaign which favored the United States, and thus when the Fort Devens inmates asked permission to reach out to the German population at home in an attempt to sue for peace, it was granted. In April 1945, the "Peace Appeal by German Prisoners of War in the US to the German People" was aired in Germany across American airwaves.

Fort Devens eventually held the third-highest anti-Nazi population of any US POW camp. Not all prisoners, however, enjoyed being guests of the American government. Given that approximately

---

[13] James Powers. *What to Do With German Prisoners.* Atlantic 11/1944. tinyurl.com/28dnkdn7.

[14] Krammer, Arnold. *Nazi Prisoners of War America.* Scarborough House/Publishers 1996.

[15] James H. Powers. *What to Do With German Prisoners.*

[16] Lamb, David. *Prisoners of Silence.* LA Times 11/30/1990. tinyurl.com/424dbbhk.

[17] Krammer, Arnold. *Nazi Prisoners of War America.*

[18] Haase, Norbert. *Anti-Nazi Prisoners War Am Prison Camps.* Traces. tinyurl.com/jhjkm4ca.

[19] Tabak, Andrew. *Fort Devens, From Boys to Men.* Andrew Tabak 2012.

400,000 enemies were incarcerated across the country, the number of escapes, 2,222, is quite low.[20] Still, captives dug tunnels, hid in the back of trucks, climbed over stockade fences, and wore disguises while simply walking out the front gate. One group in a Texas camp created dummies to place in the back row as prisoners lined up for morning inspection. Werner Richter, caught in the act, stated, "It worked fine until one of the dummies fell over."[21]

Security was tight at all POW camps. One German prisoner at Camp Myles Standish in Taunton described the futility of attempting escape. "We had no idea where we were. We had no idea there was a city of 43,000 people 4 miles away."[22] The government took measures to outline strict expectations for camp guards and staff to keep prisoners safe, even those prisoners who tried to escape. Armed guards, constant patrols, trained dogs, and stockade fences with caution lines all served to intimidate potential escapees. In his report on U-boat prisoners of war in the US, Glenn Sytko reported:

The War Department took great pains to inform all American guards that they must wait until the last possible second before firing, that they must shout "Halt" at least three distinct times, and that they must remember, above all, that a prisoner's behavior and not his proximity to the fence was the critical factor...The War Department further instructed the Camp Commandant to ensure that the POW community understood the significance of the guard's responsibility as well as the numerous variations of the word "Halt" which they might encounter. Nonetheless, by the end of the war, 56 German prisoners had risked the odds in their attempt to escape and been shot to death.[23]

Fort Devens was not immune to escape dramas. Devens POW Heinz Tonn made it to the FBI's wanted list. In 1945, the young man spent two weeks hopping rail cars on his way to Mexico before being apprehended in Missouri.[24] Toward the end of the war, Rudolph von Hyeburg's good behavior at Fort Devens netted him an assignment as a kitchen helper in a Waltham hospital where he met Gloria Sammartino of Winthrop. With her assistance, the former Afrika Korpsman escaped to New York. After being on the run for two years, Sammartino was arrested along with von Hyeburg.[25] The fortunate woman was charged with harboring an escaped prisoner rather than treason due to an April 1945 change in federal law. After spending time in jail pending trial, Sammartino was acquitted. The star-crossed couple eventually married.

Forty-five-year-old Leominster resident Fannie Welvaert was the mother of three sons and a daughter serving in the US military when she took a job at Fort Devens' Lovell General Hospital. There she met Horst Becker, a POW twenty years her junior. Together they successfully hatched an escape plan which eventually led them to a rooming house on Millbury Street in Worcester. Following a tip, Worcester police located the pair and arrested Welvaert on a charge of lewd and lascivious cohabitation. Becker was captured and returned to Fort Devens.[26] After her arrest, like Sammartino, Fannie Welvaert was convicted under the new Public Law 47, received a suspended sentence, and was placed on probation.[27]

One of the more interesting incidents of escape involved a young Massachusetts student, Dale Maple. The brilliant Harvard graduate spoke nearly two dozen languages and had an affinity for all things German, even showing up at a college costume party dressed as Hitler. In spite of being booted out of

---

[20] Garcia, Malcolm. *German POWs Am Homefront.* Smithsonian Mag 9/15/2009. tinyurl.com/bdhuj72z.

[21] Sytko, Glenn A. *U-boat men in Captivity.* Uboat.net. tinyurl.com/2s454dbh.

[22] Herwick, Edgar B. III. *Ghosts POWs Haunt Taunton Indust Park.* GBH 3/25/2016. tinyurl.com/mvmvk3z6.

[23] Sytko, Glenn A. *U-boat men in Captivity.*

[24] *Devens Prisoner Nabbed.* Morning Union 8/2/1945. Newspapers.com. tinyurl.com/whtnye73.

[25] *Winthrop Woman Harboring Prisoner.* Boston Globe 1/25/1948. Newspapers.com. tinyurl.com/zkc287rj.

[26] *Mother Harboring German.* Fitchburg Sentinel 11/13/1945. Newspapers.com. tinyurl.com/5y5vpat4.

[27] *Suspended Sentence Given Woman.* Boston Globe 1/22/1946. Newspapers.com. tinyurl.com/455m78j2.

Harvard's ROTC chapter, he joined the US Army in 1942. His superiors were less than impressed. He was assigned to the 620th Engineer General Service Company in Colorado, a rather grand title for a unit comprised of soldiers with similar questionable loyalty. In the words of Emily Breslow in her article for the *Harvard Crimson*, the Army felt it was "much better than kicking them out into society and losing track of them." In less than two years, Maple's true colors were revealed when he masterminded a plot to assist two prisoners in escaping to Mexico. Unfortunately, their car broke down near the Mexican border, and the trio was arrested. Maple was sentenced to death for aiding the enemy and desertion during a time of war. After spending seven years in prison, his sentence was commuted, and he was released.[28]

Germans were not the only prisoners arriving in the US. The 51,000 Italian POWs that were incarcerated on American soil were in a unique situation. In July 1943, Allied forces met German and Italian troops in heavy combat on the Italian peninsula. As the Allies advanced on Rome, Benito Mussolini was ousted. The new Italian government under Marshal Pietro Badoglio agreed to an armistice with the Allies, basically allowing their country to be invaded, the start of a fatal fracturing of Axis power. When Badoglio signed the agreement and a month later declared war on Germany, Italian troops in American prisoner of war camps became co-belligerents.

As a result, when the first Italian soldiers arrived at Camp Myles Standish in Taunton, they received somewhat better treatment than their German counterparts. Former soldiers of the Third Reich were heavily guarded (no POW ever escaped from Myles Standish) and wore black uniforms with a large, easily identifiable white "P" on their backs. German POWs were assigned to difficult work details, shown pictures of concentration camps, and spent all of their off hours in a stockade.[29] Those who cooperated with their captors and completed an Intellectual Diversion Program (American civics, history, and English language lessons) received a certificate of achievement. However, the camp commander was instructed: "POWs presently interned at this camp who are determined as being pro-Nazis and obstructionists to the Intellectual Diversion Program [should] be segregated and removed."[30]

For the Italians, daily life was much easier. By February 1944, it was decided that these co-belligerents posed less risk than their German counterparts, and the US Army began forming Italian Service Units. These former enemies were given access to work in the community, much of it for the benefit of the military, wore uniforms with a badge indicating "Italy," and received a salary. The first ISU to operate in the United States was assigned to work at Franklin Park in Boston. Soon projects expanded to road construction, loading supplies bound for Europe at the Boston Port of Embarkation, and tending Victory Gardens on the Boston Common. Eventually, passes into the community were issued, and men were able to attend church services or, as was the case in Taunton, join local Italian residents for a family dinner.[31] Historian William F. Hanna describes the top-secret Camp Myles Standish as "the worst-kept secret in the world." Many Italians snuck out under the fence with such frequency that "Taunton buses at the time would make a stop at the camp's main gate, and then at two different holes in the fence."[32]

---

[28] Breslow, Emily R. *Harvard to Treason.* Harvard Crimson 3/3/2011. tinyurl.com/4bupsczt

[29] Hanna, William F. *Friends and Enemies.* Bridgewater Review 11/2014. tinyurl.com/tmmcb5re.

[30] *Report Field Service Unit, POW Camp, Camp Myles Standish* 10/24/1945.

[31] Kratz, Jessie. *ISUs.* Pieces of Hist, NARA 7/21/2020. tinyurl.com/bdds86s5.

[32] Nichols, Christopher. *Crowd turns out ... Camp Myles Standish.* Taunton Daily Gaz 3/17/2012. tinyurl.com/muapjjzs.

Italian Service Unit co-belligerents unloading freight
at the Boston Port of Embarkation. WWII.[33]

Acceptance of these co-belligerents was not universal. Outside of the Italian American community, word was spreading about the relaxed treatment of Italian POWs. The general public wasn't happy. Carson's Beach in Boston was the scene of a skirmish when a sailor visiting the beach threw a rock into the Camp McKay POW compound, knocking a prisoner unconscious. One of his compatriots then jumped over the fence, and a fight ensued with guards attempting to protect the inmate from the crowd of angry Americans.[34] The Camp Myles Standish Civilian Executive Committee in 1944 praised the work of the Italians and suggested that people outside of the camp should be made aware of it. The answer was clear. "Military and civilian personnel <u>will not discuss</u> with any other person or newspaper the work the prisoners are doing or of any of their activities."[35]

Animosity gradually relaxed, and Italian POWs spent an increasing amount of time in the community, many forming lasting relationships and after the war returning to Taunton permanently. By war's end, 3,000 German and 4,000 Italian prisoners of war had spent time at the camp. Today a grotto dedicated to the Virgin Mary and constructed by Italian prisoners of war is one of the few reminders that a POW camp, or for that matter Camp Myles Standish, once existed in Taunton.

---

[33] *ISU BPOE.* Pub domain photo. 6524095 NARA Boston. tinyurl.com/4purze5k.

[34] *Bathers, Italian Prisoner in Melee.* Boston Globe 7/14/1944. Newspapers.com. tinyurl.com/3za3wsyk.

[35] *Minutes, Civilian Executive Comm.* 7/28/1944.

Grotto dedicated to the Virgin Mary on the grounds of
former POW Enclosure, Camp Myles Standish.

The Geneva Convention was anything but clear in its expectations for the use of prisoners as laborers, an important issue due to the diminishing amount of manpower on the home front. POWs couldn't have anything to do with war related operations. They couldn't build bombs or tanks or airplanes. But what about the trains that carried the parts to the ammunition factories, or producing the steel that would go into the building of those trains and those weapons? The loopholes were vast, too much for the US to handle. At the end of 1942, a committee was established to examine the issue. Their conclusion was a loosely constructed reinterpretation of Convention regulations filled with loopholes of its own. Soon another board was be established to untangle the knots. In the meantime, civilians struggled to keep up with the demands of agriculture and industry.

German prisoners had initially been allowed to work within camps on tasks such as cooking and laundry. With reinterpretation of the Geneva Convention, strict rules began to relax, and the scope of jobs began to expand. Fort Devens POW Walter Meierson of Austria repaired Army gas masks and sewed patches on uniforms.[36] At Camp Myles Standish, during off hours, prisoners were allowed into the carpentry shop where they made toys for the Red Cross to give away at Christmas time.[37]

The Geneva convention permits captors to work their prisoners...First call upon all prisoners of war is for maintenance at army camps. They can be used for any work not directly related to the war effort. Second call is for outside agricultural emergencies. Prisoners at Edwards work in the service departments, clearing brush, repairing roads, keeping up Otis field. They can be seen any day with axe in the brush or with shovels on the roadsides, working measuredly and steadily, while armed guards watch from a distance. The installation on Cape Cod is not likely to grow because prisoner manpower at present is equal to all apparent needs.[38]

---

[36] *German POW returns to Fort Devens.* UPI Archives. UPI 7/22/1987. tinyurl.com/d9nj6tfa.

[37] Downing, Terence. *POW Camp Boss, Prisoners Meet at Grotto.* Taunton Daily Gazette 5/31/1983.

[38] *Life in Edwards Stockade.* Enterprise.

Italian Service Units had established a precedent allowing prisoners to work outside camp compounds, and soon Germans POWs made their way into a variety of jobs within the local community. Located in one of the richest cranberry producing regions in the country, POWs from Camp Edwards provided labor for cultivation of cranberries. One million pounds of dehydrated cranberries were produced for the military by Massachusetts cranberry growers during each year of the war,[39] ironically many processed by the hands of German soldiers. Larger crops such as New Hampshire apples or Massachusetts cabbages also benefited from prisoner of war labor. A 1944 article in *The Enterprise* reported: "Experiment with Falmouth strawberries proved how difficult it is to use prisoners on small crops. Prisoners, however, may be drawn from Cape Cod for the Maine pea or potato crop. Each agricultural emergency in New England will bring drafting of available men from the region's stockades."[40]

German POWs arrive at Camp Westover.[41]

The POW camp at Westover in Chicopee was created for the express purpose of providing labor for the farms of Western Massachusetts. Ten barracks located on two acres of camp property housed the first 250 prisoners who arrived in September 1944. Another 250 would soon follow. Although the total would reach the relatively small number of 701 POWs, their assistance in working the area's tobacco and vegetable crops was invaluable.

With so many local men in the military, farmers were often forced to rely on workers who were unused to such difficult labor or who were unacceptable for military service due to health or behavioral issues. This at times interfered with the work that needed to be done. One hired laborer on a tobacco farm told POWs he would pay them a dollar if they would slow down. Little did he know that the farmer

---

[39] DeMoranville, Carolyn J. *MA Cranberries.* UMass Amherst 2015. tinyurl.com/5n7ermm2.

[40] *Life in Edwards Stockade.* Enterprise.

[41] *POWS Camp Westover Field.* Pub domain photo. AFHRA. Maxwell AFB. Bonofilia, John C. *Hospitality Best Form of Propaganda.* Hist J MA 2016. tinyurl.com/yc6uwcw2.

was waiting on the other end of the row to put a stop to it. With significant acreage that stretched across the Deerfield Valley, Lankowski Farms supplied potatoes for Fort Devens as well as other Army and Navy bases in the Northeast. Their experience with POW labor was, like most other farms, generally positive. The Germans provided strong men, self-disciplined and responsive to authority. The farm's first group consisted of highly educated professionals, referred to by June Lankowski as "superb workers." The second group, however, was less successful. Included were several SS troopers who clashed with the family whose Polish surname was the source of derision on the part of the Nazi prisoners.

Initially security in camps was extremely tight, but the fear that POWs would overcome their guards and dissolve into the countryside never materialized, and soon the iron-fisted hold on prisoners began to relax. Manford Ruck, a POW at Camp Westover, recalled painting a bridge with two other prisoners. When the job was done, their guard decided to have a little fun before returning to camp, and cans were set up on the bridge for target practice. At his request, Ruck was handed the gun so he could take a turn. "I could just as easily have turned the weapon on him and shot him. Instead, we all spent the rest of the afternoon shooting cans off of the bridge we had just painted. It was just four guys having fun in the woods."[42]

The United States profited from the men who were once enemies. Whether working in industrial or agricultural jobs or providing for the needs of prisoner of war camps, it is estimated that the United States benefited from their efforts to the tune of approximately 230 million dollars. Italian Service Units alone are credited with having provided 90 million days of labor.[43]

There were other smaller POW camps in Massachusetts, most of them in the Boston Harbor area. At the Boston Port of Embarkation, thousands of prisoners took their first step onto American soil.

German POWs board a train in Boston. World War II.[44]

Some were detained at the BPOE prisoner enclosure for health or intelligence reasons, some to await placement at specialized camps for belligerent Nazis. Approximately 1,800 Italian Service Unit POWs were housed at nearby Camp McKay, located on Columbia Point in Dorchester, and another 1,000 at Fort Andrews on Peddocks Island. Fort Strong on Long Island was the top secret home to several Nazi scientists toward the end of the war. Not quite prisoners, not quite guests, a veritable who's who of German physicists and engineers including Werner von Braun spent time there. Located on Marginal

---

⁴² Bonafilia, John C. *Hospitality Best Form of Propaganda*. Hist J MA 2016. tinyurl.com/yc6uwcw2.

⁴³ *ISU Boston*. Bost Harbor Isl Nat & State Park Blog 2/11/2021. tinyurl.com/55nb7nxk.

⁴⁴ *POWs board train Boston*. Pub domain photo. 195460 NARA. tinyurl.com/2j3knerv.

Street in East Boston, the Immigration and Naturalization Service had been in operation since 1920. During the war, a small number of Germans and Japanese entering the country with questionable identification papers or who had been identified by the FBI as enemy aliens were detained while awaiting transfer to prisoner of war or internment camps.[45]

The surrender of the Japanese in September of 1945 did not bring an end to captivity for the roughly 400,000 prisoners of war in America. Their exit had been in planning for a few years in anticipation of a victorious outcome to the conflict. What to be done about hundreds of thousands of ex-enemies once the last shot was fired became a topic of much controversy. Harvard Anthropologist Ernest Hooten: "To convert or re-educate a Nazi is impossible." Captain Joseph Lane of Camp Cascade in Iowa: "I've seen more than 100,000 Germans pass through my cage, and I know these bastards. They're no good...I hate them all and my men hate them. We want a peace that will knock them down to their knees and keep them there until they learn better."[46] In the end, calmer heads prevailed. Reeducation programs were established that avoided butting heads with opposing philosophies while exposing prisoners to American ideals. The hope was that when boats filled with ex-POWs headed homeward to rebuild a new Japan, a new Germany, a new Italy, democratic ideals would guide their reconstruction.

The road to repatriation was a rocky one. Who should go first, trouble-making die-hard Nazis or the cooperative majority of German prisoners? How could the government even consider exporting thousands of POWs essential for supporting American agriculture? European Allies were clamoring for prison labor to rebuild their war-torn countries, for many, an unpopular notion compared by some to slave trading. Deadlines for departure were set and delayed and set again, and four months after the war ended, there were still 313,000 German POWs in the country.[47] Eventually, in fits and starts, boatloads of newly freed enemies headed homeward, and in July 1946, the last German soldier in captivity left American soil.

For Japanese soldiers interned in the United States, the process was easier. Their reeducation, a program designed "...to replace their traditional Emperor-worship with a more positive philosophy..." was deemed a success by the government. Over a thousand shipped out in December 1945, and during January 1946, with the exception of a man being treated for health-related issues, the remaining POWs went home. Among them was Ensign Kazuo Sakamaki, captured at Pearl Harbor, the first American held prisoner of war. His return to Japan brought mixed reactions. "You need not feel ashamed...With a new heart, please work for a reconstruction of our beloved country," wrote one. From another: "I cannot understand how you could return alive. The souls of the brave comrades who fought with you and died must be crying now over what you have done...If you are ashamed of yourself now, you should commit suicide at once and apologize to the spirits of the heroes who died honorably."[48]

Early in 1945, the American Red Cross received a stack of identification cards from 4,000 captured American servicemen being held at a hitherto unknown German prisoner-of-war camp just west of Frankfurt. Stalag IX/B Bad Orb, which had previously been used to house Russian and Serbian prisoners, had begun receiving American servicemen captured in the Battle of the Bulge in December 1944. Other allies, including British, French, and Poles, were also in custody.

---

[45] *East Boston detention facility.* Densho Encyclopedia 7/14/2015. tinyurl.com/4fv58mnp.

[46] Rock, Adam. *Am Way: Influence Race on POWS.* UCF STARS 2014. tinyurl.com/2yf8x4j6.

[47] Krammer, Arnold. *Nazi Prisoners of War America.*

[48] Zimmerman, Dwight. *Axis POWs Am.* Defense Media Network 10/8/2013. tinyurl.com/5n8repdc.

Joy on the faces of Allied POWs after
liberation at Stalag IX/B. April 1945.[49]

Due to their hasty arrival, the camp was unprepared. Men slept on wooden floors, mostly without mattresses or blankets, in sixteen buildings with leaky roofs and broken windows. Supplies were severely lacking, and those who did have mattresses found the stuffing being used as toilet paper. At the time of a January 1945 Red Cross inspection, the men had been allowed only one bath since arrival. Food was inadequate, and helmets served as eating bowls. Many men were seen wearing nothing but underclothes, many without boots, and only twenty percent with overcoats in the midst of winter. The camp commander explained that due to the quick arrival of so many POWs, there had been little time to prepare. Conditions would improve, he said, as this was a transit camp, and hundreds of prisoners would soon be transferred to other stalags. A month later, reports stated that 400 men in a detachment of 900 were severely ill, and in spite of shipments by the Red Cross specifically to help the men of Stalag IX/B, the Americans received nothing. One report concludes, "It seems that the commandant is prejudiced against the Americans and British whose situation is very bad; the conditions of the prisoners of other nationalities are still bearable."

Three months after their first inspection, the camp population now 5,380 men, the American Red Cross sent a new report:

Stalag IX/B...No shipments since several months' supplies extremely urgently needed food, clothing, shoes, drugs...antidyptheria serum typhus vaccin[e] penicillin materiel for dressings, blankets, and utensils STOP grave danger of epidemics sanitary installations altogether insufficient soap toilet paper completely lacking STOP general apathy representatives harassed with questions high percentage deaths STOP[50]

Henry Freedmen experienced the deprivation at Stalag IX/B firsthand. Born in Boston, he was assigned as an infantry machine gunner upon joining the Army. In December 1944, while engaged in action against the enemy at the Battle of the Bulge, Freedman was taken captive. He and others were loaded aboard boxcars and shipped to Stalag IX/B. They were attacked by RAF bombers en route and arrived at the camp on Christmas Day. Henry Freedman was twenty-three years old. He was later transferred to Stalag IX/A where he would lose 55 pounds as a guest of Nazi Germany.[51]

---

[49] *POWs welcome liberators.* Pub domain photo. IWM. Wiki Commons. tinyurl.com/bdf2hb5c

[50] *Stalag 9V Reports.* 70th Infantry Div Asso. tinyurl.com/msy4r2dk

[51] *Ex-POW Freedman, Henry.* Am Ex Prisoners of War. tinyurl.com/p27bduh5.

American prisoners of war
in Europe. December 1944.[52]

After basic training at Fort Devens, Robert Mercer of Grafton was sent to Belgium. On December 10 near the Siegfried Line, out of ammunition and food, Mercer was one of a hundred men who surrendered to the enemy. He later described Stalag IX/B: "Bunkhouses very unsanitary, very crowded 75-100 men sleeping on the bare floor. Meals consisted of grass soup and very thin crackers."[53]

Donald Hildenbrand also trained at Fort Devens and served with the 397th Infantry Regiment of the 100th Infantry Division. On January 8, 1945, his platoon was besieged by artillery, mortar, and rocket fire. After volunteering to attempt a run in the hope of reestablishing communication with company command, he was captured by German soldiers. Along with other prisoners from the 397th, he was told to remove enemy dead and wounded from the battle area. After interrogation in a nearby barn, the men were put into boxcars and arrived at Stalag IX/B a week later.

Two weeks later, Hildenbrand was transferred to a construction work group 200 miles away. He recalled harsh conditions.

We slept on wooden planks covered with straw and before long, we were all thoroughly infested with lice...We worked from dawn to dusk, seven days a week...tunnels were being dug into the side of a hill, later to be joined into a larger interior enclosure for an underground weapons or armaments factory...After blasting into the hill, we loaded rock fragments into railcars and dumped the rock down the bank along a river...It was all hard manual labor, with little time to rest and nothing to eat during the workday... after work in our hut, [we] were given a loaf of dark bread usually split between ten men; occasionally, there was a cup of thin soup with some type of vegetable, and very rarely a little meat.[54]

Nearly 5,000 American soldiers were liberated from Stalag IX/B on April 2, 1945.

Hildenbrand, Mercer, and Freedman were among tens of thousands of Americans held captive by Germany during World War II. Nearly 30,000 US servicemen were prisoners of Japan. While conditions in European POW camps were unconscionable, just over one percent of prisoners died from the experience. The numbers for Japanese-held POWs, however, are shocking. Up to 40 percent perished while in Japanese custody. A uniquely horrifying statistic comes from author Linda Goetz Holmes: "Nine out of ten prisoners who died in World War II perished while in Japanese custody."[55]

---

[52] *Am prisoners along road.* Pub domain photo. 531236 NARA 12/1944. tinyurl.com/4a87pxc4.

[53] Wilson, Jayne Carroll and Keeras, Joseph E. *Wilderness to information Age: Grafton Chronicle.* Van/Go Graphics 2016.

[54] Hildenbrand, Don. *Company E, 397th to Stalag IXB.* George Marshall Fdn 4/2001. tinyurl.com/pv9xfcpm.

[55] Holmes, Linda Goetz. *Unjust Enrichment.* Konecky and Konecky 2001.

For those raised in a democracy that encourages free thinking, it is difficult to comprehend the mindset of a people whose actions resulted in the death of so many. The citizens of Imperial Japan lived under the shadow of a living god, Emperor Hirohito. Worshipped as a deity, his people slavishly carried out his heavenly dictates and upheld his honor, in the process giving rise to the notion of their divine descent. Thus, all others, especially prisoners of war, were considered inferior. Members of the Japanese military were indoctrinated into the Semjinkun code of conduct. To die in war brought honor to one's Emperor, country, and family. Being captured did not. "To live as a prisoner of war is to live without honor," stated Hideki Tojo, Japanese Minister of War.[56] For Japanese prisoners, it meant suicide. For Allied POWs, it meant beatings, torture, starvation, and beheading.

There was more than religious fanaticism at work, however. The Empire had a new world order in its sights, a Pacific realm controlled by Japan, a vision that was seriously hampered by a lack of materials and resources. Owing to the vast number of able-bodied men who now filled the ranks of the military, Japanese industry required a fresh source of manpower, and prisoners of war filled the void. At the end of the Bataan Death March, Massachusetts resident Samuel B. Moody and fellow prisoners were met on arrival at their POW camp with a portent of things to come.

A sloppy, fat Jap officer stood on a podium and addressed us in perfect English. The warmth of victory and the triumph of humiliation poured from his lips. "You are slaves of the Japanese Empire," he began. "You will pay strict attention to the command of every enlisted man and officer of the Japanese Imperial Army. You will not talk back to any man, and you will salute every officer addressing you at any time. We are your masters, and you will be treated as nothing more than slaves."[57]

By providing manpower, Japan was able to procure materials. The government entered into a circular relationship with the industrial giants of Japan. Companies such as Mitsubishi, Mitsui, and Kawasaki paid the army a fee for releasing POWs to work in mines and factories. In turn, the military loaded captives onto ships owned or leased by industry and shipped them to areas where labor was needed. At the end of the process, the government waited to acquire the equipment, weapons, and materials it desperately needed to carry out a war.

For many of those chosen to labor as slaves, their journey to work sites was a new kind of torture. Men were packed into cargo holds on ships, some so tightly they had to stand. The heat was oppressive, and the stench unbearable. Food was non-existent, and a few buckets of water a day lowered into the hold were expected to maintain hundreds of men. Buckets served as bathroom facilities. Aboard one such vessel, one prisoner remembered:

We threw our packs into the deep hold and quickly followed down the long ladder into the darkness, herded by the guards and their bayonets...The prisoners had been so crowded in these other holds that they couldn't even get air to breathe. They went crazy, cut and bit each other through the arms and legs, and sucked their blood. In order to keep from being murdered, many had to climb the ladders and were promptly shot by guards. Between twenty and thirty prisoners had died of suffocation or were murdered during the night.[58]

This was the Oryoku Maru, a Japanese "hell ship." The loss of life aboard these floating torture chambers was horrifying. Well over 1,000 men lost their lives to sickness, violence, or outright murder by Japanese guards. Perhaps equally disturbing, however, is that approximately 20,000 men lost their

---

[56] Jing, Yang. *Death of Am Marine.* Historynet 11/17/2016. tinyurl.com/rb6ck9fb.

[57] Moody, Samuel B. and Allen, Maury. *Reprieve from Hell.* Verdun Press 11/6/2015.

[58] Gladwin, Lee. *Japanese Ships Voyage to Hell.* Prologue Mag. NARA 2003. tinyurl.com/ywxfx955.

lives after hell ships were attacked by the Allies, a tragic but somehow understandable episode in the history of World War II.

Oryoku Maru sinking in Philippines. December 1944.[59]

On December 13, 1944, the Allies intercepted a Japanese message: "Oryoku Maru is part of a convoy with 2054 troops aboard." The ship was expected to depart Manila the next day, headed for Japan. Unaware of the cargo it actually carried, on December 14, US Navy aircraft struck. In defiance of Geneva Convention guidelines, like all hell ships, the Oryoku Maru bore no markings to indicate that POWs were on board. By the end of the attack, the vessel was dead in the water, and the Japanese gathered up the 1300 prisoners who had survived. In a report to the Americans, they admitted to the presence of POWs aboard the Oryoku Maru, stating that survivors would be transported to a new prison camp, and those too ill or injured would be returned to Bilibad Prison. Sadly, those fifteen men did not make it to Bilibad but were brought to a cemetery where they were beheaded or bayoneted. Over three hundred Allied heroes died on the Oryoku Maru.[60]

Two Allied survivors from the sinking of
the hell ship Rakuyo Maru. September 1944.[61]

Massachusetts native David G. Erickson made it through the attack on the Oryoku hell ship. He and other survivors were loaded onto the Enoura Maru, which departed for Formosa. On January 9, that vessel was hit by American planes while docked at Takao. Erickson and other prisoners who lived through this second attack were placed aboard the Brazil Maru, which arrived in Japan on January 29, 1945. After having survived the Bataan Death March, internment at O'Donnell and Cabanatuan POW

---

[59] *Nav station Olongapo.* Pub domain photo. USN NH95603. Wiki Commons. tinyurl.com/ymujrwte.

[60] Gladwin, Lee. *Japanese Ships Voyage to Hell.*

[61] *Survivors Rakuyo Maru.* Pub domain photo. NARA 520654. Picryl. tinyurl.com/yc339mk4.

camps, and forty-six days aboard three hell ships, Captain David G. Erickson passed away two days after arriving on Japanese soil. He is buried in the Manila American Cemetery in the Philippines.[62]

Born in Pittsfield, Robert Henry Rice was a formidable opponent as sub-captains go. While in command of the USS Drum during its first and second voyages, the Drum took out five Japanese cargo vessels and one seaplane carrier, returning safely to Pearl Harbor at the end of 1942, a patrol for which Rice would be awarded the Navy Cross. Six months later, Lt. Commander Rice was rewarded with a second brand new boat, USS Paddle. The vessel would serve its country well. During the next eleven months, Rice and his men successfully sank two Japanese cargo ships. On returning to Pearl Harbor for overhaul, he was transferred to the Battleship New Jersey. Rice was a lucky man. His new post meant that he would not be aboard the USS Paddle less than a year later when it achieved notoriety in a very different way.[63]

The Shinyo Maru headed for Manila in September of 1944 with 750 POWs on board. It bore no unusual markings when the convoy it was traveling in was attacked just north of Mindanao in the Philippines. A two-hour battle ensued. USS Paddle succeeded in striking two ships and dove to escape heavy bombardment by shells and depth charges. As the Shinyo Maru went down, Japanese guards lobbed grenades into holds and fired machine guns at prisoners. One Paddle crewman later recalled, "They had a Jap gunner who was shooting at the heads of the U.S. prisoners in the water. Japs in lifeboats were also shooting at the POWs and would not permit U.S. personnel to get aboard the lifeboats." Eighty-three men made it to the beach that day to be taken in by a group of Filipino and Allied guerrillas who arranged pickup by the USS Narwhal.[64] First Lieutenant David B. Bartlett and at least six other Massachusetts servicemen were among the 668 men who perished that day. Their remains were never recovered,[65] and the USS Paddle, whose men were unaware that they were firing on their own comrades that day, sadly achieved a dubious place in history.

During the course of the war, 134 hell ships carried roughly 126,000 prisoners headed toward labor camps. For those who survived hell ship voyages, hard labor, beatings, torture, and death awaited. Tokyo 8B Hitachi was a small labor camp that held 300 prisoners whose sole function was to work in the Hitachi Copper Mine owned by the Nippon Mining Company. One POW recalled, "I remember no incidents of brutality. Occasionally, someone got slapped around, but nothing of a serious nature." He attributed this to the presence of the Japanese Camp Commander, who had graduated from Northeastern University in Boston.[66] Clearly, prisoners of war had been indoctrinated into a world where getting "slapped around" and physical abuse were acceptable. Regardless of the level of treatment, this prisoner recalled, at the close of the war, Camp Commander Ryoichi Nemoto and his assistant in command would be found guilty of war crimes and receive combined sentences of twenty years of hard labor, respectively.[67]

Work details brought new challenges to POWs who were in poor health and underfed. One Australian recalled, "If they wanted 200 men, they had to have 200 men. The guards would deliver 200 men even if perhaps thirty of them might be on the backs of their mates. We would carry them back at night. Usually, one would die during the day."[68] On one particular morning, when a fellow prisoner, on the verge of death, failed to line up for work detail, the guard asked,

---

[62] *Hell ships Memorial Subic Bay.* Am War Memorials Overseas 2008. tinyurl.com/ykuv9m2a.

[63] *Paddle.* Allied Warships. Uboat.net. tinyurl.com/rtxjffvr.

[64] Mazza, Eugene. *USS Paddle: Sinking Am POWs.* tinyurl.com/yw5rjc6h.

[65] *WWII MA (Unaccounted for).* DPAA. tinyurl.com/mrysxfj9.

[66] *Marching to Victory: POWs.* Tru Blog. Truman PPF. tinyurl.com/35xcdyea.

[67] *POW Camp #8-B Hitachi.* Ctr for Res. tinyurl.com/39m2c3pm.

[68] *Treatment of Prisoners.* VA 2020. DVA Anzac Portal. tinyurl.com/5bch8f57.

"Why didn't you bring him?" and I said, "He's only got half an hour left," and then he started really ranting and raving...But no, I had to go back. So we went back again, and he was still alive, and we put him on the stretcher and went back. We...got over there — he was dead — and laid him down, and the...guard counted everybody, and everybody was correct, and the officer went off, and everybody was quite happy, so we then struggled and took Dusty back to the cremation pit and cremated him.[69]

The men were often brutalized by guards for little or no reason, considered as nothing more than replaceable slave labor. Samuel Moody of Lynn recounts being on a Bilibad Prison crew sent to work at nearby docks. He recalled a scene at the waterfront after a prisoner had made a mistake.

I spotted a Jap officer strike another officer in the mouth. The ritual was on. A lower officer was called to the second officer. He was chewed out and then cracked in the face. He turned around and called the name of the nearest sergeant. The sergeant responded. The sergeant was yelled out. Then came the inevitable slap. We knew it was coming. The sergeant cracked his nearest corporal. The corporal, in turn, grabbed the closest Jap private. The private was whacked. That was our signal...We ran to the nearest place of shelter on the dock to use as a bathroom. Always a new prisoner, who hadn't seen the system work, was nearest to the last whacked Jap soldier, the American got belted, and the ritual was over.[70]

Men assigned to work crews did their best to pay back the Japanese. Sabotage was rampant.

Mitsubishi factory at Mukden.
Note tank turrets on the floor. 1947.[71]

At Mitsubishi's Mukden factory complex, blueprint lines were drawn just a bit off, and lathes that should have turned out bullets shut down after iron filings were sprinkled into gearboxes. "We're pretty sure that none of the parts that we made was any good," said Erwin Johnson, a Mukden survivor.[72] POWs disconnected wires under dashboards and switched spark plug cables in motor pools, moved railcar labels around to send them to the wrong destination, and ran boilers at excessive temperatures, then watched them explode.[73] "The guys spent most of the time figuring out a way to mess them up," stated former POW John L. Stensby, who proudly recalled his efforts at a Mitsubishi shipyard.

---

[69] *Stan Arneil.* Audio transcript. VA 2020. DVA Anzac Portal. tinyurl.com/4zesm4yh.

[70] Moody, Samuel B. and Allen, Maury. *Reprieve from Hell.*

[71] *Mitsubishi Industries-Mukden.* Pub domain photo. Fenical, Martin. USASC. Truman PPF. 348550508 NARA. tinyurl.com/33abnwsc.

[72] *POWs as Japan saboteurs.* AP 10/5/2012. tinyurl.com/2n2f88a4.

[73] La Forte, Robert. *Resistance Japanese Prison Camps.* JAEAR 2003. JSTOR, tinyurl.com/zk33vtj4.

I was working on a big ship. The bow that hits the water first you weld those two plates up. I cranked the transformer way on down, so it wasn't hot enough to really weld. The next day, we had a day off. The following morning, there was that ship sunk in the waves.[74]

Staff Sergeant Henry John Wilayto of Belmont and a group working on the docks in the Philippines unscrewed the caps off 55-gallon drums of alcohol, turned them upside down, and, with the help of the Underground and some dynamite, blew a ship right out of the water in Manila Harbor.[75] Each act was a risk. Prisoners who were caught were subject to beatings or death, but to most, it was worth the risk. Hokaido POW Major James Devereaux explained it like this: "The main objective of the whole Japanese prison program was to break our spirit, and on our side was a stubborn determination to keep our self-respect whatever else they took from us."[76]

Conditions were inhumane at labor camps throughout the Japanese Empire. At one Kawasaki site, prisoners were made to work after being forced to stand at attention in the cold for fourteen hours. Those who collapsed were rifle butted in the head. At the infamous Omuta Mine, owned by the powerful Mitsui family, unpredictable beatings were daily fare, many of them meted out by unstable guards, veterans of the slaughters in China and the Rape of Nanjing. One of the more dangerous duties was pulling pillars. Tunnels were held in place by columns of coal, and when the tunnels had been emptied, prisoners had to knock out the pillars with hopes that the ceiling wouldn't crash down upon them. More than one POW was crushed beneath the rock, and one was dragged out by fellow workers and made to lie unattended on a cold stone floor for five hours before a doctor was allowed to attend him.

Mitsubishi had the onerous distinction of operating seventeen hell ships. The industrial giant operated factories, mines, and docks across Japan. Located in the mountains of northern Honshu, Sendai POW Camp No. 5 is remembered for its frigid conditions. Salvind Tobia of Southbridge was one of 351 prisoners[77] who walked two miles up a slope using a rope to guide them through blinding wind and snow into a mine where icicles hung from ceilings. Barracks were allowed two hours of heat a day, and pneumonia was rampant among the men.[78]

Over 10,000 prisoners of war were utilized as slave labor to support the profits of private industry in Japan. The exact number of Allied deaths suffered at their hands will never be known. The government of Japan eventually apologized for their treatment of POWs, and in 2015, Mitsubishi made a statement accepting responsibility for their actions. Seventy years after the war ended, they were the first Japanese company to do so. Mitsubishi, Mitsui, and Kawasaki outlasted the conflict perpetrated at the hands of their government, and all three companies remain in operation today (the city of Boston has purchased nearly 150 railway cars from Kawasaki since the 1990s).[79]

The stories of those who survived are haunting. Joseph R. Manella's fateful journey toward a Japanese prisoner of war camp began the day after Pearl Harbor was bombed when he joined the Army Air Corps. The young man from Milford was sent to Texas for bombardier school, where one of his early training flights went off course and ended with Manella blowing up a gas station. As a member of the 308th Bomber Group, he participated in several missions in Chunking, China. On September 15, 1943,

[74] *John L. Stensby, Sr. Collection* 1939. VHP. LOC. tinyurl.com/3r9rw8n5.

[75] *Henry John Wilayto Collection* 1940. VHP. LOC. tinyurl.com/3r9rw8n5.

[76] La Forte, Robert S. *Resistance Japanese Prison Camps WWII.*

[77] *Sendai POW Camp #5-B.* Ctr for Res. 255anches.com. tinyurl.com/27jmcrxa.

[78] Holmes, Linda Goetz. *Unjust Enrichment.*

[79] *MBTA Commuter Rail Exec Summary.* Dbperry.net. tinyurl.com/3mr6euey.

half of his ten-member crew lost their lives after being shot down during a bombing run. Manella remembered helping a man into a parachute and pushing him out of the plane before putting his own on.

I got pretty shot up but somehow managed to bail out with a defective parachute. Miraculously, the chute worked but pulled me left, then right, up and down, as I descended with enemy fire buzzing around me but missing because of my zigzagging fall. If I had to die, I wanted it to be quick, clean, and easy, but that was not meant to be. After falling into a rice paddy, I was rescued by natives who got me to a local hospital where my wounds were attended to.

He was captured the following day.[80] For the next three years, Manella endured the hellish conditions of a prisoner-of-war camp in Changi, Singapore. In 1943, after the fall of the British-held base at Singapore, a ten-square-mile area around the Changi Jail was used to incarcerate nearly 12,000 prisoners. Originally constructed to hold 600, 50,000 captives were held at Changi Prison during the war. Many were housed there awaiting transfer to work projects such as the Burma-Thailand railway.

Overcrowded conditions at Changi. April 1942.[81]

The men of Changi Prison were tortured and abused. Manella recalled the day a guard threatened to decapitate him[82] and another incident when he was about to be killed. When asked why he shouldn't die on the spot, the Lieutenant replied that he was a star player for the Boston Red Sox. It saved his life. For some time afterward, he and other prisoners, weak and ill, were forced to stage baseball games for the enjoyment of their jailers.[83] Lack of food was a way of life, and prisoners were fed a handful of rice a day. Decent men were forced into extreme measures to survive, picking up food along the road or catching and killing the cats that frequented the kitchen area of the camp. "I took that cat, slammed it against the wood, killed it, and skinned it." If men were sick enough, they were allowed to go to the camp hospital. Manella remembered such a day, sick with "malaria and vomiting in front of guards who passively waited for him to die."[84]

Through sheer strength of will and unwavering faith, Lt. Joseph Manella survived. When Changi Prison was liberated in September 1945, he headed home. Manella spent the remainder of his life devoted to his country and his church, becoming a Lieutenant Colonel in the Air Force Reserve and a much-loved deacon at Sacred Heart of Jesus Church in Milford. He passed away in 2020 at the age of 101.[85]

---

[80] Matondi, Michael. *Lifetime of Service.* Sacred Heart Bulletin. tinyurl.com/yc2uny2a.

[81] *AWM.* 4/09/42. Pub domain photo. AWM. Picryl. tinyurl.com/4vjmhdkm.

[82] Petrishen, Brad. *Vet survived POW camp.* Milford Daily News 4/7/2014. tinyurl.com/yc2uny2a.

[83] Matondi, Michael. *Lifetime of Service*

[84] Petrishen, Brad. *Veteran survived POW camp.*

[85] *Joseph Manella.* Consigli Ruggerio 7/1/2020. tinyurl.com/35ayxu6t.

On the very same day that Joseph Manella became a member of the US Army, the Japanese began an offensive that would result in the loss of tens of thousands of lives. The Philippines and MacArthur's Far East Forces stood between them and the establishment of a Japanese-dominated new order in Eastern Asia. Thus, as part of their master plan, less than twenty-four hours after the attack on Pearl Harbor, the invasion of the Philippines began. The battle was ferocious. In spite of being outgunned and under-supplied, the Allies fought for five months, continually losing ground and being forced to fall back. Heroically, they held out until early April. Corregidor would stand for another month.

Surrender of American troops at the Malinta
Tunnel on Corregidor. May 1942.[86]

"A terrible silence settled over Bataan about noon on April 9." So wrote General Jonathan Wainwright, who was in command of the Army in the Philippines. When the call came to surrender that day, approximately 75,000 Allies, the single largest surrender in American history (excluding the Civil War), threw down their arms. What followed was an event that forever illustrates the standard by which Japan treated POWs in World War II. The prisoners, the majority of whom were Filipino, were forced to walk sixty-five miles in extreme heat with little food or water. Men who fell or stopped to drink from a puddle could expect immediate death. Periodically, Japanese soldiers would tie men to a post or a tree and shoot them as a warning to others. There is no way to accurately determine just how many brave men lost their lives during the Bataan Death March. Estimates indicate as many as 10,000 souls never made it to the prisoner-of-war camp at the end of the journey.

After training as an Army Air Corps mechanic, Samuel E. Moody of Lynn found himself in the Philippines, and in April 1942, when Bataan fell, the Master Sergeant made the long trek up the peninsula with fellow prisoners of war. He recalled his experience in his memoir, *Reprieve From Hell*. "I remember Manila and the March. I saw soldiers being stomped upon. I recalled a head being sliced from its neck and rolling aimlessly in its own blood. I thought of buddies being kicked in the groin until they vomited up their own insides."

---

[86] *Surrender Am troops Corregidor.* Pub domain photo. 535553 NARA 5/1942. tinyurl.com/46vtz9y7.

Prisoners during Bataan Death March. May 1942.
Samuel Stenzler (left) died at Camp O'Donnell, Frank Spear
(center) was executed at a POW camp in Japan, and James
Gallagher (right) perished during the Bataan Death March.[87]

There would be no respite for those who survived the Death March. Prisoners were housed in a former Philippine training base, Camp O'Donnell. While the facility operated for only eight months, it was long enough for the Japanese to cause the death of approximately 2,000 Americans and 26,000 Filipinos. Conditions were inhumane. Prisoners were fed two handfuls of maggoty rice a day. One water spigot served the entire camp population. Medical care was non-existent. Moody recalled being asked to operate on a young soldier whose wound had become infected. He had no experience, but sensing the wound was life-threatening, he did his best to remove the dead flesh. The young man died three days later. It was a low point for Moody.

Somehow, dying didn't seem difficult. I would only have to put my head down and tomorrow would be in a new world. I wanted to be away from the pain and the thirst and the hunger. I could achieve it. It was easy. So many others had done it before. I tried to die. I asked myself to die. I let my body fall limp against the ground...I knew that I would never see another day.

Moody slipped into sleep, and when he awoke, five other men lay nearby. Every single one was dead. He alone had survived the long, desperate night. "I knew at that instant I was going to live...I had tried to die and couldn't. Others had tried, and they had...A Greater Power had chosen me to make it." Three days later, Staff Sergeant Samuel Moody was loaded onto a truck and sent to Cabanatuan, a different kind of hell.[88]

When Army Chaplain William Leonard, a native of Dorchester and later Professor of Theology at Boston College,[89] arrived in the Philippines in 1945, World War II was winding down. A ravaged Manila was once again in the hands of Americans, and many prisoners of war were enjoying their first weeks of freedom. Leonard was pleased to find fellow Massachusetts priest John J. Dugan among them. Dugan was a Boston boy, born in South Boston, and a graduate of Boston College High School and Weston College. He served for many years as a chaplain at Boston City Hospital. Recollections of his experience during the war are peppered with fond memories of meeting people from back home. Dugan was already a member of the Army Reserves when he was called to active duty in 1940 and sent to the

[87] *March of Death.* Pub domain photo. 532548 NARA. tinyurl.com/3cxuzfcu.

[88] Moody, Samuel B. and Allen, Maury. *Reprieve from Hell.*

[89] Feldhedge, Gary. *William Leonard.* Liturgical Pioneers 2021. tinyurl.com/mrxx2v8x.

Philippines.[90] While evacuating with the patients and staff of the 12th Medical Regiment on April 9, 1942, Bataan fell, and he became a prisoner of the Japanese Empire for the next 34 months.

Due to a bout with malaria, Dugan was in the hospital when the Japanese herded thousands of captives northward along the Bataan peninsula. During his stay, the Japanese decided to move all nurses to Corregidor. Bridgewater native Helen Cassiani was one of them. She met the priest on the final day at the hospital, and in a strange coincidence, they would meet again three years later back in Massachusetts.

After being moved to several different camps, Dugan finally landed at Japanese Military Prison Camp No. 1, known as Cabanatuan, where he would spend his final twenty-seven months as a prisoner of war. His extraordinary story, *Life Under the Japs*, paints a vivid picture of daily life in Camp No. 1. Food, ever scarce, was a common topic. Having previously been fed a diet consisting completely of two servings of rice a day at the hospital, it was a hopeful sign that at Cabanatuan, the men received three. The extra rice was never enough, however, and carabao, dogs, snakes, and rats were at times added to the menu.[91] (Samuel Moody recalled, "Anything that was food went into the pot…When meals were ready, the sign was posted, 'Fitch's Kitchen. Stop Your Bitchin.'")[92] On occasion, local residents were allowed to sell food to prisoners. More than one member of the Filipino underground risked his life in this way to bring information back and forth to the camp.

Cabanatuan prison hut.[93]

Prisoners were put to work clearing fields and planting crops. According to Dugan, more than a thousand men labored at the farm daily. Most of the food was taken by the Japanese. A small amount, often rotten, went to the prisoners. It was a difficult detail. Men weakened from malnutrition, ill with malaria and other diseases were still expected to toil in brutal heat seven days a week, many of them dropping in the fields from exhaustion. POWs were brutalized by guards who used clubs to beat them for little to no infraction of the rules. Dugan described a favorite trick of the Japanese, tripping a man, then kicking him in the stomach and face. He recalled witnessing an incident when a Marine sergeant had been told to board a truck by a guard. When a second guard came along, displeased that the Marine was there, he brutally punched the man in the ear with his fist. The Marine was still struggling with the after-effects when Dugan saw him two years later. The worst punishment, however, was doled out to those who dared to escape. One man was killed in an attempt; his body was displayed in front of prisoners as a lesson in what would happen should they try the same. The soldier had sustained inhuman treatment at the hands of the Japanese. Captives were told that for every man who escaped, nine others would be shot.

---

[90] *Jesuits Freed.* CS&T 2/1945. CNA. tinyurl.com/udn3rhbp.

[91] Dugan, John and Duffy, Joseph. *Life Under the Japs.* New Eng Province Hist 8/24/2016. tinyurl.com/u2f589hb.

[92] Moody, Samuel B. and Allen, Maury. *Reprieve from Hell.*

[93] *Cabanatuan hut.* Pub domain photo. US Army. Wiki Commons. tinyurl.com/2s39jsaa.

Somehow in the midst of this hell, the men maintained a strong sense of morale. The Japanese flag, displayed prominently in the compound, was the source of hatred and foul language, serving not to demoralize but to boost morale. Men found entertainment to sustain them, holding variety shows and enjoying the ridiculousness of the propaganda-laden Manila Tribune provided by their keepers. In spite of the efforts of the Japanese to crush their captives, the men remained strong and resolute. "The Nips never counted on the American spirit and the American sense of humor," said Dugan. "The combination is unshakable."

POWs celebrate the 4th of July in a Philippine POW
camp. Discovery would have meant death. July 4, 1942.[94]

Dugan described his religious duties as well. An old Army cook stove served as the altar for his first mass at Cabanatuan, but it is his account of a midnight Christmas service during his first year of captivity that is the most memorable. Held in the open air under a moonlit sky, nearly 6,000 men, the entire population of the camp, attended. A choir sang, priests delivered a sermon, and Father Dugan narrated to the non-Catholic congregation. Dignitary seating at the front held POW officers as well as the Japanese camp commander. For those in the hospital unable to attend, Fall River native Father Alfred D. Talbot held a separate service.

In the fall of 1944, a glimmer of hope appeared in the skies over Cabanatuan. Navy bomber groups began flying over on their bombing runs to Clark Field. Japanese sentries did their best to dampen spirits: "Too bad for American planes. When they returned to carriers, they did not find them. Japanese Navy sank all the carriers." Outwardly, prisoners were stoic. Showing any reaction would result in a beating. Emotions ran from fear (most assumed that when the Americans arrived, their captors "would wipe us out to a man") to enthusiasm over the "Yanks and tanks" that were on the way. The Japanese issued a stern warning: stay in camp or be shot. However, soon, news filtered in from new prisoners and the homemade short-wave radio hidden away in the camp...Americans were on the ground at Lingayen Gulf, fifty miles away.[95]

---

⁹⁴ *POWs celebrate 4th July.* Pub domain photo. 531352 NARA. tinyurl.com/ys5ucn4z.

⁹⁵ Dugan, John and Duffy, Joseph. *Life Under the Japs.*

Coast Guard landing barges in Lingayen Gulf carry the
first wave of invaders to Luzon. January 1945.[96]

The story of the Great Raid on the Japanese prisoner-of-war camp at Cabanatuan is awe-inspiring. The Warfare History Network relates how this tale of unbelievable heroism may have begun when a diminutive nineteen-year-old Army Ranger from Iowa dared to speak up to the legendary General Douglas MacArthur. Young Galen Kittleson was a man of few words. The longest dialogue the soldier ever engaged in during the war, the story went, was when he said to a fellow Ranger, "Let's go to chow." Yet Kittleson had the bravado to approach MacArthur and ask when he planned to rescue the survivors of the Bataan death march. The General responded with, "You be ready when the time comes."[97]

When MacArthur arrived to reclaim the Philippines in the fall of 1944, the enemy began to move, abandoning prison camps in their haste to escape. The viciousness of the Japanese toward the Allies seems to have known no bounds as they sought to exterminate those who had been interned. At Palawan, prisoners were ushered into a building that was doused with gasoline and set on fire. Others were randomly shot or bayoneted, set on fire, and buried alive. Kittleson's concerns were well-founded. Shortly after the war, it was discovered that an order had been issued from the War Ministry in Tokyo regarding the disposal of prisoners: "Whether they are destroyed individually or in groups, and whether it is accomplished by means of mass bombing, poisonous smoke, poisons, drowning, or decapitation, dispose of them as the situation dictates. It is the aim not to allow the escape of a single one, to annihilate them all, and not to leave any traces."[98]

The moment Kittleson was waiting for came in January 1945. Thirteen Rangers and a group of Filipinos moved out across Japanese-held territory toward Cabanatuan, followed later by Col. Henry Mucci's band of Rangers, rebels, and Alamo Scouts. It was a deadly situation. Intelligence indicated the presence of 5,000 Japanese in the vicinity of the camp and up to 300 more within the prison. On the evening of January 29, Mucci made final plans. "Remember," he said, "these boys have been in that shit hole beaten and starved for nearly three years. If they can't walk to the river, carry them. We don't leave

---

[96] *Landing barges Lingayen Gulf.* Pub domain photo. Ted Needham. 26-G-3856. 513215 NARA. tinyurl.com/mwpvzbav

[97] Sasser, Charles. *Great Raid Cabanatuan.* Warfare History Network 4/2019. tinyurl.com/mrt6bbt8.

[98] *Masaharu Homma and Japanese Atrocities.* Am Experience. PBS. tinyurl.com/mpasfm5a.

one of them behind. Not a single one...Go with God—and bring our boys home. They have not been forgotten."

The following night, the rescuers began snaking their way through the 700 yards of turnip and sweet potato fields surrounding Cabanatuan. Lt. John "Frank" Murphy of Springfield and his 6th Ranger squad approached the main gate.[99] Twenty yards from their target, they were discovered. A skirmish ensued, and within minutes, the gate was in control of the Americans. Down the road at a bridge, a battle between Filipino rebels and Japanese reinforcements had just begun. At the other side of the compound, 1st Platoon C Company, under the command of Lt. William O'Connell of Boston,[100] rammed through the gates.

Father Dugan's account of the liberation at Cabanatuan reveals confusion, heroism, disbelief, and gratitude. When a vicious barrage of gunfire suddenly ripped through the dark night, many prisoners stood in shock and disbelief. Dugan stated, "We were convinced that the Nip guards were wiping us out." The Japanese commander came running out to see what was happening and was "dropped in his tracks with a dozen bullets in him." By the time the firing stopped, not one Japanese was left alive. In the silence, a voice suddenly yelled out, "We're Americans! You're free!"[101] One of the men liberated later recalled, "I think I was the first American out of the prison camp. The first thing I knew, I was standing outside with a big Yank. His name was Capt. Prince of Seattle, Wash. The first thing I did was to grab the captain and hug and kiss him right there."[102]

It was over in twenty-eight minutes. Two Rangers lost their lives, and all of the Filipino rebels had survived. In one of the largest POW rescues of the Second World War II, 512 Allied prisoners of war were carted or carried or walked or hobbled to freedom. Galen Kittleson survived the war, served in Vietnam, and rose to the rank of Command Sergeant Major in the U.S. Army Special Forces.[103] A grateful nation awarded Prince and Mucci the Distinguished Service Cross. Prince would later say, "We all worked together. I had no bigger impact than Colonel Mucci. The only reason the story has any legs at all is because we saved people in addition to beating up the Japanese. The heroes of the thing are the POWs."[104]

Cabanatuan POWs celebrate after
liberation. January 30, 1945.[105]

[99] *Banquet Honor Capt Murphy.* Springfield Daily Repub 1/13/1946. Newspapers.com. tinyurl.com/mrccz6v6.

[100] *Murphy Springfield Hero.* Boston Globe 2/3/1945. Newspapers.com. tinyurl.com/5n6uc337.

[101] Dugan, John and Duffy, Joseph. *Life Under the Japs*

[102] Barber, Mike. *Leader of Great Raid.* Seattle P-I 8/24/2005. tinyurl.com/mnrahumc.

[103] Sasser, Charles. *Great Raid Cabanatuan.*

[104] Barber, Mike. *Leader Great Raid.*

[105] *POWs celebrate.* Pub domain photo. US Army. Wikipedia. tinyurl.com/dj3avtcm.

For two POWs from Massachusetts, the story wasn't quite over yet. Lt. William E. Galos of Lexington and Sgt. Joseph H. Horan of South Boston seem to have had a cosmic connection. When Galos was wounded during battle in the Philippines, Horan, a medic, found him and brought him to a combat hospital. The two would meet again on the Bataan Death March when Galos was "viciously stabbed by a Japanese bayonet," and once again, Horan stepped in to help. When the long line of men made it to Camp O'Donnell, Galos and Horan were assigned to the same barracks. They were soon moved to the POW camp at Cabanatuan and would remain there until their rescue in January 1945. Back in the States, the two men were separated, and Galos was discharged. Their story doesn't end here. In October, an unexpected reunion took place when Galos made a visit to Cushing General Hospital in Framingham to visit Father John Dugan and discovered that Joseph Horan was a patient at the very same hospital.[106]

Father John J. Dugan was awarded a Bronze Star and Army Commendation Ribbon. He returned to his beloved Massachusetts and spent two years as Chaplain of Cushing Hospital in Framingham. After suffering a heart attack in December of 1964, he passed away. Father Dugan's Commander-in-Chief had "called him for his eternal reward."[107]

Yoshimura Hisato, a physiologist in Unit 731, had a special interest in hypothermia...Hisato routinely submerged prisoner's limbs in a tub of water filled with ice and held them there until the limbs were frozen solid and a coat of ice was formed over the skin...the limbs made a sound like a plank of wood when struck with a cane. Then he tried different methods for rapidly thawing the frozen appendage, such as dousing limbs with hot water, open fire, or leaving the subject untreated overnight to see how long it took for the prisoner's blood to thaw it out.

These were the "marutas" or logs, a name used by their captors for the men and women who endured torture at the hands of the Japanese in the name of medical research. Major Shiro Ishii had been conducting biological warfare experiments on Chinese captives in Manchuria since the 1930s. It is reported that none of Ishii's subjects from this laboratory survived.

With the advent of war, a fresh source of laboratory specimens, Allied prisoners of war, became available. A new facility for research was opened not far away in Harbin and named the Epidemic Prevention and Water Purification Department, commonly known as Unit 731. Better still, in nearby Mukden, a POW camp with 2,000 inmates operated for the benefit of a Mitsubishi industrial facility. Nearly 1,500 of these prisoners were American. They would become a ready source for Ishii's research. A pool of 200 prisoners was maintained at Unit 731 to be used as human guinea pigs. Here, both men and women were subjected to horrific medical experimentation. Vivisection, freezing and thawing, and infection with pathogens such as syphilis, bubonic plague, and cholera were among the tortures endured by victims.[108]

---

[106] *Bataan Trio at Framingham.* Boston Globe 11/1/1945. Newspapers.com. tinyurl.com/37cwchy5.

[107] Dugan, John and Duffy, Joseph. *Life Under the Japs.*

[108] Bozu, Joel et al. *Med Aspects Biol Warfare.* OSG, AMEDD 2018. tinyurl.com/3xddm67y.

Unit 731 Complex[109]

Much controversy existed following the war as to the veracity of claims that Americans and other Allies had actually been used for experimentation. Yet numerous reports from G.I.s bear witness to suspicious treatment by their captors. Prisoners testified to seeing Japanese medical personnel moving through barracks at night, giving injections to sleeping men, some of whom were found dead the next morning. One group was given oranges to eat and became desperately ill afterward. Many were moved to areas where they were injected, and data on symptoms were collected.[110] Most victims did not survive to tell their stories.

To be fair, proof of Ishii's work was sketchy. The Japanese went out of their way to destroy evidence at multiple sites as the end of the war approached. No prisoner at Unit 731 was left alive. One Japanese nurse recalled victims' bodies, bones, and body parts being hastily buried,[111] buildings were dynamited, and records were hidden away. The United States appears to have taken allegations of atrocities seriously enough to investigate. Here, too, however, the Japanese covered their tracks. Chelsea, Massachusetts native Lt. Col. Murray J. Sanders, a bacteriologist assigned to the U.S. biological warfare unit in Maryland, was sent to Japan one month after the war ended to investigate. Sanders conducted a series of interviews with the help of an interpreter. When he realized that denials routinely referred to their work as "defensive research" rather than biological warfare, which was clearly criminal, he became suspicious, soon discovering that his interpreter had been employed at Unit 731.[112]

It cannot be said that all of the approximately 3,000 men and women who died at the hands of the Japanese in Unit 731 rest in peace. When the subject of bacterial warfare and human experimentation was brought up at the Tokyo War Crimes trial in 1946, it was discounted due to lack of evidence. Yet a post-war classified US document stated: "Independent investigation conducted by the Soviets in the Mukden Area may have disclosed that American prisoners of war were used for experimental purposes of a BW (biological warfare) nature and that they lost their lives as a result of these experiments." Transcripts of the Soviet War Crime Tribunal clarify the nebulous "may have" statement in the American report:

Prosecutor: Did Detachment 731 study the immunity of Americans to infectious diseases?
Unit 731 officer named Karasawa: One of the researchers of the detachment...told me...that he had come to Mukden to study immunity among American war prisoners.

[109] *Unit 731 Complex.* Pub domain photo. Bulletin Unit 731. Wiki Commons. tinyurl.com/y6578nfc.

[110] Holmes, Linda Goetz. *Unjust Enrichment.*

[111] *Unit 731.* Guardian. tinyurl.com/yufwvrhj.

[112] Brody H et al. *Japanese inhuman experimentation* 4/2014. NLM. tinyurl.com/ypc6mprf.

Nevertheless, it is accepted today that the United States brokered a deal with the Japanese government. Murray Sanders became a controversial figure when it became apparent that the decision to sweep Unit 731 atrocities under the rug was prompted by General Douglas MacArthur. Several years after the war, Sanders admitted that he had played a major role. During his 1945 interrogation of Unit 731 personnel, the Lt. Col. understood that he was being lied to and turned to MacArthur for advice on how to proceed. The General told him to offer anything and get as much research data as he could. What was offered was immunity.[113] Shiro Ishii was absolved of his crimes and lived out his relatively short life peacefully. Other Unit 731 colleagues spent their remaining years unhindered by their pasts, among them a governor of Tokyo,[114] an assistant head of the Japanese Medical Association, two directors of Japan's National Institute of Health, and a chairman of Japan's Olympic Committee.[115]

In 1945, Tadao Ishimaru was chosen to work on Cherry Blossoms at Night, a Japanese biological warfare plan to use kamikazes to carry plague-infected fleas onto American soil. San Diego was the target. In an interview with the *Los Angeles Times* in 1995, he stated: "I don't want to think about Unit 731... Please let me remain silent."[116] Five decades after the war, Ishimaru wanted to forget. If only it were that easy for the thousands of souls who lived and died in the horror of Unit 731.

When the war was finally over, former prisoners headed home in both directions, some to the United States and some to the devastation of their war-torn countries. For those held captive on American soil, the experience was often remembered in a positive light. Rupert Mezroth had pleasant memories of his time at a POW camp in Florida and eventually emigrated to Greenfield, Massachusetts, where he opened a printing company.[117] One German POW held at Fort Devens maintained a correspondence with Devens Mess Sergeant George Provias after the war, thanking him for his "sincere and peaceful character."[118] Kazuo Sakamaki wrote of his four years as a prisoner in the United States:

My steps were these...failure, capture...attempts at suicide, failure again, self-contempt, deep disillusionment...desire to learn and yearning for truth...freedom through love, and finally, a desire for reconstruction. I claim no credit for this transformation. I wish to preach to no one. I only hope that this will show to all...that man is capable of being made anew...The key to it all [is] the concept of democracy. I learned it as a prisoner. It was the best education of my life.[119]

For Americans returning from POW camps abroad, some were able to put the past behind them while stoically enduring devastating physical and emotional scars. Many sought retribution. Some sued the Japanese industrial giants that had enslaved them. Former POW Frank Bigelow, who was held at the Omuta Prison Camp, stated, "Justice is long overdue...." Bigelow was injured at a Mitsui Mining Company site after a rock fell on him while working 1600 feet below ground. After gangrene set in, his leg was amputated without anesthesia, using a hacksaw, razor blades, knives, and four men holding him down. "And what do I think the company owes us? My leg, a couple of years of our lives...Most of all, they owe us an apology."[120]

[113] Brazil, Jeff. *Truth on Ailing POWs*. LA Times 3/20/1995. tinyurl.com/356m5yps.

[114] Jung, Romeo. *Unit 731*. Dangerous World. Baskin Eng. UCSC 3/25/2018. tinyurl.com/yc45cvyn.

[115] Gold, Hal. *Japan's Infamous Unit 731*. Tuttle Publ 2019.

[116] Kristof, Nicholas. *Unmasking Horror*. NYT 3/17/1995. tinyurl.com/55t57fd8.

[117] Heisler, Barbara. *Returning to America*. GSR 2008. JSTOR. tinyurl.com/4jkmeeyh.

[118] Huntley, Tanna. *Unlikely Friendship*. Fort Devens Museum Newsl 2022.

[119] Kramer, Arnold. *Japanese POW Am*. PHR 1983. JSTOR. tinyurl.com/34hpfkp9.

[120] *World War II POWs*. Senate Comm Judiciary 6/28/2000. tinyurl.com/bdd8jnkj.

Allied POWs, after being liberated at
Omori Prison in Japan. August 1945.[121]

The US government welcomed returning POWs, ensuring decent medical care and back pay. Thanks to the War Claims Act of 1948, using money taken from Axis government coffers, former prisoners received additional compensation for time spent in captivity. Yet there was a dark side to the government's response. Many GIs were forced to sign a gag order to prevent information about their experiences from becoming public. Bigelow recalled, "We were each handed a paper…We were told to read and sign and keep our mouths shut, and I am just putting that politely."[122]

By the end of the war, 130,000 Americans had been held as prisoners of war. Approximately 14,000 perished in captivity, 11,000 of them in Japanese custody. In addition, it will never be known how many of the 73,000 souls still listed as missing died as prisoners of war. Their courage defies description. They were then and will forever be heroes. "When death was preferable," wrote Brig. General A.S. Blackburn of those who survived, "these men dared to live."[123] Thankfully, 116,000 came home.

---

[121] *POWs cheer rescuers.* Pub domain photo. 520992 NARA. tinyurl.com/yhduxv6z.

[122] *World War II POWs.* Senate Comm Judiciary.

[123] Holmes, Linda Goetz. *Unjust Enrichment.*

Chapter 13

Servants of God

What am I doing here…I love peace so passionately and hate war
so utterly…yet here I am in the midst of it, feeling that it is right for me to be here and that, indeed, I
could be nowhere else…
Chaplain Russell Cartwright Stroup
Pacific Theater of Operation[1]

In March 1945, Task Force 58 was positioned 100 miles from Japan, its mission to strike critical targets like Itami and Kobe Harbor in support of the offensive on Okinawa. Their efforts were not without resistance, for in the early morning hours of the nineteenth, a Japanese twin-engine bomber swept out of the clouds, untouched by USS Franklin's anti-aircraft guns, and dropped a pair of 550-pound bombs on the ship. Nearby aboard the USS North Carolina, Robert Palomeris recalled the events of that horrific day.

I rushed to my battle station on the bow, uncovered my gun, put a magazine in it, had it cocked and ready to fire, but I couldn't fire because the USS FRANKLIN was dead ahead of us. This plane came in dead ahead of the FRANKLIN, and I watched the whole thing. He came right on down over the carrier, whose flight deck was loaded with planes, and dropped two bombs. They just absolutely annihilated everything…. The FRANKLIN had pulled out of its line in front of us, on fire and things going off, guys in the water. I never saw so many sailors in the water, some dead, some alive and hollering, and we started throwing everything we could get our hands on: life jackets and rafts, shark repellents.[2]

A declassified Navy report describes the attack in great detail. USS Franklin, "Big Ben," was in the process of refueling some of the thirty-three planes on her deck. Twenty-two more rested below, with forty-five already aloft. Two bombs scored a direct hit on the flight deck, blasting holes in the armored decking as large as fourteen by eighteen feet. A gigantic gasoline explosion followed. Clouds of smoke fumed upward off the deck. Planes were blown off the ship. Bombs waiting to be loaded blew up where they sat or rolled into craters in the deck, detonating in the hangar below. Small caliber ammunition popped and whizzed around the crew. As fires raged, smoke and heat filled compartments below, making escape nearly impossible.[3] The attack on the Franklin resulted in some of the worst loss of life experienced by a US Navy vessel since the start of the war. Big Ben never sank on that fateful day and made it to port on March 24, 1945. By then, approximately 800 brave souls were lost, and another 300 were wounded.

---

[1] Snyder, Jeremiah. *Let Us Die Bravely.* Undergrad Res J. CU 2009. tinyurl.com/3ya62xp5

[2] *USS Franklin Tragedy.* Battleship North Carolina. tinyurl.com/2zjdxusx.

[3] *Franklin Damage Report 9/1946.* NHHC. tinyurl.com/etmm6faa.

Attack on U.S.S. Franklin. March 19, 1945.[4]

The heroism of the men of USS Franklin is humbling. For their bravery and sacrifice that day, more than 1,000 Purple Hearts were awarded, along with 19 Navy Crosses, 22 Silver Stars, and 116 Bronze Stars. Two men received the Congressional Medal of Honor. One of them was Joseph T. O'Callahan, a claustrophobic, nearsighted, thirty-nine-year-old from Worcester. Born in Boston, he became a Jesuit priest while teaching at Boston College, and by 1938, he had moved on to the Mathematics Department at Holy Cross College. Several months before the outbreak of war, O'Callahan, believing that he could do more good as a Navy chaplain than as a teacher, joined the US Navy. In March of 1945, now a Lt. Commander, O'Callahan reported for duty aboard the USS Franklin.

Seventeen days later, the ship came under attack. Father O'Callahan arrived on deck to find the Franklin full stop in the water, flames, twisted steel, wounded and dead everywhere. He quickly organized the men to fight the fires, yelling, "Lads, lads! Want to save our happy home?" When dangerous fumes began pouring out from an ammunition handling room, O'Callahan guided a party to shoot water into the opening, then led men to toss out the shells before they exploded. As they were handed from sailor to sailor, men responded with, "...praise the Lord and dump the ammunition." A smoke-covered O'Callahan signaled to Captain Gehres that the situation was under control. When a hot 500-pound bomb rolled across the deck, a group of sailors stopped it from falling into a hole where it would surely have exploded. Two officers, nerves frayed, failed to disarm it until O'Callahan walked up and calmly stood there with arms folded while the officers completed their task.[5]

O'Callahan seemed to be everywhere that day. He encouraged men to action, shepherded wounded to safety, took hold of fire hoses, tossed ammunition, and administered last rites. According to Naval History and Heritage Command, "The image of the cross, painted on his helmet, became etched into the memories of those who watched as he moved through the carnage with his head slightly bowed as if in a constant state of prayer."[6]

For his selfless actions that day, O'Callahan was awarded the Congressional Medal of Honor, the only chaplain in World War II and the first Navy Chaplain in history to be so honored.

A valiant and forceful leader, calmly braving the perilous barriers of flame and twisted metal to aid his men and his ship, Lt. Comdr. O'Callahan groped his way through smoke-filled corridors to the open flight deck and into the midst of violently exploding bombs, shells, rockets, and other armament. With the ship rocked by incessant explosions, with debris and fragments raining down and fires raging in ever-increasing fury, he ministered to the wounded and dying, comforting and encouraging men of all faiths; he organized and led firefighting crews into the blazing inferno on the flight deck; he directed the jettisoning of live ammunition and the flooding of the magazine; he manned a hose to cool hot, armed

---

[4] *USS FRANKLIN.* Pub domain photo. USN. 520656 NARA. tinyurl.com/4xe2hvye.

[5] *O'Callahan Wins MOH.* New Eng Hist Soc 2022. tinyurl.com/ycyxajn3.

[6] Foster, Jeremiah. *Franklin III.* NHHC 11/21/2019. tinyurl.com/3x4368b6.

bombs rolling dangerously on the listing deck, continuing his efforts, despite searing, suffocating smoke which forced men to fall back gasping and imperiled others who replaced them. Serving with courage, fortitude, and deep spiritual strength, Lt. Comdr. O'Callahan inspired the gallant officers and men of the Franklin to fight heroically and with profound faith in the face of almost certain death and to return their stricken ship to port.[7]

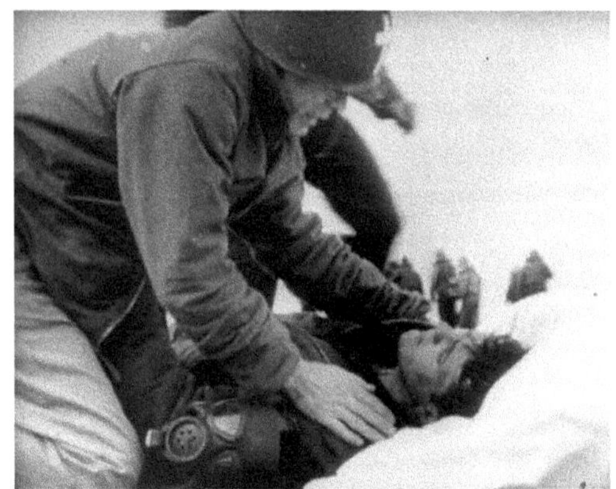

Lt. Commander Joseph T. O'Callahan gives last
rites after the attack on USS Franklin. The young
man in the photo survived. 19 March 1945.[8]

On May 17, 1945, as the tortured remains of the Franklin lay in her berth at the Brooklyn Navy Yard, a ceremony was held on her deck to remember those who were lost and to honor those who had risked so much to save the lives of their comrades. Among the crowd, Joseph O'Callahan's mother was approached by Franklin's Captain Gehres. "I'm not a religious man," he said. "But I watched your son that day, and I thought if faith can do this for a man, there must be something to it. Your son is the bravest man I have ever seen." Joseph O'Callahan survived the war and came home to Holy Cross. He passed on in 1964 and is buried in the College of the Holy Cross Cemetery. The USS O'Callahan was commissioned in his honor in 1968.[9]

O'Callahan was one of thousands of chaplains who served their country during times of war. Throughout history, governments have waged war under the umbrella of righteousness provided by a deity who supposedly supported their cause. The United States, "one nation under God," was no different. Feeling the need "...to implore the blessing of Heaven upon the means used for our safety and defense," George Washington's request for a chaplain corps in the Army of Independence was granted. The presence of God was essential to the nation at war. Asking armies to kill required men of sound mind as well as body, and chaplains were tasked with keeping trained killers connected to a sense of greater purpose and to their souls.

By the time of the attack on Pearl Harbor, the nation, clearly unprepared for war, was also unprepared to minister to its fighting men. The Army and Navy combined counted approximately 200 chaplains in their lists. Filling the ranks with men of the cloth was not easy. Members of the clergy could not be drafted, and throughout the war, the military had to rely on volunteers. More complicated was the attitude of various denominational governing boards toward war. During the Great War, a surge of patriotism had swept the nation, and churches made a concerted effort to lend their support. As America approached a second international conflict, the attitude of churches, as with the largely isolationist

---

[7] *Joseph O'Callahan.* Stories of Sacrifice. MOH Soc. tinyurl.com/f9fhjkwx.

[8] *80-G-49132 Joseph O'Callahan 3.* Pub domain photo. NHHC. tinyurl.com/4tx3edja.

[9] *Joseph T. O'Callahan Wins MOH.* New Eng Hist Soc.

population, swung in the opposite direction. Embracing clerical involvement in the military was slow. By 1943, however, their philosophical differences were somewhat resolved, and chaplains, though never filling quotas, were widely dispersed across all theaters of operation.

Regardless of the military's high expectations for candidates (the requirement of four years of college and three of seminary training would exclude a significant number of African American clergy), men left the comfort of family, home, and parish to join up. In the little town of North Conway, NH, Episcopal priest Roger Warren Barney opted to enlist when the war's hungry need for men caused his flock to nearly disappear.[10] Others joined from a sense of patriotism, many as an act of conscience. Certainly, Jewish Chaplains had a personal stake in the conflict. Chaplain David Max Eichorn noted, "One-fifth of our number lie in martyr's graves."[11]

The first step toward active duty was training. For the Navy, chaplain school operated out of Newport Naval Base in Rhode Island. The Army utilized Fort Benjamin Harrison in Indiana until early 1942 when it was moved to Harvard University. It would remain there until the end of the war and be relocated to Fort Devens. In addition to clerical duties, clergymen learned basic first aid, participated in gas mask drills, and underwent rigorous physical exercise. Some, bound for specific assignments, jumped out of airplanes. Conveying the realism of what was to follow was more difficult, and there is no doubt that most members of the clergy who enlisted were unprepared for the harsh reality of war.

Once chaplain training was completed, many clergymen were assigned to army and navy bases or military hospitals. However, most found their way to combat zones. Here, their jobs and lives changed significantly. No longer were services held in cozy chapels or lofty cathedrals but on ships, clustered under palm trees, in barns, altars placed on the hood of a jeep, often surrounded by the sound of battle. Father John Foley of Boston College recalled, "...serving my Mass on the boat deck aft, flush against the side of an invasion boater up against an AA gun mount shield."[12]

With a canvas tarpaulin for a church and packing cases for an altar,
a Navy chaplain holds mass for Marines at Saipan. June 1944.[13]

One of the more moving accounts occurred during the horrific battle for Iwo Gima. When a Marine suggested the possibility of climbing to the top of a mountain peak at the end of the island and raising the American flag, Marine Chaplain Charles Suver promptly responded: "You get it up there, and I'll say Mass under it." Five days into the fighting, after a Marine platoon led by Lt. Ray Whalen of

[10] Piehler, G. Kurt. *Religious Hist Am GI WWII.* UNL 2021.

[11] Jeremiah Snyder. *Let Us Die Bravely.*

[12] Duffy, Joseph. *To Love and Serve.* New Eng Province Hist 2014. tinyurl.com/4n6uc9vu.

[13] *Tarpaulin for church... 6/1944.* Pub domain photo. 532525. NARA. tinyurl.com/2tu948k6.

Watertown[14] successfully fought their way to the summit, Father Suver celebrated Mass on the pinnacle of Mount Suribachi.[15]

Mass atop Mount Suribachi on
Iwo Jima. February 1945.[16]

The role of chaplains was multi-faceted, and those who served stateside kept just as busy as their colleagues overseas. In 1942, at a massive ceremony in Post Office Square in Boston, Navy Chaplain Joseph Canty, a native of Taunton and former pastor of St. John's Church in Attleboro, provided a blessing. "May God speed the completion of the righteous task that lies before you," and 500 newly sworn-in recruits were whisked off to war.[17] Chaplain Frank R. Morton was assigned to the First Naval District out of Newport. He tended to his flock at Coast Guard stations from Nantucket to Watch Hill, arriving by Coast Guard cutters, picket boats, and jeeps.[18]

Close to the battlefield, chaplains were charged with seeing to the spiritual needs of their flock, attempting to somehow instill a sense of morality in those who fought. Beyond the issues of killing and death, men yearned for wives and girlfriends often while being unfaithful. Abstinence and venereal disease prevention were frequent topics. They provided encouragement for those about to go into battle, mailing last letters home to loved ones, or kneeling in prayer crouched on the crowded deck of a Higgins boat. Many chaplains worked at hospitals or acted as public relations liaisons with the local population.

Others settled for nothing less than following their men into battle. Connecticut native Paul Redmond was ten years older than the average paratrooper when he became the first Marine Chaplain to join the Raiders. Chaplains, too scarce and valuable to be risked, were generally excluded from the opening wave of battle. Redmond, however, insisted he be allowed to join his comrades. "These are my boys. They will need me most out there. I'm going with them."[19] Chaplains who opted for combat went wherever their men did, moving from foxhole to foxhole, dragging wounded away from danger, assisting medics, and offering prayers. Ignatius Maternowski, a thirty-two-year-old Catholic priest from Holyoke, was assigned to the 82nd Airborne Division. On June 6, 1944, Maternowski parachuted out of a plane along with his regiment and landed in northwest France. As he attempted to assist wounded soldiers, a German bullet struck him in the back, making him the only chaplain to lose his life on D-Day.[20]

[14] Hurwitz, Hy. *Iwo Flag Planting.* Boston Globe 3/16/1945. Newspapers.com. tinyurl.com/56j6mre5.

[15] Moriwaki, Lee. *Rev Charles Suver.* ST 4/15/1993. tinyurl.com/2yhkzzb3.

[16] *Mass Atop Suribachi.* Pub domain photo. NH104583 Iwo Jima Op. NHHC. tinyurl.com/38ajwf8b.

[17] *Recruits Post Office Sq.* Boston Globe 10/15/1942. Newspapers.com. tinyurl.com/238d8pz4.

[18] *Navy Chaplain to Air.* Transcript-TG 1/7/1944. Newspapers.com. tinyurl.com/2y43s4sz.

[19] Dorsett, Lyle. *Serving God and Country.* Berkley Publ Group, Penguin Group 2012.

[20] Gelinas, Samuel. *D-Day hero.* Daily Hampshire Gaz 6/7/2024. tinyurl.com/33ykjw6k.

Father Maternowski during paratrooper training.[21]

Perhaps their most troubling task was tending to those who would never again see the break of dawn. Chaplains stood in the midst of battle, comforting those who would soon pass on, performing last rites, and, after the battle, conducting services for the dead. They surveyed long lines of bodies to record names and sent final messages home to families. Honoring the fallen was a sacred duty, and many chaplains went to great lengths to locate those lost, often in spite of danger. Father Francis X. Murphy of Natick recounted his experience in New Guinea with the *Boston Globe* in 1944:

We spent a whole day moving down the south coast of the island in an outrigger canoe. Then, it took another full day to penetrate the jungle. By the light of the tropic moon filtering through the palm fronds and dense jungle bush, the natives pointed out the rough mound of earth surmounted by a crude cross on which hung an aviator's goggles. We opened the shallow grave and removed the body of an American flyer, carefully shrouded in his parachute, and took it back to the base for a Christian burial.[22]

One Chaplain described the difficulty experienced in recovering a fallen soldier because Germans had booby-trapped the body. Another, Father Sixtus O'Connor, would pray at the graves of nearly 3,000 concentration camp victims.[23] On Iwo Jima, where historian Norman Cooper speculated "nearly seven hundred Americans gave their lives for every square mile," the burial chores were staggering. Chaplain Edgar Hotaling, a graduate of the Andover Newton Theological Seminary in Newton, stated: "Most jobs you can get used to. But this one is different. Every man you bury is a fresh tragedy."[24] Even the enemy was respected in death. As the Battle for Bataan raged, Chaplain Albert Talbot of Fall River came upon a Japanese soldier who had been taken prisoner. The man was in his final moments of life, and Father Talbot accommodated his last wish of being baptized into the Christian faith.[25]

---

[21] *Ignatius Maternowski.* Pub domain photo. US Army. Lucas, Kenneth. *Fr. Maternowski* 9/26/2019. Friars Memoriam. tinyurl.com/yjwc4ymp.

[22] Riley, Arthur. *Help in Pacific.* Boston Globe 2/8/1944. Newspapers.com. tinyurl.com/2s47cbya.

[23] Piehler, G. Kurt. *Religious Hist Am GI WWII. UNL* 2021.

[24] Dorsett, Lyle W. *Serving God and Country.*

[25] *Chaplain Baptizes Jap.* Berkshire Eagle 8/29/1942. Newspapers.com. tinyurl.com/2d5nt7zt.

Grave marker carved by Marines
on Iwo Jima. 1945.[26]

The extraordinary diary of Father John P. Foley provides an unforgettable account of the life of a Navy Chaplain in World War II. The Jesuit priest taught at Holy Cross College in Worcester before becoming a Dean at Boston College. Shortly after the outbreak of war, he joined the Navy. His journal entries portray the excitement, violence, and emotion experienced not just by Foley but by the men in his care. In the fall of 1942, as he made his way toward Morocco in a naval convoy that included the Battleship Massachusetts, rough seas caused so much turbulence that his head crashed into the wall while he was resting in his bunk. He observed other ships rocking so fiercely that he could see ten feet below the waterline. The ship came under attack, and depth charges fired off day and night. "Our ship is a floating arsenal," he wrote. "If she is hit, the report will be that she 'disintegrated.'" Mass followed one round of general quarters. "Overhead is the blue canopy of the sky. We have no walls broken by stained glass windows, just sterns and bows; we boast no marble inlaid floor...just a wooden deck...and lines that are whistling in the wind." A sailor stopped by, he recalled, to request that the priest send a message home to his wife, "just in case I am plowed under."

Saturday night, November 7, they approached the shoreline as the enemy launched a devastating attack. Around him, Foley saw planes strafing and heard shells screaming overhead while nearby ships boomed out a counterattack. Quietly, matter-of-factly, he wrote of three casualties. Members of a commando party gathered around him prior to embarking on a covert mission to cut a sub net. "May the blessing of Almighty God...descend on you..." Still later, men headed ashore in a launch amidst a thirty-foot surf. Soon, seven wounded returned, one stating, "I would sure appreciate a prayer." By afternoon, wounded men and bodies began flowing in. One man was struck over the heart and survived when the bullet pierced a bible and a picture of his daughter, leaving him with just a bruise. Another Huffstutler, four days later, made his final trip ashore to the cemetery at Blue Beach in a landing craft along with the chaplain, "machine guns...cases for 48 rockets, 4 lbs. of TNT, racks six on either side..." Graves were being dug by prisoners of war, and when the plots were ready, Americans on one side of the priest and POWs on the other stood at attention. "Eternal rest grant unto them, O Lord..." Finally, the war ended. "Thank God this needless bloodshed is over, in at least one section of a bloodstained world..." Father John P. Foley returned to Boston College after the war and went home to his God in 1995.[27]

---

[26] *127-GW-305-11514 Battle Iwo Jima.* Pub domain photo. USMC. NHHC. tinyurl.com/mryrzrx5.

[27] Duffy, Joseph. *To Love and Serve.*

The position of chaplain was recognized by the Geneva Convention. Men of God were classified as non-combatants. As such, they were to be considered neutral, protected by allies and enemies alike and did not carry weapons. Many clergy themselves, however, violated the Geneva Accord. Warren Wyeth Willard was a gun-toting "chappie." As a minister prior to the war, he founded Camp Good News in Forestdale, Massachusetts. After joining the Navy, he was sent to the Pacific Theater of Operation, where he accompanied his men into the fighting at Tarawa and the Gilbert Islands.[28] On Guadalcanal, he reportedly roamed back and forth on the beach, yelling, "I'm Chaplain Willard, and you can't shoot me!" Willard was the only member of the clergy on Guadalcanal who survived.[29] He was credited with serving more consecutive days under constant enemy fire than any chaplain in the history of the US Navy and Marine Corps."[30] He would be awarded the Navy Legion of Merit for his service. The citation reads:

On November 21, while attached, at his own request, to an assault battalion, which landed under extremely heavy enemy fire, the boat in which he was riding was hit, and several men were killed and wounded. After administering to the men...he made his way to the beach despite continual enemy fire. There, he aided in evacuating and caring for the wounded and giving spiritual comfort to the dying. On November 22 and 23, when the beachhead had been secured, he immediately organized parties and personally directed the collecting and burying of the majority of the dead...When the battalion was ordered to reembark he asked permission to remain to finish the task, but his request was refused... His untiring efforts and devotion to duty under the most adverse conditions were in keeping with the highest traditions of the United States Naval Service.[31]

After the war, Chaplain Willard spent several years as Director of Evangelism at Wheaton College before heading back to school to earn a law degree. He later returned to the pulpit at the Third Baptist Church of Barnstable and ended his career as minister of the First Presbyterian Church of Waltham. The final chapter in the life of this energetic and inspirational man ended at age 94 in Sandwich, Massachusetts, in the year 2000.[32]

With not enough chaplains to go around, meeting the demands of those who served required a redefinition of who exactly fell under which ministry. The majority of clergy were Catholic or Protestant, while the number of those of the Jewish faith fell far short. When war broke out, there were no rabbis in the ranks of the US Army or Navy. The country itself counted only about 1,000 rabbis total, and as Philip Bernstein, in his article, "Jewish Chaplains in World War II," pointed out, over half of those were ineligible due to age, health, or educational qualifications. By the war's end, 309 rabbis would serve.[33]

In the meantime, chaplains had to broaden their thinking...all who served, regardless of denomination, were accepted as part of God's flock. Overcoming this problem appears to have been seamless. Men eagerly sought out chaplains as men of God, less than as men of any particular church. Chaplain Roger Barney, raised in Dorchester,[34] recalled with admiration a Catholic priest who went into combat to deliver sacrament to a large number of men, noting a remarkable number of Protestants who sought "the Body and Blood of Christ."[35] Father John Foley of Boston recalled an officer who approached him prior to battle:

---

[28] *W. Wyeth Willard.* ReCollections. Wheaton Coll Arch 2/2/2010. tinyurl.com/3fve884s.

[29] Boutilier, Emily Gold. *Courage Under Fire.* Brown Alumni Mag. 5/3/2007. tinyurl.com/2jkystc8.

[30] *W. Wyeth Willard, Leatherneck.* ReCollections.

[31] *W. Wyeth Willard.* Leatherneck Mag. 1980. Hildebrand, Jim. Marines and Corpsmen Tarawa & Guadalcanal. tinyurl.com/2eu3p5yt.

[32] *W. Wyeth Willard, Leatherneck.* ReCollections.

[33] Bernstein, Philip. *Jewish Chaplains WWII.* AJYB 1945. JSTOR. tinyurl.com/ywct653p.

[34] *Roger Barney and Jane Barney Papers.* U Mich. tinyurl.com/49t3ax3a.

[35] Piehler, G. Kurt. *Religious Hist Am GI WWII.*

"I control the lives of two hundred men tomorrow, Father...I'd like to feel there was someone more powerful than I helping me to make the right decisions. I'm a Protestant, but there's no Protestant chaplain aboard. Would you give me your blessing?"
"Kneel down, son."[36]

Stories of selflessness, humility, and self-sacrifice among military chaplains are common in the annals of World War II history. After their liberation from Cabanatuan, Holy Cross alumnus Father Eugene O'Keefe asked Hugh Kennedy, a fellow Jesuit if doctors had found anything wrong during his first post-POW physical exam. Kennedy responded, "Yes, a little dandruff." In addition to severe malnutrition, the priest was suffering from dysentery, malaria, beriberi, scurvy, and poliomyelitis.[37] Nowhere are these traits more clearly illustrated than in the story of the Four Chaplains.

John Washington was born into poverty, grew up in a tough New Jersey neighborhood, and found his way to the priesthood in 1935. After Pearl Harbor, the Navy rejected his application as a result of poor vision, so the determined priest tried the Army. Covering his damaged eye during the examination, he passed the physical and was accepted. Washington requested placement in a war zone. George Fox struggled with a traumatic childhood at the hands of an abusive father. After winning several medals for his actions as an Army medic in the First World War, Fox entered Boston University's School of Theology, eventually becoming a Methodist minister. Following Pearl Harbor, he joined the Army and returned to Massachusetts for training at Harvard. Like his father, Alexander Goode became a rabbi. He was inducted into the Army after being rejected by the Navy and sent to Harvard's Chaplain School. Clark Poling was the sixth in a long family line of ministers. He lived in Massachusetts for a time before becoming a pastor in the Reformed Church of America. He joined the Army and was ordered to the European Theater. All four men were sent to Camp Myles Standish to await deployment. Unknown to the four chaplains, the stage had been set for one of the most inspiring and enduring legends of World War II, the tragedy of the USS Dorchester.

The former cruise ship was a frequent visitor to Massachusetts on her regular route from Miami to Boston. With the outbreak of war, the Dorchester was stripped down and refitted to become a troop transport. Her 1943 mission was to carry lumber, mail, and over a ton of assorted goods to Greenland. Her most important cargo, however, was the approximately 700 soldiers who had recently processed through Camp Myles Standish in Taunton. In late January, Convoy SG-19 left Newfoundland and headed eastward. This was U-boat territory, and on February 2, the convoy commander notified vessels that a submarine was in the area. Dorchester Merchant Marine Captain Hans Danielsen addressed those on board: "Now hear this: Every soldier is ordered to sleep in his clothes and life jacket. Repeat, this is an order! We have a submarine following us...If we make it through the night, in the morning, we will have air protection from...Greenland."[38] Tragically, the Dorchester would soon be gone.

History has recorded numerous reports from survivors of the incident. In the early morning hours of February 3, the Dorchester was struck by a single torpedo. The explosion was not heard by convoy vessels nearby. Engines immediately ceased to function, lights were extinguished, and a heavy ammonia smell spread through the ship. A foghorn distress call was sounded, six blasts, then silence. There was no more steam. Though lifeboats were on board, many had been destroyed by the explosion, and others were inaccessible, locked in ice. Men slid down ropes to get to boats or jumped into the water to swim toward rafts. Many would not survive the frigid water. Navy gunner Roy Summers ran toward the stern but stopped when he saw rotating propellers rising up from the water, snuffing out the lives of those who

---

[36] Dorsett, Lyle W. *Serving God and Country.*

[37] Giblin, Gerard. *Woodstock Letters* 11/1960. BC. tinyurl.com/yc332p3c.

[38] Clifford, James. *No Greater Glory.* AHF. tinyurl.com/2295yryc.

had just leaped overboard. He had survived the sinking of the USS Chatham in August. Summers witnessed two chaplains handing out life vests.

Not far away, Father Washington gave absolution to soldiers as they abandoned ship. One private tried unsuccessfully to convince the priest to go with him. Walter Miller heard someone say he couldn't find a life vest. "Here's one, soldier," came a reply, and George Fox took off his life jacket and gave it to the man. Lt. Mahoney nearly returned to his quarters to look for gloves but was stopped by Rabbi Goode. "Don't bother Mahoney. I have another pair. You can have these."[39] After going overboard, Pvt. William B. Bednar remembered, "I could hear men crying, pleading, praying...I could also hear the chaplains preaching courage. Their voices were the only thing that kept me going."[40] Other survivors report the chaplains all gave up their life vests to save the lives of those on board. In the last moments, the four men were seen standing together on the deck of the dying vessel, praying with arms linked.

The four chaplains of the USS Dorchester[41]

It took less than half an hour for the Dorchester to sink beneath the waves. Nearly 700 souls, including Father John Patrick Washington, Rev. Clark Vandersall Poling, Rabbi Alexander David Goode, and Rev. George Lansing Fox, slipped quietly away into the annals of history. Within a week, Camp Myles Standish in Taunton held a memorial service for the hundreds of soldiers who, a short time earlier, had passed through their gates. In 1944, the Four Chaplains were awarded Purple Hearts and Distinguished Service Crosses. U-boat 223 sustained no damage during the attack on the Dorchester, but less than a year later, along with half of her crew, would meet her end in the Mediterranean at the hands of British destroyers.[42] The sinking of the Dorchester is remembered as one of the worst losses at sea in World War II.

Four days later and approximately five hundred miles to the east, another tragedy was about to unfold. The SS Henry R. Mallory, along with Convoy SC-118, was headed from Halifax to Iceland. She carried trucks, tanks, supplies, and 381 members of the Marines, Navy, and Army. Also aboard were seven Army Chaplains. Lt. Horace Gravely was a much beloved Methodist minister from South Carolina who impressed colleagues during their training at Harvard with his refusal to drink alcohol. David Youngdahl from Minnesota had been assigned to an artillery regiment stationed at Camp Myles Standish early in 1942. He and Texan Ira Bently were both Baptist ministers and Valmore G. Savignac was a thirty-two-year-old priest from Providence, Rhode Island. Captain Gerald J. Whelan was a Christmas

[39] Clifford, James. *No Greater Glory.*

[40] *Four Chaplains.* VWMF. tinyurl.com/3zmsnf6z.

[41] *Fox, Goode, Washington, Poling.* Pub domain photo. Four Chaplains Day. USAF. tinyurl.com/2s3kv7zp.

[42] *U-223.* Uboat.net. tinyurl.com/ycx4bedk.

baby, born and raised in Roxbury, where he attended the parochial school at the Redemptorist Church of Our Lady of Perpetual Help. Rev. Ernest W. MacDonald was also a Massachusetts boy, a native of Boston who grew up in Quincy, attended Thayer School in Braintree, and graduated from Andover Newton School of Theology. He was thirty-seven years old. Father James Liston, also thirty-seven, hailed from Chicago.

All seven chaplains, as well as the four chaplains from the Dorchester, were stationed together at Camp Myles Standish prior to shipping out. David Max Eichorn, who would later become the first rabbi to enter Dachau Concentration Camp, was also at the Taunton camp. Before sailing, Father Whelan visited his family, bringing along a few friends from Myles Standish, including Liston and John Washington. Liston and Whelan left for Halifax the next day. Washington would follow a few days later on the ill-fated Dorchester.

On February 7, 1943, German sub U-402 located Convoy SC-118 in waters southwest of Iceland. USS Mallory had fallen behind. Just before 7 a.m., a torpedo slammed into the ship's starboard side, followed immediately by explosions that blew off hatch covers and fatally damaged the engine. In thirty minutes, the ship was gone, leaving behind survivors floundering in the frigid water. Only three lifeboats made it off the ship.

Aboard the Mallory, Father Gerald Whelan had just approached the lifeboats when a voice with an Irish lilt yelled out from below, "Jump, Father, jump!" It was Joe Reilly, a young man from Gloucester who had befriended the priest a few days before. Whelan recalled, "I knew he would know how to run a boat because every mother who gives birth to a boy in Gloucester takes him down to sea immediately and gives him oarlocks." "Joe," the priest told him, "let's you and me start saying a rosary. We need help." The seas were running high that day, with the air temperature around 50 degrees and the water temperature much colder. Even if men had made it off the ship, many would perish from hypothermia. The chaplain remembered waves up to forty feet, so high "...that we could look down on the skipper...of our rescue ship, that's a good 35 feet out of the water! And then we drop down to a point where you could see the ship's belly and the screw propellers churning empty air."

The sinking of the Mallory went unnoticed by other members of the convoy, including Roy L Raney, Captain of the Coast Guard Cutter Bibb. Raney was more than qualified for the job. He'd begun his career as a Navy pharmacist mate and moved on to the Coast Guard. He headed Coast Guard Air Station Salem before assuming command of the Bibb. In January 1943, the cutter left the Boston Navy Yard to join Convoy SC-118. Four hours after Mallory's sinking, the Bibb encountered a lifeboat. Commanded to keep up with the convoy, Raney deliberately disobeyed the order and went in search of survivors.[43]

Nearby, the USS Ingham arrived to assist, a crewman remembering, "I never saw anything like it, wood all over the place and bodies in life jackets...never saw so many dead fellows in my whole life."[44]

---

[43] Hartwell, Joe. *Sinking of USS Henry Mallory 2/7/1943.* tinyurl.com/227s29y2.

[44] *Bibb 1937.* USCG 2/23/2020. tinyurl.com/uau2nkv2.

Commander Roy L. Raney, USCG[45]

On the deck of the Bibb, Lt. Henry Keene was assisting survivors onto the ship when he heard Raney yelling, "Someone get that dammed dog!" Below, floating on a raft, was Rickey, a pet of Mallory's cook, George K. Dunningham of Winthrop. Keene threw a rope around himself, lowered down to the raft, and picked up the dog. Once Rickey was on board, he returned to his work of saving human lives.[46]

Over two hundred men were rescued from the frigid waters of the Atlantic that day. Captain Raney received the Navy Commendation Ribbon for saving the lives of the men of the USS Mallory. He later commanded USS Wakefield, making thirteen trips across the Atlantic carrying US servicemen to Europe and returning with German prisoners of war, and received a Bronze Medal for his efforts. Thankfully, Roy L. Raney returned from the war and, in 1954, became Commander of the First Coast Guard District in Boston.[47] Lt. Keene would also receive recognition. The American Humane Society and the Society for Prevention of Cruelty to Animals honored the Lieutenant for his valiant rescue of Rickey, the dog.[48]

Survivors from SS Henry R. Mallory being
picked up by USCGC Bibb. 1943.[49]

U-402 had a successful run on that cold February day. Under the command of Captain Seigfried von Forster, six ships from Convoy SC-118 were sent to watery graves, and a seventh followed the next

[45] *CDR Roy L. Raney, USCG cutter Bibb.* Pub domain photo. USCG. Facebook. tinyurl.com/mtacf359.

[46] Webster, W. Russell. *Someone get that damned dog!* Capt W. Russell Webster *11*/1996. tinyurl.com/5ys3dccb.

[47] *Vice Admiral Roy L. Raney.* USCG.

[48] Webster, W. Russell. *Someone get that damned dog!* 12/1996. USNI. tinyurl.com/3aacjw9a

[49] *Raft USCGC Bibb.* Pub domain photo. USCG. Hartwell, Joe. *SS Henry Mallory.* Rootsweb.com 10/10/2000. tinyurl.com/efpdrr2h.

day. The sub captain's luck ran out eight months later when U-402 was sent to the bottom with all hands by the American escort carrier USS Card under the command of Captain Arnold Isbell.[50] Sadly, Isbell, who is credited with ten U-boat kills, would not survive the war. While awaiting his next assignment, command of the USS Yorktown, he was temporarily placed on board another Essex class aircraft carrier, USS Franklin, where his life tragically ended along with over 700 other heroes.[51]

February 7, 1943, remains one of the blackest days in the annals of US Army Chaplain history. Five chaplains, Rev. Horace Gravely, Father James Liston, Rev. Ernest MacDonald, Father Valmore Savignac, and Rev. David Youngdahl, lost their lives in the sinking of the USS Mallory. Ira Bentley survived and, after discharge, returned to his home state of Texas, where he continued his career as a Baptist minister. Gerald Whelan also returned to the States after the war, eventually founding a new parish at Lookout Mountain in Georgia, where he passed away in 1985. He and Admiral Roy Raney remained friends for the rest of their lives.

At the end of the day, these servants of God were just men. They, too, had left home and family; they, too, stood amidst the whirring bullets and crashing bombs, and they, too, watched their comrades die. They counseled those who suffered from the emotional trauma of battle while they were suffering, too. Chaplain Hiro Higuchi wrote to his wife about the struggle to maintain control during the war. "...it's just hell—undreamable goriness and fear..." Seeing bodies of fallen warriors lining the roadway on his way to the front, he stated: "A few more weeks of this and I shall go mad." Maintaining a sense of humanity and "loving thy neighbor" was a challenge. Higuchi stated: "The more I come across German brutality—the less I like them and wish they were really wiped out of the map." From Chaplain Leo Weigel: Germans were "a menace that should be exterminated because [they] will not be checked any other way." And Chaplin Charles Suver who said mass on Iwo Jima: "I often found myself cursing (under my breath) the Japs and [I came] pretty close to hating them. Had any of them walked into the hospital tent, I would have been among the first to shoot..."[52]

Nothing, however, prepared these men of God for the depravity of the concentration camps. Max Eichorn, who served at Sinai Temple in Springfield for a time, was the first rabbi to enter Dachau and perform a religious service there.[53] He recalled walking in the footprints of Jewish martyrs. "We cried not merely tears of sorrow. We cried tears of hate." In an incredibly moving and courageous piece he wrote while at Dachau for the Jewish Welfare Board, he stated:

We stood aside and watched while these guards were beaten to death, beaten so badly that their bodies were ripped open and innards protruded. We watched with less feeling than if a dog were being beaten. In truth, it might be said that we were completely without feeling...These evil people, it seemed to us, were being treated exactly as they deserved to be treated. To such depths does human nature sink in the presence of human depravity.[54]

There were other chaplains whose names and stories are less recognizable. Father William J. Gallagher served at parishes in Worcester, Rochdale, Millville, Athol, and Baldwinville. During World War II, he worked with the French Resistance to help Allied prisoners escape from Nazi held territory. When he passed away at age 95 in 2012, he was the oldest priest in the Worcester Diocese.[55] Massachusetts born Jean Cossette saw extensive action in Europe, participating in five battles, and twice

---

[50] *U-402.* Uboat.net. tinyurl.com/5djzsb2n.

[51] *Arnold Jay Isbell.* Uboat.net. tinyurl.com/5b5amd29.

[52] Bernstein, Philip S. *Jewish Chaplains WWII.*

[53] Eichhorn, David Max. Encyclopedia.com. tinyurl.com/jfbs7m3t.

[54] Dorsett, Lyle W. *Serving God and Country.*

[55] *Fr. Gallagher, oldest priest, dies.* CFP 12/20/2012. tinyurl.com/3hrf2s4a.

earning a Bronze Star for bravery.[56] Father John McGovern of Boston was present as graves were dug at the first cemetery established in France in World War II. The coastline at Vierville-sur-Mer had been the scene of horrific fighting when the first wave of Operation Overlord hit Omaha Beach. More than 2,000 heroes lay temporarily interred in graves at the foot of a cliff awaiting burial at a permanent cemetery when the Chaplain conducted mass there.[57]

Rabbi Judah Nadich offers a prayer during a Jewish New Year celebration in London. To his left is Col. Moses Strock of Boston, Chief of Dental Services, Fifth General Hospital. 1943.[58]

Rabbi Judah Nadich enlisted in the US Army after Pearl Harbor and became the first Jewish Chaplain assigned to the European Theater. In 1945, after witnessing the horrible living conditions of former death camps prisoners, he was appointed by General Eisenhower as a special advisor on Jewish affairs. In this position, he was instrumental in securing relief for thousands of Jews who had been displaced by the war. Nadich later spent ten years as rabbi at Congregation Kehillath Israel in Brookline.[59] In 1939, the 40-year-old auxiliary Bishop of Boston was named Military Vicar for the United States. Having been rejected by the military who decided he was "too short, had a bad disposition and was not attentive to orders," Cardinal Francis Spellman, a native of Whitman, advocated for American involvement in the war and was a vocal supporter of those in uniform, making multiple trips to visit troops throughout his career. After the war, he became Archbishop of New York.[60]

[56] *Men In Service.* Fitchburg Sentinel 1/11/1946. Newspapers.com. tinyurl.com/yn7usfnt.

[57] *European Theater.* Chaplain Kit. tinyurl.com/2yvwxzuv.

[58] *Jewish New Year 1943.* Pub domain photo. IWM. Wiki Commons. tinyurl.com/5fkmvk6r.

[59] Levin, Shira Nadich and Levin, James. *Judah Nadich.* B'Nai Jeshurun. 10/4/2014. tinyurl.com/yt8d4hv9.

[60] *Cardinal Francis Spellman.* American Legion. tinyurl.com/y3293vnf.

By the end of World War II, over 10,000 members of the clergy had served as chaplains in all branches of the military. They sustained the third highest percentage of casualties of any group in the service of their country, and earned 2,453 decorations including one Congressional Medal of Honor.[61] After the war, Admiral Chester Nimitz, who held chaplains in high regard, uttered words that provide a lasting and fitting tribute for these servants of God.

By his patient, sympathetic labors with men day in, day out, and through many a night, every Chaplain I know contributed immeasurably to the moral courage of our fighting men. None of this effort appears in the statistics. Most of it was necessarily secret between pastor and his confidant. It is for that toil in the cause both of God and country that I honor the Chaplain most.

A chaplain celebrates mass for Marines on Guam.[62]

---

[61] *Combat Chaplains.* U-S-HISTORY.COM. tinyurl.com/2yz4ppn5.

[62] *Mass on Guam.* Pub domain photo. Chaplain Corps UA 17.01. NHHC. tinyurl.com/hauahcpk.

Chapter 14

Women at War

Women who stepped up were measured as citizens of the nation, not as women...This was a people's war, and everyone was in it.
Col. Oveta Culp Hobby
Director, Women's Auxiliary Army Corps[1]

Natalie Hays Hammond was a bit of a free thinker. Creativity ran deep in the Hammond family. Her brother, John Jr., was an inventor who'd been mentored by Thomas Edison and dabbled in radio waves so successfully that he earned the title, "Father of the Remote Control." In the 1920's, brother John built Hammond Castle in Gloucester, a town which Natalie would later call home. The young woman found a place in the world of art as a painter, collector, and costume and set designer.

When war broke out in Europe, Hammond decided to travel to England to organize civilians in defense of their country. The British Government said no thank you. Not to be put off, Natalie turned to residents of her town and formed the Gloucester Civil Patrol. The mission of the group was to prepare young women to handle air raids in the event that Gloucester was attacked. Unfortunately for Natalie, enemy bombers seemed to show little interest in the fishing town, so the organization came to an end. She switched to teaching communications and transportation skills to the women of Gloucester in the hopes that they would reach out to other communities and share their knowledge. This time, the project was a hit, and Natalie quickly promoted herself to colonel. In spite of bumps in the road (due to membership, which included many socialites, obeying orders wasn't always a priority, and the Abercrombie & Fitch designed uniforms were a little pricey for the average member), Governor Saltonstall gave thumbs up to the newly named Massachusetts Women's Defense Corps in May of 1941.[2]

Natalie Hayes Hammond[3]

---

[1] Hobby, Oveta Culp. *Women who stepped up...* Quote. *Oveta Culp Hobby.* Texas Originals. tinyurl.com/nhf5mrdp.

[2] *WWII Women's Defense Corps.* Cape Ann Mus Lib & Arch. tinyurl.com/2db6pk7d.

[3] *Natale Hayes Hammond.* Pub domain photo. LOC 2014719297. Wiki Commons. tinyurl.com/62yy6c55.

Eight months later, over 100 MWDC schools were operating across the state. Women were trained in first aid, transportation, communications, canteen management, and air raid precautions. During a March 1942 event in Maynard,

The women conducted a drill involving a convoy of twelve cars. The women drove to a rendezvous site in Clinton, where their final test was a tire change. Mrs. Louis Boeske was complimented for her speed at this skill. She replied that she had spent many years in and around cars with her husband.[4]

By the end of 1942, however, trouble was brewing. One *Boston Globe* article reported that members had expressed concerns over "bitterness" and "squabbling" within the organization. Complaints also mentioned that the Women's Defense Corps had "too much 'Boston' and "too much 'society.'"[5] (Members were encouraged to join the physical training course at the Elizabeth Arden Salon on Newbury Street in Boston.)[6] In spite of the controversy, praise for the first-ever women's defense group in the country flowed in, and membership continued to grow. It all came crashing to a halt when reports began to surface that a few members had used Defense Corps gasoline to attend a private function at the Copley Plaza Hotel in Boston. J.W. Farley, Director of the State Public Safety Committee under whose umbrella the MDWC now fell, was not amused. Hammond was ousted and, to really throw fire at the fumes, replaced by a man.[7]

Hammond did her best to prove the adage, "Hell hath no fury like a woman scorned." From the Berkshires to the Atlantic shore, newspapers put out article after article tracking the feud between Hammond and her nemesis, Farley. Hundreds of Defense Corps members resigned in protest, MWDC guards were posted at the doors of Hammond's office, and furniture and files were removed. Farley made his opinion of the former director clear: "Miss Hammond was suffering from the Hitler complex—a complex of field boots and favorites."[8] By the time all the roaring and thunder died down, Hammond was still out, relegated to the role of assistant to the new commander, and the Women's Defense Corps began to fade as new organizations offered more attractive roles for women who wanted to serve.

The concept of using women in support roles during wartime was not new to the United States. As far back as the Revolutionary War, women acted as nurses, seamstresses, and cooks for the Army. Nearly a thousand women would support troops during the War Between the States. The role of women changed in World War I. For the first time, they became part of an Army Nurse Corps, the Navy inducted women as yeomen for clerical work, and "Hello Girls," telephone and switchboard operators, became members of the Army Signal Corps. At the outset of World War II, recognizing the important work being done by women in England, the Secretary of War moved forward with a similar plan for the US Army. Development went quickly until it hit a sizable obstacle...Congress. Enter the indomitable Representative from Massachusetts, Edith Nourse Rogers.

The decision made by Edith's parents to move from Maine to Lowell changed the young eleven-year-old's life. Her father, a mill manager, exposed his bright, inquisitive daughter to the blue-collar world of the textile industry, an experience that would influence her for the rest of her days. Educated at Rogers Hall, a private school in Lowell, she married lawyer John Jacob Rogers. Rogers served in the US House of Representatives for a dozen years before passing away at age forty-three. One week later, Edith launched a campaign to replace her husband in Congress.

---

[4] *Women and WWII.* Maynard Life Outdoors/Hidden History Maynard, 7/31/2019. tinyurl.com/44bdh8e8.

[5] *Defense Corps Resent Boston Domination.* Boston Globe 1/21/1943. Newspapers.com. tinyurl.com/ynen9rjd.

[6] *Arden Salon.* Photo caption. Boston Globe 11/18/1941. Newspapers.com. tinyurl.com/ywpsm9yn.

[7] *Lane Heads Women's Defense Corps.* Daily Item 1/9/943. Newspapers.com. tinyurl.com/ypjw54am.

[8] *Public Safety Hearing.* Berkshire Eagle 3/12/1943. Newspapers.com. tinyurl.com/bdhj88ra.

Rogers certainly wasn't the front runner. No woman had ever been sent to Washington from Massachusetts, and it seemed unlikely she'd be the first. In the Republican Primary, she faced well known politician James Grimes, who had previously held a seat in the Massachusetts Senate. On the Democratic ticket, the sole candidate was Bostonian Eugene N. Foss, a wealthy businessman whose record had more than its share of ups and downs. Enrolled at the University of Vermont, he failed to achieve a degree. He lost his bid for a position in Congress several times, running as a Republican and later switching to the Democratic Party. Finally successful in his bid for governorship of Massachusetts, he spent three terms in office before being defeated for reelection. An interesting conversation between Grimes and Foss appeared in the *Boston Globe* prior to the primary.

"Jim," said Gov. Foss, "it looks very much as if you will be my opponent on the Republican-end in this fight, and I congratulate you...But however, I shall cut down your majority severely in the last analysis, as the count of the votes will show."
"Of course, Governor," replied Ex-Senator Grimes, "there is no question about my winning both the nomination and the election, and I hope you and I will be just as good friends after the contest as we are today..."[9]

Unfortunately for the pair of swaggering politicos, things turned out a bit differently. Rogers wiped out Grimes in the primary, taking 13,000 of the 15,000 votes, and when the special election was held, Foss went down with only 28 percent of the votes. Edith Nourse Rogers became the first woman from Massachusetts to enter the hallowed male-dominated halls of Congress, commenting, "I hope that everyone will forget I am a woman as soon as possible."[10]

Having visited field hospitals during World War I, Rogers understood the exhaustive efforts of nurses at war and knew what women had to offer. She quickly joined the effort to include women in the Army. On May 28, 1941, she addressed the House of Representatives.

It is proposed to employ the Women's Army Auxiliary Corps in noncombatant service in positions for which women are better qualified than men, and on such other duties to assist in the national defense...intelligent women can be used to release intelligent men for more intensive work...providing a means to the women of the country to demonstrate their patriotism...

She suggested an organization made up of 25,000 female volunteers, ages 21-45, to act in a variety of roles: pharmacists, technicians, therapists, clerks, cooks, chauffeurs, messengers, and instrument repairers. Perhaps the most radical expectation in the bill was that women should actually be paid for their work. In addition to a salary, women would receive medical care, compensation for injuries, and be provided with uniforms. They would not be enlisted members of the Army but a separate branch, the Women's Army Auxiliary Corps, whose mission would be to support the Army.

The space of time it took for the bill to come to a vote was filled with often heated debate. At its core were two seminal issues. The first, stated in no uncertain terms by Clare Hoffman, Congressman from Michigan, was that women belonged in the home. The second concern unsurprisingly dealt with men. The possibility existed that women would replace men in the workplace, a somewhat understandable notion in 1941, as women were doing just that, making a remarkable impact on industries engaged in war production. Congressman Frank Hook of Michigan went one step further, stating that men would lose their dignity if women joined the Army, and his colleague, Andrew Somers of New York, described the bill as "revolting... to [his] sense of Americanism" and "decency."[11]

---

[9] *Foss Visits Grimes.* Boston Globe 6/12/1925. Newspapers.com. tinyurl.com/2ftn59be.

[10] Wasniewski, Matthew, Ed. *Women in Congress.* Comm House Admin House Reps. US GPO 2006.

[11] Karamcheti, Meena. *WAAC At Tradition.* Menlo School. tinyurl.com/yx5af3aw.

When Congress reconvened on March 17, 1942 following a lengthy discussion encompassing twenty-eight pages of the Congressional Record, Rogers emerged victorious. Sixty-seven percent of members voting including 100 percent of the Massachusetts delegation approved the bill, and the Women's Army Auxiliary Corps (WAAC) was born.[12] President Roosevelt signed the bill into law two months later, and Texan Oveta Culp Hobby was appointed to lead the new organization.

Congresswoman Edith Nourse Rogers: the
first woman to formally open and close a session
of the US House of Representatives. January 1929.[13]

For most women, the experience was new and different and exciting. Many went into roles which reflected their former lives as civilians. Mary Regan, a former Grafton teacher from West Roxbury, became an instructor for new WAACs.[14] Alberta Holdsworth gave up a successful job as an underwear buyer at Jordan Marsh to join up and became a member of the first graduating class of WAACs. She was assigned to Washington, D.C. to work in the Army's Service Supply Group.[15] Others found new skills. Chelsea native Thelma Sherman Kardon enjoyed the experience and stepped up to the challenge. Kardon would later say, "The training was fantastic. It put me on my shoulders, told me what to do. I took everything in..."[16] She served in the Military Police.

Francis Keegan Marquis of West Newbury was a graduate of Simmons in Boston. The young woman showed an early interest in women's issues and worked for Boston's Franklin Square House. Keegan joined the WAACs in July of 1942 and led one of the first US Army women's expeditionary forces in World War II. The 149th WAAC Post Headquarters Company was assigned to Eisenhower's headquarters in Algiers. The North Africa campaign was still ongoing, and women went to work with anti-aircraft guns and bombs booming around them.[17]

Mary Hallaren of Lowell achieved a first for the Army. In July 1943, Capt. Hallaren commanded the very first WAAC battalion to be assigned to Europe. Their impact was so important to the war effort that the decision was made to recruit American women living outside of the United States. Lucille N.

---

[12] *WAACs.* Cong Record House 3/17/1942. CONGRESS.GOV. tinyurl.com/ymd84b2f.

[13] *Congresswoman makes history.* 01/01/1929. Pub domain photo. LOC. Picryl. tinyurl.com/2y5rywjz.

[14] *Nell Giles Finds WAACS...* Boston Daily Globe 9/10/1942. Newspapers.com. tinyurl.com/3mknfnj8.

[15] Giles, Nell. *WAACS Entrain for Posts.* Boston Globe 9/16/1942. Newspapers.com. tinyurl.com/4yavy997.

[16] *Thelma Kardon.* IA's WWII Stories. IA PBS 2006. tinyurl.com/bddbzvyw.

[17] *Frances Keegan Marquis.* West Newbury. Westnewbury.org. tinyurl.com/4p7a79mb.

Hall of Auburndale, living in England at the time, became the first. Most WAACs worked in clerical positions, but the role played by telephone operators was crucial. Navigating complicated networks of phone lines, women transmitted orders from headquarters to commanders in the field. The timing was crucial. WAACs like Sally McCaffrey of Jamaica Plain and Laura Carson of Chicopee Falls worked long, tension-filled hours in all types of weather conditions, with one group operating in a flooded wine cellar.[18]

The WAACs were up and running, but Edith Nourse Rogers wasn't done yet. She continued to advocate for women in the Army, and in July 1943, with the approval of Franklin Delano Roosevelt, the WAACs became the Women's Army Corps, no longer auxiliary but an official part of the US Army Reserves. Approximately 100,000 women served as WACs in domestic and overseas roles during the war. Rogers had paved the way for women in the military. The flood gates now opened, the Navy, Marines, and Coast Guard would soon follow suit.

One of the first official photographs of women in the military,
(L-R) US Army Nurse Corps, US Navy Nurse Corps, US Navy
WAVES, and US Army WAACs. Lt. Alberta M. Holdsworth
of Boston stands at the far right. 1942.[19]

In 1917, Secretary of the Navy Josephus Daniels found a loophole in the one-year-old Naval Act which allowed "all persons who may be capable of performing special useful service for coastal defense" to become members of the Naval Reserve. For Daniels, whose country was about to enter the First World War, that meant using women to take over the jobs of men who were needed at sea. Less than three weeks before Congress declared war, women began enlisting. These Yeoman (F) or "Yeomanettes" were primarily assigned to clerical duties, but soon afterwards their role expanded. It seems women were capable of driving trucks and fixing them, breaking codes, and making munitions. By 1921, their services no longer needed, the last yeoman was discharged.

In spite of their positive track record during the Great War, as the US moved closer to its next conflict, the Navy didn't exactly welcome women with open arms. Admiral Chester Nimitz was hesitant when approached by Edith Nourse Rogers about establishing a female branch of the Navy. He opted to check with departments under his command. Only two gave a thumbs up, and it was observed that others

---

[18] *WAC in ETO.* Lone Sentry. LONESENTRY.COM. tinyurl.com/3ztxs8vd.

[19] *Uncle Sam's nieces.* Pub domain photo. Office War Info 1/1/1942. LOC. tinyurl.com/ysvv6zzk.

"...would prefer to enroll monkeys, dogs, or ducks." However, the WACs were making a positive impact on public opinion, and the Navy saw the handwriting on the wall. Soon, Secretary of the Navy Frank Knox requested that women be allowed to enlist in the Naval Reserves. Much debate followed. Congress preferred women to form an auxiliary group like the WACs. From Edith Nourse Rogers' home state, Senator David I. Walsh of Clinton was a force to be reckoned with. A former Massachusetts governor and long-time member of the United States Senate, Walsh had no problem voicing his opinion. When it came to women in the Navy, his opinion fell somewhere in the vicinity of American society and civilization in general, meeting an apocalyptic demise should women be allowed in.[20]

For advice the Navy turned to the Dean of Barnard College, Virginia Gildersleeve, a well-known educator and activist for advancing the role of her sisters in society. She established a long-lasting relationship with Massachusetts native and Barnard professor Elizabeth Reynard, who summered with her on Cape Cod. Gildersleeve would spend the latter part of her life in Centerville.[21] Her efforts on behalf of the Navy paid off. With a stroke of the pen in July 1942, the President created Women Accepted for Volunteer Emergency Service. While the WACs had laid the foundation, their status was as an auxiliary group that worked alongside the Army. WAVES were actual members of the US Naval Reserves.

WAVE Mary Lyons of Wilbraham on
duty in New York City. WWII.[22]

Waiting in the wings was Mildred McAfee, President of Wellesley College. Shortly after creation of the WAVES, McAfee took a leave of absence from the College and became the first woman in American history to achieve officer ranking in the US Navy. She was appointed Director of WAVES, and one of her first acts was to select Elizabeth Reynard as second in command. (The young woman had been approached by the Navy several months before to find a name for the new group. Thankfully, Reynard nixed suggested "swans," "gobettes," and "sailorettes" in favor of the more nautical "Women Accepted for Volunteer Emergency Service.")[23] Lt. Reynard was given a crucial task, to find a location suitable for the Navy training program. After visiting naval sites across the country, Reynard determined that the best choice for officer candidates was Smith College in Northampton, Massachusetts.

---

[20] Godson, Susan H. *Waves WWII*. USNI 12/1981. tinyurl.com/yde5n9eb.

[21] McCaughey. *Virginia Gildersleeve*. CU 1981. tinyurl.com/3c2awth5.

[22] *Mary Lyons* 1/1/1943. Pub domain photo. 80-G-27800 NARA. NHHC. tinyurl.com/mvcze7cz.

[23] Godson, Susan H. *Waves WWII*.

Lt. Commander Mildred H. McAfee.[24]

The campus wasn't quite ready when the first WAVES arrived for training at the new United States Naval Reserve Midshipmen School in August of 1942. Bunk beds were still being moved into dormitories. Dining facilities were limited at the college, so the nearby Hotel Northampton volunteered for the job, and the now-empty dining halls became classrooms. Studies prepared women for technical jobs in communications, navigation, and mechanics, for a specific few cryptology, and for all, Navy protocol. Just like men, they were being prepared to assume official roles as officers of the United States Navy. If the men learned to identify enemy aircraft, so did they. Standards were high for these women, and one would later recall how taxing final exams were. Apparently, the story went, the first WAVES officers had outscored their male counterparts at Annapolis, so the Navy upped the ante for the women. Said Alex Asal, in an article for Smith College, "The WAVES, it seems, were supposed to relieve men for sea duty, not show them up."[25]

WAVES officers marching down
Garden Street in Cambridge. 1943.[26]

The Navy operated specialty schools across the country where women trained after their initial indoctrination into the service. Harvard and Radcliffe in Cambridge held Supply Corps courses. At Lakehurst, New Jersey, Kathleen Scott Robertson, a native of Norwood, became a parachute rigger. The task performed by the PRs was crucial. Proper packing, repairing, and maintenance of parachutes translated into saving lives. The Navy made the questionable assumption that women were well suited to this job due to their innate ability to operate sewing machines. (Apparently, 90 percent had never used one before). What the Navy did not believe, however, was that women were capable of passing the course

[24] *Mildred McAfee.* Pub domain photo. USN. NARA 80-G-K-13616-A. NHHC. tinyurl.com/3j69t7et.

[25] Asal, Alex. *Learning to Be Navy.* Smith College 6/11/2019. tinyurl.com/33j49796.

[26] *Waves Cambridge, MA 1943.* Pub domain photo. NHHC. Bedell-Burke, Margie. *WAVES Marching Cambridge.* Women WWII. tinyurl.com/6wbzkfjm.

final exam, which called for a parachute jump using chutes they had packed themselves. Thus, they were excluded from the jump. This didn't sit well with Kathleen, one of the first seven women to enlist in the WAVES. Eventually earning the right, in 1944, she became the first WAVE to successfully execute a 2,000-foot free-fall parachute jump from a Douglas R4D.[27]

The contribution made by WAVES during World War II is astounding. They assumed roles in medicine, aviation, technology, meteorology, and communications. WAVES were used as gunnery and navigation instructors for men. By the end of the conflict, nearly 100,000 women had served. Smith College had done its part, training over 8,000 women for the Navy, 200 of whom graduated from Smith.[28] After the war, Mildred McAfee married Rev. Dr. Douglas Horton, Dean of the Harvard Divinity School, returned to her post as President of Wellesley College, and became nationally recognized for her ecumenical work. She passed away in New Hampshire in 1994. Elizabeth Reynaud returned to Barnard College and became an author. She died at age 64 and is buried beside Virginia Gildersleeve in Bedford, New York.[29]

The US Coast Guard falls under jurisdiction of the Department of the Navy during times of war, so when FDR established a women's reserve branch for the Navy, a similar organization for the Coast Guard soon followed. The journey to admit women into the organization seems to have been a bit less tortuous than for the Army and the Navy. WACs were already at their posts and WAVES at Midshipman School by the time the first recruits made their way to Oklahoma for training. (The first officers trained at Smith College.) They were known as SPARS, an acronym for the Coast Guard motto, "Semper Paratus Always Ready." The name was chosen by their director, Lt. Commander Dorothy Stratton, who felt that WORCOGS (Women's Reserve of the Coast Guard) was a bit confusing. The former dean at Purdue University who had been a member of the initial class in Northampton was appointed as the first SPAR on November 23, 1942, one day after the program was signed into law.

Most SPAR recruits were 22-years-old with a high school education, most officers twenty-nine with a college degree, and according to the US Coast Guard, "The chances were good that she came from Massachusetts, New York, Pennsylvania, Illinois, Ohio or California."[30] Requirements for the job were pretty much standard among female reservists.

59 inches in height, 95 pounds in proportion to general build. Defective vision not due to organic disease is acceptable, provided it is corrected with glasses to 20/20 or better for each eye. Applicants must be able to distinguish whispered words at 15 feet. Teeth must meet specified standards.

As with most other branches of the military, the majority of women assumed clerical duties. Many SPARs, however, became boatswains mates, coxswains, and radiomen. A few worked as pharmacist's mates. Aviation opportunities were limited. Less than fifty women became parachute riggers, navigators, and air traffic controllers. The big history-making story for SPARS in Massachusetts, however, involved the quaint town of Chatham, Massachusetts.

A Coast Guard station had operated along the Chatham shoreline since 1872. With the onset of war, the station was very much in the business of scanning the horizon for U-boats. In 1942, with the development of the LORAN navigation system, the Chatham Coast Guard Station became the site of Unit 21, part of the country's ultra-secret LORAN network. (Following his long tour of duty with the Coast Guard in the Pacific, Roger Kehm of South Dakota was sent to District Coast Guard Headquarters in Boston for reassignment to Unit 21. Kehm had never heard of the Unit, and when he asked where it

---

[27] *Kathleen Culp.* FL Womens Hall Fame. tinyurl.com/54seskvp.

[28] Asal, Alex. *Learning to Be Navy.*

[29] *Elizabeth Reynard.* Find Grave ID 25898265. 4/9/2008. tinyurl.com/4dwr4sjw.

[30] *SPARS.* USCG. tinyurl.com/2u8tsm68.

was located, he was told Fredrichsdal, Greenland. Even three months after the war ended, LORAN was still a well-kept secret.)[31]

Soon after Unit 21 was up and running, it occurred to the Coast Guard that there really wasn't any reason why women couldn't monitor LORAN information. So in 1944, Lt. Vera Hamerschlag and eleven women under her command arrived in Chatham. Hamerschlag had been introduced to the LORAN during its development at the MIT RAD Lab, and she and a second SPAR were sent to the school for a crash course. Secrecy was of the utmost importance, so much so that all notebooks and coursework were confiscated at the end of each day, and even the instructor had no idea why these two women had joined the all-male classes. One male Coast Guard officer speculated that they had qualified for the job because of their "ability to keep their mouths shut."[32]

SPAR Anita Freeman was stationed at
CG Unit 21 in Chatham. WWII.[33]

When the SPARS arrived in Chatham, the station was staffed completely by men. Within one month, all but one would be replaced by women, and, six months after that, he too would be gone. The tiny fifty by thirty-foot building held an operations room, sleeping quarters, office space, and repair shop. Outside, a 125' mast supported the station antenna. SPARS were issued guns and given the order to shoot any unauthorized person who entered the building. They worked 24 hours a day receiving and recording signals every two minutes. It is reported that the all-female unit was the only one of its kind in the country.

Despite the need to conceal the work of Unit 21, the presence of the SPARS did not go unnoticed. Radioman 3rd Class Anita Freeman recalled, "Everybody hated us. They thought we were snobs because we couldn't talk to anybody."[34] Apparently, not everyone. The Detroit native would marry Sulli Eldridge[35] and remain a resident of Cape Cod, working in her daughter's Chatham restaurant, Sandi's Diner, for twenty-five years.[36] Radio technician 1st Class Marina Simmons married her husband Ray in

[31] Kehm, Roger. *Roger Kehm LORAN service.* LORAN history. tinyurl.com/ms9nxu8.

[32] *Long Blue Line.* My CG. USCG 3/12/2021. tinyurl.com/bdbn8ra7.

[33] *Anita Freeman.* Pub domain photo. *Long Blue Line.* My CG. USCG 3/12/2021. tinyurl.com/bdbn8ra.

[34] *Long Blue Line.* My CG.

[35] *Anita Freeman Eldridge.* FamilySearch. tinyurl.com/um7ky977.

[36] Foster, Stephanie. *On the job with Mom.* Cape Experience. Cape Codder 5/6/2005.

May of 1944 at the local Methodist Church.[37] J. Richard Kraycir of the Chatham Marconi Maritime Center stated: "There was no question that a war was going on if you lived in Chatham. The Navy was at the RCA station, the SPARS were busy at the Coast Guard Station, RADAR was being erected on Stepping Stones, and the hotels were filled with military personnel. Blackouts were in force, the USO was in town, and of course, there was a very busy laundry for uniforms!"[38]

During World War II, 10,000 women enlisted in the US Coast Guard Reserves. They were stationed in every USCG district with the exception of Puerto Rico. By 1946, the SPARs had disbanded. They had accomplished much, and their lives were changed forever. "I wanted to stay," said one former SPAR, "but unlike male servicemen who were offered the opportunity to re-enlist, we women were told we had to get out."[39] To honor their service, in 1944 the USCG cutter SPAR was launched with homeports in Boston, Woods Hole, Maine, and Rhode Island.

SPARS, Boston USCG District.
VJ day, 1945.[40]

In 1834, Congress placed the proud men of the Marine Corps along with the separate but equal sailors of the Navy under one umbrella, the United States Department of the Navy. Marines (the name literally referring to the sea) had been going to war on American ships since 1775. Marines have fought alongside John Paul Jones, raised swords on the shores of Tripoli, and stood their ground at Chateau Thierry and Belleau Woods. And for over two hundred years, the US Navy has provided the transportation that enabled Marines to place boots on the ground in battlefields across the globe. The association has been so successful that today Annapolis produces officers for both groups, and it is rumored that all good sports-loving Marines root for the sailors at the annual Army-Navy football game.

Therefore, when FDR signed the law allowing women to enlist in the Naval Reserves, included in the legislation was a provision for the Marines. Only the framework had been established, however. The Marines had no plans, nothing on the drawing board, and they weren't ready to accept women into their ranks just yet. The leading opponent was none other than Marine Corps Commandant General

[37] *Long Blue Line.* My CG.

[38] *Chatham WWII.* Cape Cod Mus Trail 9/2020. tinyurl.com/3absmjuk.

[39] Military Spouse Team. *Women of WWII.* Military Spouse. tinyurl.com/34zarev8.

[40] *Bos personnel VJ day.* Pub domain photo. USCG 190530-G-G0000-3018. tinyurl.com/2u8tsm68.

Thomas Holcomb. His opinions on the subject were so well known that an incident which occurred at a dinner party on the evening that Holcomb changed his mind have become legend. When the General rose from his seat to announce that he planned to welcome women into the fold, a portrait of Archibald Henderson, 5th Commandant of the Marine Corps, promptly fell off the wall and landed smack on the table in front of him.

The war was less than a year old, and the General was facing mounting pressure to find enough Marines to send into battle. The evidence provided by the WAC and WAVES programs in freeing up able-bodied men was irrefutable. So, for the good of the Corps, he forged ahead and addressed the issue with the Secretary of the Navy, stating women should be used in noncombatant roles, thus releasing men for combat duty. Unexpectedly, he became somewhat of a champion for the women, who were, after all, Marines. When searching for a nickname for the group, the General rejected "Glamarines," "Dainty Devil-Dogs," and "Sub-Marines." "They are Marines. They don't have a nickname, and they don't need one…They inherit the traditions of Marines. They are Marines." In a very no-nonsense Marine way, they became known as WRs (Women Reservists).[41] Entry of women into the world of the all-male Marines wasn't without growing pains. When Holcomb learned that WRs were being referred to as "BAMs" ("Big-Ass Marines"), he responded strongly: "Officers and men of the Marine Corps treat members of the Women's Reserve with disrespect…This conduct…indicates a laxity in discipline which will not be tolerated."[42]

The Corps had moved cautiously toward the issue of women in their ranks (picture walking in stockinged feet over broken glass in a darkened room), and by the time Holcomb accepted women, the Marines had some catching up to do. They approached Anne Adams Lentz, who had been consulted on uniform designs for WACs, to assist in creating outfits for female Marines. The former Holyoke resident had been a designer for Best & Co. in New York.[43] The collaboration was successful, and nearly six months after the legislation was signed by FDR, Anne Adams Lentz became the first woman inducted into the United States Marine Corps Reserves.

Two weeks later, Ruth Cheeney Streeter became the second. A native of Brookline and graduate of Bryn Mawr College, Streeter was a licensed pilot who felt she had something to contribute to the war effort. At age 47, she approached the Womens Auxiliary Ferrying Squadron. After being rejected four times due to her advanced age, she decided to try the WAVES but opted not to accept a grounded position as a flight instructor. Shortly afterward, on the recommendation of Virginia Gildersleeve, General Thomas Holcomb offered Streeter the position as head of the Marine Corps Women's Reserve.

The Marine Corps began routinely accepting women into their Reserves in February of 1943. It was good timing. The Japanese had just been evicted from Guadalcanal at the cost of 1,600 Marine lives and nearly 5,000 wounded. Approximately 1,000 women who would "Free a Man to Fight" joined the Marines during the following month.[44] The first step for Women Reservists was training. Falling under the Department of the Navy, WR officers trained in the WAVES programs at Smith College and Mount Holyoke College in South Hadley. Ernestine Stowell was a senior at Mount Holyoke when the Marines arrived. She was so impressed that she joined the Corps after graduation. Stowell worked in intelligence during World War II and remained with the Marines for thirty years, retiring in 1981 with the rank of Colonel.[45]

<hr>

[41] *It's Your War Too.* Nat WWII Mus 3/13/2020. tinyurl.com/mp4m2xs3.

[42] *Marine Corps Women's Reserve.* Pritzker Military Mus Lib. tinyurl.com/ur8z25ua.

[43] *Lenz Designs Uniforms.* Transcript-TG 12/29/1943. Newspapers.com. tinyurl.com/ytv6weuy.

[44] Stremlow, Mary. *Free Marine To Fight.* 1994. MCHC. tinyurl.com/3c84hs6m.

[45] *Ernestine Stowell.* Beers Story Funeral Home 7/27/2017. Legacy.com. tinyurl.com/7mu9vvj6.

The first group of Women Marine Corps Officer
Candidates at Mount Holyoke College. 1943.[46]

Massachusetts women made significant contributions to the Marine Corps. In addition to Lentz and Streeter, E. Louise Stewart, a graduate of Wellesley College, was one of the first five women to join. She became a poster child for recruitment when her picture was featured on the cover of Collier's magazine in 1943.[47] Charlotte D. Gower held a degree from Smith College. During the war, Gower was recruited by Wild Bill Donovan for his secret Office of Strategic Services and, with the founding of the CIA in 1947, became one of its first officers. Winchester native Julia Hamblet became a Marine in April 1943 and trained with the first class at Mount Holyoke College. She spent six years in the Corps, rising to the rank of Colonel. In 1946, she was named director of the MCWR.[48]

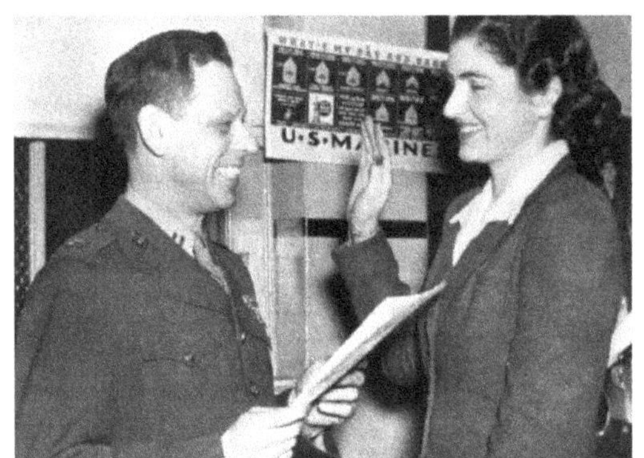
Julia Hamblet is sworn in as a US Marine
Corps Women's Reservist. 1943.[49]

By the end of World War II, the roles filled by the women of the Marine Corps Women's Reserves were diverse thanks to Major Streeter, who at the outset asked that WRs be trained in "anything except heavy lifting and combat." The National Parks Service reports on the dizzying list of their accomplishments:

...radio operators, photographers, parachute riggers, motor transport drivers, aerial gunnery instructors, cooks, bakers, Link trainer instructors, control tower operators, motion picture technicians, automotive mechanics, teletype operators, cryptographers, laundry managers, post-exchange salespersons and managers, auditors, audio-visual librarians, assembly and repair mechanics,

---

[46] *Women Marine Candidates.* Pub domain photo. USMC. Wiki Commons. tinyurl.com/yc7hr9wk.

[47] *E. Louise Stewart.* WMA 8/6/2013. tinyurl.com/k9b6xprs.

[48] Schudel, Matt. *Julia E Hamblet.* Wash Post 4/25/2017. tinyurl.com/yj3kwyca.

[49] *Julia E. Hamblet.* Pub domain photo. USMC. Stremlow, Mary. *Free Marine to Fight.*

metalsmiths, weather observers, artists, aerial photographers, photograph analysts, chemists, postal clerks, musicians, statisticians, stewardesses, and writers.[50]

The Marine Corps Women's Reserves was disbanded in September 1946, and over 18,000 women hung up their uniforms and made their way home.

It can only be supposed that Hannah Lincoln Harkness had a wild streak. As a child, Nancy, as she was called by her father, had a habit of jumping out second-story windows into snowbanks. In spite of their disapproval, the young lady from Michigan convinced her affluent parents to pay for flying lessons, and by the age of sixteen, Harkness had her pilot's license. Flying wasn't exactly a popular hobby for teenage girls in the1930s, so when the peaceful campus of the prestigious Milton Academy in Massachusetts was disrupted by the buzz of a low-flying aircraft, no one suspected that it was one of their own young ladies. Apparently, Nancy had decided to do a fly-by over a local boys' school with a quick side trip to the Academy but came in low, knocking shingles off the chapel roof.[51] "The Flying Freshman" moved on to Vassar, but her life took a serious turn when the Depression hit, and she was forced to drop out. Unwilling to leave her love of flying behind, she took a job in Boston selling airplanes. Soon afterward, she met and married Robert Love, founder of Boston's Inter-City Air Lines, and became a pilot for the company.[52]

A *Boston Globe* article announced the nuptials. "Miss Harkness, who is barely over 20 and who is little and very pretty, can smile wisely to herself. For now, she wears a sizable and very sparkling diamond ring on her left hand, and she is engaged to the president of Inter-City Air Lines, Robert Love, son of a New York banker." There was so much more to Nancy Harkness, however than a ring on her finger. The Bureau of Air Commerce (forerunner to the Federal Aviation Agency) saw a use for her talents and hired her as a test pilot. When the Air Marking Program was created to provide pilots with navigational markers on easy-to-see buildings and land formations, Nancy was called to help out. In Massachusetts alone, nearly three hundred markers were placed by Harkness.[53]

By 1942, Nancy had been considering ways for female pilots to contribute to the war effort for quite some time, and she developed a plan to use women to transport planes from production lines to military bases, thus making more men available for active duty. She knew of nearly fifty qualified female pilots. "I really think this list is up to handling pretty complicated stuff. Most of them have in the neighborhood of a thousand hours or more, mostly more, and have flown a great many types of ships." General Hap Arnold's opinion was clear: "The use of women pilots serves no military purpose."[54]

Harkness, however, had several things working in her favor. She had the support of Lt. Col. Robert Olds, who was in the process of setting up a Ferrying Command using male pilots. She was persistent, and, unbeknownst to her, she had Eleanor Roosevelt behind her. Long a supporter of women taking on new roles in society, the First Lady had been approached by aviator Jackie Cochran with a pitch to allow female pilots to operate in support roles in the military. On September 1, 1942, in her syndicated newspaper column "My Day," Roosevelt wrote:

The CAA [Civil Aeronautics Authority] says that women are psychologically not fitted to be pilots, but I see pictures every now and then of women who are teaching men to fly...It seems to me that in the Civil Air Patrol and in our own ferry command, women, if they can pass the tests imposed upon men, should have an equal opportunity for non-combat service. I believe in this case, if the war goes on long enough, and women are patient, opportunity will come knocking at their doors. However, there is just a chance

---

[50] Stremlow, Mary. *Free Marine To Fight.*

[51] McCutcheon, Mary. *Love Plying the Sky.* Milton Mag 3/22/2017. tinyurl.com/yaf24ach.

[52] Brady, Janis. *Migrant Story.* NPS 4/6/2022. tinyurl.com/2rwhncy9.

[53] *Nancy Harkness Love.* Vassar Encyc. Vassar. tinyurl.com/3hw7k4ta.

[54] *Establishing Women's AF Service Pilots.* Am Experience PBS. tinyurl.com/4yp28ehv.

that this is not a time when women should be patient. We are in a war, and we need to fight it with all our ability and every weapon possible. Women pilots, in this particular case, are a weapon waiting to be used.[55]

Cochran proposed training female pilots to perform a variety of domestic military aviation tasks, while Love's simpler idea was to use already established pilots to work with the Army Air Forces Ferrying Command. Under pressure from FDR and the First Lady and facing a shortage of pilots as war raged on, Hap Arnold caved in, and Love's plan was given the green light. The Women's Auxiliary Ferrying Squadron (WAFS) was established with Nancy Harkness Love at its head. Two months later, Cochran was named Director of the Women's Flying Training Program. By summer of 1943, both groups having proved successful, they merged to create the Women's Airforce Service Pilots (WASP).

Nancy Harkness Love[56]

Among their many jobs, women pilots towed sleeves behind their planes, allowing anti-aircraft gunners to practice shooting, basically turning themselves into targets. One vital role was as a test pilot for aircraft that had undergone repair, a task so dangerous that many men refused to take it on. They learned to pilot attack planes and bombers and ferried them from factory to Army Air Force bases. Nancy Love was familiar with B-17s. She and her co-pilot, Betty Gillies, became the first women to fly the heavy bombers. In 1943, Britain asked for a shipment of 100 of the aircraft, and Love said yes when asked if she wanted to be the first woman pilot to complete an inter-continental flight for the military. Unfortunately, Hap Arnold got wind of it. A PBS article reports: "As Love started the engine on the B-17 and was about to taxi down the runway, an officer came screeching down the runway in a jeep with an urgent telegram in hand. The message was from Arnold. It read: 'CEASE AND DESIST, NO WAFS WILL FLY OUTSIDE THE CONTIGUOUS U.S.'" The General feared backlash should a female be shot down by the enemy.[57] Apparently, Nancy Harkness Love, a veteran of hundreds of flights, was still just a woman after all.

In some ways, the story of the WASPs is not exactly the proudest moment in Army history. In spite of their contribution to the war effort, members faced resistance. The Bullock Museum of Texas, location of the first WASP training airfield, reported, "Male instructors...wondered publicly if the women could really fly these military planes, and male pilots worried privately that they could."[58] On the evening of August 23, 1944, Mabel Rawlinson was killed during a training exercise at Camp Davis in North Carolina. She had logged over 200 hours of flight time with the WASPs when her engine cut out, and her plane crashed landed in trees at the end of the runway. She died, unable to extricate herself from the cockpit when it erupted in flames. The Army did not honor her with a military funeral nor with a flag to

---

[55] Roosevelt, Eleanor. *My Day 9/1/1942.* E. Roosevelt Papers. tinyurl.com/8jjzu4fm.

[56] *Nancy Harkness Love.* Pub domain photo. NARA 535755. Picryl. tinyurl.com/2jd68tma.

[57] *Nancy Harkness Love.* Am Experience PBS. tinyurl.com/5yymfbpk.

[58] *Women AF Service Pilots.* Bullock Mus. tinyurl.com/4896ydk3.

drape the coffin, which was shipped home at the expense of her family. As with many of the other thirty-seven WASPs who lost their lives in service to their country, their sister pilots chipped in to pay for her funeral.

WASPs at pilot training school in Texas. Second
from the left is Dorothy Erhardt of Bridgewater.[59]

In the end, members of the Women's Airforce Service Pilots were championed by an unlikely source. In March 1944, General Hap Arnold appeared before Congress in an effort to officially recognize WASPs as members of the US military. He stated that the women were better qualified than their male counterparts, better trained, and more willing to fly dangerous assignments than men. He preferred WASPs over the civilian pilots who flew with the Civilian Air Patrol. Unfortunately, in May, Arnold suffered a heart attack and was consigned to a sick bed. Without their powerful and vocal supporter and in deference to negative public opinion, Congress denied the request.[60]

In December 1944, the Women's Airforce Service Pilots disbanded. The 1,000 women who served as WASPs left a distinguished record. They had qualified to fly over 75 different aircraft models, operated jet and rocket propelled airplanes, and piloted over 60 million miles. While women served as reservists in the Army, Navy, Marines, and Coast Guard, WASPs were the only group denied official military status, unable to receive health insurance or take advantage of the GI Bill, and failed to receive recognition.

Following the war, life went on. Many WASPs tried to find jobs as pilots, most failed. Flying was still a man's job. Some opted to stay airborne as flight attendants. Others found their way into the private sector and quietly carried on with their lives. Ruth Adams had taken her first flying lesson at an airfield outside of Worcester,[61] graduated from Wellesley College, and worked for a time at Boston's Museum of Fine Arts. She returned to school after the war and became a psychiatrist.[62] Lois Dobbin Auchterlonie spent over thirty years as a writer at Raytheon in Massachusetts.[63] And the remarkable Nancy Harkness Love moved to Martha's Vineyard with her family, keeping in touch with her fellow pilots, advocating for their acceptance by the military, and passed away at the age 62. In 1977, President Jimmy Carter granted veteran status to members of the group, and in 2009, President Barach O'Bama awarded Congressional Gold Medals to the WASPs of World War II.

---

[59] *Pilot school.* Pub domain photo. NARA 4A-22689-K3616. Johnson, Caroline. *Photos WWII Women Pilots.* NASM, Smithsonian 8/10/2018. tinyurl.com/muwfuzs2.

[60] Wilson, Jessica. *Waiting in Wings.* SLC 5/2015. tinyurl.com/ykfa5bph.

[61] *Ruth Adams.* CAF Rise Above7/20/2022. tinyurl.com/yc2r7fyz.

[62] *Ruth Adams.* Am Legacy Mus 8/31/2013. Facebook. tinyurl.com/5ymdtbcb.

[63] *Lois Auchterlonie.* Skagit Valley Herald 2013. Legacy. tinyurl.com/3aeh48yz.

The accomplishments of women in the military during World War II are staggering. They had served in the Army, Navy, Coast Guard, and Marines and laid the foundation for women in the soon-to-be-created Air Force. Over 350,000 had done their part. Perhaps their greatest achievement, however, was finding their way in a man's world, successfully proving that they possessed abilities that, in truth, had been there all along. They changed the face of the military and of American society. SPAR Jane Ashcraft Fisher would later write: "Women did not just 'free a man to fight.' They learned that they could do what a man could, and be accepted for it."[64]

While the planned outcome for women's groups in the military was demobilization by 1946, it was generally expected that ending enlistment and suspending re-enlistments would naturally bring a close to the WACs, WAVEs, and Women's Reserves. (The WASPS program was terminated in 1944, and SPARs came to an end in 1946.) As the deadline approached, the Army and Navy began to consider keeping women on board. A vague period of limbo ensued, some women being granted leaves, others urged to re-enlist when the opportunity arose, while the Army and Navy attempted to make them a permanent of the military. It took two years, but in 1948, President Harry S. Truman signed the Women's Armed Services Integration Act making it possible for women to serve as regular members of the United States Armed Forces.

And what of Edith Nourse Rogers? The extraordinary Congresswoman from Massachusetts spent thirty-five years in the House of Representatives, passing away in Boston at the age of 77 in the midst of her final campaign. She had been a champion of veterans, blue collar workers, and women, never fearing to cross party lines, and never forgetting that she was the voice of the people of Massachusetts. A wonderful profile of Rogers and her career appears in an unlikely document. In May of 1943, a "most confidential" memorandum was sent to the Foreign Office in London from Professor Isaiah Berlin. It is no secret that Churchill was often impatient with what he viewed as the American habit of dragging their feet when it came to involvement in the war. Berlin was sent to the British Embassy in Washington, D.C. to report findings that might assist the British government in lighting a fire under the Americans.

The document, which arrived at the Foreign Office, included information on members of the US Senate and House of Representatives Foreign Affairs Committees. It is at times, an amusing document filled with Berlin's impressions of those who shared power with FDR. The words "Anglophile" and "Anglophobic" are peppered throughout the document, along with his brutally frank appraisals. "Carter Glass of Virginia is very old and frail and something of a legend in the South...He cannot have many years of active service before him." (He lasted until 1946.) Due to a recent election, two members of the House Committee had been replaced, one being the isolationist, "highly eccentric George Tinkham," Congressman from Boston. Of the forty-eight members of the Senate and House Committees, only two members were women, and only one was from Massachusetts...Edith Nourse Rogers. Her entry reads:

Edith Nourse Rogers of Massachusetts. In Congress since 1925. She was an Isolationist up to and including the Lend-Lease, after which, however, she swung in behind the President on all major foreign policy measures. Though she is likely to continue her support, she will only do so after she has convinced herself that America's own best interests are thoroughly protected and that the Administration is not trying to "put something across." She is regarded in Congress as a capable, hard-working, and intelligent woman. A pleasant and kindly old battle-axe but a battle-axe.[65]
It seems entirely probable that the "old battle-axe" would have approved.

There was one group of women who moved seamlessly into the realm of war without much fanfare or distasteful debate. Where there is war, there will be wounded, and where there are wounded,

---

[64] Ryan, Kathleen M. *Beyond Kinship.* Academia 2009. tinyurl.com/4v3ej29c.

[65] Hachey, Thomas. *Am Profiles Capitol Hill.* WI Mag History 1973. JSTOR. tinyurl.com/y336v4mn.

there will be nurses to care for them. As early as 1775, Congress approved the request of General George Washington to pay women to provide nursing care for the Continental Army. By 1901, the Army embraced the role of women nurses and founded the Army Nurse Corps. Similar to an auxiliary agency and but not an official part of the regular army, nurses did not hold rank or grade and received unequal compensation. The work of these dedicated women led to significant changes. The Army Reorganization Act of 1920 granted relative rank. They could be appointed as lieutenants and captains and wear insignia, but their authority fell below men who held the same rank.

The path for women of the Navy Nurse Corps began in 1908. Fifteen years later, they were issued uniforms and in 1930 received retirement pay. Lacking in rank, nurses were referred to by the title, "Miss," a situation which Sec Nav Frank Knox felt created confusion. He approached Congress, and in 1942, Navy nurses were granted relative ranks. Pay increases followed, although salaries fell below their male counterparts in the Navy.

When bombs dropped on Pearl Harbor, the Army had less than 1,000 nurses, the Navy even fewer. As men rushed to war, so did nurses in numbers so great that a crisis resulted. Civilians were left without adequate care, and the pool of nurses that the military could pull from was significantly reduced. The Red Cross stepped up, recruiting 71,000 nurses for the military during World War II.[66]

Cadet Nurse Corps poster. World War II.[67]

The government established the United States Cadet Nurse Corps. Supervised by the Public Health Service, over the next five years, 85 percent of nursing schools in the United States participated in the government-funded program. Women ages seventeen to thirty-five were encouraged to join with a promise of free room, board, uniforms, and employment. In return, women were required to serve in a nursing capacity until the end of the war. In Massachusetts, 9,000 women, including Mary Maione of Hamilton, Eleanor Wyckoff of Lynn, Betty Beecher of Weymouth, Dottie Hall of Westford, and Evelyn Benson of Brookline, became USCNC nurses.[68]

The war began early for the nurses of the Second World War. Teresa Maude Duggan of Boston joined the Navy in 1930 and was lucky enough to be transferred to a hospital ship docked in an island paradise. The USS Solace was equipped with two operating rooms and over 400 beds. The tropical

[66] *WWII and Red Cross.* Am Red Cross. tinyurl.com/5a7njr4p.

[67] *Be Cadet Nurse.* Pub domain photo. NARA. Picryl. tinyurl.com/mtzp82fj.

[68] Poremba, Barbara. *WWII cadet nurses.* Salem News 7/1/2022. tinyurl.com/mrxr4nsp.

climate and relaxed atmosphere made it a somewhat idyllic billet. On one Saturday evening in December, for example, a formal dinner with dancing was held on the deck of a nearby battleship, the Arizona.[69] The next morning, the world exploded.

Aboard his ship anchored at Pearl Harbor, Edward F. Borucki of Holyoke was preparing to go to mass when general quarters sounded. "General quarters, man, your battle stations...Japanese planes attacking Ford Island." Borucki completed his assigned task, closing eight watertight compartments, and headed to his next detail, the hospital.[70] Nearby, USS Solace waited to receive victims of the attack. From its mooring at the end of Battleship Row, the staff and patients witnessed the terrifying events of December 7, 1941. The Solace navigator was at breakfast when he spied the USS Utah beginning to list, thinking it was some type of drill. Utah had actually been hit by two Japanese torpedoes. Seeing commotion in the harbor, the chief of Solace's medical services, Capt. Erik G. Hakkanson headed toward the deck with his movie camera. Hakkanson's video capturing the Japanese attack and subsequent destruction of the Arizona is perhaps the best-known footage of the outbreak of World War II.[71]

The crew of the USS Solace responded immediately. Motor launches were sent to the Arizona, and within thirty minutes, the ship began receiving victims. Plucked from the oil-soaked waters of the harbor, three-quarters of the survivors had suffered serious burns. One surgeon recalled, "Many were so seriously burned as to be unrecognizable." Some arrived "with fuel oil matting together scraggly clumps of singed hair, clothing charred or completely gone, hands and forearms denuded of flesh, dark and claw-like." Teresa Duggan and her colleagues wore life preservers as they worked. She remembered, "At first, I was frightened. But after that, we were so busy, and I had so much to do I was no longer afraid, although there were moments when I did think it might be my last day on Earth."[72]

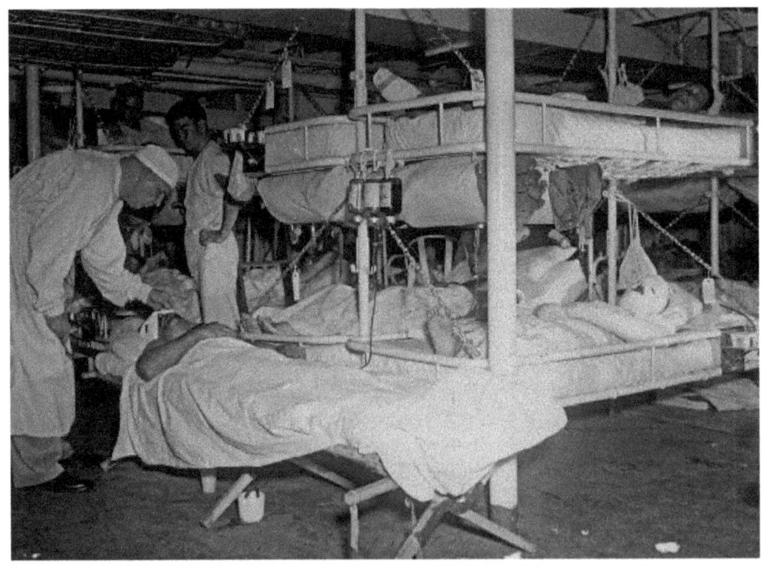
Navy surgeon caring for casualties. USS
Solace, Pearl Harbor. 7 December 1941.[73]

By the final hours of December 7th, more than 200 casualties had received treatment aboard the Solace. Two months later, the ship with Duggan aboard was reassigned to the South Pacific. Teresa

---

[69] Milbrath, Gwenyth. *Nurses Pearl Harbor.* MEDCoE 10/2016. Gale Academic Onefile. tinyurl.com/utwsnsp2.

[70] *Former Newsie Back.* Transcript TG 2/28/1942. Newspapers.com. tinyurl.com/smfapdvp.

[71] *Solace II.* NHHC 4/3/2020. tinyurl.com/4b9fwww6.

[72] Milbrath, Gwyneth Rhianon. *Nurses of Pearl Harbor.*

[73] *Surgeon USS Solace.* Pub domain photo. NavSource. BUMED 09-5043-31. tinyurl.com/5n6b286w.

Duggan would go on to achieve the rank of Lt. Commander and retire in 1951 after more than two decades of service in the United States Navy.[74]

Twenty-nine Navy nurses were stationed at nearby Hospital Point. It was hard not to notice that they were under attack. Japanese planes flew in just above the flag pole, so low that observers could make out the faces of pilots. Ten minutes after bombs started flying, a Japanese plane crashed into the hospital's laboratory building. Nurses set about preparing wards, releasing those who could manage on their own. One officer cut off his own cast "and hobbled towards his ship." Injuries were slightly different here than on the Solace. Only half presented with burns while most had received shrapnel and bullet wounds. Shock was almost universal. By nightfall, 961 patients had been treated, 313 would never go home again.[75]

The Army was on Oahu as well, where a total of 150 nurses manned three hospitals. The largest army airfield in Hawaii, Hickham Field, was an easy target due to its location just a few blocks from the harbor. Sgt. Edmond E. Bunoski of Williamstown, was in the barracks when he noticed smoke billowing from the Arizona.

The noise sounded like the thousand pounders. It made a terrific jar. We thought it odd because there were no operations from Saturday noon through the weekends. Someone shouted, "Jap planes." Even then it seemed inconceivable though we saw them dropping bombs. We couldn't believe it. It was peacetime...We watched helpless and unarmed as the planes dropped fragmentation bombs and machine-gunned the barracks. A car was coming out of a side street...The plane headed over it, and three or four people...jumped under it. A bomb hit, and it started burning. The men were wounded and couldn't crawl from under the wreck.[76]

Military barracks after Japanese attack on
Hickham Field. December 7, 1941.[77]

The nurses stationed at the Hickham Field hospital had difficulty keeping up with the influx of patients who were laid out on the ground or on the porch awaiting treatment. One survivor recalled watching a nurse move from patient to patient administering morphine. "The blood ran on the floor. She

[74] Evans, Dorothy. *Teresa Duggan.* Tampa Bay Times 11/30/1985. Newspapers.com. tinyurl.com/4j9jrfue.

[75] Milbrath, Gwyneth Rhianon. *Nurses of Pearl Harbor.*

[76] *Williamstown First 250 Years.* Williamstown House Local History 2005.

[77] *Pearl Harbor Attack.* Pub domain photo. 330-PS-2355 USN. NMUSM. Picryl. tinyurl.com/bders69a.

showed me where it came up over the soles of her shoes."[78] Like nearly all nurses on the eve of war, training in first aid had not prepared them for removing chunks of shrapnel or dealing with triage. This would change.

Lena Lizza Southerland of Willimansett recalled little of the attack. Awakened in her room by the cry for nurses, she went directly to the Schofield Barracks operating room, where she stayed until 10 p.m. while the battle raged around her. Helen O'Neill and Margaret Fallon of Holyoke both joined the Army Nurse Corps in April 1941 and, after a brief billet at Camp Edwards, were transferred to Hawaii and Schofield Barracks. Second Lt. Fallon was on duty on December 7 and witnessed the attack. She went out to the porch to watch the bombing of Wheeler Field. "Those who got into the air did a grand job," she recalled, "and every man who could get his hands on a gun. Unfortunately, many were machine-gunned while asleep in their beds."[79] Robert J. Guilotte, one of seven Williamstown men at Pearl Harbor that day, received a special citation for leaving his hospital bed to help transport wounded by ambulance.[80] Several patients had seen the rising sun on the attack planes, and Fallon knew this meant war. Others were unaware of the tragedy that was unfolding. Nearby, a group of nurses gathered outside, waving as planes, which they assumed were American, took part in maneuvers.[81]

Five miles away at Tripler, seventy-six nurses began receiving victims within half an hour of the first attack. They administered morphine and tetanus shots, carefully making note of each on a toe tag. Soon patients were arriving so fast, they switched to writing an "M" or a "T" on patient foreheads. Bombs dropped on Wheeler Air Field, and nearby Schofield Barracks was strafed. One nurse had little experience with severe trauma. While treating a patient with bullet wounds in his chest, the doctor instructed her to plug up a hole with her finger. The patient died, and Ziesler stated, "I know now what shrapnel is."[82] Less than a day later, the nurses of the Philippines would have similar stories to tell.

For many, joining the Army or Navy Nurse Corps meant travel to exotic locations. The Philippines was high on the list. Like the nurses of Hawaii, few women were prepared for the horror that unfolded on December 8, 1941. The Japanese attack began at Clark Field and Fort Stotsenberg, fifty miles north of the Philippine capitol. When the call came in to Manila's Sternberg Hospital asking for nurses to help, Helen Cassiani raised her hand. The young woman had graduated from Bridgewater High School and was the first woman to enlist in the US Army Nurse Corps from her hometown.[83] "Cassie" was 24-years-old and had been in the Philippines six weeks when she arrived at Stotsenberg. It was a scene of horrific destruction, and she and her team found their way to the hospital in darkness by following the cries of those who had survived. The next morning, the attack resumed, and Cassiani and her colleagues took shelter in an empty swimming pool.

The Philippines was about to fall, however, and by the end of December, the Army evacuated all of its nurses in Manila to Bataan and Corregidor. For some reason unclear to history, eleven Navy nurses were left behind, and on January 2, 1942, these women became prisoners of the Japanese Imperial Army. Cassiani ended up at Hospital #1 on the Bataan Peninsula. The threat of attack was constant, and during surgery, Cassie and her team often had to duck under the operating table until the bombing stopped. Casualties kept pouring in. One surgeon recalled:

---

[78] Milbrath, Gwenyth. *Nurses of Pearl Harbor.*

[79] *Nurse Tells of Pearl Harbor.* Holyoke Daily Transcript TG 4/16/1942. Newspapers.com. tinyurl.com/4e92bkyb.

[80] *Williamstown. First 250 Years 1753-2003.* Williamstown House of Local History.

[81] *Nurse Tells of Pearl Harbor.* Holyoke Daily Transcript TG.

[82] Milbrath, Gwenyth. *Nurses of Pearl Harbor.*

[83] Cline, Sara. *Bridgewater nurse band of angels.* Enterprise 11/10/2017. tinyurl.com/m2pwef8d

...the zzz-zzz-zzz of a saw as it cut through bone...the plop of an amputated leg dropping into a bucket, the grind of a rounded burr eating its way through a skull...Rivulets of sweat washed away the nurses' rouge and powder, leaving only lipstick to match the ruby-red blood.

Cassie was glad for the exhausting work. "I was thankful for the hard physical labor. The work gave me...the weariness to put [my mind] to sleep." Supplies were growing short, malaria and dysentery were rampant, and the number of patients continued to rise. Cassiani took a hard, cold look at the situation. "I put my cards on the table. We were losing on Bataan. There was no convoy. We were indeed expendable. You'd have to be pretty dumb not to know that this was it, buddy."[84]

General Jonathan Wainwright, in charge of Bataan and Corregidor, knew the end was near. Wainwright was an unlikely hero. He had been stationed at Camp Devens in Ayer on the general staff of the Massachusetts based 76th infantry division and followed them to war in 1918. A thirty-four-year veteran before he was farmed out to a post in the Philippines, Wainwright was too old to fight, a heavy drinker, walked with a limp, and was a member of a dying breed, the US Cavalry. To his credit, he was knowledgeable about the Philippines, having fought there in 1909. He was also part of the team that in 1921 developed a plan for defense of the island nation in the event of a Japanese attack. War Plan Orange called for American troops to pull back and hold Bataan and Corregidor for six months, when reinforcements and supplies would be sent.

Now in December of 1941 and under attack, no relief was forthcoming. In spite of the fact that he commanded an army of starving, disease-stricken soldiers with dwindling supplies and outdated weapons, Wainwright and his men stubbornly held out. Duane Schultz, in his biography of Wainwright, stated he "led a series of delaying actions that disrupted the Imperial Japanese timetable for conquest of the Pacific."[85] The effort took its toll, however, and on April 4, Wainwright notified his superior officer that his men were "so weak from malnutrition that they have no power of resistance."[86] In his safe and comfortable headquarters in Australia, General "Dugout Doug" MacArthur was unimpressed and sent orders informing Wainwright that there would be no surrender. Unable to hold out any longer, Bataan fell on April 8, 1942.

Wainwright pulled his line back again, leaving behind over 70,000 Americans and their Allies who would become known forever as the heroes of the Bataan Death March. The final desperate battle for the Philippines would take place on Corregidor. With his remaining 3,000 men in place on the island, Wainwright established headquarters in the Malinta Tunnel. Built into a hill located at the eastern side of Corregidor where the land tapers down to a narrow peninsula, the huge tunnel complex would be home to Helen Cassiani and the nurses of Bataan for the next several weeks. They joined a staff already in place in the tunnel's makeshift hospital. It was a place of stifling heat and humidity with an appalling stench, but it offered more protection than the jungles of Bataan. As the Japanese continued their assault on the Philippines, Corregidor suffered brutal bombings. One bomb landed at the Malinta Tunnel entrance, killing more than a dozen. Cassiani lost control briefly when she rushed to the gate to assist, and a severed head rolled to her feet.[87]

In Washington, Army Chief General George Marshall and Secretary of War Henry Stimson were watching. As the death toll mounted, they approached FDR, who drafted a message to Wainwright:

My purpose is to leave to your best judgment any decision affecting the future of the Bataan garrison. I have nothing but admiration for your soldierly conduct and your performance of your most difficult

---

[84] Norman, Elizabeth. *We Band of Angels.* Random House Trade Paperbacks 2013.

[85] Schultz, Duane. *Hero of Bataan.* St. Martin's Press 1981.

[86] Taylor, John M. *Dreadful Step.* HISTORYNET 2/21/2010. tinyurl.com/bdctxfsj.

[87] Norman, Elizabeth. *We Band of Angels.*

mission and have every confidence that whatever decision you may sooner or later be forced to make will be dictated only by the best interests of the country and of your magnificent troops...[88]

The President, respectful of the chain of command, required that the message be sent to MacArthur, who should then forward it to Wainwright. MacArthur chose not to do so. Stimson had had enough. He overrode MacArthur and sent the message to Wainwright himself. Corregidor and its brave men and women held out until May 6 when the Philippine nation was surrendered to the Japanese. The nurses of Bataan and Corregidor became prisoners of the Japanese Empire. Before surrendering, they hastily signed their names on a piece of paper and left it behind in the hopes that they would be remembered. Wainwright along with most of his men would follow his brave comrades on the long road up the Bataan peninsula.

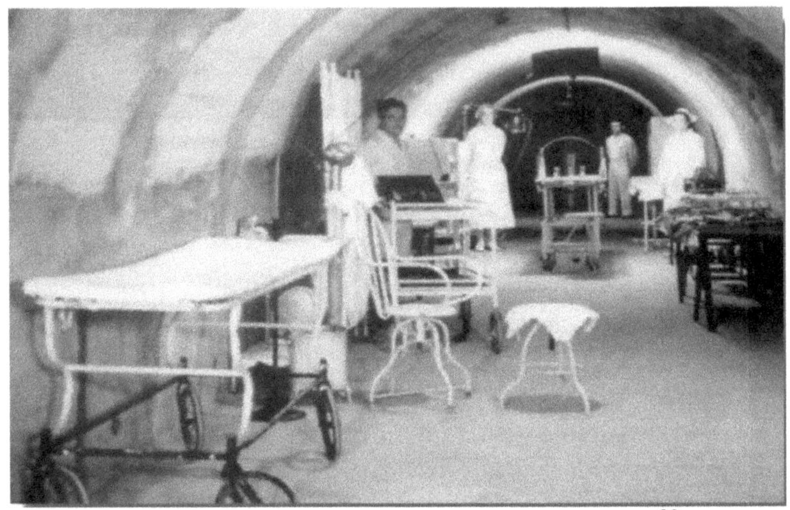

Underground hospital ward at Corregidor.[89]

The stories told by the Angels of Bataan and Corregidor are remarkably short on details from their time in captivity. References to lack of medicine, food, and death from disease and malnutrition are most often described in generalizations. Their hesitance to share the cruel reality of their experiences speaks volumes about these heroic, dedicated women. Like Helen Cassiani and most of her colleagues, Letha McHale of Dorchester, a tiny five-foot-tall Angel of Bataan, spent three years at Santo Tomas Internment Camp. Born in Stoughton, Letha weighed in at 68 pounds by the time she was freed.[90] Lt. Anne B. Wurts of Leominster was also at Santo Tomas. She had traveled to the Philippines in 1941 as part of the Army Nurse Corps, and within a few months, Corregidor fell. She later described her life as a prisoner of war in just a few words: "It wasn't good."

Anne's father, Edward Wurts, had received just two messages from his daughter in three years. But now, in March of 1945, Anne was coming home. On her arrival, she agreed to an interview with the *Fitchburg Sentinel*. The courageous nurse, "whose steady eyes the Japs had failed to blink," gave a stunning account of events that unfolded on February 3, 1945.[91] The night before, Japanese guards had rolled several barrels with kerosene-soaked rags under the staircase at the camp hospital, a sure sign that the nurses would soon be murdered. The next day, planes began flying overhead, and machine gun blasts

---

[88] Schultz, Duane. *Hero of Bataan.*

[89] *Hospital Corregidor.* Pub domain photo. *Military Nurses Philippines.* GGNRA Archives. NPS. tinyurl.com/23tr9nkj.

[90] Nelson, Trudy. *Dorchester Nurse Jap Prison.* Boston Globe 3/25/1945. Newspapers.com. tinyurl.com/568yntd3.

[91] *Anne B. Wurts.* Fitchburg Sentinel 3/3/1945. Newspapers.com. tinyurl.com/5x2fns2s.

erupted. The nurses were ordered to their rooms, the smell of gasoline everywhere, while they waited for an explosion.[92] Wurts recalled:

Suddenly, we heard tanks. Their motors sounded different than the Jap tanks we were accustomed to. When they got to the main gate, they stopped. We heard voices – American voices. Then, one of the tanks roared, and down came the big woven rattan gate. Searchlights on the tanks played around the yard, and then the machines rumbled up close to the buildings. Out poured the prisoners, weeping, shouting, chattering, everyone anxious to touch, to feel the texture of the armor that had saved us.

The sixty Japanese guards that remained after the attack held over 100 prisoners hostage until a release was negotiated, granting them safe passage out of the camp. "Did the Japs swagger, or were they crestfallen?" she was asked. Her response: "I don't know. By that time, I'd seen all the Japs I wanted to, and I didn't look at them."[93]

Army nurses rescued from Santo Tomas
Internment Camp, Manila. 1945.[94]

Unbelievably, all seventy-seven Angels of Bataan and Corregidor survived their wartime ordeal. They had overcome illness, malnutrition, lice, and rats, while demonstrating courage and dedication equal to the strongest of men. General Wainwright would say, "Never forget the American girls who fought on Bataan and later on Corregidor…Their names must always be hallowed when we speak of American heroes."[95] For their sacrifice and bravery, the women received Bronze Stars. They made their way home to live out their lives, most not willing to admit to the heroic role they had played. When greeted by a crowd on her return to Boston, Helen Cassiani remarked, "What's all the excitement about? Are all these people hanging around to see me? I haven't done anything special."[96] "She didn't speak about the war," her son, Mark Nestor, would later say. "She had gone and come back, and that was enough said."[97]

---

[92] Norman, Elizabeth. *We Band of Angels.*

[93] *Anne B. Wurts.* Fitchburg Sentinel.

[94] *Nurses rescued Santo Tomas.* Pub domain photo. US Army. Wiki Commons. tinyurl.com/zmew2vx8.

[95] *Susie Pitcher.* #Veteranoftheday. VA News 7/28/2023. VA. tinyurl.com/yxhwmce2.

[96] Ross, Leonora. *Bridgewater Nurse Freed.* Boston Globe 3/3/1945. Newspapers.com. tinyurl.com/27vsvavf.

[97] Cline, Sara. *Bridgewater nurse band of angels.*

Helen Cassiani spent the remainder of her days in the town of her birth. She passed away in her eighty-fifth year and was laid to rest in Bridgewater, Massachusetts.[98] Anne Bronson Wurts returned home to resume a career in nursing, eventually making her way to California, where she lived till the age of 96.[99] For Jonathan Wainwright, life took an unexpected turn.

Wainwright had earned the respect of those under his command. He had been known to pick up a rifle, lead his men into battle, and limp with his troops through the jungles of Bataan. In July 1942, with Wainwright now a prisoner of war, General George Marshall approached Congress requesting that he be awarded the coveted Medal of Honor. Unfortunately, his superior officer disagreed. MacArthur placed the blame for the fall of Bataan and Corregidor squarely on Wainwright. Marshall turned to Secretary of War Henry Stimson, who favored ignoring MacArthur. After an investigation regarding the veracity of MacArthur's inflammatory claims against Wainwright questioned "General MacArthur's judgment where matters of personal prestige are concerned," the matter was dropped. It was best to avoid a scandal for an army at war.

General Jonathan Wainwright spent three years and eight months as a prisoner of war, believing himself to be a failure to his country. He was liberated in August of 1945. Soon, "the Hero of Bataan" would be made a four-star general, awarded the Congressional Medal of Honor, and stand emaciated and solemn on the deck of the Battleship Missouri as the Empire of Japan came to an end.[100]

In the European Theater of Operations, nurse recollections varied little from those of their Pacific sisters. They remembered cold temperatures and snow rather than the heat and rain of the tropics. They wrote home to their families from Normandy and Anzio and Antwerp rather than Guam and Tarawa and Burma. Their letters, always censored, were short on details. Kathleen Garneau of Turners Falls had been with the Army at Normandy and now, in November 1943, was traveling eastward through Europe with Patton's army. She wrote to her parents:

The war, to all appearances and reports, is still going full blast, much against the opinion of so many people back home who prophesied a speedy victory. They only read the headlines and not the slaving and effort that brings about even 'routine' victories. Our advance in this sector has been rough and plenty slow lately, and the boys have paid dearly for our breakthrough, which was a long time coming.[101]

Her assessment was prophetic. The tortuous Battle of the Bulge was just one month away.

Katherine Flynn Nolan, wearing a heavy backpack, was 24 years old in July 1944 when she jumped off a transport into the water at Utah Beach and nearly drowned.[102] The Worcester native was stationed close to the battlefield with the 53rd Field Hospital. Their job was to arrive at a site and set up a hospital, often with the battle raging around them. Nurses and doctors were expected to patch up the wounded and send them back into battle or off to a hospital further away from the front. Nolan recalled arriving in a small village in the Netherlands. It was bitter cold. In fact, she recalled nurses wrapping themselves in blankets while they worked. "I've been cold since the Bulge," she said.

The work was exhausting as a seemingly never-ending line of patients made their way through the hospital, and nurses rarely knew what became of the men they treated. During his brief stay at the field hospital, Hamilton Greene earned Nolan's praise. "He was in a lot of pain, but you wouldn't know it. He always had a smile on his face...he really helped me with the other patients because he had such a great sense of humor. You would never believe anything was wrong with him. But his wounds were

---

[98] *Helen Nestor.* Find Grave ID 208986300 4/12/ 2020. tinyurl.com/6anctyx9.

[99] *San Mateo City CA Obit Death Notice.* GenealogyBuff.com 11/4/2010. tinyurl.com/uk6wh5s7.

[100] Schultz, Duane. *Hero of Bataan.*

[101] *Nurse Sees No Speedy Victory.* Recorder 11/13/1944. Newspapers.com tinyurl.com/4bstaecp.

[102] Stamberg, Susan. *Kate Nolan.* NPR 5/28/2004. tinyurl.com/23khzjj7.

worse than some of the others." Greene, a native of Boston, was an artist and war correspondent who had sustained abdominal wounds from machine gun fire.[103] Nolan was pleased to find her name mentioned in a 1945 article for *The American Legion Magazine*. It was written by Hamilton Greene, and it meant that he had survived. He would later be present at the Japanese surrender.[104] The 53rd Field Hospital moved eastward toward Germany along with the troops, and soon concentration camp survivors became patients as well. Katherine Flynn Nolan earned five battle stars and was awarded the Legion of Honor by the citizens of France.[105]

Easthampton, Massachusetts, native Louise Mesh Fleming had a rather unusual nursing experience during her time in Europe. The young woman graduated from Cooley Dickinson Hospital School of Nursing in Northampton and joined the Army Nurse Corps. Fleming served for a time at Lovell General Hospital at Fort Devens before being transferred to Italy. At the 300th General Hospital, the staff was charged with patching up the injured well enough to ship them back to the States. Naples had already fallen to the Allies, and Fleming described a city "ravaged and war-torn." Like many of her sister nurses, she hesitated to talk about her experiences. "I will not talk about the sadness. There is another side to war, too. I'm not belittling the heartache, sorrow, and death that occurs. But there is also a time when beauty appears."

The beauty she referred to came from an unexpected source...babies. With the arrival of the Allies, love was in the air in Naples, and so many infants were being born that the hospital set up a maternity ward. "Sanded-down orange crates became cribs, Coke bottles became baby bottles. It was the cooperation of every department that made the delivery of the first baby possible," Fleming recalled. "The newborns brought joy into our lives where sorrow had recently been."[106] Louise Fleming's positive outlook served her well. She returned to Massachusetts after the war and passed away in Westfield at the age of 105.[107]

Frances Slanger experienced the horrors of D-Day when she came ashore at Normandy four days after the battle began. The former Roxbury resident and graduate of Boston City Hospital School of Nursing[108] was one of several Massachusetts nurses in her unit, including Elizabeth Powers of Lowell, Christine Cox of Prides Crossing, and Margaret Bowler of Westfield. Five weeks and 3,000 casualties later, the nurses were stationed in Belgium when Slanger decided to write a letter to the Stars and Stripes describing her experience.[109]

We had several articles in different magazines and papers sent in by grateful GIs praising the work of the nurses around the combat zones. Praising us – for what? We wade ankle-deep in mud – you have to lie in it. We are restricted to our immediate area, a cow pasture or a hay field, but then who is not restricted...Sure we rough it, but in comparison to the way you men are taking it, we can't complain nor do we feel that bouquets are due us. But you – the men behind the guns, the men driving our tanks, flying our planes, sailing our ships, building bridges – it is to you we doff our helmets. To every GI wearing the American uniform, for you we have the greatest admiration and respect.

...after taking care of some of your buddies, comforting them when they are brought in, bloody, dirty with the earth, mud and grime, and most of them so tired. Somebody's brothers, somebody's fathers, somebody's sons, seeing them gradually brought back to life, to consciousness, and their lips separate

[103] Saunders, David. *Hamilton Greene.* Pulp Artists 2012. tinyurl.com/2hv3wx42.

[104] Howard, Henry. *Our WWII Story.* Am Legion 5/21/2020. tinyurl.com/5n3w7u5c.

[105] *Katherine M. Nolan.* Naples Daily News 3/12/2019. Legacy. tinyurl.com/mtky98fa.

[106] Simison, Cynthia G. *Another side to war.* MASS LIVE 7/1/2018. tinyurl.com/yayksfxx.

[107] *Louise Fleming.* Find Grave ID 236079686 1/21/2022. tinyurl.com/yrvdbvv4.

[108] Ullian, Jessica. *WWII nurse's words echo.* BU Bridge 9/10/2004. BU. tinyurl.com/4jhpf4m4.

[109] Cowan, Ruth. *Army Nurse Dies.* Boston Globe 11/22/1944. Newspapers.com. tinyurl.com/bdf98dh4.

into a grin when they first welcome you. Usually, they say, "Hiya babe, Holy Mackerel, an American woman" – or more indiscreetly, "How about a kiss?"

These soldiers stay with us but a short time, from ten days to possibly two weeks. We have learned a great deal about our American boy and the stuff he is made of. The wounded do not cry. Their buddies come first. The patience and determination they show, the courage and fortitude they have is sometimes awesome to behold. It is we who are proud of you, a great distinction to see you open your eyes and, with that swell American grin, say "Hiya, Babe."[110]

The newspaper editors were impressed, and in early November, published her work, unaware that Slanger had been killed the day after she wrote the article. Frances Slanger, the first American nurse to die in the ETO from enemy fire, was 31 years old. She rests in the town where she grew up, Roxbury, Massachusetts, and in 1945, the hospital ship Frances Y. Slanger was launched to honor her memory.

By the end of World War II, 59,000 women had served as nurses in the Army and another 11,000 in the Navy. They experienced combat, were held as prisoners of war, and lost more than 200 of their own to the ravages of war.

An Army nurse, prepares an IV injection
by the light of a kerosene lamp. 1944.[111]

Their sacrifice and dedication are honored by this statement from First Lieutenant Anne Sosh Brehm, who served with the Army Nurse Corps in China, Burma, and India. "Let the generations know that women in uniform also guaranteed their freedom. That our resolve was just as great as the brave men who stood among us, and with victory, our hearts were just as full and beat just as fast–that the tears fell just as hard for those we left behind."[112]

Other Massachusetts women achieved fame for their research, inventions, bravery, and some, for their looks. Here are a few of their stories. Born in Vermont, Mary Doyle was a teenager working as a telephone operator when she was approached by an artist who asked if she would be interested in sitting

---

[110] *Frances Slanger.* NMAJMH. tinyurl.com/yvs8ek3z.

[111] *Army Nurse WWII.* Pub domain photo. US Army. Wiki Commons. tinyurl.com/3ykxzfpy.

[112] Lockwood, Martha. *Wilma L Vaught.* 3/21/2013. AF. tinyurl.com/yc6esnwf.

as a model for him. All she had to do was dress up in work clothes, place one foot on a copy of Mein Kampf, and hold a riveting gun on her lap. The money was good. The job paid ten dollars, so she agreed. On May 29, 1943, Mary Doyle appeared on the cover of the Saturday Evening Post, and Norman Rockwell's "Rosie the Riveter" made history. Doyle later became a dental hygienist, married Robert Keefe, and moved to Whitman, Massachusetts.[113]

Borderlands State Park in Easton and Sharon is located on property formerly belonging to Blanche Ames Ames. Born in Lowell and a graduate of Smith College, this extraordinary woman married wealthy shovel company owner Oakes Ames and, in 1910, built the mansion that stands today at Borderlands. Blanche Ames was not just another pretty face. A restless inventor, she developed a hexagonal lumber cutter, designed environmentally friendly toilets, and bred disease-resistant turkeys. During World War II, she patented a gadget that used balloons and wires to snare the moving propellers of enemy airplanes. The military approved of the device, but the war ended before it could be put to good use. An outspoken activist, Blanche promoted birth control and women's rights. She passed away at her Borderlands estate at the age of 92.[114]

Marion Armstrong became the first female intelligence cartographer. An avid student of geography, she attended Clark University in Worcester. Geography, it seems, was developing into an important field for the country at war. After being approached by a visiting professor, she and fellow student Henry Frieswyk moved to Washington, D.C. to become members of a newly developed OSS program involving cartography.[115] The Office of Strategic Services was in the business of providing information, and maps were most definitely essential information. Working out of the abandoned Ford's Theater, 22-year-old Armstrong and her team created a three-dimensional map of Italy. The relief map, the first of its kind to be used in the European Theater of Operation, was made specifically for Eisenhower during planning for the Sicily campaign.

Marion Armstrong Frieswyk[116]

Over the course of the war, OSS cartographers produced over 8,000 maps, including two globes so large that when one was needed for the Yalta conference, it couldn't be loaded onto the plane and had to be sawed in half. The OSS ceased to function at the end of World War II, but the Map Division was retained, and in 1947, the Central Intelligence Agency, including a Cartography Division, was

[113] *Mary Doyle Keefe*. Carmon Funeral Homes 4/21/2015. tinyurl.com/4w6yk6xf.

[114] *Blanche Ames*. Lemelson-MIT tinyurl.com/yb4zhv6e.

[115] *Marion Frieswyk*. Jefferson Funeral Chapel. tinyurl.com/58j8cut2.

[116] *Marion Frieswyk*. Pub domain photo. *Marion Frieswyk*. CIA 3/30/2020. tinyurl.com/543w4fzy

established. Marion was still on board. She remained with the CIA until the 1950s, working with the head of her division, her husband, Henry Frieswyk.[117]

Mary Sears developed an interest in all things aquatic as a child while exploring Heard Pond near her home in Wayland. After graduating from Radcliffe and earning degrees in biology and zoology, Sears entered the field of oceanography at a time when it was a male-dominated profession. Her first exposure to Woods Hole Oceanographic Institute occurred when she worked as a research assistant to the Institute's first director, Dr. Henry Bigelow. It was the beginning of a very lengthy and successful association. Prohibited from going to sea with her fellow Woods Hole researchers (bad mojo...no women allowed on board), in 1941, she accepted a job investigating guano birds in Peru while traveling *aboard a ship.* Not surprisingly, Davy Jones wasn't nearly as outraged about a woman on board as were the crew of Woods Hole's Atlantis, and Sears made it safely home to a country at war.

By the time she arrived, the Institute had been cordoned off with barbed wire, was under guard, and the staff severely depleted as men headed off to war. Anxious to do her patriotic part, she applied to the WAVES and was rejected. Shortly afterwards, Woods Hole was approached by the Navy's Hydrographic Office requesting a scientist be released to work with them. According to author Catherine Musemeche, "the only one...deemed nonessential to the pressing wartime research taking place in the lab...was Mary Sears." Granted a waiver, Sears became a member of the WAVES in January 1943.

Lt. Sears became head of the Navy Hydrographic Office's newly created Oceanographic Unit. Her first big assignment came when World War I ace Eddie Rickenbacker spent three weeks awaiting rescue after his plane crashed in the Pacific. Why had it taken so long to find him? Sears went to work, and a month later her paper, "The Drift of Objects under the Combined Action of Wind and Current" was presented to her superiors.[118] "Submarine Supplements to the Sailing Directions," which assisted submarines to hide under water by using water temperature data, soon followed. The efforts of Mary Sears, recognized by some as the first oceanographer in Navy history, saved countless lives during World War II. She retired from the Navy in 1963 and passed away in Woods Hole at the age of 97. In 2000, the US Navy launched the Oceanographic Survey Ship, Mary Sears in her honor.

By the end of World War II, more than 350,000 women had served in official government positions. Ninety had been held as prisoners of war, 565 received Bronze Stars for heroism, sixteen were awarded Purple Hearts, and approximately 500 had made the ultimate sacrifice.[119] They served their country as spies, pilots, inventors, correspondents, researchers, code breakers, and healers. They laid the foundation for those would follow as official members of the country's military force. During debate on the proposed 1948 Women's Armed Services Integration Act, the question arose as to why women should be allowed into the military on an equal footing with men. General Dwight D. Eisenhower responded simply and eloquently: "We need them."[120] After the war, most women returned to the lives that had been laid out for them before the conflict, most fading into anonymity, while holding their stories of courage, determination, and sacrifice in their quiet, private memories.

...though women tend to lose their identity, so closely are their lives woven into the warp of history, they are, nonetheless, co-makers of history...

Ruth Considine[121]

---

[117]Eder, Mari K. *Girls Who Stepped Out of Line.* Sourcebooks 2021.

[118] Musemeche, Catherine. *Mary Sears' Pioneering Research.* Women Shaped History. Smithsonian Mag 2022. tinyurl.com/39shxx9z.

[119] Martin, Kali. *It's Your War Too.* Nat WWII Mus 3/13/2020. tinyurl.com/mp4m2xs3.

[120] Lopez, C. Todd. *Female Service Members Excelled.* DOD 6/12/2023. tinyurl.com/mw8emk3h

[121] Considine, Ruth. *"...though women tend to lose their identity."* Quote. Sachse Bown, Mary Ann. *Aunt Ruth's Pioneer Women.* What's New at KanColl. tinyurl.com/2mwvb89d.

Chapter 15

Aftermath

So many dead. So many maimed. So many bright futures consigned to the ashes of the past. So many dreams lost in the madness that engulfed us...the survivors of the abyss sat hollow-eyed and silent, trying to comprehend a world without war.
Eugene E. B. Sledge[1]

April 14th, 1945
Dear Mrs. Roosevelt:
Our beloved President is dead...I myself could not believe it. We came as thousands of other people from Europe. We were born in Germany, we are American citizens now. To us President Roosevelt was America. His smile, his charm, his noble personality was symbolic of everything this our country stands for...This letter may never reach you, it does not matter. There are in the little town of Adams four people who will pray for the soul of this great man every day and thank the Lord that such a man was born.
Ernest A. Spicker, M.D.
Adams, Massachusetts[2]

FDR was dead, felled by a cerebral hemorrhage at his Warm Springs, Georgia retreat on April 12, 1945. In Massachusetts, a *Worcester Telegram* editorial stated, "Franklin D. Roosevelt was a casualty of this war as truly as if he had been killed on the field of battle."[3] Three hours after his death, Harry S. Truman was sworn in as the 33rd President of the United States. The following day, the former president's body made a final journey to the White House where a simple service was held, and on the 15th, Franklin Delano Roosevelt was laid to rest at his family home in Hyde Park, New York.

A national day of mourning was held, and shops and businesses shut down. War plants remained in operation. Schools closed, many like Fairview's Memorial Junior High School after students participated in ceremonies featuring a selection of FDR's favorite hymns. Mayor Edward Bourbeau of Chicopee ordered City Hall closed, and flags hung at half-staff.[4] Other communities followed suit. In Holyoke, Robert Gillette respectfully displayed his thirty-two-star American flag. Purchased by his grandfather during the Civil War, the flag had flown following the deaths of Presidents Lincoln, Garfield, McKinley, and Harding.[5]

The mourning period allotted to Franklin Roosevelt seems hasty, but time was of the essence. Truman cautioned, "We are still a nation at war."[6] Yet hope was in abundance. On the very same day that newspapers screamed out the news that FDR was gone, the *Berkshire Eagle* front page headline read, "Ninth Army Drives 15 Miles from Berlin."[7]

In Europe, the end came quickly. Two weeks later, Mussolini was executed by his own countrymen, his body strung upside down at a gas station in Milan. On April 30th in the Fuhrerbunker

---

[1] Sledge, E. B. *With the Old Breed*. Presidio Press. Random House 1981.

[2] *Letter Ernest Spicker to Mrs. FD Roosevelt*. 1945. US Army Quartermaster Museum.

[3] *Quotes Today's TG 4/13/1945. Way We Were, Worcester, MA*. Historical Briefs 1992.

[4] *South Hadley*. Transcript-TG 4/13/1945. Newspapers.com. tinyurl.com/ycyd7a8z.

[5] *Oracle*. Transcript-TG 4/14/1945. Newspapers.com. tinyurl.com/2r5kx6kd.

[6] *Battle Okinawa*. Nat WWII Mus. tinyurl.com/mvu4jsst.

[7] *Truman Takes Up FDR's Tasks*. Berkshire Eagle 4/13/1945. Newspapers.com. tinyurl.com/mr2et8n4.

located below Berlin streets that were now swarming with Russian soldiers, Adolph Hitler committed suicide. He had outlived his enemy, Franklin Roosevelt, by eighteen days. Hirohito would have his reckoning four months later.

On May 7, 1945, the Third Reich came to an end when General Alfred Jodl signed an unconditional surrender. It was a small, understated ceremony. (Eisenhower disdained theatrics.) At Allied Headquarters in Rheims, France, two German officers huddled over a table while Jodl affixed his signature to the document. Representatives of the Allied nations stood close by, including three high ranking American officers, one of them Springfield native General Harold Roe Bull. Eisenhower did not attend. He waited in a room nearby and received his former enemies briefly after the signing. Did they understand the terms and significance of what they had just agreed to? They each answered "yes" and were escorted out. The fighting in Europe had ended.

General Alfred Jodl signing
the surrender of Germany. 7 May, 1945.[8]

Most of the country reacted with calm rejoicing. Massachusetts was no different. Bells rang and church services abounded. At Fort Devens, personnel gathered on the parade ground as the base chaplain led them in prayers. For thousands of Devens prisoners of war, work continued on schedule without incident.[9] The celebration was a bit more spirited in Rochdale. Chester Woodcock proudly reported that locals stuffed a dummy, "hung the cuss over Mill Street...and put a sign on him saying HITLER – KAPUT – JAP – RATS – NEXT." Things got a bit out of control when they started throwing rocks and set Hitler on fire. Thankfully, everything seems to have settled down. "Jimmy Weir was going to wake up the whole village that night, but something must have gummed up the works."[10]

General Evangeline Booth of the Salvation Army believed it was all premature anyway. She was convinced Hitler was alive and hiding out in Boston.[11] Springfield set aside funds for celebration in anticipation of VE Day. When the moment came, however, the "City of Firsts" remained quiet. Too many of their boys were still at war.[12] The Mayor of Leominster had planned ahead, banning observance of the anticipated victory in Europe. Schools and businesses were told to remain open. While he expected residents to offer prayers of thanksgiving, Mayor Mathias LaPierre stated, "VE-day is the beginning of the end, but we still have before us the grim struggle in the Pacific."[13] Ruth Jordan of Grafton echoed his sentiments. She celebrated VE Day by writing to her son, George H. Jordan Jr., who was serving with the 68th Armored Infantry Battalion in Europe.

---

[8] *Jodl signs surrender.* Pub domain photo. NARA 195338. Wiki Commons. tinyurl.com/2fbrzxxy.

[9] *Prisoners Fort Devens Kept At Work.* Fitchburg Sentinel 5/8/1945. Newspapers.com. tinyurl.com/mpmjnjmh.

[10] Woodcock, Chester C. *We Hung Hitler Then Burnt Him.* Rochdale News 1945.

[11] *Hitler Alive... in Boston.* Boston Globe 9/10/1945. Newspapers.com. tinyurl.com/2zkv2xzc

[12] *V-J Celebration Springfield.* Republican 8/9/1945. Newspapers.com. tinyurl.com/53jeer3r.

[13] *Leominster Bans Celebration.* Fitchburg Sentinel 4/3/1945. Newspapers.com. tinyurl.com/bde34rpe.

We surely wish our V.J. Day could be proclaimed very soon. Today has been so very different from the day the Armistice was signed in the first World War. Today has been a very serious one, and aside from the relief to know that the fighting is over in Europe, everyone is anxious to hear from, and know how their boys are...and we realize the struggle ahead of us with Japan.

Mrs. Jordan was unaware that her son had been killed in Germany eleven days earlier.[14]

And so the war continued. When the battle for Iwo Jima had ended a few weeks earlier, 27,000 Marines and Navy were dead, wounded, or missing, one of the costliest battles in Marine Corps history. Fighting moved on to Okinawa, thought to be the last battle before the military set its sights on Japan. Nearly three months and 50,000 casualties later, the island was in American control. The cost to Japan was much greater. Over 100,000 lost their lives in battle or by suicide. The march to Japan had become a bloodbath.

In Washington, Truman met with the Joint Chiefs to consider the country's next step. Given the fanatical response at Iwo Jima and Okinawa by Japan's dying army and Hirohito's own expectation that his people fight to the death, surrender seemed unlikely. Truman's options were sobering. He could either attack the Japanese homeland or drop the newly developed atomic bomb. Casualty figures for the invasion were discussed. MacArthur projected 95,000 dead and wounded on the southern half of Kyushu alone. Other estimates ranged as high as a quarter of a million. While the debate continued, 370,000 Purple Hearts[15] and 250,000 body bags[16] were ordered in preparation for what was expected to be the bloodiest invasion in history.

On July 26, 1945 after talks between Britain, the United States, and Russia, the Potsdam Declaration demanding unconditional surrender was sent to Japan. The terms were somewhat generous considering the death and destruction the country had caused. Enemy forces were to disarm and return to their homes. Peacetime industries could remain operational. "The alternative for Japan is prompt and utter destruction." For Hirohito and his minions, the proposal was unacceptable.

In the early morning hours of August 6, 1945, Commander Paul Tibbets and the crew of the Enola Gay took off from an airfield on Tinian and headed northwest toward Japan. On board was an atomic bomb. Tibbets waited until the B-29 was in flight before informing the crew of their mission. "We are on the way to drop a special weapon on a target today, which (happens) to be Hiroshima. The blast and the explosion are going to be big as hell. You've never conceived anything like what we are going to see." He then offered cyanide to the crew in case things went wrong. All but two declined.[17] Just after 8 a.m., approximately 70,000 Japanese citizens and most of Hiroshima ceased to exit. Silence came from the government of Japan.

Back on Tinian, a second B-29, Bockscar was being prepared. At the controls was Major Charles W. Sweeney, born in Lowell, and a resident of North Quincy. Sweeney had piloted his plane, the Great Artiste when it accompanied the Enola Gay during the bombing of Hiroshima. An atomic bomb with a plutonium core was loaded onto Bockscar. Its target was the industrial city of Kokura. Unlike the Enola Gay, this flight would experience challenges. Due to stormy conditions, Sweeney ordered the bomb to be armed shortly after take-off in order to pressurize the cabin and climb to an altitude above the lightning. Escort aircraft were delayed, forcing the plane to circle for nearly an hour, a concern as the reserve fuel tank was inaccessible due to a malfunction. Cloudy weather conditions over Kokura obscured their vision, and enemy fighter planes began firing at the B-29. After three runs over the target,

---

[14] Wilson, Jayne and Keeras, Joseph. *From Wilderness to Information Age.* Van/Go Graphics 2016.

[15] Polmar, Norman and Allen, Thomas. *Invasion Most Costly.* USNI 8/1995. tinyurl.com/2k2rv34w.

[16] Andrews, Andy. *Decision to drop Bomb.* Yellowhammer News 12/5/2016. tinyurl.com/546d3t8m.

[17] Riley, Eddie C. *Enola Gay Mission.* AF 12/19/2003. tinyurl.com/muya2bm6.

Commander Frederick Ashworth of Wenham, the mission weaponeer, made the decision to switch to the secondary target, Nagasaki. Just after 11:00 a.m., taking advantage of a brief gap in the cloud cover, the second atomic bomb was dropped, immediately obliterating 43 square miles of the city.[18]

Major Charles W. Sweeney. 1945.[19]

Sweeney's troubles weren't over. Fuel tanks were at a dangerous level. Anticipating an emergency landing, he ordered air rescue crews to be notified. There was no response. The plane barely made it to an airfield in Okinawa. Unable to alert the control tower by radio, flares were fired to warn of their approach. As Bockscar's engines were about to fail, Sweeney dropped the plane down onto the runway and skidded to a stop directly behind a B-24 preparing for take-off. They had seven gallons of fuel left.[20]

In Massachusetts, immediate reaction to the use of atomic weapons was subdued. Perhaps due to lack of information about nuclear weapons or horror at the devastation resulting from the bombing, newspapers handled the events from a rather abstract perspective. The *Daily Item* of Lynn reported that a local 21-year-old, Bruce Stockbridge, had been working on the bomb unbeknownst to his parents. Apparently, it came as somewhat of a surprise to the young GI too.[21] In Holyoke, the *Transcript-Telegram* noted that paper from the local Marvellum Company was being used in the production of atomic bombs.[22] An editorial in the *Springfield Daily News* speculated what would happen if the bomb had been in Japanese hands. "The imagination does not need to go farther back than Pearl Harbor."[23] However, in a scan of Massachusetts newspapers during the days following the bombings, there is a decided lack of emotion. The prick of conscience over use of the atomic bomb that would worm its way into twentieth century dialogue was by and large absent. For whatever reason, the often fractious residents of the Bay State were strangely quiet.

One day after the bombing of Nagasaki, Hirohito agreed to surrender...but not unconditionally. Japan would accept the Allied proposal with one addition…that surrender would not compromise his status as a Sovereign Ruler. Apparently, Japan could go down, but Hirohito sure as hell wasn't planning on going with it. Americans were informed of Japan's tentative agreement and its attempt to negotiate. In this case, the people of Massachusetts felt free to air their opinions. "The Japs won't fight much longer, anyhow, with or without their Emperor," said a Brookline man. "We only invite trouble by keeping him

---

[18] *Bombing Nagasaki.* Manhattan Proj. DOE. tinyurl.com/y84r9927.

[19] *Charles Sweeney.* Pub domain photo. NARA. Picryl. tinyurl.com/3hj5cu43.

[20] *Bockscar Flight Path.* Atomicarchive. tinyurl.com/yndk3n8w

[21] *Lynn GI Work Atom Bomb.* Daily Item 8/7/1945. Newspapers.com. tinyurl.com/2s4ard7m.

[22] *Holyoke Product Manhattan Proj.* Transcript-TG 8/7/1945. Newspapers.com. tinyurl.com/yx2m4etj.

[23] *If Japs Had Bomb Imagine!* Republican 8/9/1945. Newspapers.com. tinyurl.com/48ufs6ke

in."[24] From a resident of Holyoke: "It looks as if Hirohito was asking for another atomic bomb. He can have it if he wants it, and he can have it right in Tokyo."[25] One Taunton woman was a bit more adamant. "We've gone this far and can't stop now for one man. They should be wiped out – all of them – now and forever."[26]-A third atomic bomb, earmarked for either Kokura or Niigata, was being readied when Truman brought it to an end. On August 12, 1945, he accepted the Japanese offer of surrender. Hirohito, once divine, was relegated to a ceremonial figurehead.

This time, the celebration was joyous. Many Massachusetts communities attempted to keep the lid on (many prohibited the sale of liquor during VJ day festivities). In Boston, 2,600 police were called to patrol the streets. In spite of elaborate planning by communities, things occasionally got a bit out of hand. Apparently, there was some confusion on August 12 when a major news outlet announced the Japanese had surrendered when, in fact, the paperwork hadn't changed hands yet. Enthusiastic Worcester residents jumped the gun and lit a bonfire downtown so big that firefighters were unable to control it.

[27] At Greenfield's celebration, factory whistles and fire alarms sounded, North Main Street was cordoned off, and 10,000 people attended a parade and fireworks display.[28] However, members of the Greenfield Moose Drum and Bugle Corps had trouble containing their excitement and, at 7 p.m. the night before, had led an impromptu victory parade down Main Street.[29] In Adams, somebody hung Hirohito off of President McKinley's statue.[30] In Fitchburg, the party went on for forty-eight hours. Omer Couture's ice house was destroyed when authorities suspect it was ignited by a spectacular bonfire blazing nearby.[31] The boys in Spencer had some fun as well. "People were dancing in the streets, horns and whistles were blowing...Richie Lilystrom snuck into his grandma's house and stole a jar of homemade peach brandy." Apparently, somebody "borrowed" a 12-gauge shotgun belonging to Scott Gerish's father, "shot off a few rounds, then went home and went to bed."[32] Representative John W. McCormick of Boston celebrated by placing a wreath on the grave of Franklin D. Roosevelt.[33]

On the morning of September 2, 1945 in Tokyo Bay, unlike the jubilation at home, the atmosphere aboard the USS Missouri was intense. Under heavy clouds, over a thousand sailors, Allied officers, and members of the press waited. General MacArthur stood silently behind a table containing the instrument of surrender, written on parchment found in the basement of a building in what was left of Manilla.[34] Billowing above the deck was an American flag that had been flying at the US Capitol on December 7, 1941. Once the sixteen members of the Japanese delegation were on board, opening remarks were made. A representative of Hirohito's government and a leader of the Japanese Imperial Forces solemnly approached the table and signed the surrender document. Next up was MacArthur. Behind him stood General Jonathan Wainwright and British General Arthur E. Percival. Percival had been taken prisoner after the fall of Singapore and Wainwright after Corregidor. The men had been liberated two weeks earlier and now stood somber and dignified, humiliating reminders of Japanese brutality, as MacArthur handed each a pen that had been used in signing.

---

[24] Lerner, Leonard. *Fight Until Hirohito Is Out*. Boston Globe 8/11/1945. Newspapers.com. tinyurl.com/exafvppu.

[25] *Shout Sing*. Transcript-TG 8/14/1945. Newspapers.com. tinyurl.com/2ak6vcu9.

[26] Lerner, Leonard. *Fight Until Hirohito Is Out*.

[27] Taylor, Robert. *New England Home Front WW II*. Yankee Books 1992.

[28] Severance, Charles Sidney. *History Greenfield*. Higginson Book Co 1954.

[29] *V-J Night Found Outlet*. Recorder 8/15/1945. Newspapers.com. tinyurl.com/b7uth4x4.

[30] *Local Celebration*. No Adams Transcript 8/15/1945. Newspapers.com. tinyurl.com/35shhf5t.

[31] *V-J Celebration Climaxed*. Fitchburg Sentinel 8/16/1945. Newspapers.com. tinyurl.com/2c4fs3zn.

[32] Civin, Marty. *Memories*. Marty Civin 2008.

[33] *Wreath on Grave Roosevelt*. No Adams Transcript 8/15/1945. Newspapers.com. tinyurl.com/3apmtc69.

[34] *Japanese Sign Surrender*. Video Transcript ARC ID 39079. NARA. tinyurl.com/mt9cc99f.

General Douglas MacArthur signs the surrender document on the
USS Missouri. Behind (L-R) are Lt. General Jonathan
Wainwright and Lt. General A.E. Percival. September 2, 1945.[35]

Nimitz, representing American military forces, then stepped forward and signed the document under the watchful eye of Admiral Bill Halsey and Rear Admiral Forest Sherman of Melrose, Massachusetts. One by one, leaders of the Allied nations affixed their signatures and made their mark on history.

Admiral Nimitz signs the surrender document on the USS Missouri.
Behind (L-R) are General MacArthur, Admiral Halsey,
and Rear Admiral Forest Sherman. September 2, 1945.[36]

There was only one small hitch in the ceremony that day. MacArthur had planned for a show of American air power to appear above the proceedings. A flock of B-29s was scheduled to gather not far from Tokyo Bay, pull into formation, and then fly over the Missouri. One aircraft, the City of Kankakee, arrived a bit early, and its pilot suggested that they take a quick spin over the Japanese shoreline to view the devastation. However, when the plane headed back to the rendezvous point, they were unable to locate the formation of B-29s due to overcast skies. What they could see, however, was the Battleship Missouri. Crew member Jack E. Ryan of Lexington recalled:

Lock [the pilot] *dropped the plane to an altitude of about 300 feet. Roaring over the ship's decks and guns approximately 100 feet off its port side...Captain Lock "rocked" the plane's wings as it passed the Missouri to acknowledge the ceremony's participants. We were very low, and the Missouri was on my side. I could see all of the sailors dressed up in their whites – long lines of them two or three ranks deep,*

---

[35] *MacArthur signs surrender*. Pub domain photo. NAID 520694. tinyurl.com/24xcbkje.

[36] *Nimitz Signs Surrender*. Pub domain photo. NAID 348666413. Truman PPF. tinyurl.com/ysjemyz6.

a hundred or so in each line...I could see the table with men seated and apparently signing something, but I couldn't see who was doing the signing – American or Japanese.[37]

The big show was late starting. On the deck of the Missouri, the signing had concluded and an anxious MacArthur leaned over to Admiral Halsey, whispering, "Bill, where the hell are those airplanes?" MacArthur would later write, "At that moment, the skies parted and the sun shone brightly through the layers of clouds. There was a steady drone above and now it became a deafening roar and an armada of airplanes paraded into sight, sweeping over the warships..." Above the 258 ships that swarmed around the Missouri in Tokyo Bay, 465 B-29's, and 399 Hellcats, Corsairs, Helldivers, and Avengers appeared overhead.[38] It was a massive flexing of American muscle, perhaps a last exclamation point to the war or perhaps a warning to what remained of the Japanese Empire. The horror that was the Second World War was finally over.

Aircraft fly in formation over USS Missouri
during surrender ceremonies. September 2, 1945.[39]

The first proof of what had happened came in 1944 when the Russian Army surrounded Majdanek in the town of Lublick, Poland. Within days, word of a German prison complex made it into the media, and the world began to discover the depth of the depravity of Hitler and the Nazis. It was just the beginning. Six months later, Auschwitz, where a million innocent victims had been murdered, was liberated. It was January 1945, and the war was still raging. The soldiers who had opened the gates of hell wouldn't be home for months. It was left to members of the press to tell the story.

Victor O. Jones had been reporting since his days at Harvard. In 1944 while working at the *Boston Globe*, he was sent to the European Theater as a war correspondent. Like many others, he had heard rumors of death camps, but the descriptions were so extreme, so "fiendish" that he dismissed them. However, when the Russians invited members of the press to tour Majdanek, Jones was among them, and his skepticism quickly disappeared. The story was heavily covered by the press, and initially Jones hesitated to report on it as there was no New England angle to the story. But by April of 1945, Jones felt it was necessary to "bear witness," to verify what others had already reported. Now that the Allies were deep within Germany, "the full horror of their crimes is apparent everywhere." He wrote, "From this city I can take you on a short jeep drive in any direction and show you sights that will make you physically ill."

---

[37] *John Ryan.* Rogers Funeral Home 9/9/2017. tinyurl.com/bdc7mdtd.

[38] Graff, Cory. *Final Mission.* Smithsonian Mag 9/2020. tinyurl.com/mpfc76kp.

[39] *F4U's FR6F's fly surrender ceremonies.* Pub domain photo. NAID 520775. tinyurl.com/bdf228a8.

Jones told of political prisoners incarcerated there. One man's ability to reason had ceased to function, his mind trapped in a pattern of hatred. He would scratch a few lines into the dirt, point at it yell "Hitler," then violently jump on it until exhaustion set in when he sat down for a few minutes of rest only to begin again. Another would soon be dead from dysentery. Too weak to sit up and shaking so badly he had to hold his jaws to talk, the man said proudly, "They wanted me to collaborate with their puppets. I wouldn't do it." Of those whose only crime was to worship in the Judaic tradition, he said simply, "And then there are the Jews, and, for what few of them are left, the Nazis deserve the deepest concoctions of Hell." Jones had another important point to make, however. "This ends for all time [the] notion that only small groups [are] guilty."[40]

Otto Zausmer apparently felt the same. Zausmer left his native Austria prior to the Anschluss and settled in Boston, taking a job with the *Boston Globe* in 1941. While reporting from Czechoslovakia shortly after VE Day, he visited a camp where Germans, the same Germans who had annexed the Sudetenland and settled into a territory that did not belong to them, were awaiting transport back to Germany. "Now they are driven from their homes, deprived of their jobs, herded into barracks, living on a diet of potatoes, bread, black coffee, and cabbage." He found conditions distressing but "realized that this place was a sanatorium compared with Dachau, Buchenwald or Mauthausen." Zausmer interviewed several of the inmates and found many had developed selective amnesia. When asked what she knew of Nazi camps, a young English teacher screamed, "We had nothing to do with them, and besides, anybody taken to a German concentration camp was guilty in some way." The reaction wasn't uncommon. Zausmer recalled the response of a German nurse when shown pictures of concentration camps. "This is just propaganda, and besides, people sent to concentration camps were asocial."[41]

In her book, *I Refused to Die,* Susie Davidson collected the stories of several Massachusetts men who saw the camps first hand. Leo Barry of Hyde Park remembered the smell. "As we neared the town of Dachau, a stench began to permeate the air, which was indescribable." James B. Aitken of Quincy and South Yarmouth was one of the first to enter Dachau.

What we found was beyond belief. There were lines of railroad cars full of dead bodies at the entrance to the camp. At the stockade, we saw thousands of displaced persons in striped uniforms behind the fence. We saw the gas chambers, the furnaces for cremation, and piles of thousands of dead, naked bodies. It was terrible.

Sol Feingold, raised in Chelsea, was a member of the Army's 42nd Rainbow Division when he approached Dachau. He remembered seeing a white flag flying above the camp. "But the soldiers were very incensed by what they saw—they came across the bodies in the boxcars, and shot some of the SS." Roxbury's Phil Minsky arrived at a small camp nearby that was used to hold inmates until they could be shipped to the ovens at Dachau.

The smell of burning flesh hit us right in the nose. We could not believe what we were seeing. There were bodies strewn about...the striped clothing was still smoldering, and the bodies half burned...We were probably there only a half hour after the SS troopers had fled while shooting any inmates who had tried to get out of their coops. They also set fire to the straw mats the inmates had slept on.
Minsky reflected, "We were experienced soldiers, having been in combat, and we thought we'd seen everything...But we had never seen anything like this."

Six million Jews died at the hands of the Nazis. Many of those who lived made a point of sharing their stories in the hopes that this horror would never happen again. Several of them were from Massachusetts. Israel Arbeiter was in a slave labor camp in Starachowitze, Poland, when he was struck

---

[40] Jones, Victor O. *Views Nazi Horrors.* Boston Globe 4/21/1945. Newpapers.com. tinyurl.com/yn7b26vv.

[41] Zausmer, Otto. *Globe Man Prague.* Boston Globe 8/26/1945. Newspapers.com. tinyurl.com/bds6r58z.

with typhus. Those who were too ill to work had no usefulness to the Nazis, and in the night, the prisoners in quarantine with Arbeiter were called outside. "That night in that barrack, there were 87 people. 86 were killed. I am the only one who came out of there alive." Sylvia Hack was twenty-five when she was sent to Birkenau. She remembers stepping on dead bodies at night when she got up to go to the bathroom and envying them. "They didn't have to see the things I was seeing."[42] After her father was murdered, Rena Finder and her mother were removed from the Krakow ghetto and placed in the concentration camp at Plaszow. She was ten years old. Finder recalled sitting next to her friend when the girl suddenly fell over, murdered by camp commander Amon Goth, who was known to use prisoners for target practice from the balcony of his quarters. She was sent to work at the nearby Emalia factory owned by Oskar Schindler, who would eventually save her life and that of more than 1,000 Jews. Rena Finder and her mother survived, but by then, most of her family were gone.[43]

Today, there are approximately 245,000 Holocaust survivors left. Most found their way to Israel, and many to the United States. Nearly 1,800 live in the Boston area.[44] The New England Holocaust Memorial in Boston was dedicated in 1995. It is inscribed with the words of Buchenwald survivor and Nobel Peace Prize recipient Elie Weisel. "We cannot give evil another chance."[45]

One day after the attack on Pearl Harbor, the Imperial Japanese Army moved to Singapore. The British, under the command of Lt. General Arthur Percival, maintained the Alexandra Hospital, which was overflowing with wounded Allied servicemen. On February 14, 1942, a Japanese soldier approached the hospital. A British officer went out to meet him, pointing to the bright red cross on his armband. The man pulled out his gun and fired. For the next hour, Japanese soldiers roamed the hospital, randomly shooting and bayoneting staff and patients. Following the slaughter, 200 men were rounded up and crammed into an outhouse. The next day, on the pretense of providing water, men were pulled out in small groups and summarily executed. One hundred more died that day. Unable to mount a strong defense and low on supplies, Percival surrendered. He would spend the remainder of the war at the dreaded Changi Prisoner of War Camp.

Capitulation was not enough for General Tomoyuki Yamashita, the Tiger of Malaya, leader of the Japanese troops. For roughly three weeks, his soldiers embarked on the Yamashita-ordered "sook ching," the systematic purging of Chinese from the population of Singapore. The killing was indiscriminate, and an estimated 50,000 died. In 1944, the general was moved to command the Japanese forces in the Philippines. Here, according to the International Crimes Database, thousands of civilians were raped, tortured, and murdered by the men under Yamashita's command.[46]

On September 2, 1945, the war over, the Tiger of Malaya emerged from the jungles of the Philippines and was taken into custody. As per instruction of President Truman, those responsible for commission of war crimes were to be held accountable. One month later, Yamashita's trial began in Manila. It was perhaps the most important of all those to come. The proceedings, however, were held on shaky ground. Unquestionably, those who would sit in judgment had a monumental ax to grind. (In fact, when Yamashita formally surrendered, sitting across the table from him was General Arthur Percival.) The concept of war crime trials was not new. In this case, however, Yamashita was not charged with a single act of violence but rather failure to control the men under his command while they carried out heinous acts. Was this a legitimate crime? Also, MacArthur had assigned a military commission to hear the case. The question of whether or not this group had legal jurisdiction became a problem.

Yamashita was convicted and sentenced to death, coincidentally on the fourth anniversary of the attack on Pearl Harbor. It was the first verdict to be decreed by a World War II war crimes tribunal.

---

[42] Davidson, Suzie. *I Refused to Die.* Ibbetson Street Press 2005.

[43] Rosinski, Jennifer. *Survivor speaks out.* Boston Globe 5/21/2006. Newspapers.com. tinyurl.com/yz83fpky.

[44] Solis, Steph. *Bos home to Holocaust Survivors.* AXIOS Boston 1/24/2024. tinyurl.com/5n89kyzy.

[45] *Memorial.* New Eng Holocaust Mem. tinyurl.com/2jbpun4j.

[46] *Yamashita v. Styer.* Intl Crimes Database 2013. tinyurl.com/3xsk2ne8.

Yamashita would not go quietly. His three defense attorneys brought the case before the US Supreme Court. One of them was A. Frank Reel of Cambridge. In an interview with the *Boston Globe,* Reel stated his opinion that Yamashita, "a quiet, modest old fellow," was a "fall guy" for his superior, General Tojo, and had been denied a fair trial. All the witnesses hated him, Reel claimed, recalling one woman who was prevented from bringing a bag of rocks into the courtroom to throw at the General. "We were rather glad, though, because defense counsel sat right next to Yamashita, and her aim might have been poor."[47]

General Yamashita (back right) stands behind
his defense counsels, including A. Frank Reel
(front right). October 1945.[48]

On February 4, 1946, a front-page article in the *Boston Globe* read, "Yamashita Must Die."[49] The Supreme Court had rejected his appeal. Chief Justice Harlan F. Stone, raised in Amherst, presented the opinion, and one after another, Yamashita's arguments went down. The military commission appointed to stand in judgment had the legal right to adjudicate the defendant's actions. Then, this earth-shattering ruling: "The law of war imposes on an army commander a duty to take such appropriate measures as are within his power to control the troops under his command for the prevention of acts which are violations of the law of war..."[50] One US Judge Advocate referred to the trial as "one of the most far-reaching and important in the history of world jurisprudence."[51] Its implications would have a massive impact on the upcoming war crime trials at Nuremberg and Tokyo, where defendants would be indicted for crimes committed by those who fell under their leadership.

Nineteen days later, the fierce Tiger of Malaya, stripped of medals and insignia and wearing American Army clothing, climbed the steps to the hangman's noose. He used his last words to pray "for the Emperor's long life and his prosperity forever." Tomoyuki Yamashita died an unrepentant criminal, stating, "I do not feel ashamed before God for what I have done..."[52]

When Yamashita met his end, the German war crimes trials had yet to begin. Nuremberg had been chosen as the location, the site of the numerous rallies that laid the foundation of the Third Reich, the site where Nazi race laws were first revealed, and a site almost sacred to the German people. The key players for the Allies had been chosen. Chief among them was Francis Biddell. Educated at Groton and Harvard in Massachusetts and a longtime summer resident of Wellfleet, Biddle was appointed as US

---

[47] Sullivan, Donal. *Lawyer Describes Trial.* Boston Globe 2/21/1946. Newspapers.com. tinyurl.com/3k8armh9.

[48] *Yamashita and Defense Counsels.* Pub domain photo. USASC. NAID 348544604. Truman PPF. tinyurl.com/4yun4hsd.

[49] *Yamashita Must Die.* Boston Globe 2/4/1946. Newspapers.com. tinyurl.com/4wtmh4rr.

[50] *In re Yamashita 1946.* Justia, US Supreme Court. tinyurl.com/2z9pj8h9.

[51] *Trial to Set Precedent.* Republican 10/18/1945. Newspapers.com. tinyurl.com/4v9zt6d3.

[52] *Yamashita Dies on Gallows.* Boston Globe 2/23/1946. Newspapers.com. tinyurl.com/43wxbh6k.

Attorney General by FDR. During his tenure, he famously attempted to silence racist Catholic priest Charles Coughlin, supported Roosevelt's decision to intern Japanese Americans, and successfully prosecuted members of the German espionage operation, Pastorius. In 1945, Truman appointed Biddle to serve as the chief American judge for the first of thirteen International Military Tribunal trials to be held in Nuremberg.

The prosecution was headed by US Supreme Court Justice Robert H. Jackson. Other members of the team included Thomas F. Lambert, resident of Needham and professor of law at BU and Suffolk University. Lambert would prosecute Nazi party chief Martin Bormann (who was tried in absentia as his whereabouts were unknown). A graduate of Williams College and Harvard, Brig. General Taylor Telford was placed in charge of the High Command Trial, better known as the General's Trial. He would replace Jackson as chief prosecutor after conclusion of the first trial. Joining them was Major Frank B. Wallis of Beverly. His job was to present the Nazi Chain of Command before the court.

Dr. Leo Alexander of Newton was also a participant in the trial. With specialties in neurology and psychiatry, he held prewar positions at Worcester State Hospital, Boston City Hospital, and Harvard Medical School. He was sent to Nuremberg as medical advisor to the chief prosecutor. Alexander studied the psyche of Nazis on trial for war crimes and reported his findings.[53] "All this pain and suffering produced absolutely nothing of value. Men with the knowledge of these defendants must have known their experiments were unscientific, more designed to torture and kill than to produce discoveries."[54]

While strategies were being planned, the nuts and bolts of the trial needed to be addressed. The site chosen, the Palace of Justice, had sustained minimal damage during the war. However, renovation was necessary to prepare for the onslaught of trial participants, members of the press, and spectators. For this, Daniel Kiley was chosen. The young man from Roxbury, who in his youth had frequented the Arnold Arboretum as his favorite go-to dating spot, would become a legend in landscape architecture. His design skills were noticed by his superiors during his time in the OSS, and Kiley was sent to Nuremberg to refurbish the courthouse.[55]

Renovation of the courtroom at Nuremberg.[56]

Planning also included space for the defendants. Conveniently located very near the Palace of Justice was a prison. To safeguard those being held, a passage was built, providing access to the court. Guards were assigned. Among them was William H. Glenny of Granby. Born in Holyoke, Glenny later spoke of his experience at Nuremberg. Prison cells were spartan with "only a bolted cot, a chair and a table that was collapsible. No shoes, no belts, no conversation." He recalled his first look at Hermann Goering and commenting that he wasn't such a big man, unaware that the Reich Marshal spoke English.

[53] Coughlin, William. *Leo Alexander.* Boston Globe 7/23/1985. Newspapers.com. tinyurl.com/3vpf9e5u.

[54] Jones, Victor O. *Globe Man in Nuernburg.* Boston Globe 1/31/1947. Newspapers.com. tinyurl.com/5354s94x.

[55] Martin, Douglas. *Dan Kiley Dies.* NYT 2/25/2004. tinyurl.com/4av55e78.

[56] *Courtroom Nuremburg.* Pub domain photo. U.S. Army. Wilford, Melissa. *Trials Tribulations.* US Army 9/2009. tinyurl.com/39ta25ds.

"Once, he was taken out of his cell and had to go by me, and as he came by, he slowed down and gave me a dirty look. He starts with my shoes and comes up slowly. I could swear the hair on my head was coming up." After being a first-hand witness to the trials and the verdicts that followed, Glenny felt the proceedings had been "...fair and just...There's a limit to how far a soldier can go in carrying out orders."[57]

War crimes defendants at Nuremberg.[58]

Emilio DiPalma of East Longmeadow and Holyoke was at Nuremburg as well. He was a battle-hardened nineteen-year-old when he was assigned to guard the prisoners' cells. Later, he was moved to the courtroom to stand behind the defendants. He remembered Hermann Goering as annoying. The Reichsmarschall continually asked for water. DiPalma would fetch it, hand it over, and Goering would hand it back. "Bah, Americanish." Finally losing patience, the young man filled a cup with toilet water, which the Reich Marshal drank, commenting, "Ahhh, gute vasser!" DiPalma felt it was "my little contribution to the war effort."[59]

Documenting the trial for the public and history was essential. Ray D'Addario of Holyoke was a member of the Army Pictorial Service when he was assigned to the International Military Tribunal. The result is a body of photographs that have come to represent the Nuremberg war crimes trials. Photos of the defendants, of Robert Jackson at the podium, and of the devastation in and around Nuremberg were disseminated across the globe. One expert on IMT history stated that D'Addario's photo of Herman Goering wearing sunglasses in the defendant's box is "...known around the world, and if one were to make a silhouette and ask random people what it was, millions would correctly say, 'Nuremberg.'" Ray D'Addario was the only photographer to remain at Nuremberg through all thirteen trials.[60]

[57] Cahill, Patricia. *Guarding Nazi soldiers.* Mass Live 3/27/2011. tinyurl.com/2h7c6zda.

[58] *Nuremburg Trials.* Pub domain photo. 540127 NARA. tinyurl.com/2kjjb5fb

[59] Richer, Alanna Durkin. *Lives Lost: Vet Guarded Nazis.* Wbur, 5/28/2020. tinyurl.com/3xztcemr.

[60] Hevesi, Dennis. *Raymond D'Addario.* Boston Globe 2/19/2011. Newspapers.com. tinyurl.com/2s9j4sef.

Ray D'Addario at Nuremburg Trials. 1946.[61]

On October 16, 1946, ten defendants were executed in the gymnasium of the Palace of Justice prison. Two had escaped the hangman's noose. Robert Ley, Hitler's labor boss, committed suicide before the trial began. (A contributor to the *Berkshire Eagle* had much to say about Ley's death, calling him "a bull-necked straw boss whose guilt-crazed mind drove him to suicide." Apparently, the city of Nuremberg had sent a bill for $4.09 to the Allies to pay for Ley's funeral expenses. "For a prize example of two-bit German arrogance, that would be hard to beat.")[62] Hermann Goering opted for a cyanide capsule. Ray D'Addario was upset that his request for access to the hangings was denied. He later stated: "Today, I'm very, very happy that I didn't see the execution."[63]

Sgt. Joseph Malta of Revere, however, had a birds-eye view. While serving as an MP in Europe and after hearing of the existence of German concentration camps, he volunteered to assist in hanging the Nazi criminals. "These were the ones that gave the orders," said Malta. "They weren't sorry for anything." By the time the trials were over, he participated in the execution of sixty Nazi officials. Malta's take on his grim role was unapologetic. "It was a pleasure doing it...I'd do it all over again."[64]

Five months after opening statements in Nuremberg, the Tokyo war crimes trials began. It had been a lengthy period of preparation. Dissension among the eleven countries participating in the International Military Tribunal Far East (IMTFE) caused a delay in the start of proceedings. Leading the American prosecution team was Rhode Island native and Harvard graduate Joseph B. Keenan. The tough, larger-than-life attorney had made a name for himself during the prosecution of the Machine Gun Kelly gang and for his involvement in drafting federal kidnapping laws after the Lindbergh baby case. Keenan was a self-assured, good old boy who played politics with the likes of J. Edgar Hoover and FDR. As Arnold Brackman pointed out in his history of the Tokyo trials, Keenan was a competent attorney, but: "His knowledge of Asian affairs...did not extend beyond chow mein." More than one of his colleagues felt, "He did not measure up to the job."[65]

John W. Fihelly from Plymouth no doubt concurred. Fihelly had been called to Tokyo by Keenan specifically to handle Hideki Tojo's cross-examination. The former Boston attorney interviewed the Japanese Prime Minister, the most high-profile defendant, fifty-one times at Sugamo Prison. In the days just preceding Tojo's interrogation in court, the two attorneys met multiple times to discuss strategy.

[61] *Ray D'Addario.* Pub domain photo. US Army. Wiki Commons. tinyurl.com/579zembf.

[62] *Accounts Payable.* Berkshire Eagle 8/17/1946. Newspapers.com. tinyurl.com/26v2aetb.

[63] Hevesi, Dennis. *Raymond D'Addario.*

[64] *Joseph Malta.* Find Grave ID 125040151. 2/11/2014. tinyurl.com/y493h7de.

[65] Arnold C. Brackman. *Other Nuremburg.* HarperCollins Publishers 1989.

Twenty minutes before Tojo was to take the stand, Keenan spoke to Fihelly. Keenan was in, and Fihelly was out. The Chief Prosecutor promised he would begin the questioning and later on, defer to Fihelly. But when the moment came, the court would not allow a second prosecutor to step in. Keenan's interrogation was a disaster. "It was the consensus in Tokyo that Tojo had handled Keenan very well," said Fihelly in a *Boston Globe* interview. Interpreters reported Tojo using insulting language with Keenan[66] and successfully finding multiple opportunities to justify his actions. Said one observer, "Tojo had a good morning hanging of Keenan."[67] Keenan's response to the Fihelly issue reeked of sour grapes. "This is not the type of controversy I care to engage in, especially with a subordinate who was dispatched to aid me and who left peremptorily without completing his mission."[68]

It wasn't the only controversy involving Keenan. Truman had appointed John P. Higgins of Jamaica Plain to represent the country as the American judge on the IMTFE panel. Higgins, who had attended BC, BU, Harvard, and Northeastern, had been Chief Justice of the State Superior Court for nearly ten years.[69] Keenan, hoping for a candidate whose reputation equaled that of the men already appointed to the bench, was appalled. "With all due respect to Judge Higgins," wrote Keenan, "he is...known only locally in his state [and] would not constitute an appointment comparable to the foreign members who have been nominated." For an extra shot of disapproval, he added, "...the Superior Court of Massachusetts...does not in the eyes of others reach the dignity of the U.S. District Court."

Five months later, Keenan's comments, including a cable describing the judge as a "distinct embarrassment," somehow made their way to Higgins, who quickly resigned. It appears, however, that Higgins may have been less of a problem for others than for Keenan. The entire team of prosecutors agreed that MacArthur should prevent Higgins from resigning.[70] But the damage had been done, and by July 25, Higgins was back in Boston, telling reporters, "Because of recent deaths among [State Superior] court membership...in fairness to the people of the Commonwealth...I could not remain away for such a long period."[71] Higgins was replaced by Myron Cady Cramer who had been originally suggested as a candidate by Keenan.

Defendants and counsel, Tokyo War Crimes Trial. 1946.[72]

Twenty-eight Japanese officials were placed on trial. The man at the top of the war crimes list, Hirohito, was conspicuously absent. It was feared that to put the emperor on trial would shake the foundations of Japanese society and cause serious complications in establishing a new government.

[66] Hurwitz, Hy. *When Prosecutors Fall Out.* Boston Globe 2/11/1948. Newspapers.com. tinyurl.com/4ndbkdv3.

[67] Lowe, Peter. *Embarrassing necessity.* 7/2018. ResearchGate. tinyurl.com/49xatyuy.

[68] Beech, Keyes. *When Prosecutors Fall Out.* Boston Globe 2/11/1948. Newspapers.com. tinyurl.com/2htztdkf.

[69] *Chief Justice to Represent US.* Boston Globe 2/2/1946. Newspapers.com. tinyurl.com/2tufesu8.

[70] Arnold C. Brackman. *Other Nuremburg.*

[71] *Higgins Home From Trial.* Boston Globe 7/25/1946. Newspapers.com. tinyurl.com/452xsppv.

[72] *Tokyo War Crimes Trial.* Pub domain photo. US Army. Meck, Holly. *Tokyo Trials.* USAHEC 11/18/2010. tinyurl.com/bdz2y4eu.

MacArthur, in charge of the trial, stated: "Destroy him and the nation will disintegrate."[73] Hideki Tojo, at the center of the show, would have to answer for the attack on Pearl Harbor. Also of high interest were the two men who had signed the surrender document on the deck of USS Missouri. One of them, Yoshijirō Uzemu, Imperial Army Chief of Staff, was condemned to life in prison but died two months into his sentence. The other was Mamoru Shigemitsu.

Less hawkish than his co-defendants, Shigemitsu presented a bit of a problem. While serving as Japanese foreign minister during the war, he had advocated for peace. Unfortunately for Shigemitsu, a vengeful world looking for retribution sought to hold him accountable. On his defense team was George A. Furness, a lawyer from Brookline, Massachusetts. A former Army major, he was experienced in defending war criminals, having been assigned to the trials in Manilla in October of 1945. One of his defendants was General Masaharu Homma, the man responsible for the Bataan Death March.[74]

Furness went the extra mile for his client. After his death sentence, he arranged to have Homma's wife meet with MacArthur. She shared her belief that the world would experience "a great loss...if her husband were executed."[75] The world disagreed, and less than a month later, Homma met his end via firing squad. Furness would show the same level of determination for Shigemitsu. Shortly after the verdicts were read, Furness and a fellow defense attorney filed an appeal with the US Supreme Court questioning the legitimacy of the Military Tribunal. The appeal was struck down, the verdict upheld, and Shigemitsu was sentenced to seven years in prison.

In order to assist the prosecution, the government called upon those who had survived incarceration by the Japanese. Thousands of letters were sent to former POWs.

Dear Sir,
War Department records indicate that you were held as a prisoner of war by the Japanese. It is believed that you may have been a victim, witness, or have knowledge of war crimes committed by the Japanese. To do justice for those who suffered so much... it is necessary that every returned prisoner of war make his information of record in writing.[76]

Two of the men who provided affidavits were from western Massachusetts. Wayne A. Nelson of Springfield was twenty years old when he was taken prisoner near Manilla.[77] He somehow survived the Bataan Death March and, for the remainder of the war, was held in some of the most infamous Japanese POW camps, including Fukuoka, O'Donnell, and Cabanatuan.[78] Harold T. Irving of Holyoke was serving in the Philippines when war broke out. With the fall of Bataan, he escaped into the jungles and fought with local guerrillas for over a year before being captured by the Japanese. Surprisingly, Irving's testimony was used by the defense. Prison guard Yoshika Yagi was on trial for brutality against prisoners of war. Irving's testimony stated that the guard was of even temperament, a "happy-go-lucky fellow, always smiling."[79]

In May of 1945, Mrs. Angie Moody of Lynn received a yellowed Filipino bakery invoice with a message written on the back. "Dear Mother and Family: Received your letters...I am well and happy and getting along fine under these conditions. Miss you all very much." It was signed, "Your loving son, Samuel B. Moody." The twenty-one-year-old Army Air Force mechanic had survived the fighting on

---

73 *MacArthur to Chief of Staff US Army.* Office Of Historian. DOS. tinyurl.com/kzzkj63v.

74 *Defend Signer of Surrender.* Boston Globe 1/28/1947. Newspapers.com. tinyurl.com/st2432j3.

75 *Capt Takes Mrs. Homma to MacArthur.* Boston Globe 3/11/1946. Newspapers.com. tinyurl.com/3wa98byh.

76 Gunn, Damon. *Letter War Dept 2014.* Guise, Kim. *Pacific POW Witness.* Nat WWII Mus 4/28/2021. tinyurl.com/44rvkjfe.

77 *Prisoners Interrogated.* Republican 8/31/1946. Newspapers.com. tinyurl.com/4n7vkrcj.

78 *Wayne Nelson.* Central Maine.com. Kennebec J 10/30/2010. tinyurl.com/2s3z3rje.

79 *Sgt Aids Defense of Guard.* Transcript-TG 5/14/1946. Newspapers.com. tinyurl.com/yn764ze4.

Bataan, retreated to Corregidor with Wainwright, and then disappeared. When the letter from Samuel Moody arrived, the family hadn't heard from him in nearly three years. The document, found in an abandoned prison camp near Luzon, was intended as a public relations tool to be broadcast over Japanese airwaves. Since then, however, Moody and his fellow prisoners had been moved to Japan, and his whereabouts were unknown.[80]

Unbelievably, five months after the letter arrived, Samuel Moody came home. He had survived the Bataan Death March, been torpedoed on a hell ship bound for Japan, endured beatings, and lost sight in one eye. The Sergeant was back in Lynn, but not for long. The government chose Moody to tell his story at the Tokyo War Crimes Trial. "After 1244 days as a prisoner of the Japanese, I had come to Japan to testify against my tormentors...My job was to relate truths about Japanese officers—and these were truths that would forever prevent these animals from claiming they were part of the nobility of man."

Moody's testimony was limited to what one Japanese defense attorney referred to as the "so-called Bataan Death March." "I chuckled within myself without cracking a trace of a smile...These twenty-eight accused, who to me were responsible for every beating I took, were being granted the fullest rights and privileges of our laws. It seemed very strange."

Sgt. Moody told his story in bits and pieces in response to questions from the prosecution and defense counsels. One particular exchange stood out in his memory. Defense Attorney Logan asked: "Do you know anything about any orders that were given to the highest-ranking officer on that march?" Multiple objections were voiced by the prosecution. Logan rephrased the question several times. Each time, Moody related anecdotes from his experience until he was finally forced to admit, "I know nothing about any orders about the death march." He immediately knew what he had done. As he walked out of the courtroom, Moody looked over at the defendants. "Instead of hate, I felt pity for these men. Justice made me admit things helpful to their case. In the end, I knew this same Justice would tighten the rope around their deserving necks."[81]

It did. In November 1948, the verdicts were read. Six men would spend the rest of their lives in prison. Seven, including Hideki Tojo, former General of the Imperial Army and Prime Minister of Japan, would hang. In the weeks preceding the execution, a letter arrived at MacArthur's headquarters. Tojo's wife, accepting that her husband would die, requested his body be released to her. Noting that "respect for the remains is not only an old custom of the East but is also a stern rule of Buddhism...." How ironic that she was expecting respect from the Allies for the man who had callously caused the death of thousands of their comrades.[82]

In the early hours of December 23, the condemned men met in a small Buddhist temple in Sugamo Prison. They sipped wine and cheered for a prosperous future for Japan. Tojo and two others shouted, "Banzai!" Only Seishiro Itagaki, former Minister of War, expressed remorse. One by one, they climbed the steps of the scaffold, and one by one, they died.[83] The bodies were quickly transferred to a crematorium in Yokohama, and shortly afterward, their ashes were placed in seven different Jeeps, transported to unknown locations, and scattered. What was left of the Prime Minister, clothing, notebooks, fingernail clippings, a few strands of hair,[84] his glasses, and his false teeth,[85] was returned to his wife. One Athol columnist shared his thoughts on the executions: "So far as Tojo and his evil colleagues are concerned, having failed their emperor by not winning the war, they should have

---

[80] *First Note in 3 Years.* Daily Item 5/8/1945. Newspapers.com. tinyurl.com/565y68vb.

[81] Moody, Samuel B. and Allen, Maury. *Reprieve from Hell.* Pickle Partners Publ 2015.

[82] *Secrecy Tojo Execution.* Athol Daily News 11/26/1948. Newspapers.com. tinyurl.com/4vwjsmet.

[83] *Tojo Defiant Near End.* Berkshire Eagle 12/23/1948. Newspapers.com. tinyurl.com/3tafp984.

[84] *War Lords Death.* Republican 12/23/1948. Newspapers.com. tinyurl.com/bkz558zz.

[85] *Tojo Glasses, False Teeth.* No Adams Transcript 12/23/1948. Newspapers.com. tinyurl.com/487c8twc.

committed harikari, according to the Japanese code of honor. As a matter of fact, Tojo did try but didn't quite succeed. The Allied Tribunal has done a better job."[86]

Finally, it was time for the boys to come home. Since VE Day, 52,000 had arrived in Boston, but millions more were waiting. Planning had been in the works for months, and in September 1945, Operation Magic Carpet commenced. Over 700 ships, including aircraft carriers, Victory and Liberty ships, and passenger liners loaded with exhausted and excited GIs, headed stateside. Boston was expected to see 1,500 each day for a year.[87] Newspapers that had previously contained column after column of KIA or MIA now listed those who were headed home. On December 27, 1,541 members of the Yankee Division stepped off the Lewiston Victory onto the dock in Boston. Seven other ships carrying fellow members of the 26th Infantry were expected in other East Coast ports on the same day.[88] When the Queen Mary pulled up to her berth, aboard were over three hundred homeward-bound men from the greater Boston area.[89]

USS Aiken Victory arriving in Boston with
1,958 troops from Europe. July 1945.[90]

The following February, she would carry eighty war brides from England to their new homes in the US.[91] General Norman Cota of Chelsea, who would be remembered for his heroic deeds at Normandy, arrived alongside those of lesser rank, men like Corp. Leslie E. Williams of Greenfield, who carried scars from his wounds along with three battle stars,[92] men whose names would largely go unnoticed by history but who had unflinchingly stood their ground before the enemy just the same.

They were moved swiftly, not into the arms of loved ones, but to the next stage of their journey. Once off the boat in Boston, the men boarded trains for the short ride to Camp Myles Standish, where they would spend several days undergoing medical checkups and sifting through reams of paperwork. Those in need of medical care found their way to Camp Edwards. The Falmouth base was already feeling

[86] MacKenzie, DeWitt. *MacKenzie's Column*. Athol Daily News 12/23/1948. Newspapers.com. tinyurl.com/mr2xtyhh.

[87] Potter, John. *Thousands GIs Return*. Boston Globe 6/17/1945. Newspapers.com. tinyurl.com/skwd7mwk.

[88] *YD Troops Arrive*. Boston Globe 12/27/1945. Newspapers.com. tinyurl.com/mc9nkn96.

[89] *Men Arriving Queen Mary*. Boston Globe 8/2/1945. Newspapers.com. tinyurl.com/muam96cv

[90] *Aiken Victory arriving Boston*. Pub domain photo. Pvt Frederic Murphy. HAER. Wiki Commons. tinyurl.com/42zyryyt.

[91] *Brides, Babies on Queen Mary*. Boston Globe 2/6/1946. Newspapers.com. tinyurl.com/ycy2bdrf.

[92] *Devens Releases County Men*. Recorder 1/21/1946. Newspapers.com. tinyurl.com/598xmhrj.

the crunch caused by troops who had returned earlier in the year. Its convalescent hospital, which treated 1,300 patients in March, was expected to soon hold 6,000 beds.[93] Fort Devens handled those ready for discharge. All three bases were overextended. On just one day in early September, 1,000 men arrived at Devens for separation, joining the crush of those already standing in line.

Write your name on a white tag and tie the tag to the button on your left breast pocket. When your name is called out, go to the counter where your Army records are...Personal items such as clothing are retained by the soldier. Army equipment like weapons, tents, backpacks, and web gear are turned in... Many times at a separation center, you see shoulder patches from every corner of the world as soldiers from different units are mixed together in the rush to out-process...

The last stage began with signing your discharge papers...The final formality was a graduation ceremony of sorts. In the chapel there was an invocation by the chaplain. He gave a speech about what you, as soldiers, had done, how grateful your nation was, and how you should now go out and resume your lives as good citizens of a free country. Names were called out, and discharge folders issued with a congratulatory handshake. Music played on the chapel organ as you walked out the door back to life as a civilian.[94]

They came home to a country that was about to experience a revolution. Change was in the air. So was love. Four million returning servicemen and women would give birth to the "baby boom." In 1946, 3.4 million bundles of joy made their way into the world, 20 percent more than the previous year. The numbers kept going up and up. After the stork made 4 million visits in 1964, things began to quiet down.[95] That's a lot of bronzed baby shoes.

But it wasn't just footwear on the minds of post-war industrialists. Grim pessimists predicted the healthy economy would slam shut along with the wartime factory doors. Optimists pointed to the potential of a sudden influx of workers into a nation where factories were already up and running. The transition to a peacetime economy was gradual. In March 1946, 62 percent of those listed as unemployed in Massachusetts were veterans.[96] In May, the *Fitchburg Sentinel* reported 3,000 people without jobs, 2,200 of whom were veterans. One year later, unemployment continued to decline, with only 1,600 jobless vets reported.[97] The government had invested heavily in Massachusetts during the war, and the economy of the Bay State fared better than many other parts of the country. Always rich in industry, thousands of workers who built the ships that went to war and produced everything from bombs to shirts now brought their skills to a burgeoning Bay State marketplace.

This time, rather than the hungry military clamoring for goods for the boys overseas, it was the consumer that drove the economy. What about all those babies, for example? They needed toys, right? During the war years, metal, rubber, and wood were rationed as toy manufacturers turned out war materials. Christmas was a bit low-keyed, and Santa struggled to find gifts for under the tree. Massachusetts was home to several well-known toy companies. (In fact, Winchendon was known as the Toy Town.) In 1946, the N.D. Cass Toy Company of Athol noted record sales,[98] and Pressed Products of Holyoke was doing so well that it split into three groups, one of them a toy and novelty division. Its product line featured a walking dog, a tractor model, and the Eff-An-Bee Patsy doll.[99]

---

[93] *Hospitals Increase Population.* Transcript-TG 3/9/1945. Newspapers.com. tinyurl.com/st7ejjp5.

[94] Tabak, Andrew. *Fort Devens, From Boys to Men.* Andrew Tabak 2012.

[95] History.com Eds. *Baby Boomers.* History.com 6/7/2019. tinyurl.com/cy7wduxw.

[96] *Vets Idle MA.* Berkshire County Eagle 3/27/1946. Newspapers.com. tinyurl.com/yc3c4fjj.

[97] *Unemployment Decreases.* Fitchburg Sentinel 5/15/1948. Newspapers.com. tinyurl.com/3u9adw8v.

[98] *Do You Remember.* Athol Daily News 12/10/1946. Newspapers.com. tinyurl.com/mp6w9r2j.

[99] *Holyoke's Industries.* Transcript-TG 8/26/1946. Newspapers.com. tinyurl.com/bdfk77dv.

Even Santa had to make changes during
the war years. Christmas 1940.[100]

The name of the game in postwar toys was plastics. Eight balls, silly putty, and hula hoops all hit it big during the post-war era. Dolls were now constructed with soft plastic body parts. Enter Betsy Wetsy. The doll had been in production since the late thirties. Put a bottle in her pouty little mouth, squeeze in some water, and voila! Betsy's diaper needed changing. Holyoke's Eff-An-Bee folks had a problem with this. They'd been making Dy-Dee, a tinkling tot who blew bubbles, since 1933. They took Betsy's manufacturer, Ideal Toy Company, to court. Unfortunately for Pressed Products, the judge ruled that bodily functions fell outside the domain of the courts. Following Pearl Harbor, doll production had come to a halt, and Betsy had to hold her water until the end of the war when she surged ahead of Dy-Dee and into the hearts of baby boomers across the country.[101]

Plastics roared into the postwar world, changing everything from rope and radios to boats and furniture. Life got easier for wives in the kitchen when a chemist from Shirley invented a product that revolutionized food storage. After working at a plastics company in Leominster during the war, the man found a use for polyethylene, a recently developed substance used in the manufacture of radar. He melted it, molded it, and created a line of products ranging from butter dishes to bowls with burping lids. Earl Tupper became a millionaire by marketing his Tupperware through private sales rather than retailers, and Tupperware parties became an American phenomenon.[102]

---

[100] *Santa Claus and cannons.* Pub domain photo. LOC. tinyurl.com/42bvnzk3.

[101] Izen, Judith. *Betsy Wetsy and Tiny Tears.* DOLLS Mag 4/4/2024. tinyurl.com/5n93r3jk.

[102] *Earl Silas Tupper.* PBS Am Experience. tinyurl.com/36yaxzx8.

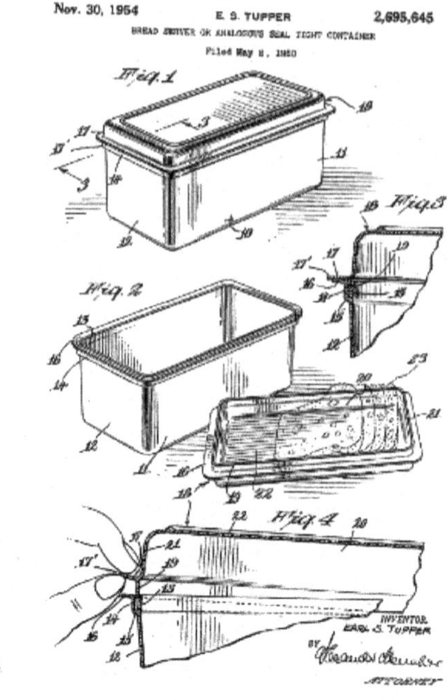

Patent drawing of a seal-tight
container filed by Earl S. Tupper. 1950.[103]

Perhaps the biggest boon to the postwar economy was construction of new homes. In 1946, Harry Truman predicted that 2.7 million houses would be built by the end of 1947. He aimed a little high, but there was good news anyway. The building industry exploded after the war, and 1947 housing starts more than quadrupled over 1945. All across the Bay State, construction was booming. Leominster anticipated an all-time high in home construction, outbuilding the town's 1920's record by half a million dollars.[104] Joseph F. Kelly of Arlington, former Navy Seabee commander, took advantage of the housing market and surplus of veterans. His company sought to hire former Seabees and vets to work on 105 house lots in the Allendale area of Pittsfield.[105] Housing developments were planned across the state, hoping to attract veterans who had access to government-sponsored home loans. Gilbert Barr of Newton saw combat in France, Germany, and Italy before returning home with a Purple Heart in his pocket. While overseas, his wife was forced out of their apartment and had to move in with family. It was less than ideal. Fortunately, Gilbert was able to purchase a home in Oak Hill Park Veterans' Development Housing,[106] a 140-acre site slated to contain 412 homes.[107]

The most popular design for these buildings, the ranch, was a simple, rectangular, two or three-bedroom box with a picture window in the living room and, for pricier homes, an attached garage. Nine out of ten houses constructed during the postwar period were ranch houses.[108] Simple in design and definitely more attractive than the surplus Quonset huts that were popping up, the ranch house was relatively affordable. In Winchester, for example, you could pick up a ranch house with fireplace, electric kitchen, and a tiled bathroom for $13,900.[109]

---

[103] *Seal tight container.* Pub domain image. USPTO Picryl. https://tinyurl.com/2w8aw9nz.

[104] *Leominster Home Construction.* Fitchburg Sentinel 9/3/1948. Newspapers.com. tinyurl.com/9p2c5a3y.

[105] *Seabees CMDR Offers Jobs.* Berkshire Eagle 7/13/1946. Newspapers.com. tinyurl.com/4avaa4ck.

[106] Riley, Arthur *Owning Home.* Boston Globe 11/22/1948. Newspapers.com. tinyurl.com/bdzxhmwd.

[107] *Salvucci Preparing Sites.* Boston Globe 11/22/1948. Newspapers.com. tinyurl.com/bdzxhmwd.

[108] Kviklys, Laura. *1950's Ranch House.* NPS 4/2015. Newspapers.com. tinyurl.com/bdh6fez3.

[109] *Winchester Special.* Real Estate, Boston Globe 10/30/1949. Newspapers.com. tinyurl.com/5e9smswh.

How people spent their hard-earned cash in the feel-good postwar era began to change. For four long years, Americans had worried, and toiled, and gone without, and now they wanted leisure time. What better way to get away from it all than to travel? Six months after the surrender, the *Boston Globe* warned, "New England May Expect Rush of Motoring Vacationists—Travel Facilities to Be Strained."[110] Businesses along the Mohawk Trail made plans to take a chunk of the $500 million expected to be spent on travel. John Treadway of Williamstown felt regional development was essential because tourism "is our bread and butter." North Adams sought to assert its place as the number one city along the Trail. Mayor Bowes warned that the shack town which had sprung up on the top of Mt. Greylock was detrimental to tourism and needed be cleaned up. No problem...Florida, Massachusetts Selectman Donald Canedy announced that the zoning laws on the agenda of the upcoming town meeting would address those nasty eyesores.[111]

Souvenir shop along the Mohawk Trail, 1941.[112]

Cape Cod hoped to keep tourism bucks rolling in after the peak summer months. Art exhibits, dog trials, and horse shows were scheduled for early fall, and $6,000 in prize money awaited golf tournament winners. For fishing enthusiasts, a tuna derby was planned. It was huge. Weigh in stations were located in eight Cape Cod communities, and an array of prizes would be awarded for long fish, many fish, heavy fish, and first fish. Not to overlook female vacationers, one lucky lady would take home the gold for the heaviest tuna caught by a woman.[113]

One popular leisure pastime which experienced a resurgence after the war was board games. In Massachusetts, some manufacturers had no trouble transitioning from ammunition and airplane parts to games. Parker Brothers of Salem still relied on its prewar staple, Monopoly. During the war, the British manufacturer of Monopoly had been granted permission by Germany to include the harmless looking board game in POW first aid packages. Little did they know, the company was working with the Secret Service to hide a map, compass, and small tools inside the game.[114] After the war, Parker Brothers expanded its line to include a game first created in England, Clue. (That explains the whole Colonel Mustard mustache, monocle thing.) At the opposite end of the state, Springfield's Milton Bradley halted war production and ramped up its board game business. One of its postwar products was developed to occupy the time of young polio victims during an outbreak in the 1940s. Candy Land remains popular today.

[110] *New Eng Motoring Vacationists.* Boston Globe 4/14/1946. Newspapers.com. tinyurl.com/4w35jfkx.

[111] *Mohawk Trail Tourist Business.* No Adams Transcript 6/25/1947. Newspapers.com. tinyurl.com/3xs43jfm.

[112] *Souvenir shops Mohawk Trail.* Pub domain photo. LOC. tinyurl.com/3jjkpz95.

[113] *Cape Cod to Greet Visitors.* Boston Globe 8/15/1948. Newspapers.com. tinyurl.com/599vrtmu.

[114] *Get Out of Jail Free.* ABC News/17/2009. tinyurl.com/xn3dmwft.

Monopoly 1935-1941.[115]

     For those who enjoyed reading, there was a shift in literature trends. Non-fiction works about World War II celebrated its heroes, relived the horror of battlefields, dissected the government's role, and recorded the history of the conflict. Shrewsbury's Roscoe Blunt, recipient of a Purple Heart and Bronze Star, wrote of his combat experiences in Europe. *Foot Soldiers* received critical acclaim for its realism.[116] William Shirer reported from Europe during the war and spent his retirement years in Lenox, Massachusetts. His book, *The Rise and Fall of the Third Reich,* sold millions of copies. Always a popular form of entertainment, movies like *They Were Expendable* and *Run Silent, Run Deep* now brought the graphic reality of war to the American public. In 1947, the Best Picture Oscar went to *The Best Years of Our Lives,* which depicted the experience of returning veterans. Massachusetts resident Harold Russell, who lost both hands while serving in the US Army, earned Best Supporting Actor and Special Achievement Oscars for his work.[117]

Harold Russell. 1946.[118]

---

[115] *Monopoly.* Pub domain photo. Lucianomarq. Wiki Commons. tinyurl.com/5cksr3mb.

[116] *Roscoe Blunt.* Britton Funeral Homes 2011. tinyurl.com/2rbhvhjv.

[117] *Handless Actor Two Oscars.* No Adams Transcript 3/14/1947. Newspapers.com. tinyurl.com/bdehe3ws.

[118] *Harold Russell.* Pub domain photo. Samuel Goldwyn Co. Wikipedia. tinyurl.com/5hewvfev.

Massachusetts made its mark in the field of science and medicine during World War II, and advances continued into the post-war era. One development in particular would change the face of American society. The Baby Boom, which could be considered too much of a good thing, gave rise to an interest in contraceptives. Dr. Gregory Pincus was a biologist whose work on in vitro fertilization had cost him his teaching position at Harvard. In the early 50's, he developed a birth control pill in a carriage house on the grounds of the Experimental Foundation for Biology that he co-founded in Shrewsbury. It was a controversial move. Birth control was illegal in Massachusetts, and a huge no-no with the Catholic Church, but the concept seemed to be popular with women. For one trial, eight hundred volunteered. "We couldn't get enough pills," recalled researcher Edris Rice-Wray. "As soon as we got started, everybody wanted to get on it." The FDA was less than enthusiastic, dragging its feet through the post-war period into the 60s before approving the contraceptive.[119]

Not just Massachusetts, but the world was changing as well. There should have been calm across the globe, but what resulted from the upheaval of World War II was a period of destabilization. The sun had finally set on the British Empire, and countries around the world struggled to establish their own independent identities. China was ripped apart by a brutal war of ideologies as Chiang Kai-shek and Mao Tse Tung wrestled for control. Stalin was on the move, gobbling up as much of Europe as he could get away with, and the term "Cold War" began making its way into the vernacular. The Middle East, where Palestine was about to be partitioned, is still unstable today.

In 1945, in an attempt to ensure that the world would never have to endure another global conflict, the United Nations was established. Several Massachusetts towns were hopeful for a shot at the UN headquarters location. For a time, Boston was a serious contender for the site. What about Lenox? It was great for winter sports, and officials hinted that building an extra ski tow wasn't out of the question. Orange, with its three-runway airport and access to all that crystal clear Quabbin water, was hoping for a chance.[120] Camp Myles Standish in Taunton, a short train ride from Boston and with an abundance of soon-to-be empty buildings, was definitely in the running.

The United Nations opted for New York City, and Massachusetts was left with the question of what to do with the Taunton facility. In 1946, Governor Maurice Tobin purchased the camp from the government for one dollar. Noting that hundreds of children with cognitive disabilities were on waiting lists for state care and training, he ordered that an institution to meet their needs be developed at the fArmy camp. The Paul A. Dever School operated on the site until 2002. Today, the former military base is the site of the Myles Standish Industrial Park.

Camp Edwards remains in the hands of the military. In 1947, the Air Force became its own individual branch and eventually assumed control of Edwards, renaming it Otis Air Force Base. The camp still functions today as Joint Base Cape Cod. Westover's history is similar. In 1947, the air base passed into the jurisdiction of the Air Force. It played a major role during the Berlin Airlift of the late 1940s and later became a Military Air Transport Service Base covering the Atlantic region. During the Cold War, Westover served as a Strategic Air Command base and became a high-priority target of the Soviet Union. A secret underground bunker was built in Amherst to be activated in the event of a nuclear attack.[121] The base has been involved in conflicts from the Korean War through the Vietnam era, and in operations in the Middle East. Today, Westover is the largest Air Force Reserve Base in the United States.

---

[119] Emanuel, Gabrielle. *Birth control pill invented.* Wbur 5/24/2023. tinyurl.com/ycxsjckh.

[120] *Orange Site UNO.* Athol Daily News 12/14/1945. Newspapers.com. tinyurl.com/ywvw2bat.

[121] Whittemore, Katharine. *Debunking the Bunker.* Amherst Coll 5/9/ 2017. tinyurl.com/3dr8axar.

Westover Air Force Base. 1976.[122]

    In 1946, Fort Devens was deactivated. With the popularity of the GI Bill, the University of Massachusetts utilized space to provide education classes for returning servicemen and women. Soon, however, Devens would once again act as a training base, this time for soldiers bound for Korea. Fort Devens officially ended its role as an active-duty installation in 1996.

1995 photo of Fort Devens barracks from the air.
All barracks have since been demolished.[123]

    Other former government installations were put to good use in Massachusetts. Squantum Point Park is located on the site of the former Naval Air Station Squantum. A museum and casemates can be visited at Fort Taber/Fort Rodman in New Bedford. Wompatuck State Park, on the grounds of the Hingham Naval Depot Annex, offers hiking, biking, and camping, and the Springfield Armory has been designated a National Historic Park.

    These aren't the only remnants of World War II left behind in the Bay State. In Wellfleet in 2015, a 14-inch projectile was found buried at Marconi Beach. Sgt. William Qualls of the Massachusetts State

---

[122] *Westover AFB*. Pub domain photo. USAF. Wiki Commons. tinyurl.com/mr2jze4e.

[123] *Fort Devens from air*. Pub domain photo. USGS. Wikipedia. tinyurl.com/aekjevtu.

Bomb Squad reported finding a torpedo in Provincetown and a depth charge in Gloucester.[124] In 2010, the fishing boat E.S.S. Pursuit was forced to anchor off New Bedford while it waited to be decontaminated. Several crew members had become ill after chemical weapons were hauled aboard along with a load of clams.[125] As late as March 2024, a gun with a live round and a hollow bazooka shell were pulled out of the Charles River in Needham.[126] None of this should come as a surprise as the government used the waters off Massachusetts as a dumping ground after World War II; some munitions were pitched overboard, some loaded aboard ships and sunk.

A more dangerous legacy can be found in the water and soil of Massachusetts. In 1980, a federal Superfund was created for cleanup of the country's most critical areas of contamination. Owing in part to the historically immense bulk of industry in the Bay State, much of it dating from the World War II era, and in part to numerous former military sites, by 2015 the EPA had identified thirty-two Superfund sites in Massachusetts. Camp Edwards sits on an aquifer which provides water for Cape Cod and was placed on the Superfund list in 1989 after toxins were identified in the water supply. The Watertown Arsenal was added in 1994.

While not identified as Superfund sites, many other areas have been placed under the watchful eye of environmental agencies since World War II. New Bedford Harbor was designated as a trouble spot when genetic changes in the local fish population were noted. Since then, one million cubic yards of soil have been removed.[127] In 1980, several dozen barrels of toxic waste were discovered on the grounds of the former National Fireworks Company in Hanover. Soil and water samples tested positive at twice the minimum level necessary to qualify as a Superfund site.[128] Within the former Hingham Naval Depot property, ten different areas of hazardous soil and groundwater containing an assortment of explosives, munitions, and toxic substances had to be dealt with. Clean-up is expected to conclude in 2031.[129] Other sites that have fallen under the scrutiny of the Environmental Protection Agency include former military sites in Natick, Bedford, Fort Devens, and at South Weymouth Naval Air Station and Hanscom Air Force Base.

By the time the troops returned at the end of the war, they had earned the respect of a grateful nation. Veterans were held in such high esteem that many would be elected to honored places in the government. Following Harry Truman, the next eight presidents all served in the military during World War II (although Jimmy Carter was enrolled in the wartime accelerated program at Annapolis). Two men born in Massachusetts would ascend to the White House, John F. Kennedy (Brookline) and George H. W. Bush (Milton). Many veterans served in postwar government positions in Massachusetts as well. Henry Cabot Lodge Jr., a decorated war hero, returned to the US Senate seat he had given up in 1944 in order to serve his country. Lodge defeated popular David I. Walsh, who had been in the seat for over two decades. Edward Brooke returned from the European Theater of Operations to become the Massachusetts Attorney General before moving on to the Senate. Paul A. Dever, Navy vet, and Francis Sargent, who walked away from war carrying a Bronze Star and Purple Heart, became governors of the Bay State.

The United States underwent sweeping social changes in the postwar period. Women who had parachuted out of planes, built ships, and were now consigned to the home, planted the seeds of discontent that would become the Women's Liberation movement of the sixties.

---

[124] Herwick, Edgar B. *Explosives washing ashore.* WGBH News. World 7/31/2015. tinyurl.com/v46va6wm.

[125] Lindsay, Jay. *Chemical hauled in clam boat.* SouthCoast TODAY. Standard Times 6/8/2010. tinyurl.com/3j3pxrmt.

[126] Johnson, Malcolm and Klein, Asher. *Explosive fished from Charles River.* 10 Boston 3/7/2024. tinyurl.com/yc62pjrh.

[127] *New Bedford Harbor Cleanup.* EPA 2/9/2024. tinyurl.com/mbrpkm4x.

[128] Trufant, Jessica. *Hanover fireworks site.* WICKEDLOCAL.com 9/27/2019. tinyurl.com/y4vcmctd.

[129] *Hingham NAD.* Bombs In Backyard Series. ProPublica 2017. tinyurl.com/5ak6wn8t.

Women welding a destroyer escort hull
plate. Boston Navy Yard. 1943.[130]

Black Americans who had served their country were no longer content to be held down, nor were the thousands of African Americans who had migrated to the industrialized North to fill wartime jobs. The conflict and unrest that arose fed into the bubbling cauldron of Civil Rights that would explode in the late fifties. Boys from the backwoods, from the country, and from cities and towns across America were on the move as well. In the words of a popular World War I song, "How ya gonna keep 'em down on the farm after they've seen Paree?" There was a sense of restlessness in the air. WAC Sgt. Mary Callahan of West Roxbury had concerns about returning to her job as a fourth-grade teacher. "I don't know how I'm going to like it. My tastes may have changed in the Army."[131]

To assist veterans in their quests for new lives, Congress passed the Serviceman's Readjustment Act. John F. Kennedy described the "G.I. Bill" at a 1946 speech in Magnolia, Massachusetts. His words laid out expectations that those who had offered up their lives for their country should be granted full measure in the American way of life which they fought to defend. The legislation included unemployment insurance, home loans, and funding for education. It was a step that would have a major impact on American society.

By the 1940s, many colleges had become elitist institutions inhabited by the wealthy and well-connected, with few opportunities for those of limited means. The acceptance process was described by Harvard President James B. Conant: "Instead of demonstrated ability to profit from a college education...accidents of geography and parental income have played the dominating role." Conant called it "undemocratic."[132] All that was about to change.

Over two million veterans enrolled in higher education through the G.I. Bill. These were not the pliable prewar teenagers sitting in quiet awe of their learned teachers. These were adults who had lived through war. They declined to be treated like eighteen-year-olds and were tough, independent, and self-assured enough to challenge the reasoning and assumptions of their professors. It was a spirit that would change the approach to education, resonate with the youth of the fifties, and emerge full blown in the turbulent rebellion of the sixties.

Born in Charlestown and a resident of Weston, Warren Seavey, a longtime Harvard law professor, was atypical for his time and a good fit for the postwar revolution that was about to take place. Seavey was himself rebellious, or irreverent, or both. His approach to teaching challenged the provincial methodology of Harvard's revered past by simply asking his students, "Why?" He treated colleagues

---

[130] *Women welding hull plate.* Pub domain photo. BOSTS 14958-5. *BNY WWII.* Bost NHP. NPS. tinyurl.com/yzunva5u.

[131] DiPesa, Betty. *WAC WAVE Schoolmarms Again.* Boston Globe 9/11/1945. Newspapers.com. tinyurl.com/5aubzw79.

[132] Chauncey, Henry. *Letter to editor. What People Talk About.* Boston Globe 2/16/1945. Newspapers.com. tinyurl.com/3rd5ache.

and students in the same manner (unthinkable) and insisted upon asking his charges questions without verifiable answers (annoying).[133] For better or for worse, Harvard made him the Faculty Advisor for Servicemen. Believing "that men returning from war were more than the sum of their test scores...he went rogue," wrote Joshua Prager in a *Boston Globe* article. Even though he lacked the authority, he knew that legally, if he told someone Harvard would accept them, the college would have to do just that. His typical response to a veteran's query was, "You are just the sort of man we want. When you are released from the service, come to Cambridge, and we will be glad to take you in."

Applications to Harvard had increased five-fold since the surrender, and the university tried to contain Seavey's enthusiasm for veterans, one of them stating, "...a large group of incompetents will pull the standards down." It didn't have much of an effect. Early in 1946, a uniformed naval officer, hoping to enroll, made his way to the Professor's office. After describing his academic record, the man asked, "Do you want any credentials?" "No, I don't need them," answered Seavey, who accepted him on the spot. Warren Seavey had a major impact on the acceptance practices and pedagogy of Harvard University. The returning servicemen who gained entrance thanks to Seavey earned the respect of many. Harvard Law School Dean Erwin Griswold described them as "the most unusual and probably the best student body" the Law School had ever had.[134]

When the sound of guns and weeping finally quieted, authorities began the grim business of tallying up the cost. In terms of lives, the National World War II Museum estimates 60 million souls were lost. No one will ever know. The people of Europe paid dearly for the ambitions of Hitler and the Nazi party. In Germany, nearly 9 million lost their lives, while its Axis partner, Italy, accounted for 457,000 deaths. The cost in Russian lives is unfathomable...24 million men, women, and children gone. Numbers for the Pacific War are equally horrific. It is impossible to determine how many died in China. The Japanese began their slaughter of Chinese civilians well before the war, and by the time of surrender, as many as 20 million may have disappeared. Over 2 million members of the Japanese military, along with more than a million civilians, died during the war.[135]

In terms of monetary expenditure, the United States tops the list at 341 billion dollars (approximately 6 trillion today), outspending her closest competitor, Germany, by 71 billion dollars. In spite of its ego maniacal superiority complex, Japan could only find 56 billion dollars with which to supply its war machine. Even Italy, at 94 billion, spent more. Great Britain, fifth on the list, provided 120 billion.[136] For America, whose economy, technology, and industry had outpaced enemies and allies alike, the Second World War firmly established it as the number one superpower in the world.

Most of those who had caused this appalling conflict earned their just rewards. Hitler and Goering died by their own hands, Mussolini was killed by his own people, and Tojo hung on the scaffold of his enemy. Hirohito, emperor, supreme ruler, descendant of gods, was demoted. So was his horse. One of Hirohito's famous white horses, Hatsushismo, was discovered in a stable in Tokyo and taken to a farm in Oklahoma where he spent the remainder of his life surrounded by decidedly less than divine farm critters.[137] In addition to the war crimes trial in Tokyo, 5,000 other Japanese criminals were brought before tribunals, and 900 were sentenced to death. After the first hangings at Nuremberg, twelve other trials sentenced 85 defendants to prison terms and 12 to death.

The Allied leaders, the larger-than-life men who had guided the free world to victory, would continue to make history after the war. Winston Churchill fell from power with his party in 1945, remained active in government, and returned to the Prime Minister role in 1951. He spent the remainder

---

[133] Keeton, Robert E. *Warren Seavey.* Harv Law Rev 1966. JSTOR. tinyurl.com/27h4nec4.

[134] Prager, Joshua. *Warren Seavey and Students.* Globe Magazine. Boston Globe 12/25/2022. tinyurl.com/2ky588rx.

[135] *Worldwide Deaths WWII. WWII History.* Nat WWII Mus. tinyurl.com/4rb8bspt.

[136] *World War II Cost.* Parramatta Hist Heritage, City of Parramatta 2020. tinyurl.com/3jnf5kkf.

[137] *Steed Down to Earth.* Berkshire Eagle 8/19/1946. Newspapers.com. tinyurl.com/bpamhzmd.

of his life lecturing, painting, and writing, published a six-volume history of World War II, and won the Nobel Prize for Literature in 1953. Churchill passed away in London at the age of 90.

The Prime Minister was a man of wit, outspoken and often controversial. Though initially critical of FDR's hesitancy to join the war, the two men became close friends and allies. This was not the case with Stalin, the third member of "the Big Three." Churchill understood the importance of bringing Russian resources, namely 30 million men, into the fight, but he never trusted the Russian leader, always remembering Stalin's alliance with Hitler in the Tripartite Pact. Owing to Churchill's fear of a postwar Russia turning its sights on Britain, two months after VE day, he ordered planning for Operation Unthinkable, an attack on Red Army strongholds in Poland and Germany. Churchill was right to be concerned. As soon as the war was over, Joseph Stalin showed his true colors, emerging as a lethal dictator much like Hitler, the man who had caused the death of millions of Russians. Stalin's rule over his Communist regime would last until 1953, when he was felled by a stroke.

Stalin's neighbor, Chiang Kai Shek, held the reins in China until he was ousted during a Chinese civil war led by Mao Zedong. Communism was on the march. Harry S. Truman was not FDR, but he had ended the war and managed to gain enough popular support to win a second presidential term in 1948. His popularity hit a wall, however, when Chairman Mao's Army invaded South Korea. This war would bring down another American hero.

Five years after the last shot was fired in World War II, Truman ordered American troops to stop the spread of Communism on the Korean Peninsula. In command was the man who had been Supreme Allied Commander in the South West Pacific Theater, General Douglas MacArthur. Truman was not a fan, privately referring to him as a prima donna. Even Eisenhower, who had served with the General, stated, "I studied dramatics under him for five years in Washington and four in the Philippines." However, MacArthur was capable and wildly popular, partly because of his successes and mostly because of the incessant public relations campaign waged by the General to nurture his image.

As the conflict progressed, China moved its army closer to the Allied line, and MacArthur pushed for the authority to attack. But looming large behind the Chinese was their ally, Russia. Truman hesitated to become embroiled in another expansive conflict in Asia, particularly one that could launch a third world war. The President told MacArthur to prepare for a cease-fire...the Secretary of State would soon begin peace talks. The General took matters into his own hands, publicly announcing he would offer to meet with the Chinese and threatening a possible Allied invasion if they refused to cooperate. Truman exploded. "I'll show that son of a bitch who's boss. Who does he think he is—God?" MacArthur continued his behind-the-scenes politicking, sending a letter containing decidedly snarky comments aimed at Truman to one of his chief supporters, US Representative Joseph W. Martin from Massachusetts.[138]

The letter, added to the General's long history of failing to obey his Commander in Chief, was enough for Truman. He fired MacArthur. It created a firestorm, fanned by the old soldier who most definitely was not planning to just fade away. He addressed Congress, went on a speaking tour, and delivered the keynote address at the Republican Convention in 1952 where he hoped for the presidential candidate nod. (Eisenhower was chosen instead.) The General spent his later years as a Remington Rand Corporation board member and passed away at the age of 84. He is buried in a marbled and columned tomb in Norfolk, Virginia, a far grander resting place than that of George Washington, John F. Kennedy, or Harry S. Truman.

MacArthur's counterpart in Europe fared better. Much respected by his colleagues, his men, and his country, Dwight D. Eisenhower followed Harry Truman into the White House. Truman had witnessed the rise of the Cold War, which in 1953 landed squarely in the General's lap. Eisenhower did a relatively good job of quieting the situation, calming the Red Scare in the United States by beefing up anti-espionage laws, expanding the powers of the FBI to investigate Communist activities, and working

---

138 MacArthur, Douglas. *Letter to Joseph W. 3/20/1951.* Cvce.eu. Univ LU. tinyurl.com/4f5vvp8k.

behind the scenes to discredit Senator Joseph McCarthy. He was a military man first and foremost, however, and when it came to Communism, his message to Russia was clear. Keep it to yourself. He placed nuclear weapons in European NATO bases conveniently close the Russian homeland. He kept the boiling tensions of the civil rights movement in check, and brought an end to the Korean War. Eisenhower retired to his farm in Gettysburg, Pennsylvania, and passed away at the age of 78.

Harry S. Truman weathered the war and led the country into a prosperous postwar economy. He desegregated the military and integrated women into the armed forces. He had been integral in the destruction of Germany and Japan, yet implemented the Marshall Plan to help rebuild Europe and sent over two billion dollars in aid to Japan. He established the Truman Doctrine, pledging US support to any democratic nation that comes under threat of authoritarianism. In spite of what Truman accomplished for the country and the world, he left office with an approval rating of only 30%. His presidency, however, has withstood the test of time. In a 2021 C-Span survey of presidential historians, Harry S. Truman, Dwight D. Eisenhower, and Franklin Delano Roosevelt are ranked as three of the top six most effective presidents in American history.[139]

President Harry S. Truman[140]

After the initial news of Japan's surrender, the people of Massachusetts quickly turned their thoughts to the postwar world. Strangely, having lost so much and so many, their thoughts did not turn to retribution. They were busy welcoming their sons and daughters home, worrying about the economy, and praying for lasting peace. They looked not to the dark days of the past but toward a brighter the future. On the day following Japan's surrender, an article appeared in the *Springfield Daily Republican* containing a prayer written by a local veteran who had been wounded in the First World War and lost his only son in the second.

---

[139] *Pres Historians Survey 2021.* C-SPAN 2022. tinyurl.com/3pznpwmj.

[140] *President Truman.* Pub domain image. Truman PPF NAID 348309927. tinyurl.com/rbbbhzjw

---

[141] *Prayer of Thanksgiving.* Springfield Daily Republican 8/15/1945. Newspapers.com. tinyurl.com/28y47u9w.

Chapter 16

In Remembrance

They fought together as brothers-in-arms. They died together, and now they sleep side by side. To them, we have a solemn obligation.
Admiral Chester W. Nimitz

It was 1943. The bulk of Germany's oil resources were produced by refineries in and around Ploiesti, Romania. It was a rich target, and the Allies developed a plan to destroy the area, a bombing mission with a twist. Up until then, bombers had been used for precision bombing from high altitudes. For Operation Tidal Wave, a mass of B-24s would take off from North Africa, swoop in low over Ploesti, and drop their payload. On August 1, five bomber groups headed toward the target, and plans began to fall apart. Several planes lost direction. The Germans intercepted Allied communications, and anti-aircraft guns and barrage balloons waited for the approaching planes. As bombs dropped on targets, explosions sent flames upward to engulf the B-24s, and smoke clouded visibility. The damage was only temporary. After repairs and rebuilding, oil once again began to flow from refineries into the German war machine.

Second bombing of Ploesti. May 31, 1944.[1]

Ploesti would continue to be a high priority target for the Allies, and after an attack in 1944, the site never fully recovered. However, the loss of life and materials during Operation Tidal Wave was extensive. Besides the fifty-two bombers destroyed, 310 men lost their lives on what would become known as "Bloody Sunday." Among them was 27-year-old lst Lt. Alfred W. Pezzella of Newton.

In November 1917, General John Pershing observed the burial of three American soldiers who had been killed in a raid in France. In his memoirs, he recalled the service held by a French general at the graves under the sound of distant guns. "This joint homage to our dead...seemed to symbolize the common sacrifices our two peoples were to make in the same great cause."[2] The experience made a lasting impression on General Pershing, who would later publicly state: "I believe that, could these soldiers speak for themselves, they would wish to be left undisturbed where, with their comrades, they

---

[1] *Bombing Ploesti.* Pub domain photo. US Army. LOC. Wikipedia. tinyurl.com/a697kssc.

[2] Pershing, John J. *My Experiences in WW.* 1931. Arcadia Press 2019.

fought the last fight… I recommend that none of our dead be removed from Europe…" Teddy Roosevelt concurred. The body of his son, Quentin, a pilot who had died a hero's death in an air battle behind enemy lines, remained in France. Initially, public opinion swung behind these two well respected American leaders, and soon hundreds of families began requesting their loved ones remain in Europe.[3]

Much debate followed in the court of public opinion. An article in the *Springfield Union* asked, "Shall the American dead in France be disinterred and brought back to America, or shall their bones be allowed to remain permanently in the soil of the country where they fell?" Rumor abounded that many families had expressed their desire to journey to Europe to retrieve their fallen, leading to criticism that only the wealthy would have the privilege of paying their final respects. Discussion continued to snowball, and by the end of 1919, 100,000 letters had reached the War Department imploring the return of loved ones.[4] The government acceded to their wishes, and within five years, 46,000 heroes lost in World War I were repatriated.

Thus by the Second World War, the precedent was set. But to bring those home who died before the end of the conflict was impossible. All available resources were required for the war effort, and that included the space that it would take to ship thousands of coffins home. In addition, many were buried in areas where combat still raged.

Graves of fallen US Marines on Tarawa
before headstones were prepared. November 1943.[5]

It certainly would have been more convenient to let them rest in one of the many cemeteries overseas. However, more than half of families wanted their loved ones returned. One group was particularly vocal. The list of Gold Star mothers in Massachusetts was growing, and many wanted their boys brought home. Joseph J. Brown of the 5th Armored Division had been killed in Germany in 1944, and his mother, Mildred Brown Wolfram of Holyoke, asked Gold Star Mothers to telegraph their leaders in Washington. "Don't let them tell you they want to be with their comrades," she stated. "Do they think Gold Star Mothers can cross the ocean every time they want to place flowers on their son's grave?"[6]

In 1946, Congress approved the Return of the Dead Program. The concept was still controversial. Richard Happel of Pittsfield had strong opinions about returning the dead. "No other nation in the world even contemplates so cold and clammy a project as lugging their war dead home." Happel had a suspicion that the government's choice to return fallen servicemen was the result of a lobbying effort on

---

[3] Hatzinger, Kyle J. *Establishing Am Way of Death.* UNT 2015. UNT Digital Library. tinyurl.com/4kb5tatc.

[4] Haskin, Frederic *American Dead.* Springfield Union 12/12/1918. Newspapers.com. tinyurl.com/mua5p4bh.

[5] *Graves Tarawa.* Pub domain photo. USN. NAID 520722. tinyurl.com/2suhr4xk.

[6] *Mother Urges Return of Bodies.* Republican 2/12/1946. Newspapers.com. tinyurl.com/2sbux47r.

the part of casket manufacturers who stood to gain $800 per coffin. He stated: "It seems a pity that the little bit that remains of them cannot be spared the indignity of being pulled and hauled across two continents, just because some clever operators put over a fast one."[7]

Happel was right about one thing. It would prove to be an expensive endeavor, over 2.6 billion dollars in today's currency. The effort expended by the government to bring home the fallen was nothing short of extraordinary. A promise had been made to those who fought: "The final disposition of our soldiers' remains, in accordance with the wishes of their loved ones, is an inherent obligation of the Government as the final gesture of a grateful country to those who paid the supreme sacrifice." It was a promise the United States took seriously.

In 1947, over 10,000 workers began repatriating the dead. Newspapers that had carried happy stories of those who survived, now wrote about those who had come home to their eternal rest. In October 1947, the Liberty ship, Joseph V. Connolly, was the first to arrive, carrying the remains of 5,600 who had perished.[8] In January 1948, the Army transport, Cpl. Eric G. Gibson, arrived in Brooklyn carrying 1,753 coffins. Aboard were the bodies of Roger Kane (Cherry Valley), Alfred Gomez (Onset), and Alfred Cordes (Great Barrington) along with comrades in arms from forty-three Massachusetts cities and towns who had made their final journey home.[9] By 1951, over 170,000 men and women who had lost their lives in World War II were laid to rest on American soil. Regardless of the government's efforts, however, thousands of heroes would never return.

Not all heroes came home. Burial aboard
USS Liscome Bay, 1943. WWII.[10]

The work of the Return of the Dead Program continues. Instead of the dog tags formerly used as the primary identifier, today the American Graves Registration Command relies heavily upon DNA. It is this remarkable tool that helped to bring Alfred Pezzella home. On August 1, 1943, as the Lieutenant's B-24 dropped its load of bombs over Ploesti, the aircraft was struck by enemy fire. The wings were damaged, it began leaking fuel, and lost altitude. The B-24 rolled over, crashed, and burst into flames. There were no survivors. Those who were lost in the action were interred in a cemetery in Ploesti and later removed to an American military cemetery in Belgium. Several years later, the AGRC set about identifying the DNA of the previously unknown soldiers from the Ploesti raid.[11] On October 20, 2023, an aircraft touched down on the tarmac at Logan Airport in Boston, and after eighty years, Lt. Alfred W. Pezzella came home. He had fought and died in the service of his country, earned a Distinguished Flying

[7] Happel, Richard. *Ghoulish Lobby.* Berkshire Eagle 9/18/1947. Newspapers.com. tinyurl.com/4a7kvtms.

[8] *Joseph V. Connolly.* NavSource Online 10/23/2023. tinyurl.com/34jz56ux.

[9] *Bodies Bay State GI's Arrive.* Boston Globe 1/21/1948. Newspapers.com. tinyurl.com/5n8m6kr8.

[10] *Sea burial.* Pub domain photo. 11/1943 USCG. Wikipedia. tinyurl.com/47auf323.

[11] Wells, Ray. *Alfred W. Pezzella.* AAMB 9/14/2023. tinyurl.com/47d2mr4b.

Cross with Bronze Oak Leaf Cluster, a Purple Heart, and the Air Medal with Four Oak Leaf Clusters. He is buried among heroes at the Massachusetts Veterans National Cemetery in Bourne.[12]

Customs associated with burial during war have changed over the course of American history. During the War of Independence, churchyards or family graveyards received the fallen. The unspeakable death toll of the Civil War, more than 600,000 lives lost, created a crisis...how to bury the dead. Battle survivors, wounded or weary, were unable to remove the hundreds of comrades who hfad fallen, so hastily dug unmarked graves became part of the landscape of every battlefield. While fighting raged, cemeteries sprang up near battlegrounds and hospitals, and soon Abraham Lincoln ordered development of national cemeteries. One site, located on the grounds of Confederate General Robert E. Lee's home, became Arlington National Cemetery.

Today there are 158 national cemeteries in the United States, one of them in Massachusetts. Located in Bourne on 749 acres formerly belonging to Otis Air Force Base, the Massachusetts National Cemetery was dedicated in 1980. With more than 77,000 graves, it is one of the largest national cemeteries in the US. Two Congressional Medal of Honor recipients (Richard DeWort, Korea, and Jared Monti, Afghanistan) are buried here. It is also the final resting place of Lt. Commander Fred Christensen of East Falmouth, the last American World War II flying ace. In Germany, he shot down twenty-two enemy aircraft including the six German planes which he knocked out during a battle that lasted two minutes. Christensen did not fly solo. His co-pilot was Sinbad, a stray black cat he'd picked up along the way. For his efforts, he received the Distinguished Flying Cross, a Silver Star, and the Air Medal. He passed away at age 84 in Northborough.[13]

Capt. Fred J. Christensen Jr. 1944.[14]

A second World War II pilot whose honorable service has been colored somewhat by the events of history is Major General Charles Sweeney of Milton. On August 9, 1944, Captain Sweeney flew his B-29, Bockscar, to Japan and dropped an atomic bomb on Nagasaki. The Japanese agreed to surrender the following day. Years later, Sweeney wrote, "I took no pride or pleasure then, nor do I take any now, in the brutality of war, whether suffered by my people or those of another nation. Every life is precious. But I felt no remorse or guilt...The true vessel of remorse and guilt belonged to the Japanese nation."[15] Sweeney died at age 84 and is buried in the Massachusetts National Cemetery. His gravestone reads, "Great Patriot."[16]

In several instances, the federal government has acquired soldiers' lots, the resting place of veterans in private or community cemeteries, and placed them under the care of the National Cemetery

---

[12] *Alfred Pezzella.* Brasco & Son Mem Funeral Home. tinyurl.com/2kps8r8y.

[13] Marquard, Bryan. *Fred Christensen.* Boston Globe 4/10/2006. Newspapers.com. tinyurl.com/yp2hs7n3.

[14] *Fred Christensen.* Pub domain photo. USAF. Wiki Commons. tinyurl.com/ysaxcb3p.

[15] Howe, Marylyn Sweeney. *Am's Last Atomic Mission.* War's End. tinyurl.com/bde7znen.

[16] *Charles William Sweeney.* Find Grave ID 9113703. 7/17/2004. tinyurl.com/45vmvmux.

Administration. Woodlawn Cemetery Soldiers' Lot in Ayer contains the graves of fifty-two soldiers, most of whom served at Fort Devens. The lot was purchased shortly after World War I, and the last burial occurred in 1931. Also under federal care is the Fort Devens Post Cemetery. Formerly known as Malvern Hill Cemetery, veterans of six American wars rest there. The remains of nearly two dozen German and Italian prisoners of war can also be found here[17] , including Capt. Frederich Steinhoff who committed suicide in the Charles Street Jail in Boston after surrendering his U-boat.

Grave of Frederich Steinhoff, Fort Devens.

As the population of World War II veterans began to age, it became clear that more burial sites would be needed, so the federal government chose to fund state managed cemeteries. In 2001, the Massachusetts Veterans Memorial Cemetery was consecrated in Agawam. Located on sixty acres of former farmland,[18] by 2016, over 7,000 veterans had chosen this location as their final resting place.[19] Nearly two decades after the town of Winchendon dedicated 210 acres for a burial ground, it was designated a state Veterans' Cemetery,[20] and an unusual memorial can be found at the site.

When the German army unexpectedly broke through Allied lines at what would become known as the Bulge, fighting was fierce. To fill in the ranks and provide cover, the 333rd Field Artillery Battalion, a segregated unit of African Americans, was called forward. It experienced devastating losses. Half of its soldiers were killed or wounded. A handful of men were able to find shelter with the help of a local resident near the town of Wereth. After being betrayed by a neighbor, the men were taken prisoner. Unfortunately, their Nazi captors were members of the Waffen SS, a group firmly entrenched in master race and racial inferiority dogma. For these eleven African Americans, it would be a short captivity. According to the National World War II Museum:

At 7:00 p.m. on the evening of December 17, the SS men drove their captors into the forest. There they savagely tortured their victims with rifle butts and bayonets before cutting off many of their fingers and running over them with vehicles—whether before or after the Americans were dead is impossible to say. Then they moved on, leaving the bodies behind.

What makes their story even more painful is that the American government chose to overlook the death of these heroes. When the discovery of the atrocities at Wereth and Malmedy (which occurred on the same day) were reported by investigators, Congress chose to sweep aside the slaughter of the African American troops while acknowledging the victims of the Malmedy massacre. It wasn't until

[17] *Fort Devens Cemetery.* NCA 9/3/2021. tinyurl.com/4tmpyr2c.

[18] *State dedicates cemetery.* Cape Cod Times 4/23/2001. tinyurl.com/3kyzv6cy.

[19] Urban, Cori. *Agawam Veterans Cemetery.* MassLive 5/27/2016. tinyurl.com/yckfduue.

[20] Gershon, Livia. *Cemetery dedicated.* Gardner News 6/8/2005. tinyurl.com/yxzy6dm5.

2017 that the government officially recognized the sacrifice of the "Wereth Eleven."[21] They wouldn't have to wait quite that long in the state of Massachusetts, however. Working with the Central Massachusetts chapter of Veterans of the Battle of the Bulge, nearly a decade before, the Massachusetts Veterans Memorial Cemetery in Winchendon erected a monument to the men who died at Wereth. They were from Alabama and not one had a connection to the Bay State. They were simply eleven heroes who died in the service of the country and were deserving of honor and respect.[22]

Private and community cemeteries throughout the Bay State contain the graves of veterans who served in all wars. Those who have been awarded great medals rest near those who quietly risked their lives or made the ultimate sacrifice in service to their country. Many of those who achieved fame are buried in Massachusetts.

Chester W. Nimitz Jr., son and namesake of the Commander of the US Pacific Fleet, was a naval hero in his own right. A member of the US Navy Submarine Service, Nimitz was stationed on the USS Sturgeon at Pearl Harbor on December 7 and later became Executive Officer on the USS Bluefin. A recipient of the Navy Cross, three Silver Stars, and a Bronze Star, Nimitz, who resided in Needham, is buried in Oak Dale Cemetery in Wellfleet.[23]

Pulitzer Prize winner Art Buchwald, a native of New York, served as a US Marine in the Second World War. After a difficult childhood, he called this experience, "the best foster home he ever had." He served as a munitions handler during several Pacific island campaigns. Postwar, Buchwald became an author, journalist, and newspaper columnist and was noted for his unique and ever-present sense of humor. West Chop Cemetery in Tisbury is the final resting place of this great American humorist.[24]

In 1993, one of the most famous voices in the Bay State was laid to rest in Temple Emeth Memorial Park in West Roxbury. Johnny Most, NBA broadcaster for the Boston Celtics, participated in twenty-eight missions as an aerial gunner on a B-24 in World War II, service for which he earned seven medals.[25] Most was a published author and poet. Among the works he left behind is a poem composed while visiting the graves of those who fell on VE day.

I stood among the graves today and swept the scene with sight.
And the corps of men who lay beneath looked up to say good night.
The thunder still, the battle done, the fray has passed them by;
And as they rest forever more, they must be asking, 'Why?'[26]

It was Memorial Day 1945, and 10,000 people had come to the Boston Common to remember those who had fallen. Five hundred troops stood at attention as Maj. General Sherman Miles read the citation, "For conspicuous gallantry and intrepidity at the risk of life above and beyond the call of duty..."[27] Private Elden H. Johnson of East Weymouth was 23 years old when his platoon was ambushed near Valmontone, Italy.

Braving the massed fire of about 60 riflemen, three machine guns, and three tanks...he stood erect and signaled his patrol leader to withdraw...Pvt. Johnson advanced beyond the enemy in a slow, deliberate walk. Firing his automatic rifle from the hip, he succeeded in distracting the enemy and enabled his 12

---

[21] Lengel, Ed. *333ʳᵈ Field Artillery*. Nat WWII Mus 8/21/2020. tinyurl.com/23b92rr6.

[22] Feifer, Jason. *Winchendon to honor AL Soldiers*. Telegram Gaz 8/16/2006. tinyurl.com/mt5t454n.

[23] *Chester Nimitz Jr*. Find Grave ID 6522592. 6/18/2002. tinyurl.com/3zxar229.

[24] Daly, Chris. *Art Buchwald*. Prof Chris Daly's Blog 5/1/2014. tinyurl.com/3trxpjkz.

[25] *Johnny Most*. Find Grave ID 6876576. 10/25/2002. tinyurl.com/y467fb4h.

[26] *Johnny Most*. Wikipedia 3/24/2024.

[27] *Heroes Honored*. Boston Globe 5/31/1945. Newspapers.com. tinyurl.com/yz8adczf.

comrades to escape. Advancing to within five yards of a machine gun, emptying his weapon, Pvt. Johnson killed its crew. Standing in full view of the enemy, he reloaded and turned on the riflemen to the left, firing directly into their positions. He either killed or wounded four of them. A burst of machine-gun fire tore into Pfc. Johnson and he dropped to his knees. Fighting to the very last, he steadied himself on his knees and sent a final burst of fire crashing into another German. With that, he slumped forward dead. Pvt. Johnson had willingly given his life in order that his comrades might live.[28]

Elden Johnson was awarded the most precious honor which his country could bestow upon him, the Congressional Medal of Honor. Established during the Civil War, it is recognized as "an honor bestowed upon only the most honorable." Of 3,538 Medals of Honor awarded thus far, tiny Massachusetts, with a land mass smaller than forty-four other states and 18 percent of the population of the most populous state, ranks third in the number of recipients.[29] During the Second World War, 472 members of the military received this prestigious honor. Here are a few of their stories.

Elden H. Johnson[30] William G. Walsh[31]

Joseph R. Julian[32] James Montross Burt[33]

During the assault of a hill on Iwo Jima, February 27, 1945, Marine Corps Gunnery Sgt. William G. Walsh and his company came under heavy machine gun fire. Sgt. Walsh fearlessly led the charge up a steep rocky slope, making it to the ridge. When a Japanese grenade fell into the trench where Walsh and his fellow soldiers sheltered, Walsh immediately threw himself upon the bomb, saving his comrades at the cost of his own life. Born in Roxbury, 22-year-old William Walsh was laid to rest among other fallen heroes at Arlington National Cemetery.[34]

---

[28] *Elden Johnson.* CMOHS Stories Sacrifice. tinyurl.com/v2sucrjk.

[29] *MOH Statistics and FAQs.* CMOHS 2024. tinyurl.com/4tds3ezb.

[30] *Elden Johnson.* Pub domain photo. Wiki Commons. tinyurl.com/mwbwntw6.

[31] *Walsh WG.* Pub domain photo. USMC. Wiki Commons. tinyurl.com/3jke9pws.

[32] *Julian JR.* Pub domain photo. USMC. Wiki Commons. tinyurl.com/ecpre979.

[33] *James Burt.* Pub domain photo. US Army. Wiki Commons. tinyurl.com/w2evjmvc.

[34] *William Walsh.* CMOHS Stories Sacrifice 2024. tinyurl.com/5as67v55.

One week later on Iwo Jima, another Marine made the ultimate sacrifice. Born in Sturbridge, Joseph Rodolph Julian and his comrades were pinned down by machine-gun and mortar fire when he made the decision to execute a one-man assault on the enemy. Hurling grenades into a nearby pillbox, he killed two Japanese, seized a discarded rifle, and dispatched the remaining five. The sergeant then disabled two more enemy nests located in caves. His last action was to grab a bazooka and wipe out the remaining pillbox. Joseph Julian was awarded the Medal of Honor in 1945.[35]

Company B, 66th Armored Regiment, whose target was a large German garrison near Aachen, was under the command of Lee resident James Montross Burt. Over a period of ten days, the captain displayed heroic courage in directing his men during the assault. On October 13, 1944, the group fell under heavy fire. Disregarding personal danger, Burt jumped down from his tank, walked to the front of the line, and "calmly motioned his tanks into good firing positions."

On the following day, seeing a nearby infantry commander in trouble, he left his shelter to move seventy-five yards through enemy gunfire to assist the seriously wounded man. While the battle raged, he advanced his tank into enemy lines on three occasions to direct firing or for reconnaissance. Twice, his tank was knocked out from under him, and twice, he climbed into another tank and carried on. In spite of having been wounded, he rescued injured comrades and continued a devastating assault on German forces. "Capt. Burt held the combined forces together, dominating and controlling the critical situation through the sheer force of his heroic example."[36] For the action, which he described as "the most hair-raising experience of his military career," James Montross Burt was awarded the Congressional Medal of Honor.[37]

Massachusetts is the home to many Medal of Honor firsts. William H. Carney was a former slave who escaped north with his family and joined the Massachusetts 54th Infantry. In 1863, he became the first African American Medal of Honor recipient for his heroic actions at Fort Wagner in South Carolina. Carney return to the Boston area after the war and is buried in New Bedford.[38] Born in Boston, Joseph DeCastro had a difficult childhood, ending up for a time at the State Reform School in Westboro. During the Civil War, he joined the Army and fought at Gettysburg. In spite of being wounded twice, DeCastro, of the 19th Massachusetts Infantry, captured the flag of the 19th Virginia Regiment and earned the Medal of Honor.[39] The 18-year-old was the first Hispanic to be so honored. In 1946 when Thomas O'Callahan received the Medal of Honor, he became the only chaplain from Massachusetts to receive the precious award. For his heroic actions aboard the USS Franklin, the mathematics professor from Holy Cross became a legend. O'Callahan was the first US Navy chaplain in history to receive the Congressional Medal of Honor.

A wide variety of medals have been awarded throughout our country's history to mark the accomplishments of military personnel. In 2009, the Massachusetts Medal of Liberty was created to honor Bay State men and women of the military who lost their lives in the line of duty. The town of Milford experienced much loss during World War II, and several of its citizens have received the state's Medal of Liberty. Edward C. Bagnoli was a 31-year-old Sergeant in the US Army when he was killed in action in France on June 25, 1944. Back at home on that fateful day, his son, Edward Charles Jr., was born. Private First Class Thomas F. Rogers, also in the Army, died at age 21 in May of 1944 while serving in General Mark Clark's Fifth Army. On that day, he wrote to his mother: "The going is rough, but I'll be home for Christmas."[40]

---

[35] *Joseph Julian.* CMOHS Stories Sacrifice 2024. tinyurl.com/3ea45953.

[36] *James Burt.* CMOHS Stories Sacrifice 2024. tinyurl.com/y6fxf35c

[37] *Town To Honor Burt.* Berkshire County Eagle 9/19/1945. Newspapers.com. tinyurl.com/mvyvks66.

[38] *William Carney.* Blog Posts. MOHS 12/9/2022. tinyurl.com/2pn7rprj.

[39] Jowdy, Laura. *MOH Recipients Hispanic.* Blog Posts. CMOHS 9/15/2021. tinyurl.com/2s3u2456.

[40] *Medal Liberty Heroes.* Citizens for Milford. tinyurl.com/mr4xfz67.

Massachusetts Medal of Liberty[41]

At a moving 2023 Memorial Day tribute in Northampton, eight World War II veterans were honored. Massachusetts Medal of Liberty recipient Edwin Nartowicz served in North Africa, Italy, and Sicily. He saw combat at the Battle of Monte Cassino, where the Allies suffered over 50,000 casualties. Nartowicz, a few months shy of his 100th birthday, was thrilled with the honor. "It's the greatest thing that's ever happened to me." Pearl Judd received the medal for her father, William Adams, who was killed in France in 1944. "It is absolutely indescribable and so overwhelming. I feel now that he is very definitely not forgotten."[42]

A ceremony in Springfield in 2019 was particularly poignant. PFC Francis E. Drake Jr. lost his life during the battle on Guadalcanal and was buried, unidentified, in a field. He was 20-years-old. The government informed Drake's mother that they were unable to locate his body. In 2011, while digging on his property, a resident of the island discovered human remains, and seventy-five years after being killed in action, Private Drake came home. He was awarded a Purple Heart, the Silver Star, and the Massachusetts Medal of Liberty.[43] Francis E. Drake was the first Springfield Marine to lose his life during World War II. He is buried in the Massachusetts Veterans Cemetery in Agawam.[44]

---

[41] *MA Medal Liberty.* Pub domain photo. MA Nat Guard. tinyurl.com/yc493x4p.

[42] Merzbach, Scott. *Definitely not forgotten.* Hampshire Gazette 5/29/2023. tinyurl.com/bdcuxmj5.

[43] *Marine killed WWII awarded Medal Liberty.* WWLP.com 8/14/2019. tinyurl.com/ycs9ttfw.

[44] *Francis Drake Jr.* Find Grave ID 18436297 10/17/2017. tinyurl.com/yj47s8em.

Each year, citizens of the United States celebrate an important national day of remembrance, Memorial Day. Following the Civil War, General John A. Logan, head of the Grand Army of the Republic, formally designated May 30 as a day for "strewing flowers, or otherwise decorating graves of comrades who died in defense of their country," hence its earliest title, Decoration Day. During the interwar years, Memorial Day became a more festive occasion with parades and picnics which seemed to reflect on the American way of life while remembering those who had protected it. But with the outbreak of World War II, a solemnity fell once again upon the proceedings. Six months after the attack on Pearl Harbor, Shelburne Falls paid tribute to their fallen, and Rev. Frederick Duplissey addressed the crowd.

We find ourselves this day a part of another war that we did not want, and as we remember our heroes of another day, we also have close to our hearts those who have answered the call and gave their lives for our safety and a new pledge grows within us, or at least it should, that we...will see this business through to victory, that a lasting peace and the abundant life shall be a reality.[45]

Some speeches, like that of Rev. McAuliffe in Adams, were more emphatic. "If the veteran dead whose memories were being honored could only speak, they would warn Americans to beware of the forms of government that have betrayed Europe, and they would say that it was not for such forms of rule that they fought and died."[46]

The people of Boston have not forgotten those who made the ultimate sacrifice. Since 2010, flags have been placed on the Common each Memorial Day in memory of Massachusetts servicemen and women who lost their lives in service to the country. In May of 2024, over 37,000 American flags remembered the fallen.[47]

In many towns and cities, it became popular to place permanent reminders within the community to honor those who died in World War II. One of the more common memorials in Massachusetts is naming a street intersection after a veteran. In 1943, the town of Hull dedicated a square on Nantasket Ave. in honor of Sgt. James W. Richardson who fell in North Africa.[48] Two brothers, James and Cornelius Downing, are remembered by a square in their name at the corner of Park Ave. and Lowell Street in Arlington.[49] Jesse Arnold Silva Square is named after the first serviceman from Provincetown who was lost during the war. The 27-year-old paratrooper was killed in the Italian Campaign in February 1944.[50]

Statues are a common method of paying tribute. A likeness of General George S. Patton stands on the Esplanade near the Hatch Shell in Boston. Many communities pay tribute to multiple conflicts in a single monument or space. Leominster's Monument Square recognizes veterans of many conflicts, including World War I and Vietnam, and the more than eighty residents who died in the Second World War. Less typical, a fountain located on the common in Worcester recalls the 518 citizens who lost their lives in World War II. Even more unusual, a few cities have named bridges after those who have fallen. The Pearl Harbor Memorial Bridge in Lowell is dedicated to those who lost their lives on December 7, 1941. Among them were Clifton Edwards aboard the USS Curtis, John Targ aboard the USS Arizona, and Arthur Boyle at Hickham Field.[51]

---

[45] *Tribute To War Heroes.* No Adams Transcript 6/1/1942. Newspapers.com. tinyurl.com/57d37jrs.

[46] *Adams War Dead Honored.* No Adams Transcript 6/1/1942. Newspapers.com. tinyurl.com/mshj6zw5.

[47] Kwangwari Munashe, and Becker, Kaitlin. *MA commemorates Memorial Day.* 10Boston 5/27/2024. tinyurl.com/fns457yh.

[48] *Square Dedicated.* Boston Globe 5/31/1943. Newspapers.com. tinyurl.com/yahn4c57.

[49] *Square Dedicated.* Boston Globe 4/25/1946. Newspapers.com. tinyurl.com/ykbssyak.

[50] *Town Square.* Town of Provincetown. tinyurl.com/43wjpdbm.

[51] *Monuments Memorials.* Lowell Mem Aud. tinyurl.com/bdee85zh.

Memorial to fallen heroes of WWII.
Lawrence, Massachusetts.[52]

One of the more notable memorials in the Bay State marks the heroism of a Medal of Honor recipient who was born in Washington, D.C., enlisted in Wisconsin, and perished in the service of his country over 8,000 miles away from Massachusetts. Cassin Young graduated from the US Naval Academy in 1916. His entry in the Annapolis yearbook described the young sailor:

TEDDY is a cute little devil, but the last is far more appropriate than the first, for ever since his early days here, Teddy has been getting into trouble at pretty regular intervals, but he has, however, managed to get out of trouble at equally regular intervals...Teddy isn't brilliant; he's too irresponsible to be considered one of the more capable men in the Class, but he's got his nerve with him, and that alone should pull him through many a situation.

On December 7, 1941, Young was in command of the repair vessel, Vestal, moored beside the Battleship Arizona. As the Japanese attack began, he hurried to man an anti-aircraft gun, but when the forward magazine of the Arizona exploded, Young was blown off the ship. Quickly climbing back aboard, he safely guided Vestal away from the inferno and ran her aground, where she would later be recovered. For his bravery that day, Cassin Young became one of sixteen Medal of Honor recipients present at Pearl Harbor. Less than a year later, while in command of the heavy cruiser San Francisco at Guadalcanal, the Captain was killed when a Japanese shell struck his ship.[53] In 1943, a grateful nation commissioned the destroyer USS Cassin Young. She survived two kamikaze attacks and seven actions in the Pacific. Today, one of only four remaining Fletcher class destroyers, this memorial to the heroism of a young naval officer from Washington, D.C., can be found at the Charlestown Navy Yard.

Without question, the largest Massachusetts memorial to those who served can be found at Battleship Cove in Fall River. Home to five National Historic Landmarks, Battleship Cove has been in operation since 1965. The destroyer, Joseph P. Kennedy, Jr., was launched in Quincy in 1945. Named after a Bay State native and brother of a future president, Lt. Kennedy lost his life in August 1944 while on a mission to destroy V2 rocket launching sites. The ship proudly served during the Korean War and went to her final berth in Fall Fiver in 1974. The submarine USS Lionfish was commissioned in 1944 and saw two tours of duty in the Pacific during World War II. Decommissioned at the Boston Navy Yard in 1953, she is a memorial to the courageous sailors of the US Naval Submarine Force.

---

[52] *WWII Mem Lawrence* 1/2012. Pub domain photo. Daderot. Wiki Commons. tinyurl.com/2e77p9th.

[53] *Cassin Young.* Lucky Bag. USNA Mem Hall 11/3/2023. tinyurl.com/54bv2snp.

Battleship Massachusetts leaving the
Fore River Shipyard. 1942.[54]

On June 12, 1965, the Battleship Massachusetts made her final voyage. With the gentle nudging of tugs, BB-59 moved up the Taunton River to her new home in Fall River. As the ship arrived, it passed under the towering, incomplete Charles M. Braga Jr. Memorial Bridge, honoring the first Fall River native to perish in World War II. Braga lost his life aboard another battleship, the Pennsylvania, at Pearl Harbor.

The crown jewel in the Battleship Cove collection holds eleven battle stars and has earned her place in history for never having lost a man during combat. The heaviest ship ever constructed at the Fore River Shipyard in Quincy, USS Massachusetts, was commissioned in 1942. Dubbed "Big Mamie," the Massachusetts was active in both the European and Pacific Theaters throughout the war. During her first tour in November 1942 off the coast of Casablanca, she destroyed the French cruiser Jean Bart, firing the first 16-inch shell of the war. The bulk of her service was in the Pacific, where she engaged the enemy in the Gilbert, Solomon, Marshall, and Palau Islands, continuing on to Iwo Jima and Okinawa in 1945. In July of that year, while engaged in bombing an enemy ironworks facility in Japan, she fired the last 16-inch shell of World War II. USS Massachusetts was stricken from Navy records in 1962 and has since become a permanent memorial to Braga and the hundreds of thousands of heroes who served their country in World War II.

In 1919, President Woodrow Wilson established a national day of remembrance to mark the end of the First World War. In honor of the cessation of hostilities on the eleventh hour of the eleventh day of the eleventh month, Armistice Day would be held on November 11 of each year. By 1954, however, the country had been involved in two more major conflicts, and President Eisenhower proclaimed that Armistice Day would forever be known as Veterans Day. "On that day, let us solemnly remember the sacrifices of all those who fought so valiantly, on the seas, in the air, and on foreign shores, to preserve our heritage of freedom, and let us reconsecrate ourselves to the task of promoting an enduring peace so that their efforts shall not have been in vain."

When the guns of the Second World War fell silent, tribute to the 16 million Americans who served began flowing in. President Harry Truman stated, "Our debt to the heroic men and valiant women in the service of our country can never be repaid. They have earned our undying gratitude." Over 400,000 of them made the ultimate sacrifice. Massachusetts had done its part and sent 342,401 of its sons and daughters to war, the ninth highest number of all forty-eight states. Of those, 6,572 never came home.[55]

As painful as it can sometimes be to see a yellowed picture in a family photo album, to stand beside a grave, flowers in hand, or to look upon the American flag knowing its stripes have been stained

---

54 *USS Massachusetts.* Pub domain photo. USN. Wiki Commons. tinyurl.com/57uduaut.

55 Stebbins, Samuel. *States Sent Troops WWII.* 24/7 Wall St 4/26/2023. tinyurl.com/bdd7snp3.

red with the blood of fallen heroes, it is our responsibility to remember. We must never forget those who fought, those whom we loved and lost, and those unknown who died for the great cause of freedom. Today, over eighty years since the bombs dropped on Pearl Harbor, we are the beneficiaries of their legacy. Let the words of General George S. Patton, spoken in Boston six months before his own death in 1945, bring us comfort: "It is foolish and wrong to mourn the men who died. Rather, we should thank God that such men lived."

Two Coast Guardsmen pay silent homage to a fallen comrade in the Ryukyu Islands. 1945.[56]

---

[56] *Coast Guardsmen pay homage.* Pub domain photo. NAID: 513229. tinyurl.com/mu56pws7

Appendix A

Those Who Fought

All that stood between civilization and the abyss of tyranny was their courage, their faith, and their devotion to duty.
Senator Susan Collins[1]

To honor those whose stories should be told...

Osea Audette

The fighting on Tarawa in November 1943 was horrific. The plan was to land on the beach, push inland, and capture an important Japanese airfield. Securing the beachhead alone would cost many lives. Twenty-seven-year-old Osea Audette from Spencer, who had made it through the terrible assault on Guadalcanal, was one of them. Casualties on Tarawa were staggering. In 76 hours, over 3,000 members of the Marines and Navy were either lost or wounded. It was a pyrrhic victory, the source of much controversy in Congress and the press for months afterward.

Back in Spencer, Osea's father, Alexander J. Audette, was not content to sit back quietly and grieve. The forty-eight-year-old grocery store owner applied to the Marines and was rejected, but in March 1945, he was accepted into the US Navy, proudly stepping up to take his son's place. Alexander Audette served on the hospital ship USHS Louis A. Milne.[2]

Sgt. Osea Audette never came home. Unfortunately, his remains have never been located, and today, he rests among his fallen comrades on Tarawa.[3]

Ben Bagdikian

"I was born during a massacre of Armenians and as an infant was carried by my father, mother, and four older sisters through an excruciating escape over frozen mountains." So began the life of the extraordinary BenBagdikian, a native of Turkey. The family found their way to Stoneham, where his father took a position as pastor of a church in Cambridge. Influenced by his frequent forays into Boston area neighborhoods, Bagdikian learned "...that the distribution of inherent talent, decency, inventiveness, and intellectual skill—as well as brutality, greed, and 'invincible ignorance'—are distributed through every level of society."[4] These lessons would be reflected in his writing, for which he would later win a Pulitzer Prize.

When war broke out, the Clark University student joined the Army Air Corps. In a March 1942 letter, Bagdikian eloquently expressed concerns regarding America's position that "we are all Right and they are all Wrong."

I have as fervent a feeling for freedom and my country as anyone on earth. And I am convinced that we must win this war and win it decisively. We will be ruthless in fighting the war and merciless in rejecting any peace that sanctions overt or otherwise international irresponsibility or forceful aggression. In that state of mind, will I kill Japanese and German soldiers and aviators. But I'll be

---

[1] Collins, Susan. *Honoring Veterans WWII*. Susan Collins 9/2/2005. tinyurl.com/mr23jhxk.

[2] Fiske, Jeffrey. *History Spencer, MA*. Spencer Hist Comm 1990.

[3] *Osea Audette*. Find Grave ID 101051551 11/21/2012. tinyurl.com/2mvwamkw.

[4] *Bagdikian, Ben*. HSL. tinyurl.com/2s4esz8a.

damned if I can bring myself to really believe that "we are all Right, and they are all Wrong." We have no choice but to fight the immediate wrong, but anyone with any understanding at all can see that no people, no large group of millions of human beings, are either worthy of annihilation or are "wrong."

Bagdikian returned home after the war, and his beliefs never wavered.[5]

Raymond O. Beaudoin

Army 1st Lt. Raymond Beaudoin[6]

Born in Holyoke, Raymond Beaudoin was a member of the National Guard when he was called to active duty in January 1941. He was with the 30th Infantry Division when they stormed ashore at Normandy.

In April 1945, Lt. Beaudoin and his platoon were headed across an open space on their approach to Hamelin, Germany, when they came under heavy attack. As his men dug in, Beaudoin chose a position closest to the Germans, keeping up heavy fire to cover his men and killing six of the enemy. Under attack from three directions and in need of ammunition and support, Beaudoin made the decision to distract the enemy, hoping that one of his men might successfully get away to find help. He crawled eighty yards over the open ground toward a deadly sniper nest, rifle and bazooka fire so intense that he was covered in debris, and bullets ripped through his uniform. Thirty feet from the enemy, Beaudoin stood up and charged, shooting two snipers and killing a third with his bayonet. Minutes later, he was killed by machine gun fire, having saved the members of his platoon. He was 26 years old. The war in Europe would end one month later. Lt. Raymond O. Beaudoin was awarded the Congressional Medal of Honor. He rests in Notre Dame Cemetery in South Hadley, Massachusetts.[7]

Edward H. Beaumont

On February 6, 1945, Holyoke's *Transcript-Telegram* reported the tragic news...the submarine Tang was "overdue from her last war patrol and presumed lost."[8] The Tang and her skipper, Commander Dick O'Kane, were already the stuff of legend when the government released the information to the public. According to the National WWII Museum, USS Tang sank "...33 enemy ships, the highest scoring

[5] Bagdikian, B H. Letter. Southwick, Albert. *WWII Correspondence Albert B. Southwick 2-6/1942*. Marshall Street 2013.

[6] *Raymond Beaudoin*. Pub domain photo. US Army 200422-A-ZZ999-301. Lange, Katie. *Raymond Beaudoin*. 4/27/2020. US DOD. tinyurl.com/2479xyuc.

[7] Lange, Katie. *Raymond Beaudoin*. 4/27/2020. US DOD. tinyurl.com/2479xyuc.

[8] *Tang Presumed Lost*. Transcript-TG 2/6/1945. Newspapers.com. tinyurl.com/5n6bkbur.

submarine in United States Navy history, making O'Kane the most successful American sub skipper of all time."[9]

During her fourth patrol, at great peril, the men of the Tang rescued twenty-two downed aviators from shallow, shark-infested waters of the Pacific. Aboard was Lt. Edward Beaumont of Worcester. Born in Paxton, the 33-year-old earned a silver star for bravery. The citation reads:

His cool manner and exceptional ability in furnishing his Commanding Officer with vital information on approaches and attacks against enemy shipping contributed directly to the success of his vessel in sinking five enemy ships...His efficiency and calmness contributed directly to the success of his vessel in evading severe enemy counterattacks, sometimes in very shallow waters. His conduct throughout was an inspiration to the officers and men in his ship and were in keeping with the highest traditions of the United States Naval Service.[10]

Beaumont's next patrol would be his last. On October 24, 1944, during operations against a Japanese convoy in the Formosa Strait, the Tang destroyed two ships before one of its own torpedoes swung around and slammed into her. Edward Beaumont, Radioman Charles Andriolo of Woburn, and seventy-six others went down with the Tang that day. Commander Dick O'Kane, who would later be awarded the Congressional Medal of Honor, and eight members of his crew were rescued and spent the remainder of the war in Japanese prison camps.

Lt. Commander Richard O'Kane (center) and aircrewmen
rescued by USS Tang. May 1944.[11]

Raymond W. Bradford

Raymond Bradford was a member of the US Army forces in New Guinea, stationed in the Hollandia supply area. While living in Whatley, Massachusetts, in 1980, he recalled a horrific bombing:

A lone Jap plane...dropped a bomb in the middle of a gasoline dump. The fire which started blew up practically all of the gasoline, ammunition, and rations on the 1,500-yard beach. Our battery – set up along the beach – lost a lot of our equipment...The fire itself was terrifying: great thunderous roars and

[9] *USS Tang.* See & Hear. Nat WWII Mus. tinyurl.com/5zjf3723.

[10] *Edward Huntley Beaumont.* Hall Valor Proj. tinyurl.com/2vx3uf2d.

[11] *USS Tang.* Pub domain photo. USN. NARA 80-G-227987. NHHC. tinyurl.com/vf52k45j.

brilliant multi-colored flashes, sending shrapnel from the ammunition hundreds of yards. Whole barrels of gasoline were blown up into the air to explode over our heads.

He spoke of the rumors that followed.

Japs were about to land from barges. Word was sent down to clear out so artillery might shell it. Another rumor – the fire had reached the poison gas dump...started a frantic scramble for discarded gas masks that made the rest of the affair seem calm in comparison. Truly a night to remember.[12]

Robert Chouinard

Corporal Robert Chouinard was hankering for fried eggs. He'd made it through battles in Austria, France, and Normandy and was hunkered down in a foxhole near Munich when he spied a farmhouse. Luckily, the woman who lived there was an American married to a German, so she gave him eggs. The following day, the temptation was too great, so he headed back to the farmhouse. This time, however, he encountered a German soldier standing in the hallway and an officer seated at a table nearby. Chouinard held up his rifle, shouting, "Halt! Don't move!" The war was coming to an end, so there was no resistance as the officer preferred surrendering to Americans rather than to Russians. The corporal alerted a superior officer. "The next thing I know, a great big herd of soldiers came out of the woods — could have been a hundred. They were there all night, right next to us. Could have wiped us out. They walked out with their hands up." The story could have ended very differently had Chouinard opened fire.[13]

The Corporal had dreamed about becoming a football player since his childhood in Newburyport. Strangely enough, he got his wish. After delaying college due to the draft, he spent three years with the Army in Europe and, at the end of the war, was sent to France to guard German POWs. A football team was formed to pass the time, coached by a Boston College graduate. It was wartime football, played in a hay field, a truck for a locker room, with German POWs for doctors. Chouinard made his way home after the war and enrolled in college, where, in an odd twist of fate, he played football for BC. He went on to become a Physical Education teacher at Salem High School.[14]

Norman D. Cota

Norman Cota began his life in Chelsea, Massachusetts. As a young man, while working in his father's grocery store, he picked up the nickname "Dutch," a name that would follow him throughout his eventful life. After attending Worcester Academy, the young man moved on to West Point, graduating early due to the outbreak of the First World War. A member of the Army Infantry, he was promoted to the rank of Major by the end of the conflict.

---

[12] *A Bicentennial History. Goshen, Massachusetts 1781-1981.*

[13] Mullins, Lisa. *WWII Soldier held his fire.* WBUR 11/11/2021. tinyurl.com/ms3vb4hd.

[14] Crowley, Ellie. *Robert Chouinard.* BC Alum & Friends. tinyurl.com/bddc4aba.

Major General Norman Cota[15]

In December 1944, the Second World War was now three years in, and Cota was called to duty of a different kind. A young private from Detroit had deserted his unit, repeatedly turning down offers to return to his post. Eddie Slovik blatantly stated, "...I'll run away if I have to go out there." It was bad timing. The Battle of the Bulge was raging, and thousands of soldiers were dead, brave men who had stood their ground and died for their efforts. The military was short on sympathy for the likes of Eddie Slovik. He was found guilty of desertion and sentenced to death by Norman Cota, who called the experience "the worst fifteen minutes of my life." Eisenhower supported his decision. Cota later stated, "If I hadn't approved it — if I had let Slovik accomplish his purpose — I don't know how I could have gone up to the line and looked a good soldier in the face."[16] Slovik's life ended by firing squad in January of 1945, the only soldier to be executed for desertion in World War II.

Cota's actions six months earlier on D-Day had already earned him a rightful place in history. Cota had been heavily involved in the planning for Operation Overlord, and as the clock ticked down toward D-Day, he was chosen as Assistant Division Commander for the 29th Infantry, one of the first units scheduled to go ashore at Omaha Beach. However, it was anticipated that the massive amount of men expected to land would create chaos on the beach, so a smaller unit, the "Bastard Brigade," was formed and placed under Cota's command.

They made land at 7:30 a.m. on June 6, 1944, and met with enemy fire so intense that it pinned troops down on the beach, causing Cota to utter his famous words, "Gentlemen, we are being killed on the beaches. Let us go inland and be killed." Seeing barbed wire barricading the top of the sea wall, he ordered a hole to be blown through it and sent his men in. The first one through went down, so Cota raced up the bluff, through the gap, and attacked the German gun emplacement on the other side. At one point, moving so quickly that he outpaced his men, Cota stood calmly waiting for them, "twirling his .45 on his finger." Finding another group making slow progress, he asked, "What outfit is this?" "5th Rangers!" came the reply. "Well, goddamn it then, Rangers, lead the way!" To this day, the Army Rangers' motto remains, "Rangers lead the way."[17]

One of Cota's more famous episodes occurred when he encountered a group of soldiers stalled outside a farmhouse in France. He approached the captain, who explained they were unable to move forward because of enemy fire coming from the building. "Well, I tell you what, captain. You and your men start shooting at them. I'll take a squad of men, and you and your men watch carefully. I'll show you how to take a house with Germans in it."

---

[15] *Norman Cota Sr.* Pub domain photo. PA Nat Guard. Wikipedia. tinyurl.com/5n7f69jt.

[16] *Deserter just desserts.* Ledger 11/4/2017. tinyurl.com/3jvx95mz.

[17] *Norman Cota.* New Eng Hist Soc. tinyurl.com/ykhhr6fa.

Cota pulled two grenades off his jacket and headed toward the farmhouse, his squad following behind. He kicked open the door, lobbed the grenades in, and German soldiers began running out the back. "You've seen how to take a house. Do you understand? Do you know how to do it now?" "Yes sir!" came the response. "Well, I won't be around to do it for you again. I can't do it for everybody."[18]

Brigadier General Norman Cota was awarded the Distinguished Service Cross in 1944 for his actions on D-Day.

For extraordinary heroism in connection with military operations against…enemy forces on 6 June 1944, at Normandy, France. General Cota landed on the beach shortly after the first assault wave of troops had landed. At this time, the beach was under heavy enemy rifle, machine gun, mortar, and artillery fire. Numerous casualties had been suffered, the attack was arrested, and disorganization was in process. With complete disregard for his own safety, General Cota moved up and down the fire-swept beach, reorganizing units and coordinating their action. Under his leadership, a vigorous attack was launched that successfully overran the enemy positions and cleared the beaches. Brigadier General Cota's superb leadership, personal bravery, and zealous devotion to duty exemplify the highest traditions of the military forces of the United States and reflect great credit upon himself, the 29th Infantry Division, and the United States Army.[19]

Cota's grandmother said in a 1945 *Boston Globe* interview, "In accepting all the medals that have been given him, he's always said that he wore them for his boys who really did the fighting and ought to get the credit."[20]

Denton W. Crocker

From his perch atop the roof of the high school in Swampscott, young airplane spotter Denton Crocker little dreamed that he would soon be a "bug chaser," slogging through the jungles and swamps of the Pacific. After graduation from Northeastern University in 1942, the Salem-born Swampscott resident was drafted into the US Army and shipped out to the Pacific. Crocker was a biologist and considered himself lucky to have a post with the 31st Malaria Survey Unit. His job in some of the most malaria-infested locations on the globe involved identifying mosquito specimens, draining mosquito breeding ponds, and making malaria prevention recommendations.

Spraying enlisted men's barracks with DDT,
26th Field Hospital. 1944.[21]

[18] *Norman Cota.* Am Policy Roundtable 6/12/2018. tinyurl.com/384tkuzp.

[19] *Norman Cota Sr.* Mil Hall Honor 2021. tinyurl.com/4f9bu9x6.

[20] *General Debarking Today.* Boston Globe 8/2/1945. Newspapers.com. tinyurl.com/y5d8x4ea

[21] *Spraying barracks DDT.* Pub Domain Photo. Hist Med. A015226. NLM. tinyurl.com/592akrru.

Yet he considered this a much safer duty than many of his Army colleagues. Crocker's memories ranged from leech bites and insect stings to being a passenger aboard a ship loaded with 500 lb. bombs while being attacked.

One time, standing in the noontime mess line, I looked toward the harbor to see a plane low to the water heading for the outermost vessel, the place where ammunition ships anchor away from the other vessels. Unopposed, the plane continued straight for its target and struck. Both disappeared in a great cloud of smoke...as I was explaining what had happened, a great blast struck us, the large mess tent shook violently, and we all ducked. A kamikaze pilot had achieved his glory, and only a disappearing cloud in the sky remained as evidence of what had happened.

A friend and "foxhole mate" said of Crocker, "Denny and I are enormously loyal to our country. We tremble with patriotism in our foxhole."[22]

Howard Cutler

In May 1943, in North Africa, Howard Cutler of West Brookfield was severely wounded in action. The twenty-five-year-old was hit by machine gun fire, a bullet entering his mouth and passing through his jaw and throat before lodging in his shoulder. He was captured by German soldiers who then carried his stretcher seven miles before loading him onto a motorcycle for transport to a German hospital. Luckily, a few days later, the British overran the facility, and the young man returned stateside.[23]

His harrowing experience earned Howard Cutler a place in West Brookfield's World War II history. The young Corporal became the town's first soldier to be drafted, first to be transferred overseas, first to be wounded, first to be captured, and, thankfully, the first to return home.[24]

Doolittle's Boys

On December 7, 1941, the Japanese bombed Pearl Harbor, and the country went to war. One month later, America decided to retaliate, and Lt. General Hap Arnold approved a plan to attack Japan. Enter James Harold Doolittle. The man who had been born to fly entered the Army as an air cadet in 1917 and never looked back. In 1925, Doolittle was awarded the Massachusetts Institute of Technology's first doctorate in aeronautics. By the time war broke out, he had flown an amazing array of aircraft, served as a test pilot, won awards, and earned a reputation as a daredevil. For his efforts, he was promoted to the rank of Lt. Colonel and assigned to lead Hap Arnold's mission to bomb Japan.

It was a crazy plan, and it was perfect for Jimmy Doolittle. His B-25 bombers were expected to take off from an aircraft carrier (bombers had never done that...they were too big), the flight distance to Japan was too far (B-25s could only fly 2,000 miles), and there wasn't enough room in the planes for the required bombs and fuel. None of it seemed to bother Doolittle. He ripped out gun turrets and non-essential equipment to make room for a heavy payload of bombs. Sure, the bombers could take off from an aircraft carrier. They just couldn't land on one. The sixteen B-25s, each with a crew of five, would simply have to drop their load on Japan and fly on to China. For this, he added three extra gas tanks, enough for 2,400 miles. The aircraft carrier Hornet was selected, and the mission was scheduled for April 1942. "They told him [Doolittle] not to go on the raid himself," remembered a member of the sixteenth flight crew, Jacob DeShazer. "It's too dangerous for a man as important as he was — but he was the first one off the carrier."[25]

---

[22] Crocker, Denton. *War On Mosquitos.* Narrative 1942. LOC tinyurl.com/ywtcthr8.

[23] Fiske, Jeffrey *Hist W. Brookfield.* W. Brookfield Hist Soc 2009.

[24] *Odd Items.* Boston Globe 7/5/1943. Newspapers.com. tinyurl.com/5arw64su

[25] *Doolittle Raiders Remember Mission.* ABC News 4/18/2002. tinyurl.com/msk7errh.

A total of eighty men volunteered to join Doolittle on the raid without any information about the mission except that it might very possibly be their last. Many of them were from Massachusetts. David William Pohl of Wellesley, a graduate of Wellesley High School and Babson College,[26] wrote home in March to tell his parents that he was going on an "extended tour."[27] The youngest of Doolittle's Raiders, he served as a gunner on the eighth aircraft to take off. Fifteen of the planes made it to their destination. Pohl's did not. China, one of America's Allies, was regarded as a safe landing place. Russia, at that time still a card-carrying member of the Tripartite Pact, was not. Crew 8 was detained when it landed in Vladivostok after running low on fuel. After being held for thirteen months, the men escaped, all five of them surviving the war.

Eugene F. McGurl, navigator of Crew 5, attended Arlington High School, Northeastern University, and MIT. After successfully striking a power station, oil tanks, and a large manufacturing plant, McGurl's B-25 made it to China. Sadly, Eugene F. McGurl was killed two months later when his plane crashed after a bombing run in Burma.[28]

Col. John A. Hilger was at the controls of the Crew 14 aircraft. Born in Texas, the pilot married Virginia Botterud of Weymouth and was living in Jamaica Plain at the time of the raid.[29] He would enjoy a lengthy career with the Air Force, retiring in 1966 with the rank of Brigadier General.

Edwin W. Horton Jr.'s B-25 was the tenth to lift off the Hornet. The crew, including the gunner-engineer from North Eastham, hit their targets and landed successfully in China in spite of being the only plane seriously damaged by anti-aircraft fire.[30] Horton remained with the US Air Force after the war and retired in 1958 after twenty-three years of service.

On May 20, 1942, "Holyoke hearts swelled with pride" on learning that one of their own, 27-year-old Lt. Carl R. Wildner, had flown with Doolittle on his raid over Japan as navigator of Crew 2. Ironically, Wildner had taken his first airplane ride out of an airfield in Springfield at age fourteen in a plane piloted by Jimmy Doolittle. He was living in Amherst at the time, where he graduated from that town's high school and the Massachusetts State College.[31] Crew 2 successfully dropped their payload and crash-landed in China. Wildner returned home safely after the war.

Crew 15 completed its mission, bombing an aircraft factory and dockyards, before ditching their B-25 off the Chinese coastline. Aboard was another Arlington boy, Howard A. Sessler. The navigator-bomber was 25 years old and a former Northeastern student when he joined Doolittle's mission. Back in Arlington three months later, Sessler claimed to have witnessed a baseball game underway as his plane passed over Kobe. He estimated the 30,000 people at the game "...heard our planes, but didn't seem to know what to do. So they kept right on with the ball game, I guess."[32] After landing in China, as Crew 15 quietly made their way toward safety, they received word that bombardier Ted Lawson had been seriously injured when the seventh B-25 crash landed. One of Sessler's crew mates, Thomas R. White, was a physician who had received his medical degree at Harvard. White tracked down the injured flyer and amputated his leg.[33] All three men would return home after the war, and Lawson would go on to pen his memories in a bestseller, *Thirty Seconds Over Tokyo*.

---

[26] Rottiers, Geert. *Crew 08 David Pohl.* Doolittle Raid 8/15/2023. tinyurl.com/2ycvzrj9.

[27] *Youth in Tokio Attack.* Boston Globe 5/20/1942. Newspapers.com. tinyurl.com/28cdfxmx.

[28] *McGurl.* Doolittle Raiders. tinyurl.com/yh4wdx68.

[29] *Seven Get Medal.* Boston Globe 5/20/1942. Newspapers.com. tinyurl.com/3f3pj4tp.

[30] Rottiers, Geert. *Crew 10 Edwin Horton.* Doolittle Raid 4/16/2023. tinyurl.com/yc2zbhue.

[31] *Holyoker Bombed Japan.* Transcript-TG 5/20/1942. Newspapers.com. tinyurl.com/mr2dr3f4.

[32] Moore, Gerry. *Navy Relief Drive.* Boston Globe 7/17/1942. Newspapers.com. tinyurl.com/4akvzhpf.

[33] Rottiers, Geert. *Crew 15.* Doolittle Raid 9/10/2023. tinyurl.com/44za8x6j.

A B-25 takes off from the deck of the USS Hornet
on its way to take part in Doolittle's Raid. April 1942.[34]

While causing minimal damage, Doolittle's Raid had a profound impact on the two nations. Isoroku Yamamoto had to reconsider his belief that an attack on the homeland by the United States was not feasible, and the Imperial Navy was forced to recall a significant number of air and naval craft from combat areas to protect the country. Japan planned its own retaliation. Four months later, at the Battle of Midway, the United States struck a blow from which the Japanese would not recover. For Americans, still reeling with shock and rage over the events at Pearl Harbor, the success of Doolittle and his men was cause for celebration. All sixteen aircraft had successfully completed their missions, and in spite of the fact that all had crash-landed (fifteen in China, one in Russia), only seven flyers lost their lives. Three men were killed in action; three were executed while prisoners of the Japanese, and one died while incarcerated. One month after the attack, Jimmy Doolittle reluctantly accepted the Congressional Medal of Honor on behalf of his Raiders.

William Driscoll

In the February 1944 edition of the Norton Spirit, an article appeared about Lt. William Driscoll. The 24-year-old had been employed in the Engineering Department of Worcester's Norton Company before joining the Army. By October 1943, he was stationed in England as part of a US Army Air Squadron. One of his colleagues, described as "a regular guy," was actor Jimmy Stewart.

During a mission in late December, the young pilot's Liberator bomber was hit by anti-aircraft fire, which ripped off the plane's rudder. In a letter to his mother, Natalie Driscoll, he spoke of the explosion, which "blasted the earphones from our heads," after which the plane went into an 8,000-foot downward spin. At some point, the bombardier and navigator disappeared. Miraculously, Lt. Driscoll and his co-pilot were able to bring the aircraft back into control, and "...with the help of God and four P-47s for protection," they made it safely back to England.[35]

The following October, Driscoll, now a captain, was flying a B-24 over England when the bomber broke up in mid-air and crashed, killing all twenty-four men on board. William Joseph Driscoll Jr. now rests in Saint John's Cemetery in Worcester, Massachusetts.[36]

The Filthy Thirteen

In June 1943, an officer approached a demolition platoon of the 101st Airborne Division, asking for men willing to participate in maneuvers with the Second Army of Tennessee. "You, you, and you,"

[34] *Doolittle Raid.* Pub domain photo. NAID 520603. tinyurl.com/5eewrhw9.

[35] *Driscoll's Escape.* Norton Spirit 2/1944. Norton Abrasives.

[36] *William Driscoll Jr.* Find Grave ID 208643570 4/2/2020. tinyurl.com/yy5tdxfc.

pointed the man as he picked out the group of "volunteers." Shortly afterward, the paratroopers dropped out of the sky and commenced their mission, causing disruption behind "enemy" lines. The men captured a communications crew, listened in on their opponent's movements, stole vehicles, and disabled others. Discovering the location of a meeting being held by enemy officers, they decorated their uniforms with bars and snuck into the tent during a briefing. Unfortunately, one of the raiders, the 17-year-old who'd come up with the plan, aroused suspicion because he looked too young to be an officer. The jig was up. His team stepped forward, and the entire tent full of Second Army officers became prisoners.[37]

Filthy Thirteen comrades prepare for a mission.
June 5, 1944.[38]

The mayhem was a specialty of this particular platoon. Pvt. Jake McNiece's Filthy Thirteen was a group of hard-drinking, hard-fighting, unruly paratroopers of the 506th Parachute Infantry Regiment. "We were a tough bunch of cookies," McNiece later wrote, "and we had been in every jail and stockade from Rome to Nome and Maine to Spain." But they weren't hardened criminals, just a handful of guys who liked to have fun, even if it meant "Army Reg's violations such as AWOL, drunk, fighting...running off with the colonel's jeep, breaking into the mess hall."[39]

While much has been made of the platoon's no bathe/no shave habits, the Mohawk "scalp lock" (McNiece was one-quarter Chocktaw and wasn't fond of head lice), and "war paint" (the Private declined to put leaves on his helmet because it was like "looking through a brush pile every time someone is trying to kill me," opting for camouflage paint instead),[40] the real story of the men of the Filthy Thirteen is their unwavering courage. As members of the first wave of paratroopers to land in Europe on D-Day, their job was to clear the way for the invading army. McNiece's men were tasked with destroying two bridges and securing another that would impede German reinforcements from entering Normandy.

Among them was George Barans of Adams, Massachusetts, who survived after being wounded early in the battle. Robert S. Cone, known as "Ragman," grew up in Roxbury. The twenty-two-year-old spent two days hiding in a hedgerow with a bullet in his arm before making his way to a nearby farmhouse. Unfortunately, the owner alerted German soldiers, and Cone was taken prisoner. Back in Roxbury, his parents received the sad news. Their son had been killed in action in Normandy. Nearly three months later, an Army lieutenant from East Boston, returning home after escaping his captors, reported meeting Cone in a German hospital. On December 4, a postcard arrived from a POW camp in Germany. Robert was alive. After eleven months, the young man returned home. Robert Cone moved to

[37] Killblane, Richard and McNiece, Jake. *Filthy Thirteen*. Casemate Publ. 2003.

[38] *Paratrooper applies paint.* Pub domain photo. USASC. NARA 111-SC-193551. Wiki Commons. tinyurl.com/cnk3d6wa.

[39] Simison, Cynthia. *Paratrooper jumped with Filthy 13*. Masslive 6/6/2019. tinyurl.com/4p2vdxhd.

[40] Killblane, Richard and and McNiece, Jake. *Filthy Thirteen*.

Hull after the war. Roland Baribeau, "Frenchie," was twenty-nine when he left his family and two children in Springfield to join the paratroopers. Sadly, after successfully landing in Cherbourg, Baribeau was killed in action. He rests among heroes in the Normandy American Cemetery.[41]

The D-Day mission was successful, but the Filthy Thirteen paid a high price. Approximately half were killed, wounded, or taken prisoner. They had displayed "competence, mutual trust, shared understanding…disciplined initiative, and risk acceptance."[42] The Filthy Thirteen had earned the admiration of the US Army and would soon capture the imagination of the American people under a new name, "The Dirty Dozen."

James M. Gavin

Rumor has it that when James Gavin was seventeen years old, he was turned down by a US Army recruiter who told him his parents would have to consent. So Gavin, knowing this would never happen, told the recruiter a sob story. He was an orphan, he said, which had been true before he was adopted. The recruiter bought it, went to a lawyer to become his legal guardian, and signed him up for the Army. Gavin became a risk-taking paratrooper, often participating in training jumps using experimental parachutes. He rose to the rank of Lt. General and, during the war, jumped with his men, fought with his men, and wrote letters home to the families of each and every one he lost. He expected his officers to be at the front of every jump line and at the back of every chow line. He participated in more combat jumps than any other US general officer, earning him the nickname "Jumpin Jim."[43]

Maj. General James Gavin receiving a medal
from Field Marshal Montgomery. September 1944.[44]

Gavin spent the four years of war in combat zones, including Sicily, Sardinia, Normandy, and the Battle of the Bulge. In May 1942, he accepted the surrender of 150,000 enemies, the entire 21st German Army. Later that day, his men opened the gates of the Wobbelin concentration camp. He later wrote: "Even our hatred for the German, deep-seated and intense as it was, was to be added to when we found the concentration camp a few miles from here. The first burgomeister (mayor) committed suicide with his family the night that I arrived. We couldn't understand why until we found the camp. Those things must never be forgotten."[45] James Gavin, who became the youngest US Army division commander in World War II, moved to Massachusetts after the war and became a Vice President of Arthur D. Little Co. in Cambridge.

[41] Simison, Cynthia. *Paratrooper jumped with Filthy 13.*

[42] Shawlinski, Robert et al. *Filthy 13.* NCO J11/29/2022. AUP. tinyurl.com/s9nvhbna.

[43] *Jumpin Jim Gavin.* WETSU 8/4/2020. tinyurl.com/4wu7p3sj.

[44] *James Gavin.* Pub domain photo. AFPU. IWM UK. Wiki Commons. tinyurl.com/s527am27.

[45] Stewart, Chad. *James Gavin.* USO 9/20/2015. tinyurl.com/y5cadw9c.

Richard W. Green

Bosuns Mate Richard Green made several appearances in his hometown paper, the Rochdale News, during World War II. Known as "Smokey," the young man seems to have used humor to get him through his experiences in the Pacific. "I'm still in these beautiful islands, talking to the coconuts," he wrote home in 1945. "The weather here is very warm, the lizards and snakes are taking salt pills daily. I've heard of people frying an egg on the sidewalk, but this is the first time I've ever seen fish wash up on the beach all fried." A more serious tone could be detected underneath the chuckles. "It's going to seem very strange, this going back to civilization. Wish I could talk to 'Bud' Morrison and get a few ideas of what to expect."[46]

George J. Hall

Apparently, 25-year-old George Hall was a rather unassuming young man. In April 1945, Hall, with only one leg, boarded a streetcar and headed to the Boston Common, where he was awarded the Congressional Medal of Honor for extraordinary heroism during the battle at Anzio.[47] On May 23, 1944, Hall's unit came under heavy machine gun and sniper fire. The young Staff Sergeant volunteered to go after the machine guns. He crawled across open ground and tossed a few grenades into the gun site, killing two Germans. Four others surrendered. After encountering a second cluster, he continued throwing grenades until five more Germans surrendered, leaving five of their dead comrades behind. Hall turned his attention to a third group of gunners but was struck by an artillery shell, nearly severing his leg. "As soon as I saw what had happened to my leg, I knew I couldn't go forward anymore," Hall said. "Every time I tried to drag my leg, the pain was so great I had to give up. I yelled for a medic, but there was so much noise nobody could hear me…So, I pulled my sheath knife out and cut through the two tendons that were holding my leg on."[48] His unit was able to eliminate the final group and continue its advance. Hall's Medal of Honor citation reads, "For conspicuous gallantry and intrepidity at risk of life above and beyond the call of duty."

Army Staff Sgt. George John Hall.[49]

[46] *Smokey Green Finds Pacific Hot.* 3/1945. Vol. 2. Rochdale News.

[47] *Speed Brother Home.* Boston Globe 2/17/1946. Newspapers.com. tinyurl.com/mptu8jwd.

[48] Lange, Katie. *George J. Hall.* US DOD 5/23/2022. tinyurl.com/ua7pj5z8.

[49] *George Hall.* Pub domain photo. US Army 220517-A-DO439-082. Lange, Katie. *George J. Hall.*

Sadly, George Hall passed away in February 1946 from a condition he had developed in childhood. He was the first Medal of Honor recipient to die since the close of World War II.[50]

Charles A. Harris

Gunners Mate Charles "Bucky" Harris of Watertown was assigned to a Motor Torpedo Boat in the Pacific Theater. These small, fast vessels, known as Patrol Torpedo or PT boats, carried machine guns and torpedoes and were like annoying hornets, dodging in and out of enemy-held waters to harass shipping, interrupt supply flow, destroy mines, and sink landing craft. Roughly 600 PT boats were built by the Elco and Higgins companies during World War II, and they were, according to the National Park Service, considered expendable.[51]

In the early morning hours of August 1, 1943, in Blackett Strait in the Solomon Islands, twenty-year-old Bucky Harris, sleeping on the deck of his boat, suddenly awoke to see the bow of a Japanese destroyer bearing down on him. He was able to don his life vest before being thrown into the water. His leg was severely injured, and weighed down by a heavy sweater and boots, Harris was having trouble staying afloat. Nearby was another member of the crew who had been badly burned. Somehow, in the darkness, the PT boat captain found the men and attempted to bring them back to what remained of the vessel. Harris, however, was exhausted, telling his commanding officer to leave him behind...he was too tired to swim. "For a guy from Boston, you're certainly putting up a great exhibition out here," Lt. John F. Kennedy replied. He helped Harris remove his sweater and boots, placed the burned man's life jacket strap in his teeth, and guided the men to a remnant of the boat.[52]

The crew of PT-109, including Harris and William Johnston of Dorchester, was rescued a week later. Harold William Marney of Springfield, who had been manning the turret when the boat was rammed, did not survive.[53] Lt. John F. Kennedy, of course, would make history once again in 1961 when he became the 35th President of the United States. Very few Higgins PT boats survived the war, and one of the last remaining Elco, PT-617, today sits in her final berth at Battleship Cove in Fall River.

John J. Hennessey

In 1939, John Hennessey of Waban was heading down the road to a promising career with the US Navy when he opted to resign so he could join a band of mercenaries operating in Asia. It sounds a bit shady, but the actions of Hennessey and his fellow Flying Tigers have become legendary. Two years before, 43-year-old aviator Claire Chenault, who, according to NPR, seems to have had a bit of a prickly personality, was shown the door labeled "early retirement" by the US Army. Not willing to give up flying, he found his way to the Chinese Air Force on the eve of a bloody war with Japan. Chenault wrangled the sale of 100 Curtis P-40s from the US and managed to coerce nearly as many members of the US military to pilot them. Hennessey and his fellow flyers first saw combat shortly after Pearl Harbor when their base was attacked by Japanese bombers. The Flying Tigers successfully shot down nine out of ten of the enemy's planes with the loss of one, which crash-landed after running out of fuel.

[50] *Speed Brother Home.* Boston Globe,

[51] *PT Boats WWII.* NPS 10/21/2022. tinyurl.com/jn2dpezc.

[52] Mosteller, Roy. *Charles Harris.* US Navy Mem. tinyurl.com/49x54j35.

[53] *Harold William Marney.* USN Mem. tinyurl.com/4v9jh5r2.

A Chinese soldier guards Flying
Tigers aircraft somewhere in China.[54]

Chenault's group flew missions over China, Burma, Rangoon, and Thailand and is credited with downing 299 enemy planes with a loss of just twelve of their Tigers. In April 1942, with America at war, the Flying Tigers were made an official part of the United States Army Air Force. Hennessey stated, "The Japs have a healthy respect for the A.V.G.'s. When they heard the American Volunteer Group would be dissolved on July 4 to release pilots for duty at home, they ordered their flyers not to attack the Chinese until after July 4!"

The Newton High School graduate returned home following his service with the Flying Tigers after having achieved a place in their history. "My plane was so old," stated Hennessey, "that I got the record for forced landings—13 while in China."[55]

George Hursey

Cpl. George Hursey was a 20-year-old from North Carolina when he watched Japanese planes roar down from the skies over Hawaii. "We were on a hill overlooking Pearl Harbor, and you could see everything. One of the battleships blew up in our faces," he remembered. "All hell was breaking loose."[56] His artillery unit responded immediately, taking part in the furious battle that followed. Hursey survived unscathed. Eight months later, his experience at Guadalcanal was "100 times worse." Hursey recalled water that had pooled on the ground, turning blood red, and the last few moments of his time in battle when he was hit by shrapnel. He returned stateside to a new assignment at Camp Edwards on Cape Cod, where he trained artillerymen.[57] On November 5, 2019, George Hursey, a longtime resident of Brockton and one of the last Pearl Harbor survivors in Massachusetts, passed away. He rests among heroes at Massachusetts National Cemetery in Bourne.[58]

Waino Jyringi

Waino Jyringi was a textile worker living in Rochdale when he was inducted into the Army at Fort Devens on March 23, 1942.[59] The following year, the village began publication of *The Rochdale News*, a small newspaper to be sent to members of the Armed Forces. Throughout the remainder of the

---

[54] *Chinese soldier guards planes.* Publ domain photo. NAID 535531. tinyurl.com/3ny69uxh.

[55] *Flying Tiger China to Waban.* Boston Globe 8/4/1942. Newspapers.com. tinyurl.com/2e6u4xsc.

[56] Reyes, Max. *Pearl Hrbr survivor dies.* Metro. Boston Globe 11/10/2019. Newspapers.com. tinyurl.com/ms33wsfp.

[57] *George Hursey Dies.* Pearlharbor.org. 11/22/2019. tinyurl.com/k6bpy6dm.

[58] *George Hursey.* Russell Pica Funeral Homes. tinyurl.com/mtycfubh.

[59] *Waino Jyringi.* WWII Army Enlistment Records. FamilySearch. tinyurl.com/4za7rfwb.

war, Jyringi was featured in the newsletter several times, giving the reader a glimpse into the Sergeant's life with the US Army.

In January 1945, Jyringi, located in the Philippines during the rainy season, described watching enemy engagements in the air. The newspaper reported that Jyringi "gets a thrill watching plane dogfights, likens it to a football game, and cheer[s] wildly when a Nip is shot down." The Rochdale Fire Department was offering a prize to the first hometown soldier to make it to Tokyo. Jyringi reported that he was "edging nearer"[60] to winning the $50 bond.

Two months later, a Bronze Star was awarded to Technician Fourth Grade Waino Jyringi, Field Artillery, United States Army:

*For meritorious service in operations against the enemy on the island of Leyte, P.I., from 12 December to 21 December 1944. Technician Jyringi, while acting as a radio operator in an artillery forward observer team, completely operated his radio in exposed positions during the advance of the 3rd Battalion, ***Regiment from Catayon to Valencia. The communications established by him enabled his battalion to continually furnish effective artillery fire on enemy positions and materially aided the Infantry's advance.*[61]

Jyringi's experience in the Army was not without humor. In a letter dated March 1945, Boatswain's Mate Richard W. Green wrote to Jyringi:

Dear Wink: Being a Seabee I don't have much time to write, but I'll knock off work long enough to congratulate your outfit and the swell job you have done. But I'd like to ask you "doggies" to do us Seabees a favor. In the future, when you invade an island, please don't be so rough; take it easy. We Seabees spend months building roads and accommodations for you fellows, and then you fellows, instead of coming nice and quiet, always tear up things. Of course, we don't mind rebuilding the roads, but we have enough to do keeping ahead of the "Japs," at the rate they are retreating, they will probably catch up to us and interfere with our work. So in the future, just come in nice and quiet. We have living quarters and theaters all set up for you; why destroy them? Pal – Smokey.[62]

Elias Jyringi must have been a proud father. Another son, Sergeant Aarne Jyringi, with an Army Air Corps squadron in Corsica, received an official commendation in 1944 for his efforts. His commanding officer wrote:

In addition to being a good soldier, your son Aarne has been especially valuable as an airplane sheet metal craftsman. While he has never been in position to perform spectacular feats which make for medals and publicity, he has done his part in making many such things possible...you can be mighty proud of your son and what he has contributed to one of the finest branches of the service, the Army Air Corps.[63]

In July 1945, the newspaper reported that the Waino had been wounded in action in the Philippines. A bullet struck his wedding band, and the damaged ring was mailed home as proof.[64] Waino Jyringi, Bronze Star and Purple Heart recipient, along with his brother, made it home at the war's end. He passed away in 2004 while still a resident of Rochdale.[65]

---

[60] *Rochdale News* 11/2/1944 Vol 2. Rochdale News.

[61] *Bronze Star Waino Jyringi.* Rochdale News 3/1945 Vol 2.

[62] *Advice from a Seabee.* Rochdale News 3/1945 Vol 2.

[63] *Aarne Jyringi Receives Commendation.* Rochdale News 9/1944 Vol 1.

[64] *Rochdale News* 7/1945 Vol 2. Rochdale News.

[65] *Waino Jyringi.* Morin Funeral Home 10/18/2004. tinyurl.com/ckewdbcx.

<u>**Alfred Williams Kinsman**</u>

The Battle of the Bulge was less than 24 hours old, and Battery B, 285th Field Artillery Observation, was moving eastward through Belgium. It was eight days before Christmas 1944 when the battalion suddenly ran into a group from the German 1st Panzer Division under the command of 29-year-old SS Officer Lt. Col. Joachim Peiper. Outgunned and out-manned, Haverhill's Alfred Kinsman and his fellow soldiers surrendered. What followed was a crime so heinous that the name "Malmedy" has since become synonymous with Nazi brutality. Approximately 120 Americans were gathered together in a field and, under orders from Peiper, machine-gunned. Eight-four perished. Survivors would later recall seeing Waffen SS walk amongst the fallen, shooting those who showed signs of life. The damning evidence would be discovered a month later when the bodies of the victims were found; forty-one were shot in the head, and ten showed rifle butt head injuries.[66] Private Michael Ward of Charlestown was one of the lucky ones. In a letter home a month later, he wrote, "I can tell you now where we were stationed when the breakthrough came. It was the small town of Malmedy northeast of Liege. A lot of things happened there that aren't even fit for print!" Much of Ward's letter was censored anyway.[67]

Fallen heroes at Malmedy. 1944.[68]

Sgt. Alfred Kinsman, 25 years old, was laid to rest among the fallen heroes of Malmedy at Henri-Chapelle American Cemetery in Belgium.[69] Joachim Peiper had a different fate. He and seventy-three members of his SS unit were placed on trial for war crimes and found guilty. Peiper's punishment was execution. Five years later, his sentence was commuted, and in 1956, he was released from prison. However, the men who died at Malmedy would have retribution. After discovering that the former Nazi was quietly living in their midst, information about Peiper's history was distributed. In 1976, Joaquim Peiper was burned to death when French anti-Nazis set fire to his house in Traves, France.

---

[66] *Massacre Malmedy.* JVL. tinyurl.com/ffu55mre.

[67] *Horrors of Malmedy.* Boston Globe 1/24/1945. Newspapers.com. tinyurl.com/3rmscp9d.

[68] *Soldiers slain Malmedy.* Pub domain photo. NARA 196544. Wiki Commons. tinyurl.com/3r6uvh89.

[69] *Kinsman Alfred.* AWMO 2008. tinyurl.com/ys9zyxmk.

<u>Ruth Evelyn Black Koczela</u>
<u>Leonard Stanley Koczela</u>

Born in 1921 in the tiny village of Searvilles, a section of Williamsburg, Ruth Evelyn Black was attending State Teachers College of North Adams when war broke out. Drawn to the war effort, she joined the WAVES in 1943 and was sent to a post at US Naval Communications in Washington. Ruth Black was a code breaker.

Leonard "Paul" Koczela of Adams was also a student at the Teachers College when he met Ruth. Theirs would be a long and complicated courtship. After joining the Navy, he was stationed on the transport ship USS Elmore. In January 1944, Elmore was in the Kwajalein Islands. Elmore's assignment was to carry the 1,600 Marines aboard to shore and bring back the dead and wounded. In a painful memory, Paul recalled trips to the beachhead to drop off Marines and, on the following trip, finding many of those same men dead and floating in the water.

Paul returned from war, married Ruth in 1946, and, like the new Mrs. Koczela, became a cryptographer with the National Security Agency. They spoke little of their experiences during the war, both still conscientiously adhering to their oath of secrecy. Paul passed away in 2003. After the war, Ruth became a homemaker and substitute teacher, tried skydiving at 89, and went on safari at 91.[70] She passed away at age 101.[71]

<u>John MacPhee</u>

"I'll never make that beach," thought 22-year-old John MacPhee of Sandwich as he slogged through the water on Omaha Beach with thirty-six pounds of dynamite and an M-1 rifle on his back. It was June 6, 1944. He knew that "if you get hit in the water, you're done for," so in spite of 100 pounds of gear and a heavy, water-soaked uniform, he pushed forward onto the beach. That was as far as he got. At first, it was a shrapnel hit, then bullets ripped into both of his legs. The humerus in his right arm shattered, and his time in combat was over. MacPhee, one of the lucky boys on the beach that D-Day morning, was sent home. He would spend the rest of his life with an arm that never quite worked right and three bullets still lodged in his body. Said MacPhee, "If you're in combat for one minute, you're in combat for a lifetime. Believe me."[72]

<u>Stephen J. Manella</u>

Waltham's Corporal Stephen Manella kept busy during his time at Fort Dix in New Jersey. In July 1944, using "mystic numbers and magic names," he and his buddies came up with the date when the Second World War would end. The statistics looked like this:

	Churchill	Hitler	Roosevelt	Il Duce	Stalin	Tojo
Year born	1874	1889	1882	1883	1879	1884
Age	70	55	62	61	65	60
Years in Office	4	11	11	22	20	3
Took Office	1940	1933	1933	1922	1924	1941

Astonishingly, the numbers for each leader tally up to 3,888. By applying a formula consisting of numerical nonsense and mathematical mumbo jumbo, Manella predicted that the war would end at 2 p.m. on September 7, just a few months away. Of course, his calculation was a little off (by approximately

---

[70] Pregent, Dennis G. *Berkshire Patriots*. Writeway Publ 2023.

[71] *Ruth Koczela. 2023*. Legacy. tinyurl.com/mr38ve6a.

[72] Maxwell, Trevor. *Everyone has story*. Cape Cod Times 6/7/2002. tinyurl.com/j3ucmxju.

fourteen months or 61 weeks or 427 days, give or take the mumbo jumbo), but his mathematical prowess had earned him fifteen minutes of fame in the pages of the *Boston Globe*.[73]

<u>William A. McKean</u>

On his very first day in combat, Braintree resident Capt. William McKean earned a Silver Star. The twenty-six-year-old was cutting wires on a bridge outside Cherbourg when, according to a *Boston Globe* report, he "ran amok" with a hatchet. McKean had taken cover under the bridge during an artillery attack and, while there, began removing enemy demolition charges. When a group of Germans attempted to stop him, he successfully killed or captured all five. An artillery rocket landed nearby, "...so close he was spitting blood for five days, but refused evacuation." McKean was also the recipient of a Purple Heart for shell fragment injuries. "You know, you pick them up here and there," stated McKean.[74]

William A. McKean returned after the war having earned a Silver Star with Oak Leaf Cluster, a Purple Heart with three Oak Leaf Clusters, a Bronze Star, an American Campaign Medal with Oak Leaf Cluster, a Combat Infantryman Badge, and a Master Parachutist Badge.[75] He rose to the rank of Colonel and passed away in 1989.

<u>Joseph E. Muller</u>

Joseph E Muller, a native of Holyoke, was a member of the US Army Infantry when he saw action in the Pacific. On May 16, 1945, the 77th Infantry Division was engaged in battle on Okinawa. By then, the war in Europe was over, and the surrender of Japan was only three months away. For his sacrifice that day, Muller was awarded the Congressional Medal of Honor. His citation reads:

When his platoon was stopped by deadly fire from a strongly defended ridge, he directed men to points where they could cover his attack. Then, through the vicious machine gun and automatic fire, crawling forward alone, he suddenly jumped up, hurled his grenades, charged the enemy and drove them into the open, where his squad shot them down. Seeing enemy survivors about to man a machine gun, he fired his rifle at point-blank range, hurled himself upon them, and killed the remaining four. Before dawn the next day, the enemy counterattacked fiercely to retake the position. Sgt. Muller crawled forward through the flying bullets and explosives, then leaping to his feet, hurling grenades, and firing his rifle, he charged the Japs and routed them. As he moved into his foxhole shared with two other men, a lone enemy, who had been feigning death, threw a grenade. Quickly seeing the danger to his companions, Sgt. Muller threw himself over it and smothered the blast with his body. Heroically sacrificing his life to save his comrades, he upheld the highest traditions of the military service.[76]

In August 1946, the Berkshire Eagle reported on a simple ceremony that took place in the home of Mrs. Mary St. Germain in Holyoke. With "reverent respect for the memory of a gallant soldier, tinged with a note of deep patriotism," and with the "thanks and admiration of the American people," the Congressional Medal of Honor was awarded to Sgt. Joseph E. Muller. Next to his mother stood her two other sons, who had gone off to war but had thankfully returned.[77]

---

[73] *Figures WW's End.* Boston Globe 7/20/1944. Newspapers.com. tinyurl.com/mrew5ma2.

[74] Jones, Victor. *Kelly Tells Stories.* Boston Globe 3/5/1945. Newspapers.com. tinyurl.com/2r77vx6f.

[75] *William A. McKean.* US Army OCS Alumni Asso. tinyurl.com/457t2can.

[76] *Joseph Muller.* Stories Sacrifice. CMOHS. tinyurl.com/mu7px3fr.

[77] *Mother Given Son's Medal.* Berkshire Eagle 8/19/1946. Newspapers.com. tinyurl.com/5n8585wd.

Paul C. Powers

Paul C. Powers, Jr. was stationed in Europe with the 377th Infantry Regiment, 95th Infantry Division, in December of 1944 when the platoon he was leading encountered heavy enemy fire. Under a hail of gunfire, the Technical Sergeant from Spencer crept forward toward a German machine gun nest, pulled the pin on a grenade, and tossed it into the pillbox. Within moments, a machine gun appeared at the portal of the pillbox. Powers grabbed the barrel and yanked it out of the opening. He then dropped another explosive into the ventilator shaft. Nine Germans threw down their arms and surrendered.[78] Powers' "personal bravery and zealous devotion to duty" earned him the Distinguished Service Cross.[79]

Robert W. Sanders

Robert W. Sanders was valedictorian of his graduating class at Brewster High School and was 22 years old when he enlisted in Boston. He was a gunner with the Army Air Force in Europe when he wrote home. "It doesn't matter whether I'm dead or alive. I just want to come home." That wish would be denied him. On August 22, 1944, during his fiftieth mission ("the magic number to get back stateside"), Robert Sanders was killed when his B-24 crashed during a bombing run over Vienna.

His mother, Ruth, was devastated, unable to respond to multiple government inquiries about where she would like her son's remains to rest. For the remainder of her life, Ruth Sanders rarely spoke of her loss. In the words of Rob Sanders, nephew of the fallen airman, it was "the family taboo." Yet Rob, a Harwich firefighter, was driven to honor his uncle's memory. He wanted to find him.[80] Fifty-five years after the tragic loss of Robert Sanders, his nephew's search came to an end when the family was notified that Sanders' remains lay at rest in the Ardennes Cemetery in Belgium. His citation reads:

Robert W. Sanders
Staff Sergeant, U.S. Army Air Forces
779th Bomber Squadron, 464th Bomber Group, Heavy
Date of Death: August 22, 1944
"Time will not dim the glory of their deeds."[81]

John F. Thornell, Jr.

Capt. J. F. Thornell. 1944.[82]

---

[78] Fiske, Jeffrey. *History Spencer, MA.* Spencer Hist Comm 1990.

[79] *Paul Powers.* Hall Valor Proj. tinyurl.com/5djz5p2e.

[80] Lord, Robin. *Wish echoes across decades.* Cape Cod Times 5/23/2001. tinyurl.com/azf5n4rk.

[81] *Robert Sanders.* ABMC. tinyurl.com/yt7txh5c

[82] *Capt. Thornell.* Pub domain photo. Am Air Mus. Wiki Commons. tinyurl.com/2wrzwfk2.

In July 1944, First Lieutenant John Francis Thornell, Jr. of East Walpole, was awarded the Distinguished Service Cross.

For extraordinary heroism...in aerial combat against enemy forces on 8 May 1944... Lieutenant Thornell, with complete disregard for the odds against him, led a fight against a vastly superior force of enemy fighters in the vicinity of Nienburg, Germany, and dispersed the enemy, attempting to intercept a friendly bomber formation...he attacked three enemy fighters and, by courageous flying and skillful gunnery, destroyed two of them. Later, Lieutenant Thornell was attacked by a lone enemy fighter whom he outmaneuvered and destroyed, bringing his total for the day to three enemy airplanes destroyed. The outstanding courage, coolness, and skill displayed by Lieutenant Thornell upon this occasion reflect highest credit upon himself and the Armed Forces of the United States.[83]

The Army recognized pilots who downed five or more enemy aircraft in combat as "Aces." Thornell is credited with downing seventeen enemy aircraft, earning him the rare designation of Army Air Force Triple Ace. He remained with the Air Force after the war and retired as a Lieutenant Colonel in 1962.[84]

Uno Who

This amusing letter signed "Uno Who" was sent by John Gunther Jr. to his parents in Rochdale. Whether or not he was the author is unclear. Written under the heading "CENSORED" with a date and place recorded as "Who Cares," it is a clever look at the role of censors in World War II.

Dear Friend – Also the Censor:

After leaving where we were before we left for here, not knowing we were coming here from there, we would have arrived here, or we could have arrived someplace else. But we are here, however, and not there, although I am not quite sure where "there" would have been in view of the fact that we are here instead of there.

The weather here is just as it always is at this season, because this is the season for that kind of weather, although I must say that it is not at all like the weather where we were before we came here because that was where we were instead of where we are now. The journey here was neither long nor short, but we had a lot of fun in the kind of conveyance in which we came.

The people here look just like they do, and have the characteristics for the type of people they are. However, I must say, they do not in the least resemble the people in the place from which we came, although that is to be expected, because, as I told you, we are not where we were anymore because we are now here.

We came here in the same manner in which everyone comes here from where we were, and the distance was the same for us as it is for everyone else who makes the same journey. Naturally, we had to bring all of our clothes with us because we can't wear here what we used to wear there, but we might leave here and head for some place like it was there. It is quite a new experience for me, because it is not in the least like it was where we were before we arrived here.

---

[83] *John Thornell.* AAMB. tinyurl.com/3db467mu.

[84] *John Thornell.* Hall Valor Proj. tinyurl.com/ydmfphvm.

It is, in all probability, time now to end this somewhat newsy letter before I reveal too much valuable information. The Censor, you know, might be a spy.
Love,
Uno Who[85]

David K. Weiner

When David Weiner stepped up to receive his diploma from Worcester's South High School, his future was filled with uncertainty. The country had gone to war six months before, and he dreamed of becoming a fighter pilot in the Army Air Corps. In February of 1943, he was called to duty and inducted into the Army at Fort Devens. His journey with the military would land him not in the cockpit of an airplane but fighting with the infantry in Europe. Weiner would later describe his experiences in combat with chilling eloquence.

It's strange how similar going into combat is to, say, graduating from college or, getting married or having a first child. In all of these, there are so many firsts in things that you encounter. In combat, there is the first sound of live shells whistling overhead, looking for a site to create massive destruction, and the first time you have a German in your sights and wonder whether you have the will to pull the trigger. Also, the first time you see a dead soldier on the ground with maggots feeding on his recently living flesh, and the first time a close friend is killed by a bullet that could have hit you instead. Also, the first time a bullet misses you but hits your buddy. And, in combat, after the first time, there is the second time...and the third...and the fourth...and the fifth.... Soon your mind determines what you are going to become: a hollow-eyed automaton fighting and waiting for your turn to die or a casualty with no will or mind left to carry on the fight to live.

One day, walking in formation down the main street of one of the towns we had just captured, I saw an undamaged German tank standing at the side of the road. Sitting on top was a German soldier looking straight ahead. I wondered what our officers were thinking, allowing such a danger in a town so recently taken. It was not until I had passed the tank and looked back that I saw that one-half of the soldier's head had been blown away. It was a frightening sight, but, I am sure, just what the newly liberated townspeople must have wanted it to be for any remaining Germans or their collaborators.

Exactly three years to the day after the Japanese attacked Pearl Harbor, Weiner was wounded in northeastern France, struck by shrapnel in the chest and legs. His days in combat were over. The young man from Worcester returned stateside, spent time in a rehabilitation hospital, and was discharged in August 1945.[86]

Chester C. Wenc

Chester "Chuck" Wenc of Grafton served with the 106th Infantry in the ETO and fought at the Battle of the Bulge. Many years later, Wenc described his experience, reflecting on the difference between a German and an American soldier.

American soldiers were smarter and more innovative...Americans had access to guns back home, primarily for hunting. Americans had cars and knew how to repair them, whereas Germans were lucky to have bicycles. Americans developed a sense of Yankee ingenuity, relied on the buddy system, and

---

[85] *Censor Loses Job.* Rochdale News 11/1944 Vol 2.

[86] *David K. Weiner.* Longmeadow, MA. tinyurl.com/24nsdzat.

worked in a spirit of togetherness. If an American officer was killed, the next-ranking soldier assumed command. German soldiers were trained to take orders from the officers only and didn't know what to do or how to react if their commanders fell in the line of duty.[87]

Wenc was one of eleven members of the Central Massachusetts Chapter of Veterans of the Battle of the Bulge to receive the prestigious Chevalier de la Legion d' Honneur and was a recipient of a Bronze Star for valor in battle. He passed away in 2017 at age 92.[88]

Robert W. Woodward

The twenty-eight-year-old Harvard grad from Rockland made it onto the beach at Normandy when he spied a German pillbox. Woodward crawled into a nearby tank and directed it to shoot at the gun emplacement, successfully stopping some of the gunfire. It wasn't enough for Woodward. He climbed out of the tank and, "completely exposed to enemy fire at a range of less than 300 yards," ran toward the pillbox, firing pistols into the openings. Twenty-three Germans gave up. For his actions that day, Robert Woodward added a Distinguished Service Cross to the Purple Heart and Silver Star that he had already earned.

The captain, however, preferred to talk about his run-in with seven Germans in a Lincoln Zephyr. A few months after D-Day, Woodward and two other soldiers were chasing a German vehicle along the back roads of France when a Lincoln Zephyr full of Germans whizzed by. The jeep changed course to pursue it, firing at it. "But bouncing along in a jeep, you can't hit much. It was just like one of those rides in the movies." The jeep just couldn't keep up, and the car sped off, without realizing that there was a major roadblock ahead. US Army tanks lumbered down the road in a line that stretched for miles. Woodward recalls seeing the Lincoln weaving in and out of the tanks while being fired upon. Eventually, the front tire took a hit, and the car landed in a ditch. The Germans climbed out and opened fire, "to the great surprise of the tank guys...What the heck, they were in the middle of a whole armored division, so a fat chance they had. But that was a hot one, seven Germans trying to drive through the whole lst Army in an auto."[89]

Marines plant the American flag on Guam. July 21, 1944.[90]

---

[87] Wilson, Jayne Carroll and Keeras, Joseph *Wilderness in Information Age: Grafton Chronicle.*

[88] *Chester Wenc.* Roney Funeral Home. Worcester T & G 6/20/2017. Legacy.com. tinyurl.com/4nc7xsn8.

[89] Holt, Carlyle. *Men Decorated Heroism.* Boston Globe 9/28/1944. Newspapers.com. tinyurl.com/ykvh5mms.

[90] *Am flag Guam.* Pub domain photo. USMC. DOD. tinyurl.com/mtyy8rsf.

World War II
Medal of Honor Recipients
From Massachusetts

*They said we were soft, that we would not fight, that we
could not win. We are not a warlike nation. We do not go to war
for gain or for territory; we go to war for principles, and we
produce young men like these.*
Harry S. Truman

Raymond Ovila Beaudoin
US Army
Born Holyoke, Massachusetts
Medal of Honor Action:
Hamelin, Germany, April 6, 1945
Killed in Action

James Montross Burt
US Army
Born Hinsdale, Massachusetts
Medal of Honor Action:
Wurselen, Germany, October 13, 1944
Died February 15, 2006

William Robert Caddy
US Marine Corps
Born Quincy, Massachusetts
Medal of Honor Action:
Iwo Jima, March 3, 1945
Killed in Action

Arthur Frederick DeFranzo
US Army
Born Saugus, Massachusetts
Medal of Honor Action:
Vaubadon, France, June 10, 1944
Killed in Action

George John Hall
US Army
Born Stoneham, Massachusetts
Medal of Honor Action:
Anzio, Italy, May 23, 1944

Died February 16, 1946

Robert Murray Hanson
US Marine Corps
Born Lucknow, India
Resident of Newtonville
Medal of Honor Action:
Bougainville Island, November 1, 1943 – January 24, 1944
Killed in Action

Elden Harvey Johnson
US Army
Born Bivalve, New Jersey
Resident of East Weymouth, Massachusetts
Medal of Honor Action:
New Valmonte, Italy, June 3, 1944
Killed in Action

Joseph Rodolph Julian
US Marine Corps
Born Sturbridge, Massachusetts
Medal of Honor Action:
Iwo Jima, March 19, 1945
Killed in Action

Charles Andrew MacGillivary
US Army
Born Prince Edward Island, Canada
Resident of Quincy
Medal of Honor Action:
Woelfling, France, January 1, 1945
Died June 24, 2000

Frederick Coleman Murphy
US Army
Born Boston, Massachusetts
Medal of Honor Action:
Siegfried Line, Saarlautern, Germany, March 18, 1945
Killed in Action

Joseph Timothy O'Callahan
US Navy
Born Boston, Massachusetts
Medal of Honor Action:
Near Kobe, Japan, March 19, 1945

Died: March 18, 1964

Everett Parker Pope
US Marine Corps
Born Milton, Massachusetts
Medal of Honor Action:
Peleliu Island, September 19, 1944
Died: July 16, 2009

John Vincent Power
US Marine Corps
Born Worcester, Massachusetts
Medal of Honor Action:
Kwajalein Atoll, February 1, 1944
Killed in Action

Ernest William Prussman
US Army
Born Baltimore, Maryland
Resident of Brighton, Massachusetts
Medal of Honor Action:
Near Les Coates, France, September 8, 1944
Killed in Action

William Gary Walsh
US Marine
Born Roxbury, Massachusetts
Medal of Honor Action:
Iwo Jima, February 27, 1945
Killed in Action

William Hale Wilbur
US Army
Born Palmer, Massachusetts
Medal of Honor Action
Fedala, Morocco, November 8, 1942
Died December 27, 1979

Edward G. Wilkin
US Army
Born Burlington, Vermont
Resident of Longmeadow, Massachusetts
Medal of Honor Action
Siegfried Line, Germany March 18, 1945
Killed in Action[91ii]

---

[91] *Stories of Sacrifice.* CMOHS. tinyurl.com/mry7r89m.

ABOUT THE AUTHORS

Jeffrey Proctor studied and wrote about naval history
for more than twenty years. In 2018, he created VETERANSREMEMBER.COM to interview military veterans and preserve their stories. He authored several novels under the name J.P. Burke, including *Duchess* and *The Man in the Wormhole*. In 2019, he published *BLADES,* a biography of USN chopper pilot, Don Broderick. Jeffrey was a graduate of Emerson College and resided in Massachusetts. Sadly, he passed away in 2021 before this book, his final work, could be published.

Paula Fitch Proctor holds degrees from Worcester State
College, Anna Maria College, and UMASS Lowell. After a career teaching science and sixth graders and working as an administrator, she retired to apparently become an author. Paula's shared love of history with her son, Jeffrey, led to their collaboration on *Massachusetts at War.* She is a lifelong resident of Massachusetts.